Also by
the Same Author

*The Fatal Crown*

Simon & Schuster
New York  London  Toronto  Sydney  Tokyo  Singapore

# Beloved Enemy

The Passions of
Eleanor of Aquitaine

A Novel

# Ellen Jones

SIMON & SCHUSTER
Rockefeller Center
1230 Avenue of the Americas
New York, New York 10020

This book is a work of fiction. Names, characters, places and incidents
are either products of the author's imagination or are used fictitiously.
Any resemblance to actual events or locales or persons, living or dead,
is entirely coincidental.

Copyright © 1994 by Ellen Jones

All rights reserved,
including the right of reproduction
in whole or in part in any form.

SIMON & SCHUSTER and colophon are registered trademarks
of Simon & Schuster Inc.

Designed by Hyun Joo Kim
Manufactured in the United States of America

1   3   5   7   9   10   8   6   4   2

Library of Congress Cataloging-in-Publication Data
Jones, Ellen.
Beloved enemy: the passions of Eleanor of Aquitaine: a novel/Ellen Jones
p.   cm.
1. Eleanor, of Aquitane. Queen, consort of Henry II, King of England,
1122?–1204—Fiction. 2. Henry II, King of England, 1133–1189—Fiction. 3. Great
Britain—History—Henry II, 1154—1189—Fiction. 4. Great Britain—Kings and
rulers—Fiction. 5. Queens—Great Britain—Fiction. I. Title.
PS3560.O4817B44   1994
813'.54—dc20        93–42290 CIP
ISBN  0-671-87279-6

# ACKNOWLEDGMENTS

The verse by Bernart de Ventadour, that appears in the page of epigraphs preceding the prologue, is translated from the *langue d'oc* by Claude Marks and appears in his book, *Pilgrims, Heretics, and Lovers, A Medieval Journey,* Macmillan Publishing Co., Inc. New York, 1975.

The verse from the cansos by William IX, Duke of Aquitaine, is also translated by Claude Marks and appears in the same book as mentioned above.

The lines by William IX, Duke of Aquitaine, that appear on pages 63–64 and 563 are from *Songs Of The Troubadours,* edited and translated by Anthony Bonner, Schocken Books, New York, 1972.

The lines on pages 261 and 277 by Bernard de Ventadour are also translated by Anthony Bonner and Claude Marks, respectively, and appear in the books mentioned above.

I would like to gratefully acknowledge my supportive agent, Jean Naggar; the unfailingly brilliant Susanne Jaffe, editor extraordinaire; Prof. Marie Ann Mayeski, Professor of Theology at Loyola Marymount College, for her historical expertise; Lyn Stimer for her invaluable help, patience, support, and incisive suggestions; Lisa Rojany for her eagle eye and validation. Lastly, and always, to Mark, who made it all possible.

# AUTHOR'S NOTE

This story is a work of fiction set against the backdrop of actual events of history. The characters, with few exceptions, are real and have their place in history. Many of the incidents depicted actually occurred; others, based on rumor and legend, may or may not have occurred. Chroniclers of the twelfth century do not always agree, nor do later historians who bring their own interpretations to past events. I have taken my own liberties with dates, locations, and the nature of various events.

*Beloved Enemy*

# Main Cast of Characters

House of Aquitaine

| | |
|---|---|
| WILLIAM, | IX Duke of Aquitaine, VII Count of Poitou, the "First Troubadour." |
| WILLIAM, | his son. Later X Duke of Aquitaine, VIII Count of Poitou. |
| ELEANOR, | eldest daughter of William, X Duke of Aquitaine, granddaughter of the "Troubadour." Later Duchess of Aquitaine. |
| DANGEREUSE, | Mistress of the "Troubadour." Eleanor's grandmother. |
| PETRONILLA, | Eleanor's younger sister. |
| AGNES, | an Abbess of Saintes, Eleanor's aunt, her father's sister. |
| RAYMOND, | Prince of Antioch, Eleanor's uncle, her father's younger brother. |
| RALPH DE FAYE, | Eleanor's uncle, her mother's brother. |
| CONON, | an equerry. |
| MASTER ANDRÉ, | a cleric in Poitiers. |

House of Capet

| | |
|---|---|
| LOUIS, | the VI, "The Fat," King of France. |
| LOUIS, | the VII, his son, King of France. |

## HOUSE OF NORMANDY AND ANJOU

| | |
|---|---|
| HENRY II, | Duke of Normandy and Count of Anjou, King of England. |
| GEOFFREY, | Count of Anjou, his father. |
| MAUD, | Countess of Anjou, his mother. |
| GEOFFREY, | Henry's illegitimate son. |

## PEERS OF THE CHURCH AND CHURCHMEN

| | |
|---|---|
| ABBESS OF FONTEVRAULT, | an abbey for monks and nuns. |
| ARCHBISHOP OF BORDEAUX | |
| ABBÉ SUGER, | advisor to King Louis VI and VII. |
| BERNARD OF CLAIRVAUX, | Abbé of Citeaux. |
| THEOBALD OF BEC, | Archbishop of Canterbury. |
| THOMAS BECKET, | an archdeacon of Canterbury, Chancellor of England. |

## THE BROTHELS

| | |
|---|---|
| YKENAI, | called Bellebelle, a whore. |
| GYTHA, | her mother and a whore. |
| MORGAINE, | a Welsh whore. |
| GILBERT, | a brothelmaster in Southwark. |
| HAWKE, | a brothelmaster in London. |

## OTHERS

| | |
|---|---|
| BERNART DE VENTADOUR, | a troubadour of Aquitaine. |
| ROBERT DE BEAUMONT, | Earl of Leicester, Co-Justiciar of England. |
| RICHARD DE LUCY, | Co-Justiciar of England. |
| WILLIAM FITZ-STEPHEN, | secretary to Thomas Becket. |
| HANS DE BURGH, | a Flemish knight. |
| IVO, | a woodman in the village. |
| ELFGIVA, | an alewife in the village. |

*To live with a woman without danger is more difficult than raising the dead to life.*

—St. Bernard of Clairvaux
*Sermons on the Canticles*

*The most persistent hate is that which doth degenerate from love.*

—Walter Map, 12th Century
*De Nugis Curialium*

*In full agreement and consent,*
*'Tis thus true lovers' love must be.*
*Two wills can only find content*
*In absolute equality.*

—Bernart de Ventadour
*Limousin Troubadour*

# Eleanor of Aquitaine
# Family as of 1161

Eleanor of Aquitaine m. (1) 1137 Louis VII

Marie
b. 1145

Alix
b. 1150

Eleanor of Aquitaine m. (2) 1152 Henry II = Ykenai

| William | Henry | Matilda | Richard | Geoffrey | Eleanor | Geoffrey |
|---------|-------|---------|---------|----------|---------|----------|
| b. 1153 | b. 1155 | b. 1156 | b. 1157 | b. 1158 | b. 1161 | (bastard) |
| d. 1156 | | | | | | b. 1155 (?) |

Robert the Pious
King of France
996 —1031

Henry I
King of France
1031 — 1060

Robert
Duke of Burgundy

Adela
m. (1) Richard,
Duke of Normandy
m. (2) Baldwin V,
Count of Flanders

Philip I
King of France
1060 — 1108

Audiard
m. Guy Geoffrey
Count of Poitou

Matilda
m. William the
Conqueror,
Duke of Normandy
King of England
1066 — 1087

Louis VI
King of France
1108 — 1137

William IX
Count of Poitou
Duke of Aquitaine

William Rufus
(no issue)
1087 — 1100

William X
Count of Poitou
Duke of Aquitaine

Henry I
Duke of Normandy
King of England
1100 — 1135

Louis VII King of France

Maud
m. (1) Emperor Henry V
(2) Geoffrey of Anjou

Eleanor of Aquitaine

Henry of Anjou
Duke of Normandy
Count of Anjou
King of England

# Poitou,

# 1130

*E*leanor stood before the abbess's oak table hiding her fear behind the deceptively sweet smile and innocent expression she always assumed in the presence of Authority. The abbess had not yet arrived but the very chamber itself contained a forbidding air that seemed to emanate from the tapestried walls, the silver candelabra, the carved oak chest, even the flickering ivory tapers. It was a hot August afternoon but inside these quarters there was a chill.

Eleanor had no idea why she had been summoned from the schoolroom. Images of recently broken abbey rules flocked into her mind: climbing an apple tree in the orchard, snatching a loaf of bread from the kitchen after Compline, letting a flock of chickens out of their pen to run loose over the grounds, stealing out of the dorter after Matins—too many to count. She prided herself on seeing how many rules could be broken before the Abbess of Fontevrault found out.

The door opened behind her. With unsteady fingers, Eleanor smoothed down the skirt of her black convent gown, made sure the white cap was tied securely under her chin.

"Sit down, my child." The abbess appeared on the opposite side of the table.

Framed in a stark white wimple, the stern face with its long aristocratic nose looked benign, almost kindly. So unusual was the abbess's expression that instinctively Eleanor knew this summons could not concern her misdeeds. Apprehension fluttered like a cluster of moths in her belly. Once she was seated, her eyes encountered the grim scenes of martyred saints depicted on the crimson-and-blue wall hangings. She quickly looked away.

"My child, I fear I have bad news for you," the abbess said in her calm voice. "This morning an equerry arrived from the ducal palace in Poitiers to inform us that death has claimed your mother and brother." She crossed herself. "I deeply mourn your loss but urge you to remember that your mother and brother are with the Queen of Heaven now. *Requiesant in pace.*"

Her mother. Dead? And little William, barely two years old? It could not be true. Eleanor tried to picture her mother, whom she had not seen since she came to Fontevrault a year ago. All she could conjure up was a gentle, retiring shadow trying to make her behave in a proper manner. But for seven of her eight years, that shadow had remained steadfast as the morning sun, predictable as the evening star. Impossible to imagine life without her. It must be a mistake. Eleanor opened her mouth to say as much but the words stuck in her throat.

"You may be excused from your lessons for the remainder of the afternoon," continued the abbess. "I know you will want to pray in the chapel, and Sister Cecile waits outside to accompany you."

"But I must go home." The words came in a strangled croak. "At once. It—it may not be true."

"I think we may assume it is. Always best to recognize the truth sooner rather than later. Your father thought it best that you stay here for the nonce. Apparently matters are unsettled in Aquitaine at the moment and—"

"Everything is always unsettled in Aquitaine," said Eleanor. "I cannot stay. My sister, Petronilla, will need me, and then—and then there is the funeral . . ." She could not go on.

"In such hot weather the funeral will not be delayed."

"I want to see the equerry."

"Of course. He is being looked after in the guest quarters." The abbess rose to her feet. Tall and imposing in her black habit, she exuded such a commanding aura that resistance tended to shrivel in her presence. Now, she swooped around the table like a great winged bird, settled in front of Eleanor, and tilted her chin in talon-like fingers.

"Your studies should not be interrupted. You are proving to be an exceptional student since your rebellious attitude and frivolous behavior have lessened. After a very bad start I am pleased with your progress over the last year."

Her eyes, gray as a pond in winter, held Eleanor in a steady gaze.

"Far better not to brood unduly over your loss. 'Idleness is the enemy of the soul,' sayeth St. Benedict. Study diverts attention. After all, you are a maid of eight years, no longer a babe to be coddled. What says Holy Writ? 'The Lord giveth and the Lord taketh away. Blessed be the name of the Lord.' "

"But I want to go home," Eleanor whispered, barely listening.

"There is no more to be said." The abbess paused, as if debating with herself, then seemed to come to a decision. "Now, I want you to pay close attention to me. Eleanor!" The talons shook her chin with such impatience she winced.

She began to speak, obviously choosing her words with care. "Your only brother is dead. Once your esteemed grandfather, Duke William, has passed on, your father will inherit the duchy of Aquitaine. But after him, who is left? Only you and your younger sister. Unfortunately, your father's reckless nature and outspoken temperament are well known. Should anything happen to him— Heaven forfend—you, as the eldest child, follow next in line to inherit Aquitaine. Naturally one assumes your father will marry again and have other sons, but meanwhile . . ." The abbess released Eleanor's chin.

Confused, Eleanor could not take in the import of the words. "Marry again? You mean—a new mother to replace mine?" The possibility of such a betrayal was so shattering she felt quite breathless.

"Come, don't look so astounded. Duke William is getting on in years now, and God will soon call him to His bosom. But your father has many years left—if his headstrong spirit can be bridled— and is sure to want a male heir for Aquitaine."

"Instead—you mean instead of me?" The world teetered on a knife-edge. A bottomless pit yawned beneath her. An unknown mother? New brothers to replace little William? Total strangers ruling in Aquitaine? The chamber whirled, and Eleanor grasped the polished wood of the table in front of her.

"That is the way of the world. Not that I approve this time-honored custom that favors sons to inherit their fathers' lands. Women are just as capable. That is to say women of some education."

The chamber righted itself. The abbess swooped to the door.

"I don't want a new mother," said Eleanor in a fierce voice she did not herself recognize. "Or a new brother. You said—if that doesn't happen then would Aquitaine be mine?"

A long silence ensued, during which Reverend Mother regarded Eleanor thoughtfully. "What I said was that you are, at the moment, next in line. Although the likelihood of you ever ruling the duchy is indeed remote, there is no law in Aquitaine forbidding women to inherit."

Eleanor stared at her. "So—so I could then?"

"Anything is possible. But if you want to be a successful duchess, you will need your wits about you. The English king Alfred put it very well: 'Unlettered king, crowned ass.' This applies to any ruler. Therefore, it behooves you to continue your education . . ."

Despite the turmoil bubbling inside her, Eleanor shot the abbess a grudging look of respect. Reverend Mother always got her way in the end. Nor, Eleanor realized, did she disagree. *After* her journey to Poitiers she would most certainly return to the convent to continue her studies. If she was going to prevent Aquitaine from falling into the hands of a stranger, she would indeed need her wits about her.

The Vespers bell sounded.

"Go now." The abbess opened the door. "Pray to Our Lady for what you want. She knows how to answer our prayers." A fleeting smile touched her mouth. "I will join mine to yours."

Instantly, the severe look returned. But Eleanor, who from the beginning had regarded Reverend Mother as the most formidable opponent ever encountered, knew that she had found an unexpected ally.

After going to the St. Benoit Chapel with Sister Cecile, where she tried her best to pray, Eleanor said she did not want any supper, and went to look for the equerry. She ran alongside the high stone wall that enclosed the abbey, past the fish pond, vegetable garden, granary, mill, and dovecote. In the hazy distance she caught a glimpse of the monks' quarters, separate from the nuns', and a long line of black-robed figures heading for the refectory.

She reached the guest quarters where she found Conon, a young equerry with hair like thick straw, who served her father. He lay asleep on a pallet, his black boots covered with dust. Eleanor prodded him with the toe of her shoe. He woke with a start.

"Is it true? Are my mother and brother really dead?"

Conon stumbled to his feet. "Yes, Mistress." He bowed his head and crossed himself.

"How? No one sent to tell me they were ill."

"There was no time, as it was very sudden and unexpected. Your mother and brother went on an excursion one afternoon. It was very hot, the food they had with them may have spoiled—several servitors also fell ill and died. All that is known is by the next morning both had fever and complained of severe stomach pains. The physicians could do nothing. Within a fortnight both had died."

Tears appeared in Conon's eyes. Eleanor felt a heavy weight settle on her chest.

"Your grandparents are inconsolable. The entire court is plunged into mourning. It is feared your sister may pine away, so great is her grief. Duke William has even composed a lament in honor of the sad occasion." Conon wiped his eyes and began to hum a few notes.

"And my father?"

Conon put a hand over his heart and closed his eyes. "Undone by grief. My lord has not touched food or drink for a sennight. He weeps constantly. Mistress, you have never seen such despair. It is feared he will die of a broken heart—even now they are readying his coffin—"

It was the typical Aquitainian way of describing events, most of which could be discounted. Still, there was probably a kernel of truth in Conon's tale. In such a state her moody, unpredictable father might do anything—Eleanor suddenly had a vision of him surrounded by the slew of well-born women who attended her mother. All eager to comfort him, to become the next duchess when her grandfather, Duke William, died. Her blood froze. She *must* return without delay.

"Do take me with you when you leave, Conon."

"But I understood from Duke William that you were to remain."

"Please, Conon." Her lower lip began to tremble. He had to take her. He could not refuse. "Surely you see that I cannot stay here now."

"What will the duke say if I disobey his orders? Moreover, I travel first to Châtellerault to inform your uncles. Now, if I had a valid reason to take you with me . . ."

Eleanor closed her eyes, gasped, and held both sides of her head between her hands. "I will go from my wits if I cannot go home—I may fall mortally ill . . ." She began to sway back and forth.

Conon nodded. "Very well, Mistress, I will tell the duke that with my own eyes I saw you fall into a dead faint, and fearing for your life I undertook to disobey his orders. But in the event he does not accept this, you must intercede on my behalf."

"I promise. Thank you, thank you." Weak with relief, Eleanor threw her arms around the equerry. She was going home.

When Eleanor arrived in Poitiers three days later, the castle was in its usual state of uproar, almost exactly as she had left it a year ago.

"I'm so glad you're here, Nell," said six-year-old Petronilla without surprise when Eleanor appeared in the courtyard, covered with dust from the journey. "Maman and William have gone away and aren't ever coming back." Her sister's face was streaked with dirt and her eyes rimmed with red. "No one tells me what to do now." She threw herself into Eleanor's arms. "I knew you would come."

Eleanor's whole world had tumbled apart, yet here everything appeared the same. The courtyard was still crowded with servants drawing water from the well; hens squawked loudly; falconers aired their charges; fewterers walked the greyhounds and wolfhounds back and forth. Everyone crowded around her offering sympathy; even the fat cook waddled out to hug her.

After searching through the castle, Eleanor finally found her father in the stables. A giant of a man with azure eyes and a head of corn gold hair, he gave her a gloomy, puzzled look.

"Aren't you supposed to be at Fontevrault, Nell?"

"I—uhh—I felt I should come home, and persuaded Conon to take me. It wasn't his fault."

He nodded absently. "Perhaps it is for the best. I don't know what to do about Petronilla. Not much of a homecoming, I fear." He patted her affectionately on the head, then gave her a big hug. "I'm glad to see you, Daughter. Your poor mother—and little William— both gone." He began to sob.

"I know, Father." She could not bear to see him so distraught.

He gave a tremulous sigh and wiped his eyes. "What will I do? I must have an heir." He bit his lip and shook his head. "Well, I'm off to the Limousin. The barons there are causing unrest, worse than usual. Those conniving bastards can certainly pick their moment. And the whoreson king of France has ordered your grandfather to appear before him to answer one of his ridiculous charges. Between ourselves, mind, the duke is unwell, not up to either journey, so I must go in his place. What a coil. You must look after yourself, and Petronilla too."

"What are you doing here, Nell?" asked her grandfather, Duke William, that night at supper in the great hall of the Maubergeonne Tower.

"Reverend Mother—Reverend Mother thought I should come home."

Her grandfather's hair, once bright as sunlight, was now faded. His face, usually bronzed from wind and weather, looked pale and old. Duke William, whom everyone affectionately called the Troubadour, glanced at her from blue eyes not quite as piercing as they once had been. "Expressly against my instructions? I think not. If you must lie, at least learn to do it with more finesse. Still, I am glad to see you, child. I hear you are Fontevrault's prize pupil now. Well done."

He turned to the guests at the high table. "For a while I feared Nell might be booted out of the abbey school. Unruly behavior, I was told." He rolled his eyes. "Distracting the worthy monks from their prayers more likely, if she's any granddaughter of mine, eh, poppet?" He kissed the hand of a lady seated beside him—she had embroidered green ribbons plaited into her braids—winked at a smiling beauty across the table, and, although Eleanor could not be sure, squeezed the thigh of a noble's wife sitting on his other side.

"Really, my lord," said the archbishop of Poitou in a disapproving voice.

Eleanor suspected that if her imperious grandmother, closeted in her own quarters which she rarely left, had been present, the duke might have been more restrained. When everyone joined in the laughter that followed, she felt confused. She had come home to protect what was left of the world she had known. Her father and Petronilla were distraught, but otherwise the atmosphere was as gay and carefree as she remembered. Why did no one mourn her mother? Inside her chest a dam burst. Tears flooded down her cheeks. For the first time it was blazingly, horribly real. Her mother was dead.

There was a moment of silence except for the sound of her sobbing. She could see all the heads at the table turn toward her.

"It's a great shame about your mother and brother." Duke

William crossed himself. "Tragic. But 'Least said, soonest mended.' Pay attention to people when they are alive, I always say, not after they're gone. We must find you a new mother, my child, the sooner the better. Your father needs to sire an heir, and—"

Eleanor choked on a sob which silenced him.

The conversation continued. No one was paying any attention to her now. Eleanor brushed the tears from her eyes and looked around for her father's younger brother. Raymond would surely understand and comfort her. But he was not at the high table, nor had she caught a glimpse of him since she had returned.

"Where's Uncle Raymond?"

"Gone to King Henry's court in England to seek his fortune," said her grandfather. "In truth, my incorrigible young son had dallied with one wife too many. There was an irate husband at his heels, and he barely escaped over the border into Anjou." He sighed. "Let us hope the English court has a sobering influence, and that Raymond will grow more circumspect with age."

"I doubt it! How far can the apple fall from the tree?" someone shouted in a voice slurred with wine. "In any case, the English king has so many of his own bastards hanging about that he sets a poor example."

Duke William repressed a smile. "Shocking. Perhaps I should have sent Raymond to the papal Court?"

A great burst of laughter followed this.

"Really, my lord, a most unsuitable conversation before the child." The archbishop of Poitou looked down his nose.

"Quite right, quite right. The worthy archbishop is trying to help me lift the ban of excommunication I've labored under all these years." He gave Eleanor a sly wink. "In exchange I have promised to mend my ways. Whatever one has done during one's life, it is prudent to expire in the bosom of Holy Church."

Duke William, the Troubadour, began to strum his lute and sing a canso of his own composing in the slightly cracked but always thrilling voice that Eleanor loved. Tonight, however, even her grandfather's music could not dispel her loneliness and heartache. She had been very fond of her uncle Raymond, only eight years older than herself and a jolly companion. She missed him almost as much as she missed her mother.

Her grandfather finished his song with a flourish of chords and much applause. Then: "What was I saying?"

"You mentioned the bosom of the Church," said the archbishop with a complacent smile.

"Ah! Less alluring than some bosoms I've known, I must confess. Speaking of which," said Duke William, and he started on one of his stories.

While the hall rocked with laughter, the archbishop, red as a squawking gobbler, grabbed Eleanor's hand and half-dragged her, protesting, from the hall.

Over the next few weeks Eleanor became increasingly aware that she might as well have stayed at Fontevrault. No one paid her any attention, including her father. He had returned after ten days, morose and frustrated, having lost a skirmish with the battling nobles of the Limousin. He stormed about the castle, refused to attend the French king's summons in the duke's stead, and made himself thoroughly disagreeable. Fulfilling Eleanor's worst fears, the attendant women spent much of their time trying to console him.

"One of those silly peahens is hoping to marry him," Eleanor said, watching Petronilla stuff her mouth with marchpane.

They were in the kitchen, where the fat cook always made them welcome.

"Don't want him to marry again," said her sister, spittle dribbling down her chin. "No one tells us what to do now. I like that."

"You'll make yourself sick with all those sweets," said Eleanor. "I don't want him to marry again either. No one can take our mother's place. Reverend Mother says I'm now the heir. If father gets another son I won't be."

"I would rather Aquitaine belonged to you, Sister, than anyone."

Eleanor reached over and kissed Petronilla's sticky cheek.

Shortly after her father's return, Eleanor's grandmother, Dangereuse, her mother's mother, asked to see her alone. Uncle Raymond had told Eleanor that Dangereuse had been married to one of Duke William's vassals when the duke carried her off many years ago and installed her as his mistress in Poitiers. At the time he was married to Philippa of Toulouse, mother of his seven children, who created a storm of protest. The resulting scandal was such that in order to achieve a degree of respectability, Raymond said, his father hastily married his mistress's daughter by the vassal to his eldest son, then sixteen years of age. Eleanor was their first child.

Although its exact nature eluded her, Eleanor knew that her

grandparents had committed a grave sin—which the Church was still trying to rectify. She had heard the servants gossiping in corners that against all reason and God's judgment, the wayward grandmother still kept a siren hold on Duke William of Aquitaine. The adulteress did it by witchcraft, they whispered, by magic potions and spells. Not that Eleanor believed this. Still, it endowed Dangereuse with an air of mystery that made Eleanor more than a little afraid of her.

On a hot afternoon the last week in August, she climbed the winding staircase to the top of the Maubergeonne Tower where Dangereuse had her own quarters. Eleanor had not seen her grandmother since returning from the abbey—one only visited her when summoned. The chamber floor was covered with rushes mixed with crushed gillyflowers and ivory lilies. Silver basins and jugs graced the gleaming oak tables. Clad in a robe trimmed with miniver and ermine, her still-beautiful grandmother lay on a canopied bed under an embroidered green-and-gold coverlet. Her luxuriant chestnut hair, streaked with wings of white, cascaded over her frail shoulders. She extended one languid white hand. In the other, she held a silver mirror, turning it this way and that while she examined her narrow face with its high cheekbones and unnaturally pink lips.

"I am glad to see you, child." Eleanor kissed the proffered hand which smelled deliciously of rose water. "I hope all those nuns haven't flogged the spirit out of you?" She gave Eleanor a penetrating look. "I can see they have not. It is safe for you to return to Fontevrault before too long, and continue your education."

When Eleanor started to protest, Dangeureuse held up an imperious hand. "Do not argue. Important for a woman to be lettered. It makes her equal in knowledge. Knowledge is power."

Still looking at the mirror, she licked a finger and smoothed down one arched eyebrow. "How do you find your father? I have hardly set eyes on him."

Tears of bitterness welled up in Eleanor's eyes. "My father is always gone and when he's not he's in a foul mood. My grandfather ignores me. The servants who are supposed to tend us are always off gossiping. I miss my mother."

"So do I, but life must go forward." She put down the mirror and peered at Eleanor. "Sweet St. Radegonde, I hope you are not going to start feeling sorry for yourself. There is nothing I hate more than a whining female. If you do not care for the way things are, change them."

She ran distasteful fingers through Eleanor's thick tangle of chestnut curls. "Just look at you! What man will pay attention to a dirty, unkempt ragamuffin? Wash your hair with vinegar." She ran a veined hand over Eleanor's cheeks and forehead. "Such exquisite skin, like ivory and peaches, but I see spots and freckles. Too much sun and too many sweetmeats."

"No one notices what we eat or if we eat at all."

Dangereuse rapped Eleanor sharply across the knuckles. "The first lesson you must learn is that it is a woman's business to get herself noticed."

"But how?

"How? How?" With a contemptuous snort, her grandmother picked up the mirror again. "Those that must ask will never know."

"My father talks of marrying again. Having sons."

Dangereuse shrugged and pulled a face at the mirror. "What of it? Men always talk of marrying and having sons. Apart from war and seduction it is their only other occupation."

"But I could not abide a new mother—or brother."

"Of course not." She gave an amused cackle. "You would be pushed aside then for good, wouldn't you? I suspect you want the duchy for yourself."

"No! I mean, yes—I mean, I do want—"

Her eyes, pale green flecked with brown, oddly tilted at the corners like a cat—or a witch—silenced Eleanor with a withering glance.

"Foolish child! So full of yourself. How can you know what you want? What do you understand of such matters? In three centuries of rule, despite its vast array of riches, the duchy has always been a source of trouble and strife to its dukes. Aquitainia, the Romans called it, for the many rivers that abound. Hah! Rivers of blood would be more apt."

"I would hate strangers ruling here," Eleanor whispered, baffled by her grandmother's words. "I love the duchy."

"So do I. Which makes us both fools. But you will not get much joy from this paradise, I assure you." Dangereuse sniffed, then shrugged. " 'Wild goose never reared tame gosling.' What else did I expect?" After a significant pause she picked up the mirror again and examined herself. "In the absence of a male heir, women may inherit in Aquitaine. Thus, there is no reason—no legal reason— why, if your father does not marry again and produce a son, you should not have the duchy. If you are clever enough. Which remains to be seen." Her gaze left the mirror and raked Eleanor's face. "To get what you want you must take matters into your own hands. But to do that you must first get yourself noticed. If, as a female, you cannot accomplish such a simple task then I wash my hands of you." She leaned forward until her face almost touched Eleanor's, who felt her heart thump. "I may not leave my own quarters, but I cast a long shadow, child. When I speak, my lord listens—"

There was a knock on the door and Duke William entered, carrying a bouquet of pink summer roses. Her grandmother quickly waved Eleanor away.

"My dearest, how lovely you look today, quite like a young maid. Nell paying you a visit, is she?" He sat down on the bed, took Dangeureuse's frail hand in his, and laid it tenderly against his cheek. "I had a sudden longing to see you with roses in your hair."

"William," murmured her grandmother, her face suddenly youthful and radiant.

They gazed at each other while the duke snapped off the heads of several roses and began to twine them in her hair. Eleanor knew they had forgotten her presence. She crept to the door of the chamber passionately wishing that someone, someday, would love her as much as her grandfather loved her grandmother.

She was out the door when she heard Dangereuse call out to her, "Tell my new chaplain, Master André, to start teaching you how to read and write Provençal. One may as well be prepared for all eventualities. In the unlikely event you surprise me."

During the next few days, Eleanor wandered distractedly about the castle, half-expecting any moment to meet her mother round the corner of a passage, see her presiding at the high table, or sewing with her women in the solar. Despite the fact that she had bathed in a hot tub of water and washed her hair with vinegar, she was still ignored.

She ate what she wanted—omitting sweetmeats—and did as she pleased. When she fell ill after stuffing herself with unripe apples, no one seemed very concerned. She rode her pony over forbidden fences, half-hoping she would fall and hurt herself so someone would pay attention. She persuaded the head falconer to teach her to fly sparrow hawks, and no one stopped her. When she and the steward's son were caught buck naked together examining each other's differences, the steward thrashed his son, but just warned her to start behaving like the lady she was. As far as she knew he never told anyone of the incident. Her father and grandfather, constantly preoccupied with the never-ending troubles in Aquitaine and their bitter quarrels with Fat Louis of France, appeared to have forgotten her existence.

She could think of no way to remind them.

One day her father left on a journey to Bordeaux.

"Please let me go with you," she begged.

"What would I do with you? I have vassals to tend to, revenues to collect, cases to judge—" He shook his head.

To her surprise Eleanor missed Fontevrault: she missed her lessons, the harmonious surroundings, the sisters gliding through the grounds like a flock of black starlings. Most of all, to her even greater astonishment, she missed the calm, authoritative presence of Reverend Mother. Her only consolation was the instruction she received from Master André, the young chaplain.

One day about a month after she had returned from Fontevrault, sour-faced Aunt Agnes, one of her father's five sisters, arrived from Maillezais, ten leagues distant.

"Just look at you, Eleanor," she said, marching into the chamber where Eleanor and her sister slept. "When was the last time you put on a clean gown? I've a good mind to take you and Petronilla back home with me. Your grandfather's court is no place for untended children." She sniffed. "You've only that wicked old grandmother to guide you, which is like the blind leading the blind."

Eleanor and Petronilla exchanged fearful glances. Everyone knew Aunt Agnes hated Dangereuse. She had never forgiven her father's mistress for displacing her own outraged mother, Philippa of Toulouse, who, heartily sick of her husband's amorous exploits, had repaired to Fontevrault Abbey, where she had died—of frustrated rage rather than grief, wagged malicious tongues. Aunt Agnes had made Eleanor's mother's life miserable by cruelly reminding her that not only the Church—which had excommunicated both the duke and Dangereuse—but even the easygoing Aquitainian nobles had been shocked by their duke's scandalous behavior. The fact that Duke William continued to live in open adultery with his mistress only added more coals to the simmering fire of Aunt Agnes's disapproval.

Her father returned from Bordeaux, and the next day a huge number of guests arrived from as far away as Champagne and Anjou. When Eleanor slid into her place at the high table her grandfather was in the middle of a story.

". . . so my friends, though my life has been a most colorful one, having gone on crusade and seen something of the world, fought battles which I usually lost, kept the warring factions of this duchy in one piece, my happiest moments have been spent either pursuing, seducing, or writing songs about women. As you know, to appease the Church I agreed to give all that up and mend my ways. My only consolation is that the Christian heaven will turn out to be like the Moslems'—filled with beautiful houri."

There was much sympathetic laughter.

Then her father told about his troubles in Bordeaux, how his vassals in Angoulême resisted his authority, and the difficulties he had in getting his rents collected all over the duchy.

Tonight, decorated with lady slipper and blue larkspur, strewn with fresh green rushes, the hall looked particularly festive. The ladies sparkled in gaily colored gowns, trailing long sleeves; gold ornaments glittered on their breasts. Jugglers tossed silvery balls into the air; acrobats turned handsprings; jongleurs sang Duke William's songs about lovely domna who bestowed their favors upon worthy knights.

But Eleanor, sitting at the high table, was miserable. In order to make herself more presentable, she had bathed again in a wooden tub of hot water, found a reasonably clean gown of buttercup yellow, and plaited her hair with a silken gold riband.

Her grandfather held up his hand. The singing came to a stop, the entertainers moved back from the center of the hall.

Duke William began to strum his lute. A visiting troubadour from Moorish Spain danced into the center of the hall and accompanied her grandfather by snapping his castanets in time to the music. The air was blue with smoke and thick with the scent of roast game; dogs scavenged for bones under the trestle tables; pages dashed up and down the hall, refilling goblets of wine, carrying smoking slices of meat.

Overcome by a sudden impulse she could never after explain

even to herself, Eleanor jumped up on the wooden bench and climbed onto the long, white-clothed table. She started tapping her feet to the rhythmic sounds. For a moment there was silence; she could see every head turn toward her, catch the looks of amusement and incredulity. Her heart leapt like a doe in flight, and for an instant she thought of scrambling back onto the safety of her seat. But her gaze collided with that of her astonished grandfather, his hand briefly paused on the lute strings before continuing to play, then moved on to meet her father's dumbfounded blue stare. Both men looked as if they had never seen her before.

Slowly Eleanor raised the skirts of her gown, higher and higher up her yellow-stockinged legs, until her knees then her skinny thighs were revealed. She twirled and dipped, stepping over and around the silver salt cellars, platters of game, roast fowl, and baked fish, the silver bowls of ripe peaches, nuts, and sweetmeats.

"Hola! Hola! That's my girl." Her grandfather shouted his encouragement. A look of pure delight crossed his face, and for an instant she glimpsed the golden rogue of legend. "Look at Nell, my friends, the *gai saber* runs in her blood! Here is a true daughter of Aquitaine!" He rose to his feet with a flourish, quickening the tempo; the castanets followed.

The *gai saber*—the joyous art of the troubadours—ran in her blood! Duke William had given her the highest compliment he could bestow. Eleanor's father began to clap his hands, and soon the entire hall was laughing, applauding her, crying out their admiration.

"Disgraceful," Eleanor heard Aunt Agnes grumble over the din. "Flaunting herself like a strumpet."

Eleanor, vibrant, joyous, filled with an intoxicating sense of power, did not care. At last, at last she was the center of everyone's attention.

When the music stopped her father looked up at her. "Splendid, splendid. I had no idea, my girl! How old are you now?"

"Eight."

"How time passes! I've been neglecting you, Nell. We must spend more time together."

"As Dangereuse was just reminding me, until you marry again and have a son, Nell is your heir, William, don't forget that," said her grandfather. "She may as well start learning what it means to inherit Aquitaine"

"Oh yes. I want to be the heir, Father. Please, please, please don't marry again." She climbed down into his lap, twined her arms around him, and nuzzled his neck.

There was more laughter. Duke William took one of Eleanor's hands and kissed the tips of her fingers. "Now there's a temptress for you, eh? Who can resist? Speaking of temptresses, that reminds me, did I ever tell you about the time I met these two randy sisters . . ." He was off again on one of his stories.

For the rest of the evening Eleanor remained on her father's lap, cradled within the warm circle of his arms, so full of happiness she did not think she could contain herself. What her grandmother had said was true: In order to get what you wanted, it was necessary to take matters into your own hands.

From that moment on her life changed. Aunt Agnes left Poitiers without her, predicting dire consequences for Eleanor's future. Eleanor returned to Fontevrault but whenever she came home she was always the center of attention, petted and spoiled by her father and grandfather, who taught her to play the lute and sing a few of his songs.

Her grandmother died a year later when Eleanor was nine. Duke William followed her within six months. Eleanor's father became Duke William X of Aquitaine. There had been several half-hearted attempts on her father's part to find a suitable wife, but for one reason or another nothing had come of his efforts—thus far. People shook their heads and said it was the will of God.

When she was ten the new duke took Eleanor with him on a progression through his duchy.

"All the vassals of Aquitaine must now pay homage to me as their overlord, just as I myself will have to pay homage to the king of France, God curse him," he told Eleanor. "I want you to see for yourself what is involved."

Followed by the usual retinue of scribes, clerks, scullions, cooks, troubadours, and knights, she rode on her father's horse in front of the saddle, at the head of the long column. After trotting through the forests of Poitou, they visited the armoury at Blaye, then the Abbey of Saintes where Aunt Agnes, now widowed, had become a nun.

She had lost none of her sourness. "This child should be home learning needlework and how to make simples, not making progresses through the duchy. You will rue the day, Brother."

Fortunately, her father paid no attention to his tiresome sister and they continued their journey. In village after village she watched him collect his rents in the form of pigs, chickens, sacks of flour.

At the grape harvest in Cognac, Eleanor treaded the grapes with the villagers, while her father supervised the loading of casks from last year's harvest onto the carts.

"Come back next year, little duchess," the people called out when she left, doffing their caps to her. "Now you are one of us."

"Little duchess," she repeated to herself, cherishing the words.

Next they visited the purple hills of the Limousin, where Eleanor met the quarrelsome barons she had heard so much about, watched her father renew their oaths of loyalty, and judge a case between two petty lords over water rights. When she sang a few of her grandfather's songs for these fierce nobles, they cheered her.

"You have the great gift the Troubadour had," her father said as they turned southwest toward the capital, Bordeaux. "You know how to win over your subjects."

Eleanor was not sure what gift he meant, but she noted that her father's quick temper and sometimes rash behavior did not endear him to his vassals.

By September they returned to Poitou. They stopped first at the fishing village of Talmont, perched on a rocky headland that overlooked the sea, where her grandfather had kept his falcons. Here she listened to her father talk to fishermen about boats and nets and how large a catch might be expected that season.

"You see how varied each part of our duchy is," he said, lifting her down from his horse. "And you have not yet seen half of Aquitaine. From Poitou to the Pyrenees, the people are all vastly different."

Taking her hand he led her to the edge of the cliff. It was very hot, the sky a bowl of burning blue. Not a breath of wind stirred the air. The duke turned away from the gently lapping waters that washed the red rock and pointed to the far-off hills melting into a silver horizon.

"The dukes of Aquitaine have ruled here since time out of mind, Nell. And we will go on ruling as long as we keep ourselves from being swallowed up by greedy overlords like the king of France, and hold our unruly vassals in check. We belong to ourselves and always have. This land is in our blood and we can never be free of it."

Duke William bent down and picked up a piece of rust-colored rock lying on the cliff's edge. It shimmered like a gem in the sun.

"On this very cliff where we now stand, the Romans founded a village; the Goths forged weapons from the flint rock; the Arabs rode their stallions to the cliff edge." He solemnly pressed the rock into her hand. "This is the most affluent fief in all Europe, a sacred trust passed on from generation to generation. I intend to marry again and have a son. But through some extraordinary stroke of fate, should this priceless jewel become yours, heed my words, and guard our heritage well."

A male heir. Eleanor had hoped that if she loved her father enough, she might somehow avert that dark cloud hanging over her life.

It could not, it must not happen.

Thus far Our Lady—and other spirits perhaps—seemed to be answering her prayers.

From the moment she made the decision to dance on the table, felt the surge of power crest like a rolling wave within her, Eleanor had known in the very marrow of her bones that her destiny and Aquitaine's were bound together for all time. She must protect it, love it, die for it even, whether she would or no.

# Part One

*Aquitaine, abounding in riches of every kind.*

—Ralph of Diceto

*The Poitevins are full of life, able as soldiers,*
*brave, nimble in the chase, elegant in dress,*
*handsome, sprightly of mind, liberal, hospitable.*

—Twelfth-century *Pilgrim's Guide*

*With the sweet coming of the spring*
*When woods turn green and birds do sing,*
*Each one in his special tongue,*
*The verses of his newest song,*
*'Tis fitting that each man should seek*
*That which his heart does most desire.*

—William IX, Duke of Aquitaine,
VII Count of Poitou:
The First Troubadour

# CHAPTER 1

# Bordeaux, Aquitaine, June, 1137

*E*leanor was suddenly awakened from sleep by the sound of horses' hooves ringing against the tiles of the courtyard. Riders arriving at Bordeaux in the dead of night, long after the city gates were closed, usually heralded ominous news: an uprising somewhere in Aquitaine, a sudden death—unless—perhaps her father had returned from his pilgrimage to St. James of Compostela in Spain!

Slipping naked from the bed she shared with her younger sister, Petronilla, Eleanor ran lightly across the carpeted floor to the narrow window of the turret chamber and pushed it open. The scent of honeysuckle and night-blooming jasmine rose on the June air, heady, almost overpowering. A pale shaft of moonlight crept over the buttressed walls of Ombrière Palace, illuminating the squat tower that housed Eleanor's quarters, and outlining the riders below.

Two dark figures dismounted, ringed immediately by a score of grooms and palace guards.

"Wake the Duchess Eleanor and the archbishop," called a familiar voice which Eleanor recognized as belonging to Conon, her father's equerry.

This was followed by the sound of booted feet thundering across the courtyard.

"Where is Duke William?" A guard's voice echoed the question in Eleanor's mind.

The reply was inaudible as riders, grooms, and guards vanished from view. Eleanor's heart jumped. Where *was* her father? She waited a moment longer to see if more riders would appear. The courtyard remained deserted, ghostly under flowing black clouds that now obscured the moon.

Eleanor turned from the window then stopped short. For a moment she felt her heart freeze, the breath catch in her throat. *Duchess* Eleanor? Had Conon actually said that? Holy Mother—she clapped a hand over her mouth, swallowing a scream. No. She must have imagined it. Barely awake, her wits were still dulled with sleep.

But something was afoot. In her mind she heard her dead mother's soft, sweet voice cautioning her against unseemly curiosity, the tendency to meddle where she might not be wanted. Most unmaidenly behavior for the eldest daughter of the House of Aquitaine. "But this matter—whatever it is—concerns me," Eleanor whispered under her breath. "I know that it does. Please understand."

Careful not to wake her sleeping sister, she ran across the faded Syrian rug her grandfather had brought back from his crusade to the Holy Land, snatched the first thing she saw—an ivory gown that lay crumpled on the floor—and hurriedly pulled it over her head. A candle end still sputtered. Trying to ignore the apprehensive ache in her breast, Eleanor picked up the silver holder, glided past the sleeping bodies of her attendant women, and slipped out the door of the chamber.

Her bare feet made no sound against the cool stone as she flew along the passage, spun down the winding staircase, and slowed to a halt before the open doors of the great hall. Yawning servitors were just lighting torches in their iron sconces. The flames cast flickering shadows over the stacked trestle tables and wooden benches, lending an eerie glow to the scenes of falconry and hunting depicted on the heavy tapestries covering the stone walls.

Torchlight illuminated the rotund body and tonsured head of the archbishop of Bordeaux, deep in conversation with the two equerries, Conon and Roland.

Her heart thumping, Eleanor blew out the candle then marched resolutely into the hall.

"Where is my father?" she asked in a tremulous voice.

The archbishop exchanged quick glances with the equerries. "My poor child—I was going to wake you but felt I should hear—good heavens, you are not dressed! Most unseemly. Go back to your chamber and clothe yourself properly."

Ignoring the archbishop, she steeled herself to ask again: "Please—where is he?"

"I bring sad tidings, Mistress." Conon faced her with bent head. "Duke William—may God give him rest—is dead of a fever."

Dead of a fever. Dead of a fever. Dead of a fever. The senseless words beat like a drum roll in her head; Eleanor could not take in their import. Impossible that that great affectionate giant of a man, bursting with life, should be suddenly extinguished like a candle flame. She wanted to run screaming to her bed, hide under the bed-clothes, and turn back these unforgiving moments; pretend she had never heard Conon's shattering words. But she was rooted in place, compelled to hear each last agonizing detail.

"Where?" she whispered.

"In Santiago, Spain. We buried him there not ten days ago then rode straight back to Aquitaine with the news. With his last breath the duke urged us to keep the matter secret."

Tears sprang to Eleanor's eyes. "His death secret? Why?" Her voice was barely audible.

"Why?" Conon paused in obvious surprise, exchanging another look with the archbishop. "Because of you, my lady, of course."

His words made no sense. "I don't understand."

"Once word of his death is spread abroad, my child," said the archbishop, "every greedy and ambitious lord in Europe will light upon the duchy like a flock of vultures. While those covetous vassals within Aquitaine's borders will converge upon Bordeaux like bees to nectar."

Eleanor looked from the archbishop to Conon to Roland.

"She doesn't understand, Your Grace," Roland said. "It's the shock."

The archbishop snapped his fingers. "Bring your new mistress a goblet of wine," he said when a servant appeared.

"I know this is a terrible tragedy, Eleanor, but you must pull your wits together. You are a great prize now. Many will want to marry you, by force if they cannot have you any other way. He who possesses you, possesses Aquitaine. You and the duchy are now in-separable."

The prelate's words cut through her anguish. Stunned, she took an involuntary step backward. When the servant offered her a goblet of wine she could barely hold it, downing it in shocked aquiescence.

"Now, my child, we will decide what to do when you are more appropriately dressed."

"What—what else did my father say, Conon?"

Conon withdrew a roll of sealed parchment from beneath his hauberk. "Duke William has charged us to deliver this message to King Louis of France without delay."

For an instant the hall and its occupants reeled. A message for her father's greatest enemy? Had the world suddenly gone mad?

When the walls and wooden beams of the ceiling had righted themselves, Eleanor saw that even the archbishop looked stunned.

"Do you know what this message contains?"

"Only too well, Your Grace," replied Conon, his voice laced with bitterness. " 'Eleanor will be your duchess now,' the duke said to me with his dying breath. 'She is barely fifteen years of age and my heart trembles for her safety. I must leave her and the duchy in someone's keeping until she marries. Louis of France is overlord of Aquitaine; he will find her a suitable husband.' Thus spoke the duke. This is what the message contains."

Conon stuffed the roll back inside his hauberk.

*"Benedicamus Dominum!"* The archbishop shook his head in disbelief as he crossed himself. "It is quite beyond my comprehension. I assume the poor man felt this was the only way to protect Aquitaine from the vultures. Desperate times require desperate measures." He crossed himself again. "Perhaps, at the hour of his death at least, the duke was graced with wisdom. After an unruly life, filled with acts of folly, this was God's blessing on him. Perhaps we are wrong to judge him. But France? Come, my sons, you must have a goblet of wine and some cold meat or you will never survive the journey to Paris."

He snapped his fingers and ordered a servant to bring some bread and cold meat for the equerries.

He pointed a finger at Eleanor. "Go now and do as I bid you."

Ever since the demise of both her brother and mother seven years earlier, Eleanor had known that with her father's death she would one day become duchess of Aquitaine and countess of Poitou—unless he married again, which he had not done. While she had wanted, one day in the far distant future, to become duchess of Aquitaine, she had never imagined that day would come so soon. Not when she was still so young, so—so untried. The thought of shouldering all her father's burdens filled her with terror.

When her mother had died Eleanor had mourned her loss, inconsolable without that gentle, self-effacing presence, admonishing but always loving. But then she still had her father, her grandfather, and grandmother to share her misery. Now she had no one but her younger sister, who always looked to Eleanor to nurture and comfort her.

For a moment she was robbed of all breath. How could she sustain this second loss? She felt so alone, so small, so unfit to bear the yoke of Aquitaine.

". . . what kind of husband will the king provide, I wonder," the archbishop was saying now. "It is such a risk."

Husband? The word and its implications cut through the engulfing fog of despair. A stranger in her bed? In her duchy? It was impossible that her father, in his rightful wits, would ever have placed her fate in the hands of a man he despised as much as the French king. Her family had never trusted their overlords any more than they trusted Holy Church. No. Despite all the warnings about vultures descending on her beloved Aquitaine, she did not want or need a husband. The thought was so hateful that Eleanor felt her whole body tremble. Outrage warred with grief.

"It must be a mistake, Conon," she said. "As His Grace pointed out, my father was desperate at the end, so concerned for my safety that this blinded him to what he was doing. I beg you, please do not carry this message to Louis of France."

The archbishop clucked like an old hen. "Not carry the message to France? My child, what can you be thinking of? The word of a dying man is sacred. Whatever our personal feelings, Conon must do as the duke ordered."

"His Grace is right, my lady. The duke was fully alert and quite clear on this point. It was an agonizing decision but he did it to protect Aquitaine—and you."

A servant refilled her goblet. She held it in both hands, clinging to it like a spar, then downed the wine again, almost choking on the bitter dregs. She had to do something. What could she say that would make them listen?

"I—" She took a deep breath. "I am—I am the duchess of Aquitaine now. Well, you said so yourself, didn't you?" She paused, desperately hunting for the right words. "I—yes, I—hereby order you not to go to France with this message. We will find another way to protect both the duchy and myself."

The two equerries and the archbishop stared at her as if she had two heads. Suppose they ignored her words? Refused to do her bidding? How had her father and grandfather before him summoned the power to make themselves obeyed?

"The child is young yet headstrong and frivolous, spoiled, as we all know. At this moment she is undone by grief," said the archbishop in a severe voice. "How can you heed her words? Do as the duke bade you, my good fellow."

"Conon, Roland—" Holy Mother, what could she say? What magic incantation could she call upon to sway their hearts? Body shaking, palms damp with her own sweat, Eleanor hesitated.

"For three hundred years my family, whose roots go back to Charlemagne and beyond, have ruled in Aquitaine. When I speak, it is not just my voice you hear, but the voice of all the dukes that have ever ruled this land."

She saw the equerries look at each other then at the archbishop. Eleanor felt herself sway with relief when she saw Conon and Roland drop down on one knee and bow their heads.

"As you will, my lady. I am your man," Conon said.

"And I," echoed Roland.

"By the Mass, I hope your vanity is satisfied, you foolish, selfish child," said the archbishop in an icy voice. "You have just abandoned Aquitaine and yourself to the first brigand who comes along with a show of force. This is your father's headstrong behavior all over again."

Her relief was short-lived. The prelate's words filled her with dread. Could he be right? Was Louis of France the wiser solution? A ray of dawn sunlight streamed through the open doors of the keep and into the hall accompanied by a brisk morning breeze. She shivered, aware now of her light gown, and how unsuitable she must look.

"Please wait," she said in a faint voice. "I will be right back."

She walked out of the hall with all the dignity she could muster. Before she dashed up the staircase she heard the archbishop's voice echo across the threshold.

". . . every inch her grandfather and father's child. Willful and concerned only with her own desires. I fear it is bred in the bone. The worm in the fair apple."

Inside the chamber her sister and the women were still sound asleep. Despite her need to seek solace in her younger sister's arms,

Eleanor could not bring herself to wake her: soon enough Petronilla would hear about their tragic loss.

She tip-toed across the Syrian rug to where a pole protruded from the wall next to an ornately carved chest. From the pole hung several tunics and gowns. Atop the chest rested an inlaid wooden box. Its lid gaped open revealing a tumble of gold and silver necklaces, jewel-studded brooches, and ornate rings. A flash of rust caught Eleanor's eye. Digging into the box, her fingers curled around the rust-colored stone her father had given her so long ago at the fishing village of Talmont, and which she had saved. She lifted it out, her father's words ringing in her ears ". . . this priceless jewel become yours. Guard our heritage well."

Eleanor passed a shaking hand over her forehead. Against all the odds, what she had always wanted had come to pass: Aquitaine was now hers. But for how long? Would King Louis, a greedy overlord and her father's enemy, try to swallow up the duchy himself if she defied him? If she followed her father's wishes, what kind of husband would the French king provide for her? Eleanor was wise enough to know she would have absolutely no say in the matter.

It might be a man old enough to be her grandfather, or a child of eight. The dreadful possibilities made her flesh crawl. Which was the greater evil? The devil one knew about or the devil one didn't know; the king of France or Aquitaine overrun by—what had the archbishop said?—brigands, unscrupulous vassals. Where could she turn? God? He would only tell her to follow the archbishop's advice. Stifling a sob, Eleanor sank to her knees beside the chest, closed her eyes, and asked her blood for guidance.

When she finally opened her eyes again, she knew what she had to do.

# France,

# 1137

*L*ouis the Fat, King of France, lay half-dozing as he attempted to fight off the virulent effects of a persistent flux of the bowels, his third such attack in less than a year. As Paris lay sweltering under an unseasonably hot June, he had been taken to a hunting lodge on the outskirts of the city where it was somewhat cooler. Here, in a crowded chamber, servitors vainly tried to swat away the dark swarm of flies clustered thickly on the oaken table and bed, on pewter pitchers of fetid wine, even on Louis's bloated body.

Through slitted eyes he could see one black-robed physician taking his pulse with the aid of a sand-glass, while another examined his urine, swirling it round and round in a silver basin. The stench of excrement and unwashed flesh hung over the chamber like a shroud.

His eyes closed and he was about to drift off into sleep when a voice startled him awake.

"Sire, I have important news. Couriers from Bordeaux have just now arrived to tell us that Duke William of Aquitaine has died in Santiago, Spain."

The voice belonged to Abbé Suger, his chief advisor. Louis forced his eyes open and tried to speak. Although his debilitating illness had not impaired his wits, sometimes he could not force his weakened body to obey the dictates of his reason.

"Give thanks to God and all His Saints," he finally croaked, even as his heart burned with a fierce joy. The most unruly, rebellious, and stubborn of his vassals was dead. "It is nothing less than a miracle."

A palsied hand made the sign of the cross while his mind leapt to embrace the full significance of the abbé's news. "If Duke William is dead then who—let me think—didn't the son die some years ago? So there is only the young daughter?"

"Eleanor. She inherits all of Aquitaine and Poitou. And that's not all," Abbé Suger said. "These couriers say that with his last breath the duke begged you, as overlord of Aquitaine, to find the daughter a suitable husband."

The King tried to raise himself then groaned, shaken by a spasm of pain. The physicians hurried forward.

"Sire, let us bleed you again—"

"Imbeciles, there's hardly any blood left in my body now."

One of the physicians held out a goblet. "Wine mixed with juice of poppy—"

"Will put me to sleep when I most urgently need to stay awake. Bring more servants to help me sit. I feel stronger. This news has done more for me than all your accursed potions and bleeding." He waved them away. "Go on."

"Naturally Duke William would have been concerned," Abbé Suger said. "As always, his lands seethe with unrest. And when his death becomes known—"

"I am not an idiot, Father," Louis interjected. "Why else would Duke William have entrusted the girl to my care? There was no love lost between us. He gave her to his overlord for one reason only: to protect the duchy from his own vassals and other lords hoping to make themselves wealthy by marrying the heiress of Aquitaine."

He licked bloodless lips. "So rich a prize must not be allowed to slip through our fingers." The king's eyes met the rheumy blue gaze of his advisor. "We must get there first." A sly chuckle escaped through rotting teeth. "A suitable husband, you say? Who could be more suitable than my son, Louis, heir to the throne?"

He managed to lift a swollen arm. Bloated fingers resembling thick white sausages grasped Abbé Suger's shoulder. "Think on it! Since time out of mind the rebellious dukes of Aquitaine have flouted the authority of king and Church. Now their troublesome reign has come to an end. Only a maid stands between the French crown and the most affluent fief in all Europe. A miracle!" He lay back, panting heavily; the speech had exhausted him.

A score of servitors arrived to hoist his massive bulk into a sitting position against the pillows. After he sipped some wine, Louis's color improved and his voice became stronger.

"My son and a huge force of knights should leave at once for Aquitaine. The wedding must be celebrated at Bordeaux as soon as he arrives. We dare not wait for the mourning period to be over. Where is the boy now?"

The abbé coughed. "In the cathedral, Sire."

"God's wounds, I need not have asked. The boy is still more oblate than future king." He pointed an accusing finger at Suger. "This is your doing, Father, now you must undo it. Accompany him to Bordeaux. Prepare him for marriage. Make a man of Louis."

The king knew the accusation was unfair. If the boy was not ready to become a husband—or a monarch for that matter—it was hardly the abbé's fault. Bred for the cloister not the crown, only the accidental death of his eldest brother had catapulted Louis from the monastery to heir to the kingdom of France.

Abbé Suger rose slowly to his feet, a frown creasing his forehead. After a moment's hesitation he spoke:

"There is the matter of consanguinity, Sire. You are aware Louis and Eleanor are related in the third degree? The marriage will need a dispensation from the pope himself, which may take—"

"I don't care if they are related in the first! I want Aquitaine and I want it now! Before someone else gets it. Haste is the main issue here. Stop putting obstacles in the way; you can supply the necessary dispensations. The primary thing is to get Louis wed." His eyes narrowed. "If you are fool enough to mention this—this unimportant fact of consanguinity, then it will become the scandal of Europe. Let sleeping hounds lie."

Abbé Suger, looking extremely uncomfortable, cleared his throat.

The King glared at his advisor. "May God give me patience, I can see by your face there is more to come. All right, what now? Get it out. Get it out."

"It concerns the young duchess."

Louis raised his brows. "The maid is deformed? Addled in her wits? Resembles a toad? Cursed with a harelip?"

"On the contrary, the maid is rumored to be too beautiful for her own good, unusually intelligent for one of her sex, and lettered as well." The abbé's disapproval was evident in every word he uttered. "It is also said that she is hot-headed, frivolous, and mettlesome, not amenable to control. You may recall that her mother died when she was a child. There was only that adulterous grandmother as a womanly influence, God save us." He signed himself.

"Worse than no influence at all."

"Exactly, Sire. The father and all his court have indulged her, allowing the child to run wild. She has been taught that Aquitaine is her trough and she may swill from it as she pleases." There was a meaningful pause. "Nor is she a dutiful daughter of Holy Church."

Louis shrugged impatiently. "Have you ever known an Aquitainian who was? The duchy is a hotbed of heresies—" His black brows suddenly came together in a single hirsute line. "By God's wounds, do you say she is unchaste?"

The abbé pursed his lips. "I have not *heard* that she is, only that the creature has stirred more than one heart to folly. However, with these southern women—" He shrugged. "What concerns me, Sire, is her moral character, the problems she may present in the future. Such an undisciplined influence might well have an evil effect upon our innocent Louis and, subsequently, on France itself."

Louis's eyes became hard black slits in his puffy face. "Are you suddenly grown deaf? How many times must I say it? With this marriage Aquitaine falls effortlessly into the royal power of France. So long as she is still virgin, nothing else matters. Do you understand that? Nothing, nothing, nothing!"

He glared at one of the guards by the door. "You, rout my son out of the cathedral. Tell him to make ready to leave at once for Bordeaux."

The guard hesitated. "Now, Sire?"

"No, next week, next month, next year! May God give me strength, I'm surrounded by imbeciles and fools! Oh never mind! Just do as I say."

He turned back to Abbé Suger, his breath coming in short gasps. "Do you tell me that—this daughter of Eve, member of an inferior sex, still hardly more than a child, is of any real concern to you? That between us we cannot tame this wild eaglet long before she becomes queen of France?" Suger turned red; Louis smiled. "Good. Now go."

When the abbé had bowed himself out of the chamber, Louis closed his eyes. The encounter had robbed him of his strength.

Still, the prospect of Aquitaine becoming a French possession was sure to breathe new life into his ailing body. Indeed, even now, he felt a frisson of anticipation pulse through his veins. Although he had made glib assurances to Suger, he had hidden his own disquiet, a disquiet related not only to a sense of his own mortality, but grave concern for his realm as well.

At his death—which he feared might come sooner rather than later—the old order of things would pass. It always happened in a new reign. Then what? If only he could look into the future. Heavenly Father, he prayed, do not let me die. Not yet. Not for a long time to come. With a shy, devout, inexperienced youth and a willful, tempestuous maid at the helm, what will happen to France?

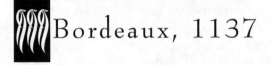

# Bordeaux, 1137

"My father only put Aquitaine in the French king's safekeeping and asked him to find me a suitable husband—in time," said Eleanor, her voice trembling with mingled anger and fear. "How can I agree to marry his son, or anyone else for that matter, when I'm still in mourning?"

Aghast at the news that the French prince was on his way to Bordeaux not six weeks after her father's death, Eleanor was still sitting in the straw-filled cart that had brought her from the small vineyard outside Bordeaux into the courtyard of Ombrière Palace.

"Such haste is unseemly, but God will understand," said the archbishop of Bordeaux in an agitated voice. "King Louis feels that he cannot properly protect Aquitaine unless you are closely allied to the Capet family. It is really a great honor he bestows upon you."

His nose wrinkled in reproof as he took in her skirts bunched up around her knees, purple grape juice dribbling down her chin, smeared across her mouth, and staining her bare legs.

"Although I doubt if the French king would be so eager to have you if he saw you like this. Still treading the grapes at your age! Disgraceful."

Eleanor ignored this. He had been criticizing her behavior as far back as she could remember, and she had never paid the slightest attention. "How can you call this enforced wedding an honor, Your Grace? Protect the duchy! The French king has always coveted Aquitaine for himself."

Grieving for her father, struggling to accustom herself to the overwhelming task of trying to replace the late duke, Eleanor had been treading the grapes with the other inhabitants of Bordeaux when the equerry Conon had appeared with the unwelcome news that Prince Louis had left Paris with an escort of five hundred knights. He was on his way to Bordeaux to marry her and she must return to the palace at once.

"Five hundred knights! Fat Louis of France does not give me much choice in the matter." She prayed she would not disgrace herself by suddenly bursting into tears. "Do my feelings, my grief, count for nothing in this matter?" A foolish question, as she already knew the answer.

The archbishop threw up his hands in a gesture of impatience. "*Your* feelings? We are all grieving. By God's wounds, what do one's feelings have to do with the matter?" He folded his arms across his black-robed chest. "What do you think it means to be a duchess? To do just as you please? Have everyone jump when you give an order? You have a vast inheritance in your keeping. To rule is also to serve, to bend to the will of others as needful."

Eleanor shot him a defiant glance. "I don't recall my father bending to the will of others." Except when he was forced into doing so, echoed a small voice in her head.

"Naturally not," the archbishop said in a dry tone. "That was one of the reasons he was an incompetent duke. Of course he was forced to—well, no need to go into that now. In any case he is not an example to follow, my child. Your grandfather, on the other hand, however disgraceful his personal morals may have been, knew how to yield with grace when the occasion demanded." He paused. "Or so he was able to make others believe. A great gift."

Eleanor felt a lump rise in her throat. Her charming Troubadour grandfather. Who would rather have conquered women than enemies. Hadn't her father once said she possessed her grandfather's gift?

"We waste time. There is much to discuss." The archbishop gestured imperiously at the driver. "Take this cart back to the vineyards."

When the cart didn't move, he frowned. "Well, go on, boy, go on. Did you not hear me?"

The boy driving the cart looked questioningly at Eleanor. An unexpected glow of triumph spread through her, warming the chill in the pit of her belly, giving her a surge of courage. She gave a tiny shake of her head.

The equerry, Conon, spoke for the first time.

"Now that word of your father's death is no longer secret, Lady, the French king is anxious to move quickly and I, for one, thank God for his haste, no matter how unseemly." He glanced at the archbishop. "We didn't want to alarm you, but there are rumors of an uprising in the Limousin, and indications that your vassals there intend to march on Bordeaux, take you captive, then marry you by force." He signed himself. "In truth, you *don't* have much choice in this matter."

"You should have told me." The surge of courage diminished. Bile rose in her throat.

The barons of the Limousin! Her childhood had been haunted by their continual unrest.

"But I do have a choice," she said bitterly. "Rape, and then a forced marriage by my own vassal, or an enforced marriage to the French prince, and then a rape blessed by Holy Church. I feel just like Queen Radegonde must have felt with the Franks pursuing her."

"I would hardly call you a candidate for canonization, my child," said the archbishop.

Six centuries earlier, this learned queen had fled the kingdom of the Franks and her brutal husband. She was later consecrated as a nun and founded the Convent of Ste.-Croix in Poitiers. St. Radegonde, now a patron saint of Poitiers, was one of Eleanor's favorite heroines.

If only she too could run away. Tears spurted to her eyes and to avoid shaming herself, Eleanor jumped down from the cart and walked a few steps away. Across the river, in the far distance, she watched the line of dark blue hills melt into the blazing sapphire hue of the sky. Closer to view were the purple vineyards she had just left, a winding river, and a herd of cows placidly grazing in a nearby field. In truth, she was just like St. Radegonde. A martyr to—behind her she heard a discreet cough.

"If I may interrupt your reflections, Lady?"

She brushed away the tears and turned. "Well?"

"There is another aspect of this business that has not been mentioned," said Conon. "The most important part." He paused. "One day you will be queen of France."

"I?" She could not grasp the meaning of his words.

"Yes, Lady, who else? No one, not even the great Troubadour himself, would have dared aim so high." With his usual dramatic flair Conon flung himself down on one knee. "On that auspicious day, on that most glorious occasion, every one of your loyal vassals—I among them—will sleep sounder in his bed knowing that Duchess Eleanor—*Queen* Eleanor—rules in Paris."

Queen? The thought took her breath away. It was impossible to imagine. Until this moment she had not realized the full implications . . . Queen Eleanor! She silently repeated the title to herself.

She felt Conon's and the archbishop's steady gaze. After a long pause she asked, "How old is this French prince and what does he look like?"

The archbishop let out a long sigh and signed himself.

"Sixteen. A year older than yourself. Of pleasing appearance, they say, isn't that so, Conon?"

"It is as His Grace says, Lady. The prince is indeed pleasing. Though, in truth, 'pleasing,' does him scant justice. Comely is more apt. Did I say comely?" Conon closed his eyes and staggered back a few steps. "Mere words fall far short . . . Never have I seen a youth so fair. His beauty is beyond—"

"Yes, yes. But what does he look like?"

"Blue-eyed, with silver gilt hair like all the Capets. Pleasant and modest as befits a youth fresh out of the cloister."

Conon thought for a moment. "Also malleable, was my impression. Quite docile in fact." He gave her a significant glance.

Malleable. Of all that had been said, that word leapt out at her. Conon understood her dilemma far better than the archbishop. A malleable husband would not attempt to interfere too strongly with Aquitaine; a malleable husband would not try to control or overpower her. As Queen of France she would be able to protect her domains.

And the prince must be pleasing to look upon. Conon might well exaggerate but he would never tell her an outright lie. An image of a knightly figure, dashing and debonair, rose before her. The Limousin barons, she recalled with distaste, were dark-visaged, portly, and smelled strongly of garlic.

"There will be a lot to do to prepare for the wedding before he arrives. When I come back we can decide on the guests." Eleanor jumped up on the back of the hay-filled cart. "All right, Jean, I am ready."

"By God's wounds, where are you going?" the archbishop called as the horse pulled the cart away.

"To help finish the grape harvest."

All the way back to the vineyards while the cart bounced over deep ruts in the road, Eleanor thought about her decision. Had she done the right thing? Not that she really had any other choice, but still . . . she could change what she did not like, as her grandmother had advised so long ago. What else had the canny old woman said? To get what you want you must take matters into your own hands. Until the death of her father six weeks earlier, Eleanor thought she had what she wanted: a life of merriment, frolic, and idle romance. Free from care and concern. One day, of course, to inherit the duchy; one day, an idyllic love and marriage with some appropriate suitor. But all that was now changed.

Her own hopes and desires must be subordinate to the welfare of Aquitaine now. The duchy had to be kept inviolate. Free from harm. Surely a queen of France would be able to accomplish that? As if in a dream, Eleanor remembered how desperately she had wanted Aquitaine, never imagining there might be a price to pay. In some dark corner of her mind she could hear Dangereuse laughing . . .

CHAPTER 3

"I think I see him." Petronilla was leaning precariously
out the window of the turret chamber in Ombrière Palace.

"See who?" Eleanor asked.

Indifferent to the excited voices of female attendants and relatives packing boxes, stuffing leather saddlebags with shoes, jeweled
headbands, and woolen stockings for the journey to Paris, Eleanor
sat on an embroidered stool, and looked into a hand-held silver mirror while a serving woman brushed out her long mane of curly
chestnut hair.

"You know perfectly well. The French prince, who else? Come
and look."

Eleanor, clad only in her oat-colored linen shift, did not stir. Now
that the dreaded moment was at hand she was reluctant to see the
heir to the French throne. Her sister's excitement only made matters worse. She stared disconsolately into the mirror. Large hazel
eyes, tilted at the corners and fringed by thick sooty lashes, stared
back at her from the soft oval of her face, their usual sparkle
dimmed. The full lips that one troubadour had compared to crushed
summer wildberries were turned down in a pout. Even her skin
lacked its characteristic amber glow. She let the mirror slip to the
floor.

"Nell! Do stop sulking and come look."

Eleanor sighed and got to her feet. The scent of musk oil in the
chamber was overpoweringly sweet, the disorder oppressive. Piles
of scarlet, emerald, and azure gowns and tunics, velvet cloaks, and
leather shoes were strewn over the wide bed and carved wooden

chest. Amid a profusion of brooches set with pearls and lapis lazuli, gold and silver chains tumbling out of ivory caskets, a bracelet studded with rubies stood out. It reminded her of huge drops of blood.

Steeling herself, Eleanor joined Petronilla at the window. Beneath a burning blue sky, the chivalry of France had converged on the east bank of the Garonne River that ran beside the old Roman wall confining the city of Bordeaux. Under the fluttering blue-and-gold banners of the fleur-de-lis were a seemingly unending host of knights, barons, heralds, squires, and standard-bearers.

Eleanor shielded her eyes from the morning sun. "Which one is Louis?"

"You see that group of men?"

While royal retainers pitched gaily colored pavilions in the meadow beyond the city, several figures had detached themselves from the horde and were now walking down to the river where a flotilla of boats waited to ferry them across.

"The sun strikes sparks from the head of one of them. It must be a crown."

Now Eleanor could see that in the center of the group was a tall slender youth in a black cloak with a gold circlet on his head. She caught a glimpse of fair hair, a blur of undistinguished features, although at this distance it was hard to tell exactly what he looked like. Could that really be the French prince? Her heart sank. The overall impression was so—so bland, so unlike the splendid golden cavalier that had filled her hopeful dreams.

"He reminds me of a large, harmless rabbit," she said to Petronilla, wrinkling her nose.

The women in the chamber tittered.

Petronilla, a brown-haired, green-eyed version of Eleanor with a full-breasted body that belied her thirteen years, looked solemn. "A rabbit in holy orders would be more apt. What kind of a husband will he make, I wonder?"

"Stop teasing, Petronilla," said Aunt Agnes, recently arrived from the abbey at Saintes. "Eleanor has made a most illustrious marriage. Pray to the Holy Mother that you are only half as fortunate."

"I intend to marry for love, Aunt." Petronilla stuck out her tongue when the aunt turned away.

"I never heard such nonsense." Aunt Agnes, an unlikely sister despite her black habit, swung round again, hands on her ample hips. "Marriage is a business contract and has little to do with romance.

Fief marries fief. Such are the realities of life, and sensible women do not imagine otherwise. You've been listening to too many of your grandfather's songs."

"But grandmother went with grandfather for love," Petronilla pointed out.

"Love! Love! The girls of today think only about carnal love!" Aunt Agnes scowled. "With all that nonsense about romance and dalliance you listen to, it's no wonder you both have such alarming ideas. When your mother died— may God rest her sainted soul—I told your father once if I told him a hundred times, William, you let these girls run wild. Speaking of that wicked grandmother, she never became duchess of Aquitaine, did she? In fact, she had no official standing at all, and was denied the respect and authority accorded a wife."

"She never seemed to mind. What was it she often said, Nell?" Petronilla put a hand over her lips as she tried to keep from laughing.

"Ah—let me see—a woman rules her world from between her legs?" Eleanor kept a straight face at the outraged look that crossed her aunt's face. In fact, it had not been her grandmother who said that but her grandfather, and for years she and Petronilla had tried to work out its meaning.

"Disgusting! You should have your mouths washed out with salt and vinegar!"

"A woman wields little authority in any event, Aunt," Petronilla continued. "It's Nell's husband, that rabbity prince, who will rule here in Aquitaine."

"Indeed he won't," said Eleanor. "Aquitaine is mine."

She looked beyond the walls of Bordeaux to the far horizon, a silver ribbon glinting in the morning sun. One day she would wear a crown—but it could never compare with being duchess of a land at least twice the size of France. A lump rose in her throat, and she was seized with an aching desire to stretch out her arms and hold the entire duchy in a fierce embrace.

"Aquitaine is mine," she repeated. "It will never belong to anyone else." And, to her surprise, she felt her spirits lift.

"I don't see how Nell could ever love the rabbit prince." Petronilla threw herself on the bed and lifted her arms above her head. "She will have to make a cuckold out of him in order to find any joy in life."

"Petronilla!" Aunt Agnes crossed herself. "What a wicked,

shameful thing to say. Ask the Holy Mother's forgiveness."

Eleanor left the window, flung herself on Petronilla, and began to pull the thick plaits of her hair. "Of course I won't put horns on the poor prince. Not unless he's membered like a rabbit too." She held up her thumb.

Giggling, she collapsed on top of her sister and soon the two of them were rolling on the bed choking with laughter. The other ladies joined in the mirth. Even Aunt Agnes could not repress a salty chuckle.

"Well, really, it does not do to take them too seriously," she said. "After all, they're just children."

When Eleanor was presented to the young prince in the great hall of the palace that same afternoon, she could hardly keep a straight face. Unfashionably clad in a dark blue tunic with a silver cross hanging from his neck, Louis was tall and broad of shoulder, with fair hair, a pointed beard, and docile blue eyes. Upon closer inspection his slight overbite did, unfortunately, confirm her impression of a startled hare. It was obvious he was instantly enraptured, could hardly take his eyes off her, which was gratifying—although she had come to take such attentions for granted.

A Benedictine cleric of middle years, frail-looking and thin, with a watchful expression on his sallow face, stood protectively next to the prince. This must be the famed Abbé Suger, advisor to King Louis the Fat, and a prelate of enormous influence. Eleanor had heard that he was the one who wielded the true power in France.

He was clearly less impressed with her than was Louis. Hazy bluish eyes narrowed as the abbé took in the scarlet and gold-embroidered gown with its long sleeves trailing the rushes, the tight bodice that clung to her slender body, outlining her uptilted breasts and narrow waist. Even the sparkling jewels around her throat and wrists, the narrow gold fillet set with seed pearls that held in place the cascade of chestnut hair flowing down her back, seemed to give him offense.

"I'm delighted to meet you at last." Eleanor forced herself to smile at Louis as if she had waited for this moment her entire life. Whatever her feelings, Aquitainian hospitality must always be observed. "There's a lovely feast prepared in your honor and the finest troubadours and jongleurs have come from all over the duchy to entertain us."

Louis blushed, then turned to Abbé Suger, who shook his head. "Prince Louis should really fast today. He has had a long journey, fraught with danger, and has not attended a proper Mass for two days. A day spent in prayer will do him good. Tomorrow will be time enough to start the marriage celebrations."

"But the feast is part of the prenuptial ceremonies." Eleanor's dark eyebrows met in a frown. "All my vassals and relatives, not to mention the guests, will be most offended if their new duke-to-be is not present."

"Louis is an unworldly son of Holy Church," Abbé Sugar said with a fond glance at the prince. "He knows little of feasts and entertainment, as befits one raised in a cloister."

"If he is to become duke of my duchy would it not be politic for him to familiarize himself with Aquitainian mores?" Eleanor asked, keeping her voice gentle. If at all possible, she was determined to behave like her diplomatic grandfather rather than her irascible father. "As Duchess of Aquitaine I would be grateful if he would attend."

"Perhaps, Father, it would be best if I followed the customs," Louis said softly. "After all, we are guests in this land, and it would not do to give offense."

So he had a tongue! Eleanor smiled. She held out a graceful hand, the fingers sparkling with rings. After a moment's hesitation Louis took it carefully in his sweaty palm, as if it were a precious relic that might break in two. Abbé Suger bowed, and stepped back, but not before she had seen a flash of enmity in his eyes.

"Was the journey truly 'fraught with danger?' " she asked in a whisper half-meant to be heard.

"Perhaps that is an exaggeration. There was some grumbling among the peasants and burghers in a few of the French towns. You see, my father had levied a special tax to finance the marriage."

"You forget our reception in Limoges, my son," said the abbé, his eyes on Eleanor. "There were several outbreaks of violence, quickly suppressed by our troops. Not everyone in your duchy, Mistress, is pleased by this alliance with France. In my opinion, it is only the presence of our army that prevents the lawless vassals of Aquitaine from open rebellion."

Sweet St. Radegonde, the old man had ears like a fox. Still, what he said was probably true. Aquitaine was no more pleased at having a French duke than she was. She supposed she should be grateful that the Limousin barons had been suppressed, but in fact she was irritated by the Franks' interference in her affairs. She would have to make that very clear to Louis—at the propitious moment.

Eleanor watched Louis glance from Abbé Suger to herself, thrown off balance by the antagonism he sensed between them. It was not an auspicious beginning, but she had no intention of letting the abbé rule her future husband's life—nor hers—not if she had anything to say about it. Instinct told her that if she were to protect Aquitaine, Louis must be weaned away from the influence of this overbearing cleric.

With Louis seated next to her at the feast, Eleanor presided over the white-clothed high table set with the finest gold salt cellars and jewel-encrusted silver goblets her grandfather had brought back from the crusade. The great hall of Ombrière Palace was hung with huge silken tapestries depicting scenes of love and dalliance in forest glades, and decorated with freshly picked summer flowers and newly spread green rushes. It was also overflowing with guests from Aquitaine, Champagne, Blois, and Anjou, even as far away as Spain. There was hardly room between the trestle tables for the servitors and pages to trot back and forth between the hall and kitchens.

"There must be well over six hundred people here, perhaps a thousand if you include those outside the palace." Eleanor heaped Louis's trencher with mullet, lobster fried in egg, rice cooked with almond milk and cinnamon, morsels of roasted peacock, cranes, geese, and slices of pork, hot from the turnspit.

She watched Louis pick at his food, nibbling cautiously at a bite of pork and barely tasting the ruby-colored wine from her very own province of Gascony. "Aren't you hungry?"

Given the enormous appetites of her grandfather and father, she found this unmanly behavior far from reassuring. Down the table she caught sight of Petronilla stuffing lobster into her mouth to keep from laughing, her eyes signaling What-did-I-tell-you? Eleanor made a face at her then looked around the hall, warmly nodding at relatives and smiling at a vassal-lord from the Quercy, waving at another from the Perigord—all of them known to her since childhood.

Unexpectedly she met the cornflower blue gaze of a stranger

seated at the far end of the table. He was extraordinarily handsome, with red-gold hair and fair skin. Also sumptuously dressed in
a green-and-blue tunic, gold-embroidered mantle, and blue cap,
from which protruded a sprig of yellow broom. He raised his jeweled goblet to her with a disarming smile. Her pulse quickened and
she smiled back. It was then she noticed that he seemed to be holding something in his lap. A dog, perhaps? She could not see clearly.

She leaned toward the archbishop of Bordeaux, who sat on her
right. "Who is that lord with the broom in his cap?"

"Count Geoffrey of Anjou. You will recall that shortly before
your father—may he rest in peace—went on pilgrimage to Spain, he
joined the count in his initial effort to reclaim his wife's duchy of
Normandy from Stephen of Blois."

"Yes, I remember." So this was the man referred to as Count Geoffrey le Bel. Anjou was her nearest neighbor to the north; its borders marched with that of Poitou. "Surely Normandy is not yet
won?"

"Not yet. But a slight wound in the count's foot forced a temporary return to Angers. It is a great honor that he came all the way to
Bordeaux to pay his respects."

Eleanor was about to turn her attention to her other guests when
a loud scream brought her eyes back to the count. What she had
thought was a dog turned out to be a little boy of about four years
of age with reddish hair and an angry scowl. Count Geoffrey, obviously discomfited, was talking rapidly into the child's ear. As
Eleanor watched, the boy shook his head vigorously, screwed up his
eyes, and screamed again with such violence that his plump little
face turned purple.

The count, his own face now bright red, stood up and slung the
child over his shoulder like a sack of flour. As he limped past
Eleanor, the boy's blazing gray eyes met hers. Unexpectedly he
grinned. Eleanor grinned back, then blew him a kiss; absurdly, she
felt a conspiratorial bond had formed between them. The cunning
little rascal had contrived the entire episode. His dramatic exit, followed by sympathetic laughter, had gotten everyone's attention. It
was exactly the same way she might have behaved at that age.

The archbishop lifted up his head and sniffed. "Trust the lively
young sprig of the House of Anjou to create a stir," he said. "I hear
the young Henry is headstrong and self-willed, just like his Norman

mother, and after that exhibition I can well believe it. I shudder to think what he will be like when grown."

"A force to be reckoned with, I imagine," Eleanor said.

By the time the fruits, figs, and berries had been served, the silver pitchers of red and white wine emptied, the men had loosened their belt buckles and slipped off their fur-lined surcoats. The women drowsed. Even the dogs, stuffed with scraps, lay panting under the tables in the July heat. The steward blew a silver horn, servitors cleared the center of the hall. Several troubadours entered the hall and began to play their instruments. As the sounds of viol, rebec, and pipe reverberated across the hall, many Aquitainian lords left their seats and began to perform rustic local dances.

After a time, the rhythm changed as the click of castanets struck a new sultry beat. Eleanor's blood responded and she rose from her place, threading her way past the tables toward the center of the hall. The Lord of Ventadour joined her, and accompanied by the enthausiastic clapping and singing of her vassals they danced the fandango, a lively new dance that had crossed the Pyrenees from Moorish Spain. Whirling, dipping, spinning, Eleanor felt the blood pound in her ears, the rhythm of the music drumming through her entire body. Everyone's attention was upon her; all eyes turned in her direction.

Flushed and breathless, she finally returned to the table. Abbé Suger's eyes almost popped from his head, while Louis was apparently struck dumb.

Eleanor sipped from her goblet of wine. "Do you have dancing and troubadours in France?"

"Prince Louis has never danced, naturally," the abbé said with a severe expression. "Nor does he listen to such—such bizarre sounds. Liturgical music, of course, is quite another matter."

"Can Louis not speak for himself?" Eleanor arched her eyebrows.

"As Father Abbé says, I'm unfamiliar with such pastimes, Your Grace."

"Oh please, Louis, do call me Eleanor. After all, we will soon be sharing the same bed."

Louis lowered his eyes and blushed to the roots of his hair. Abbé Sugar's look told her he thought the remark highly indelicate.

At that moment an expectant hush filled the hall as a troubadour strutted proudly into the center to kneel before Eleanor with an elaborate bow.

"We are most honored to have the great Cercamon attend our prenuptial feast," she said in a loud voice.

The troubadour tuned his lute and, in a melodic voice of piercing sweetness, began to sing a planh, or lament, for her father. Reminded again of her great loss, Eleanor felt tears prick her eyes. There was a respectful silence in the hall when he had finished, and more than one southern baron unashamedly wiped his eyes.

"What would our beloved duchess like to hear?" the troubadour called out.

Some demon took hold of her and before she could weigh the consequences said, "The canso of the infallible master first and then the two sisters."

There were loud guffaws, knowing looks, and expectant smiles from the Aquitainian nobles. Cercamon raised his brows, gave her a conspiratorial smile, and tilted his head to one side.

"I will now sing several cansos written by the First Troubadour, our very own, much beloved ninth duke of Aquitaine, whose colorful, adventurous life was, in truth, the measure of the man." He paused. "His cansos reflect a few of these—adventures."

"Forgive me but I'm not familiar with the life of your grandfather," Louis said in a respectful voice. "To what glorious deeds does the minstrel refer?"

Eleanor watched Cercamon pluck a few strings. "He reminds us that the duke devoted most of his time to either pursuing, seducing, or writing songs about women. He thought of love as a game, you see, like chess, between two equal partners."

Louis wore an expression of complete bafflement. Abbé Suger made a hissing sound, reminding Eleanor of a snake she had once trod on. Her mother would have considered what she had just done quite wicked; her grandfather would have highly approved. Sometimes she felt torn between these two influences, but the older she grew, the more her grandfather's blood seemed to prevail. If she could have called back her thoughtless words she would have done so, but Cercamon had already started.

*I am called the 'infallible master'*
*for there is no woman who, after a night*

*with me, will not want me back the next day;*
*and, I may say, I am so knowledgeable*
*on this subject*
*that I could easily earn my living thereby*
*in any marketplace.*

There was a roar of approving Aquitainian laughter. The French contingent looked decidedly uncomfortable, and Louis was so pale Eleanor feared he might swoon. Abbé Suger's mouth had fallen open in horror.

Cercamon continued his recital with the familiar ballad of how Duke William took two licentious sisters to bed for eight days. The hall rocked with bawdy mirth and gusty shouts of encouragement.

Cercamon next sang a canso he had composed, he said, in honor of their glorious duchess. Her skin, kissed by the warm sun of Aquitaine, resembled the flesh of a ripe peach. Her luminous eyes sparkled like the waters of the Garonne; her hair was luxuriant as the flowering chestnut, her lips as soft as the petals of the rose, her body as supple and slender as a young willow, her breasts as firm and round as apples of ivory. But, alas, he could only worship her from afar.

Thank the Holy Mother he had added that. The troubadour's words could not help but remind Eleanor that Cercamon knew whereof he spoke. Six months ago she had allowed the slender, curly-haired minstrel to kiss her briefly and fondle her breasts before she laughingly pulled away when his eyes became glazed with lust.

While the Aquitainians continued to stomp the floor in appreciation, the French were obviously discomfitted. Louis's eyes were closed and he seemed to be praying. When Abbé Suger's outraged gaze met hers, Eleanor knew she had made a serious enemy. Had she allowed Cercamon to go too far? Probably so. On the other hand, these people must take her as she was.

What a curious race were these cold, bearded Franks, virtually unkempt barbarians compared to the elegant, clean-shaven Aquitainians with their lavish dress, long curling locks, and insatiable capacity for enjoyment. Had the French forgotten how to laugh? Was all pleasure condemned as sin? An icy sliver of foreboding touched Eleanor's heart. Soon she must leave Aquitaine and a way of living she cherished. What sort of life could she make for herself among these alien northern strangers?

She glanced at the table where the elegant count of Anjou now sat without his son. Odd, but the one person with whom she had felt the most rapport was not Louis, her future husband, but the rebellious young Henry of Anjou.

# CHAPTER 4

"*I* can't do it," said Eleanor. "I won't do it."

Clad in shimmering white, a snowy veil upon her head, Eleanor stood in the center of the turret chamber surrounded by Petronilla, her women, and all the visiting female relatives. They stared at her as if she had gone mad—which in a way she had.

"All brides are fearful the day of the wedding," said Aunt Agnes in a brisk voice. "It's natural. In truth, if you were not fearful, I for one, would be gravely suspicious."

Eleanor sighed. "I'm not fearful. I simply know that I'll be miserable if I marry him."

"How many times must I tell you that no one marries for happiness!" Aunt Agnes turned to the other relatives. "This is the result of being brought up by men, especially my father—whose head was always in the clouds—and not exposed to a woman's influence, where the realities of life would have been taught her."

"Nell," said Petronilla in an anxious voice. "Everyone is waiting for you. It's too late to change your mind now. You must go through with the wedding."

"Happiness comes from serving your husband, bearing him children, and doing your duty as a wife and mother," another female relative said.

The chorus of agreement that followed reminded Eleanor of a group of clucking peahens.

She walked over to the bed, almost tripping on the long white train, and sat down. "No."

Aunt Agnes threw up her hands. "If I told her father once I told him a hundred times: the child has no mother to guide her; you impose no restraints. She will grow up to be willful and assertive, altogether unwomanly. But would he listen?"

Her mother. The familiar lonely ache spread through Eleanor's chest. Her mother would have understood, not forced her into a marriage every instinct she possessed warned her would be a disaster.

Aunt Agnes sat down beside her. "Listen to me, Niece." She lowered her voice. "Once you've provided an heir or two for France, no one will give you much thought. Then, between ourselves as married women, mind, you may please yourself and who's to know?"

Eleanor couldn't decide whether to laugh or cry. Why did women make such a public show of virtue but follow their own inclinations in secret, hiding behind a curtain of respectability? Men at least behaved with less deceit.

"People will always take notice of me, Aunt. I am Duchess in my own right, and one day I will be queen. I have no intention of, one, becoming a mere brood sow for the French dynasty, and two, letting Louis run affairs in my duchy while I sit idly by doing nothing."

"Doing nothing?" Aunt Agnes, along with all the female relatives in the chamber, looked at her with their mouths agape.

Finally, her aunt shook her head in disbelief. "Worse and worse. Of course you will be doing something. In truth you will be doing everything! Who do you think runs matters? Men? Of course not. Women! Why, without us every castle, fief, and manor in Aquitaine would fall apart tomorrow. Who do you think organizes the households, the servants, sees to the food, clothes, wounds, illness, the raising of children—"

"If the men are at war or on pilgrimage and we're besieged, who do you think prepares the boiling pitch, the hot oil—" interjected another relative.

"I even ensure that my lord's armor is kept oiled and polished, his arrows sharpened, and his bow strings taut—" said an elderly cousin.

There was another chorus of agreement.

Aunt Agnes sniffed. "Why should it be any different in France? You will do everything but, of course, your husband will hardly be aware of it. My dear departed lord—may God assoil him—never made a decision in his life—and never knew that he didn't. That is women's lot: you do the work but never receive the acknowledgment. Such is the way of the world."

Eleanor could not keep from laughing. "But that isn't sufficient for me. If I run my duchy I want everyone to know it. To take notice of me. I will not hide my light behind a husband's vanity."

"Humph. What say the old saws? 'Gentleness is better than haughtiness,' and 'No galling trial until one gets married.' Meanwhile, what will happen to Aquitaine? If you are not in Paris to keep an eye on the duchy, do you think Louis of France will? Or anyone else? What do you think it means to be a duchess? A life of singing, frivolity, and dalliance? Your subjects are depending on you to look after them, never forget that." She shook a warning finger in Eleanor's face. " 'If the head cannot bear the glory of the crown, better be without it.' "

Eleanor got up and walked to the turret window. Below, the courtyard was thronged with people, their upturned faces reminding her of daisies straining toward the sun. Someone caught a glimpse of her and pointed, shouting. Instantly she drew back. Forget? How could could she ever forget? In the end everything always came back to Aquitaine. Even the glory of the French crown.

She turned and straightened her veil with resigned fingers.

A short time later when she and Louis led the wedding procession through the cobbled streets of Bordeaux to the sound of bells pealing and horns blaring, it was all Eleanor could do to keep a smile on her face. Only her cheering subjects lining the streets prevented her from giving way to the misery and frustration welling up inside her. She barely noticed the housefronts proudly displaying gaily colored banners and wreaths of pink, white, and yellow flowers, hardly felt the warmth of the July morning, was indifferent to the blaze of blue sky and fragrant air.

She paid no attention to Louis, a silent shadow marching beside her, except to note that his clothes were appropriate for the occasion. He wore a white linen shirt, a purple pelison of cloth and silk trimmed with fur and embroidered in gold thread around the neck and sleeves, a deep purple tunic and mantle of the same color also edged in fur. A golden chaplet crowned his pale hair. The gems flashed brightly in the morning sunlight.

Inside the Cathedral of St. André, hundreds of white tapers had been lit; incense lay like a stifling fog; the sound of chanting monks was overpowering. Enclosed in a suffocating web of doubt and loneliness, Eleanor knelt before the archbishop of Bordeaux. Was her aunt right? Would she feel less miserable now, more accepting of her fate, even well-disposed toward Louis if her mother had lived to guide her? For the first time in years, her heart yearned for what might have been, for the reassurance and comfort she had once known—and might never know again.

The archbishop was frowning at her, she could delay no longer. In a faltering voice edged with misgivings Eleanor exchanged her vows with Louis who, taut with anxiety, fumbled his marriage lines and dropped the ring.

After the main part of the ceremony ended, the archbishop intoned the Te Deum and, when the choir had finished the prayer of thanksgiving, pronounced a special blessing over them.

"Let this woman be amiable as Rachel, wise as Rebecca, faithful as Sarah. Let her be sober through truth, venerable through modesty, and wise through the teaching of Heaven."

The ceremony dragged on. Finally the Agnus Dei was sung. Louis advanced to the altar and received the kiss of peace from the archbishop. Now he was supposed to turn and at the foot of the great crucifix embrace her, then transmit the kiss of peace. He gingerly put his arms around Eleanor's waist but forgot the kiss. There was a moment of stunned silence, but he had already released her before she could remind him.

After the ceremony they bent their heads to receive the golden diadems that gave them official status as duke and duchess of Aquitaine. When Eleanor looked at the timid Louis—his resemblance to a rabbit was even more pronounced today—and compared him to the handsome, impetuous giants that had been her father and grandfather, she knew she could never think of him as the real duke. In her mind *she* was both duke and duchess, the heroic savior of her duchy. After all, by marrying Louis, hadn't she saved her beloved Aquitaine from falling into the hands of her own unscrupulous vassals or greedy foreign nobles? The thought cheered her. It was done; she was now a princess of France and must make the best of it.

The wedding festivities were held at the Ombrière Palace. At Eleanor's order, the walls had been hung with red and green silks, and the floor strewn with roses and lilies picked fresh that morning. In the center of the high table a roast swan, dressed as if it were still alive, with gilt beak and silvered body, rested on a bed of green pastry marked with little banners.

According to custom Louis was handed a great silver goblet. His hands trembled as he drank, and in passing the goblet to Eleanor he spilled some. She looked down. The ruby-colored drops of wine looked like blood against the dazzling white of her gown. Like the omitted kiss of peace, it was a sinister omen.

They were only two hours into the feast when Abbé Suger, who had been absent, hurriedly approached the high table.

"I've just received word that there is unrest and fighting in the Limousin which could easily spread to Bordeaux," he said. "As I told you when we arrived, Madam, the barons there are displeased by this alliance with France, and the moment our troops left, trouble began. Although it means ending the festivities and postponing the wedding night celebrations, it would be best if we headed north to Poitou at once. I've already ordered our camp to be struck and the packhorses loaded."

"But there is no need to leave," Eleanor said, surprised at his sense of urgency. "The barons of the Limousin are always causing unrest."

In truth, there were uprisings, troublesome vassals, and skirmishes in the duchy almost all the time. It was a way of life in Aquitaine and no one took it very seriously. Besides, she looked forward to the wedding night. Despite all the indications to the contrary, should Louis somehow miraculously prove himself a satisfying lover there was some hope for their happiness. She clung to that remote possibility like a talisman.

"That's as may be," Abbé Suger said, "but I cannot take the chance of running into difficulties with your vassals. Suppose a major battle were to ensue in the middle of the wedding night ceremony?"

"Perhaps you're right," Eleanor said slowly. "If we can avoid bloodshed we should do so."

"*Benedicamus Dominum!* I'm glad to see you're not like your hot-tempered father—may God forgive him his sins—he rarely avoided bloodshed."

Eleanor bit back a hot rejoinder. "Unfortunately, my father's temper too often ruled his judgment. But I've learned from his mistakes. If diplomacy will serve, use it. Violence is only a last resort in my opinion."

Abbé Suger raised skeptical brows but let the matter drop. What Eleanor had not said was that it was quite in order for her father to put down a rebellion in his own lands, but she could not bear the thought of French knights spilling one drop of hot Aquitainian blood. Far better to postpone the consummation of the marriage.

On the journey north to Poitou, Eleanor slept as she always had with Petronilla, who confided to her that she had fallen passionately in love with the seneschal of France, Ralph of Vermondois.

"But he's three times your age, with grandchildren!"

"What does that matter? This is true love."

"Oh, you're always imagining yourself in love with someone, usually unsuitable," Eleanor said. She would have to keep an eye on her flighty sister.

On the second day of the journey they were overtaken by the count of Anjou and a small group of his knights near Angoulême. His son was perched on the saddle in front of him, and when Geoffrey reined his horse to a stop, young Henry clamored to get down. Eleanor pulled her roan mare to a halt and Louis was forced to do the same.

"How pleasant to see you again, my lord," said Eleanor, her heart quickening at sight of the handsome count. "Do you ride with us awhile."

Geoffrey smiled down at her. "There is nothing I would enjoy more, but I must return to Angers at once to prepare for another attack on Normandy."

"I understand. We will miss your company, won't we, Louis?"

To Eleanor's embarrassment Louis mumbled something inaudible and looked away. He seemed ill at ease, uncertain of how to conduct himself when others were present. She gave Geoffrey an apologetic smile which he returned with a sympathetic look.

"Come along, Henry," he called to his son, who had disappeared into the bushes along the side of the road.

Henry reappeared with a bunch of ivory lilies, wilting from the heat, clutched in his grubby fist. He trotted up to Eleanor and solemnly presented them to her, looking up into her face with wide gray eyes and a tentative smile.

"Why, how thoughtful!" Eleanor took the flowers, touched by the child's gesture. "Thank you, my lord." She smiled back, reconfirming the bond they had formed at the feast in Bordeaux.

Suddenly overcome by shyness the boy ran to his father, who hoisted him up onto the saddle.

"You've made another conquest, Lady," said Geoffrey with a laugh and a meaningful look.

He rode on ahead with his party. Little Henry, peering around his father, waved until he was lost in a cloud of dust.

"What a charmer is young Henry of Anjou," said Eleanor. "He will break many a heart when he grows to manhood."

Louis said nothing.

Five days later when the royal procession crossed into Poitou, Eleanor rode ahead with Louis, eager to show him the wondrous sights so familiar to her. If she could instill in him a love of her native land it would go a long way toward establishing cordial relations between them. Although Louis dutifully followed her lead, she had no idea what was going through his mind because he continued to remain virtually tongue-tied. Eleanor began to find his silent, retiring demeanor irritating.

He had no reaction to stately castles surmounting cropped hilltops, fortresses rising over stone-faced cliffs, green marshes or cool streams. The only time he showed any interest was when they visited the Abbey of St. Maixent.

On a balmy morning in early August, six days after they had left Bordeaux, they came in sight of the Clain River that encircled the ancient walled city of Poitiers, capital of Poitou. Streaks of white cloud stretched across a deep blue sky; a dazzle of sunlight illuminated the red roofs and spires of the town. From the Church of Notre Dame la Grande the bells rang for Sext. Eleanor's heart quickened with anticipation at the familiar sound.

"This is my favorite city in all Aquitaine," she told Louis.

She was tempted to stop at the bottom of the hill and visit the monastic church of Montierneuf where her grandfather lay buried, but thought better of it. The roistering, wenching Troubadour would have thoroughly disapproved of Louis.

She spurred her horse forward and rode to the top of the hill. The gates of the city were thrown open, and they made their way along narrow streets, squawking chickens, and squealing piglets scurrying out of the way. Men doffed their caps; women bobbed a curtsy and smiled their welcome. One plump woman ran out into the street with something in her arms. She bent her knee to Eleanor and handed her a square of lace neatly folded.

"Dame Marie, did you make this for me?" She took the lace in one hand. "How beautiful! I cannot thank you enough. How fare your children? Did little Jean recover from his ague?" She prodded Louis riding beside her. "Dame Marie is the finest lace-maker in Poitiers, Louis. Have you ever seen anything like this?"

"In Poitiers?" Dame Marie gave Eleanor a slightly affronted look. "In all of Poitou, Madam, at the very least."

Eleanor laughed. "Of course. Probably in all of Aquitaine, if truth be known."

Dame Marie beamed. Louis looked blank; what was the matter with him? Perhaps—was it possible he was dull-witted and people had kept it from her?

"Master Grimbold, how thoughtful of you. Has the pain eased in your leg since your fall last year?" she asked a tall man leaning on a cane who proudly presented her with two wheels of round white cheese. "Master Grimbold makes the tastiest cheeses in Poitiers— in all of Poitou. Don't they smell wonderful, Louis?"

An elderly white-haired man was the next to approach her. He slipped a newly made leather bridle into her arms, which were now so full of gifts that Eleanor called for a groom to help carry them.

"Old Raoul, how kind. Louis, have you ever seen more exquisite workmanship? Tell me, did your mare give birth to a filly or a colt?"

After she had received more gifts and exchanged a stream of pleasantries with the townsfolk, Eleanor waited until they were out of earshot before turning to Louis.

"Cat got your tongue? Why didn't you respond?"

"I—can't think what to say. Do you really know these simple people?" Louis's look of astonishment was almost comical. "To think you can actually remember their names." It was the very first question he had originated.

"Of course I know them. I traveled with my father all over the duchy year after year since I was ten, and never forget a face or a name. These are my subjects, after all, and Poitiers the city I know best. Did you never travel through France with your father?"

"I? Oh no, I rarely left Paris—or the cloister."

The cloister. She kept forgetting about the cloister. What kind of a king would he make, she wondered, if he knew neither his country nor his people?

"As you will officially become count of Poitou, it might behoove you to get to know these people," she said, not reassured by his look of dismay. "I will help you in every way I can," she added, impulsively reaching over to touch his hand.

They reached the town square, thronged with Poitevins who tossed flowers on the bridal couple and greeted their new countess with roars of welcome. To her delight Eleanor was lifted from her mare and carried upon the shoulders of her cheering subjects to the Maubergeonne Tower, part of the ancestral palace of the counts of Poitou.

She immediately dragged a bewildered Louis through the grounds to see her favorite haunts: the garden of fruit trees heavy with rosy pears and amber peaches; the stable of Arab stallions and the falcon mews. She even introduced him to Master André, her old tutor. Ignoring Louis's diffident reaction to everything, Eleanor arranged a feast, summoning the city's most renowned troubadours and jongleurs for the evening's entertainment. She was determined to bring this dull and retiring prince to life, whether he liked it or not.

After all, this *was* a rather special night: at long last the marriage was to be consummated.

# CHAPTER 5

# Poitiers,

# 1137

hat evening, at the high table in the great hall of the palace, Eleanor presented Louis with a gift.

"This exquisite goblet belonged to my father," she said in a little speech she had prepared. "He inherited it from his father, the Troubadour, who always claimed that it was the gift of a Moorish princess."

She held out the goblet. Carved out of a single piece of rock crystal mounted in jewel-set gold, it was one of her most prized possessions. Before Louis could accept the gift, Abbé Suger snatched it from her grasp as if it were a red-hot coal.

"I will take this—for safekeeping."

Before Eleanor could protest, her attention was diverted by the appearance of a huge pasty carried into the hall by the chief cook and two servitors. They laid it proudly on the table in front of Louis.

"Open it," Eleanor said, handing Louis her own knife.

He looked at the abbé, who nodded. An expectant murmur ran around the hall as Louis rose and tentatively poked a small hole in the pasty. The guests snickered.

"Is that the best you can do?" someone called. "I hope you fare better with Lady Eleanor."

There was a chorus of ribald laughter.

"Our Countess needs a man, remember," someone else shouted.

"Aye, the lusty blood of the Troubador runs in her veins."

The hall rocked with mirth. Louis, crimson with embarrassment, seemed unable to move. Taking pity on him, Eleanor took the knife from his hand and boldly slashed open the pasty. Scores of little birds fluttered out, flying wildly about the hall.

"That's it, that's the way. You'll show the French prince a thing or two, Lady." The entire hall applauded.

Eleanor smiled broadly and waved, then turned in expectation to the entrance doors where a handful of falconers waited, hawks on their wrists. At a nod from her they unhooded their birds. Within moments the feasters, shouting their delight and encouragement, scrambled from their seats, and tried to dodge the hawks who pounced upon their prey, bringing the little birds down in the middle of the trestle tables. The dogs began to bark and jumped up after the hawks. The hall was in an uproar what with mingled screams and laughter, blood and feathers scattered everywhere.

Louis grew so white, Eleanor feared he would be sick. Was the nobility of France so backward they did not have this form of entertainment? What *did* the Franks do except fight and pray?

Finally the wedding feast was over. Eleanor and Louis were solemnly led into the huge chamber that had been her father's and grandfather's before her, going all the way back three hundred years, she told him. The chamber was lit by fifty white candles in silver holders and hung with garlands of pink summer roses and pale blue forget-me-nots. The archbishop of Bordeaux blessed the nuptial bed and sprinkled holy water over the chamber to dispel any demons who might be lurking in the corners—for it was well known that such spawn of the devil were drawn to carnal acts.

After the traditional ceremony of putting the couple to bed had been completed, Eleanor's attendants, with much giggling, departed. Petronilla flashed her a knowing look and took her leave. Repressing a smile, Eleanor slipped out of her ermine-trimmed robe and settled herself in the wide crimson-canopied bed. To her surprise, Louis, still dressed in his robe, suddenly hopped out of bed and knelt on the white-and-gold cushion at the prie-dieu in a corner of the chamber—a prie-dieu Eleanor had last seen used by her late mother.

Be patient, Eleanor reminded herself, trying to ignore the silken caress of lilac-scented sheets against her skin. Make allowances for his upbringing. Don't rush matters.

But, like her forebears, the hot blood of Aquitaine ran in her veins, blood that could be traced in a direct line to Charlemagne,

she thought with pride. Exposed from the cradle to the varied plea-
sures of earthly love, particularly in the example of her wanton
grandparents, Eleanor had always looked forward to losing her
maidenhead.

From the moment she had danced on the tabletop as a child and
held everyone's attention, she had learned a valuable lesson about
the impact of feminine power. When she grew older there were
friends of her father's and others, like the troubadour Cercamon,
drawn to her alluring beauty like moths to candle flame. She knew
every male who saw her wanted to taste her ripe lips, hold her firm
high breasts in their hands, and press themselves against her taut
slender body. They reminded her of panting hounds, their tongues
hanging out, crawling on their bellies for approval. From the time
she discovered her power over men she enjoyed teasing them while
keeping herself aloof. In truth, their whimpering eagerness filled
her with scorn.

Only once had she herself come close to being scorched by Cu-
pid's fire.

Last winter a comely troubadour with bronzed skin from Moorish Spain had visited her father's court at Bordeaux, where he created a sensation with his deep caressing voice and the pulsating
rhythm of his castanets. His hot black eyes had raked her body with
such intensity that Eleanor felt as if he had undressed her. After entertaining the guests in the hall he had taken Eleanor outside and,
despite her struggles, masterfully kissed her on the lips in the
moonlit gardens surrounding the palace. Claiming that she was the
most beautiful creature he had ever set eyes on, he declared that he
would fall mortally ill if he could not possess her. Eleanor knew that
this was the very least compliment an accomplished troubadour
would pay any reasonably attractive female if he did not wish to be
accused of extreme discourtesy.

But, unlike the others, even Cercamon, he had been more per-
suasive, less reverent, and before she could stop him, he had forced
her lips to open under his. By the time he had succeeded in sliding
his hand up the silky skin of her thigh, his fingers just starting to
explore the mysteries of her sex, Eleanor, entranced, had no will to
stop him. She often wondered what might have happened if her sister had not discovered them—much to Eleanor's vexation. For days
afterward she would grow moist between her legs, remembering the
delicate touch of his seductive fingers.

The candles had begun to sputter before Louis finally left his de-
votions and returned to bed, jolting her out of her tantalizing rever-
ies. He looked pale and resigned, reminding her of a lamb going to
slaughter; before disrobing, he blew out all the candles, then
slipped into bed. Trembling, he curled up beside her. Her body,
warm and aroused, instantly grew chill. Sensing his terror she tried
to pity him but only succeeded in feeling repelled.

"I'm not fragile, Louis," she whispered. "There is no need to be
afraid." She forced herself to open her arms, gathering him up as if
he were a frightened puppy. "What ails you? Do you not find me desirable?" A foolish question, for already she could feel his member
hardening against her thigh.

"You're an angel of loveliness," he said in a strangled voice, instantly withdrawing from her embrace. "But Holy Church teaches
that for a man to desire his wife is as great a sin as adultery. I never
thought to be married—and—and—"

"In your heart you regard our bedding as an act of fornication
despite the fact we are married?"

Taking his silence for assent, Eleanor did not know what to say.
That a man should be mortified by his own virility, the instinctive
surge of his natural desires, was beyond her comprehension. This
must be the Church's doing, she thought bitterly. Such harsh and
unnatural doctrine had never taken hold here in the sensuous south,
and, in fact, was one of the many reasons why her forebears had so
consistently resisted the influence of zealous churchmen who railed
against sin.

When Louis still made no move to touch her, Eleanor finally took
his hand and laid it gently on her breast. He snatched away his fingers as if they had been scalded. Instead he kissed her with shy reverence on the cheek. Like a brother. For Eleanor, who longed to be
taken masterfully in passion, it was a gesture that made her flesh
crawl. What could she do?

"Surely even the Church wants an heir for France," she said. If
nothing else he would at least have dynastic impulses.

"Yes. That is true."

Thank the Holy Mother. Here, at last, was a chink in the armor
of his resistance. "Well, then, let us provide one. It is our duty."

Her words seemed to inspire him with courage. Screwing his eyes
shut, Louis clumsily mounted her in a kind of worshipful awe, cautiously poking about in all the wrong places. It might have been

amusing if it hadn't been so utterly disappointing. That he was finally able to enter her at all was a tribute to her knowledge of carnal matters. Upon encountering her maidenhead, however, Louis grew terrified and would have withdrawn if she had not gently encouraged him, biting her lips to keep from crying out in pain as his tentative thrusts finally deflowered her. Thankfully it was soon over.

"You're a Christian martyr to endure that ordeal. I pray the Holy Virgin make you fruitful."

So that we do not have to do this very often, she added to herself. Louis had not said the words but she heard them as clearly as if he had shouted them from the battlements. If this night's work was a foretaste of things to come, she could only agree.

Climbing out of bed, he pulled on his robe and again knelt at the prie-dieu. Her sense of disappointment deepened. Her father's prize stud stallion was more adroit than the heir to the French throne. She tried to stifle her resentful thoughts as she shifted uncomfortably in the bed. Perhaps in some way she was at fault? Eleanor had never experienced such a sense of failure before. Her lower parts felt sore and she could feel a trickle of moisture between her legs that she assumed was blood. At least there would be visible proof on the sheets that she had been a virgin on her wedding night, which vicious minds like her Aunt Agnes's had not expected to be the case. Not that Louis would have known the difference. With a sigh of regret she remembered the sensuous touch of the troubadour from Moorish Spain.

Bitterly disappointed, Eleanor cried herself to sleep, while Louis, oblivious, remained at the prie-dieu. When she woke in the morning he was still there, sound asleep on his knees.

In an effort to forget the dismal events of the previous night, Eleanor spent the next day planning a feverish round of merriment for the coming weeks: hawking and hunting parties, more feasting, dancing, and entertainment.

She was in the courtyard, showing Louis her prized white gyrfalcon, when a group of French nobles thundered into the courtyard of the palace. One of them jumped from his horse and knelt before Louis.

"My prince, it is with deep regret that I inform you that death has finally claimed the king of France."

"My father, dead?" Stricken, uncomprehending, Louis looked first at Abbé Suger then at Eleanor.

"My poor Louis, what a calamity," said the stunned prelate. Then, collecting himself, he carefully went down on one knee. "Your Majesty, may I express my condolences on our most grievous loss."

At that moment Eleanor knew that the last vestige of her carefree childhood had gone forever. Was it only three months ago that she had been the thoughtless, indulged daughter of the duke of Aquitaine? And now—the realization was overwhelming—now she was Queen of France.

# CHAPTER 6

# Paris, 1142

Shivering, Eleanor walked along the narrow chill passage so dimly lit she felt as though she existed in a world of perpetual twilight. Even after five years she still could not adjust to the inhospitable atmosphere and cold gray drizzle of France after the gracious warmth and sunlit vistas of Aquitaine.

Eleanor remembered her first shocked view of this ancient seat of the kings of France, unable to believe that the crumbling gray stone fortress, rusty tower gate, and fortified bridge Louis was pointing to with such pride was a royal castle, or that this tiny island in the Seine was the very heart of the French kingdom.

Even Paris had been a shock. In Poitiers she had looked forward to seeing this city, having heard that it was the most popular center of learning in Western Europe, famous for its lectures on philosophy and theology which attracted a wide number of students and a host of brilliant teachers.

What Eleanor had not heard was that the French capital was a jumble of noisy, cramped streets, whose overhang of narrow wooden houses blocked out any ray of sun. Pigs and goats foraged everywhere for food while street vendors rudely jostled the passersby as they urged them to buy buttery waffles and spicy turnovers carried in baskets covered with white cloths. Nor had she expected the all-pervading stench of rotting food and human refuse that clung to everything, even following her into the castle itself. Worst of all she was not prepared to find the Parisians so humorless and argumentative, lacking any sense of style; so different from the pleasure-loving, carefree Aquitainians.

On this chill September evening, Eleanor entered the great hall which, despite the flaring torches set into the walls, looked as cheerless and forbidding as did everything else in the castle. Made even more grim by the dark blue-and-gray tapestries covering the walls, the scenes of martyrdom and tormented sinners only added to the bleakness.

The royal family—Louis, the queen dowager, and his cousin, Ralph of Vermandois, seneschal of France—were seated at the high table along with Petronilla, the ubiquitous Abbé Suger, and a guest. Eleanor's heart sank. Holy Mother, not again. The guest, an all-too-frequent visitor, was Bernard of Clairvaux, Abbé of the Cistercian monastery at Citeaux.

As Eleanor approached the table, she could hear the Cistercian monk make one of his dark pronouncements.

"His lectures smack of heresy."

"Whose?" Eleanor made a place for herself at the table.

"Peter Abelard's, my dear." Louis gave her a welcoming smile.

"Is he back in Paris? I would like to attend a lecture given by the great Abelard," she said.

"On no account may you attend, my dear," Louis said. "Most unseemly for the queen to be glimpsed at one of his lectures."

"Most unseemly," echoed the prim queen dowager. She made no secret of her disapproval of her son's frivolous wife, who had displaced her in importance.

"Why? Everyone tells me Abelard is one of the most gifted scholars in Paris and an inspired speaker."

"As you know, we open our gates to the students in the warm weather," Louis continued, not answering her question, "and I should have no objection to your listening to theological lectures from within our own gardens, or even the occasional trip to the Left Bank, which you have already visited—but not to hear Abelard."

It was on these rare trips to the Left Bank of the Seine that Eleanor had had her only glimpse of the raw intellectual excitement for which Paris was famous, the vitality so lacking at Louis's court and in her own life. Teachers and students hotly debating, the clash of beliefs, the passionate voicing of new ideas had enthralled her.

"Beware the man who values mind above spirit," Bernard's voice intoned. "What says Proverb Ten? '. . . in much talking thou shalt not avoid sin,' and it is also writ: 'A wise man is known by the fewness of his words.'"

An austere holy man dressed in a simple white cassock belted with a knotted rope, Bernard claimed to disdain riches and worldly pomp. Generally considered to be a saint—only death was necessary to make it official—he wielded enormous influence among the courts of Europe. Although he declared he preferred the peace of the cloister, it appeared to Eleanor that the devout monk spent far more time meddling in the affairs of the world than he did within monastery walls.

"I don't understand your objection, Father. Is it because Abelard views the Trinity in terms of divine attributes rather than divine persons?" she asked in a mock-sweet voice, more to provoke the cleric than because she really cared. "Or because he advises us to question everything?"

Despite the fact that she was curious to hear what his debates were like, Eleanor's main interest in the teacher-monk Abelard was due less to his eloquence from the lectern than a romantic aura resulting from an earlier scandal involving the novice, Héloise. The idea of a priest passionate enough to break his vows with a nun had won Eleanor's wholehearted approval.

"You are familiar with Abelard's work?" Louis looked shocked.

Bernard slowly turned his smoldering dark gaze toward Eleanor. "That is obvious, my son." He paused while his eyes swept over her crimson gown with its full sleeves that trailed the rushes, then up to the gold-and-pearl pendants dangling from her ears, to settle on her oval face framed by a white wimple and topped by a gold crown.

"My tutor in Poitiers is very enlightened in his tastes."

Everyone at the table stared at her as if she had just sprouted horns and a tail.

"Your tutor allowed you to read the works of Abelard?" Louis was clearly aghast.

"Poitou is known for diversity rather than orthodoxy, my son." Abbé Suger crossed himself.

"All of Aquitaine is a breeding ground for heresy," said Bernard.

This was one way of looking at it, Eleanor thought. The comparative openness and tolerance of southern society *was* receptive to various spiritual and intellectual influences.

"That is going a bit far, perhaps," she said. "Certainly, we take a broader view—"

"Broader view?" Bernard raised scraggly brows. "There are only believers, heretics, and infidels. Nothing else."

"I certainly don't take such a narrow view—" she began.

"Indeed, that is only too evident. Beware, Madam, beware the consequences of your own unbridled nature." Bernard jabbed a warning finger at her. "Like your father you have a restless spirit, but in the end Holy Church forced him to submit. It would behoove you to take heed and learn from his example."

Furious at this public rebuke, it took every ounce of willpower Eleanor possessed not to retaliate with a hot retort. *You* personally forced him to submit, Eleanor longed to say. *You* brought about my father's excommunication. *You* made him change the course of his life, a change that resulted in his ill-fated pilgrimage to St. James of Compostela—and an untimely death. You, Bernard of Clairvaux, are responsible and I will never forgive you for it. She contented herself with the knowledge that she would hear Abelard lecture with or without the Church's—or anyone's—approval.

Later that evening, while Louis, as usual, was on his knees in the chapel, Eleanor, still fuming, was walking along the twilit passage back to her quarters when she heard high-pitched giggles coming from the chamber where Ralph was housed as a guest. The laughter sounded suspiciously like Petronilla's who, Eleanor knew, continued to harbor a persistent infatuation for the lord of Vermandois. A giant of a man, with dark curly hair and a bronzed craggy face, Ralph was undeniably appealing, but married, with a granddaughter Petronilla's age. She had warned her sister not to involve herself with this unsuitable lord and cause a scandal.

The door of the chamber was slightly ajar and Eleanor cautiously pushed it further open, then stopped in surprise at the sight that met her eyes.

Petronilla was sitting on the red-canopied bed clad only in her chemise, which had been pulled down to reveal naked breasts, round and plump as pink cabbages. Beside her Ralph, breathing heavily, gazed raptly at her half-clothed body. Eleanor knew she ought to march straight into the chamber and loudly protest this seduction of her sister—except she knew which one had undoubtedly initiated the seducing. In any case she could not bring herself to move.

Ralph now proceded to fondle Petronilla's voluptuous bosom with huge hairy hands, rubbing his thumbs over her delicate nipples. Petronilla lay back on the bed, pulling Ralph down beside her.

Eleanor felt her breath come in little gasps. Ralph buried his face in Petronilla's breasts while she took one of his hands and slid it up under her chemise. Obviously this game was not new to either of them. Eleanor was uncomfortably aware of her pounding heart and a feeling of moisture between her legs.

Whatever Ralph was doing under the chemise, it was causing Petronilla to moan and squirm in obvious delight. The lord of Vermandois, whose mouth was otherwise engaged, began to wheeze so strenuously through his nose Eleanor feared he might do himself an injury. Really, the wretched man sounded as if he might expire at any moment. Unable to bear the sight one moment longer she withdrew.

Trembling with unsatisfied longings, drenched in sweat, Eleanor shut the door and leaned against the passage wall to collect herself. After a moment's pause she marched resolutely into the royal bedchamber. Dismissing her women, she quickly undressed, rubbed oil scented with rose petals over her breasts, belly, and hips, then climbed into the blue-canopied bed, pulling the coverlet over her naked body.

When Louis walked into the room she gave him her most inviting smile. He undressed and got into bed beside her. About to blow out the candle she stayed his hand and threw off the coverlet.

"Don't be in such a hurry," she said, twining her arms about his neck. "You haven't been near me for weeks."

"Oh—I hadn't realized—" He blushed and unwound her arms. "I take communion tomorrow. You know I can't—come near you during the three days prior." He averted his eyes. "Cover yourself."

For answer she brought his mouth down to hers and kissed him, forcing open his unwilling lips. She took one of his hands and laid it firmly on her breast. Left to himself, Louis never fondled her bosom nor kissed her with his mouth open; he entered her only briefly and withdrew right after he had spilled his seed. For a tantalizing moment his hand curled over her breast, before he withdrew it.

Normally, when he resisted, Eleanor could not bring herself to pursue the issue, simply as a matter of pride. But tonight she took his reluctant hand and slowly slid it down her satiny skin until it rested on the fringe of bronze hair between the juncture of thighs and belly. Louis caught his breath. Eleanor saw his eyes furtively dart to where his hand lay. She opened her legs; for an instant his fingers hesitated, then impelled by a force of their own he started to touch her.

The Compline bell sounded. Louis snatched his hand away.

"Do not lie there thus—your nakedness is unseemly," he said in a thick voice.

"No, it's entirely natural—if you were a natural husband."

"What do you mean?"

Eleanor sat up in the bed. "What I mean is that if we continue in this fashion, I will go from my wits."

He looked genuinely bewildered. "I don't understand."

"I'm never satisfied, never fulfilled. I have needs—"

She stopped at the horrified expression on Louis's face, the deep crimson that stained his features.

"My dear," he began in an agony of embarrassment. "You know that I love you as a good Christian husband should love his wife, but when you speak like this I fear for your immortal soul. How often have I told you that desire in a woman is the work of the devil? No chaste or religious-minded wife would have carnal longings. Abbé Suger once told me that if a man loved his wife too ardently, it is a sin worse than adultery."

"Perhaps that is why I cannot conceive a child—Abbé Suger is always in our bed!"

Louis crossed himself, slipped out of the bed, and went to pray at the prie-dieu. Eleanor, unspent as always, watched him with mingled anger and despair. Any mention of a child always provoked the same reaction. After he had taken communion he would undoubtedly bed her—after a fashion. The only way Louis was able to copulate with her at all was if she lay absolutely still and unmoving, like a marble statue, with no show of feeling. Why did she continue to make the effort?

If matters continued thus, she would end up an embittered, frustrated woman, a stranger to the joys of love, the comforts of marriage. Eleanor wanted to scream. It was simply not fair that the silly, wanton Petronilla should effortlessly experience what she was so ripe to enjoy. Both daughters of the hot-blooded south, Eleanor wondered if this heritage was not proving more of a curse than a blessing.

She must find a way out of this coil.

Bored to distraction, Eleanor haunted the stalls of Paris. Every dirty cobbled street loudly blazoned its own speciality: the cloth merchants' street, the bakers' and goldsmiths' streets, the street of the Jews, where money was loaned and exchanged. Her continual purchases of bolts of sendal and wool, costly jewels, scented oils from the East and other luxuries, eventually resulted in a major upset between herself and the queen dowager.

"I can no longer live in the same quarters with this—this extravagant sorceress," Louis's mother screamed one evening, after Eleanor had returned from the marketplace with a gold and ruby ring.

Louis shifted from one foot to the other.

"Louis, are you going to allow this woman to insult me?"

The queen dowager turned on Eleanor. "I'm leaving the palace, do you hear? You've not only bewitched my son, you wicked creature, but your extravagance will bring France to ruin."

Eleanor igonored her irate mother-in-law. "Louis, how can you stand by and permit this?"

"Your mother is right, Louis," said Abbé Suger with a dark look at Eleanor. "Even your council accuses the queen of beggaring the treasury. You must put a stop to her behavior."

But Louis, pale and mute as always when confronted with any sort of unpleasant situation, could deny her nothing—of a material nature anyway. Ignoring his council, his mother, and Abbé Suger, he continued to indulge her, as if trying to make up to her for his failure to please at night.

The queen dowager vacated Paris in a shower of accusations and dire predictions. Aware of his waning influence, Abbé Suger came less and less often to the palace, and was seen more and more in the Church of St.-Denis, which he was in the process of restoring. Despite his frugal attitude toward her spending, Abbé Suger himself spent lavishly on new stained-glass windows and other embellishments for his favorite project.

Thus, in the end, Eleanor felt she had achieved some sort of victory.

It was a poor substitute for love, however, and made her wretched existence no easier to bear.

Several months later, Geoffrey of Anjou paid one of his infrequent visits to Paris after a recent triumph in Normandy.

"You will notice a difference since your last visit two years ago, my lord," Eleanor said, pleased, as always, to see him.

She stood in the entrance to the great hall proudly pointing out the changes she was making in the castle: new tapestries worked in blue and scarlet wools graced the stone walls, a half-completed hearth that would have a chimney to funnel the smoke.

"*Grâce à Dieu*, the hall will be virtually transformed," Geoffrey said. "This castle used to remind me of a dungeon."

"Perhaps that is why I always felt like a prisoner."

"And now? Are you still in need of being rescued?" Geoffrey's cornflower blue gaze sent a shiver of anticipation through her.

"If I were?"

"I would feel obligated to rescue you."

Eleanor led him down the passage and up the winding staircase to the solar, where a troubadour was strumming his lute.

"I also intend to broaden the narrow window slits to let in more light." A servitor offered them silver goblets of wine on a wooden tray "And the wine is now imported from Bordeaux and Gascony—which makes it drinkable."

Geoffrey smiled as he took a goblet. "That's not all you've imported. I hear there is a veritable parade of troubadours, knights, and jongleurs streaming into Paris from Aquitaine. And surely these are new." He nodded at Eleanor's ladies, flitting about the solar like colorful hummingbirds, chatting, laughing, singing along with the minstrel. "I must congratulate you."

Their eyes met; Geoffrey's hand brushed against hers as if by accident. Her heart raced and she did not move away. Suddenly aware her ladies were watching, Eleanor felt her cheeks burn and stepped back.

The Vespers bell summoned them to evensong. Eleanor led the way out of the solar and down the passage.

"How is your charming son? He must be nine or ten by now."

Geoffrey slowed his step. His handsome face twisted into a grimace; he shrugged elegant shoulders. "My charming son, Henry, is with his mother in England these days. Although I worry about his welfare in that war-torn land, it is something of a relief. Subduing Normandy is easier than trying to subdue Henry."

Eleanor laughed, vividly remembering the connection between herself and the gray-eyed scamp at her wedding feast, then again when he had presented her with a bouquet of lilies on the road to Poitiers.

"Do you go often to Aquitaine?" Geoffrey asked as they continued on their way to the chapel.

"Seldom. Louis doesn't like me to go without him, and he dislikes going so—" she gave an eloquent shrug. "I miss my duchy—I cannot tell you how deeply."

"It strikes me that you are not very happy, Madam."

Unexpectedly, her eyes filled with tears. Geoffrey reached out as if to touch her, then withdrew.

The next day when Count Geoffrey was leaving, Eleanor wished she could find an excuse to keep him longer. In the courtyard he bowed over her hand, his eyes caressing her in a manner that sent a wave of heat through her body. She was aware that Louis, standing next to her, had stiffened.

With an aching sense of loneliness she watched the Angevin lord mount his black stallion and ride off into the gray drizzle of the autumn day.

Luxurious quarters, entertainment from morning until night, gay companions, were no compensation for the vast emptiness inside her heart. Even a stolen visit, when she dressed as a page to hear Peter Abelard lecture, had not relieved the monotony for long. In fact, she had been disappointed after a while and found the arguments boring. Did it really matter whether a sow led to market was led by the rope or the man? She was still restless, still wretched, and still a prisoner. What could she do?

"What you need is a lover, Nell," said Petronilla one afternoon as they lounged on Eleanor's bed in the solar.

"But I'm not quite ready to take that step. Too dangerous. You know what happens to adulterous queens?"

"Annul the marriage? Banish you to a convent? That wouldn't happen to you, you're duchess of Aquitaine! Besides, you'd have to be caught first."

"Everyone watches me. I know Bernard of Clairvaux is just waiting like a hawk, ready to pounce if I do anything that even looks suspicious."

"You can't imagine the joys you're missing, Sister."

The growing scandal of Petronilla and her elderly lover, Ralph, provided the only real excitement in Eleanor's life. Apart from occasional mild flirtations with her own troubadours or visiting nobles like Geoffrey of Anjou, her most vital connection to the passionate existence she craved was through her sister's adulterous affair.

But Louis was shocked and humiliated by the behavior of the two lovers. "Ralph is married to the sister of the count of Champagne, who is a powerful vassal of mine. He is most distressed by these events and by rumors that Ralph will seek an annulment. This— this disgraceful affair must cease."

They were in their own chamber preparing for bed. Louis had just risen from the prie-dieu.

"What are you saying?" Eleanor cried, already under the fur-lined, blue and gold–embroidered coverlet. "They are in love, never will they be parted. It's naught to do with the count of Champagne. How can you be so unchivalrous, so lacking in romance?"

"But, my dear, the count has complained to the pope, who has upbraided me for allowing such adulterous behavior under my own roof. Ralph is my cousin, I can't very well condone—"

"Why, why, why are you so spineless?" Eleanor threw herself on the lace-trimmed cushions and pounded her fists on the coverlet. "Show a little mettle! Stand up to the pope, to the count! Assert yourself. Behave like a fearless knight for a change."

Eleanor knew she sounded like a shrew but did not care. If only once Louis would act like a true king, the strong gallant she so longed for him to be! Reminding her as usual of a cowed, bewildered puppy, Louis crept under the coverlet and curled up on his side of the bed. Why had God cursed her with such a husband? What had she ever done to deserve such a wretched life? How long could she go on before exploding?

A month later Bernard of Clairvaux unexpectedly arrived at the palace, demanding to see her.

"After five years of marriage, your failure to bear a child is the talk of Paris," the monk said, when they met in the Chapel of St. Nicholas. "Like everyone else, I'm concerned for the future of the realm."

It was a concern Eleanor shared and she did not object to discussing it, even with this meddling monk. For once he might be able to do some good.

"Louis still thinks of himself as a future priest and finds every excuse imaginable not to bed me," she said. "Sundays, Wednesdays, and Fridays he is forbidden to lie with me, then again forty days before Easter or Christmas, as well as three days before communion. You know how often Louis takes communion? So you see it is hardly my fault. I am more than willing."

"King Louis behaves as a devoted son of Holy Church, but I will

write to His Holiness in Rome. I feel certain that upon my recom-
mendation he will grant dispensations to King Louis in this matter.
The weal of the kingdom is at stake." Abbé Bernard's gaze bored
into hers. "More than willing, you say? What does that mean exactly?"

"What you think it means, Father." A sudden urge to shock this
unshakable, devout churchman took hold of Eleanor. "I am young
and ripe for the marriage bed."

"I'm sure you are aware that carnal desire, even for a husband, is
held to be sinful. Relations between husband and wife are not intended for pleasure but for the sole purpose of bearing children.
However, with the disgraceful example set you by your adulterous
family, what else can one expect but wanton cravings?" His eyes
narrowed. "Do you attempt to solace yourself in order to relieve
your unholy lust?"

Eleanor was intrigued. "No. There are ways to do that?"

A look of disgust crossed Bernard's ascetic face as he signed himself. "Unfortunately, the devil has endless means at his disposal to
entice the unwary. It relieves my mind that you are ignorant of such
matters."

Eleanor assumed an air of maidenly innocence. "Totally ignorant. You must tell me what—what these means are so I will be sure
to avoid them."

"You must never, never touch yourself—with an object or otherwise."

"An object?" Eleanor did not have to feign a look of incredulity.

For the first time Abbé Bernard looked uncomfortable. "I have
heard that Satan often uses a candle as his instrument of temptation."

With an exclamation of pretended horror Eleanor crossed herself.

Before she left the chapel Bernard showed her the penitential
codes. He pointed out that though a great number of lines were devoted to the sins of adultery, sodomy, and bestiality, by far the
greatest was devoted to the sin of self-abuse as practiced by laymen.
Because she read Latin, Eleanor noticed a whole other section that
appeared to deal with self-abuse as practiced by the clergy, before
Bernard quickly closed the book. She repressed a smile. So men of
God were not immune to the same needs that pricked her own flesh.

"Curb your carnality, woman," warned Bernard, "lest you fall
into the sin of onanism, or self-abuse, which I consider to be worse

than adultery. I will give you a forty-day penance and I enjoin you to pray to the Holy Virgin, day and night, to make you fruitful. I also advise a pilgrimage to a holy shrine."

After this discussion, Louis was granted dispensations that permitted him to bed her five days of the week, although he rarely took advantage of this relaxation. Eleanor, on the other hand, found ways, unsatisfactory as they were, to temporarily dispel her own torments. This led her to wonder, not for the first time, if the strictures of the Church did not, in practice, often lead people to the very sins they wished to prevent.

Eleanor did not conceive but had no intention of visiting a holy shrine nor of observing the forty days of penance. Quite unexpectedly another solution offered itself.

One day in late autumn, as she shopped with her women in the marketplace at a draper's stall, she overheard two well-dressed Parisian women talk of a visiting seeress, a gypsy woman from Moorish Spain, who was reputed to have success as a teller of fortunes.

When Eleanor returned to the palace she ordered one of her servitors from Poitiers to return to the marketplace and discreetly inquire about this gypsy. After several hours he returned with the information that the woman did indeed exist and where she could be located. The seeress spent much of her time traveling throughout Europe, he said, and had come to Paris in secret. In the south, gypsies were readily accepted. In France, Eleanor knew that the Church was particularly hostile to the seeress's race as well as to the gypsies' gift of second sight, which the Holy Fathers deemed witchcraft.

Eleanor dismissed the servant, sent for Petronilla, and persuaded her to accompany her on a visit to the seeress.

A week later when Louis was out of Paris to inspect a newly installed stained glass window at Chartres, Eleanor and Petronilla slipped out of the palace one chill November evening after dusk. Innocent of jewelry, fustian cloaks covering plain linen gowns, they looked like ordinary women of burgher status. Two Poitevin grooms and the servitor from Poitiers, sworn to secrecy, accompanied them on foot.

Eleanor had rarely explored Paris after dark. There were not many people abroad, she noticed, and those who were seemed anxious to avoid them. This gave the whole venture an added spice of danger and excitement. They passed through dark twisted alleys until they came to a narrow wooden house on a winding street beside the banks of the Seine. The dark street was filled with river fog; the light from a sickle moon cast mysterious shadows on the ground. They knocked and the door was immediately opened by a handsome youth with dark hair and swarthy skin who said he would take them to his grandmother.

Petronilla was afraid and refused to see the seeress, preferring, she said, to wait outside the chamber with their attendants. Also fearful, but still determined, Eleanor entered alone. The seeress, wearing many skirts in violet, rose, and deep purple colors, was seated on a divan piled high with cushions. A brass lamp burning a naked flame lay on a low table in front of her. She motioned for Eleanor to sit on a stool on the other side of the table. The woman's face was in shadow but she appeared to be very old. Her head was loosely covered with a black shawl, and Eleanor glimpsed golden hoops dangling from her ears.

"What I want to know—" Eleanor began in a trembling voice.

"I know what you want, granddaughter of the Troubadour," the woman interjected in a heavily accented tongue.

Eleanor was shocked into silence. How did the woman know who she was?

The woman chuckled softly, pleased at the effect she had created. "Your grandfather and father were always kind to my people, which is why I consented to see you. Give me your hand." She stretched out an arm ringed almost to the elbow with jangling gold bracelets.

Eleanor held out a shaking hand. The woman grasped it in warm brown fingers, surprisingly strong and reassuring. A moment later Eleanor found herself telling the old woman everything about her marital relations with Louis and her fears that with such a husband she would never produce a son.

"You will have many sons," the old woman said in a crooning voice, gazing into Eleanor's palm. "It is written here quite clearly. But not with the man to whom you are now wedded." She looked up. Above the flickering flame her eyes, bright as ebony beads, met Eleanor's. "Much about you is revealed. For instance, in the ignorance of youth you seek to lose yourself in love, to burn with passion's flame. Beware, for such a love carries within it the seeds of its own destruction and may well be your undoing."

The old woman's words reminded Eleanor of Bernard of Clairvaux, and she was tempted to close her ears.

"Beware, as well, of a need for power, which—"

"Where is this man who will give me sons?" Eleanor interjected. She had not come to hear a sermon. "When will I meet him? Is it to be soon?"

The seeress smiled and let go of Eleanor's hand. "Not very soon, I think. At the moment he is only nine years old." She paused. Her smile faded; her eyes closed. Swaying back and forth in a kind of snakelike trance her words came forth in a soft hiss.

"Child of the sun, you will undertake many hazardous journeys and suffer much heartbreak, beyond that of most women. Four— yes, four kings will you know and two alien lands, but the road ahead is filled with treachery and stained with blood." Her voice became silent.

After a few moments the gypsy opened her eyes and held out her hand.

Deeply shaken, Eleanor dropped several silver coins into the curled fingers. "Your words—what do they mean?"

The seeress's eyes, opaque and unblinking, held Eleanor's. "I speak that which I see; meaning is beyond my powers. But this I know: You have been given the strength to bear what must be borne. Others who cross your path may be less fortunate. You cast a long shadow, Lady—and will endure."

Eleanor rose to her feet and stumbled out of the room as in a dream. All the way back to the castle the seeress's words drummed through her mind. From some far-off place she sensed a breath of anguish, an aura of impending doom so faint, so fragile, a heartbeat later she wondered if she had ever felt it at all.

# CHAPTER 7

# England,
# 1143

The cart bounced over a rut in the road. Henry of Anjou, jolted awake, poked his head up through the straw to see a pearly dawn break over the wooded English countryside. He pushed aside a wooden cage of clucking chickens and several wheels of white cheese then sat up, rubbing the sleep out of his eyes. They had left Wallingford at Matins. Surely they should be nearing London by now?

"Are we getting close?" he called softly to the driver of the cart.

Old Anson turned his black-capped head and glowered. "Keep your head down, Master Henry, for Lord's sake, how many times must I tell ye we be in enemy territory? Aye, soon be there by me reckoning."

London! At long last he would finally see for himself this noble and celebrated city that his mother had told him about, the city which, more than any other, represented his birthright. When Henry had heard that London lay less than a day's journey from Wallingford where he was currently staying with his mother and uncle, he had been determined to see it for himself—despite the ongoing civil war between his mother and the cousin who had usurped her throne, King Stephen. Due to the danger involved he had been strictly forbidden to leave the castle grounds.

The dawn mist was just starting to burn off and Henry, wide awake now, inhaled deep breaths of the spring air as he looked around him. The trees were still barren of leaves but there was the loamy scent of sap rising and the earth had already put forth young green shoots. As far as he could tell the road was deserted.

"There's no one about to see me, Anson," Henry said.

"Sleeping, wasn't ye? We passed a party o' pilgrims a ways back, a cart or two going to market same as us, and a litter accompanied by armed knights. Next time could be a band o' the king's Flemish mercenaries. Suppose they stop us and ye get caught? Can't ye get it through ye head, Master Henry, there be skirmishes raging all about us! Now if ye don't keep down like I says we goes straight back to Wallingford." He leaned over to spit on the ground. "Must've been addled in me wits to ever let ye and Master William talk me into this harebrained foolishness."

Henry gnawed at his lip. The old man was quite capable of doing what he said. "I'll be careful."

The only response was a doubtful snort.

Henry prodded his cousin, William of Gloucester, with his elbow. "Wake up. We'll soon be there."

William, eldest son of Henry's uncle, Earl Robert of Gloucester, sat up with a yawn, scratched his crop of nut brown hair, and rubbed the sleep out of his eyes.

"God's eyes, mind where you go." Henry carefully moved a straw basket of eggs. "Anson'll kill us if we upset his precious eggs." He lowered his voice. "He saw some armed knights ride by and now he's talking about Flemish mercenaries. I think he's scared."

"Of course he's scared. Do you blame him?" William shivered. "This journey's filled with danger. Even though you seem to regard it as nothing but a lark."

Henry, loath to admit the possibility of any real danger, wished he had kept silent. He watched the fields and undulating downs stitched with countless hedges stretch away to the purple horizon. Not once in all the days of cajoling and finally bribing Old Anson, chief wheelwright in the village of Wallingford, to take William and himself to London had he given serious thought to the possible consequences of getting caught. Of course, he *knew* London was held by his mother's arch-enemy, King Stephen, but the fact had no real meaning for him.

Aware that he was able to persuade most people into doing what he wanted, the risks involved did not concern him. Or so Henry's father, the count of Anjou, never tired of telling him over and over and over again. Thoughtless. Reckless. Foolhardy. These were only a few of the count's favorite expressions when it came to his son and heir. It was a good thing he paid them so little mind or he would never make *anything* happen.

"Well, I'm not," Henry said with an air of defiance.

"Not what?"

"Afraid."

"You would be if you had any sense. If you'd lived here these past four years, instead of only a few months, you'd have reason to be afraid, let me tell you."

"I didn't think you were a coward, Cousin."

William threw a fistful of straw at him. "Hold your tongue, boy. You're only ten. I'm thirteen and soon to be knighted. Treat me with proper respect or I'll make you sorry."

Henry scowled, hating to be reminded of his age. Had it really been so long as William said? He reckoned on his fingers: Stephen usurped his mother's throne in 1135; she had set sail for England in 1139 to reclaim it. It was now 1143. Four years. His cousin was right.

Henry watched William collapse on the straw and stare at a pale blue sky streaked with wisps of white cloud. "God's teeth, if my father ever finds out about this I won't be able to sit for a week." He glanced at Henry. "And if your mother gets wind of it—in truth, Cousin, I'd rather deal with my father ten times over than explain to my aunt Maud why I let you talk me into risking our lives just to show you London. I might even prefer dealing with the Flemings."

The cart swayed as it labored up a hill. Below lay the green and blue reflection of the Thames River. Henry knew exactly what William meant.

Yesterday, when his mother and uncle had suddenly been called away from Wallingford, leaving William and himself in the care of an overburdened castellen, Henry had decided the time was ripe for his planned escapade. Such a moment might not come again. But the possibility, remote as it was, of having to face his formidable mother was so daunting that he instantly retreated from the thought.

He sent William a sullen look. "I'm supposed to be heir to the throne, king of England one day. I just want to see London, my future capital. Is that so terrible, I ask you?"

"God's teeth! Do you forget that London is violently opposed to your mother and all things Angevin? What do you think would happen if King Stephen got his hands on you?"

Since Henry had never entertained such a possibility he had no ready answer.

"Well, I'll tell you, blockhead," William continued. "You'd be held for ransom; the war would be over; your mother's cause lost, and all the misery and fighting we've endured over here on your behalf would have been for nothing. Do you understand? Nothing! My father's lands would be confiscated, your mother would never be queen, and even if Stephen let you live, you would never be king of England."

There was a note of bitterness in William's voice that Henry had never heard before. He wondered if his cousin blamed his mother for returning to England to fight for her crown, thus plunging the country into civil war.

"You shouldn't have come if you think it's so dangerous."

"Someone with sense had to look after you."

Henry threw himself on William and began to pummel him with both fists. William punched him in the nose with such force Henry could hardly breathe.

"I don't need any looking after," Henry said, gasping. "Nor to be kept out of danger. I was sent here to be a rallying point for my mother's supporters. Everyone knows I'm going to be king of England one day. How can anything happen to me?"

"Ye'll find out quick enough, young master, if there be one egg cracked or a hen hurt. Stop that fighting at once or—" Anson broke off and listened intently. "What be that noise?"

There was the sound of many hoofbeats coming up swiftly behind them. Henry sat up. All he could see was a great cloud of dust.

"Must be enemy troops," William said, peering into the distance. "Certainly not my father's men this close to London. Jesu, suppose they stop us?"

"Suppose they do?" Henry rubbed his aching nose. "We're just farm boys going to market. Why would we interest Stephen's troops?"

"Now I told ye lads what to do if we be stopped," Anson said quickly. "Keep down in the straw and mayhap ye won't be seen."

A few moments later a large troop of Flemish mercenaries came up directly behind the cart. Anson pulled at the reins and the horse swerved sharply off the road. Henry and William sank into the straw while the troop trotted past. One of the soldiers at the end of the column slowed and rode up alongside the cart.

"Vat ye got here, old man?" He had a thick Flemish accent.

"Just eggs, cheese, and chickens to sell at market in London, good sir," said Anson.

Henry could hear the tremor of fear in his voice.

"Yah? Und this?" The soldier had removed his sword from its scabbard and parted the straw. "Are these lads for sale too?"

A few of his companions chuckled. To Henry's horror the soldier deliberately lifted his sword high and brought the point slowly down toward William, who, petrified, reminded Henry of a rabbit looking at a stoat.

He sat up and glared at the soldier. "Stop that. You might hurt him."

"Listen to the cockerel crow!" The soldier gave him a wolfish grin. "Yah, I might hurt him—and vat vould you do about it?"

The sword continued down, missed William's leg by no more than an inch it seemed to Henry, passed through the wooden cage, and speared a chicken, who squawked loudly then abruptly stopped as the sword went through its innards.

The soldiers laughed uproariously while their companion withdrew his sword, wiped off the blood on William's jerkin, and returned it to his scabbard.

"Be thankful it vasn't you, little cockerel," he said to Henry.

The troop passed in a flurry of dust. Anson steered the horse and cart back onto the road. "By me faith, God was watching out for us," he said in a trembling voice. "Gave me a fair turn that did. If we wasn't so close to London I'd turn back, I would. Master William, ye no be harmed?"

"He's fine," Henry said, noting that William was incapable of speech. Flecks of blood dotted the straw and were splattered over the chickens, who screeched to high heaven. "I'll see you're reimbursed for that chicken, Anson."

The only reply was a grunt.

Henry looked at his cousin in concern. A smear of crimson stained his tan jerkin; his face was the color of new cream. He looked as if he were fighting back tears.

"Whoreson Flemish pigs." Henry gnawed his lip in frustration.

The king had imported the Flemish mercenaries and their captain, William of Ypres, from Flanders, to help fight the Angevin forces. Henry knew from his mother and uncle that they were con-sidered little better than animals, hated and feared by both sides.

"One day I'll make them sorry," he said.

William suddenly turned and began to throw up over his side of the cart. Henry, pretending not to notice, looked intently at a tur-reted manor house clothed in ivy, then a wooden cottage with a roof of thatched reeds.

The Fleming's taunt, "little cockerel," echoed mockingly in his ears. How he would have liked to retort in kind, even run the bas-tard through if he'd had a sword. Sometimes it seemed like he would be ten years old forever, that he could not grow up fast enough. God's eyes! One day he would be taken seriously. One day, nobody would dare to mock him. The first thing he would do when he became king of England was get rid of such filthy scum as the Flemings.

*When* he became king, he repeated to himself like a talisman, not even allowing himself to think, *if*. From as far back as Henry could remember, he had known he would inherit his father's counties of Anjou and Maine, and fall heir to his mother's crown in England and her duchy of Normandy: twin legacies passed on to her by her father, the late King Henry.

If there were any justice in this world, his mother would be on the throne this very moment. Her father had forced his magnates to swear homage to her and honor her as queen after his death. What the nobles had done instead was to allow his mother's scheming cousin, Stephen of Blois, to usurp the throne at the king's death. More than half the loyal barons broke their sworn oath and crowned Stephen king.

Henry, only two at the time, had been unable to grasp the far-reaching implications of what had occurred. But his heart had un-derstood only too well that his safe and well-ordered world, as well as everyone's around him, had been turned upside down. For the next few years, bewildered and upset, he had witnessed his mother veer between anguish and icy rage, his father storm angrily about the castle, swearing vengeance. Everyone had trusted and loved Stephen of Blois, his uncle Robert had said again and again. The re-sult of Stephen's betrayal had made a searing impression, one that Henry knew would mark him for life.

From that moment on, Henry was well aware that he had never fully trusted, nor taken for granted, anything or anyone—except

his mother and father, of course. Behind a loving friend who swore
the most sacred oath, there might well hide a treacherous heart.
Nor had he forgotten the pain of being separated from his parents
when, four years ago, his mother had sailed to England to reclaim
her throne, and his father had set off to capture Normandy from
Stephen's forces. Fortunately his father had sent for him in Angers,
and the last year had been spent in Rouen before sailing to England
to join his mother.

His father had made good headway; Normandy was almost re-
captured. But in England the civil war between King Stephen and
his mother still raged like a pestilence, with never an end in sight.

A brisk wind sprang up, ruffling the straw in the cart. The road
dipped, leaving the wooded hills behind. In the distance Henry
caught another glimpse of the Thames and a huge tower.

"That's Westminster," said William, pointing. His face, though
still pale, was now composed.

"You're—feeling better?"

"Yes. Fine. Thank you for—for trying to help." Embarrassed, he
slid his eyes away. "I hope I would have done—that is to say, had the
courage to do the same."

Henry felt a glow of pride at this unaccustomed praise from his
older cousin. It lessened some of the guilt he felt for having brought
about the situation. He could just hear his father: "If you'd thought
about the consequences in the first place you wouldn't have need-
lessly endangered three lives."

The road suddenly dropped again. Below, mill wheels turned in a
small river that flowed into the Thames. Farther on a wooden
bridge led to a gate in the city's walls. Henry caught a sweeping
view over the massive walls of the city and into the teeming thicket
of chimneys and houses. A variety of sounds assailed his ears: the
guards shouting on top of the walls, the throngs at the gates clamoring for entrance into London.

Old Anson crossed the bridge, skirted the city wall, and took a
lane to the left that led to open ground. The bells from all the
churches in London rang the call to Terce as he pulled the cart to a
stop.

"This be the market site o' Smithfield," he said. "It be as far as I
go. If ye want to get into the city ye'll have to walk through Aldergate there on ye own." He pointed some distance away. "I'll sell me
produce and be ready to leave no later than Nones. Ye be back by

then and we'll return to Wallingford. By Nones, mind. And be care-ful in London."

Henry and William jumped down from the cart. By the time they reached Aldergate they found themselves amid a great crowd of people, horses, and carts. His heart pounding with excitement, Henry looked up at the eighteen-foot-high walls and the double swinging doors of heavy oak, reinforced with iron. Surmounting the gateway was a blood-stained human head fixed upon a pike. Ravens clustered about the eyeless face.

"Is this a sample of the king's justice?" Henry could not help re-press a shudder.

"More likely his Flemish captain's. Stephen's too soft for any real justice." William looked warily around them. "Do you stay close to me. I'm familiar with London and can show you the sights. On your own you won't know where to go and are sure to get lost."

They passed through the gates and entered the city. The street they were on, fully ten feet across, Henry marveled, led to Newgate Street, William told him, and St. Paul's churchyard where a great cathedral was still undergoing construction. Henry, trying not to gawk at everything he saw, wondered if it would be completed by the time he became king. The air, smelling of fish, ale, wool, and dried leather, was intoxicating.

They turned down another street and followed an alley that led to the quays. The haunting calls of the boatmen, shrill cries of eel-wives selling their wares on the bridge, had a strange, almost mag-ical sound that stirred Henry's blood. My city, he thought. This is my city.

"Here's a public cookshop," William said. They stopped and bought a cone of roast chestnuts and two ham-and-eel pasties.

Munching on their pasties Henry and William wandered about the quay. Both upstream and down, Henry could see row upon row of docks and wharves where burly seamen, coarse smocks pulled up over their belts, loaded and unloaded cargo from moored ships.

William pointed in a lordly gesture. "These boats sail to and from Nantes, Flanders, Normandy. Even the Levant. You have to admit, Cousin, both Anjou and Normandy are mere backwaters compared to London."

Henry merely grunted, unwilling to state how impressed he was, but relieved that William seemed quite his old superior self again.

"We'll have time to cross London Bridge before meeting Old Anson at Smithfield," William said.

Just as they stepped onto the bridge a band of youths ran past pursued by a group of soldiers. Henry was knocked to his knees. By the time everyone had rushed by, Henry's chestnuts were scattered over the ground and William had vanished. A group of small, ragged urchins swarmed over the wooden planks, scrambling to pick up the fallen chestnuts. His hose torn, his blue jerkin muddied, Henry picked himself up. At least he still had his pasty.

There was such a press of people coming and going across the bridge that Henry was swept up in the crowd. He was almost halfway across before he was able to stop and catch his breath. Still no sign of William. Obviously his cousin had been pushed one way and he another. Should he go look for him? No. William boasted of his familiarity with the city; he was bound to be fine. Henry would ask the way back to Smithfield when the time came and all would be well. In truth, it was far more exciting to be on his own.

He took another bite of his pasty and leaned over the wooden railing. A sharp river wind brushed his hair and blew salt spray into his face. Suddenly he felt someone sidle up beside him. Henry turned his head. Standing next to him was a girl. She looked to be his own age as far as he could tell. A faded yellow gown, much too big for her, hung on her skinny frame; her face was streaked with soot and her hair was a jungle of thick black curls. She also smelled strongly of spoiled fish, sour ale, and even more unpleasant odors. Henry moved away from her, but she didn't seem to notice as she stared intently at the swirling muddy waters below.

"Look there! Quick! Do ye see him?"

"See who?"

"That great silver fish. Long as me arm he be with big green eyes."

Henry peered into the water. "I don't see any fish. It's too muddy to see any. Furthermore, I never even heard of a fish that looks like that."

"Well, he be there right enough. If ye knows how to look."

Her garbled speech, different from any he'd heard, was barely understandable, her voice harsh to the ear with a kind of lilt to it.

"Is this your idea of a jest?" He gave her a suspicious glance. "I don't believe any such fish exists so don't try to tell me somebody caught one." He took another bite of his pasty.

"Ooh no. Ye could never catch him. He just be there to look at."
Her eyes followed his hand.

"Are you hungry?"

She nodded and he handed her the eel-and-ham pasty.

She almost snatched it from his hands, rewarding him with a
smile. Immediately her face was transformed. Now Henry was
aware of enormous dark blue eyes and little white teeth. Under the
soot and grime he imagined she might look quite pleasing. He
watched while she took a dainty bite.

"Ooh, grand that be," she said, gravy dribbling down her chin.

"I'm glad you like it." He paused. "My name is Henry. I'm visiting my mother here in England."

"Don't ye have no father then?"

"Of course I have a father. Everyone has a father."

She stared at him in silence for a moment. "Where ye father be?"

"In Rouen at the moment. He's count of Anjou but acting as
duke in Normandy—until I can take over for him." He stole a
glance to see how she reacted to this.

The girl nodded and took another bite of the pasty. "Normandy.
Where's that then?"

"Across the Channel. Near France."

"I hears tell of France. Ye been there?"

"No." Henry paused. "But I met the French queen."

"Ye never!"

"By God's eyes, I did! I even gave her flowers."

She stared at him, her enormous blue eyes glowing with admiration. "Be she—beautiful like they all says?"

Henry, who only remembered an overall impression of loveliness, smiled. "Indeed."

She sighed. "Ye be here for long?"

"Not too long. My father relies on me, you know."

She nodded again and handed him back the pasty with dirty fingers, the nails caked with mud. "I knows right off ye wasn't from
London, o' course, but I never met no foreign person before. That
must be why ye talks so funny-like. I be named Bellebelle."

Henry swallowed, pleased that she accepted everything he said
without question. "You can keep the pasty. I'm not hungry. What
an odd name."

"It do be different. Me mam says I be christened Ykenai—a
Saxon name, but folks all calls me Bellebelle." She stuffed the rest

of the pasty into her mouth and waved toward the far side of the bridge. "I be from Southwark."

She finished eating, licked the crumbs from her fingers, wiped her nose with her forearm, then leaned companionably over the railing with him. Together they watched a group of boys tilting in small boats. Perched in the prow and holding lances, the youths skimmed across the water toward a shield hanging from a pole. They hit the target and fell into the river. Henry and Bellebelle laughed along with everyone else.

"I comes here every chance I gets," Bellebelle said. "Whenever I can get me mam to take me."

"Where is she now?"

Bellebelle gestured toward a group of women in gaily striped cloaks huddled together farther down the bridge. Henry noticed that some passersby shouted remarks at the women but he was too far away to hear what was said. One man even threw what looked like a dead fish at them.

"Why are they being treated like that?"

Bellebelle scuffed a worn shoe on the wooden plank; her eyes clouded over, her face grew flushed, and she did not answer.

Behind them a sudden commotion shifted Henry's attention. Approaching were two of the soldiers he had seen earlier with a youth in tow, obviously drunk. They were driving him along with harsh blows and whenever he faltered or stumbled they kicked him with their heavy boots. The boy had tears running down his face.

"There's no call to treat the wretch that way," said Henry. "He's too flown with ale to walk properly."

"Them's the king's Flemings," Bellebelle whispered. "Best stay out o' their way."

The accursed Flemings again. Henry stepped forward. One of the soldiers stopped, gave him an insolent stare, then pushed him aside. Everyone on the bridge scattered as far away from the soldiers as possible. Henry, feeling the first flush of rage wash over him, was about to stand his ground when he felt a surprisingly strong hand grab his arm and forcefully yank him back to the railing.

"Are ye daft?" The fear in Bellebelle's voice was palpable. "This be London and the Flemings has a free hand. Ye can't do nothing. No one can't do nothing." She paused. "But ye would've tried, wouldn't ye?"

"One day it will be different," Henry said between his teeth, swallowing his anger as the soldiers moved on. "Believe me it will. When I'm king of England there won't be any need for bloody heads on the gates, and I will see justice done to poor creatures like that."

Bellebelle nodded, looking at him in awe. "O' course ye will, cause ye don't have no wishbone where ye backbone ought be. Anyone can see that."

He smiled at the odd phrase, noting that she hadn't even questioned what he'd said about being king. "Thank you. I'd best be going. I've lost my companion and need to get back to Smithfield. Can you tell me how?"

Bellebelle gave him detailed directions then looked over the railing again, resting her chin on her hands. Henry squinted his eyes, staring into the water.

"I see the fish," he said.

Bellebelle turned and gave him a radiant smile.

When Henry reached Smithfield, the bells were just striking Nones. William was waiting and so relieved to see him that he pounded him on the back.

"God's teeth you had me worried. I looked for you everywhere. What happened to you?"

Henry shrugged. "Nothing, really."

All the way back to Wallingford while William talked about his adventures with a would-be pickpocket, Henry thought about Bellebelle and London and the Flemings. There had been an odd feel to the city, something he couldn't quite name. Certainly he'd never been aware of that feeling in the cities of Angers or Rouen. It was like—yes, he had it now—like a ship with no one at the helm.

When he was king, Henry decided, anyone who walked into London would know immediately that someone was in control, guiding the ship.

# CHAPTER 8

# Southwark,

# 1145

"*They* want ye now, Belle." It was the tavern keeper's voice calling from inside the tavern.

Bellebelle, standing on the tavern steps, felt her stomach plummet. Why was she so fearful? After all, she had always known what was going to happen, had often felt impatient for it to be over. But now that the moment was here . . .

She stared at the streaks of white cloud that swept across a gray-blue sky, the fading sunlight glinting on the White Tower across the river in London. The end of a brisk February day, but just the beginning for her. A salt wind whipped across her face, bringing with it the sickly smell of rotting fish and slops that always hung over the Bankside in Southwark. Above her head Bellebelle could hear the dirty tavern sign, The Bishop's Hat, creak and sway on its leather hinges as usual, but this afternoon it had a scary groan as well.

"Belle! Gilbert be calling for ye and ye don't want to cause no trouble. Not today."

She pretended not to hear.

The tavern and adjoining brothel-house sat side by side on a small incline back from the street; from where she stood, over to the right, Bellebelle could just glimpse the priory roof of St. Mary Overie, where Morgaine had taken her to Easter service last year, and the tall spires of the parish churches of St. Mary Magdalene and St. Margaret soaring toward heaven. Over to her left was the wooden bridge that spanned the river, then the Strand where the herring boats were moored, and beyond it the tidal stream where vessels from foreign ports rode at anchor.

Whenever she walked on the bridge, Bellebelle always looked for the boy, Henry, she had met two years earlier. He was the only person with whom she had ever shared the secret of her magic fish. Month after month, when she was able to persuade her mother or one of the other whores to take her, she had searched all over the bridge for him. But, to her great disappointment, she had never seen the boy again. Of course she was almost fourteen years of age, too old for such things now. In truth, the last time she had gone to the bridge, six months ago at least, she hadn't caught so much as a glimpse of the fish.

"Come along now, Belle," Arnolf, the tavern keeper, called again. "I know ye hear me. No use putting things off."

With a shiver of fear, Bellebelle turned and reluctantly entered the tavern, lit as usual by smoking candles. At night it was a fearful place, filled with rough voices, screams, and wild laughter. Daytimes, however, the tavern was usually quiet, except for the rattle and call of the dicing players crouched in a far corner of the room. This afternoon Bellebelle barely noticed the trestle tables and wooden benches with their handful of drinking men. She ignored the invitations of two sailors, peg-tankards of ale in their fists, standing at the long wooden counter that ran half the length of the tavern, and brushed aside the half-drunk patron who reached out to grab her.

"I hope all goes well, lass," said old Arnolf, as he knelt in front of a row of wine casks resting on low wooden racks.

"Surely I'll draw a fine one," Bellebelle said, forcing a brave smile. "Gilbert says they'll all be gentlemen of means."

"Gilbert! He's a brothelmaster, lass. Only a fool would believe the likes o' him." He shook his head. "Eh, you'd see the good in the devil himself, Belle." Arnolf lowered his voice. "Means or no, there be noblemen as rough and vicious as them sailors, make no mistake. That knave ought to be whipped raw, selling off your maidenhead like it were a catch of herring. Eh, I suppose ye were lucky Gilbert waited this long."

She did not reply, for Old Arnolf had voiced Bellebelle's deepest terror. From years of listening to the whores she knew that some customers could be rough and hurtful. Especially the big, hulking creatures from the docks. The whores dreaded such men, but Gilbert, the brothelmaster, forced them to accommodate all customers. Except on one rare occasion, which Bellebelle had never forgotten. Her mother, Gytha, had refused to service a man because of the size of his member, saying it would kill her. Gilbert had beaten Gytha for not doing as he bade her, but Gytha said she would rather suffer the beating than the member.

Bellebelle pushed the horrid incident from her mind, walked slowly out the back door of the tavern, and lingered in the small dirt yard that separated the tavern from the back entrance to the brothel-house. She dreaded the moment when she would have to enter the downstairs room of the brothel and face an unknown group of customers who were there for the sole purpose of bidding for her maidenhead.

All the whores assured Bellebelle that she was wondrous fair to look at. The glances of the men in the brothel and tavern tended to make her believe this. But the men assembled this afternoon were of a different class, wealthy and more particular—or so Gilbert had boasted. Such men did not usually visit the Bankside stews of Southwark. What if none of them liked how she looked, and refused to bid? She was anxious to please, and skilled enough with what the whores had taught her, she felt certain, to satisfy. But if no one wanted her, Gilbert would not keep her on. How would she survive? She desperately wanted to succeed. How else could she ever realize her dream of—

"What in God's name be keeping ye?" Gilbert stood in the doorway to the brothel-house. With a menacing glare, he crooked an impatient finger. "Get in here now and be quick about it."

Bellebelle scuttled across the yard and followed Gilbert into the back room of the brothel. Inside, his face now wreathed in smiles, Gilbert slid behind a table. Facing him stood a group of ten men.

"Here she be," Gilbert said in the oily voice he reserved for the customers. "Take off ye clothes, girl, but keep ye chemise on."

Her heart pounding, Bellebelle averted her eyes from the men. With shaking fingers she took off her worn black shoes and woolen stockings, aware of their lustful gaze watching every move. She forced herself to repeat silently her mother's constant words of admonition: "Lust is naught to be feared, but used to ye own advantage. When ye don't see it, then ye needs worry."

"As ye can see, Bellebelle here be a vision of unsoiled loveliness, a virgin pure as a nun," Gilbert was saying to the men. "But the lucky gentleman as wins her maidenhead won't be disappointed, that I promise ye, for she be a virgin with a lifetime of experience.

Her mam be me finest whore and the girl's been in training, so to speak, since she been born." He gave a lecherous wink. "Learned her trade with her mother's milk."

"You mean to say she's known nothing but the brothel-house?" There was no mistaking the shock in the man's voice. "What a terrible fate for the lass."

"That's right, nor never likely to know nothing else neither. As for a terrible fate, well now, I daresay that be a matter of opinion. She might be dead: I could've thrown her to the dogs to eat, or dumped her into the river, but I kept her out of the goodness of me heart."

And for the coins ye be about to pocket, Bellebelle wanted to say as she slowly pulled the faded blue gown over her head. If Gilbert had a heart she had never seen hide nor hair of it.

Shivering in her faded chemise, Bellebelle paraded back and forth in front of the men.

"All right now, ye've all had yourselfs a good look," Gilbert said. "Let's see the money first and then we'll open the bid."

While the men, arguing among themselves, emptied their purses onto the table, Bellebelle crept to a corner of the room and sat on a stool. She did not want to hear herself being auctioned off like a catch of herring, so she forced herself to think of something else.

From as far back as Bellebelle could remember, she had always wanted to better herself: by which she meant, if anyone had asked, that she did not want to lead her life in the same manner as her mam had done. Her earliest memories were of Gytha sprawled half-naked across a wooden frame bed, reeking of ale and weeping, complaining of how bad her life was. On those rare occasions when Gytha lay alone, Bellebelle would creep into the bed under the dirty gray blanket of unwashed wool and wind her tiny arms around her mam's neck in an effort to comfort her. More often, however, Gytha was joined by a succession of strangers, men who heaved and grunted over her unresisting body, then threw several coins onto the bed before putting on their clothes and leaving. They rarely paid attention to Bellebelle silently curled up on a straw pallet in the corner.

Her mother's chamber was her place of business as well as their home. It contained a large frame bed, rickety oak table, two scratched wooden stools, and a chest, also of oak, which held their few belongings. In addition there was a charcoal brazier, an iron cauldron of water, and a heap of worn linen towels that always looked dirty.

One night that Bellebelle would never forget, a comely man clad in a black cloak fastened at one shoulder with a heavy silver clasp, noticed Bellebelle in her corner. He reached into the purse fastened to his jewel-studded black belt then bent to give her a silver coin.

"Here," he said in a kindly voice, lifting the tangle of black curls from her dirt-streaked face as he stared into her large, dark-blue eyes.

She had never seen such a well-favored man before in the brothel.

"What a beautiful rose to bloom in such a dungheap. No low-born country lad sired this gosling, I'll warrant, nor foreign soldier either, if I'm any judge. Do you know the father, Gytha?"

"Oh, aye, a fine gentleman he were, my lord, a Norman like ye-self," her mother said, a note of bitterness creeping into her voice. "She be his spitting image. Even he could see that. Promised he'd care for the babe, and for a while he come back regular to see her. Sent money for her keep when he couldn't come hisself. Then he come no more. Never 'eard from him again."

"The country's been beset by civil strife these many years," the man replied. "Did it never occur to you he might be dead?"

Gytha shrugged. "Either way he be gone. As for beauty, what'll that get the lass, eh? A life in the stews is all, same as me. Better she were born dead, I say."

"May God forgive you for that." The man gave Bellebelle a sweet smile as he crossed himself. "Perhaps He has a different future in mind for her. What are you called, child?"

"Ykenai or Belle."

"I gives her the old Saxon name of Ykenai, but she were born on the last bell of Matins, Michaelmas Eve," said Gytha, "so's the whores call her Belle."

"*Une belle Belle.*" The man chucked her under the chin.

"Bellebelle." She repeated it with a shy smile.

The name had stuck. Although she never saw the man again, the incident took on a particular significance in Bellebelle's mind for two reasons: it was the first time she became aware that her father was a particular man her mother remembered, not a faceless, grunting stranger. This unknown father had come back to the brothel to see her, even sent money for her. In her own eyes she became a different person.

The second reason was that the man had said God might have a different life in mind for her. It was the first time such a possibility had occurred to Bellebelle, and she tucked it away deep in her heart where it comforted her like a charcoal fire on a frosty morning.

"The likes of him can preach of a different life," Gytha started wailing the moment the man had gone. "But what else can a whore's brat be but a whore—for as long as you be mistress of your looks." She snatched up a steel mirror, the treasured gift of a regular patron, and carefully examined herself.

With her cloud of pale gold hair, violet-blue eyes, and milky skin, her mother was the most beautiful creature Bellebelle had ever seen. Pure Saxon, Gilbert said. Bellebelle passionately wished she looked more like her.

With a discontented sigh, Gytha threw down the mirror and reached for the wooden pitcher of ale that stood on the scarred oak table near the bed. Bellebelle, who had wanted to ask her mother about this unknown father, knew that her mother had, as usual, forgotten she was there. Soon Gytha would be too flown with ale to make any sense. The moment passed and Bellebelle never again found either the right time or the right words to ask her.

There were no other children in the brothel-house, which was unusually small as it held only five or six women. The larger houses often had as many as twenty whores. Gilbert, the brothelmaster, ran the house, controlled the women, arranged for their customers, and beat them for disobedience or not pleasing the men they serviced. On such occasions Bellebelle would stop up her ears so she would not hear their screams. When the whores were idle they spent their time gossiping among themselves, so she became well aware of what a hard life they led: on the street they were forced to wear striped cloaks so that their profession would be instantly recognized. This subjected them to cruel jeers and taunts, often worse. Their freedom to come and go as they pleased was restricted by the brothelmaster, to whom they were virtually slave-bound. They could not leave the brothel-house of their own accord, but Gilbert was at liberty to throw any one of them out at his whim when they grew too old or worn out to be of use, or when they were suspected of having the burning sickness in their female parts.

Belle knew that her mother was Gilbert's most popular whore. He gave her only the better class of customers: city burghers, the few petty lords that sometimes came to Southwark, prosperous country farmers, knights from across the Channel, and the like. The rough dockside men, sailors, and other rogues of Southwark he kept for his less well-favored doxies.

Most of the time Gilbert ignored Bellebelle, until one day about two years ago. Gytha had sent her to the cookshop down the road, an outing she always dreaded. The cookshop lay in the center of a huge yard filled with treacherous potholes, mud puddles, and squawking chickens. Wreaths of black smoke curled upward into the sky and the air was always filled with the odor of baking bread and roasting meat. Skinny barefoot children played in the puddles; haggard women, fretting babies in their arms, gossiped among themselves. They always eyed her darkly, looking hungrily at her basket filled with hot eel pasties, a long wheaten loaf, and roast fowl.

"Slut's brat," they taunted. "Bastard. Who's ye father, eh?"

Bellebelle did not understand why the women called her names or the other children refused to play with her, sometimes driving her off with stones and offal. She quickly ran through the yard, her basket swinging from her arm, and did not pause for breath until she was in sight of the brothel-house and tavern.

On this particular morning, Gilbert, a short man with a fat paunch and greasy hair, was standing by the door watching her. A look came into his little pig eyes that gave her a queasy feeling in the pit of her belly.

"Ye be growing up, little one," Gilbert said, leering at her. "Come'ere." Without waiting for her to comply, he ambled over to her and ran a dirty hand over her flat bony chest.

"What ye think ye be doing?" said a sing-song voice behind her. "Belle be too young for that, not yet come into her courses."

Turning her head Bellebelle saw Morgaine, the Welsh whore, approaching the brothel-house. She was dressed in a clean but faded blue gown under her striped cloak. Her mane of shaggy brown hair fell in a thick braid down her back; around her neck glittered a silver crucifix and a necklace of shiny blue stones marked with a strange design.

"She be growed soon," Gilbert said. "In a few years time she'll be me prize, she will, a real beauty." He paused. "Though there's some would like her just as she be." He ran a thick white-coated tongue over dry lips. "If this be the house down the road there," he continued, jerking his thumb to the left, "she'd naught be virgin still. But

I doesn't hold with children fornicating. Spoils 'em when they starts too young."

Morgaine fingered the bone-handled knife, its blade honed to a sharp edge, that she was never without. "It'd kill Gytha if ye tried to sell Belle before time. Just ye leave the lass be, look ye. Mayhap she'll not want to follow in her mam's footsteps." She fixed Gilbert with a penetrating stare from her deep-set brown eyes.

Bellebelle watched Gilbert shift from one foot to the other. Even though Morgaine worked for him, she made him uncomfortable—as she did everyone.

"Don't be daft. What else would the lass do? What else be she fit for?" He ran his eyes over Bellebelle and rubbed his hands together. "She'll fetch a good price first man as has her. Virgins always does. Time she earned her keep."

A hot wave of resentment clogged Bellebelle's throat. She had been earning her keep in one form or another—emptying slops into the river, fetching and carrying, sweeping up—ever since she could walk.

Despite her dreams of bettering herself, Bellebelle had still not come up with any other means of earning her livelihood. Her mother had just begun to instruct her in the business of being a whore, telling her about men, how to arouse them if they were timid, for instance, or unable to perform. A customer who not be satisfied wanted his money back, Gytha warned, and would cause trouble. Therefore she must be mistress of all the tricks of her trade. Bellebelle was just now learning how to suck and rub on a customer's private parts.

Morgaine tousled her dark curls. "Don't mind the greedy old goat," she said, as Gilbert shuffled off. "Just don't let him catch ye alone, look ye."

Bellebelle had already become adept at evading the lecherous fingers of men who tried to catch her alone, but she smiled her understanding. Morgaine was her favorite whore.

Stolen from her family in the Welsh mountains at fifteen, she'd been sold to the brothel two years ago. Bellebelle had heard her mother say that Morgaine possessed a secret remedy, known only to the women of her Welsh tribe, for shrinking and restoring muscle tone to her female parts. It was her boast that she could make a man spew in minutes. She was popular among the customers, but the other whores feared her for she supposedly cast spells and had the gift of healing and second sight. Behind her back, Gilbert referred to her as the Welsh witch.

"I just come from that fat pig of a priest at St. Mary's," said Morgaine. "Wouldn't give me communion again. 'Not unless ye gives up ye sinful, wicked life,' he says, may St. David curse him."

Unlike the other whores, Morgaine always attended Mass whenever Gilbert permitted her to leave the brothel. The priest always refused to give her communion but she kept returning anyway. It was from Morgaine that Bellebelle learned the few simple prayers she knew: the Hail Mary and the Lord's Prayer. In addition she had taught Bellebelle a few Welsh runes that sounded like gibberish but which she chanted on nights when the moon was full.

"If I not want to work in the brothel, Morgaine," Bellebelle asked, "where else could I go?" She sat on the wooden steps and pulled her yellow smock over her knees.

The bawd gave her a startled look. "By St. David, I don't know, lass. Can't imagine what I were thinking of when I said that to Gil. Mayhap there'd be work for ye in London—selling herring or hawking other food on the streets." She paused before adding doubtfully, "I suppose ye might marry one o' the men round these parts."

Bellebelle thought about this. She had seen the herring sellers and eel-wives trudging about the Bankside in all sorts of weather, their backs bent under the heavy wooden trays slung across their shoulders. They looked old and shriveled before their time, far worse than the whores. When she thought of the rough dockside men, coarse and vicious, the sailors who came to the brothel, she shuddered.

"Mayhap I'd rather be a whore," she said slowly. "If ye gets a customer to like ye well enough to take ye away from the Bankside stews, then mayhap it be possible to save enough money and leave off early on, 'afore ye gets old."

Morgaine gave her an indulgent smile. "And what would ye do then?"

"I don't know." Bellebelle knit her brow, trying to explain what she meant. "Lead an easy life where people be nice to ye. Not always be having to please."

"That's naught but a dream, Belle, best put it behind ye. No life be easy. No female's life leastways. Hard work, not much joy, and ye looks don't hardly last whether ye be a whore, herring-seller, or a fine gentlewoman dropping babies every year. Even the womenfolk in me tribe was old and worn out 'afore their time. For us, one life be much like another, I expects." She snorted, her nostrils flaring. "And ye always be having to please, look ye. Some of us gets paid for it and some doesn't, that's all."

Morgaine sighed. "Time ye understood these things proper, lass."

Bellebelle chewed her lip. She'd rather be paid for it.

"Well, mustn't grumble, eh, Belle? We got ourselfs a roof over our heads and food in our bellies. Just ye remember, lass, whatever ye does, do it proper. Don't never get no wishbone where ye backbone ought be."

Morgaine gave an embarrassed laugh and punched Bellebelle playfully in the ribs. "Listen at me, will ye? They'll have me preaching the sermon at St. Mary's next 'stead o' that whoreson priest. Go on now, take ye basket upstairs."

Although Bellebelle waited expectantly, the next two years brought no visible change to her life. The civil war between the Empress Maud and King Stephen of England continued to take a great toll on the country. Despite the conflict that raged outside, inside the narrow world of the brothel-house nothing ever changed. Except that she was growing up.

One day she noticed that she had begun to sprout breasts, her hips were rounder, and shortly thereafter she started her monthly flux. Her mother complained that she stank like a slops bucket, forced her into a wooden tub of water, scrubbed the filth off her face and body, and washed the lice out of her hair. When she had dried her off Gytha stepped back then stared as if she had never seen her before.

Bellebelle picked up her mother's steel mirror and, somewhat fearfully, gazed into it. A stranger looked back at her. What had happened to the skinny runt, all eyes and tangled hair? Wonderingly, she touched the delicate oval of her face. Here was a young girl with soft ringlets, black as a moonless night, that fell well below her shoulders. Against her milky skin, now pink from the scrubbing, her eyes gleamed like dark blue stars. Gytha suddenly burst into tears. Bellebelle couldn't imagine why, but she was so used to Gytha's weeping and tantrums she no longer sought reasons for them.

As unlike her fretting, anxious mother as day from night, Bellebelle was grateful for her serene, cheerful disposition that, along with her looks, she decided must have come from the father who had been a fine Norman lord.

One morning Gilbert caught her alone in the chamber. Bellebelle had been tidying up Gytha's usual mess of clothes strewn over the bed, wet linen towels hanging over the furniture, and half-filled wooden cups of ale lying across the floor. He had crept into the chamber, approached her from behind, and before she could stop him caught her around the waist. His stinking breath in her face made Bellebelle want to vomit and she struggled to free herself. When his hands clutched her small round breasts she began to scream and kick behind her at his legs. He let go just as Gytha and Morgaine rushed into the chamber and routed him out with curses and threats. He denied he had any intention of ravishing her— though he had every right to do so if he wished—he just wanted to find out if she were ready.

"And she be ready," he announced. "A real beauty, she's big enough now to earn her way proper. Fondlin' and suckin' on the customers don't bring in enough for her keep."

"She be too young," Gytha said, sniffling. "Can't be more'n eleven. Ten more like."

"She do get younger each year to hear ye tell it. That lass be all of thirteen, close to fourteen more like, if she be a day," Gilbert said. "I remembers when she be born even if ye lost what wits ye had in the ale jug. No more delays now, Gytha. She earns her keep like a proper doxy or I sells her down the road, I does."

The threat silenced Gytha.

"I'll get me best and richest customers together and put her maidenhead up for sale. Highest bidder wins her. She'll make me rich, she will."


"Sold!"

Gilbert banged a heavy fist down on the table. "To the gentleman from London. The goods to be delivered tomorrow night. Ye be a most fortunate man, Sir, most fortunate."

Bellebelle, startled out of her memories, jumped. She had almost forgotten where she was or what was happening.

"C'mere, girl." Gilbert beckoned her.

She walked over to the table, trying not to shrink from the look of disappointed lechery reflected in nine pairs of eyes. Steeling herself, she cast an anxious sideways glance at the man who had won the right to break her maidenhead.

Suddenly Bellebelle felt giddy with relief. He was youngish, plump, with a ruddy face. The fur-lined cloak, black velvet tunic, and gold chain around his neck indicated to Bellebelle that he was prosperous. He gave her a timid smile which she returned.

Quickly slipping on her clothes, she left the room, anxious to tell her mother that the gentleman who won her seemed the kind that would be easy to please. In truth, Bellebelle realized in surprise, she was now actually looking forward to tomorrow night when her life as a working whore would begin at last.

CHAPTER 9

The following morning all the whores crowded into Bellebelle's tiny chamber. Newly scrubbed, the cubicle contained a charcoal brazier, a wooden bed with a thick straw mattress, rickety stool, one bucket for slops, another for water, and a scarred wooden chest. It was the very first place that belonged entirely to her and she loved it.

The day was unusually mild for midwinter. Bellebelle, perched on the stool, watched Gytha lounging on the mattress in a white chemise and coarse wool stockings, sipping from a wooden cup of foaming ale. Since sun-up the whores had been telling tales of how they lost their maidenheads, and giving Bellebelle the benefit of their experience.

"Always vash your lower parts, yah, mit vite wine or fresh animal piss," said a buxom whore newly arrived from Flanders.

"We drinks mostly ale here. Gilbert would never give us white wine. Anyways, vinegar and water be just as good. But I've taught the lass all that," Gytha said. "What herbs to use and when. Belle don't want to be caught out like I was with her."

"Ye must always pretend to be pleased," said a plump girl, Agnes, with a giggle, making a place for herself on the bed. "I often close me eyes and gasp loudly as if I would fair swoon away."

"Some fools'll believe anything." Morgaine appeared in the doorway. "More important to beware of men as has a touch of the devil in them, look ye." She crossed herself and then held up two fingers in the ancient sign to ward off evil.

"Like that funny customer who wanted to be whipped?" Belle-belle looked questioningly at her mother, shuddering at the memory of Gytha standing over the man, beating him with a soft calf whip which he himself had brought, while she fondled his private parts as he howled in pleasurable pain.

"No. T'weren't no harm in him," said Gytha, "nor the poor soul as had me put him in rusty leg irons 'afore he could do anything. But there be a few like to cause pain, though Gilbert don't favor suchlike."

Bellebelle knew that Gilbert's establishment did not provide really hurtful practices as did some other brothels on the Bankside.

"Honest fornication, that's what I be selling," Gilbert often proclaimed with a righteous air. "None o' those devilish perversions for me. I don't 'old with children under twelve, boys o' any age, nor nothing that draws blood. No heavy violence, says I, or out ye goes."

"I seen that Londoner as won ye, and he don't have an evil look. I asked me runes to be certain." Morgaine smiled reassuringly at Bellebelle, who knew that the Welsh whore kept a wooden box of stones with strange markings on them similar to the blue necklace she wore.

The other whores crossed themselves upon hearing about the runes. Bellebelle did not know why they feared Morgaine and her magic stones. How was this different from the power they said lay in the crucifix?

"O' course he might be one of those as wants ye to call him father or brother, or calls ye by the name of one of his sisters, or his mother," Gytha said. "Daft in the head but t'ain't no harm in them neither. Each to his own, says I."

She giggled. "Morgaine, ye remember that funny old man who called us all Sister Mary and blessed us afterward?"

"The one turned out to be a country priest? I'll not soon forget him." Morgaine rolled her eyes. "We had to pray 'afore and after. Fair wore out my knees it did."

"Then 'afore he left he tries to get us all to give up our sinful life," Gytha said.

Morgaine snorted. "Give up our sinful life, says I? Why the bishop o' these parts would fair starve if we was to do that. Who do ye think Gilbert pays his rents and license fees to? I asks. Bishop o' Winchester, that's who. They all be alike, them churchmen, preachin' against sin with the one hand and collecting the wages of sin with the other."

"Strangest one I ever had could only be pleasured if I stood naked 'afore him and wrung the neck of a chicken," Gytha said, shaking her head in wonder. "Gilbert charged him double, to pay for the chicken, then sells the dead bird to the cookshop."

The whores burst into laughter but Bellebelle felt sick to her stomach, hoping she would never have to hurt anyone as part of her duties—either man or bird. She enjoyed taking care of people, and liked to give pleasure, but she could not bear the thought of causing pain. Hopefully, the man who won her would want nothing unusual.

That night when the rich burgher from London, whose name was Jehan de Mornay, appeared, he was far more anxious than Bellebelle. When she stood naked before him, her flesh glowing in the light of a single candle, he stared at her as if caught in a spell. His hands trembled as they touched her budding breasts. Bellebelle, who had been steeling herself for a rougher assault, felt surprised—and relieved—at how gentle he was. He spent a long time examining her body and caressing it, before finally entering her.

She was prepared; he was slow and careful, but still it was painful, more painful than she had expected, and Bellebelle could not keep from crying out when he broke her maidenhead. Moments later he spilled his seed. Thank the Holy Mother, it was over. Jehan seemed embarrassed by the blood-spattered sheets and distressed at Bellebelle's obvious discomfort. She was grateful he was so concerned, and when he left without making another attempt, she wept with relief.

When Jehan had gone, she washed herself with the vinegar and water Gytha had provided for her. Bellebelle quite liked Jehan but the whole business, despite all her knowledge, was far worse than she had imagined. How could the whores endure it night after night, year after year?

"Mustn't grumble, lass," said Morgaine later, applying a healing ointment to Bellebelle's afflicted parts. "I knows ye hated it, but it could've been even worse, look ye. The tales I could tell—" she shook her head and crossed herself. "St. Mary Magdalene watches out for whores and she was with ye tonight."

The other whores assured her she would get used to it and not even think about what was happening. But Gytha cried and cried, then drank herself into a dead faint. Bellebelle spent the rest of the night holding her mother in her arms.

To the envy and amazement of the whores, Jehan de Mornay arranged with Gilbert that Bellebelle should be his private doxy while he was in London. Neither Gytha nor Morgaine, the queens of the brothel, had ever received such an offer. Gytha was torn between fits of jealousy and bursts of pride. Bellebelle accepted her good fortune as a matter of course. After all, she had dreamed of something like this happening, and now it was coming true. She saw it as the first step in realizing her plan of getting out of Southwark.

Despite the civil war that continued to rage between King Stephen and his cousin, the Empress Maud, Jehan's business interests often took him across the Channel to Normandy and Paris. When he was gone, Bellebelle was free to accept other customers— which she did only when Gilbert forced her. While Jehan was in London he came to Southwark two or three times a sennight, bringing her a continuous stream of gifts.

For the first time in her life Bellebelle had new clothes, not an old gown cast off by either her mother or one of the other whores. Her first new gown was of pale cream sendal with long flowing sleeves to wear under a blue wool tunic bordered in red and green around the hem. It was very fashionable in Paris, Jehan explained, where Queen Eleanor set the style. In addition, he bought her gold and black leather shoes, white woolen stockings, a gold brooch set with seed pearls, and a black cloak striped in red, the hood and inner lining covered with gray squirrel fur. Never in her life had she seen anything so wondrous. When Bellebelle was alone she sometimes stroked the fur as if the animal were still alive.

In addition to gifts, Jehan also brought her news of the world across the Channel.

"There have been serious disturbances in Outremer. Pope Eugenius III dictated a bull urging King Louis and all his faithful vassals to protect Eastern Christendom from possible infidel attack," he told her one night in early March. "The Holy Father promises them remission for their sins. It is said Louis will go to appease God, who has failed to grant him a son. In a hundred and fifty years of Capet rule there has always been a male heir."

"What sins could he have committed that God would not grant him a son?" Bellebelle gave him a puzzled look. They were sitting on her bed eating roast chestnuts which Jehan had brought her from London.

Jehan shrugged. "Despite his reputation for saintliness, King Louis is far from being a saint—in my opinion. Take the affair of the queen's sister, Petronilla, and Ralph of Vermandois, for example." He clucked disapprovingly. "Surely you have heard? It was the talk of Paris."

"I doesn't remember. What happened?"

Jehan settled himself more comfortably on the bed. "Ralph was married to the sister of the count of Champagne. A very powerful lord. He persuaded three bishops to annul the marriage—with Louis's connivance it is said—so he could wed Petronilla. The enraged count of Champagne appealed to the pope, who not only excommunicated the adulterous pair, but Louis as well!"

Bellebelle nodded. She had heard about excommunication from Morgaine. "So that be why he must appease God?"

Jehan threw a dried-up chestnut across the chamber. "In part. It gets worse. Goaded, so they say, by Queen Eleanor, to take action against the count of Champagne, Louis invaded the count's lands, and set fire to the houses and huts in the town of Vitry." Jehan's voice dropped to a hush. "Thirteen thousand inhabitants fled into the sanctuary of the cathedral, but the flames spread to the roof, which caught fire. All those trapped inside perished." He crossed himself.

Bellebelle gasped aloud. "How horrible! Poor souls. No wonder the king wants to make amends."

Jehan sighed. "Louis has fallen into a deep melancholy, I hear. Mortifies his flesh and will not eat. Apparently impressed with this evidence of true remorse, the pope has just granted Louis a full pardon and restored him to the bosom of the Church."

"Do the Franks hold this against him?"

Jehan shook his head. "The French love Louis. In truth, everyone blames Louis's queen, Eleanor of Aquitaine. If she had not backed her sister's sinful cause, people say, none of this would have happened. There's vicious gossip against her, especially from the Church, who has always hated her from the day she married Louis."

Bellebelle popped a chestnut into her mouth. "Why does they hate her?"

"The prelates say she influences Louis against them, and behaves in a manner unbecoming to the wife of a reigning monarch."

Bellebelle felt a spurt of sympathy for this French queen, who was not the only one having difficulties with the Church. After all, Morgaine was always in trouble with the priest at St. Mary's. "What do the Church object to? Besides the—the affair of her sister."

"What don't they object to! The most recent example is the queen's desire to join the crusade—if it ever occurs. She has threatened to prevent her vassals in Aquitaine from going—which, as duchess, is her right—if she cannot go too. It's the talk of Paris."

"Has you seen her? What do she look like?" Bellebelle bit into another chestnut.

"Beautiful beyond belief." Jehan kissed his fingers. "With the face of an angel, a body to match, and the presence of—of the queen that she is. Louis makes a poor show beside her." He went on to describe Eleanor in glowing detail.

Bellebelle, who could tell that Jehan, though disapproving, greatly admired the French queen, was stunned by his words. She was unable to imagine a woman who had so much power she could get her own way with men. It was men who ruled the world; women counted for nothing.

"The Frankish barons and the Church also resent the fact that Eleanor is duchess of Aquitaine in her own right," Jehan continued. "So much power should not be in the hands of a woman, they say."

Bellebelle shook her head. "I doesn't understand. If Mary can be the Queen of Heaven in—in her own right, like you said, what be wrong with Eleanor being duchess?"

Jehan chuckled. "It seems logical if you look at it that way, but don't let the priests hear you."

Bellebelle sighed. How she would love to meet this fascinating and strong-minded queen! Impossible, of course. But even knowing that somewhere such a woman existed was a kind of comfort.

From then on, whenever Bellebelle prayed to the Holy Virgin, an image of Eleanor of Aquitaine, as Jehan had described her, always appeared in her mind. The French queen became like her very own magic stone, a protection against the fears and evil of the only world she knew.

# CHAPTER 10

# Paris,

# 1145

*O*ne sunny afternoon in March of the year 1145, Eleanor was lounging in her solar in the refurbished Cité Palace. Her ladies were clustered around her while an Aquitainian troubadour sang a *joi d'amour.*

The steward entered with the news that Bernard of Clairvaux had arrived at the palace and requested an audience with her.

"I don't wish to see him," she said with a twinge of unease. "Make my excuses. Conduct him to the king instead. He is sure to be in the chapel."

The steward bowed and left.

Eleanor hoped he would hold firm to her instructions. The Cistercian monk was quite capable of persisting until he got his way. He did not recognize obstacles, she had observed, only challenges to be overcome. What could Bernard want with her this time? It was probably to do with the pope's intention to recapture Eastern Christendom from the infidel. The Holy Father was preaching another crusade and urging the Franks to take a leading role. Eleanor had told Louis that if he would not let her go, she would refuse to let the Aquitainian knights take part. The interfering abbé had no doubt got wind of this. Sometimes she wondered if he had spies listening at doors all over Europe.

The last time they met the monk had publicly called her a wayward daughter of Eve who had bewitched the gentle Louis and led him from the path of righteousness. She seethed at the memory.

"Abbé Bernard insists on seeing you alone, Madam," said the steward, reentering the solar. "Short of forcefully ejecting him—I do not see what I can do." He gave her a helpless look.

"I understand."

With a sigh of resignation Eleanor nodded her head, then dismissed the troubadour and her ladies. She decided to remain seated in her chair with its high carved wooden back and arms. She was queen. Let the abbé come to her. She smoothed the skirts of her crimson tunic and adjusted the cream-colored coif around her head. While she waited she watched the afternoon sunlight stream in through the enlarged window slits, bathing the chamber in a golden glow.

Abbé Bernard stalked into the solar, pale and stern as an Old Testament prophet, his cowled white habit hanging loosely from his gaunt frame. He looked more emaciated each time she saw him. The abbé took a few steps toward the armchair then stopped. Bending his tonsured head, he fixed his dark gaze upon her. Eleanor felt skewered by those great burning eyes; for what seemed an endless moment they stared at each other across the space of the solar. Neither tried to hide their enmity.

Despite her intention to make the monk come to her, Eleanor was mortified to find she had risen from her seat and was walking across the chamber. Bristling with resentment, she felt suborned by a will as strong as her own. No, stronger than her own.

When she stood before him, defiantly refusing to bow her head or modestly cast down her eyes, he addressed her in the low melodious voice that had transfixed hundreds of admirers.

"You must cease your constant meddling, Madam, your pernicious interference in affairs of state. What says Holy Writ? 'Turn away from your own will.' Your blatant encouragement of your sister's adultery, as well as inciting the king to invade Champagne, has set a disastrous example. It is France who suffers."

"France? How does France suffer?"

"If you do not see how then you are less intelligent than I give you credit for. What says Proverb Ten? 'Death and life are in the power of the tongue.' Do you deny that your influence over Louis resulted in his excommunication?"

Eleanor prudently held her tongue. Secretly she was proud of her influence over Louis. She could not directly control the affairs of France, but through her husband it was possible to create almost any effect she desired.

"Do you deny that your gross interference resulted in the death of thirteen thousand innocent people?" Bernard's voice heightened in intensity.

Trust him to rub salt on the still-raw wound of Vitry. How many times must she be reminded of the ignominious part she had played in that disastrous incident?

"Who could have foreseen such terrible results?" Eleanor said, signing herself. "But you cannot hold me responsible. It is typical of Louis to turn what should have been a minor invasion into a full-blown holocaust. A swift march into the count's lands, a show of strength, a brief skirmish would have been sufficient."

Bernard compressed his lips into a tight line. "You would do better to examine your own conscience, Madam, rather than criticize your husband. Remember Proverb Sixteen. 'There are ways that seem to men right, but the end thereof plunges down to the bottom of hell.' "

"You think I haven't searched my conscience? But in my opinion Louis stabbed himself in the foot with his own sword. Just as he did in Aquitaine." If he quoted one more proverb, Eleanor thought, she would scream.

"Aha! *Benedicamus Dominum!* Now we come to it," said Bernard with a look of triumph on his face. "You have never forgiven Louis for what he did in Poitiers, have you? You would sacrifice the welfare of France for the sake of that heretical, pleasure-loving sewer you prize so dearly!"

Eleanor stiffened. Everything he accused her of was true. Even now, remembering the sequence of events, she was filled with an impotent rage at what had happened two years ago when rebel leaders in Poitou renounced the king of France's authority and declared themselves a free city. She had been ready to leave at once for the duchy but Louis forbade her. Despite her entreaties and those of the vassal who had brought the news, he had remained adamant. It was the only time she had failed to persuade Louis to do her bidding. In the end, armed with letters from her and explicit instructions on how to handle the rebels, he had marched into Poitiers.

The result was total disaster. Louis had ignored everything she said. Instead of even attempting diplomacy, he had caught the rebel leaders unaware and punished them by hacking off their hands. Outraged and despairing, Eleanor had done what she could to salvage the situation and restore order, but the political wounds inflicted on Poitou had gone deep. She knew that if she wanted to keep what remained of the Poitevins' goodwill, she must never again allow Louis to visit the duchy unless she herself was present.

"I see you make no attempt to deny this, Madam!"

"Why should I deny it?" She gave Bernard a challenging look. "No, I have never forgiven Louis for his savage, senseless cruelty, his total lack of judgment, and I never will."

The monk turned his back on her and stalked over to the window slit, his arms crossed over his chest. "Do you know what the people say about you?"

"No, but I'm sure you will tell me."

He suddenly swung round and pointed an accusing finger at her. "It was an evil day for France, they say, when the Aquitainian sorceress married their beloved Louis. They despise you, Madam. Can you blame them?"

Eleanor, who had had no idea she was so hated, felt as if he had struck her, but would have died rather than let him see it. "I have done nothing to earn their displeasure. I think you go too far."

"On the contrary, Madam, I've not gone far enough. Done nothing, you say?" Bernard counted on his fingers: "One, and most important, you've failed to give the kingdom an heir. Two, your frivolous behavior, your constant meddling, is the scandal of all Europe. Three, it is no secret that your loyalty to Aquitaine is far greater than your loyalty to France. Have I not just heard evidence of that? Four, there are persistent rumors that you have put horns on your husband! What says Holy Writ? 'Go not after thy lusts.'"

Eleanor felt her cheeks burn, for even though the rumors of infidelity were untrue, the desire had been there.

"Do you have nothing to say? Am I to take your silence for an admission that these charges are true?"

She faced the monk with head held high. "The charge of adultery is an outrageous, vicious lie. Who dares to accuse me? Let the coward do so to my face. As for lack of a child, I thought *you* were going to change Louis's ways. If anything he has grown worse."

For a moment Bernard said nothing, his expression unreadable. "I'm relieved to hear these rumors are unfounded. There was much gossip when Louis dismissed that love-smitten minstrel from your court, and I have heard that Count Geoffrey of Anjou was overly attentive on more than one occasion . . . Remember Holy Writ: 'Pleasure brings punishment, and necessity wins a crown.'"

Eleanor steeled herself to remain courteous. "The bounds of propriety were never exceeded—in either case." This, thank the Holy Mother, was absolutely true. The minstrel had composed and sung to her a song that exceeded Louis's idea of good taste and, consequently, he had been sent back to Aquitaine. Geoffrey of Anjou had been attentive. If the opportunity had offered itself . . . Fortunately it had not.

"As you are well aware I did have a word with the pope, and he granted Louis a few dispensations," Bernard continued. "But now it is obvious to me that the fault lies elsewhere."

He wagged his finger at her. "Daughter of Belial, you must repent of your ways: Cease agitating against the Church and France; obey your husband as St. Paul commands, and set your foot on the path of righteousness, lest your shameful actions wreck this realm!"

His eyes bored into hers and she took a backward step.

"You disgust me, you and your women, laden with gold and silver, walking with mincing steps, bosoms thrust forward in a most unseemly manner, garnished and decorated in a fashion more fitting for a temple than a God-fearing court. Are you not ashamed?"

So the austere Bernard was aware of bosoms. Far from being ashamed Eleanor was intrigued.

"If you will agree to do what I say, and, in addition, abandon your sister's sinful, wanton cause, I promise, in exchange, to intercede with Our Lord to make you fruitful." Bernard paused. "It is well to remember that a barren queen can always be put aside—a word in the right ear—"

Stifling her anger, Eleanor was tempted to tell him it was ridiculous to threaten her—but was it entirely an empty threat? It might be wise not to put such a threat to the test where Bernard was concerned. Nor did it seem possible that this arrogant monk could in any way change her barren state. On the other hand there were many who could attest to his miraculous cures.

Eleanor thought quickly; in an instant her decision was made. Ralph and Petronilla must pursue their own course and fend for themselves—without further help from her. She would persuade Louis to make peace with the count of Champagne and return all the lands he had taken. As to what Bernard called her meddling—well, she could be less obvious about that. Not even Louis would realize where his ideas originated.

Effecting a modest demeanor, Eleanor lowered her eyes and clasped her hands to her breast. "Father, if by using your holy influence you can help me to have a child, I will do all that you wish."

A sudden treacherous thought entered her mind that made her blush. She totally despised this holy cleric. But if ever she found a man whose will and strength of purpose were equal to that of Bernard of Clairvaux, whose capacity for passion and zeal were not directed only toward God and saving souls—she did not let herself finish the thought.

"Very well, my child, I will do what I can. Sons are what France needs but, in addition, caring for your children will also keep you occupied and put an end to the rumors that you intend to accompany Louis on a crusade to the Holy Land. By God's wounds, what an outlandish idea!" He paused. "Be an obedient wife and the Holy Virgin is sure to answer our prayers. What says—"

"What Holy Writ says, Father, is that 'A wise man is known by the fewness of his words.' "

The austere lips twitched. Eleanor decided to ignore the thrust about the Holy Land. One thing at a time. She bestowed on Bernard her most charming, her most irresistible smile. The abbé gave her one last burning glance that told her he was not fooled for an instant; he knew very well what was in her sinful mind, and this only confirmed his belief that she was an evil corrupter of men. But she sensed that behind the iron wall of his judgment, hidden deep beneath the mask of the zealous monk, what little remained of the old Adam was not altogether displeased.

Louis made peace with the count of Champagne. By year's end, Eleanor at twenty-three gave birth to her first child, a daughter, called Marie after the Queen of Heaven. It was not the son she and Louis so desperately needed but it was a start. Eleanor, who had longed for a babe, was puzzled and not a little guilty to find that she had so little maternal interest in this weak and puling infant. She would never have believed herself to be such an unnatural mother, and this unexpected reaction greatly disturbed her.

Louis decided that in order to deserve a son he must do more to cleanse himself of sin. The incident at Vitry was never far from his mind, and he still wore a hairshirt and prayed day and night in the chapel.

"If I go on pilgrimage to the Holy Land, do penance at Christ's tomb, and remain celibate until then," he told Eleanor, "surely God will grant us a son."

Eleanor gave him a withering look. "I see. Being celibate for several years is the best way to beget a son?"

Louis frowned, not comprehending. Such reasoning was wasted on him.

Then, as if in response to Louis's intention, word arrived in Paris from Eleanor's uncle Raymond, the prince of Antioch, that the infidel Turks had captured the Christian state of Edessa. Raymond wrote that not only was Antioch in danger, Jerusalem itself was in dire jeopardy. He begged his niece to urge her husband to help the threatened Christian states. Suddenly the pope's entreaties to take action took on a new and personal significance for both herself and Louis.

"In addition to aiding your uncle, here is my chance to purify my soul and lead a crusade against the enemies of Our Lord," Louis said to Eleanor, tears of joy in his eyes. "I will ask the pope to let me lead this magnificent venture."

Now that her own family was involved, Eleanor also found herself stirred as she had not been before. She remembered her grandfather entertaining his court with tales of his exploits, amorous and otherwise, on the first crusade to the Holy Land. It was this experience, which had brought Duke William into close contact with the exotic Moslem world, that helped influence him to compose the songs and music that earned him the title of the First Troubadour.

Eleanor became more determined than ever to accompany Louis on this pilgrimage. Uncle Raymond, her father's younger brother whom she had not seen since she was a child of seven, was in trouble and pleading for aid. Raymond had been one of her staunchest allies; she remembered her disappointment upon returning home from Fontevrault to find him gone from Aquitaine. Of course she had heard about Raymond's adventures at the court of King Henry of England, then his travels to the East and his eventual marriage to a princess of Antioch. How she longed to see him again.

Little Marie was cared for by an army of nurses and did not need her. Most importantly, here, at last, was a chance to satisfy that craving for excitement and intrigue that continued to plague her. For the first time since she had become Queen, Eleanor felt she had something to look forward to.

• • •

"I've told you before that you cannot go with us, my dear," Louis said.

"Out of the question," echoed Abbé Suger.

Other members of Louis's council looked at Eleanor askance and muttered among themselves.

They were all gathered in Louis's council chamber on a cold day in February in the year 1146.

"Either I—and my women, of course—accompany you on this pilgrimage, Louis, or I will forbid the Aquitainian knights from joining you, just as I warned you I would. They will listen to me, and you cannot force them with threats and punishments as you did in Poitiers."

Louis paled, as he always did when she mentioned what he had done in Poitiers. He sent Abbé Suger an imploring look. The abbé, whom Eleanor knew disapproved of the pope's venture, no longer made the slightest effort to hide his dislike and distrust of her.

"Such a journey is most ill-advised, Madam. I do not think Louis should go. What will become of France if he is killed or maimed? As for yourself—"

"I've decided to go, Louis," Eleanor said, ignoring Abbé Suger. "If you persist in your objections, you are aware of the consequences. Let me remind everyone here that many noble women were present on the first crusade. Even today the roads of Aquitaine are always thronged with pilgrims en route to Compostela, many of whom are women. My grandfather himself told me that the Margravine Ida of Austria raised her own troops and rode at their head."

The council members looked at each other in dismay.

"I believe she was lost during the massacre," said Abbé Suger. "It is something to think upon."

The Troubadour had said Ida was captured by a powerful sultan and disappeared into his harem, a far more romantic fate.

Several days later Louis told her his council and the Church had reluctantly agreed to her joining them.

Eleanor herself went to Aquitaine to gather those knights and ladies she intended to take with her, and to appoint a loyal vassal who would manage affairs in her absence. In the duchy she was surprised by unexpected resistance from several of her chief vassals, who reminded her that their fathers and grandfathers had considered the first crusade a destructive venture: lands had been mortgaged to raise money and more men had died than returned. Why then should they risk their lives for strangers?

Eleanor finally persuaded a number of her barons to participate. Still there was only a half-hearted response, not only from the southerners but the French vassals as well. Solidly behind the crusade and worried by the lack of volunteers, the pope sent an urgent appeal to Bernard of Clairvaux, who agreed to speak at an open assembly in the hillside town of Vezelay in Burgundy on the thirty-first of March. The news brought such a multitude that a platform had to be set up outside the church so that everyone could hear him. Looking frailer than ever, the redoubtable Bernard addressed the huge crowd in a voice of thunder, urging everyone to forget their personal differences and unite against the infidel to free the Holy Land.

"All sins will be forgiven," he cried. "There will be an everlasting reward in heaven for those who take up the cross." Next to him lay a huge pile of red felt crosses. Bernard held one up. "A red cross on his tunic will be the sign of the crusader."

There was a great roar of approval from the crowd. Louis, overcome with religious fervor, fell weeping to his knees and prostrated himself before the Cistercian monk. Eleanor, moved despite herself, also vowed to take the cross.

Bernard raised skeptical brows. "I have noticed you are most pious, Madam, when your own interests happen to coincide with those of Holy Church."

After receiving her cross, Eleanor and several of her more daring companions vanished from the hillside. They returned some hours later. Astride white horses, dressed in crimson boots and white tunics, bright red crosses prominently displayed across one breast, they created a sensation. Swords held aloft, they galloped through the crowd, exhorting the faint of heart to follow God's call. There was little the shocked Bernard could do as a host of recruits fell all over themselves to take the cross.

Soon the entire crowd of barons, knights, churchmen, and humble folk were clamoring to get their crosses. The sun had set and darkness fallen, but still the people came.

Originally intended to begin in the spring of 1147, the crusade was delayed by enormously complicated preparations: taxes had to be raised all over Europe to pay for the gigantic enterprise; decisions made as to whether to travel by land or sea.

It was June of 1147 before the great host finally assembled at the Abbey of St. Denis outside Paris. Pope Eugenius III himself was there to invoke God's blessing upon the crusaders. As far as the eye could see there was a vast army of knights from Brittainy, Burgundy, Normandy, Paris, and Champagne, as well as Eleanor's vassal knights from Aquitaine. Foot soldiers had been gathered from every hamlet, town, and farm. In addition there were bishops, chaplains, barefoot pilgrims, beggars, and even felons, all hoping for salvation. Strings of horses led an endless train of arms, armor, catapults, battering rams, and movable towers. Wagons groaned under the weight of food and pavilions.

Eleanor was aware that men looked with disapproval at the huge numbers of her own retinue of lady companions, their maids, and troubadours; not to mention the vast array of carts to hold chests of bedding, robes, gowns, jewels, cooking and washing utensils, barrels of Gascon wine, and other necessities Eleanor had insisted they could not do without. Even pet falcons, strapped to their mistresses' wrists, had not been forgotten, despite Bernard's specific injunction not to bring them.

"Do you intend to loose the falcons against the infidel," asked Abbé Suger pointedly, "while the troubadours lull the enemy into submission?"

Eleanor disdained to answer, relieved that the abbé would be left in France, managing the realm in Louis's absence. Despite the many complaints about her entourage and the vast amount of baggage, Eleanor had no intention of letting anyone spoil this journey. Filled with anticipation, she felt certain she was setting forth on a glorious adventure; one destined to change her life.

# CHAPTER 11

# Southwark, 1148

To everyone's surprise, Jehan de Mornay remained Belle-belle's faithful customer. The whores said his devotion wouldn't last, but three years after breaking her maidenhead, he still came regularly to the brothel-house. He had taken no steps to remove her from the Bankside but then again she had not dared to raise the issue—and probably never would. She was only sixteen or seventeen—no one knew for sure—with many good years still left her, said Gytha.

One afternoon in mid-July, Morgaine and Bellebelle crossed the river into the city of London. They had persuaded Gilbert to let them have a few hours off and after much grumbling he had agreed, provided they were back to service the evening customers. The air was cool, the day filled with sunshine, the sky a clear blue dotted with puffs of white cloud.

Bellebelle sauntered slowly across the bridge, dressed in a blue-and-white striped cloak over a new rose-colored gown that Jehan had brought her, a small leather bag of coins tied round her waist underneath her chemise. A group of youths were out on the river tilting in small boats. She was reminded of the boy, Henry, she had met so long ago, and wondered, as she had so often before, what had happened to him. She paused for a moment to look over the railing but the fish was nowhere to be seen.

Morgaine grabbed her hand, hurrying her along, only slowing when they reached the Strand. Bellebelle, who had not been in London for almost a year, was amazed at the number of open stalls and taverns lining the streets. At least twice as many as she remembered. There was so much more to see now that her eyes hardly knew where to look first. Red-cheeked citizens, after a brief glance at their striped cloaks, good-naturedly jostled Bellebelle and Morgaine aside to stand in line at the public cookshop which sold coarse meats as well as quail and pheasant,

Caught up in the air of excitement, Morgaine and Bellebelle visited the stalls, eagerly eyeing bolts of wool and silk, leather boots from Spain, strings of onions and garlic from Brittainy.

"Ye'd never think there be a war going on," Bellebelle said. "Not here in London leastways."

Morgaine nodded. "It do be like Gilbert say. War or no war, some things goes on no matter what. Trade, food, and whoring."

By the admiring looks cast in her direction, Bellebelle was sure that, except for the striped cloak, no one would ever guess she was a whore, especially one from the Bankside stews.

"Come on now. We don't want to run out of time."

To Bellebelle's surprise, Morgaine seemed to have a particular destination in mind, darting down one twisted street after another. Finally she asked for directions and they came to a narrow lane.

"This be it. Gropecuntlane."

"Why we here?"

"It do be the home of a famous brothel, not like Gilbert's place and them rotten stews." Morgaine's eyes sparkled with excitement. "Different type whores work here."

"How different?"

"Well, the girls would 'ave better conditions to work in, wouldn't they? Only service rich or noble clients, I suppose, which means ye earn more money. All like Jehan only better."

They started slowly walking down the lane, which grew wider as they approached a row of tall wooden houses smeared with black, red, and blue paint.

Morgaine pointed out a wooden house with closed blue shutters that looked like a private dwelling, yet was different in some way from its neighbors. Down the lane stood a tavern with a freshly painted sign picturing a crowned blue cock. Next to the tavern was a cookshop, wreathed in a haze of smoke. Compared to Gilbert's brothel and the Bankside this area looked less dirty and not as dangerous.

"Look! That must be it." Morgaine nudged Bellebelle in the ribs. "What would ye say to working in such a place? That'd be grand, eh? A lass as looks like you wouldn't have no trouble finding work here. Shall we go in and have us a look round?"

Bellebelle stared at her in disbelief.

Morgaine laughed. "Cat got ye tongue?"

"How could I leave me mam? Ye know how she be needing me."

"O' course I does," Morgaine said in a soothing voice. "We just be seeing what it be like, look ye, that's all. Not a word to Gil or ye mam, but I be trying for a way to get ye out of Gilbert's stew, Belle. I knows ye been wanting that for donkey's years." Morgaine shot her a quick glance. "When the right time comes, I mean."

Church bells rang the hour of Nones.

"Didn't know it be so late. We must be off now, Belle."

All the way across the bridge, Bellebelle could think of nothing but Gropecuntlane. The idea of servicing only noble or wealthy clients like Jehan, in pleasant surroundings, opened up a whole new world. Her head buzzed with the possibilities. If a whore worked hard in such a place she might be able to make a lot of money, save some of it, and leave the brothel before she became too old or worn out. If she could find a way to take Gytha with her, find a small place to live out of Southwark . . . her dream of bettering herself suddenly seemed within reach.

"Gilbert'll take a stick to us," Morgaine said, practically running now. "We best hurry."

Bellebelle's heart sank. She'd forgotten about Gilbert. He would never, never allow her to leave. He owned her as he did all the other whores. She remembered the chilling tale Gytha had once told her about a doxy who tried to leave the brothel-house. Gilbert had caught her and beat her so cruelly she was marked for life. The poor drab could no longer work and was thrown out into the street to beg for her daily bread.

They reached the brothel just as the sun began to set. The tavern next door was already filled with the sound of drunken laughter and curses. Bellebelle noticed five horses being watched by grooms in livery.

When they entered the brothel-house, Gilbert grabbed Bellebelle and fairly shoved her up the stairs.

"Why you been gone so long, eh?" he asked, his eyes narrowed in suspicion. "Well, never mind that now. Got a party o' knights drinking in the tavern. A Fleming be with them, seems to be in charge. Ordered a fine supper from the cookshop, and then called for five o' me best whores. Ye both be needed. Look sharp now, girls, and make yourselfs ready."

This evening there was an unusual air of excitement about the brothel. In the passage upstairs, the whores, dressed in clean chemises, could hardly conceal their eagerness, except for Gytha, who was already in her cups and oblivious to what was going on.

The whore from Flanders followed Bellebelle into her cubicle while she hurriedly removed her cloak, gown, and bag of coins. When she was clad only in the oat-colored chemise, she splashed water on her face from the cauldron.

"Your mam's been svilling ale all day, yah. She be getting vorse, Belle, like she don't care no more if she be alive or dead." Her voice dropped to a whisper. "I caught her vashing herself out three and four times today with vater and vinegar, and scratching herself like a bitch mit fleas. You know vat dat means !"

Bellebelle looked at her in horror. The burning sickness! Each whore dreaded it, lived in constant fear of it, and knew that its onset meant the end of her life as a whore—if she got caught—or, in some instances, an early death.

Bellebelle had no time to question her further. There came the sound of bawdy laughter at the bottom of the stairs and she barely had time to arrange her hair, pinch her cheeks to make them look redder, and smile in the foolish way customers seemed to expect.

Her heart pounding, Bellebelle stepped out the door.

Gilbert, carrying a lighted torch, was puffing up the stairs. Of the five men who followed him, only one caught Bellebelle's attention. Around his neck he wore a silver chain from which hung a large silver medallion set with five green stones that blazed with fire in the torchlight. His fixed smile and dead eyes made Bellebelle feel sick to her belly. Beside her the Flanders whore gasped.

"*Meine Gott!* It's him—"

Bellebelle could see she had gone pale under the painted crimson of her cheeks. "Who?"

"Dat von—dat Fleming—" She pointed a fearful finger at the man with the silver medallion. "l know dat devil in Bruges. Varn whoever—"

One of the knights approached them with a snigger. "Which milk cow's got the biggest udders?"

The Flanders whore immediately pulled down her chemise revealing pendulous white breasts.

The knight reached out and fingered a rouged nipple. "This one's for me."

Her relief visible, the Flanders whore and the knight disappeared into her cubicle. Another knight picked the plump, giggly whore Agnes.

To Bellebelle's dismay she saw the Fleming's gaze immediately fasten on Gytha. He pointed a languid finger at her and something flickered deep within the snakelike eyes. Suddenly Bellebelle felt overwhelmed by a sense of foreboding so intense she almost cried out. Even without the warning she would have known, instinctively, that this man was not like the others, but one of those with a touch of the devil in him.

Bellebelle tried to signal her mother but Gytha, unsteady on her feet, paid no attention and, Fleming in tow, lurched into her cubicle. Too late. Morgaine, who had overheard the Flanders whore's warning, pressed Bellebelle's hand.

"Me room is close by ye mam's and ye be next door," she whispered hurriedly. "Keep a sharp ear out for anything that sounds— out of the way, look ye. Take this." She slipped Bellebelle her bone-handled knife.

Bellebelle nodded and instinctively hid the knife behind her, wondering what she was supposed to do with it. In truth, she didn't really know what Morgaine meant. In the brothel-house there were all sorts of odd sounds that were a natural part of the surroundings. How could she recognize one that was really unusual?

There was no time for further thought as her customer walked toward her. A stout man approaching his middle years, he gave Bellebelle a weary smile. Once inside the cubicle he threw himself down on the bed with a sigh, and asked Bellebelle to take off his boots and massage his feet. She did as he said, first laying the knife on the table next to the bed. Thus far, she could detect no noise from her mother's room next door.

The customer, who told her his name was Ralph, did not appear to notice her uneasiness or lack of attention. Instead, thank the Holy Virgin, he seemed more eager to talk than to swive her. He explained that he had ridden in from York with his own men and one Hans de Burgh, who commanded a troop of the king's Flemish mercenaries.

"De Burgh," she repeated distractedly, to show she was listening.

"A proper bastard if ever there was one. Christ, the tales I could tell you! The man's no better than an animal, like most of them are, but de Burgh's mother is Norman which makes it all the harder to understand. However, the king dotes on his Flemings so we must put up with them."

Bellebelle forced a smile, continuing to massage his feet while she tried to listen for any sounds that might be coming from next door. Suddenly, she realized that the man he was speaking about might well be the Fleming with her mother.

"Be he here?" she asked.

"Yes, of course. De Burgh's the man wearing a silver medallion set with emeralds. The one who took the flaxen-haired doxy."

Bellebelle's fear increased. If even his companion called him an animal . . .

"We defeated a raiding party of Scots in York," Ralph was saying now, "and just returned to London for reinforcements to take back north with us. There's a major battle expected with the king of Scotland and his great-nephew from Normandy, Henry Fitz-Empress . . ."

Bellebelle nodded, not really taking in what he said. Fortunately, a whore was never expected to answer.

Ralph gave a huge yawn. "I'm getting too old for these campaigns, by God. Perhaps you wouldn't mind if I just—" He fell sound asleep right in the middle of his sentence.

Relieved, Bellebelle quickly got up from the bed and crept over to the wall. Pressing her ear against it she listened carefully. For a while she could hear nothing, yet her uneasiness grew. It dawned on her that it was the total absence of any noise at all that was so frightening. Suddenly she heard a low chuckle that froze the blood in her veins. Then absolute silence.

Later, she could not remember picking up Morgaine's knife which she must have done, for when she slipped out of her cubicle and quietly opened the door to her mother's, it was gripped firmly in her hand.

The sight that met her eyes was out of some impossible hellish nightmare. Gytha, gagged tightly with one of her own stockings, her hands tied above her head with the other, was spattered with blood. Her eyes were wild with terror, her face contorted in a frozen scream. Her legs twitched and jerked, while the Fleming, naked, crouched on his knees over her body. A twisted smile on his face, he slowly and methodically dug into her flesh with a long knife.

No time to call for help. This devil was hurting her mother and must be stopped. Instinct flung her headlong into the cubicle; her body hurtled toward the bed with the speed of an arrow. As de Burgh scrambled off Gytha's body, Bellebelle's arm took on a life of its own, raising itself high above her head. With all the strength she possessed she brought her arm down, driving the point of Morgaine's dagger deep into de Burgh's side.

His hands shot out, gripped Bellebelle's throat with iron fingers, squeezing until she felt the chamber begin to spin. Then, his eyes glazing, he suddenly toppled sideways over Gytha's body.

Bellebelle, gasping for air, rolled him off the body and onto the floor. Her mother's eyes were now closed, her face slack. She had fainted. Kneeling beside her, Bellebelle tore the suffocating gag from her mouth, undid the stockings, and, weeping and choking, tried to staunch the blood oozing in rivulets down her naked body. To her horror, she could see that Gytha had also been burned with a candle, for there were angry red welts and dried wax over her breasts.

A noise at the door. Bellebelle turned her head to see Morgaine, fully dressed, standing in the open doorway. She entered, closing the door softly behind her.

"I left mine asleep," she said, her eyes raking in the situation in one fierce glance. "By St. David, I knew that beast be trouble but never like this." She walked over to de Burgh's body and looked down at the waxy face. "Holy Mother of God, have ye killed him then?"

Killed him? Uncomprehending, Bellebelle stared at the inert form. Had she actually killed de Burgh? Stricken, she looked at Morgaine.

"I—I doesn't know."

"Looks dead to me." She prodded him with her foot.

"Dead? But I—"

"Ye must leave, Belle. At once. His men'll be through soon and come lookin' for him. It won't take them long to learn who the culprit be, look ye. They'll be after ye quick as lightning and if they catch ye—" Morgaine crossed herself. "They can see what he done but he be the king's man, and ye and Gytha just be whores. They'll pay Gilbert to keep his mouth shut and who's to know?" She touched Bellebelle's bruised throat. "Here." She pulled the necklace of blue stones from around her neck and slipped it over Bellebelle's head. "For protection against the evil forces o' darkness."

"Me mam—I can't leave her."

Morgaine bent to examine Gytha's prone body, lifted her eyelids, then nodded. "Thank the Holy Virgin she fainted, or she'd be screaming to high heaven and ye'd have no chance to escape. We'll look after her, Belle, don't be feared. She's been cut up and burned but nothing that won't heal in time. It do look worse than it be. Ye saved her from . . . never mind."

She gave Bellebelle a push. "Grab your things, only what ye can carry easy like. Get over to London if ye can. To Gropecuntlane. They'll take ye in, like I told ye. Don't show ye face in Southwark. This be your chance, lass! Take it. Go now, d'ye hear? Now!"

Bellebelle's last sight of the cubicle was of her mother's bruised body; Morgaine coolly pulling out the knife from de Burgh's side, carefully wiping the blood-stained blade on the bed-sheet, and tucking it away under her skirts.

In a daze, Bellebelle ran out of the chamber. The passage was empty. She softly opened the door of her own cubicle. Snoring fitfully, the customer, Ralph, slept on. Hastily she rinsed her bloody hands in the cauldron of water, tied the bag of coins round her waist under the blood-stained chemise, slipped on the clothes she had worn earlier that day, stuffed a few belongings into a straw basket, then tip-toed out of the cubicle.

Numb with fear, her throat aching, she stood irresolute for a moment, not knowing what to do. Then the sound of giggles and lusty male laughter sent her scurrying to the top of the stairs.

With a last fleeting look of anguish at her mother's door, Bellebelle carefully crept down the stairs, crossed the tiny hall, and cautiously opened the door a crack. The shouts and singing from the tavern would cover any noise she made. Pushing the door all the way open she peered out. A short distance away she could see the outline of the horses and the grooms talking among themselves. A picture of her mother's burnt and cut body swam before her eyes and for a moment she swayed unsteadily. Sounds from above now, someone pounding on a door, and raised voices. With a prayer to the Holy Virgin to keep her safe, Bellebelle turned and ran down the dark passage that led to the back entrance.

She slipped through the open door, raced across the dirt courtyard, then out the rear gate. An unseen silent shadow, she sped
down the deserted street, away from the brothel-house, away from
her beloved, helpless mother, away from the only life she had ever
known. The night closed round her like a warm protective cloak.
Soon she was lost amid the dark twisted alleys of Southwark.

C H A P T E R   1 2

"*T*he wound's not mortal. You'll live," the black-robed physician said upon bandaging de Burgh's body.

"No thanks to that slut who tried to kill me," de Burgh muttered. "Here, help me to my feet."

Two knights helped him to stand, his body swaying between them.

Morgaine, sick with worry over what might be happening to Bellebelle, felt a sense of relief. At least the poor lass wouldn't be accused of murder. The other whores, along with Gilbert, Ralph, de Burgh, and three other knights were crowded into Gytha's cubicle.

The physician—usually flown with ale—who lived on the Bankside and sometimes tended them, shambled over to Gytha's unconscious body. After a cursory examination he spread an ointment over her wounds and burns then turned to Gilbert.

"Did you know this one has the burning sickness? The cuts and burns will heal in time but the other—" he shrugged.

De Burgh hissed like an adder. "Whoreson! Swine!" He shook a threatening fist at Gilbert. "What kind of a hellhouse do you run here? Before I'm through, you'll be in no condition to ever run a brothel again."

"Jesu, my lord, I swear I knew nothing," Gilbert said in a whining voice, his face ashen. "Me lords." He turned imploringly to Ralph and the others. "Gytha kept it from me. How could I know?"

"Has the filthy bitch infected me, do you think?" De Burgh looked fearfully at the physician. His face, beaded with sweat, was the color of suet, his eyes bloodshot and wild.

Morgaine shuddered. He looked sick unto death, and if there was any justice in this world this fiend of Satan would die of either his wound or the burning sickness.

"Who can say, my lord?" The physician threw up his hands. "Some become infected, some do not. It lies in God's hands."

De Burgh shook off the support of the men. Before Morgaine or the others realized what he was doing, he had staggered over to the bed and picked up his curved dagger that still lay there covered with Gytha's blood. He thrust the startled physician aside, then plunged the blade into Gytha's breast.

"Stinking carrion bitch, may you rot in hell," he cried, his face contorted with rage. Then, clutching his side, he began to sway on his feet. A crimson stain appeared on the white cloth.

The knights sprang after him and dragged him away, half-fainting, to a corner of the room. The whores screamed and covered their faces with trembling hands. With a cry, Morgaine ran to Gytha, although she knew the wound had done for her. Thank the Holy Virgin the poor creature had felt nothing.

"You're well out o' this mortal coil, m'dear," Morgaine whispered as she wept over her friend's lifeless body. "None can hurt ye now." She signed herself then muttered a few words in Welsh.

After a moment she dried her eyes then pointed an accusing finger at de Burgh. "Murderer! Murderer!" She turned to the other men. "Ye been witness to cold-blooded murder. Will none o'ye see justice done?"

Gilbert, regaining courage, nodded. "Aye, she be right. First this man tortures me best whore and now he's gone and killed her. I run a respectable house, I does, ye can ask anyone on the Bankside! Never had no trouble before that madman come."

De Burgh slumped unconscious to the floor. Ralph gave him a contemptuous glance. "Madman is right. I knew that rotten scum would go too far one day. Get the swine out of here and take him back to London."

One of the knights slung de Burgh's body over his shoulder and carried him out of the chamber. The other two knights exchanged uneasy glances.

"When the king's Flemish captain hears of this he'll be ready to strangle that doxy with his own hands," said one of the knights. "This is only a dead whore of no great account, but de Burgh is valuable to the captain. We cannot let her escape."

Ralph nodded reluctantly. "No, the poor lass must be apprehended and brought to justice, though God knows she had provocation. Go after her, she's on foot and can't have gotten far. Then one of you inform the sheriff—there should be a sheriff of Southwark."

The two knights quickly left the chamber.

"What about Gytha?" demanded Morgaine. If there was a sheriff of these parts, she'd never seen hide nor hair of him. Law on the Bankside? Not bloody likely. "Will ye no see justice done for her?"

Ralph sighed. "I fear de Burgh will never be brought to justice for this murder or for any of the other evil deeds he's committed. But here's compensation for you." He poured some coins into Gilbert's palm, a few into the physician's, and the rest into Morgaine's. "Divide this with the other whores."

Morgaine threw him a contemptuous glance. Did he really think money would make up for the loss of her friend? She felt so helpless; how could she right this terrible wrong? In these lawless times, where the king's writ carried almost no weight and hundreds died daily, who would care about the murder of one whore?

The bells had rung for Lauds before Gytha's body was cleaned up. Morgaine wrapped it in a sheet to be taken the next day to unhallowed ground, where Gytha would be buried in a pauper's grave—where they would all end.

Morgaine decided that tomorrow she would make one of her now infrequent trips to St. Mary Overie, light a candle to the Virgin, whether that whoreson priest liked it or not, and pray that somewhere, somehow, Bellebelle would find a safe haven. I be proud of ye, lass, she said to an invisible Belle; ye didn't show no wishbone where ye backbone ought be.

Bellebelle had no idea where she was. She must have been wandering through Southwark for hours as she had heard the church bells strike not only the midnight hour but Lauds as well. She had decided to wait until Prime then return to the brothel-house no matter what the danger might be. Despite Morgaine's reassurances, she could not just abandon her mother. Now she found herself in a web of narrow deserted streets that looked frighteningly unfamiliar, at least in the darkness.

Her body felt sticky with sweat and she was exhausted. Unable to go on she stopped for a moment to lean against the wooden wall of a house and catch her breath. She closed her eyes and immediately saw an image of her mother's cut and burnt body, the figure of de Burgh toppling over sideways, the hilt of Morgaine's knife protruding from his side.

She had killed a man.

Bellebelle knew she had done this but could not accept the terrible impact of such a crime. How could she, the gentlest of souls, who could not bear to hurt a living thing, even an insect, have murdered a fellow creature? Filled with horror, she felt black bile rise in her throat, and she looked down at her hands.

The sound of footsteps and raucous laughter intruded on her thoughts. Turning sharply she saw a band of youths lurching down the street toward her. Clad in black, they had the carefree look of student clerics. Praying they wouldn't notice her, Bellebelle tried to flatten herself against the wall of the house.

"Oh, I say, what have we here?" a drunken voice called out as one of the youths caught sight of her. "By all that's holy, a tart! What luck."

"How can you tell?" asked another slurred voice.

"She's wearing her striped cloak, fool."

In the glow of a full moon, Bellebelle saw there were four youths, all drunk, and of a mind to make mischief. Immediately they closed round her.

"We have already paid homage to Bacchus," announced one of the youths. "Now we must honor fair Aphrodite." He belched loudly. "Lie down, O beauteous goddess, and let us worship at your—ah—shrine."

There was a chorus of laughter. Hands tore at her cloak, which fell to the ground. Bellebelle could smell their hot wine-breath in her face, feel clawing fingers scrabbling at the skirts of her gown. She twisted and turned, pushed and blindly struck out at them. Terrified, she began to scream at the top of her lungs.

Above her head there was the sound of scraping wood as shutters were flung open and an outraged voice called out:

" 'Ere, stop that at once! At once I say! The watch'll be making 'is rounds any moment now and you best be gone 'fore he returns. What's the world coming to when honest folk can't get a decent night's sleep?"

The students stopped their assault and began to hurl insults at the voice above. While they were distracted, Bellebelle ducked and shoved between them, but could not retrieve her cloak from where it lay on the cobblestones. As she dashed down the street she turned her head to see a night-capped figure silhouetted in the window empty a bucket of slops over the students. Amid the howls and curses that followed no one bothered to pursue her. She ran on, swallowed up in the darkness.

Bellebelle had finally slowed to a fast walk when she heard the click of horses' hooves some distance behind her. It must be de Burgh's men looking for her. Even in Southwark, it was unusual for travelers to be riding the streets so late. Except for the unruly students she had met no one but a few stray dogs. Clutching her basket which, somehow, she had managed to hang onto, she started walking quickly down a wide street. This looked vaguely familiar. An imposing structure loomed out of the darkness and she realized it was the bishop of Winchester's house, with its large wharf and landing-place. At least she knew where she was now.

As the pounding hooves grew closer Bellebelle turned a corner and started running. At the end of the cobbled street she turned to see two riders rounding the corner behind her. Catching sight of her they spurred their horses forward.

Looking wildly for a means of escape, Bellebelle swerved left, saw a dark narrow alley, and slipped into it. Her heart pounded, her breath sobbed in her throat, and her legs felt as if they might buckle at any moment. Just ahead lay a wooden gate leading into a yard. She ran through the gate. Beyond rose the massive stone edifice of a church. On the eastern side a narrow door lay slightly ajar. Behind her the pace of the hoof beats increased. Bellebelle sped toward the door. Half falling, she stumbled headlong through the opening.

Barely able to see, Bellebelle made her way down an aisle with row after row of pews on either side. Her shoes sounded loud as drum beats against the tile floor. The aisle came to an end; she turned a corner and saw that she had entered a small chapel. It looked familiar. Surely this was the Lady Chapel at St. Mary Overie's, where Morgaine had taken her a year ago last Easter. It must be. The church, she remembered, was near the bishop of Winchester's dwelling. Now it was deserted, a little fearsome in the semi-darkness, with its empty pews and flickering candles. Her chest heaving, Bellebelle collapsed onto a pew. With any luck at all her pursuers would not think to look inside.

When her eyes adjusted to the dim light she saw a figure some distance in front of her, and she almost screamed. The figure did not move and after a moment Bellebelle realized it was the statue of the Holy Virgin that stood in front of the altar. Candlelight illuminated gold-encrusted blue robes over a white gown and the jeweled circlet atop her wimpled head. A gold scepter rested in one hand, an orb of the world in the other.

Voices and footsteps sounded outside the chapel.

"Most unlikely you will find your fugitive tart in the church," said a strange voice, "and if you did there is naught you can do to her while she's here in sanctuary."

"Not in the church, no," replied another voice. "But if she *is* here, she'll have to come out sooner or later. When she does, the Sheriff of Southwark—whom we'll inform—will be waiting. This business is in his borough and if we cannot find the cunt tonight it is his duty to search for her and bring her to justice. We return to York with a detachment of troops to do battle with the Scottish king and his nephew, Henry of Anjou."

It must be one of the knights in Ralph's party. Bellebelle fell to her knees, clasped her hands in front of her and screwed her eyes shut tight. The knights, initially flown with wine, had only seen her in her chemise in flickering torchlight. With these other clothes on she did not look like a doxy, and they might not recognize her. Thank the Holy Mother she had lost her striped cloak, which would have given her away immediately. Now they might mistake her for a predawn worshipper.

The footsteps entered the Lady Chapel then paused.

"But if the girl's mother is still at the brothel-house surely she'll return there?" the first voice asked.

"Someone will apprehend her if she does, Father," the knight's voice answered. "T'wont do her much good though. The Fleming, de Burgh, killed the mother when he found out she had the burning sickness. The whole place is in an uproar. Can't help feeling sorry for the little cunt. De Burgh acts crazed sometimes, likes to cause pain. The mother was bleeding like a butchered sow when I saw her. The girl was only trying to protect her mother when she stabbed him. But his captain won't like it, no matter the reason."

For an instant the words did not penetrate. Gytha dead? By de Burgh's hand? But she had killed him. Surely she'd not heard right. It must be a terrible mistake. The footsteps got louder.

"What a ghastly sight for the daughter to see. May God have mercy on her—and the poor mother as well. To die like that—"

The priest—he must be a priest or the knight would not have called him father—paused. "The girl will be taken to the Clinke, I suppose? One can only hope the full circumstances of her case will be weighed before justice is meted out."

The voices sounded closer now. Bellebelle repressed a scream. The Clinke was Southwark's worst prison, with a fearful reputation.

"For a whore, Father? In these lawless times?" The knight gave a grim laugh. "She'll rot there for sure—if she lives that long. When de Burgh's Flemings return from York and have their sport with her, there won't be much left. De Burgh himself will see to that. He never forgets a slight much less a near mortal injury."

"Spare me the unsavory details."

For a moment Bellebelle felt her whole body grow slack with relief. He was not dead, just wounded! Thank the Holy Mother, she had not killed anyone. But her mother . . .

Booted feet stopped beside her pew. Frozen with horror Bellebelle could hear her breath rasp in her throat. Her heart seemed to have stopped. She knew the law forbade a person to be dragged out of sanctuary—

"Who's this?" It was the knight's voice.

Any moment now iron fingers would grab her by the arm and pull her out of the pew. But with Gytha dead, did it really matter what happened to her? If she died in the Clinke or on the streets of Southwark or by the hands of de Burgh's Flemings—what difference would it make? Her life was over.

"Ah—" there was a long pause. "I believe I've seen her here before. Hardly the one you're looking for."

There was a grunt and the footsteps continued down the aisle, retreating further and further away.

After a long silence Bellebelle opened her eyes, still expecting to see the knights in front of her, ready to haul her off to the Clinke. A plump black-robed priest with a tonsure of gray hair stood by the pew, his arms folded across his chest.

"You're the doxy they want, aren't you?"

Bellebelle gasped. "No. No. I'm not."

"Do you now add falsehood to your other sins?"

"How—how did ye know?"

He pointed to her necklace of blue stones. "I'm Father Sebastian, and I've seen that heathen bauble before, on the Welsh bawd who comes here from time to time. You're from that same evil house of the devil?"

She nodded dumbly.

"My poor child," the priest said, signing himself, "what a terrible way for you to hear of your mother's death, may God grant her mercy for her sins. I will give you sanctuary for this night but no longer. You'll fare better away from these parts in any case. The Flemings, a lawless breed, are quite capable of storming into the church and taking a felon by force, no matter what that Norman knight says." He crossed himself. "When he described what might happen to you, I found myself unable to tell them you might be the one they want. As Our Lord was merciful to the Magdalen, how could I do otherwise?"

"Thank ye," she said through frozen lips, the meaning of his words lost on her. "I be grateful for lodging."

He looked at her closely. "Come, let me give you some wine and a crust of bread. Then I will hear your confession."

Bellebelle, still carrying her basket, followed him out of the Lady Chapel into a small chamber that had a pallet and blanket on the floor, shelves stacked with wax candles and black robes. On a small table was a wooden pitcher of wine, wooden cups, and a half-eaten loaf of bread. A candle stub sputtered in a rusty iron holder.

"Father—I doesn't want any—any confession, but I can repay ye kindness with silver." Bellebelle, feeling like she was made of wood, started to lift her skirts but the priest held up his hand in a stern gesture.

"Holy Church cannot accept the wages of sin."

He tore off a chunk of the bread and handed it to her, then poured a cup of wine from the pitcher. "Give up your wicked life. That is how you can repay me. What says Leviticus? 'Do not prostitute thy daughter, to cause her to be a whore: lest the land fall to whoredom, and the land become full of wickedness.'"

She stared at him mutely, bit off a piece of bread, and slowly began to chew. It was hard and dry, difficult to swallow. When he handed her the wine she downed it at a single gulp, wondering why Morgaine spoke so harshly of this priest who had saved her from a terrible fate. At the thought of Morgaine, Gytha's body swam before Bellebelle's eyes. The numbness suddenly dissolved as sobs of anguish welled up from the very depths of her being. When she heard the cries, like the inhuman wails of a stricken animal, she did not at first recognize that they were coming from her own throat.

"Remember this," said Father Sebastian. "Had your mother lived she would have been thrown out into the streets to die a slow and painful death from the burning sickness. Despite the violence of her end, God, in His infinite wisdom, has been merciful."

Bellebelle did not know how long she wept but when at last the choking sobs came to a shuddering stop she felt drained and empty. The priest was still there, watching her.

"Perhaps it is no accident that in your hour of travail you came upon St. Mary Overie," he said. "God rest you, my child."

He left the candle stub burning and closed the door behind him.

Trembling with exhaustion, her head reeling from the wine which she was unused to, Bellebelle lay down on the pallet. Within moments she was asleep.

She woke to the sound of the bells tolling the hour of prime. Shivering in the early morning cold, Bellebelle rose, straightened her clothes, and, basket in hand, slipped quickly out of the tiny room. She wanted to be gone before the service started and anyone saw her. Her heart ached, her head felt as if it were stuffed with feathers. Uncertain where to go she crept back into the Lady Chapel and slid into a front pew. She was hungry and thirsty, but food and drink were not as important as safety. It was obvious she could never return to the brothel-house again. But where could she go? Who would take her in?

Bellebelle stared at the figure of the Virgin directly in front of her, then gasped and rubbed her eyes. What was happening? Was she losing her wits? She clapped her hands over her mouth to keep from crying aloud. Slowly, gradually, the statue began changing into that of a royal queen, cloaked in majesty, ablaze with light, her presence filling the chapel with an awesome power.

Impossible, but the figure looked like Eleanor of Aquitaine, exactly as Jehan had described her. Help me, Bellebelle cried, help me. Was that a smile on the queen's face? The chapel grew dim before her eyes. Then—the pain in her heart eased; the fear, gnawing like a rat at her belly, subsided. Morgaine's voice, as clearly as if she were standing beside her, said: "Now don't ye get no wishbone where ye backbone ought be, lass, how many times I told ye that? Get yeself over to London."

Until this moment she had completely forgotten Morgaine's words about the brothel-house in Gropecuntlane. A whisper of hope swept though Bellebelle. If she could get safely to Gropecuntlane, Morgaine had said they would take her in. The knight had repeated something Ralph said about returning to York. He and his knights could well be gone by now. The sheriff had never seen her. In the crush of dawn traffic across the bridge, she might pass unnoticed. If she hurried—suddenly, Bellebelle caught her breath, gripping the wooden pew in front of her.

Her mother's death had released her forever from the prison of the Bankside stews. Morgaine had told her to grab her chance at a better life. Now, with a clear conscience, she could do just that.

Tears of relief blurred her eyes. Thank you, thank you, thank you, she voiced her gratitude aloud in a passionate litany. When Bellebelle wiped the tears away, the vision had faded, the statue looked as it had before. The chapel was exactly the same. Only she was changed.

# CHAPTER 13

# York,
# 1148

*H*enry of Anjou sat brooding in his pavilion on the edge of the thick woods that backed the city of York. Should he give vent to his true feelings? Certainly he had every right to do so, considering how he had been cheated. When he had sailed from Normandy six months ago to be knighted by his great-uncle, King David of Scotland, he had envisioned a glorious battle against King Stephen, usurper of his mother's throne.

After landing on the English coast he had gone straight to Bristol to visit his cousin William, who had inherited his father's earldom of Gloucester, and was a staunch supporter of the Angevin cause. Accompanied by a small group of knights supplied by William, Henry had traveled the back roads from Bristol to Scotland in order to avoid royal troops as well as the vicious brigands who made the main highways so dangerous. He had been appalled at the sight of deserted orchards, half-tilled fields left idle, the smoking ruins of manors and farms, the bodies of slaughtered beasts—and men. Whether the result of brigands or the king's troops, *his* land had been desecrated. Henry could hardly wait to exact his vengeance.

After the expected battle with King Stephen, from which, of course, he would emerge the triumphant victor, Henry saw himself taking his rightful place as ruler of England in his mother's name. All had gone as he envisioned: he had been properly knighted by his great-uncle, and persuaded him to come to York with his troop of Highlanders to do battle with the English king.

Then, just a few hours ago, the Scottish king had informed him that Stephen's troops, far outnumbering his own, were heavily massed around York, with more arriving daily; they had little hope of winning even a skirmish much less a pitched battle, said his great-uncle. Sick with disappointment, Henry wanted to storm about the pavilion, throw himself on the ground, and give vent to one of his violent, screaming rages. But, surrounded by the respectful glances of the ferocious Highland lords, he held himself in check. After all he was a knight now, with a shining image to uphold.

In the strenuous effort to suppress his anger, Henry felt as if a tight helmet had been jammed down on his head; he began to gnaw his nails in agitated frustration. Cheated, that was exactly how he felt: cheated of a chance to cover himself with glory, win accolades from his great-uncle of Scotland, and impress his parents, the count and countess of Anjou. If he had been successful against Stephen he might have persuaded them to make him duke of Normandy, a title inherited by his mother but held, temporarily at least, by his father. One day he would make Stephen pay for this humiliation, one day when he was king—

"My lord, will you take some wine?" His squire, Jocelin, knelt before him holding out a wooden tray with wooden cups.

Henry grabbed a cup, downing it in one swift gulp, then stood up. "Jesu, I cannot just sit here like a penned sheep and do nothing!" He grabbed his short yew bow and a quiver of arrows which he slung over his shoulder, then searched in his scuffed leather saddlebag for an old ivory hunting horn, whose leather thong he slipped round his neck. "I am going into the woods and shoot a stag for our dinner tonight."

To his dismay six dour knights rose with him. "I would prefer to go alone. Just a short way into the forest. I don't even intend to take my horse. Just the dogs."

His great-uncle's grizzled men, all proven warriors, exchanged worried glances.

"Ach, laddie, that is to say, m'lord, but ye canna go alone—" one began.

"Stop them from following me, Jocelin. I dinna need a covey o' bloody nursemaids to follow on ma heels," Henry mimicked under his breath, fuming at the "laddie."

Followed by two enormous wolfhounds belonging to his great-uncle, he strode quickly out of the pavilion, made his way through the Scots camp, and disappeared into the thickly wooded forest. He fervently hoped he could find a stag, even a fox would serve, but he had to kill something or burst.

Great-Uncle David fully expected him to leave the environs of York by morning and find his way back to the coast, then set sail for Normandy. The idea that he must slink away from Stephen's forces like a craven cur almost made him choke with injured pride.

"God's eyes," he shouted, and kicked violently at the spongy turf with a muddy black boot. Immediately the pressure in his head lessened.

A rustle in the trees. Henry spun round, whipping out his blade from the leather sheath attached to his belt. A brown-and-white hare jumped from behind a beech tree and disappeared into the green brush. The dogs, barking furiously, sped after it. Henry sheathed his knife, called the dogs back, then fastened leather leashes round their strong muscular necks. He pushed deeper into the forest.

His soft leather boots made no sound as he stalked through the woods. A short brown cloak over a dark green tunic girded by a belt with gold clasps, a brown cap on his head, blended in perfectly with the tawny green of the thicket. Verdant moss covered the ground; majestic beeches, crowned with shiny green branches in midsummer, towered over him. Through the pillarlike trunks Henry caught a glimpse of a small clearing filled with wild foxglove, lacy ferns, and thick gorse bushes.

A branch snapped. Henry sank to his knees behind a thorn bush. The hounds growled softly. Peering out from beneath his cover, Henry saw a large brown buck bound into the clearing, head lifted, wet nose snuffing the wind. His short tail switched back and forth and one hoof pawed the ground. Not the ten-branched stag he'd longed for, still . . . Quietly Henry slipped off his bow and notched an arrow to the string. Then, loosing the dogs, he jumped to his feet and burst into the clearing. The wolfhounds leapt toward the buck, who, in the instant of flight, seemed to pause midair. Henry's bow twanged, the arrow buried itself in the buck's right flank. The beast staggered then raced out of the clearing; the hounds, giving furious tongue, tore after it.

Henry followed and a short distance away found the stag fallen to its knees, the dogs closing round it. In one quick movement Henry drew his knife across the buck's throat. Hot blood spurted from the mortal wound, the terrifed eyes glazed over. Gently he put his hand on the noble head and velvet muzzle, overcome with that momentary sense of compassion and awe that always accompanied a successful kill. For an instant, victor and victim, hunter and hunted, were joined in some ancient tribal rite of blood bondage.

Henry's anger drained away with the lifeblood of the buck; a feeling of calm came over him. As the dogs lapped the blood that was slowly seeping into the ground, he pulled the arrow out of the buck's soft flank, wiped it off on his tunic, then replaced it in the quiver.

There was a crash in the underbrush and several of his great-uncle's men appeared.

"M'lord, ye must return to the camp at once. King David says the enemy forces be blocking all roads out o' York. Ye must leave now, he says, through the woods. Tomorrow be too late."

Henry gave them a sullen look. "I'll be there directly. The buck needs to be carried back."

While the knights tied the buck's legs to a branch, Henry realized that his trip to York had been a complete waste of time. No battle, nothing to show for his efforts in persuading his great-uncle to march from Scotland to York. Perhaps, on his way back to the coast, he could persuade his cousin William to accompany him on a foray into the south of England. Even a minor battle would help. Anything to prove himself worthy of the ducal title.

Instinct told Henry that the time was ripe for him to take over Normandy. King Louis was still on crusade and could not interfere. By the time the French monarch returned from the Holy Land, he, Henry, could be solidly established, and Louis would be forced to recognize him as the rightful duke.

He was sixteen and his life was slipping by. At this rate he would never make a name for himself.

# London, 1148

Swept along by the crowd of people crossing the bridge, Bellebelle could not believe that it was only yesterday she had made the journey with Morgaine: excited, filled with hope. Today she felt penned in by bleak gray skies, an emptiness in her belly, and a desperate need to escape before it was too late. She shivered; a chill lingered on the damp river air, more like November than July, and she missed her cloak, which by law she had to wear.

When she saw a boy leaning over the wooden railing she ran over to him with an eager cry.

"Henry?"

The child turned and gave her a puzzled glance. Bellebelle backed away with an awkward smile. Was she going daft? Henry would not still be a young lad but a youth of at least fifteen or sixteen by now.

"Make way, make way for the king's troops," shouted a voice behind her.

Hooves drummed behind her. The crowd of people scattered to the railings. Fear gripped her as she recognized a party of Flemings approach. Keeping her back to the men, Bellebelle stared at the barges and rounded sailing cogs filling the Thames. The hoofbeats thundered by. When she could no longer hear them she peered into the murky waters for a glimpse of her magic fish, but not daring to linger, continued on her way.

Just as she reached the Strand the bells rang for Terce. Bellebelle ducked into a deserted alley, lifted up her skirts, and took a coin from the pouch around her waist. Famished, she bought a hot ham-and-eel pasty from the cookshop, and though it burned her mouth almost swallowed it whole. At a stall selling bolts of cloth she bargained for a soiled end piece of gray striped wool and used it as a shawl around her shoulders. With food in her belly and no longer so cold, she felt a surge of newfound confidence, certain of finding work in Gropecuntlane and eluding the Flemings.

In the next instant Bellebelle was torn by guilt and pain. Her mother had just died a terrible death, and she had not thought of her, not one time all the way across the bridge. How was it possible to feel confident? Was it because of what had happened in the Lady Chapel? Or because the priest had pointed out that her mother's death had been more of a blessing than a curse? No matter the cause, she knew that Gytha would want her to escape the Flemings and survive. Of course she would always miss her mother, but, somehow, the bone-chilling sense of horror connected with her death had lessened. For this she was grateful.

A pack of lean dogs trotted past her with a snarl. She would need a stick of some sort to protect herself, she realized, if the dogs of London were as fierce as the dogs on the Bankside. Turning off the Strand she walked down a wide street behind two carts loaded with baskets of eggs, wheels of cheese, wooden cages of hares, and squealing piglets.

Mingling with the noise of the pigs, the clatter of wheels and hooves were the cries of street-vendors selling their wares, the odors of spices, leather, and roasting nuts.

"Fine ripe cheeses from Cheshire!"

"Fresh milk! Here be fresh milk from Kent!"

"Hot chestnuts, a ha'penny for a cone."

Bellebelle passed a row of open-fronted stalls. One appeared empty but somewhere in the back she could hear the click-clack of a shuttle as a weaver moved it to and fro upon the loom. In the next stall a cobbler hammered at his last; further along, a saddler twisted his awl. In the next street, a carpenter polished one leg of a newly made stool. Bells rang everywhere: from the necks of sheep and goats being driven through the streets, in the hands of beggars, pealing from the churches.

There was a sudden commotion and Bellebelle stepped back out of the way as a hurdle drawn by two horses bumped through the street spattering mud. A man was roped to the hurdle with a round loaf of bread tied under his chin. Jeers and taunts were thrown at him as he was dragged by.

"What's he done?" Bellebelle asked the carpenter by whose stall she had stopped.

"That be baker down the street. Probably sold moldy bread or cheated on the weight of it. Law has to make a public example of suchlike, don't they?" The man threw a piece of wood at the baker.

Behind the hurdle came a cart pulled by a mule and driven by a grinning youth. In the cart was a young girl clad in a chemise and a hood of coarse cloth. She held aloft a penitential wand; her skin glowed red and prickly from the cold, and tears ran down her face. Bellebelle felt sick to her belly. She knew the girl must be a prostitute, as she had seen this kind of punishment before. The offense might be anything from being infected with the burning sickness and keeping it secret, to not wearing her striped cloak. Heartsick, she watched passersby throw clumps of mud and refuse at her.

No longer able to bear the pitiful sight, Bellebelle ran down the street and darted into a narrow alley where she stumbled on the filth-strewn surface, almost falling into a pothole. Picking her way with care, she continued down the alley, turned a corner, and saw that she had entered a wide lane that looked easier to manage. The image of the girl in the cart stayed in her mind.

The thought of such a terrible thing happening to her was terrifying. Whoring was the only life she knew, and thus far it had treated her well. But suppose the brothel at Gropecuntlane would not take her in? Suppose she had to live off the streets? Suppose— Bellebelle stopped, suddenly recognizing the houses smeared with red, black, and blue paint. Yes, there it was: a wooden house with blue shutters, exactly as she remembered.

She smoothed her hair and walked slowly up and down past the house, trying to summon the courage to knock on the door. Finally she stopped outside the tavern, uncertain what to do next. A large beefy man with a black patch over one eye stormed out the door of the tavern followed by a companion, almost running Bellebelle down in his haste.

" 'Ere, look where you be going." He stopped, his eyes narrowing. "What you doin' loiterin'? Ain't seen you 'afore, has I? Not from the brothel you ain't. I knows the bawds there and ye ain't one o' them. Plyin' ye own trade, are ye? Hawke won't like that he won't." He grabbed her roughly by the arm. "Steal them clothes too did ye? A whore, and thief to boot, I'll wager."

"No, good sir. I—I be new at the brothel." She twisted her arm away and started to run but the man caught her.

"Ah, leave the lass be, Hugo, let's eat."

"She ain't from the brothel, I tell ye. Black Hugo's never wrong. Wager she's got some money too with all them fancy clothes."

"Yes, I be from there." Bellebelle struggled wildly in the grip of his iron fingers. "Leave me go."

"We'll see who's right. C'mon. Hawke'll thank me for getting rid of ye. He don't like no poachin' on his territory."

Black Hugo dragged Bellebelle down the street and knocked loudly at the door of the blue-shuttered house. The door opened and a man filled the threshold. His head was bald, pocked with bluish stubble; a livid purple scar contorted one side of his face into a hideous pucker.

"You're not welcome here, Hugo, how many times must I tell you?" To Bellebelle's surprise he spoke partly in the accents of a gentleman, "Now if it's trouble you wants—"

"No, sir, no trouble." Black Hugo's tone had changed to a whine. "Just found this doxy loiterin' about the tavern and she claims to be one o' ye new bawds so I—"

"I never saw her before—oh, good day, my lords, I hope you were well-provided for?"

Two richly clad men appeared in the entrance preparing to leave, while the brothelmaster—Bellebelle felt sure it was he—fawned over them. One of the men, much older than the other, with gray-streaked fair hair and beard, examined her curiously.

"What a lovely creature. I haven't seen her before, Hawke, is she new? Looks less like a tart than any girl you've got. I'll take her next time." He bowed to Bellebelle and with his companion walked down the street toward the cookshop.

"Yes, my lord, I'll do that, my lord," the man Hawke called after them.

"Don't show your face here again, scum," he said to Black Hugo, pulling Bellebelle inside and slamming the door.

"Follow me."

He led her down a dark passage and into a large clean chamber furnished with a table, several stools, two large oak chests banded with iron, a bed, and a brightly burning brazier. A stack of leathery sheets, strange featherlike implements, a stone jar filled with black liquid, and a three-branched silver candleholder, a kind she'd never seen, littered the table. Hawke indicated a stool and sat down opposite her.

"I'm Hawke, the brothelmaster. Tell your tale, girl. If you lies to me I'll turn you over to the likes of Hugo and his cronies, and that's a promise, that is."

He was a strongly built man, and Bellebelle could not tell whether he was old or young. It was impossible not to look at the scar, the round hairless head, or the heavy black leather belt studded with silver that encircled his waist. Haltingly at first, Bellebelle told her story, leaving nothing out including her wounding of de Burgh. The only thing she held back was the vision in St. Mary's. Hawke's eyes, reminding her of ice in winter, never left her face.

"Hans de Burgh," he said at length. "Last year that Flemish scum marked one of me best girls so fierce she could never work no more. The whoreson's not welcome here and well he knows it. You be safe from the likes of him in Gropecuntlane. We has a favored clientele. In high places some of 'em. *Very* high if you takes me meaning."

Bellebelle didn't, but thought it best to keep silent. "Gilbert don't hold with no violence neither," she offered.

Hawke stared at her as if she were half-witted. "Does I care what Gilbert holds with? I provides everything a man wants, see? Girls, virgins, children, boys, whipping within reason—it's all one to me. But the price is steep, see, for certain practices. Arrangements made well ahead of time. All done proper-like. That's sound business."

He continued to stare at her and she felt herself cowering under his frosty gaze. "We charge the highest fees in London, girl, and we gets them, see? Only the best is good enough for Hawke's brothel."

He rose to his feet. "Take off all your clothes."

With trembling fingers Bellebelle slipped off her wool shawl, then her tunic and gown, until she was clad in her chemise.

"Are you deaf? All off's what I said. Don't have no use for a squeamish doxy."

"I—I has some money under this," she whispered.

"Does you come by it honestly?"

"Oh yes," she said and told him about Jehan de Mornay.

"I'm not interested in your money," Hawke said in an impatient voice. "Just the goods I'll be offering for sale."

When she stood naked before him he walked all around her, tapping his finger against his long yellow teeth. He prodded her breasts with an indifferent finger and a shake of his head. "A bit tight but they'll grow. What are you now, fourteen, fifteen?"

"Sixteen. Maybe more—"

"Fourteen if anybody asks. I've a good mind to pass you off as a virgin."

"But I'm not—"

"Does you think that matters? I has the means to make virgins, I does." He gave her a pitying smile. "You didn't learn much in that Bankside stew, did you? At the moment I has enough virgins so we'll leave you be."

Hawke pinched her buttocks and sighed. "Hips like a boy, and we'll have to fatten these cheeks up. Skinny shanks please no one."

Then he made her open her mouth and peered into it.

"Nothing puts the client off more than rotten teeth or stinking breath," he said with an approving nod at her even white teeth.

He then knelt on the floor and, prying her legs apart, much to

Bellebelle's disgust carefully examined her private parts. When he slipped an impersonal finger deeply inside her and probed about, she stiffened in pain and humiliation. But he paid no attention.

"All right. You ain't hiding no deformities, and I can see and feel for meself you're not infected. What's your name?"

"Bellebelle. But I were christened Ykenai."

"Does you enjoy your work?"

"I don't know nothing else. It's something I do so's I can live."

"O' course. Does I look foolish? What I mean is, does you get pleasure out of your fornication? With that fellow who give you the clothes and money, for instance."

He was watching her closely. With a shudder of distaste she shook her head. "Never. Can't think why the men does."

Once again Hawke nodded approvingly. "Good, good. Them as feels nothing, and most of you don't, make the best whores. All right, Bellebelle—no whore's named Ykenai—I don't need me another doxy, but my lord of Crowmarsh, the man you saw at the door, wants you, a big point in your favor. Now, you plays fair with me and I'll play fair with you, and that's a promise. Just remember you're not on the Bankside no more and don't tell your customers you was, see? Might put 'em off." He paused. "Oh yes, just so you knows that I'm no easy mark for whores to get round, me taste is not for women."

Was he a sodomite? Bellebelle had heard tell of these, but since Gilbert didn't cater to that trade she had never met one before. In truth, Hawke and the brothel-house itself frightened her. But even though his manner and ugly scar gave her a queasy feeling in the pit of her belly and made goose bumps on her arms, she felt that Hawke would be a better brothelmaster than Gilbert. She felt safe with him.

"I'll just make me a record here and then I'll explain the rules and regulations, how much you'll earn and all them particulars."

While she slipped on her chemise, Hawke pulled his stool up to the table, slid the silver candleholder closer to him, and smoothed a sheet of the leathery material. He took the long feather, then dipped it carefully into the black liquid. Curious, Bellebelle walked a few timid steps over to the table.

"Ain't seen no writing before, has you?"

She shook her head.

"Well, you wouldn't find no lettered men on the Bankside, now would you? This be a goosequill pen, see? This be ink. I be writing on parchment."

He began to write in a slow painstaking hand as he said aloud: "On this twenty-first day in the month of July in the year of Our Lord Eleven-Hundred and Forty-Eight did one Ykenai, called Bellebelle, formerly of the borough of Southwark, in the parish of—"

He gave her a questioning look.

"Don't rightly know. St. Mary's, I guess." Without warning Bellebelle burst into tears.

Hawke threw her a disinterested glance, then shrugged. In the flickering candlelight his scar seemed to throb like a scarlet snake. Ignoring her, he bent his head and resumed writing.

Bellebelle quickly put on the rest of her clothes. She had never felt so foolish, so ashamed, so alone. Why was she crying? She had been accepted at Gropecuntlane, a step up in the world; she was safe from de Burgh, and free of the Bankside stews. What was the matter with her? After all, she had always dreamed of bettering herself, hadn't she?

# Antioch,

# 1148

"**W**e must go by ship," Eleanor told Louis, barely able to
address her husband with civility.

After leaving Paris a year ago, what was left of the crusading
army had finally reached the Greek coast. It was now painfully evident to Eleanor that they would never reach Antioch by land.

Eleanor could hardly believe that her initial sense of excitement
and high adventure in Paris had turned into despair and near hatred
for her husband and the French. It was now obvious to her—and
everyone else—that the crusade, far from being the glorious
odyssey all had envisioned, was a total disaster. Trouble had begun
three months after crossing the plains of Hungary—and the Franks
were almost entirely to blame.

Eleanor and the captain of the Aquitainian contingent, as well
as lords of other provinces, had kept control of their knights and
foot soldiers. But the French army, disobeying Louis's orders, had
taken to pillaging farms and villages. By the time the crusaders
reached Constantinople, they had left behind them a legacy of fear
and hostility.

Since then, the near escapes, misadventures, surprise enemy at-
tacks by the Turks, and driving winter storms had all blended into
one long hideous nightmare that Eleanor preferred to forget. Louis
had turned out to be a grossly inefficient leader—but many of the
troubles, Eleanor knew, were blamed on herself and the Aquitainians. The French complained that her baggage and women slowed
them down, her frivolity was unseemly, her knights unwilling to
take orders from the French. The Franks and the Aquitainians

made no secret of their ever-growing mutual hatred. Louis's personal maladroitness was ignored.

"Yes, by ship," Louis said now in a resigned voice. They had spent the latter part of the journey arguing about almost everything, and Eleanor could see he was too exhausted to provoke another quarrel.

"But there is a shortage of available ships," replied the captain of the Aquitainian contingent. "This means that a great many of our surviving pilgrims and foot soldiers must be left behind."

"How can we leave these people to an uncertain fate?" cried Eleanor. "Surely there is something we can do?"

"Their fate is far from uncertain, Madam," the captain said. "These people will perish—unless they turn Moslem. It is the only way to survive among the infidel. But if we are to save ourselves we must reach Antioch as soon as may be."

"Become Moslems!" Louis paled and crossed himself. "Better to perish than give up one's faith."

Eleanor did not trust herself to speak. How typical of Louis. She knew perfectly well that if she found herself on the horns of a similar dilemma she would do what she had to do in order to survive. What did not bend, was broken.

The starved remnant of a great host that had once been thousands strong finally left the Greek coast. After a perilous sea voyage wracked by storms and tossing seas, they sailed into the port near Antioch. Eleanor, pale, thin from lack of nourishment, and near collapse, stood on the deck of the ship. Clinging to the rail she observed a party of knights waiting on the quay. Was Raymond among them? Eleanor, who had not seen her uncle for nineteen years, doubted she would recognize him.

A tall figure garbed in gold-embroidered purple robes, no doubt an emissary sent by her uncle, stepped forward to greet them. Eleanor saw an exceptionally handsome man with a commanding presence—and was instantly drawn to him. His hair was a mixture of dark gold streaked with bronze; his eyes the color of the sea at Talmont at midday, a soft blue tinged with green. When he smiled Eleanor's heart turned over; she could not take her eyes off him. Her interest quickened. An instant later —too late—came the shock of recognition. For one wild moment it was as if her beloved grandfather had returned from beyond the grave.

"Your Majesties, what a great honor to welcome you to Antioch," said Prince Raymond in French. Then in the soft, melodious *langue d'oc* of his native Aquitaine he added: "Despite your recent hardships, Niece, it is easy to see that you have more than fulfilled the promise of your early beauty. I've never forgotten what an enchanting child you were."

Eleanor, flushing with pleasure, immediately forgot her worn and bedraggled appearance. Louis, who did not understand the *langue d'oc* dialect, glanced uneasily from Raymond to herself, as if he could not quite believe this comely figure was his wife's uncle. Even Eleanor, despite his resemblance to her grandfather, found it hard to realize this man was a close relative only eight years older than herself.

After sending her an amused look that seemed to imply he knew exactly what she was thinking, Raymond ordered that the royal party be properly mounted for the ride into Antioch. Thereafter he concentrated all his attention on King Louis.

When they approached the walled city of Antioch, Eleanor could see a crowd of people waiting to meet them. It was a beautiful day, the sun a golden orb in a sky of such blinding blue that it hurt her eyes. The clear air was fragrant with the scent of orange blossoms. She caught glimpses of lush, green foliage, orchards heavy with golden fruit, a wide river filled with ships.

Massive gates swung open. Eager citizens and sumptuously robed clergymen cheered their entry. Inside the city, Eleanor caught her breath. Terraced gardens rose steeply against the hillside; graceful palaces revealed a glint of pink and yellow flower beds, white marble fountains, and tiled pools. The ruins of ancient Greek and Roman temples marched side by side with the soaring spires of Christian churches and the graceful minarets of Moslem mosques. On the streets she was intrigued to see Arab merchants in snowy turbans mingling freely with Christian traders. With its relaxed and easy atmosphere the city reminded Eleanor of Bordeaux, and she responded at once to its charm.

When she reached the palace and saw the well-appointed chambers that had been furnished for her ladies and herself she broke down and wept. After the harsh conditions of the past year she could hardly believe the attentive servants, silken tunics, gossasmer gowns, woven cloaks, mirrors set in carved ivory, silver basins, and perfumed soap. There had been no opportunity to bathe since leaving Constantinople, and Eleanor and her ladies spent hours in the huge wooden tubs washing each other's hair while attendant women poured steamy water, scented with rose petals, over them.

They had barely put their clothes back on when a trio of fat, dark-skinned eunuchs appeared to massage them. Eleanor's women were genuinely shocked.

"I've never heard of such people," said one of the ladies. "Nor have I ever been touched by any male other than my husband."

Even Eleanor was uncomfortable at the thought but prepared to go through with it.

"Must we remove our clothes?" she asked.

One of the eunuchs bowed and nodded. He pointed to the bed and held out a long white linen sheet.

"How do we know they are really—well—I mean—no longer men?" whispered another lady.

"Don't be foolish. Of course they aren't."

"Wouldn't we be committing some kind of sin?" asked the first.

Determined to appear far more nonchalant than she felt, Eleanor removed her clothes, folded the sheet around her and under the round-eyed gaze of her women lay face down on the bed.

The eunuch unfolded the sheet. When his strong but supple fingers kneaded her flesh with jasmine-scented oil, Eleanor immediately relaxed. His impersonal, almost indifferent touch lacked any carnal significance. He would have massaged a cow in much the same manner. In truth, his handling of her body reminded her of Louis. There was no affection, no tenderness, no desire. Louis was just like a eunuch. It would have been funny if it were not so tragic.

After doing little more than sleeping and eating for almost three days, Eleanor felt almost restored to her normal self. Certainly she looked better than when she had arrived, she decided, critically examining herself in one of the mirrors. The peach bloom had returned to her cheeks; her hair looked as if the sun were shining through it, and her hazel eyes had begun to sparkle with their usual brilliance. Although still thin, her body no longer looked like that of a fasting anchorite.

During this time Eleanor barely saw either Raymond or Louis, who was separately housed with his entourage in the prince's own palace. When she emerged from her chamber, refreshed and eager for activity, dressed in a sea green gown covered with a gold-embroidered tunic, she found herself presented with a variety of entertainment.

There was hawking and hunting, sumptuous feasts which included exotic fruits Eleanor had never heard of before: blood red pomegranates, dates, purple figs, and a long yellow fruit called apples of paradise. Instead of trenchers of bread everything was served on gold plates, accompanied by a heady, sweet wine native to the region.

Eleanor learned that Louis and his men had been provided not only with new clothes, but weapons and horses as well. As a result she assumed he was in better spirits, particularly now that the rigors of the exhausting journey were over. Hopefully, their endless bickering also would cease.

On the evening of her fourth day in Antioch, Eleanor and Louis attended a feast in the great hall of Raymond's palace, held, he said, in honor of his illustrious guests.

"My uncle is wonderously generous," Eleanor told Louis. "He has not forgotten his Aquitainian hospitality."

The Franks were being entertained by troubadours, jugglers, and a band of sinuous Saracen dancers, from whom Louis modestly averted his eyes.

"Generosity with a purpose behind it."

"What purpose?" Eleanor's spirits continued to revive at the sounds of gaiety and laughter that reminded her of her grandfather's court at Poitiers.

"Raymond wants me to postpone going to Jerusalem. He claims to be in a precarious position with the Turks. Should they attack Antioch with all their forces, he tells me, the city would fall, just as Edessa did."

"You knew that before we came, Louis. It is one of the reasons *why* we came."

Louis speared a slice of game with his knife and eyed it suspiciously. "He believes he can forestall the infidel by capturing the Turkish city of Aleppo."

Eleanor nodded. "What a clever strategy."

"Clever?"

"Of course. The Turks' defeat at Aleppo would not only safeguard the principality of Antioch as well as other Christian states but also protect the road leading to Jerusalem."

"Your uncle has been pleading his cause, I see," Louis said with an accusing look. "That is exactly his argument."

"Indeed, Raymond has told me nothing of his plans, I assure

you," Eleanor said. "It is the only course that makes sense. Surely you can see that?"

"Can I? By my faith, just because he has re-equipped us with horses and arms he thinks obligation must persuade me. It is God's will I follow, not Raymond of Antioch's."

"I was under the impression that you were following God's will when you came here to fight the infidel."

Louis glared at her, a hostile look that made her want to shake him. Sweet St. Radegonde, they were at it again, like two hounds snapping at each other, just as they had been during the past year. There was a time, not too long ago, when Louis had been her willing slave, listened to her views, and sometimes even followed her counsel. Eleanor did not doubt that Louis still adored her, but his recent losses had made him far more resistant than he had been in Paris.

There was a loud clapping and Eleanor saw that the dancers were now replaced by two jongleurs, one a dark-skinned Moor in Moorish dress, the other a flaxen-haired man dressed in the Provençal fashion.

Louis's face turned crimson. Crossing himself, he hissed through his teeth.

"Impious! A Moslem and a Christian singing together! He harbors the enemy in his own court." Louis turned his back when the two men began to play and sing a duet.

Eleanor, who had seen this pairing before at her grandfather's court, thought it quite natural. She was tempted to tell Louis about the unusual group of jongleurs she had once witnessed at her father's court in Bordeaux. Some had been Moors, others Christian, and one a Jew. Two of the Moors had been women who sang profane songs and danced, to the delight of everyone present. Jongleurs, whatever their race, were not warriors but followers of the *gai saber,* above battles, assaults and sieges. All of this would be lost on Louis, however. She could tell by the outraged, stubborn expression on his face.

It was exactly the same expression Eleanor had encountered when he insisted on going to Poitou alone. It meant Louis had made his decision and, no matter how illogical it might be, nothing would move him. A chill of foreboding pricked Eleanor. Should she warn Raymond?

Before she could act, the matter was taken out of her hands.

Eleanor spent the following day with Raymond's wife, Constance, in a lovely garden shaded by palm trees. The mosaic-tiled courtyard was strewn with rugs and cushions; low tables held silver bowls of an orange-colored fruit called apricots cooling in snow brought down from the mountains.

Into the midst of this tranquillity strode her uncle. One look at his wrathful face told Eleanor that what she feared had come to pass.

"Louis has refused to help you?"

"Yes. Constance, my dear, I would speak with my niece alone. Do you take your ladies elsewhere."

When his wife and her women had gracefully retreated to another corner of the garden, Raymond angrily pulled up several cushions and seated himself in front of her.

"I told Louis for the tenth time that the Moslems were terrified of the French army and now was the time to attack to ensure an easy victory. Your husband said he had given the matter considerable thought but must refuse. In all conscience he could not fight until he had expiated his sins against God and Holy Church by completing his pilgrimage to the sepulcher of Christ. Once he has received forgiveness he will do battle against the infidel. Can this possibly be true?"

"Indeed, I feared that might be his answer," Eleanor replied with a vexatious sigh. "I cannot tell you how sorry I am. But the man is such a pious fool that—" she threw up her hands. "Sometimes I don't know how I have endured him all these years."

Raymond's sea blue eyes searched her face. "Your unfortunate situation is all too clear to me, Niece. Nevertheless, it is rumored that you have always had great influence over your husband."

Eleanor shrugged. "In the past that has certainly been so. During our pilgrimage here, however, his affection for me has been sorely tried. We have had many bitter quarrels."

"I beg you now to use whatever influence you have left to plead my case before your husband. He *must* help us. Our very survival here in Antioch is at stake."

There was no mistaking the agitation in his voice.

Impulsively, Eleanor reached out and grasped his hand. "Of course. I'll do all I can."

Raymond gave her a slow warm smile filled with gratitude. Lifting her hand to his lips he pressed upon her palm a burning kiss that reverberated throughout her whole body. Her heart jumped; she must convince Louis to put off his pilgrimage and aid her uncle against the Turks.

That night, for the first time, Eleanor visited Louis in his private quarters at Raymond's palace. She found him at prayer in the small oratory adjoining his chamber.

"This is a pleasant surprise, Wife," he said upon completing his orisons. "But I hope you have not come on your uncle's behalf."

Surprised, for Louis was usually not so discerning, she seated herself upon one of the richly embroidered stools scattered about the chamber. "And if I have? I only ask that you hear me out. Alone." She glanced significantly at the equerries milling about.

After Louis dismissed the equerries, Eleanor motioned him to pull up a stool. "Raymond's scheme has much to recommend it. He has ruled as prince in Antioch for thirteen years and knows the ways of the infidel. Why do you refuse to join him in an attack on Aleppo, when it would speed your own plans?"

"I explained to him that I cannot undertake any campaign until I have fulfilled the vow I made at the start of this pilgrimage: to worship at the shrine of Our Lord. When I have completed that promise then I may take up arms and—and need no longer be celibate." He lowered his eyes. "But you already know this."

"What I know is that you have taken leave of your senses. The entire point of this venture was to recapture Edessa and protect Jerusalem. The opportunity to accomplish this is at hand and yet you refuse!"

Louis flushed. "I see that your uncle's silver tongue has bewitched you. Well, he has cast no unholy spells over me or my barons. We have no use for this—this corrupt, pagan potentate who dares to call himself a Christian!"

Eleanor jumped to her feet. "Dares to calls himself a Christian? After he has showered you and your men with gifts? Extended his hospitality to all crusaders in need? St. Peter's is the most beautiful Christian church I've ever seen. You said yourself, the singing of the monks was like a heavenly choir."

"Never mind what I said." Louis's lips twitched in irritation. "I am repelled by what I find here. Repelled! Indeed, Antioch does not appear to me to be in any danger whatsoever. It is a loose-living city devoted entirely to pleasure. A very Sodom of iniquity. Inside the palace Raymond himself dons slippers and loose-fitting robes like some infidel sultan. The Europeans here wear turbans, and sport beards and flowing garb like the Moslems. One can hardly distinguish between them!"

"Holy St. Radegonde, what has that to do with—"

But Louis's stream of invective would not be quenched. "Were you aware that there are as many mosques in the city as there are Christian churches? That some Christians have even intermarried with the Saracens?" His eyes were almost popping from his head. "Moslems and Christians live side by side in apparent friendship and even eat together at the palace! You saw that for yourself the other night, with the two jongleurs."

"My grandfather entertained many Moslem troubadours from Moorish Spain who visited his court. They too sang with Christian minstrels. What of it?"

"What of it?" For a moment Louis was nonplussed. "Well! But then nothing about your family would surprise me. Absolutely nothing! One need look no further than his sire to see where Raymond has picked up his heretical tendencies."

"Heretical? You *are* mad."

"It is not I who am mad." Louis crossed himself. "Only this morning I found out that many of the Christian churches have been decorated by Saracen painters! Impious! And you have the effrontery to ask me to support such a man?" His voice was edged with spite; his whole body taut with rage.

Eleanor was speechless. This was a Louis she had not seen before. His excessive religiosity had always been a sore point between them, but now it seemed to have reached a pitch of fanaticism blinding him to the very purpose of the crusade itself. Behind this Eleanor sensed a deeper enmity. The ancient hostility between Franks and Aquitainians, north and south, had been building to a climax ever since the crusade began.

No, no, no! How could she have been so blind? The tension had begun long ago; she had seen it from the very beginning of their marriage, starting with the betrothal ceremony in Bordeaux, but refused to acknowledge it for what it was. The years in Paris had exacerbated their differences, the crusade brought them to a head. Raymond represented all that the Franks hated and feared. Pleasure. Enjoyment. Sensuality. Freedom of expression. Tolerance. The encouragement of novel ideas that might threaten the status quo.

Nor was that the whole tale. At the bottom of it all, coiled like a venomous serpent, lay Louis's jealousy. He sensed her attraction to Raymond, a kindred spirit reminding her of her beloved Aquitaine. Louis's underlying hatred for all she represented had finally erupted. Eleanor knew he would never lift a finger to help her uncle.

Chilled by this knowledge, she fled the chamber. Filled with disquiet by her failure, shaken at this unexpected glimpse of her husband's true feelings, Eleanor sought out Raymond. As they walked across the mosaic-tiled floor Eleanor told him what had transpired.

"So, the king of France led thousands of people on a dangerous and lengthy journey that has already cost many hundreds of lives merely to boast he has prayed at the Holy Sepulcher?" Raymond shook his head. "It is beyond belief." He looked at Eleanor. "My heart goes out to you, Niece. Had my brother any inkling of what lay in store for you, he would never have entrusted your future to Fat Louis of France."

Remembering her initial refusal to marry Louis, Eleanor was sufficiently moved to swallow a surge of grief. Had she followed her own instincts then . . .

"Such a waste of beauty and youth and spirit." Raymond again shook his head and fell silent. When he spoke it was almost to himself. "I will not allow Louis to do this injury to the House of Aquitaine, nor to me personally. He will regret what he has done— or rather what he has failed to do. As God is my witness, he shall pay dearly for this sin of omission."

"But what can you do?" Eleanor stared at him, half fearful, half intrigued. In just this defiant manner had she heard her father threaten his enemies.

Raymond bestowed upon her an enigmatic smile.

The next morning Louis and his entourage, accompanied by Constance, paid a visit to St. Peter's Church to hear a special noon mass. After that they planned to visit an ancient monastery that lay just outside the city walls. Eleanor, furious with Louis and unwilling to join him anywhere, sent her women while she remained in the palace.

When the bells rang for Sext, she was sulking in a wooden tub of perfumed hot water. Since her arrival in the principality she had taken to bathing every other day, a luxury she had never indulged in before. But in Outremer, she had been told, both men and women went to the public baths two or three times a week. Alone for the first time since the crusade had started, the ubiquitous eunuchs and serving girls strangely absent, she welcomed this rare moment of privacy.

Closing her eyes, Eleanor lay back in the tub, aware of the mingled musky odors given off by burning incense and bowls of freshly picked anemones. The heady scent always seemed to waft through the rooms and corridors of the palace. Through the open window that overlooked the tiled court came the soothing murmur of a splashing fountain. This was followed by the soft strings of a lute. How familiar the melody sounded. What was it? Of course! "The Infallible Master," one of her grandfather's songs. Eleanor smiled in delight and began to sing aloud along with the music.

When she heard someone enter the chamber she paid no attention, assuming one of the serving girls had returned. It was not until a deep voice joined her in the chorus that Eleanor's eyes flew open.

Raymond, his robe fallen to the Persian carpet, was just getting into the tub with her.

He slid down into the steamy perfumed water but not before she had glimpsed a tall muscular body with broad shoulders and flat belly. His chest was covered with a pelt of curly bronze hair, the plumage of his manhood a deeper bronze.

"You don't mind if I join you?" he asked, as if this were the most natural occurrence. His eyes rested on her breasts, floating on the water like round shimmering pearls tipped with coral.

Eleanor, whose heart had begun to drum, slid deeper under the water. She could think of nothing to say.

"I've dismissed the servants," he said in a casual voice. "We won't be disturbed."

There was a long silence while Raymond smiled at her. "Stand up," he said softly.

Eleanor could not bring herself to comply. She shook her head.

"Surely you're not afraid?"

She nodded.

He raised his brows. "No granddaughter of the Troubadour can be guilty of false modesty." He paused. "Because I am your uncle?"

She nodded again.

"Do you feel as if I am your uncle?"

"Not—not at this moment, I don't."

"At any time since your arrival in Antioch?"

She shook her head.

"Well then? Are we not in truth two strangers who, by a fortunate stroke of fate, have found one another in an alien land? As the Moslems would say, *inshallah*—as God wills."

Eleanor was not looking at it in quite that way, but . . . She stood up in the tub, the water pouring in crystal rivulets down her body. For a long moment she watched Raymond leisurely examine her with the heavy-lidded eyes of a connoisseur. It was the first time a man had ever really looked at her naked, and Eleanor found a warm reassurance in the seasoned glance that traveled slowly and appreciatively from the arch of her neck, across the uptilted breasts, down her slender body to the silky chestnut fringe covering her sex.

"Quite, quite charming. You cannot imagine how lovely you are, sweet Nell," he said, using the name only her immediate family ever used. He reached up; one finger lightly brushed the tip of a pointed nipple.

The ripple of excitement that swept through her was so unexpected that a lump formed in Eleanor's throat. Leisurely, Raymond stood up and held out his arms. In one quick step she was pressed tightly against him. She could feel the wet hair of his chest tickling her breasts, the strength of his arms closing around her. When he bent his head to touch her lips, the slow kiss spread through her like melting honey. Although she had no mind to resist him, she knew she could not have resisted if she tried.

Famished for years, Eleanor could no longer repress her hunger for passion and affection. When Raymond carried her to the bed, casually sweeping aside a tray of figs and honied almonds, and laid her gently down upon the scented linen sheets, she was already in a fever of desire. A small part of her remained detached, reminding her that this was her blood uncle, obviously a practiced voluptuary, and she did not truly love him, but none of that mattered. She was helpless, in thrall to her own overpowering need.

"Has Louis come to your bed since arriving in Antioch?" Raymond asked, as his hands cupped her breasts, lifting them, stroking the taut flesh, watching the coral nipples become firm as pebbles.

"He has made a vow to be celibate until he prays at Christ's tomb," Eleanor whispered, her eyes closing under the mounting pleasure of his slow and deliberate caresses.

"I might have known. Pity. Still, there is more than one kind of pleasure. I doubt you have ever known any with that monk you married. Am I right?"

Eleanor, no longer capable of speech, wished he would stop talking. He had taken a nipple into his mouth, and began to tease it with his tongue, causing a wave of rapture to surge through her body. She pressed his head tightly against her breasts, savoring the feel of his lips.

"What a great hurry we're in," he said in a lazy voice, lifting his head.

His fingers slid down her hips to stroke the silken hair that lay between the apex of her thighs. When she felt him gently probe the warm mystery of her sex, she thought she would faint, momentarily embarrassed at the flood of moisture released by his touch. He bent his head to her breast again.

Caught in a whirlpool of liquid fire, Eleanor was totally unprepared for the overpowering frenzy of her response. Raymond's practiced fingers seemed to know exactly where to go, stroking, pausing just where the feeling was so exquisite. Within moments she was drowning in a wave of ecstasy that gradually spent itself upon a golden strand. A voice she did not recognize screamed aloud. Afterward she knew it for her own. But by then Raymond had stuffed a fig into her mouth.

She opened her eyes and started to laugh, almost choking on the fig. Raymond looked down at her with an amused expression.

"Sweet Jesu, that was a fire that needed quenching! Smoldering for years, if I'm any judge, and I flatter myself that I am."

Eleanor, totally at peace with her body, gave a luxuriant sigh of contentment as she stretched limp arms above her head and chewed the remains of the fig.

"I must confess I've been forced to console myself on occasion," she said. "But that, I now see, was a pale substitute."

Raymond rolled his eyes. "Like trying to put out a raging bonfire with a trickle of water. What a pity I may not introduce you to the total joys that a full consummation would provide. But since Louis does not honor your bed, that would be too hazardous. One cannot take the chance."

Eleanor propped herself up on one elbow. "Now, what would you like me to do—"

Raymond held up his hand. "Oh my dear, there is a surfeit of carnal joys to be had here in the East, where they are masters of the sensual. These joys come in various sizes, shapes, and colors, and I've sampled them all. I need nothing. To please you has given me immense pleasure."

He gave her his lazy smile that reminded her now of the boy he had been. "No pangs of conscience about Louis? Or the Church?" She shook her head. "Good. As my father used to say, these little sins of the flesh are the least of God's worries."

She smiled her agreement, wondering why it was that only fellow Aquitainians seemed to share her outlook on life. After a few moments she sat up and started to get out of bed. He pulled her back down onto the rumpled sheets.

"And where are you going in such a rush?"

"Oh, well, I thought—"

"My dear Nell, this afternoon we are not going to think but to feel, and we are going about this matter with no haste whatsoever.

There is still plenty of time. What a delightful innocent you are in these matters. That was only the beginning. There are many more fires to set alight—then quench."

By the time the bells rang for None, Eleanor had received an education in the art of love she would not have believed possible. Without actually entering her, Raymond had led her through a veritable garden of delights, teaching her to savor each one. Even Petronilla would envy her, she thought with satisfaction. She could hardly wait until she returned to France to tell her sister all the blissful details.

Her only regret—if indeed regret was the word—had been a moment when she wished that her heart was as enraptured as her body. She had been aware of a void, as if the experience, satisfying as it had been, had only rippled the surface when, in truth, she longed to be overwhelmed, shaken to the depths, possessed to the very core of her being.

Still, she was grateful for what Raymond had taught her: that in the leisurely hands of an expert minstrel, her body would respond sweetly, like a fine-tuned lute. More importantly, she knew that the feminine, sensual side of her nature, having now been fully awakened, could never be easily sublimated again. Nor did she want it to be.

"You can see what Louis has been denying you all these years," Raymond said. "Say what you will about the infidel, but when I think of all the strictures the Church has placed against the act of love, I thank God I live in a more civilized land. The Mohammedans hold that if married couples do not bed at least once a week there are grounds for dissolving the marriage!"

"If that were true in France, Louis and I would have separated within the first two weeks!" Eleanor sighed as she pulled on her chemise and gown. "How can I continue to live with that monk and not take leave of my wits?"

Her uncle, clad now in a shimmering purple robe, reclined against a heap of rose and lavender pillows while a honey-skinned serving girl—who had glided silently into the chamber only moments after she and Raymond had finished—served him aromatic wine and a fresh platter of dates, figs, and glistening slices of orange quince dipped in honey. Eleanor wondered if the girl had been listening at the door.

"Would you like to rid yourself of him?"

"Of course. But that is impossible."

"Difficult, yes, impossible, no. Have you forgotten that you and Louis are related in a degree forbidden by the church? Third or fourth cousins if I'm not mistaken."

Eleanor stared at him. She had totally forgotten—if, indeed, she had ever known they were distantly related. "But no one said anything about consanguinity at the time. The marriage was rushed through as if I were already carrying his child. Abbé Suger and the archbishop of Bordeaux must have known!"

"Consanguinity is conveniently forgotten when a marriage is desired, instantly remembered when it is no longer desirable. Someone wants to be rid of an unwanted wife and suddenly it is discovered they are third, fourth, fifth cousins!"

"But Louis would never agree to an annulment."

Raymond nibbled on a fig. "When the grounds for annulment abound? To begin with there are no heirs, only a daughter, surely evidence of God's displeasure. Secondly, Louis's conscience is bound to trouble him when reminded he is living in sin with his own third cousin. Were you ever granted a papal dispensation?"

"Never. There simply wouldn't have been time between my father's death and my marriage to Louis," Eleanor said slowly, as the possibilities became apparent. "I wonder—yes, I wonder if Louis realizes that. The subject has never come up. Not once."

"Naturally. If, in their greedy haste to acquire Aquitaine, Fat Louis of France and Abbé Suger bent a few ecclesiastical rules, who would be witless enough to call attention to it? Undoubtedly the good abbé provided makeshift dispensations, but these are no substitute for the papal dispensation required by canon law. Let sleeping dogs lie was the watchword, I'll warrant."

Eleanor was dumbfounded. To think that the means of her release had been sitting there from the very beginning! Why had she never realized it before? The issue of consanguinity was really the only door that provided escape from the prison of her marriage. Now that she had experienced not only fulfillment of the flesh but also a camaraderie of spirit, it was inconceivable that she should stay with Louis. They disagreed about virtually everything and— her thoughts hung suspended as her eyes met the cynical sea blue gaze of her uncle.

He knew exactly what was going through her mind. Her skin prickled, and she stifled a gasp, suddenly recalling what her uncle had said about Louis's insult to the House of Aquitaine, that he would regret his failure to help him. Eleanor remembered as well his enigmatic smile when she asked what he would do about it. Raymond of Antioch, seasoned voluptuary that he was, had surmised her weakness, and, with her more than willing agreement, taken advantage of this susceptibility. His carefully planned seduction had revealed to her the depths of her desperate need—the devil in her own flesh, Louis would probably call it. Anticipating that she would react exactly as she was doing, he had used her as an instrument of vengeance against her own husband.

It was a bitter blow to her pride and Eleanor felt a surge of outrage. How dare he use her, his own niece, in such a cavalier manner? And yet—how could she be angry with him? In truth, when all was said and done, Raymond had opened a locked gate which might ultimately lead her to freedom.

He rose from the bed. "Mea culpa. Mea maxima culpa. I see that I have been discovered, judged, and—forgiven." He walked over to her and, taking her hand, brought it gently to his lips. "You will never regret this afternoon's events, sweet Nell. One day you will thank me. You are a vital and intelligent beauty with a unique and glorious capacity for sensation; I envy the man you will eventually love. Believe me, you deserve better than Louis of France."

Eleanor blushed, but his words, carefully chosen she suspected, had soothed her vanity. "I agree with you about Louis. But exactly how am I to go about ridding myself of him? Abbé Suger will never allow France to lose Aquitaine."

"The abbé is an old man; he will not live forever. Time is on your side. In any case, resourceful women always find a way. You have a powerful weapon in your hands. Use it."

"You sound like my grandmother. She said a clever woman could always change what she did not like by taking matters into her own hands."

Raymond laughed. "Dangereuse was a most discerning creature! A woman to emulate—despite the fact she displaced my own mother."

Eleanor gave an impatient sigh, trying to ignore the pressure of his lips against her palm. "I swear that if I ever wriggle free of this coil I'll never marry again, but rule Aquitaine alone."

"With a lover to solace you discreetly from time to time?" Raymond released her hand, then reclined again on the bed, patting a place beside him. "That would never suit you. I am not saying you shouldn't have a lover, heaven forfend. But you need a strong husband and a brood of sons—and a land of your own to rule as well."

"I will not marry a man I don't care for." Eleanor sat down and idly picked up a slice of honied quince. "Not again."

"There are more than just your wishes to consider. You cannot manage Aquitaine on your own, you know. Fatal to try."

"Not you too! That was exactly the argument the archbishop of Bordeaux used when he persuaded me to marry Louis."

"Naturally. His main concern was Aquitaine—and it should be yours as well. With such a disparate land as ours, filled with constant unrest, you must have a man to help you rule. Come, you know perfectly well I'm right."

"I could have been a real help to Louis if he had not been so opposed to my interfering, as he called it. Sometimes he listened to me but not in Aquitaine, where I understand the people so well."

"It is precisely because you could have administered affairs in the duchy more effectively that you were prevented from doing so. It is a rare husband who is not threatened by a woman's exercise of power. A stronger man than Louis might have had misgivings. Even my father, a most enlightened man where women were concerned, never believed them to be the equal of men—except in affairs of the heart."

"And you?"

Raymond gave her one of his enigmatic smiles. "So many questions. A wise woman controls the world from—"

"—between her legs," she finished the sentence for him. "Yes, I know."

"Follow your grandmother's example." He reached over to touch her arm. "What you need is a man who not only can please you but who also possesses great strength of will—or you're apt to devour him alive." His fingers stroked her cheek. "So lovely, so contrary—Aphrodite and Artemis all in one." His hand dropped to her breast. "So desirable. But what a dreamer we have here! You want to lose yourself in a great and all-consuming love." At her look of astonishment he laughed. "You think I didn't know that? But at the same time you are not willing to relinquish one inch of your power. I fear you cannot have it both ways."

Eleanor burst out laughing. What an absurd conversation. She threw a date at Raymond, who promptly showered her with a handful of purple figs.

"Think about what I've said, Nell. Think about it seriously. Once you have an annulment your great love will show himself."

"As God wills—*inshallah?*"

"Ah, you are learning." He smiled. "And when you have found this great, transcendent passion you so desperately hunger for, remember: try not to do everything better than he does."

The bells of all the churches in the city rang for Vespers in concert with the muezzins' call to the Moslems to pray. Louis and the others should be back by now, attending the evensong service. It would be wise for her to meet them there. Eleanor stood up and walked to the chamber entrance. She opened the door, turning her head to throw Raymond a last kiss. He lay against the cushions with his eyes closed. She was neither surprised nor disconcerted to see the serving girl fall to her knees between Raymond's legs. With a smile she softly closed the door.

# CHAPTER 16

*T*he following morning when Eleanor joined Constance and her ladies to break the night's fast, she learned that during the night Raymond had received an urgent dispatch informing him of trouble on his northern borders. He had left before sunrise for a three-day inspection of the area, taking half his army with him. She was disappointed, half-hoping that there might be a repeat of the joyous events of yesterday afternoon—although she knew that such a possibility was unlikely to occur. Unfortunately, Louis was very much in evidence, and acting strangely—his manner agitated, almost hostile. Did he suspect what had transpired between Raymond and her? It seemed impossible; on the other hand . . .

"Is anything amiss?" she asked him, after they had attended the noon mass at St. Peter's and were walking back to her quarters.

"Should anything be amiss?" His face was set in grim lines and he did not address her directly.

"If I knew, I would not have asked." Eleanor paused. "You're behaving oddly."

"Perhaps I have good cause." The words were bitten off, as if he regretted having said them. Not once did his eyes meet hers.

Eleanor's throat grew dry and her heart thumped. She decided to brazen it out. "If you have something to say to me, Louis, then out with it. Stop talking in riddles."

"I think it time we left Antioch and visited Jerusalem. That is why we came."

"We came to give aid to those Christian states in danger of attack from the infidel, yet you will not lift a finger to help Raymond." She tossed her head. "I am not ready to leave Antioch. I have barely arrived."

Louis glared at her. "But *I* am ready. I order you as your sovereign and husband to obey my wishes. We will leave this—this unholy place at once."

"I absolutely refuse to go. However, you are free to leave without me."

He lapsed into one of his sullen silences. For Eleanor the remainder of the day turned oppressive, as if a heavy black cloud enveloped the palace, even the city itself. Whenever she saw Louis and his entourage, their heads were always together, and they talked in whispers. The moment they saw Eleanor they immediately broke off their conversation.

"Whatever is the matter with your husband and his party? They are behaving most strangely," Constance remarked, as they sat in the courtyard beside the white marble fountain.

So the feeling of conspiracy was not just her imagination. Something *was* afoot.

"I wish my uncle were here," Eleanor said, then immediately regretted her impulsiveness.

After a moment's silence, Constance glanced at her sideways. Was that a look of resentment in her eyes? Eleanor felt decidedly uncomfortable.

"Yes, life is always more amusing when Raymond is about. He should return within two days." Constance smiled placidly.

Repressing a stab of guilt, Eleanor wondered if she was letting her conscience play tricks on her.

The rest of the day, that night, and the following day passed without incident. Still Eleanor grew increasingly anxious. Although she could not put a finger on what was wrong exactly, Louis's hostile manner and her own intuitive sense gave her the impression she was surrounded by enemies. Only one more day, then Raymond would return.

That night Eleanor barely slept. Every few hours she awakened, filled with disquiet, only to fall back into an uneasy slumber. She woke again as the church bells tolled the midnight hour, then drifted off once more. Suddenly she heard a footfall. Opening her eyes she saw five figures looming out of the darkness surrounding her bed. She started to scream but a hand covered her mouth. Two of the figures, obviously female from the outline of their long skirts, pulled chemise, gown, and tunic over her head before she could entirely grasp what was happening. When she started to struggle, her eyes and lips were bound with cloths, her ankles and wrists tied tightly with rope. Her body was rolled up in a fur coverlet, slung over someone's shoulder like a sack of grain, and carried out of the chamber.

No one spoke. Eleanor sensed she was being removed from the palace and placed in a litter. Rage and fear warred within her. Had the Turks gained entry into Antioch? Stolen into the palace like thieves in the night, and abducted her for ransom?

The litter swayed like a ship in a rolling sea. Behind her came the muffled sound of carts and many horses, then the creak of hinges slowly opening. They must be going through the St. Paul Gate. Sweet St. Radegonde, it sounded as if the entire French army were leaving Antioch. Could it be Louis himself who had abducted her? The last sound she heard, one she was never to forget, was the call of the muezzin summoning his flock to morning prayer.

After what seemed an endless time, the cloth was removed from Eleanor's mouth, the blindfold from her eyes, and the ropes from her wrists and ankles. She found herself sitting next to Louis in the litter. When she pushed aside the curtain, the noon sun was blazing high overhead, causing her eyes to water.

"How are you, Wife?" Louis asked in a solicitous voice as he handed her a silver flask of wine. "I should tell you that we are well away from Antioch, on the road to Jerusalem."

Eleanor was so choked with rage and pain and humiliation that only hoarse incoherent sounds issued from her throat. Louis, his face pale but triumphant, gazed at her in concern. With the last ounce of strength left in her, Eleanor hit him full force across the face with the flask. Blood spurted from his nostrils.

The look of triumph in his eyes changed to one of horror.

"Why, why have you done this? Take me back to Antioch," she cried, beating at his face with her fists, tears draining from her eyes. "I will never, never, never forgive you."

Despite her screams and protests, Louis would not budge.

"Raymond is an evil, corrupt influence. You would not come of your own accord, thus, for your own protection, I was forced to take these ignominious measures before he returned. He has more men than I do and would have prevented us from leaving, I doubt not." He wiped the blood from his face with his sleeve. "Your spirits will be restored when we reach Jerusalem."

Whatever Louis had discovered about that rapturous afternoon, and how he had discovered it, would remain a mystery. But he had acted too late, thank the Holy Mother. He could take her as far away as the moon and it would not matter.

Eleanor knew that the encounter with Raymond of Antioch had changed the course of her life forever.

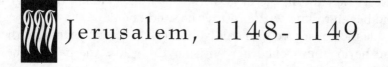 # Jerusalem, 1148-1149

Jerusalem turned out to be a fascinating city, but one which Eleanor felt certain she would always remember with bitterness.

The Persian carpets, pale blue damask hangings, inlaid marble walls, and carved ivory and wood furniture, which had been so exquisite in Antioch, were oppressive in their quarters in the Tower of David. Even the Chinese porcelain dishes, brought by caravan from the East, were no match for Raymond's gold plate.

Louis, however, could hardly contain his joy. He insisted Eleanor join him on a tour of the city's shrines, scattering alms everywhere. When he laid the oriflamme he had brought with him from France on the tomb of the Savior, he was in a state of sublime ecstasy.

Although he showered her with gifts—a delicate Persian vase, a gold cross set with rubies—as the weeks went by it became increasingly evident to Eleanor that Louis was having her watched. He either accompanied her everywhere himself or had her escorted by his own equerries. What did he think she would do? Try to flee back to Raymond? She longed to do just that but knew it was impossible. There had been no word from Antioch since she left and as time passed the lack of news became increasingly ominous.

Meanwhile she wandered restlessly about the city, momentarily distracted by the shaded courts, the narrow streets with their countless steps, the stalls of the bazaars, the camel caravans loaded with spices and perfumes. But all the while her thoughts turned to

Raymond as she relived again and again their enchanting afternoon together.

In order to put her attention on something other than what might be happening in Antioch, she joined Louis in his pilgrimage along the Via Dolorosa, listened to mass in the Holy Sepulcher, observed the spot where the Last Supper had taken place, and toiled up the slopes of the Mount of Olives. One pearly dawn they visited the Sea of Galilee.

"Look," Louis said to Eleanor as they stood on the shore watching the fishermen in their little boats. "They're dropping their nets just as they did in the days of the apostles." He fell to the ground and began to kiss with rapture the sandy bank.

Eleanor observed him coldly. In all their eleven years together he had never approached her with anything like the passion he displayed now.

"Really, Louis, how can all these ruins excite you? Everything we see is ancient and falling to pieces. A treasured monument to the holy past, I grant you, but only valuable as it reaches into the present and has something to teach us. I have seen and learned everything I'm interested in. Let us return to France."

"I'm not ready to return," he said, rising to his knees. "I was hoping the city might have a holy influence on you. Whatever you may have learned it does not strike me that you have become a more repentant and dutiful wife."

"What is that supposed to mean?"

"I think you know."

Eleanor forced herself to keep silent. Louis was continually dropping veiled hints about her behavior with one breath then refusing to clarify what he meant with the next. The situation was intolerable.

Without a word Eleanor stormed back to the waiting litter. "Take me back to the city at once," she told the grooms. "You can return for the king later." She experienced a perverse pleasure in leaving the astonished Louis stranded by the sunlit shores of the lake.

When she returned to their lodging in the Tower of David, seething with frustration and resentment, a knight from Antioch awaited her.

"Lady, I bring ill news."

Eleanor dismissed her women, called for some of the local Syrian wine, then seated herself on a cushioned divan in a chamber. Her heart was heavy with foreboding; she did not want to ask the dreaded question lest she be proved right.

"It is Count Raymond," said the knight.

She closed her eyes and took a deep breath. "Tell me."

"The tale does not make easy telling."

"Be that as it may, I would hear it all." She gripped her hands tightly in her lap. Thank the Holy Mother Louis was not with her.

"I am one of only a handful of knights who managed to escape from Antioch and make his way to Jerusalem," he began.

"When Prince Raymond returned to the palace, and found you and the king gone, he became violently angry, determined to prove to the French that he did not need them. I've never seen my lord so distraught, so unwilling to listen to reason. Exhibiting a rash impulsiveness—"

Eleanor held up her hands. "I can hardly bear to hear the rest. Sweet St. Radegonde, this sounds so typical, so characteristic of my family." Her breath caught in her throat. "Forgive me. Go on."

"Your uncle, who is a peace-loving man at heart, ignored the advice of cooler heads as if he were seized by some kind of madness, provoked beyond all reason. He senselessly attacked the Turks with a meager force of men. A massacre followed. Count Raymond was slain almost immediately. His head—" He paused while Eleanor exclaimed in horror. "Forgive me, Lady, I knew this would distress you but you wanted to hear. His head was cut off, the skull set in silver, and sent to the Caliph of Baghdad. Antioch is lost to the Turks."

Tears filled her eyes and an intolerable weight bore down upon her chest. Beyond speech, Eleanor reached out and pressed the knight's hand. Unable to stop herself, she sobbed uncontrollably. Dimly she heard the knight leave and her women enter. She felt wine being virtually forced down her throat, then, still weeping, she let herself be led into her chamber and put to bed.

It seemed like she had just closed her eyes when she opened them again. It was dusk. The candles had been lit and the chamber was filled with a soft light. Eleanor, clad only in the chemise she had worn earlier that day, slid out of bed, her body numb, her head cloudy, unable to get her bearings. Where were her women? As she stumbled toward the closed door, she almost fell against a small olive-wood table. In the center were two vases and the ruby cross Louis had given her. Without warning she was seized by such an overpowering rage that it took her breath away.

Eleanor snatched the cross from the table and raising her arm above her head brought it crashing down on one of the vases. The fragile porcelain cracked like an eggshell; violet shards flew over her, slid across the table and onto the thick carpet.

"I'm going to kill you, Louis!" a stranger's voice screamed. "I want to make you suffer as you have made me suffer." She smashed the other vase, then began to beat the table. Huge dents, smeared with a scarlet stain, appeared in the satiny wood. "Do you hear me? I'm going to kill you, kill you, kill you!"

The scarlet stains spread. Eleanor stared at them in confusion then looked down. Her chemise was spattered with scarlet; one hand was dripping blood. A piece of sharp porcelain had lodged in her palm and she had not even felt it. Quickly she pulled it out, leaving a narrow wound in the center of her hand. Dropping the cross she covered her mouth with her hands, sobbing as her body rocked back and forth, back and forth.

Somewhere, deep, deep within her, Eleanor had suspected the existence of this wild, crazed maenad who had overcome her reason. The creature was terrifying, capable of anything, and she must suppress it at all costs. She *must*. This same frenzied impulse to destroy when thwarted, to vent rage, had led Raymond to his untimely death. It was the curse of her impetuous family, and she could not give in to it and hope to survive.

She heard the sound of running feet. By the time her women burst into the chamber, stunned at the blood, ruined table, and smashed vases, Eleanor, trembling, had forced upon herself a semblance of control.

"Bandage my wound. Tidy the chamber and find out the cost of the table. Remove that cross. I never want to set eyes on it again."

After a few days the first onslaught of grief and rage had abated. By the time she regained control of her anguish and recovered a measure of composure, Eleanor was able to review the entire sequence of events with a clearer head. One outstanding fact emerged: Raymond had behaved rashly but Louis was to blame for his death.

Whenever she looked at Louis, she saw a horrifying image of Raymond's skull nailed to the gates of Baghdad. She had long been disgusted by her husband; now she began to hate him, with an icy calmness that was almost frightening.

Day after day she went over and over in her mind what Raymond had told her about dissolving the marriage, examining all the legal and political aspects involved. What had begun in Antioch as mere speculation now hardened into a deadly resolve. Eleanor promised herself that she would be rid of this monkish Frank she had married, however long it took, no matter the cost. Only by freeing herself would Raymond's death be avenged—and her own life restored.

Although she clearly remembered that the marriage contract specified that she would retain Aquitaine should the marriage ever be dissolved or Louis die, Eleanor did not dare put this openly to the test. Not yet. Any steps *she* initiated would be suspect. Not only that, there was no guarantee the contract would be honored. After all, neither Louis nor his council would willingly accept the loss of the largest fief in France. Regaining her freedom but losing Aquitaine was unthinkable. An idea began to take shape in her mind, far too soon to put into full execution, but, if she chose her moment with care, a first step could be initiated.

Early in the new year of 1149, on a bright morning in January, she accompanied Louis on an expedition to the Dead Sea, two thousand feet lower than Jerusalem. They had taken few attendants; this seemed like a propitious moment. Louis was marveling at the change in temperature—it was much hotter—and the tropical foliage, when they came upon several pillars of salt.

"Look!" Louis crossed himself, then indicated one of the pillars that wind and weather had formed into some semblance of a human shape. "This must be Lot's wife. I was told to look for it."

"What? That pillar?" Eleanor burst out laughing.

"Why not?"

"Louis, you're too credulous. It's just a pillar of salt."

Suddenly his face contorted with rage. "Ever since we arrived all you've done is mock everything sacred in this glorious city. That uncle of yours has cast an unholy spell upon you. I am glad he is dead, do you hear? Glad!"

"Murderer! Murderer! The blame for his death lies at your door."

Louis pointed a shaking finger at the pillar. "This will happen to you, make no mistake, for you have disobeyed the Lord and looked back at the Sodom that was Antioch."

Eleanor could hardly believe her ears. He was getting madder all the time. Obviously it was not the right moment to put into action the initial part of her plan. They did not speak all the way back to Jerusalem.

The next opportunity came in Acre.

Louis, having fulfilled his vow to pray at the Holy Sepulcher, traveled to Acre, the second city and chief port of the small kingdom that comprised the Holy Land. To Eleanor's disgust he allowed himself to be talked into joining an expedition against the Saracen city of Damascus. Since his arrival in the Holy Land, Louis appeared to have become even more obsessed in his desire to destroy the infidel—with or without provocation.

"It is one thing to mount an attack when Christian lives are at stake, but from what I understand Damascus has always been friendly to Christians. Why do you listen to unwise counsel?" Eleanor asked.

"Unwise counsel? The emperor of Germany? The king of Jerusalem?"

"The Germans are barbarians. You saw their vicious behavior on the crusade. King Baldwin is little better than a stripling, under the influence of his Palestinian barons. It is beyond my comprehension that you denied Raymond help against a very real enemy while you are positively eager to attack a friendly state for no reason whatsoever."

Louis ignored her. He and the others mounted an expedition against Damascus which ended in disaster. The Christian armies suffered many casualties and were forced into a humiliating retreat. Eleanor had the grim satisfaction of knowing that she had been right and Louis wrong—as usual. Not that Louis ever admitted an error. If a thought came into his mind, God put it there. If matters went awry, someone else was at fault, aided by the devil.

Shortly after Easter, Eleanor finally persuaded Louis to make preparations to return to France by threatening to leave without him. Several days before they were to leave Acre she confronted Louis right after Prime as they walked down the church steps and into a waiting litter that would take them back to their quarters in King Baldwin's palace. Louis was always the most susceptible right after mass.

"Have you never wondered, Louis, why misfortune continues to dog us?" Eleanor spoke softly, letting her tone convey doubt and anxiety.

Louis, greatly affected by his harrowing experiences since leaving France, had recently cropped his head and shaved his beard like a monk; he spent even longer hours at prayer.

"What do you mean?"

She hesitated for a moment, fearful of the risk she was about to take. "For instance, this pilgrimage has been a total disaster from beginning to end. Can you deny it?"

He stiffened and gave her an aggrieved look, unwilling, as usual, to take the slightest responsibility for his part in the whole wasted venture.

"I deny that it is my fault. Why are you always blaming me? If everyone else had done their job properly—"

"Did I say it was your fault?"

"You imply it all the time." He paused. "Why bring it up?"

"To point out what has now become obvious to me, why our lives have taken such a dismal course. Think on it: no sons. The terrible business at Vitry. No victories since leaving France. Countless dead as a result of our pilgrimage."

Although Louis still would not admit it, by now it was obvious to everyone that the crusade had been a complete failure, with only hundreds left of the thousands that had started almost two years earlier. After careful thought, Eleanor had come to the conclusion that this very failure might well prove her salvation.

"As usual, you exaggerate," Louis said.

She let the silence lengthen between them, rapidly going over in her mind yet again the arguments she had prepared in her favor.

The only grounds upon which an annulment could be granted was consanguinity or adultery. If adultery were used she could be immured in a convent and Aquitaine would be taken from her. She doubted that Louis would favor adultery. His pride would forbid it, he had no proof, and Aquitaine would erupt into total rebellion if anything were to happen to her, or France tried to keep the duchy for itself. Louis's resources were exhausted. She doubted there would be enough men returning to France to permit a widespread invasion of Aquitaine, should it come to that. Those that did return would hardly be disposed to fight so soon again.

On the other hand, Louis was often unpredictable. Her ploy was a gamble, but one she had decided to take, regardless.

"We are to blame."

Louis looked mystified. "For what?"

"Offending God."

"I have offended God?"

She heard her voice falter. Once spoken the words could not be withdrawn. "Have—have you forgotten that you and I are related within the third, forbidden degree? That we married without papal dispensation?" She paused, allowing the import of her words to sink in. "We are guilty of consanguinity. Is it any wonder that God has not smiled upon our endeavors?"

The palace appeared in the distance, the sun shimmering on its white marble walls. A look of horror crossed Louis's face.

"Consanguinity!" He signed himself. "I'm not sure I ever knew we were related in the forbidden degree. Or if I did I had long forgotten. Are you sure? After all, no one has ever mentioned it to me. But that would mean—may God forgive us—surely that would mean—our marriage may not be valid?"

"That is exactly what it does mean."

"I cannot believe—" Louis's eyes bulged in agitation. "Perhaps there was a papal dispensation. There must have been."

"When we return to France we can ask Abbé Suger, but there would hardly have been time between my father's death and our marriage to receive a dispensation from the pope."

"But why did the abbé not say something at the time? Or my father? He sent me immediately to Bordeaux when he received news of your father's death. I was too inexperienced in these matters to question . . . naturally I assumed . . . Why did no one take this into consideration?"

At his look of mingled bewilderment and dread, Eleanor almost felt sorry for him. "Greed."

"Greed?" His face was pale, his eyes haunted.

"What else? In their haste to acquire my lands, greed for Aquitaine took precedence over the dictates of Holy Church." Eleanor sighed deeply. "When I remembered this—while I prayed at the Holy Sepulcher—suddenly everything became clear—especially why we lack an heir." She heard his sharp intake of breath and patted his hand. "We cannot go on as we are."

"No. No. Certainly not." Louis signed himself again, then passed a trembling hand across his face. "We have been living in mortal sin. Certainly that is an explanation for our misfortunes."

Eleanor settled back comfortably in the litter while Louis moved as far away from her as possible. The weakness of his position was no longer lost on him, she had just made certain of that.

But she would be more certain of victory if the suggestion of an annulment came from him. Despite everything, she knew he still loved her, but Louis was martyr to a formidable conscience that gave him no peace at the best of times. Eleanor had staked a great deal, her entire future in fact, on her knowledge of Louis's character. Now it was only a question of time as to whether she had guessed rightly—or wrongly.

# Sicily–Tusculum, 1149

*I*f the voyage from Greece to Antioch had been fraught with hardship and terror, this one from Acre was even worse, thought Eleanor, clinging to the wooden rail as the vessel rolled in the pale green shallows.

Only two vessels had set sail from Acre. No more had been needed to accommodate those who were left of the mighty pilgrimage that had left France two years ago. Eleanor, unable to bear the sight of her husband's morose face another moment, had suggested they sail in separate ships, and Louis, brooding over the issue of consanguinity, aware that his marriage was hanging by a thread, agreed.

During a severe storm, the two ships—both flying Sicilian flags—lost sight of each other. Off the Peloponnesian coast, Eleanor's vessel had run straight into the midst of a raging sea battle being waged between the opposing fleets of the king of Sicily and the emperor of Byzantium. Fortunately, the Sicilians eventually routed the Greeks, and now, feeling more dead than alive, she was finally in sight of a friendly shore. Sicily. She and Louis had left Acre at the end of April. It was now July. She had not touched land for two months.

King Roger of Sicily was a Norman, and generally well-disposed toward the Franks. Eleanor knew he would welcome her.

Physically and emotionally exhausted, still grieving for Raymond of Antioch, Eleanor suddenly collapsed onto the deck. Only half-conscious, she was dimly aware that two sailors carried her to the beach. Then she knew no more until she opened her eyes to find a dark-skinned man in a white burnoose and turban bending over her.

"Open your mouth," he said in heavily accented French.

When she had done so, he lifted her head, then poured a cool drink down her throat. She gave a little choking cry. Was she still in Antioch? Jerusalem? Was this all a dream?

"Please, Madam," said a voice in Norman French. "Do not be alarmed. I am King Roger and you are safe in my palace at Palermo."

She weakly turned her head to see a tall man with a beard and a concerned look on his face.

"By God's grace, you have survived a very rough voyage and a major sea battle. Indeed, both you and the king were given up for dead. Now you are under the care of my Arab physician. He tells me that in time you will make a full recovery."

"Louis—" she whispered. The chamber began to grow hazy.

"No word has been heard of King Louis's vessel," Roger said. "Daily masses will he held for his safety."

Before she fell into a deep sleep induced by the healing draught, Eleanor wondered if God had taken the matter of her annulment out of her hands.

A fortnight later, King Roger received word that Louis's ship had landed on the shores at Calabria near Brindisi. After a slow recovery, Eleanor, accompanied by an escort provided by Roger, joined Louis in late August. Their meeting was cool but not acrimonious.

"We should travel at once to Naples, then take ship for Marseilles—" Eleanor began.

"We do not return to France," said Louis, pale and thin after his calamitous voyage. "I have decided we should go first to Rome. The issue of consanguinity must be settled once and for all lest I go from my wits. I cannot go on with this—this sin hanging over my head. If an annulment is in order . . ." He could not finish. "The Holy Father must advise us."

Eleanor kept her face impassive. It was the very first time he had mentioned an annulment! Before she was forced to bring it up. She could barely conceal her relief. But Rome? She was so used to Louis's procrastinations that she was unprepared for his sudden decision. Weak and still tired, was she ready to battle this out with the pope? Eleanor wavered. Perhaps the question should be brought to the test so she could see where matters stood. On the other hand, she had wanted to carefully read the marriage contract once again and seek legal advice before proceeding further. Perhaps even consult the archbishop of Bordeaux, who had a formidable knowledge of legal matters. Her mind flew back and forth then settled on the answer: as far as she was concerned, the outcome was already determined—however long it took. Better to know exactly what obstacles stood in the way so that she could circumvent them.

Forced to travel slowly, it was mid-October before Louis and Eleanor reached Tusculum, south of Rome, where the papal court was in residence. She had had a relapse of the exhaustion that befell her on the voyage to Sicily, and they had been forced to stop at a Benedictine monastery in Monte Cassino until she recovered enough to continue.

The papal court was housed in a gloomy fortress, as the pope had been forced to flee Rome which was threatened by imperial troops in one of the never-ending battles between the Holy See and the Holy Roman Emperor. There was none of the splendor Eleanor had expected, and a decided lack of ceremony.

"I welcome you, my children, with open arms," said Pope Eugenius the Third. "I have been kept informed of your mishaps—indeed the mishaps that have befallen this whole pilgrimage to save the Holy Land." A look of distress crossed his face. "And, indeed, your personal difficulties, as well."

How could the pope know of their personal troubles? Eleanor glanced at Louis and from the guilty expression on his face suddenly realized that he must have written Abbé Suger, who had undoubtedly informed the pope. She was furious. It was very important that her side of the tale be heard first; now the pontiff would have heard Abbé Suger's distorted version of events, which would not be to her advantage. On the other hand, she had heard that Eugenius was a kindly man, not a fanatical zealot. Perhaps she would be able to move him.

"I will speak to each of you separately," said the pope. "The king, first."

Louis followed him into a private antechamber while Eleanor was offered refreshment of spiced wine and honied sweetmeats. Within a short time, Louis emerged, his eyes red. She could tell nothing from his face.

Inside the antechamber, crudely furnished with a table and two stools, Eleanor took a seat. A papal secretary stood in one corner, a red-robed cardinal in another. The pope, in flowing white robes, sat on a makeshift throne. Eleanor knew that what she said now—in front of witnesses—would have far-reaching consequences. It was impossible to tell the pope of her contempt for her husband, her lack of physical satisfaction, her hatred of life among the Franks. She had to make him believe that her only reason for wanting their union annulled was the fact that she and Louis had displeased God. Why else had He punished them by failing to grant them an heir after twelve years of marriage?

"My marriage at fifteen, Holy Father, was rushed through without the proper dispensations," she began with a surge of confidence. "I am now twenty-seven—"

Choosing her words with care she told the pontiff exactly what she felt he needed to hear.

When she had finished he nodded. Had her plea moved him? Impossible to tell.

"So then it is only the issue of consanguinity that troubles your conscience?" Was there a particular emphasis on the word *only*? Was that a shadow of disbelief in his eyes?

"Yes, Your Holiness. Indeed, it weighs on me night and day."

"I see. A moment, please." He beckoned the secretary. "Tell King Louis to come in."

When Louis stood beside her, the pope's round face suddenly creased into a beneficent smile. "Well, my children, I have heard all you have to say. *Benedicamus Dominum!* You may both put your consciences to rest. Let me hasten to assure you that your marriage *is* valid! Under pain of anathema no word may be spoken against it, and it cannot be dissolved under any pretext whatsoever. If the lack of a papal dispensation is troubling you then you shall have one this very day! From my own lips—and shortly on parchment—I confirm that there is no impediment to your union."

Horrified, Eleanor burst into tears. She could not endure the thought of spending even one more day with Louis, and now the pontiff had just given her a life sentence behind the golden bars of the French court.

"You see, Louis, the queen is overwrought, what with the long journey, her illness, and all. This matter has obviously weighed heavily upon her heart. An heir, my son, an heir is the answer."

He rose. "I have prepared a little surprise for you. One that should gladden both your hearts."

He took Eleanor, still weeping, by one hand, Louis by the other, and led them down a hall and into a small chamber. The room was dwarfed by a huge bed, decorated with ornate gold-and-crimson hangings.

"No expense has been spared to make you comfortable, my children. These priceless hangings came from my own chamber. Sleep well. God is with you." Beaming with goodwill, he held out his ring for them to kiss. "I have stationed a guard outside the door to be sure that you are not disturbed."

Still smiling, he withdrew. Short of getting into bed with them himself, Eugenius had ensured they would spend the night together. Eleanor wiped her eyes. Nothing had gone the way she intended. If she dared to protest, both Louis and the pope would surmise her real reason for wanting to end the marriage. Her own words had been used against her and she was helpless. Defeated, for the moment anyway, she rigidly submitted to Louis's fumbling embrace. Tears flowed afresh when she remembered Raymond's sure touch.

When they departed Tusculum several days later, the pope wept copiously, heaped gifts upon them, and exhorted them to love one another. If the pope knew her better, Eleanor thought, a fixed smile on her face, he would have known that once her mind was made up nothing and no one could change it.

"An heir will result from this blessed union," Eugenius declared.

His words froze Eleanor's blood. Sweet St. Radegonde, if she bore a son she was doomed. If, however, there was another daughter . . . Then again, perhaps she was not with child at all.

When Eleanor and Louis reached the Île-de-France on a damp, gray morning in early November, a large crowd came out to greet them. The crusade had been an ignominious fiasco, yet here were Louis's subjects rejoicing as if he had won a great victory! Eleanor wondered if Abbé Suger lay behind this demonstration.

The walls of the French palace closed around Eleanor like an oubliette. According to Petronilla, dark rumors of her depravity in Antioch were flying all over Paris. Far from rejoicing, said her sister, the air in France was filled with recriminations and a demand for explanations: Why had matters gone so awry on the crusade? What, if anything, had actually been accomplished? Why had so many lives been lost? As usual, saintly Louis was exonerated. The blame for everything was somehow due to the Poitivin seductress.

Then, to make matters even worse, shortly after her return from Tusculum, Eleanor found she was indeed with child. While news of her pregnancy silenced the rumors and forced people to regard her with a new, if grudging, respect, Eleanor's own despair knew no bounds.

"You will bear a son," said an enraptured Louis. "The pope has promised me that you will bear a son."

Eleanor clung to her only hope: that she would give birth to another daughter. This would be her salvation, her pathway to freedom. Her entire future hung on the gender of this child.

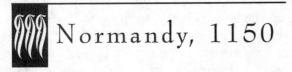 Normandy, 1150

Henry of Anjou was finally made duke of Normandy in January of the year 1150.

"And not before time," he told his squire, Jocelin, who, like himself, had a huge grin on his face. "After all, I am seventeen, a seasoned warrior, a man of judgment. This appointment was long overdue."

"Indeed, my lord. Very long."

"I was ready a year ago."

"Before that, my lord."

With a sense of satisfaction, Henry recalled what had happened after leaving York at his great-uncle of Scotland's insistence. He had made several successful forays into the south of England, picked up a host of followers, and won much acclaim. When he returned to Normandy, he had eventually been able to persuade his parents that he was now someone to be taken seriously—someone worthy of the ducal title. All that was lacking to make the title official was for him to swear homage to his overlord, King Louis of France. But there was no immediate hurry about this.

"My father says we can travel to Paris at our leisure, but I am anxious to go as soon as may be. Think on it, Jocelin, as soon as the title is official I can make plans to conquer England."

In late spring Henry and his father were ready to leave for Paris when, without warning, rumors reached Count Geoffrey of Anjou that the French king was mustering a large army.

"It is obvious he intends to invade Normandy," said the count.

"But why?" Henry, alternating between rage and bewilderment, could hardly believe his ears.

Count Geoffrey shrugged. "Whether this is due to the long-standing enmity between Normandy and France which periodically erupts or because Louis needs to assert himself after his catastrophic failures in the Holy Land is anybody's guess. Perhaps he just resents the fact that someone so young and arrogant will command the duchy. In any case we must ready our forces on the border between the Vexin and France."

Joined by Prince Eustace of England, they heard that Louis was advancing up the Seine. Henry, spoiling for battle now, was eager to engage the French king in combat. Then, at the eleventh hour, word reached them that Louis had fallen ill. All preparation for hostilities ceased; the prince returned to England. Henry, who still felt cheated by the lack of a major battle with King Stephen, was beside himself with disappointment.

When peace terms were arranged with the help of Bernard of Clairvaux, who claimed God himself had intervened to avoid bloodshed between Normandy and France, Henry gave vent to his frustration.

"Interfering old monk, why don't you go back to your cloister where you belong!" Henry shouted at the Cistercian abbé, who had appeared in his pavilion on the Vexin border.

"The violent rages of the Angevins are well known," said Bernard, his composure unruffled. "It is said of your family, 'From the devil they came, to the devil they will go.' Take heed of your demon blood, bring it under control lest it destroy you."

Henry turned purple at this and was forcefully hustled from the cleric's presence by Geoffrey and his squire.

In early summer Henry returned to Rouen with his father to consider the terms of the truce: he was to give up his claim to the Vexin, that much-disputed piece of land lying between Normandy and France; in return, Louis would officially recognize Henry as duke of Normandy.

"If Louis thinks to threaten me, he can think again," Henry said, seated with his parents in the great hall of the ducal palace in Rouen over a late supper of cold roast meats and wheaten bread. "I won't give up the Vexin."

Geoffrey and his mother began one of their heated arguments about which course he should take. Henry escaped as soon as he decently could, distressed, as usual, by the hate-filled atmosphere created by the count and countess of Anjou whenever they were together. He counted among his earliest memories his parents' bitter quarrels in Angers Castle. Henry cared for and respected each parent individually; when they were together he tried to avoid them.

"I intend to marry a woman who will be subordinate to me," he said to Jocelin. "Where the affairs of a kingdom, or matters of policy are concerned, there can only be one master. Not even the Church has the right to intervene. It is a woman's place to yield."

Although Henry loved his mother above anyone else in the world, nevertheless he highly disapproved of the forthright, independent, and sometimes overbearing manner with which she treated his father and other men. A wife, whether she be queen or empress in her own right, had the privilege of speaking her mind, the courtesy to be listened to, and her advice, if worthy of merit, heeded. After that she should behave with submission and respect, especially where her husband was concerned.

"Of course they should yield, my lord," said Jocelin. "But in my experience they rarely do."

"I will have it no other way."

The next day a party of nobles arrived from Paris and were invited to dine at the ducal palace in Rouen. They were dressed in black and wore somber expressions.

"I see you are in mourning," Henry said. "Has someone died?"

"The French monarchy, in a manner of speaking," one of the guests said.

"I don't follow."

"Have you not heard? Just two days ago the queen gave birth to another girl. There were no public demonstrations, no fires lit in celebration. The French king lies prostrate in the chapel."

"*Grâce à Dieu,* this is ill news for France," said Geoffrey thoughtfully.

"It is more like a death knell, my lord," replied another guest. "For the first time in one hundred and fifty years France is without an heir."

"This is not the propitious moment to do homage to Louis, my son," Geoffrey said under his breath. "It would be more politic to wait."

Henry shrugged. There was much to do in Normandy. He was no longer eager to pay homage to so hostile an overlord. Paris could wait.

# Paris, 1150–1151

Eleanor, trying to conceal her joy and relief, made a speedy recovery—indecently so, said the midwives who attended her—from the birth of her second child, whom she called Alix. Louis, reeling from the shock, had spent a solid week on his knees. The pope sent condolences, exhorting them to keep trying. But there was no question in Eleanor's mind that with this birth all the doubts in Louis's mind, laid to rest by the visit to Tusculum, returned with a vengeance. All she had to do was bide her time.

"Our marriage is cursed, Louis," Eleanor said, assuming a mournful expression whenever she saw her husband. "Can you not see the hand of God in this affair?" She paused, eyeing him dispassionately. Pale, gaunt, dressed in black, he had aged ten years since the news of another daughter; she felt she had shed as many.

"I mentioned an annulment to Abbé Suger. He says France cannot lose Aquitaine. He is vehemently opposed to any dissolution of the marriage."

"What good is my duchy to you when you have no son?"

Eleanor knew that many of Louis's barons also urged an annulment. Petronilla told her that they feared Louis might die before he had an heir. The only solution was to annul this marriage and try again. Louis was always indecisive; now he was maddeningly so. Eleanor realized she must be patient. A false step now would be fatal to any hope of freedom.

In January of the new year 1151, Abbé Suger, now getting on in years, fell ill and died. Louis, who had rarely taken a major decision without the abbé peering over his shoulder, was inconsolable.

"Send for Abbé Bernard," Eleanor told Louis. Instinct told her that the Cistercian monk could, unwittingly, aid her cause. He would care nothing about France's loss of Aquitaine. The spiritual realm was all that concerned him.

Before Louis could act, Bernard of Clairvaux arrived at the Cité Palace, obviously eager to step into the breach.

"This marriage is an offense in God's eyes," he told both Louis and Eleanor as they sat on their thrones in the great hall. "Abbé Suger—*requiescat in pace*—would not listen to me, being more concerned with affairs of state. Neither would the pope." He made no effort to conceal the note of triumph in his voice. "From the very beginning this marriage was cursed. I said so then; I say so now. Can you doubt this any longer?" He bent his burning gaze on Louis.

Louis turned his head to look at her. Their eyes met in a long stare. Eleanor held her breath. Holy Mother, please let him—

"No," he said, in an anguished voice. "I doubt no longer."

She had won. Now, nothing stood between her and complete freedom.

# CHAPTER 18

# Paris,

# 1151

*O*n a stifling day in August, in the year 1151, accompanied by several grooms and two squires, Henry, Duke of Normandy, and his father, Count Geoffrey of Anjou, rode toward Paris.

"Remember, when we meet with Louis of France leave the talking to me," Geoffrey said. "He is still smarting from his accumulated losses—the crusade, his failure to defeat us last year, the death of Abbé Suger. I've heard he is prickly as a porcupine."

"Hmm." Henry suppressed a yawn. "Everyone's forgotten about the crusade by now. They're more likely to remember how ill he fared in Normandy."

The count, who had finally deemed the time was ripe for Henry to swear homage, had been giving him the benefit of his advice ever since they left Rouen, and Henry was growing impatient.

"That's beside the point. I'm trying to teach you how to conduct yourself at the French court."

"Which is to do and say nothing."

"Exactly. Do not bring up the terms of the truce proposed by Louis and Bernard of Clairvaux. We must not give up the Vexin until we observe how matters lie at the French court. Be guided by me."

"I'm more interested in Paris than the court. Are the girls fair?"

Geoffrey shrugged impatiently. "The girls in Paris are made like any other. We're not going to France so you can sample the brothels but to do homage to King Louis for Normandy. Remember your position: you're a duke now." He turned his head toward Henry with a relenting sigh. "But only eighteen years of age, after all. The world is your trough; I suppose you must enjoy it while you can. But when I was only seventeen, let me tell you, I was married, burdened with responsibilities . . ."

Henry stopped listening. They were riding beside a lush green meadow backed by a rosy apple orchard. The sky was a deep hot blue; not a breath of wind stirred the apple-laden boughs. Duke of Normandy, he repeated to himself, still relishing his good fortune, still eternally grateful to his mother, the countess of Anjou—although she preferred to be addressed by her first husband's title, empress—who had relinquished her claim to the duchy in his favor.

"You're not suitably dressed, my son," the count was saying now, glancing with disapproval at Henry's scuffed black boots and shabby brown cloak. "And your mantle is far from fashionable, as I've told you. The style is for shorter mantles. You *must* get a new one made."

Henry, who never cared what he wore, shrugged. "If Louis objects, so much the better. I'm not a mincing peacock and I would have him know it." He bit his tongue and glanced quickly at his father, fearful he might have offended him. The count's preoccupation with his appearance was well known.

"I wasn't thinking of Louis but his wife. Queen Eleanor has a most aesthetic sensibility. You will regret looking so slovenly."

Henry was about to say he did not care what the queen or anyone thought, but there was something in Geoffrey's voice that bade him hold his tongue—and also intrigued him. How well did Geoffrey know Louis's wife? He eyed his father curiously. Turned out in his favorite colors of blue and green, Geoffrey sat astride his dappled horse with his usual air of nonchalant elegance. Not a hair was out of place, nor, despite the heat of the day, was there a drop of perspiration on his brow. God's eyes! Henry wiped away the sweat dripping from his forehead. How he envied his father! The count had the best seat of any horseman he knew. His horsemanship, like everything else he did, was controlled, effortless, and accomplished with panache.

Well, there was little use in wishing himself other than he was. Instead, Henry tried to recall everything he had heard about the French queen who, quite obviously, had made such a lasting impression on his father. Most important, of course, the legendary Eleanor held Aquitaine in her own right. In addition, she was reputed to be beautiful, spoiled, tempestuous—and she had announced to the world that Louis was more monk than husband. The fact that she was said to be a constant thorn in the side of Holy Church was all to her credit.

Henry also had a vague recollection of hearing about some scandal that had occurred during the crusade to the Holy Land but he couldn't remember the details. Gossip held no interest for him, and he was apt to forget what he'd heard moments after he'd heard it.

"What possessed Louis to take his wife on crusade?" he asked his father.

"What an extraordinary question. But the answer is I don't think he had a choice. He's hopelessly in love with Eleanor, always has been, and can deny her very little."

"Poor fool. It's a fatal mistake to let the heart reign in these matters."

Geoffrey threw him an amused look. "There speaks our champion in the lists of love, with all the wisdom of his mature years."

"Well, I've heard you say that women take advantage of men foolish enough to love them."

"*Grâce à Dieu,* did I say that? Then it must be true. Of course, Eleanor is not your ordinary woman."

Henry gave his father a sharp look. Again that slight change in voice. Just ahead lay the city gates, and they joined a flock of merchants, clergymen, and knights lining up to enter Paris.

"Speaking of Eleanor, let me repeat that Louis is very upset these days so please try to behave with circumspection," Geoffrey continued.

"So you already said. Upset about something other than the crusade and Abbé Suger and his failure to engage us in battle?"

They rode through the city gates and were assailed by an incessant din of voices, the mingled odors of hot roast chestnuts, spices, sizzling fat, and ripe cherries. They had to force their way through the leisurely promenade of the crowd of people. Henry was struck by the beat of the city, its air of throbbing excitement, so different from Rouen, which seemed a placid backwater by comparison.

The count raised his voice in order to be heard. "There are rumors, thick as flies, that there will be an annulment of his marriage on the grounds of consanguinity. Or that is the excuse being used. Everyone knows it is because the queen has provided no heir, only two daughters."

Henry, well aware of the devastation brought about by lack of a male heir, gave an inward shudder. Hadn't it been a similar circumstance that plunged England into seventeen years of chaos? He felt an unwitting spark of sympathy for Louis.

"An annulment means Louis will lose the wealthiest fief in France," he remarked. "Now *that* is something to be upset about."

They passed through the tower gate and across the fortified bridge. Just beyond lay the castle.

Geoffrey laughed. "Indeed. But remember, Louis also loves Eleanor. Don't judge him by your own ambitions."

Henry barely heard him. The situation had engaged his interest, and he wondered how best to take advantage of it. Such a major loss as Aquitaine would be bound to affect the future of the Capet dynasty. Might it also benefit Normandy?

"Ah, we have arrived," Geoffrey said.

They dismounted in the courtyard and entered the open doors of the keep.

While the French castle looked grim and dreary from the outside, inside it was another tale altogether. Henry was astounded at silk-cushioned stools woven with shimmering gold thread, and wonderfully worked tapestries depicting lions and dragons in glowing red-and-blue wools. There were narrow windows filled with the very new leaded glass and painted with roses, images of the Virgin and other saintly female figures. Neither Angers nor Rouen boasted anything so luxurious. Scotland, of course, was primitive by comparison. Henry carefully noted all the details of the castle so that later he could recount them to his mother.

Louis, surrounded by the bishop of Paris, Bernard of Clairvaux, and several other advisors, awaited them in the great hall seated on a high-backed chair draped with a gold cloth. Dressed in a black tunic set off by a heavy silver crucifix, the French king looked more like a prelate than a mighty monarch. His pale face resembled the underbelly of a fish, and he greeted Henry and his father with a formal courtesy that did little to hide his dislike and suspicion.

"We trust you have come to sign the treaty, my lord," said Louis in a cold voice.

"Certainly my son and I are most eager to discuss the matter, Sire." Geoffrey beamed.

"Indeed. Most eager," Henry said, noting that, as usual, his father was laying on the famous Angevin charm with a trowel. "But at the moment, Sire, we are somewhat fatigued from the journey.

Perhaps after we have refreshed ourselves . . ."

"Of course. You will be shown to your quarters at once. I will see you at Vespers and then at supper."

Two equerries escorted Henry and Geoffrey from the hall. Henry felt Louis's gaze follow him out the door.

"Thank you for taking my advice and saying nothing," said Geoffrey in a dry tone.

"Is it my imagination or does Louis hate me?" Henry kept his voice low. "What kind of bargain will he strike under such circumstances?"

"A man is known by his enemies as well as his friends. If the king of France hates you, it is because you are Norman and he fears you. A man's fear may be used against him. Never underestimate your power, my son, and always use it—with friend and foe alike."

Henry glanced at his father with respect. Sometimes it was easy to overlook the fact that beneath the count's glib charm and foppish appearance lay an astute and cunning mind coupled with a singleness of purpose that drove him straight as an arrow toward his goal.

He was about to tell his father how he felt when suddenly Henry was aware of the sounds of laughter and singing, accompanied by the strains of pipe and viol. Geoffrey paused before an open door.

"I should like to pay my respects to the queen," Geoffrey said to the equerries.

Henry, almost overpowered by a sweet, musky scent coming from the chamber, was amazed to see his father march across the threshold with assured familiarity. The music stopped; there was the twitter of excited voices.

"Why, it's Geoffrey le Bel!" cried a gay lilting voice as alluring as Eve. "What a delightful surprise. Who is that oddly dressed young man with you? Your squire? He must come in as well, I insist."

Henry did not know why he hesitated, one foot poised over the threshold, as if entering the room were a kind of special challenge that he was reluctant to meet. But he had been called a squire! This was sufficient to propel him into the chamber.

He was dumbfounded to see his father greeted by a bevy of lovely young women who surrounded him like chirping birds. Geoffrey then approached a wide cushioned bench set upon a dais. A woman sat surrounded by several troubadours kneeling before her. Over a cream-colored gown she wore a pale blue surcoat powdered with silver stars and crescent moons. Her pale amber skin glowed; luxuriant waves of chestnut hair shimmered with bronze lights. Under thick arched brows, her eyes, a mixture of glittering green and warm brown, like a forest at sunrise, sparkled with mischief and gaiety. A garland of white roses encircled her head.

"It's been far too long, *mon ami,*" she said, stretching out graceful white hands to Geoffrey as she stepped from the dais. Her fingers sparkled with pearl, emerald, and ruby rings.

"Here is my eldest son and heir, Henry, duke of Normandy," said Geoffrey, staring at the queen as one bewitched.

Who could blame him? Henry knew that he himself was falling under a spell, dazzled by the queen's beauty and charm, yes, but also something more—much, much more. A heart-stopping sense of destiny. It was as if all the days of his life had only existed to lead him to this time and this place. With every instinct he possessed Henry knew he had met a harbinger of his fate. Whether for good or ill he could not tell.

"So—this is no squire but the unruly young duke who's been troubling France." Eleanor's lips, inviting as the open half of a ripe peach, widened in a seductive smile. Her small white teeth reminded Henry of a dainty fox. "Except for his ceremonial ducal sword he is certainly not dressed like a powerful lord."

Henry felt his cheeks burn. Cursing himself for a dolt, he could not think of an apt rejoinder. "It is a great honor to meet you, Madam." The words came out in a belated croak.

"What's this? But of course we have met before," Eleanor said, cocking her head to one side.

"Impossible. I would never have forgotten," Henry said, relieved to have found his voice at last.

"Indeed? Of course you were only four or five years old at the time, and in the midst of a violent temper tantrum, so you may be forgiven."

Eleanor's women tittered; Henry looked bewildered.

"I took you to the queen's betrothal feast in Bordeaux," Geoffrey said.

Henry glowered, feeling at a disadvantage. He hated being told of events that had either excluded him or he had forgotten, although memory of the event was starting to return. His discomfort increased when Eleanor, hands on hips, lips pursed, now walked slowly around him.

"Is Normandy in such dire straits that the treasury cannot afford new clothes for its duke?"

Henry flushed crimson while Geoffrey allowed a tiny smile of satisfaction to cross his features.

"You're a far cry from the elegance of your father," she said, walking over to Geoffrey.

In what Henry took to be an intimate gesture that bespoke of long familiarity, Eleanor smoothed the count's gold-embroidered blue mantle. "Geoffrey le Bel, you must give the duke the name of your tailor. He's too barbaric for our civilized court."

Henry knew she was deliberately taunting him; it stirred him like new wine.

"With apologies to my father, but clothes alone do not make the man," he said, determined to rise to this challenge.

Eleanor widened her eyes. "Ah, so we have a philosopher in our midst. Tell me, pray, I am all ears. What does make the man?"

"I would be most happy to show you, Madam." Henry grinned. "Any time. Any place. You have only to say the word."

Geoffrey looked like a thundercloud.

Eleanor laughed. "Did you hear that, *demoiselles?* Is that a fair offer, would you say?"

The women giggled.

Eleanor's eyes clashed with Henry's like steel ringing against steel in the lists; the air between them crackled. Henry's loins stirred, the blood pounded in his head. How he wanted this woman, proud and mettlesome as a wild filly, and as far beyond his reach as a star.

Eleanor clapped her hands. "My lords, you must help us with this most intriguing question. My ladies, my troubadours, and myself are holding a most serious debate on the nature of love: Can there be true love in marriage?"

"I fear that we cannot do justice to that question at the moment," Geoffrey said in a curt voice. "We must retire to our quarters. Perhaps another time, Lady."

"I hope you will attend me later—both of you," said Eleanor, her eyes upon Henry.

Caught in the incandescent moment Henry was unable to break the spell, until Geoffrey bowed, grabbed his arm, then physically marched him from the chamber. The equerries led them to their quarters where their squires had already unpacked the saddlebags.

The count was silent but Henry felt a tension emanating from his father, and could guess the reason.

"Does something trouble you, my lord?" He decided it was better to let Geoffrey air his grievances than have them fester inside him.

"You pushed yourself forward in a most aggressive manner," Geoffrey said, rummaging through his belongings.

He lifted out a silver mirror that traveled everywhere with him, then rearranged his red-gold locks in an attempt to hide a few strands of gray hair.

Watching his father preen, Henry grudgingly admitted to himself that he was still an extraordinarily handsome man. Although his waist had thickened somewhat over the years, and his fair skin had slightly coarsened, the purity of his features was striking, his carriage was straight as a spear, and the cornflower blue of his eyes remained undimmed. "Geoffrey le Bel" still applied.

"What is that supposed to mean?"

"It means you exhibited the worst characteristics of a typical boorish Norman," Geoffrey said, "and behaved most offensively. The queen was displeased with your uncouth manner."

Henry laughed. "Displeased? On the contrary."

"I flatter myself I know the queen better than you."

"That's obvious. How much better is the question." The moment the words were out he regretted them. Too late.

Geoffrey placed the mirror carefully in his saddlebag then spun around. "Take care how you speak to me. Some matters do not concern you."

Henry felt the blood rise to his head, and threw caution to the winds. "If the king of France has personally taken against *me* because *you* have put a pair of horns on him, surely that is my concern—and my mother's as well."

Geoffrey, white with rage, swung his arm wide and cuffed him on the side of the head. "Impudent young cub! I'll teach you to flout your sire."

Henry was so taken aback that he had no time to react. By the time he did, his ear tingling from the blow, Geoffrey had marched out of the chamber. The cuff had been more insulting than painful, and he was not angry so much as astonished.

Henry had witnessed his father in some vile moods over the years, but he had never before seen him in a jealous rage. The sight did not make pleasant viewing. Eleanor must mean more to Geoffrey—a great deal more—than he had imagined. Had the French queen bedded his father? It was none of his affair, yet he felt as if someone had driven a burning spear through his vitals. One way or another, he intended to find out the truth.

# CHAPTER 19

"Is there something amiss between you and your father? You seem distant with each other," said Eleanor later that evening in the great hall.

To Henry's amazement he had been seated at the high table next to the queen, while Geoffrey was placed next to Louis. A far greater honor but one undoubtedly less pleasing to the count.

"Are you surprised?" he asked.

"Should I be?"

"I would have thought very little surprises you, Lady."

"If you think I'm responsible for any coolness between you and Geoffrey, why not come right out and say so?"

After a moment's silence Henry, aware of his surging heartbeat, turned to look Eleanor directly in the face. "How well do you know my father?"

"Not nearly as well as he would have liked." The words came readily to her tongue. Too readily? "Does that disturb you?" She met his gaze squarely. "It shouldn't. After all, everyone knows the count and countess of Anjou have never gotten along."

"I don't need you to tell me that." Henry stabbed a piece of roast venison with his knife. "In future, please refer to my mother as the empress. It is the title she prefers."

"Yes, of course." Eleanor paused. "Forgive me. I didn't mean to open old wounds." She gave him a crooked smile. "I understand about old wounds. Sometimes it helps to share them."

The new note of gentleness in her voice, the empathetic warmth in her eyes, brought an unexpected lump into his throat. Jesu, what was happening? Eleanor had somehow taken control of the conversation; its unforeseen turn was now making him feel acutely uncomfortable. He must get the reins back into his own hands. Henry swallowed, forced a smile, then flashed her a roguish look that usually reduced most females to simpering peahens.

"I would share more than confidences with you, Madam."

There was a moment's silence. "Would you indeed? How very unoriginal." The warmth was gone, replaced by the voice of the queen teasing her courtiers. "I've always heard the Normans lacked subtlety, but I hardly expected their duke to behave like—well—" She gave an eloquent shrug.

"How else would you expect me to behave? I'm a man like any other—but not a silver-tongued gallant."

"No! One would never have guessed." She peered at him flirtatiously over the rim of her jeweled goblet.

The dangerous moment was over; Henry relaxed. Eleanor's face, framed by a white muslin wimple and topped by the ducal coronet of Aquitaine, looked even more youthful and vibrant than it had earlier in the day. For a moment Henry's gaze lingered on the gold emblem of her power before passing down the slender arch of her neck. He realized that her clothes were not those she had worn earlier and felt a sudden throb in his temples. Had she changed them for his benefit—or his father's? Under a sleeveless crimson surcoat, she wore a tightly molded blue gown that revealed a slender waist and faintly outlined the nipples of her breasts. Was she wearing anything underneath? Her breasts were not large but high and firm, like a girl's half her age. Henry wondered what they would feel like in his hands.

"Stop looking at my bosom," she said in a low voice. "Everyone is watching you watching me. Particularly your father and Louis."

"I would do more than look." Henry did not shift his gaze. "Why should I make a secret of my admiration? Particularly when I know you enjoy it."

Eleanor sharply drew in her breath. "What brazen cheek! I have not said so."

"You do not need to say so."

"I find you absolutely outrageous." Her face was flushed.

"You do? From all I hear that is like the kettle calling the cauldron black."

"Are you so gullible to believe everything you hear? You should know by now that royalty attracts gossip with or without cause. However this is neither the time nor the place for such talk."

"Tell me the time and place and a herd of wild horses won't keep me away." Henry's squire offered him a silver bowl of water, and he washed the grease off his fingers. "I should warn you, however, I have no gift for inconsequential chatter."

"So you keep reminding me. I find repetition boring."

"I'm a man of action; that is where my talents lie."

"Tell me," Eleanor said, picking up the wing of a roast guinea fowl, nibbling at it, then laying it down again. "Do you never tire of bellowing your prowess? How can one know if you truly live up to the high expectations you claim for yourself?"

Beneath her bantering tone Henry discerned a shiver of excitement in her voice. His heart hammered in his chest. The tension between them, increasing moment by moment, was as intense as forked lightning.

"We could bandy words from now 'til doomsday," Henry said in a husky voice. "Accept the challenge and find out."

Eleanor gave a low throaty laugh that seemed to promise a thousand delights. When she lifted her goblet, Henry saw that her jeweled fingers trembled slightly. After a quick glance at the French king she turned back to Henry.

"Put up your lance, my lord. Any moment now Louis will arise. I will send you word of the time and place."

"Unlike your laggard husband, l have been rising for some time." He grinned, hoping she would not see how he ached to touch her. "I eagerly await your summons."

Eleanor turned pink and almost choked on her wine. She turned away and Henry, tingling from the encounter, played with the food on his trencher, too wrought up to eat.

After supper when Louis asked if he were now ready to discuss the terms of the treaty, Henry again pleaded fatigue. Eleanor had given no indication when she would send for him but he wanted to be available. Heady, as if he were flown with wine, he went into the courtyard to cool his blood. High above, a full moon paced across a sable sky, gilding the towers of the castle with a silvery light, casting dark shadows in the corners of the courtyard.

The bells of Notre Dame rang the hour of Compline. The window slits in the castle were dark, but high in the keep flickered a single flame. Eleanor's solar? Henry stared at it intently. After an hour or so, he walked disconsolately back inside the keep, up a narrow staircase, and down a winding passage to the chamber he shared with Geoffrey and their squires. He had been strenuously hoping she might have summoned him tonight.

Geoffrey appeared to be asleep, but there was something about the rigid position of his body that made Henry wonder if the count were shamming. He knew the difficulty with his father would have to be cleared up before they met with Louis. If Normandy did not present a united front, the French king would be sure to take advantage of the situation. He might demand more than the Vexin in return for acknowledging Henry as duke of Normandy. Without removing his boots Henry lay down on the straw pallet, flung an arm across his face, and with a sigh thought of Eleanor.

The alluring body, taut and sinuous as a whip, the challenging sparkle in her eyes, the peach-bloom skin were as vivid in Henry's mind as a clear-running stream in the Verte Forest outside Rouen. Was she truly getting an annulment? he wondered; had she really told him the truth about her relationship with Geoffrey?

That night he dreamed of the ducal coronet of Aquitaine, a golden circlet set with pearls and rubies. In the dream the rubies turned into drops of blood; the pearls became teardrops.

The next morning Henry woke late to find Geoffrey already gone.

"He woke at Prime and went to morning mass, my lord," Geoffrey's squire told him. "He has not yet returned here."

Henry splashed cold water on his face from a silver basin, ran a hand through the bristles of his tawny-red hair, then searched through the litter of clothes for his best mantle. A present from his mother, it was made of scarlet cloth embroidered with gold lions. Fine enough to please the most exacting queen.

"My lord, you cannot appear in public with your boots covered in mud," said the squire. "You must have dirtied them last night. Let me clean them for you."

"No time now."

The squire looked horrified. "Oh my lord, what will the count say—"

Henry grabbed the mantle, dashed out the door and through the long passage, down the staircase and into the great hall. The tables were empty but for a few knights and squires. Still standing, he downed a goblet of wine, tore the end off a wheaten loaf, and went in search of his father.

Outside in the courtyard, a servant approached and said in the soft accents of the *langue d'oc* that the queen wished to have converse with him. Henry hesitated then shrugged. If royalty beckoned he must obey. He was sure to find Geoffrey before they met with Louis. They passed a patch of summer lilies growing beside a stone bench. Henry stopped, remembering now for the first time in years that he had presented a bunch of lilies to the newly wedded French queen when she was—God's eyes!—only a few years younger than he was now. He plucked a handful of the wilted blooms and followed the servant around the side of the castle.

Eleanor anxiously paced the small antechamber. Her head was spinning with a jumble of incoherent thoughts that touched on Raymond of Antioch, the impending annulment of her marriage, her future status in Aquitaine, and, most importantly, her headlong, inexplicable attraction to Henry of Anjou. A wild impulse had come into her mind last night and nothing would dislodge it. Was she raving mad to even consider such an option? If only her uncle were here to guide and reassure her. Eleanor felt as if she were about to plunge into unknown waters that might well sink her—unless she could navigate them with a skill she had never had to use before and was not even sure she possessed.

Once the incredible idea had seized her she had spent a sleepless night trying to decide what course to follow.

Ever since the fateful meeting with Raymond, when the idea of an annulment had first been presented to her, Eleanor had known that the time would come when she would be faced with having to acquire another husband. But she had put the matter out of her mind as there were far more pressing problems that required immediate attention. Once she was a free woman, secure in Aquitaine, reliable candidates would be carefully considered. She was no longer so innocent or so foolish to believe she could rule the duchy alone—much as she would prefer to do so—because of the great dangers involved. In truth, this was exactly the position she had been in when her father died—only now she understood the potential hazards far better. But at least she would be in control. She could choose her moment; choose her consort.

Now, when she had least expected—or wanted it—the moment of choice was at hand.

Eleanor opened the door and peered out. The passage was empty. Grateful for the reprieve, she picked up a purple fig from the table and resumed pacing the chamber, astonished, no, overwhelmed at her reactions.

With the exception of Raymond of Antioch, she had been drawn to Henry of Anjou more than she had ever been to any man. When the duke was in the same room she could not look at anyone else; when he was absent she counted the moments until she would see him again. Despite his youth, it was obvious that he was already a strong, intelligent figure, and as he matured his strength would increase. He was Geoffrey's son, after all. In addition, Henry had wit, ambition, but overriding it all—Eleanor forced herself to admit it— she craved him so desperately that her body actually ached with longing. Putting aside her own needs—at least for the moment— Eleanor forced herself to look at the practical side of this choice.

Already ruler of a powerful duchy, Normandy, in time Henry would also inherit the counties of Anjou and Maine. Through his mother he was the rightful king of England. With her, Eleanor's, help—Aquitaine, after all, had vast resources—the English crown became even more of a certainty. It was politic to wed such a man, Eleanor told herself; that she found him so appealing as well was an unexpected bonus.

But did he want her? Henry lusted after her, of course. Many men did. Not that Eleanor had ever blinded herself to the equally seductive lure of Aquitaine. But did he truly want *her*? She could not endure another loveless marriage. She had always longed for love, to be swept away on the tide of an emotion stronger than herself yet still remain inviolate, in control, a free spirit. A typical Aquitainian contradiction, countered the voice of an unseen Raymond in her head, like trying to ride horses of two different colors. She could almost hear the languid yawn. It's in the blood, my dear. You'll never resolve it.

Eleanor opened the door again. The passage was still deserted.

Impulsively, she had asked to see the young duke. Now that his arrival was imminent what should she say to him? She was a duchess and a queen, used to deference, respect, and mostly having her own way.

He was eleven years younger; she had never thought to wed a

younger—Eleanor suddenly stifled a cry. Sweet St. Radegonde, what had that fortune-teller said so long ago? She calculated rapidly. Yes, yes, the times would fit! But what did it mean? Was Henry the one? Now, at this great turning point of her life, a moment that might never come again, Eleanor felt less in command of her fate than at any time in the past.

The servant led Henry through a narrow door, down a dimly lit passage, then showed him into a small antechamber. The door closed softly behind him. Eleanor, a serious expression on her face, was standing in the middle of the room. Henry gazed in astonishment at the walls, consisting entirely of glazed deep blue mosaic tile; at the floor of red-veined marble. A low ebony-inlaid table sat in front of a long divan heaped with silken cushions in vermillion, azure, and purple. On the table lay two silver goblets chased with precious stones, and silver dishes of plump blue-black and deep crimson fruits he had never seen before. Several gold-embroidered cushioned stools graced the chamber.

"I've patterned this room after one in my late uncle Raymond's palace in Antioch," said Eleanor, in answer to his wordless reaction to the chamber. She walked over to the divan, sat down, and patted a place beside her. "The figs and pomegranates I import from the East—at great expense, I might add."

"What does Louis say about that?"

"Louis has nothing to say about it. I pay for such luxuries out of my revenues from Aquitaine and Poitou."

Henry, trying not to appear as awestruck as he felt, sat down gingerly beside her. The elegance and sophistication of the queen, as well as of the chamber, made him wish that his boots had been cleaned, and an unmistakable whiff of stables less pronounced. In his own eyes he appeared clumsy and ill at ease, a ham-fisted bumpkin from the provinces. Thank God he had had the foresight to wear the scarlet mantle.

In what he felt was a graceless gesture, Henry thrust the flowers at her. He could think of nothing to say.

Eleanor gave him a questioning look then suddenly smiled.

"So you remember our second meeting. I wondered if you would. Thank you for these." She laid them carefully on the table.

Under the ducal coronet, her face looked as lovely, her body as tantalizing as he remembered. She wore the blue gown of the previous night, not entirely suitable for morning wear, Henry thought, wondering if this were meant to convey some message. His blood stirred when he realized they were entirely alone.

Except Eleanor was not in the least flirtatious this morning. On the contrary, her face was grave, her eyes intent. She appeared softer, almost vulnerable. Whatever she had in mind it was not a lighthearted tryst. Henry felt a vague sense of disappointment.

"There is so much to explain and so little time in which to do it," Eleanor began. "Forgive my boldness but I had to see you before your audience with Louis." She took a deep breath. "You've no doubt heard rumors that Louis and I are in the process of having our marriage annulled?"

"From my father. They are not merely rumors then?"

"Far from it. The details of the annulment are still being worked out but that shouldn't take too much longer. Perhaps only another six months." She paused. "Then I will be free."

Henry picked up a blue-black fig, of a kind he'd never seen before, turning it over in his fingers. Was the stem meant to be eaten? He finally popped the whole thing into his mouth, wondering why Eleanor was confiding in him. After chewing vigorously he decided that the stem was not meant to be eaten.

"Do I offer condolences or congratulations?" he asked. Where was all this leading?

"I think you already know the answer to that. The truth is I have always been miserable with Louis."

"Surely he doesn't mistreat you?" The question was ridiculous. Who would dare to mistreat this imperious beauty? Henry was growing so intensely aware of her physical presence he could hardly keep his wits about him.

"No. Unless being bored to death is considered mistreatment. It is in Aquitaine."

Henry could hear the bitterness in her voice when she talked about the king. And no wonder. It was nothing less than a crime that this charming, desirable woman should have been married to a eunuch like Louis of France. How he wished he could help her.

"When my second daughter, Alix, was born, I knew Louis would be advised to cast me off."

"I see." Henry felt flattered at her confidences but still could not imagine where the conversation was heading. Certainly not toward the seduction he had initially looked forward to.

Eleanor's hazel eyes, enormous under the dark arches of her brows, seemed to be making him some mute appeal. He wanted to respond but not knowing how shifted uncomfortably on his seat.

"My lord—Henry," she said in a tentative voice. "You see before you a woman who is no longer a maid, yet neither spouse nor widow. A woman who will soon be without protection, for according to the terms of the marriage contract, Aquitaine remains mine. You know what that means? Once news of the annulment spreads, I will be at the mercy of every ravening beast who seeks my inheritance."

Henry had heard—as who had not—of Eleanor's tumultuous marital troubles. But he had never imagined the strong-minded queen as being alone and unprotected. His heart swelled and his breath almost suffocated him.

"Madam," he began earnestly, "I had no idea you were in such straits. It would give me the greatest pleasure—that is to say—I will do all in my power to aid you."

"Few know the extent of my plight," she said with a sad smile, laying slim white fingers on his freckled hand, the palms hardened by his horse's reins, the backs pitted from the sharp beaks of his falcons.

"How may I serve you?" he asked.

She was silent for a moment, her head bent, the tips of her fingers idly stroking the back of his hand, causing Henry the most acute sensations.

"When you see Louis, I want you to agree to the treaty he desires. Give France the Vexin and let Louis acknowledge you as duke of Normandy."

Henry was astounded. Instantly suspicious, he withdrew his hand. What sort of double game was this minx playing at? Was Louis behind it? "I fail to see how this would serve you, Madam. I have no wish to lose the Vexin."

Eleanor lifted her eyes to his. "Not even in exchange for Aquitaine?"

Dumbfounded, Henry felt as if all the breath had been knocked out of him. Had he heard her aright? "Aquitaine?" he echoed lamely. "I mean—I don't understand."

"I think you do," she said in a soft voice. "I think you understand very well. I'm offering you the opportunity to marry me and become the next duke of Aquitaine—once the annulment is rendered final. If my situation were not so desperate, if haste were not paramount, I would never have approached you in this unseemly way."

Henry's first thought was what would his mother say; the enormity of the gift Eleanor offered was staggering. Duke of Aquitaine and count of Poitou—all the resources he would need to invade England. And she needed him. This legendary beauty, whose prestige and influence were famous throughout Europe, had asked for his protection! He gazed into her eyes, which, to his amazement were unnaturally bright, almost fearful. Her face had the bloomy sheen of a summer wildflower; her moist lips were parted.

Henry tried to speak but the words would not come. The blood pounded in his head as he found himself prey to an emotional upheaval he had not anticipated. Without warning, he had the sudden urge to devote himself to those luminous eyes, that beckoning mouth, to pledge his body and heart to this radiant queen who had stepped down from her pedestal and offered herself to him. He wanted her more than he had ever wanted anything in his life. How desperately he longed to express his feelings but could not. Inwardly he cursed himself, for the first time wishing he had the gift of gallantry, the golden tongue of a troubadour, the easy charm of his father.

"I have humbled myself before you," Eleanor said with a catch in her voice. "Was it a mistake? Could I have so misjudged you?"

All Henry could do was vehemently shake his head. "But why me?" His voice sounded gruff and he wondered why he was unwilling to let her see how deeply her words had affected him.

"I need a knight of rank and power. A man of strength and judgment. The fact that we are neighbors—the borders of Anjou and Poitou march side by side—is significant. One day you will be king of England. You have all the necessary qualifications, my lord, to become my protector."

"Your confidence is much appreciated but at the moment I'm merely duke of Normandy. My father is very much alive and I'm a long way from being king of England."

"With my help—the resources I can put at your disposal—you will certainly be closer to your goal. Did that thought not occur to you?"

"It crossed my mind, yes," Henry admitted slowly.

Eleanor smiled. "Thank you for your honesty."

To Henry's surprise she suddenly blushed. "And there are other reasons why I chose you. Reasons that I think you already know. My heart tells me we will suit one another."

They gazed deeply into each other's eyes. Slowly Henry bent his head and kissed her half-open mouth. He was overcome by a burning desire, a wild elation mingled with a rough urgency to take her here and now. This was his usual way with the serving girls, tavern wenches, and compliant wives he bedded. But he held back, reminding himself that he was kissing the queen of France, holding the duchy of Aquitaine in his arms. Then all thought was lost as the kiss grew deeper and deeper, plunging Henry into a whirlpool of excitement he had never before experienced.

Eleanor was the first to break away, pushing him back with trembling hands. Her breath came in ragged gasps, her body shivered as if assailed by a strong wind. He knew that she was fighting the desire to abandon herself to his ardor and this inspired him with great respect. Control in a woman was a unique quality. His mother's cool head was one of the things he most admired about her.

"Can Louis be such a fool as to have denied you marital joys?" Henry barely recognized the thick, husky voice as his own. Unable to stop himself he ran his hand over one uptilted breast. The nipple jutted out hard against his palm. "I've wanted to do that since last night." He dropped his hand.

With a shuddering sigh, Eleanor picked up her goblet of wine and curled both hands tightly round the stem. "Have we made a bargain then?" The unmistakable tremor in her voice was very satisfying. "You keep Aquitaine from the wolves and I will see to it you have the resources to take England."

"Agreed. But why must I give Louis the Vexin?"

"Because he must not suspect what we have in mind. Let him think he has beaten you. Disarmed, he will honor you as his vassal, duke of Normandy, the annulment will proceed without hindrance, and none will guess our intention until it is too late. Later, when we are wed and England is won, we will find a way to get the Vexin back."

Henry stared at her, impressed that she seemed to have thought the whole matter through. "But even when Louis is no longer your husband, the king of France is still your overlord in your capacity as duchess of Aquitaine. You may not marry without his consent."

"Once the fact of our marriage is accomplished what can he do? Louis's bark is loud but his teeth are weak. Trust me to know what

I'm doing. This plan will work, but be discreet. Do not discuss the matter unless absolutely necessary."

Henry nodded. He had a hundred questions but there was a brisk knock on the door and the same servant poked his head inside the chamber.

"The king is asking for Duke Henry, Madam."

"He is just coming." Eleanor rose.

The door closed. Henry got to his feet. It was the most momentous occasion of his eighteen years and he felt inept, in awe of this impetuous woman whom he had just agreed to wed. All he wanted to do was to take her in his arms, but she was looking at him expectantly now, obviously waiting for him to—to what?

He drew himself up, relieved that he was at least half a head taller than Eleanor. "Madam, I'm only a plain-spoken Norman but my sword will always be ready to defend you. Your honor I will guard with my life, and—and your foes will be mine."

She smiled. "A brave speech, worthy of the most silver-tongued courtier. We will do very well together."

Determined to present a chivalrous image, Henry awkwardly knelt before her. He intended to kiss her hand but somehow managed to brush his forehead against the gold filigree of her girdle instead. The next thing he knew he was outside the chamber, wiping the sweat from his brow.

His head reeling, Henry walked down the passage on the heels of the servant. Suddenly he stopped in his tracks, spun round on his toes and gave a great whoop of joy. The queen of France was to be his wife! And England—his birthright, his dream, his life's goal—was virtually within his grasp!

CHAPTER 20

*G*eoffrey was waiting at the entrance to the great hall. From his rigid stance and fixed smile Henry knew there would be rough weather ahead.

"Where have you been? I've looked everywhere for you." The count searched Henry's face. "Well, never mind that now. Listen carefully, I've thought the matter over and I think you must give up the Vexin with good grace. The most important thing is for you to be officially acknowledged as Normandy's duke. I hope you're going to be reasonable about this."

Henry smiled. "Very reasonable. In fact I agree with you."

"You do?" Geoffrey looked taken aback. "I expected a battle on my hands. What has occasioned this change of heart?"

"God's eyes, I cannot win. On the one hand you urge me to be reasonable, then when I am you find fault with that."

Geoffrey's eyes narrowed. "You've been with Eleanor. She's behind this change, isn't she?"

"Does it matter?"

The steward approached them. "My lords, King Louis is just hearing a dispute between two vassals. The case will be over in a moment. Please wait."

Geoffrey gave the man an icy smile. "Of course." He led Henry toward the open doors of the keep where rays of sunshine covered the rushes like a carpet of gold dust. Other lords, also waiting to see the French king, milled about in groups, eyeing the two Normans with speculation.

"Have you made a cuckold of your overlord?" Geoffrey's voice came out in an explosive hiss.

"Have *you*? I believe we've had this conversation before."

Geoffrey's fists clenched, and for a moment Henry thought he would strike him again. Not certain now he wanted to hear the answer, he held up his hands.

"Peace. Peace. I've no wish to quarrel with you, my lord." Henry ran tense fingers through his hair. "On the contrary, I badly need your support now."

"When have you not needed it?"

Henry took a deep breath. God's eyes, this was going to be even worse than he had imagined.

"What trouble have you managed to stir up this time?" Geoffrey's gaze bored into his.

"No trouble. Look, the situation is thus—"

"Ah, now, at last, we come to the truth."

"Once Eleanor's marriage is annulled, she and I will wed in secret," Henry said, the words tumbling out in a rush. "As duke of Aquitaine I will have all the resources I need to take England. Do I have your blessing in this affair?"

Geoffrey's eyes blazed in a face suddenly devoid of all color. His mouth worked and he rocked backward, as if unsteady on his feet. It was with great difficulty that Henry restrained himself from reaching out a hand to aid him. After a few moments he saw Geoffrey make a visible effort to bring himself under control.

"Well, you've not been idle," he said in a tight voice. "How long have you known this woman you intend to marry? A day and a half? I suspected Eleanor might soon be seeking a husband to help govern her unruly domains, but little did I dream the honor would fall to my own son. You hardly need my blessing, having managed so well on your own."

"Still, I would have it."

"It is a match far above anything I could have arranged for you," Geoffrey continued, as if Henry had not spoken. "Your mother may be a trifle upset—at first—but she will come to realize the great advantages to be gained." He paused, and after swallowing several times, added: "As do I. After all, you, your mother, and I are all slaves of ambition, are we not?" His lips stretched over his teeth in a ghastly semblance of a smile.

"There's rather more to it than that," Henry began, then stopped.

Despite his efforts to conceal it, Geoffrey still appeared so shaken Henry could not bring himself to throw more wood onto an already raging fire.

In his way Henry not only respected but loved his cool and handsome father; the fact that he was behaving more like a rival than a son troubled his conscience. It was equally troubling that he still could not tell, for certain, the exact nature of Geoffrey's relationship with Eleanor. She denied having bedded him; Geoffrey was evasive. Where did the truth lie?

"Thank you, my lord," Henry said in a low voice. "Your goodwill is important to me in this matter."

"You have always proceeded with or without my goodwill, my son," Geoffrey replied, "and success crowns all your endeavors regardless."

Henry wondered what he could do to bridge the gap, growing wider by the instant, that separated him from his father. "Do you— do you have any advice for me?" It was the only thing he could think of to say.

Geoffrey raised his brows. "Are you serious?"

Henry flushed but nodded. Geoffrey appeared in control now but there were unaccustomed beads of sweat at the corner of each temple. It was evident he was keeping himself under a tight rein.

Hands behind his back, Geoffrey began to stride back and forth before the open doors, Henry beside him. "What can I tell you? That you will have as wife a woman whom, having once seen her, every man will long to possess? But you must already be aware of that."

"What is the harm so long as she is a dutiful wife?"

"I have known Eleanor many years. She is a woman not easy to please, yet please her you must, or you will suffer the consequences. There is little love lost between Louis and myself, yet one cannot help feeling sorry for him. He has always been obsessed with his wife and to let her go will not be easy for him."

"What has that to do with me?" Henry raised his brows. "Louis has brought this state of affairs upon himself. In any case it is the loss of Aquitaine that no doubt weighs so heavily upon him."

Geoffrey gave a short laugh. "So you said the day we arrived, as I recall. You, of course, are totally indifferent to possession of the duchy, yes? Who was it just told me he now had all the resources to invade England?" He stopped a moment to scrutinize Henry's face.

"You have won Louis's wife and the wealthiest fief in his domains. Can you not spare any compassion for a man no longer in his first youth who will now lose what he values most?"

Henry felt his cheeks grow hot. Louis has lost both Eleanor and the duchy in any case, he wanted to shout, but kept silent.

Geoffrey continued to stride back and forth in front of the doors. "Then there are the rumors of her behavior in Antioch. With her own uncle."

Henry stiffened. "I'm surprised that you listen to rumor and gossip. Far better to ignore such unsavory tales, which have no truth to them."

Geoffrey paused. "If one can be *sure* there is no truth. It is important to know that your sons are *your* sons."

There was an underlying bitterness in Geoffrey's voice that sent a warning chill down Henry's spine. Deep within him stirred bleak memories of the endless conflict between his parents, his mother's tears, some secret and intangible sorrow that ate into her heart like rust into iron. Why would such unhappy thoughts surface now?

"I cannot imagine what you mean by such caveats but my sons will be mine, never fear. I know how to please a woman far better than that prickless eunuch the queen is wed to now. I find your implications offensive, my lord. Eleanor is not the kind of woman to dishonor a crown."

"You would be surprised at the kind of woman who is capable of—"

"Enough," Henry said, his body beginning to tremble as he felt one of his demon rages coming on. "Enough, do you hear?"

"Yes, all right, enough on that score," Geoffrey said after a quick look at Henry's face. "Get hold of yourself. Do you want to look like a fool in front of all these lords?" After a moment's pause he continued. "You asked for my advice, remember? Then, of course, Eleanor is eleven years older than you and—"

"What of it? My mother is eleven years older than you. By Christ, what are you trying to tell me?"

Geoffrey shrugged and turned away. "Nothing. Nothing! Suffice it to say that both your mother and Eleanor would have fared better had they been born men."

It was the last thing Henry expected to hear. What in God's name had gotten into the count? He wished now he had never sought to propitiate his father by asking for advice.

"I concede you have a point there," Henry said, "but does it matter? Do you say these pinpricks weigh in the balance against England? I like women of spirit, having known little else, and she is female enough for me."

Something about his father's attitude indicated sour grapes, a desire to destroy that which he couldn't have. Perhaps the count had not bedded Eleanor after all. Henry was surprised at the relief he felt.

"Just imagine, one day I will be duke of Normandy, duke of Aquitaine, count of Anjou and Maine—though not for a long time to come, I hope—and king of England. A veritable empire."

"And a fearful responsibility. The lord who rules is also the lord who serves. Take care lest greed for power become your master."

Henry stared at his father in amazement. "You sound like a canting cleric. What have we been about these many years except to win Normandy and England back from the usurper?"

"Had I those years to relive I might have gone about matters differently." Geoffrey came to rest before the doors of the keep and stared unseeing into the flood of sunlight.

"Come, do you tell me that you would have been content with just Anjou and Maine? An accomplished warrior and ruler like yourself?"

"In my youth, no. I too sought the English crown, remember. But now? A county is not just field and stream, rock and meadow, you know. It is also flesh and blood, bone and sinew. The dreams and aspirations of your subjects, their rages and pain, their differences and similarities. As I say, a fearful responsibility. The larger the lands, the greater the burden."

Henry, who had never heard his father speak thus, was unsettled. He felt as if he were suddenly talking to a total stranger. "What is it that makes you speak so?"

Geoffrey looked at him gravely. "Will all that land make you happy, I wonder?"

"Is this a serious question?"

With a sigh of resignation, Geoffrey shook his head. "Indeed, a foolish one. At your age I would have reacted the same. Never mind. You are your mother's son, a true Norman. I wish you well, my boy."

The steward called out to say the king would see them now.

"One last thing," Geoffrey said quickly. "If you allow yourself to become truly, deeply involved with Eleanor, never again will you be a free man."

Henry was about to ask why not but the conversation had grown uncomfortably, nay alarmingly, intimate, and he had no wish to continue with it.

"I see you don't understand," Geoffrey said. "Perhaps it's just as well."

Relieved, Henry followed his father into the hall. Within moments he had forced the matter out of his mind as he prepared to negotiate with Louis.

The homage ceremony was held two days later. Henry officially became duke of Normandy, a nominal vassal of the king of France. By this time the French court felt like a prison to him. Despite the mountains of richly spiced foods, the finest horses, troubadours, and jongleurs available, the lack of harmony in the household was painfully evident. Beneath the gay, courteous facade, hatred and tension seethed like a bubbling cauldron. It was a scene all too familiar to Henry and he wished himself well away. Even his encounters with Eleanor were disappointing, as he was unable to converse with her alone except in brief unsatisfactory snatches that left them both frustrated.

"I must return to Normandy," he told her.

"I think you should, and with all speed. The next few months will be very trying here and the less you're in evidence, the better for me. I will let you know my plans and when we should next meet." She thought for a moment. "Probably in Poitou where it will be less dangerous."

They were in Eleanor's solar, surrounded by her women. The queen was back on her pedestal, and he could do no more than bow over her hand.

"A good journey, my lord," she said, giving him a gracious smile.

Henry, who was filled with impatience at all this secrecy and intrigue, wondered if he would ever hear from her again. Their earlier conversation about marriage—God's eyes, was that only five days ago?—had taken on the unreality of a dream. Disgruntled, he returned to his quarters, and told his father that they had accomplished their mission and must make ready to leave.

"I cannot wait to shake the dust of Paris from my boots."

"Yes, the atmosphere grows more oppressive each day. I've already begun to pack," said Geoffrey.

Since the homage ceremony his father had seemed curiously indifferent to what was happening in either Paris or Normandy, and his attentions to Eleanor had markedly diminished. Impeccably clad in his favorite green tunic under a surcoat banded with gold thread, he was helping his squire carefully fold clothes into four separate saddlebags. A gold medallion engraved with the lions of Anjou hung round his neck.

"I've noticed that mantles in Paris are even shorter now. We are behind the times in Normandy. You must tell your mother to arrange for all my mantles to be shortened, oh let us say, three inches?" Geoffrey picked up his silver mirror. Squinting, he held it out in front of him, turning his head this way and that, then brushed a spot of lint off one elegant shoulder.

"Why can't you tell her yourself?"

"Ah—well, as to that, I'm not returning immediately to Rouen."

Henry's eyes narrowed. "Why not?"

"Come, Henry, I know that tone of irritated surprise." Geoffrey took a last critical look and handed the mirror to his squire. "You are officially duke now, and recognized in Normandy as a competent warrior, a strong leader from whom men may receive justice. Soon you will have England, and, apparently, Aquitaine as well. My own lands need attention too. Don't forget that."

"Isn't my brother managing Anjou to your satisfaction? I need you in Normandy."

The count sighed. "Be fair. Young Geoffrey is not very experienced. The better part of my life has been spent in securing Normandy for you, so do not begrudge Geoffrey the benefit of my advice now. He too must learn to administrate."

"Why does my brother need your advice in Anjou when the county will one day be mine? You should be giving such counsel to me, not him."

Geoffrey flushed. "*Grâce à Dieu,* but you see intrigue everywhere. That's the French influence for you. Henry, Henry, are you determined to pick a quarrel with me?" He folded a mantle and gave it to his squire. "In truth, I'm weary of arguments, sick of rebellions and battles, bored with negotiations and treaties. After thirty-seven years of doing others' bidding, I would spend the remainder of my days pleasing only myself for a change, and it pleases me at the moment to go to Angers."

It sounded entirely reasonable, but not the whole tale, not by a long bow shot. He would swear to it. Over the years, Henry had learned that the smoothly charming Geoffrey rarely gave anything away. Often he had counseled him: "If needful, say what you mean, but you don't always have to mean what you say." That was why the count's behavior had been, and continued to be, so extraordinary. With difficulty, Henry held his tongue. Nothing was to be gained by further antagonizing his father.

The next morning they left the Île-de-la-Cité. Outside Paris the road forked. One way led to Normandy, the other to the Loire Valley, Blois, Le Mans, and Angers. The day was exceptionally dry and hot, the sun a blazing orb of gold in a burning blue sky. Not a leaf stirred; the ground looked parched.

"Well, my boy, here I must leave you," said Geoffrey, reining in his dappled stallion. He appeared in much better spirits today. "I will return to Rouen in a month or two. Take care with your mother how you approach the subject of your marriage. She will not look kindly upon Eleanor."

"So you said earlier. But I don't see why not. Look at all there is to gain."

Geoffrey gave him an arch smile. "You have much to learn. What says the old saw? 'When the old cock crows, the young cock should listen.' It sometimes takes women longer to realize what is at once obvious to men. At first all your mother will see is that a strong-minded woman is trying to possess what she considers her territory."

Henry gave a mock shudder. "Yes, point taken. I just hope there is a marriage. I haven't had a private word with Eleanor since the homage ceremony."

"I shouldn't worry. Your star is ascending, my son, and neither God nor man can stop it—only that which lies in your own nature. Now, don't forget the mantles."

"Three inches. Look, father, I—"

It was too late. With an airy wave of his hand, Geoffrey, followed by his squire and two grooms, wheeled his horse around and galloped down the road leading to Anjou. Henry watched his upright figure recede into the distance. His blue mantle rippled out behind him; a blue cap embroidered with three gold lions perched precariously on his head, the ever-present sprig of golden broom bobbing up and down. The count's affection for the *planta genista* had caused him to adopt it as his, and now Henry's, surname—Planta-genet. After a few moments he disappeared into a cloud of yellow dust, but the image stayed in Henry's mind.

He had no premonition that he would never see his father alive again.

# CHAPTER 21

"Count Geoffrey of Anjou is dead, may God assoil him."
Eleanor, playing in the rushes of the solar with her young daughters, Marie and Alix, glanced up. Louis, looking like the angel of death in somber black, stood in the doorway.

"What are you saying? He left here less than ten days ago." Trust Louis to get the facts wrong. She turned impatiently back to the children.

"It's true. As God is my witness. A messenger from his son, Geoffrey, in Angers has just brought the news. Not ten leagues from Le Mans the count became overheated and stopped to bathe in the tainted waters of the Loire," Louis continued, an unmistakable note of relish in his voice. "That very night he developed a raging fever and two days later he died." He signed himself. "What says Holy Writ? 'In the midst of life we are in death.' "

Stunned, Eleanor slowly got to her feet. Geoffrey le Bel dead. It was unimaginable. After absorbing the initial shock, she wondered if word had reached Henry in Rouen. He would be grief-stricken, and she must send an immediate message of condolence. Eleanor strenuously hoped that Henry and Geoffrey had made up their differences before going their separate ways outside Paris. For a brief instant she experienced a surge of guilt, remembering that she had been the unwitting cause of conflict between father and son.

"This means that brash young upstart, Henry, is now count of Anjou as well as duke of Normandy," Louis said, watching her. "Too much power to be concentrated in the hands of one so young and impetuous. We must pray that he does not gain England as well."

"As I recall, Louis, you were only sixteen when the crown of France descended upon your inexperienced head."

Blinking back an unexpected rush of tears, Eleanor wondered what Louis would do when he discovered that Aquitaine would increase that "upstart's" domains still further. She signaled the nurse to take the children back to their quarters.

"Bernard of Clairvaux has told me that in his opinion you were far too fond of Count Geoffrey," Louis said.

Eleanor did not answer, but Louis seemed compelled to talk about the Angevin, whom he had always resented yet whose charm had beguiled him. "The abbé predicted the count would come to a bad end, and also his son."

"Is there anyone he doesn't think will come to a bad end?"

The meddling monk of Clairvaux, who had replaced Abbé Suger as unofficial advisor, now had the king's exclusive confidence. Eleanor knew Bernard distilled poison into Louis's ears at every opportunity. Mostly against her and, to be fair, not all of it false. While it was certainly true that she had dallied with Count Geoffrey over the years, flirting with him and teasing, she had never granted him the one favor he most desired.

In the monk's eyes, however, if she had sinned in her heart, the desire and the deed were virtually one and the same. Louis had told her that in his youth, Bernard had once cast a fleeting glance of admiration toward a girl. It had been winter and to make amends for this sin he had plunged himself into an icy pond for over an hour, where he almost expired before being rescued.

"Geoffrey is dead. Isn't that enough for both of you? I was raised to believe it is uncharitable to speak ill of the dead. Now, please, leave me alone. I would mourn the death of my good friend in private."

"Eleanor—" Louis began in a distraught voice. "Could we not—" His voice trailed off.

She knew the sight of those houndlike eyes, that long disconsolate face should move her to pity, but everything he did, every word he uttered, set her teeth on edge. She forced herself to respond with courtesy.

"What do you wish to say to me, Louis?"

With a despairing gesture, he left the solar.

. . .

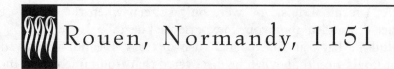

# Rouen, Normandy, 1151

In the ducal palace at Rouen, Henry wept. The unexpected death of his father was devastating. Again and again, he went over their last days together, unable to dislodge from his mind that they had not parted as friends, but as rivals for the same woman—and Geoffrey had lost. Was he somehow responsible for his father's death? Henry could not confide his sense of guilt to his mother, who was going through her own Gethsemene regarding the loss of her husband. He had the uncomfortable feeling that guilt played a part in his mother's pain as well. He did not want to know why.

All the way to Le Mans to attend the funeral and hear the will read, Henry tried to persuade himself that his father's demise had nothing to do with his actions in Paris. To imagine that it did was pure folly. Why then did he feel so ashamed?

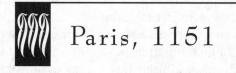

# Paris, 1151

In early September Eleanor received an angry letter from Henry, in Le Mans for his father's burial. It confirmed that he was now count of Anjou and Maine, but also mentioned a surprising clause in the count's will that left Anjou to his second son, Geoffrey, should Henry gain the crown of England. Henry was obviously outraged at this unexpected twist in what should have been a routine matter. Eleanor did not blame him for being angry, nor could she understand why Geoffrey had added the clause. In Anjou, as well as in other parts of the Continent, the eldest son always inherited the fief, county, or duchy as a matter of course. It was extraordinary that the count should have broken with precedent. The action hinted at some dark secret.

She replied immediately with an outpouring of sympathy and condolences. He did not respond but later Eleanor heard that after burying his father he had gone back to Normandy to prepare for the invasion of England. At Christmas there was another brief message from Henry, sent in secret, informing her he was having trouble getting together enough men and ships to cross the Channel. He also wanted to know, almost as an afterthought, when the annulment proceedings would occur. Then, four months passed during which Eleanor heard no word at all. Greatly disappointed, alternating between resentment and anxiety, she sometimes wondered whether the entire encounter between them had been a figment of her imagination.

The arrangements for the annulment, which had been proceeding at a snail's pace in Eleanor's view, almost came to a complete halt over the matter of her daughters.

"Of course I intend to keep Alix and Marie with me," she told Bernard of Clairvaux, Louis, and Louis's advisors, who were paying a visit to her solar. "I'm their mother and I will raise them in Aquitaine."

"As you well know, King Louis wishes to keep them, Madam," said Bernard. "They are royal children."

"Royal French children," added Louis.

"They will come with me."

Bernard raised his brows. "What has prompted this sudden burgeoning of maternal feeling? You have shown little interest in your children up to now."

"Little interest. Exactly," said Louis with a vigorous nod.

"I've shown as much interest as you," said Eleanor to Louis. "You've never forgiven them for not being boys."

She refused to meet Bernard's eyes. His accusation was only too true. She had had little maternal feeling for Marie and Alix, but she felt responsible for their welfare and had no intention of being parted from them.

There was a tense silence while Bernard fixed her with a stern look. "You may not know this, Madam, but had I had my way, the grounds for annulment of this marriage would not be consanguinity but adultery—or worse."

She composed her face into an expressionless mask. "That is a ridiculous charge. You have no reason to accuse me."

"If one were to dig deeply into your own life, Madam, I daresay much might be found that you would prefer to keep secret. Shall we put it to the test?" He paused. "You know what happens to adulterous wives? Loss of freedom—in a nunnery or remote castle—sometimes loss of life, not to mention total disgrace. I doubt convent discipline would suit you. Certainly that precious heretical duchy that means so much to you would be lost to you forever and become part of France."

Impaled on those burning eyes, Eleanor could not speak. Did he know about Raymond? What had Louis—or others—told him?

"I see that you are aware of the possible consequences. If you are wise, do not push this matter of your children. Be grateful to God that your husband is so charitable, and take a lesson from his goodness of heart. You have been allowed to retain Aquitaine. This must satisfy you. Have I made myself perfectly clear?"

Legally, of course, she was within her rights. Annulment meant the marriage had never existed, therefore the children of a nonexistent marriage might be said not to exist either. But Eleanor did not attempt to argue. In any encounter with Bernard, invariably she was the loser.

The council for the annulment proceedings was held in April of the new year 1152 at the royal castle of Beaugency on the Loire. After a host of witnesses swore that Louis was related to the duchess of Aquitaine in the forbidden degree, the archbishop of Sens rose to his feet and in a solemn voice pronounced the marriage null and void; the daughters, Marie and Alix, were to be awarded to their father. Suddenly limp, unable to move from her chair, Eleanor thought she would faint with relief. At long last, could it really be over? She stole a glance at Louis and was surprised to see his cheeks damp with tears. For an instant their gaze met. Eleanor was the first to look away, unable to bear the naked longing reflected in his eyes. That he still loved her was painfully evident.

Spurred by the knowledge that once news of the annulment was spread abroad her person and lands would be fair game, Eleanor planned to leave immediately for Poitou. She had accepted that the price of her freedom would be the loss of Marie and Alix, and, with a leaden heart, had already said her good-byes. Filled with guilt, she had convinced herself that they would be better off with Louis and his next wife—whoever that might be. Perhaps one day when they were grown she could speak to them as equals and make them understand why she had been forced to abandon them—or chosen this course as the only way out of her dungeon, would be more accurate.

Eleanor donned an ermine-lined black cloak and Cordovan boots of wine-colored leather, then hung an embossed leather sheath from her girdle. Into this she slipped a narrow silver dagger with rubies embedded in its hilt that she had bought in the bazaars of Jerusalem. It wasn't that she anticipated trouble, but it was just as well to be prepared.

Outside in the courtyard her entourage was waiting, mules and sumpter horses already loaded with her belongings. By nightfall she hoped to reach the safety of Blois, far from Louis's domains, where the royal arm could not reach her.

The Vespers bell had just sounded when Eleanor, hungry and half-asleep, approached the castle of young Count Thibaud of Blois, seeking shelter for the night. The count, a nephew of King Stephen of England, welcomed her, then, once she was safely inside his keep, announced in the most charming manner that he would not allow Eleanor to leave unless she agreed to become his countess.

She was speechless, far too tired to argue. Fortunately he took her silence for consent, and when she pleaded exhaustion allowed her to retire to her quarters immediately after supper. She had geared herself for just this possibility and then walked right into the trap like an unsuspecting rabbit. To be caught nodding like a convent maid was galling to her pride. In truth, she was not afraid of Count Thibaud, who was very young and untried, more bluster than anything else, she suspected. He should be very easy to outwit, and her seeming lack of resistance would put him off the scent.

And so matters turned out. Assuming she would not attempt to escape, the foolish count left the drawbridge lowered. In the dead of night, dagger in hand, Eleanor slipped unnoticed from her chamber into the outer bailey and out through an unguarded postern gate where her own men and horses were quartered. By dawn they were out of Blois and into Touraine. She was elated and could not wait to tell Henry how she had outwitted Count Thibaud—although this could not be considered a great feat. It was well known that the counts of Blois, though charming and comely, were not blessed with a great quantity of wits.

Despite the fact that Touraine was under Henry's control, Eleanor, wary now, sent out an advance guard to look over the region. They reported back with a rumor that Henry's younger brother, Geoffrey, planned to ambush her, take her captive, and force her into marrying him. She avoided this possible snare by taking a detour off the main road, her party then crossed the river Creuse in boats in order to put young Geoffrey off the scent.

Astride her white palfrey, Eleanor approached the borders of Poitou. The countryside, decked out in the yellow-green livery of spring, had never looked more beautiful. Above her the sky curved in a dizzying arc of palest blue. In the distance, she could see dappled slopes, black olive groves, valleys dotted with golden buttercups, and daisies turning white and yellow faces toward the afternoon sun.

Closer to view, hydrangea and magnolia trees were just beginning to put forth young green shoots. The scent of honeysuckle blew on the breeze; the sound of thrush and lark pierced the air with a throbbing sweetness. The renewal of life blossoming all around her filled Eleanor with a growing sense of promise, an awareness that after a long dry winter the sap was rising in her as well.

Despite all the obstacles Louis and his advisors had tried to put in her path, she had flung open the doors of her prison, and successfully fought for and retained control of Aquitaine, as well as the right to remarry with her overlord's consent. Thank the Holy Mother she had had the foresight to become aware of her rights, acquainting herself with the legal and ecclesiastical restrictions governing annulments. It was an almost impossible achievement, and Eleanor felt absurdly pleased with herself. Still, her recent contretemps with the count of Blois and her escape from Henry's younger brother, made it chillingly clear that to protect her duchy she would need a duke-consort. She thought wistfully of Henry and wondered where he was.

Just ahead the path led through a wooded copse. The horses picked their way through cool green glades where sunlight did not penetrate and skirted clearings filled with thistle, ragwort, wild foxglove, and bramble.

"Look, Lady," said one of the knights, as they trotted out of the copse. "Poitou."

Free! Free! Free! Her heart sang, keeping pace with the rhythm of her palfrey's hooves against the moist earth. Shackles unfettered, she was flown with the knowledge of her release, intoxicated by her hard-won independence.

They crossed the border, then followed the Vienne River as it flowed south toward Chinon, Châttellerault, and Poitiers.

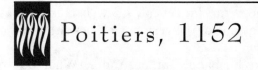 Poitiers, 1152

A day later Eleanor rounded the curve of a sharply rising hill and drew rein. Her heart leapt. Below lay the familiar walls of Poitiers. She was home. That night she spent alone with her women in her old chamber at the Maubergeonne Tower. When she woke the next morning, bursting with energy, she felt like the Eleanor of old for the first time in fourteen years.

There was an enormous amount to do in order to prepare for her wedding, which must be held as soon as possible before Louis got wind of their plans. But first she must write to Henry telling him of her safe arrival. She sought out her grandmother's old chaplain, one of her own early teachers, Master André, who could write faster than she, asking him to attend her in the small chamber at the top of the tower.

She had not visited the chamber since she was a child but nothing had changed. Surely this was the same high-backed wooden chair, worn footstool, and scarred reading desk she had known of yore? She ran her hands over them with loving familiarity, half-expecting to hear the gentle rustle of her mother's skirts as she climbed the stairs, her soft voice calling her for the evening meal. She blinked back an absurd desire to cry. What a long way she had come since those carefree golden days.

Armed with pens, inkhorn, lead, a ruler, and leaves of parchment, the now elderly chaplain clattered stiffly into the chamber and seated himself in the armchair. While he prepared himself for his task, Eleanor sank down onto the wooden bench she had sat in so often as a child. Her mother's angelic presence gave way to an image of Henry's freckled face split by an engaging grin. She remembered how his piercing gray eyes could suddenly turn warm and inviting, how intense the force of his superabundant vitality, how intoxicating the spell cast by his rough-hewn charm. Her heart leapt. She could hardly wait to feel all that restless energy . . .

"To whom is this letter to be written, Lady?"

She turned to the white-tonsured chaplain, a Poitevin born and bred, with whom she had argued all through her childhood until she went away to school at the Abbey of Fontevrault. He had taught her to read and write Provençal, knew her as well as anyone in Poitiers, and was one of the very few clerics she could not only tolerate but enjoy.

"To my next husband, Father André. What do you think of that?"

The chaplain raised unruly brows. "What I think will depend on the name of this most fortunate individual."

"Henry Plantagenet, duke of Normandy, most recently count of Anjou, and king of England in the not too distant future."

"*Benedicite!* How time passes! He must be all of eighteen years now. It seems like only yesterday that he was a naughty child creating a disturbance at your betrothal feast. And from all I hear he is creating disturbances still. But duke, count, and possibly king? Most impressive. You have outdone yourself, my child."

"I take it you think Henry a wise choice?"

He tapped a considering finger against his withered chin. "Wise? There are problems, of course. A dispensation will be required. You and the duke are as closely related as were you and Louis, all three of you having a common ancestor in Robert the Pious, King of France, in the early days of the eleventh century."

Eleanor giggled. "I know. Louis will be beside himself."

"Do I detect a note of satisfaction? For shame. Haven't you caused that unhappy monarch enough trouble, my child?"

Eleanor tossed her head. "Less than he caused me—and Aquitaine."

"This marriage to young Henry may well engender a feud between the Angevins and France that could take generations to mend. Have you thought of that?"

Eleanor rose and peered out the tiny window, bathing her face in a narrow ray of sunlight. "Normandy and France have been enemies since time out of mind, and Anjou is now ruled by a half-Norman. What is one more coal to an already raging fire? Right now Aquitaine desperately needs a strong consort." She turned back to him. "If I hadn't escaped, the count of Blois would have forced me into marriage, and Henry's younger brother attempted to lay a trap for the same purpose. And this occurred between Poitou and France within only a week's time! The future must look to itself, Father André; my concern is this duchy. I asked if you thought Henry a wise choice."

"Wiser than who? Louis of France? Most certainly so. And I would be the last person to deny that there is great need of a strong consort to protect Aquitaine. But a Norman? Will he adapt to our ways or must we adapt to his? Your people will not stand for another tyrant."

Eleanor did not answer, could not answer. She returned to her seat and looked at the chaplain with troubled eyes. When she had impulsively offered Henry her hand and duchy, she felt certain they would suit one another, above and beyond her feelings as a woman for him. She could appreciate Henry's strength, approve his vaulting ambition, and identify with his dream of ruling England.

"He has showed no signs of being a tyrant—" she began then stopped, realizing that this was no guarantee that he would not turn out to be one.

Master André was watching her carefully. "Louis of France behaved like the mildest of men—but not in Poitou when he cut off the hands of the rebel leaders, or in Vitry where he was responsible for the death of thirteen thousand innocent people."

Eleanor found she could not meet his eyes. Now that she was in the sanctity of her own domain, she felt less certain about Henry. In truth, except for his titles and lineage, she barely knew this personable youth to whom she had already committed herself.

"I suspect there will be a need to adapt on both sides," she said at last, thrusting aside a niggle of doubt.

The chaplain nodded approvingly. "Compromise is always the wise course to follow. Those that bend do not break. And it is well to remember that your father thought very highly of Count Geoffrey of Anjou; your grandfather, albeit briefly, was once married to a sister of Geoffrey's father. Thus Poitou and Anjou are not exactly strangers. How far can the apple fall from the tree?"

After a moment's pause he shot her a keen glance. "I hope you have properly thanked God and His Holy Mother for your good fortune?"

"I hardly need reminding."

"Oh, but you do. After all these years, you think I'm unaware of your attitude toward the Church? Just bear in mind that the main reason you did not lose Aquitaine to France was due to the skillful negotiations of the archbishop of Bordeaux. He saw to it that the marriage contract to Louis should stipulate that Aquitaine could only be incorporated into the kingdom of France when you had borne a son and that son succeeded on the throne."

"Yes, all right. I truly *am* grateful. Don't be tiresome."

"There is much you can teach your new husband," mused the chaplain. "The duke is mettlesome but young, not yet hardened in his ways; he can still be molded to your hand, subtly introduced to our customs and how we go about things here."

"My thoughts exactly," Eleanor said. She was about to say more but saw there was no need.

Her eyes met the old chaplain's. For an instant their disparate identities—churchman and duchess—blurred, as two Aquitainians exchanged a look of perfect understanding.

For the next few weeks Eleanor was so busy seeing to the administration of her duchy that there was little time to yearn for Henry. By prior agreement, all Louis's men were to be withdrawn from key positions in Aquitaine and replaced with her own loyal vassals. Three clerks as well as the chaplain were kept busy writing letters to her chief barons informing them that once again she was now duchess of Aquitaine and countess of Poitou in her own right and acting as such; they must once again renew their oaths of homage and fealty to her. In addition, Eleanor issued an edict declaring every act she and Louis had made together, or that Louis had made alone, now null and void.

"I intend to obliterate the last fifteen years as if they never existed," she told Master André, "and start anew."

"Is this for the benefit of your subjects, or are you punishing Louis for your unhappy life in France?"

Eleanor made a face at him but did not answer.

While letters were being written and messages sent, there was the tower to be cleaned and refurbished, her own possessions restored and polished. Everything must be made ready for the arrival of her future husband—although she had received no word from Henry and had no idea when he would make an appearance.

As the days passed, Eleanor's concern for the Norman duke was mitigated by the enormous sense of satisfaction she was achieving from finally being able to do things her way in her own duchy without male interference. Instinctively, miraculously, effortlessly, she knew exactly how to proceed without once placing a foot wrong.

One of the first things she did was to design her own seal. On one side was the figure of a bare-headed woman with outstretched arms, a falcon in one hand, a fleur-de-lis in the other. The inscription stated simply, "Eleanor, Duchess of Aquitaine." On the reverse side were the titles she would acquire when she married: Countess of Anjou, Duchess of Normandy. The figure on this side would be clad in a tight gown and a veil falling to the ground.

When Master André told her that various abbeys and convents were concerned about their rights and privileges, she acted immediately.

"Tell the abbot of Montiernuef Abbey to attend me as soon as possible."

"Lady," said the old abbot in a quavering voice, as he approached her in the great hall of the Tower the following day. "I hope you have not forgotten us."

Eleanor, seated on a raised dais, rose to her feet to welcome him. "On the contrary, I intend to renew all the abbey's privileges granted by my great-grandfather, grandfather, and father." She turned to the two clerks who attended her. "Please draw up the charter at once."

She was rewarded by a toothless smile of relief.

When the abbot of St.-Maixent complained that in her sweeping removal of all Louis's grants the abbey's woods, donated by the French king, had reverted back to her, Eleanor acknowledged her error. She instructed the clerk:

"Write the abbot that I gladly renew all his abbey's rights to those lands."

The abbot was overcome with gratitude at her prompt handling of the situation.

It was so easy, really, to keep these people happy, Eleanor realized. You listened, showed interest, and acted for the greatest good of all concerned.

One morning in mid-May, a sudden impulse took her to visit the abbey of Fontevrault near the Angevin border. She now knew a great deal more about its origins than she had as a pupil there, and what she knew appealed to her.

Founded fifty-three years ago by a Breton reformer who, as-

toundingly, believed in the superiority of women, Fontevrault had
been dedicated to the Virgin. The abbey was unique in that it
housed both nuns and monks under the rule of an abbess. Over the
years it had become a refuge for battered noblewomen escaping
from abusive husbands. Eleanor's own grandmother on her father's
side, the Troubadour's second wife, Phillipa of Toulouse, enraged at
her philandering husband and his mistress, Dangereuse, had ended
her days at Fontevrault.

"You have not visited us since you were a pupil here," the abbess
said, as they sat in her private quarters, over wine and honey cakes
baked in the abbey's own kitchens. "Of course I was much younger
then, but I remember you very well."

Eleanor laughed. "In and out of scrapes, as I recall." She paused.
"You know my marriage to King Louis is annulled?"

The abbess's face, framed by a snowy wimple, creased into a wide
smile. "Surely all Europe knows this by now."

"Of course. I had forgotten that in these parts gossip travels
faster than the wind. What you may not know, however, is that
soon I'm to marry Duke Henry of Normandy, now count of Anjou
as well, and one day king of England—or so we fervently hope."

She could not keep the note of pride from her voice.

"Indeed, I had not heard that. I wish the Holy Mother's blessing
upon you, my child." The abbess paused. "I was Alys of Anjou
when I entered Fontevrault, thus you may not know that Henry of
Normandy is my nephew. His father, Geoffrey—may he rest in
peace—was my younger brother, and for a very brief time—I was
only thirteen—I was wed to Henry's uncle, his mother's twin
brother, William, who drowned in the White Ship only days after
our wedding."

Eleanor stared. "How extraordinary. I had no idea."

The abbess smiled. "Soon I will be your aunt-in-law. I cannot
help but feel that there are so many coincidences here, the Holy
Mother must have intended our lives to intertwine."

With the exception of Petronilla, now married to Ralph and living in France, Eleanor had never sought either the counsel or company of women, despite her affection for her mother, the influence
of her grandmother, and her great admiration for the abbess—long
since dead—she had known here as a child. Winning the approval of
men had been so much more important to her survival. Now, to her
surprise, she found she wanted the approbation of this woman

whose serene presence permeated the chamber like a ray of sunlight.

"Then I take it you approve of this marriage, Reverend Mother?"

The abbess cocked her head to one side. "It is not for me to approve or disapprove, though naturally I am partial to my nephew. The duchy's welfare aside, your own heart is your best guide."

Eleanor took a sip of wine. "Not God? Or the Holy Mother?"

"Do I detect a note of skepticism?" The abbess wagged a gently reproving finger. "The Holy Mother *is* guiding us when we follow the true dictates of our heart."

It was the last thing Eleanor had expected to hear, and it disposed her to intimacy. "I will remember that." She leaned forward. "You know, I've never really had the opportunity to be my own mistress before. I must say I truly enjoy it."

The abbess's eyes twinkled. "Naturally, for now you are both duke and duchess with no one to gainsay you. The power is all yours." She paused. "Though from all I hear—and I hear a great deal that goes on in Poitou—you're using that power most wisely. It appears to me that you have the makings of a great administrator, my child. Far better than your well-meaning father, who, I often heard, frequently behaved with reckless abandon where the duchy was concerned."

At this unexpected praise, Eleanor was overcome with a surge of pleasure. In France she had been acknowledged only as a troublemaker.

"In truth, Reverend Mother, sometimes I am at a loss to understand the male way of things. Louis and his advisors complicated everything. My people can be difficult, but if one is willing to be impartial, give them generally what they want—if no harm results—and respect their differences, this business of ruling can be greatly simplified."

"I tend to agree—but do not be surprised if my nephew views the matter in a different light."

Eleanor searched the calm face before her, almost afraid to ask the abbess what she meant. "I'm not sure I understand. Is this a warning?"

There was a long pause. Then the abbess leaned forward and took Eleanor's hand in her cool dry fingers. "This is a heady time for you, my child. A golden future beckons. Just remember that a house cannot have two masters." She smiled. "Be guided by the example of St. Radegonde, the patron saint of Poitou. At a time when

Church councils were debating whether woman has a soul, she proved that a gentle female of intelligence and courage could create her own world. Through Radegonde the world of learning and transcribing manuscripts became open to us. In an age of true barbarity, she was a glowing illustration of what a woman can do."

The abbess released Eleanor's hand, rising to her feet. "And now, I fear, my duties call me."

"It is with great gladness that I, as duchess, renew all Fontevrault's privileges," Eleanor said, also rising. "In addition I would like to add five hundred silver pennies as a personal donation—let it go to the support of the abused wives and noblewomen that take refuge here."

"It is a regal gift. We are very grateful. One day, perhaps, Fontevrault can show its gratitude."

"I hardly expect to seek refuge here as the victim of a cruel and abusive husband," Eleanor said, laughing.

"No indeed." The abbess joined in the laughter.

Elated that she had discovered a friend, Eleanor left the abbey in high spirits.

A week later her formidable Aunt Agnes, who was now abbess of the Convent of Saintes, descended on the Maubergeonne Tower in high dudgeon.

"The news is all over Poitou that you have given that upstart Fontevrault a huge donation," her aunt announced.

This abbess's presence was far from serene. Her thin lips reminded Eleanor of a steel trap, and the gray hairs sprouting from her chin quivered in accusation.

"Dearest Aunt, what a pleasant surprise! Would you believe I was just about to send for you to discuss new lands and privileges for Saintes?"

Aunt Agnes snorted but allowed herself to be placated.

Shortly thereafter her mother's shrewd, mischief-making brothers appeared from Châttellerault. She promptly appointed one of them, Ralph de Faye, as seneschal of the duchy, knowing that if she gave him power he could be trusted to keep the others in line. When she heard that her troublesome neighbors, the de Lusignans, were threatening not to renew their oaths of homage to her, Eleanor invited them to a feast where she succeeded in charming them into grudging compliance.

"Matters progress well, don't you think?" she asked the chaplain.

"Exceeding well—thus far," he said.

As the weeks passed with still no word from Henry, Eleanor discovered that her memories of the young duke were growing dim. Her domains were not being threatened; she was managing the duchy's affairs with ease and skill. If the nuptial ceremony was delayed she would not be brokenhearted. Surviving on her own was far more pleasurable and rewarding than Eleanor had imagined; she was so busy that even her restless body had not troubled her. In truth, for the first time she felt released from the fetters of gender, and was amazed to realize that she was in no haste to remarry at all.

One morning in mid-May Eleanor was holding court in the great hall, listening to a series of complaints from the citizens of Poitiers. At a table close by, on a wide piece of parchment almost three feet long, a clerk recorded all decisions made.

A wealthy widow was complaining that her neighbor's pigs had broken into her garden and rooted up all her beans and cabbages.

"That is a falsehood," cried the neighbor lady. "My pigs never left my land."

"Do you have witnesses or any other proof of this offense?" Eleanor asked.

The widow sullenly shook her head.

"Unless you have witnesses there is no evidence that your neighbor's pigs broke into your garden. If you can bring at least one or two witnesses, I will hear your grievance at the next court, otherwise I must fine you for a false complaint."

Unable to stifle a sigh of weariness—the hall was very hot and she had been judging cases since Terce—Eleanor was about to ask for the next complaint when the steward, who stood at her side, bent his head.

"There is no need for you to continue here, Lady. After all, these are but trifling cases, and I or the local bailiff can easily deal with them."

"Thank you, but these are my people. After fifteen years of King Louis, they must get to know and trust me all over again. What better way than for me to dispense justice? Now who is next?"

The steward nodded then called the wives of the blacksmith and the miller, who had had a violent quarrel at the baker's oven over two missing loaves of bread. They had shouted and slapped one another, then tore at each other's hair. Their husbands had joined the fray and the local bailiff had been called in to restore order.

Repressing a laugh, Eleanor assumed what she hoped was a judicial expression.

"We cannot have such a public disturbance. It sets a bad example. The miller and the smith are fined five sous each." She glanced at the wives. "You are hereby warned that if another incident of this kind occurs the penalty will be more severe. The oven is for everyone's use and we must be charitable toward one another. Two missing loaves do not equal two stolen loaves."

As Eleanor called for the next case, she heard the sound of horses' hooves thundering into the courtyard. Moments later a groom rushed into the hall and breathlessly announced the arrival of the duke of Normandy and three companions.

She rose quickly to her feet. "That will be all for today."

Leaving the steward to dismiss the people and collect the fines, Eleanor entered the courtyard. Henry had not yet dismounted. A hooded falcon sat on one gauntleted wrist; a sprig of golden *planta genista* bobbed in his blue cap. One look at his broad shoulders, his muscular body vibrant with energy, a single hot glance from his smoky eyes, and Eleanor's heart turned over in her breast.

Before she could stop herself, she ran to his horse and stretched out a trembling hand. Henry tore off a gauntlet with his teeth and seized her fingers, almost crushing them in the force of his grip. When Eleanor felt a hot flow pass from his palm into hers, she could not remember why she had wanted for even a single moment to put off the wedding.

# CHAPTER 22

"Aunt Agnes says that I remind her of a bitch in heat," Eleanor said to Henry the day after he arrived.

They were walking in a cool section of the courtyard where the linden trees were in bud. Eleanor carried her favorite white gyrfalcon on her wrist. The bird wore a black hood decorated with seed pearls; leather jesses trailed from her feet, and silver bells tinkled around her legs.

"And is that the case?" Henry stooped to stroke several of Eleanor's greyhounds who had attached themselves to him and now followed him everywhere.

Simply dressed, his black tunic covered by a thigh-length scarlet mantle embroidered with the gold lions of Anjou, Henry looked much more presentable than he had in Paris.

After the initial excitement of seeing each other, Eleanor was aware an awkwardness had developed between them. It was hard to imagine any situation daunting enough to cast a dent in the armor of his Norman confidence, but Henry appeared ill at ease. Intimidated perhaps by being in Poitou where she reigned supreme? Eleanor had repeated her aunt's remark in an effort to break through the barrier.

Now she was pleased to see a broad grin soften his lips. "We'll just have to see, won't we?" she said with a teasing smile. "In truth, after an absence of seven months I feel I must get to know you all over again."

Henry took her hand and swung it briefly before letting it go. "I think we know each other rather better than most people in our position. Usually it is a case of Anjou-Normandy marrying Aquitaine. The people involved are rarely consulted and often have never even met, like my mother and father."

"Also Louis and myself."

"But you and I had a choice. No one arranged or forced our union." He grinned. "So if matters go awry we will have no one to blame but ourselves."

"Quite true," Eleanor said. She had never looked at the marriage in quite that light. The feeling of being in control was very reassuring.

"There is one time-honored way of getting to know each other better," Henry continued, "should you wish to make certain that all is to your liking. For myself I would like to see if Aunt Agnes is correct." He paused to raise his brows. "Though that is the last thing I would expect an abbess to say."

Eleanor laughed. "In Aquitaine even the abbesses are a different breed. As far as getting to know one another better, the castle is packed with people like herrings in a barrel. Alas, we must wait. Not too long, fortunately."

He took her hand again and brought it to his lips, letting his mouth linger on the soft palm. "No, thank God, otherwise I should never live up to your expectations."

Extraordinary. She had not expected Henry to be so discerning. She grew warm as the pressure of his lips blazed a fiery path from her palm up her wrist, arm, and shoulder to spread throughout her whole body. Uncanny that he was so sensitive to her, a quality totally at variance with his overwhelming virility, and the sense that he was poised on the string of a taut bow, an arrow ready to fly straight toward its goal.

For Eleanor the next week passed in a fever of impatience. She longed to be part of Henry's driving energy and could hardly wait for that moment.

Fortunately there was an enormous amount of detail to attend to that kept her constantly occupied, otherwise she didn't know how she could have borne the delay. Of necessity—not wanting to alert Louis to their plans—it was to be a small, unpretentious wedding. Eleanor invited only a select number of guests to the castle: the most important barons, influential clergymen, a few relatives, and several high-bred ladies who would become her attendants.

At the last moment, the archbishop of Bordeaux arrived with several canons in tow to issue the proper dispensations and ensure the validity of the marriage contract. Eleanor's astonished vassals, who had had no inkling of the wedding plans before arriving in Poitiers, were introduced to their new duke at a prenuptial feast in the great hall of the Maubergeonne Tower.

Trying to conceal her anxiety, Eleanor called for silence, and in what she hoped was a magisterial voice, addressed the guests:

"My lords of Poitou and Aquitaine. As you know, my marriage to King Louis of France has recently been dissolved. As you also may have heard, on my way home from France I was twice subjected to the threat of ambush and only just escaped an enforced captivity. These misadventures made me realize that to keep Aquitaine's sovereignty and possessions intact it is needful that I have a duke to rule with me. But one of *my* choosing." She took a deep breath; her eyes swept the assembled throng. "Here is Henry, duke of Normandy and count of Anjou, whom I have chosen as consort. A knight of high birth and great strength, whose lands border our own; a man who will help protect us from any and all dangers. Fellow Aquitainians, as you love and honor me, your duchess, please welcome him in good faith as your new duke."

Henry immediately rose to his feet. "I hope you will accept me," he said with a disarming smile. "I promise to uphold your rights even as your duchess does now. I pledge to protect the honor of Aquitaine even as I do Normandy and Anjou."

"That is more than Louis of France ever promised—or did," Eleanor said loudly, casting a worried eye over the group.

She had been prepared for an initially unfavorable reaction and was not disappointed. Expressions of shock and resentment were to be read on virtually every face. Eleanor could almost hear their unvoiced reproach: We have just thrown off the chains of one tyrant and now you wish to yoke us to another? After a few moments of hostile silence there was a sullen acknowledgment. At least there was no overt demonstration of antagonism. She prayed that her vassals' harsh reaction would soften before Henry's youthful vitality and high spirits.

"Here is no sour zealot helplessly dependent on disapproving clerics," she told Ralph de Faye, her mother's youngest brother and newly appointed seneschal, who sat next to her at the high table. "But a man of action who has already gained a reputation for himself as a shrewd and just leader."

"Hmm. All that may be true, Niece, but we are a people who hate any authority except our own, and we can barely tolerate that—as your forebears knew only too well."

"But this is a trait any Norman will understand. They are the same."

Her uncle raised incredulous brows. "Are you so blind that you cannot see we are as different from the Normans as the moon is different from the sun? If your people did not love you, they would never accept Duke Henry." He sighed and shrugged. "Well, we must hope for the best. At least you are pleased for a change."

"Oh, Uncle, you cannot know how pleased. My stormy subjects will come round in time, I doubt not."

She did not add that it was all but impossible to resist Henry's engaging charm for long.

Eight weeks after the annulment of her first marriage, Eleanor was wed to Henry Plantagenet on the eighteenth day of May in the Chapel of Notre Dame right after morning mass. Vows were joyfully exchanged; the kiss of peace given. How different was this marriage from the one fifteen years earlier! Then, dependent and innocent, she had been forced to bow to necessity and might. Now, despite the very real political advantages, she was also following her own inclinations. It was indeed a miracle.

"Well, Madam," said the archbishop of Bordeaux after the ceremony. "Thus far God has smiled on this marriage. Louis's army has not come charging over your borders but there are sure to be consequences to so illustrious an alliance. The merging of Aquitaine, Anjou, and Normandy under a single rule reduces France to one third its former size, more than sufficient to cause Louis not only alarm, but the most bitter humiliation."

She felt sorry for Louis, of course she did, but deep in her heart Eleanor could not deny a certain twinge of satisfaction when she recalled all the years of misery she had suffered at his hands.

A small feast had been prepared, and Eleanor's favorite troubadour, Bernart of Ventadour, entertained the wedding guests until well into the afternoon. The atmosphere was subdued, with nothing of the humor and ribaldry of her first wedding. But Eleanor, who had eyes only for Henry, was not concerned. Her subjects would come round. Give them time.

Finally Henry turned to her. "Have we not had sufficient songs and poetry? I think now we may leave the guests and please ourselves."

To her surprise Eleanor felt herself blushing like a convent maid as she experienced a quiver of anticipation. "Don't you like our music, my lord?"

He shrugged. "Well enough. But in truth, jongleurs, troubadours, games of chivalry, and the like are not to my taste. There is too much to be accomplished for me to waste my time on nonessentials."

Before Eleanor could take in the implications of the remark, Henry added, "Let us hope my appreciation of other pursuits will more than make up for this lack."

She promptly forgot his first remark.

A few hours later Eleanor and Henry were finally alone in the turret chamber of the Maubergeonne Tower. Here they had been put to bed by Eleanor's attendants and blessed by the archbishop of Bordeaux. The long-awaited moment was finally at hand and she had expected to feel rapturous, but from the moment the chamber door closed, Eleanor's sense of anticipation had abruptly vanished. Lying naked in the great bed, the chamber softly lit by tall white tapers, she felt enfolded in a web of anxiety.

For the first time Henry would see her unclothed, and for the first time she wondered how his eighteen-year-old eyes would view her twenty-nine-year-old body. Eleanor had always taken her beauty and desirability for granted, much as she took her position of royalty for granted. In her own eyes her body, lithe and firmly slender, had changed but little over the years despite the birth of two children. But Henry's youth suddenly made her uncertain. Suppose he did not find her fair? Suppose she did not please him? Suppose—

"God's eyes, what are you thinking about?"

"Blow out the candles."

"Blow out—why?"

"Please. Just blow them out." Eleanor turned her head away.

"Not unless I'm told why." Henry reached over, grasped her firmly by the chin, and turned her head back toward him. "Tell me."

"You'll think I'm too old."

"Too old? For what?"

"I'm serious."

"So am I, by Christ! Too old for what?"

"To please you," she whispered.

Henry stared at her in astonishment. "God's splendor, I wonder if I shall ever understand women. Well, there's only one way to find out, isn't there?" He threw back the blue coverlet exposing both their naked bodies.

She screwed her eyes shut tight and held her breath. In the long silence that followed, Eleanor could hear only the pounding of her heart, and feel a rasping dryness in her throat. Suddenly she felt Henry's lips nibbling at her ear.

"If I were one of your clever idle troubadours I might be able to describe your perfection as it deserves, but being just a simple country Norman, I can only show you."

His mouth came down hard on hers. Weak with relief and gratitude, Eleanor wrapped her arms around Henry's heavily muscled body. After Raymond's seasoned expertise, she had wondered how she would respond to Henry's youthful ardor. Raymond had been smooth and silken, a goblet of mellow Gascon wine in the purple dusk of a desert night, a tender melody sweetly strummed by a master player, infinitely skillful, always remote.

By comparison Henry was rough, raw, demanding. His lips forced hers to open; his hands explored her body as if he were invading a foreign country. His fingers grasped her breasts, squeezing them, rubbing the points against his palm until she almost screamed. When his lips traveled down from her lips to her nipple he sucked so hard she cried out in protest.

But Henry was in the moment, his attention wholly with her, every part of him involved. His excitement was so intense it poured off his body in rivulets of heat, fueling her own. It grew ever stronger, gaining momentum, consuming her body in a conflagration of desire. In her dreams Eleanor had imagined Henry touching her gently, expertly, as Raymond had done, worshipping her body with the practiced ease of a long-known rite. Instead he threw himself upon her with the force of a conqueror mounting an attack. He was larger than Louis, but after a moment's adjustment she opened to receive him.

Suddenly, at last, she felt all the hard pounding energy that was Henry Plantagenet plunging inside her like a primitive force of nature. It was terrifying. Wait, Eleanor cried out, wait, stop. Anticipating her own undoing, she pounded her fists against his back then tried to thrust him aside. Henry paused for the space of a single heartbeat, then renewed his assault, penetrating deeper and deeper through layer after layer of resistance. Her cries were drowned out, the voices in her mind silenced by a sensation so excruciating, so unexpected, so overwhelming that terror and pleasure merged, became one. Her last thought before the whole world crested, crashing out of control, was that Henry had not just taken possession of her body but violated the deepest recesses of her being.

When Eleanor slowly opened her eyes, the chamber was bathed in pale pink light streaming in through the narrow window. Was it really dawn already? The events of the previous night passed hazily through her mind. Had it all really happened or was it only a glorious dream? But no dream could have produced this delicious feeling of peaceful joy. With a sigh of deep contentment she turned her head to find Henry propped up against the pillows reading a book.

"What are you reading?" she asked in a sleepy voice.

"Good morning, slug-a-bed," Henry said, carefully closing the book and laying it beside him. "A fourth-century Roman handbook on war that belonged to my father. Are you ready to get up?"

"Get up?"

"Yes. Time is limited and I want you to show me Poitou before I leave."

Henry leapt from the bed and began to pull on his drawers and hose. Eleanor watched him with a smile. She would have preferred to wile away the day in Henry's arms but his energy was contagious.

"Why is time limited?" she asked. "Surely we can please ourselves. There is no need to leave for a few months I hope."

"A few weeks is more likely. Unless Louis causes trouble here, I must return to Normandy and continue my plans to invade England."

"Oh, Henry, a few weeks?"

Henry walked over to the bed, threw back the coverlet, and pulled Eleanor to her feet. "Don't you want to be a queen again? Meanwhile, I'm here now. Let us make the most of it." He kissed her. "Did I tell you that I've never spent a more fulfilling night?"

"Nor I. Oh, Henry, nor I." Flown with happiness she flung her arms around him, wanting to prolong the moment forever.

The chapel bells rang the hour of Prime. Henry kissed the top of her head and disengaged himself.

"Best that I remove myself from temptation. I will see you in the chapel." With a grin he tucked the book under his arm and left the chamber.

• • •

A short time later Eleanor joined him in the chapel. To her amusement, Henry paid no attention to the service but alternately read his Roman book, whispered bawdy nonsense in her ear to make her laugh, or asked questions of the seneschal who sat on his other side. After mass he bounded out of the chapel and raced into the great hall to break his fast. The moment the chaplain had finished grace Henry gulped down a goblet of Gascon wine, tore off the end of a wheaten loaf, and was back on his feet before Eleanor had barely started.

"Meet me in the stables before Sext," he said, then grabbed the old chaplain, Master André, by the arm. "I want you to tell me the whole history of Aquitaine. Now. You can eat later." Before he could protest Henry had led the astonished cleric out of the hall.

"Sweet St. Radegonde, has a whirlwind landed in our midst?" asked Eleanor's uncle in a grumbling voice. "What a life he will lead you, Niece."

"Nell looks as if she will thrive on such a life," said Aunt Agnes with a tart sniff. "She glows like a candle. Just remember, my child, all flesh is grass."

Whatever that meant. But Aunt Agnes was certainly right about her thriving. When Eleanor remembered the frustration of bedding with Louis compared to the ecstasy of last night . . .

The next two weeks were spent in a blissful round of passionate nights, days crammed with activity. When word of the nuptials was spread abroad, troubadours and knights flocked to Poitou. As the marriage seemed to be gaining acceptability and the general atmosphere became increasingly festive, Eleanor arranged for more elaborate celebrations. She had the great hall decorated daily with spring flowers, the floor strewn with fresh green rushes mixed with horehound, myrrh, and coriander.

In the evenings tall white tapers in silver sconces cast flickering shadows over tables set with snowy clothes and great silver salt cellars. Jeweled goblets sparkled with wine from Bordeaux and Gascony. To tempt Henry's indifferent palate, she had ordered a variety of dishes: roast swans decorated with leaves and red-and-blue ribbons, peacocks in their feathers, sole, oysters, and sperlings. There was a profusion of sauces spiced with sage, cumin, garlic, and dittany, as well as silver dishes of candied fruit, figs, and tarts.

Every night jugglers tossed balls and knives into the air; acrobats turned handsprings. Troubadours sang *chansons de geste, joi d'amour,* and the bawdy love songs of Eleanor's grandfather. Story-tellers wove spells with their tales of King Arthur, Charlemagne, and Roland; beauteous Helen of Troy, crafty Odysseus, his faithful wife, Penelope, and the enchanting siren, Calypso. To Eleanor's delight Henry had never heard these tales before and was suitably impressed. The legend of Odysseus, in particular, caught his fancy. With the exception of a single incident, no ripple of discord marred the harmony of Henry's visit.

One night Bernart de Ventadour introduced a new song he had composed in honor of the beautiful duchess of Aquitaine. When he came to the lines " . . . if she but graciously consent one night, while shedding all her clothes, to set me in some chosen place and make a necklace of her arms," there were murmurs of praise and loud clapping. The Aquitainians were connoisseurs of the *gai saber* of the troubadours and made a great show of their appreciation.

Pleased, Eleanor turned to Henry, expecting him to be equally appreciative. His face was a deep crimson and the expression in his eyes frightened her.

"Henry, what is it? Are you unwell?"

"Is there any truth in what that whoreson says?" he asked between clenched teeth.

At first Eleanor did not understand. "What who says?"

"Have you shed your clothes for that rogue?"

"Don't raise your voice. Of course not. Are you mad? Bernart is a great troubadour and this is how troubadours entertain, singing courtly love songs to the lady or duchess of the castle."

"Not to my duchess he doesn't. Order him to stop."

His attitude reminded her of Louis and Eleanor felt a chill. "I will do no such thing. These *joi d'amour* are the custom here, a tradition started by my own grandfather; you must know that by now. No one attaches any significance to them except as a form of the *gai saber.*"

To her horror Henry seemed to lose all vestige of control. He fell to the ground; a white froth bubbled around his lips; his eyes bulged.

"The duke seems to be having a fit of some kind," said her uncle, his voice laced with alarm. "Perhaps we should carry him to the solar and have a physician examine him." The seneschal's mouth fell open. "Sweet St. Radegonde, listen to him, he cannot know what he is saying."

By this time Henry was writhing on the ground, kicking his legs and mouthing incoherent abuse. The object of his violence appeared to be both troubadours and Aquitainians. Suddenly he gnashed his teeth and began to chew the rushes. Truly terrified, Eleanor signaled for Bernart to stop singing. It took four large guards to lift the thrashing duke and carry him out of the hall.

By the time the white-bearded physician arrived, Henry had become calmer. After examining him, the physician recommended that he be bled to let out the foul humours.

"Is he seriously ill? What can have caused this?" Eleanor asked, badly shaken. She glanced at Henry lying on the bed. The deep purple color was fading from his face and his body was no longer twitching uncontrollably. "It is as if a demon possessed him."

The physician shrugged. "They say the Angevins are a devil's brood but I leave such matters to the priests. In my opinion this demon has been brought on less by the devil than by a deep displeasure."

Eleanor stared at him. "What do you mean?"

"I mean only that displays of this kind may have won the duke favorable attention in the past. My advice, Lady, is to let the matter go. Say nothing; do nothing, lest you cause more harm than good. Such behavior may solace him in some way we cannot understand. I will bleed him now."

Concerned, Eleanor followed his advice. When Henry recovered, it was as if nothing had happened. He made neither excuse nor apology, nor did he ever refer to what had occurred. After a few days Eleanor wondered if she had imagined the whole scene. What she hadn't imagined, however, was that Henry had ultimately gotten his way. She had hurriedly sent Bernart to Bordeaux; the other troubadours were more circumspect in the lyrics dedicated to her.

"He hasn't changed much, has he?" Aunt Agnes remarked before returning to Saintes.

"I don't know what you mean," said Eleanor.

"Have you forgotten his display at your betrothal feast in Bordeaux?"

"No. But I do not see the connection."

Aunt Agnes gave her a withering look. "If you would know the man, observe the boy."

After she left, Eleanor grew thoughtful. A new aspect of Henry's character had been revealed, at least to her. Eleanor wondered if she would ever truly know the man she had so hastily married. Henry was a mixture of so many contradictory qualities it was like living with four or five men at once. In bed he was a constant revelation. After having initially established who was master, he turned out to be both tender and affectionate, quite willing to let her take the lead if she wished. He was also an apt pupil, soon practicing all the arts Raymond had shown her. If he applied them with more zest and less skill, what did it matter? Not since her childhood could Eleanor remember such a period of uninterrupted happiness.

Unlike Louis, Henry, who had had a diverse education on both sides of the Channel, was deeply interested in everything. Music and song were wont to leave him indifferent but history, political matters, and people fascinated him.

"You never told me that your grandfather threatened to build for his convenience a special brothel in the shape of a nunnery and install an entire order of whores under a harlot-abbess," he said to Eleanor with a rougish grin as they rode together, exploring the countryside beyond the city gates.

"He loved jests," Eleanor said. "Everyone adored the Troubadour—except his long-suffering wives, of course. I believe his first wife was your father's aunt. A very short-lived marriage, I'm told. His mistresses, on the other hand, he treated like queens. What was your grandfather like?"

"I don't recall him, unfortunately. But he was not a jesting man. Feared and respected rather than adored. Although he had plenty of mistresses too."

"Is that typical of most Normans?" Eleanor glanced at him out of the corner of her eye.

"Which? The fear and respect or the mistresses?"

"Take your choice."

"Well, my grandfather kept England and Normandy under iron control," Henry said. "Can the same be said of your grandfather? According to your chaplain he hardly ever won a battle. Most of his life, so legend goes, was spent pursuing women, seducing them, and writing songs about his conquests! By God's eyes, what kind of sons will we have with such a heritage?"

"The conquest of women is surely more civilized than the conquest of land."

"More enjoyable certainly." Henry rolled his eyes suggestively then jabbed a finger at her. "One day I will remind you of those words, Nell. However, had I known of these frivolous qualities in your blood I would have thought twice before aligning myself with the decadent House of Aquitaine."

Eleanor stuck out her tongue at him.

In addition to his scholarly pursuits Henry loved to hunt with hawk or hound. He was immensely pleased whenever his gyrfalcon brought down a larger bird than Eleanor's. Since hawking was simply a pleasure, not a game to be won or lost, she was happy to let his bird beat hers.

"My mother once got the better of my father in falconry," Henry told her one afternoon as they rode, falcons on wrists, to hunt crane. "It was only days after they had met, an isolated incident, but he never forgot it. Years later he would bring it up."

"It's only a sport. Why did it matter to him?" Eleanor was surprised, and grateful that she had never known this aspect of Geoffrey le Bel.

"Oh, I can readily understand why. In the hunt, in battle or political affairs, even with women—" he slid his eyes toward her—"a man plays to win. Always."

"So do women. But some things are more important than others, surely? It sounds as if your mother was more than a match for Geoffrey."

"In truth, my mother could best my father in most things." A brief frown creased his brow. "For instance, she was a much better chess player. He always resented it and she learned to let him win."

Eleanor pulled her horse to an abrupt stop. "Let him—Would you expect me to do the same?"

"I? But the issue would never arise with us, my dearest Nell," Henry said with an innocent smile. "There is nothing you can do that I cannot do better."

"Oh, such arrogance! Such outrageous male vanity!" Henry looked at her face then quickly spurred his horse forward; she rode furiously after him.

Henry's indefatigable energy was a constant source of amazement to her. He rose before Prime every day no matter how hard or long he had made love the previous night. Always restless, he rarely sat except on horseback, and only briefly at meals, where he ate and drank sparingly, never noticing what food was set before him.

Eleanor, blissfully happy, sometimes wondered if Henry was as happy as she was.

"Can you tell how much I love you?" she asked him one night when they had just finished making love.

She lay on her back with his head between her breasts.

"Of course," he murmured in a drowsy voice.

"And you? Do you feel the same?"

"About what?"

She pulled at his hair. "You know perfectly well: loving me."

Henry rolled away from her with a sigh. "Why is it necessary to discuss these things?"

He always shied away from any talk of his feelings.

Certainly Henry behaved like a man in love—in bed at any rate. Yet sometimes she felt compelled to hear him say so.

"It isn't. Not if it makes you uncomfortable."

"Well, it does." He propped himself up on one arm and regarded her thoughtfully in the flickering light of a single candle. "Why do women always want to hear about how much you love them? Don't I show you how I feel?"

"Often you do. What other women do you refer to?"

Henry looked exasperated. "God's eyes, I was referring to women in general! Do I ask you about the men you might have known?"

"There's only Louis—to speak of."

"That's not what I've heard, but I don't plague you with questions, do I?"

Eleanor turned her head away. She had not told Henry about Raymond, nor did she intend to, and since their first meeting in Paris he had never again asked her about Geoffrey. Thank the Holy Mother there was no revelation she need fear where the count of Anjou was concerned.

"I should hope you don't listen to scurrilous gossip put about by my enemies."

"Of course not," Henry said in a testy voice. "On the other hand you seem rather experienced for a woman who has known only an inept semi-monk. One might wonder why."

"What does that mean?"

"It means that the less said about our past conquests, the better."

Eleanor was ashamed of the fact that she felt jealous of every female Henry had ever known intimately. Including his mother who, up until now, had been the only important woman in his life. Or so she surmised.

"My father once told me that he would prefer never having to see a woman out of bed," Henry said, glowering at her. "I, on the other hand, enjoy women for their company and conversation, even their advice. But perhaps he had a point! In fact there is only one way I know to silence you."

He rolled toward her and began to kiss her with warm hard lips that sent ripples of desire throughout her body. The ardor of her response always excited him the more. The nipples of her breasts, always prominent, became even more so when Henry teased them with his thumb and forefinger, or took them into his mouth. She had been embarrassed to express her pleasure aloud until she realized how much he liked this.

When Henry slid his hand between her parted legs, Eleanor felt her entire body tremble. His touch was so exquisite that her body twisted and turned in ecstatic rhythm with the pulse of his fingers. After a few moments, Henry entered her deeply, moving very slowly, stopping, moving again, teasing, tantalizing, all the while kissing her open mouth. She was lost in a churning sea under a blazing canopy of stars. With each thrust and roll she sailed up the wave then down into the trough, up and down until she could bear it no longer. The waves pitched her impossibly high, the stars fell, and she screamed aloud, drowning in bliss.

One of the most astounding things about Henry was that he took such an intense satisfaction in creating these powerful effects upon her. Sometimes she wondered if this did not mean more to him than his own pleasure.

Their idyll was abruptly terminated by a letter from Henry's mother in Rouen. Eleanor had found an old shield of her grandfather's painted with the likeness of Dangereuse and was in the midst of showing it to Henry.

"My grandfather claimed—so the tale goes—that he wanted his beloved mistress over him in battle as he was over her in bed—"

A dust-covered messenger raced into the hall and handed Henry the missive. "From Normandy, my lord. Most urgent."

The Empress Maud wrote that the strategic castle of Wallingford was under siege, and his supporters in England urged the duke to invade at once without delay. Two hours after receiving the message, Henry was packed, his horse saddled.

"Must you go?" she asked, knowing the answer. He had already put off the invasion once in order to come to Poitou and marry her.

"Achieving my life's goal is at hand—surely you can understand the need for me to leave." The lover was gone, replaced by the hard-headed man of affairs.

"Understand and share it. Still, I will miss you."

"And I you." They were standing in the courtyard. "When next we meet I may be king-elect of England. That thought should console you in my absence. Now, if Louis should attack, there are sufficient forces in Aquitaine to hold him at bay. I'll need all the men I can muster to guard Normandy and Anjou and invade England as well. If I require more men and ships, you will send them?"

"Of course," she replied.

The realization that, in England, he would be going into battle terrified her. She could not bear the thought of losing him but knew better than to mention it. Henry would not take kindly to a fearful, whining woman. For an instant she clung to his solid frame, sensing his impatience to be gone.

A moment later he had disentangled himself from her embrace, mounted his horse and, followed by his few attendants, galloped out of the courtyard. He did not look back. Her eyes brimming with unshed tears, Eleanor wondered if he had already forgotten her.

# CHAPTER 23

# Wareham, England, 1153

*E*ngland! At long last!

Beside himself with excitement, Henry jumped from the wildly rocking ship and splashed through the icy green water until he reached the shore. Even though his legs were numb with cold it was all he could do not to rush headlong down the beach, shouting aloud for sheer joy.

"What day is this?" he called to one of his knights.

"The sixth morning in January, my lord."

A day to remember. He could almost visualize what the future chroniclers would say: On this sixth day of January, in the year of Our Lord, 1153, did Henry, duke of Normandy and Aquitaine, count of Anjou and Maine, land upon England's shores at Wareham to deliver the realm from the usurper, King Stephen.

A chill wind lashed about Henry's ears as he stood on the empty beach watching his forces disembark. All thirty-six ships carrying one-hundred-forty knights and three-thousand foot soldiers had safely survived a stormy Channel crossing. Hugging his body to keep warm, Henry stomped up and down on the hard sand. Not nearly enough men, his mother had warned him, but with a sure instinct he had known he would be able to pick up the rest in England. He had been unwilling to leave before ensuring Normandy and Anjou were sufficiently manned, as he suspected that in his absence Louis might attempt another foray on Normandy, despite the failure of his initial attack a few months ago.

Upon Henry's return to Rouen from Poitiers, Louis had ordered him to appear before the royal court to answer for his conduct in

marrying Eleanor without permisssion of his overlord. Henry had
sent spies into Paris who returned with the news that Louis was in-
censed at what he considered his vassal's betrayal. Henry decided to
ignore the summons. When he failed to appear, Louis and his army
had crossed the borders into Normandy. Prominent among Louis's
confederates were Henry's own brother, Geoffrey, jealous of
Henry's increasing rise to power, and his old enemy, Prince Eustace
of England.

"By joining Louis, Geoffrey obviously hopes to defeat me and
keep Anjou for himself," Henry had told his mother.

He smiled grimly when he remembered how he had trounced
Louis's forces with such vehemence that the French monarch had
retreated hastily back into France. Eustace had been recalled to
England. His mother, as formidable in her wrath as an entire army,
had dealt with his brother so soundly that Geoffrey had gone to
ground in one of his castles and caused no further difficulty. For the
moment all lay quiet in Normandy.

Henry did not expect trouble in Aquitaine, but if trouble appeared he trusted Eleanor, already pregnant with their first child, to
deal with it. At his request she had left Poitou in the hands of her
uncle Ralph, a competent seneschal, and traveled to Anjou, so that
their first son would be born in Le Mans, his own birthplace. At the
same time—as Henry could no longer trust his brother—she would
act as a replacement for himself in Angers, yet still be close enough
to Poitiers so that she would be aware of any difficulties in her own
duchy.

Whenever he thought of Eleanor a wave of heat flooded his body,
warming him despite the freezing weather. Unaccountably, no matter the time or place, his heart would swell, his loins stir, and, much
to his amazement, he often found himself talking to her in his head.
With the exception of his mother and the nameless wenches he had
bedded, Henry had had little to do with women. At times, what he
felt for Nell—he could not bring himself to use the word love—was
so intense that his need to resist this feeling was almost as overpowering.

Initially Henry had been dazzled by the sparkle and wit of
Eleanor's personality, impressed by her wealth, intoxicated by her
beauty, suborned by her overwhelming sensuality, and stimulated
by her intelligence and worldly knowledge. He had been in such a
fever to possess her that he could hardly contain himself.

Henry could not put his finger on the exact moment when he had become hopelessly bound by her spell. All that he knew was that when he left Poitou he had begun to care so deeply it disturbed him. There was something—not shameful exactly, but unmanly—in caring so strongly about a woman, almost as if his very survival were being threatened. For the first time he understood the story of Samson and Delilah in Holy Writ. As a result he had resolved never to let her or anyone else know the depth of his need. Resolutely, he now thrust all thoughts of Eleanor from his mind.

Against the driving wind he could hear his men call out to one another as they waded through the surf to the damp sand. Undaunted by the weather, Henry looked with possessive pride at the rolling green sea as it crashed onto the shore, the gray skies heavy with impending rain, the struggles of his men to secure the tossing ships. What did the elements matter? Wind and rain were merely another challenge to be met and conquered. He was riding the crest of the wave now; nothing and no one could stand against him.

Soon, soon this would be his beach, his sky, his water, his land. Even the freezing salt air was like a benediction upon his upturned face.

The men began to lead the great destriers ashore, then the baggage. When men, gear, and horses were all unloaded, Henry turned toward the town of Wareham. As they pushed against the howling wind, one of his advance guard, a knight he had sent on ahead to explore the territory, met him before they entered Wareham.

"All is quiet, my lord," the knight reported. "There is a chapel over there." He pointed toward a spire just visible through the swirling mist. "The folk inside are celebrating the Feast of the Epiphany at mass."

"An auspicious day! Let us join them," Henry said, striding toward the spire. "We've made a safe crossing and have much to be thankful for."

Inside the chapel he had just knelt and signed himself when he heard the voice of the priest reciting from scripture:

"Behold the Lord, the ruler, is come and the kingdom is in his hand." Henry's men stirred and looked wonderingly at him. His heart leapt in triumph. There was no doubt in his mind that the priest's words referred to his landing in England. Surely this was a symbolic sign from heaven that God smiled upon his endeavors.

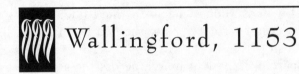 # Wallingford, 1153

Six months later, Henry, reining in his horse on top of a hill, was less sure. Like Job, the Almighty appeared to be testing him.

He had decided upon a strategy of gradual approach to attack the beleaguered Wallingford, which lay deep within royal territory. It had been his intention to draw off the besiegers by attacking other castles, forcing King Stephen to withdraw his troops to aid them. A few months at the most, he had reasoned, then he would relieve his supporters and fight the decisive battle with the king.

Now it was July and the outcome still undetermined. Removing his helmet, Henry slitted his eyes against the shroud of mist obscuring his view. Where in God's name—yes, there it was. A dark mass looming up like a giant's fist out of the winding sheet of dense fog. Wallingford. Where his enemy King Stephen waited. The veil of swirling gray suddenly lifted to admit a pale morning sun. Below, Henry could now see the gorge of the Thames River. Above it hung the huge fortress, three bastions on its north side and two on the south. On the western flank the main entrance was approached by a drawbridge while beneath the tower a heavy iron portcullis defended the gateway. Although the last time he had been here was as a young lad, the castle was exactly as he remembered.

Beneath the keep lay the town itself, the spires of its parish churches rising like needles from the cluster of thatched roofs and barns. Outside the curtain walls, the king's forces covered the open country of the Thames valley like a blight: pavilions, siege-engines, horses, and clumps of armed men were scattered everywhere. A strong wooden tower resting at the foot of the bridge over the Thames effectively blocked all supplies into Wallingford.

Henry's jaws tightened. "God's eyes! The first thing we must do is demolish that tower and victual the castle. A miracle the garrison has held out as long as it has."

"But the men have ridden all night, my lord," said Robert de Beaumont, earl of Leicester, whose recent defection from Stephen's side to his own had brought thirty midland castles into his camp. "They must eat and rest."

"Not until we have done what we came to do." Henry ignored the plea in Leicester's voice. "Now the end is finally in sight and you ask me to stop?"

In his desperate, impatient march across the southwest of England, Henry had forced men and horses through driving rain, slippery mud, and swollen rivers until they dropped on the road from exhaustion. Nor did he need Leicester to tell him the condition of his troops. Henry knew only too well that his men, wet and hungry, shivered with cold and staggered from weakness, scarce able to hold their weapons. Was he not in a similar condition? But castle after castle had fallen to him. More and more defectors from Stephen's side had swelled his ranks. How could he let up now? When he was so close? If he was merciless to his men, he was no less so on himself.

I'm on the eve of a great victory, he explained to an invisible Eleanor. I may not cease until it is won or I die in the attempt. You understand, Nell.

"But my lord," said Leicester. "It's inhuman to drive the troops this hard. You cannot expect—"

"Expect, expect?" Henry hissed the word through clenched teeth. "Let me tell you what I expect. That those who serve me are more than human, that they will rise to unimagined heights of valor and strength. If their limbs ache from weariness, if their bellies groan with hunger, what does that signify when our cause is just?" He fixed the earl with a steely gaze. "And our cause *is* just. There is no room in my camp for weaklings or the faint of heart."

"I am your man, my lord," replied Leicester in a barely audible voice.

Henry clamped his helmet firmly back upon his head, and waving an arm for his troops to follow, started down the muddy slope toward the castle and the glorious battle that now, at long last, awaited him.

"Stephen's barons claim they will not fight, my lord. At this very moment a furious debate rages inside the royal pavilion between the king and his advisors."

Henry, sitting in the great hall of Wallingford two days later, could scarcely believe the evidence of his ears as he looked up at Robert of Leicester, who had just approached the high table.

"Not fight? Men sworn to serve their anointed king? It is nothing less than treason. Does Stephen agree?"

From somewhere in the hall Henry could hear the sound of a rebec and the plaintive voice of a minstrel. He must send for that impertinent troubadour Eleanor had dismissed. Bernart something. He would know how to compose stirring *chansons* of derring-do.

"On the contrary, King Stephen is violently opposed to them. But the king is under pressure from his magnates, the archbishop of Canterbury, and his brother, the bishop of Winchester, to reach an accommodation with us." Leicester paused. "Everyone is sick unto death of this conflict. Magnates and clergy alike want peace."

Down the line of trestle tables echoed a chorus of agreement.

A dull pain throbbing in his temples indicated to Henry that one of his headaches was on the way. Although he had every reason to rejoice, as he and the leaders of his army were feasted, he felt frustrated. Did everyone suppose that because the enemy was now driven back across the Thames and supplies once again reached the castle, he would be satisfied? Well, he wasn't, Henry brooded. Routing a host of troops back across the river was a far cry from the valiant clash of arms he had expected. He had been waiting to fight Stephen since his knighting by the king of Scotland four years ago. This time no one was going to cheat him of his chance at valor and glory.

His cousin William, earl of Gloucester, leaned across the table.

"This war claimed my father's life. You have not lived here as we have, Cousin, you cannot know how terribly the people have suffered. How we all have suffered."

"So you told me on our hair-raising trip to London when I was ten years old; I have never forgotten." He laid a hand on his cousin's shoulder. "But am I not here to relieve everyone's misery by defeating the usurper?" Henry removed his hand to tear off a wing of roast fowl. "Make no mistake, William. I will avenge my uncle's death and all the other deaths by doing battle with Stephen. Now, there's an end to it. Will someone get rid of that *trouvère* before I go mad?"

From the corner of his eye Henry saw his cousin of Gloucester exchange a glance with Leicester. His gaze switched back and forth between them. What were those two plotting? He was about to speak when Leicester took a deep breath, obviously steeling himself.

"My lord, last night some of us met secretly with Stephen's barons—"

Hands balled into fists, Henry jumped to his feet.

"Please!" Leicester's voice rose. "Let me finish, I beg you. In truth, we would do almost anything to avoid further bloodshed. A compromise has been suggested which the magnates of both sides may look upon with favor. Just listen to—"

But Henry, the blood beginning to pound like an anvil in his temples, was beyond listening. They were trying to thwart him, cheat him of his longed-for battle. Any moment now the bubble of crimson rage would burst inside his head and he would lose control.

"There will be a battle, I tell you." He heard a stranger's voice shouting at the top of his lungs. "By God's eyes, there will be a battle between Stephen and me if I have to challenge him to single combat!"

Henry raced down the hall and flung himself out the door. Behind him the silence in the hall was like death.

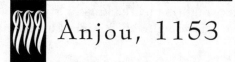 Anjou, 1153

In Angers, Eleanor waited for news of her husband. She had heard of his safe landing in England, then nothing further. But even lack of news could not dim her radiant happiness.

"Sometimes I'm so happy it frightens me," she told Petronilla, who had finally joined her. "At any moment I may wake to find it is all a glorious dream and I'm still married to that French eunuch, suffocating in that gilded Parisian dungeon, with Abbé Suger and Bernard of Clairvaux as my jailers."

"Do not speak ill of the dead," said Petronilla, subdued and far more serious since the death of her elderly husband, Ralph. She signed herself.

They were walking arm in arm on the flintstone ramparts of Angers Castle. Looking out over the red roofs of the city, Eleanor could see beyond the old Roman walls to where the converging Loire and Mayenne rivers sparkled like blue-green jewels in the July sun.

"Not only do I finally feel fulfilled as a woman," she continued, ignoring her sister's remark, "but l am also with child, and Henry sufficiently trusts my judgment to appoint me his deputy in Angers."

"There is no question that you are blessed, Sister," said Petronilla.

"I know, I know!"

Behind her came the melodic sounds of a rebec and the lilting voice of Bernart de Ventadour following at a discreet distance. Eleanor threw him a brilliant smile over her shoulder.

Petronilla frowned. "You show that troubadour too much favor. There is talk that he has become infatuated with you."

"In six weeks time I shall be delivered of a babe—a son—that should stop tongues wagging." She gently patted her rounded belly. "There is little I can do about his infatuation even if I wanted to— and I don't. It's all quite innocent as you are well aware." She laughed. "But you know how I adore being adored."

Petronilla wagged a cautionary finger. "Prudence, prudence. No breath of scandal must reach your husband's ears. Not after what you told me."

A picture sprang to Eleanor's mind of Henry thrashing wildly about on the rushes shouting imprecations at Bernart. She shivered, retreating from the grotesque memory.

"I've done nothing to be ashamed of," she said, amused but sad that the once-flighty Petronilla should be the one to preach caution. "Henry will be most pleased when he hears how well I've done in his capital."

Unwittingly, Eleanor had fallen in love with Angers. Upon her arrival she had not known what to expect and was pleasantly surprised to find it a mellow city of ancient churches and monastic schools, where philosophy and poetry had long flourished under the benign rule of the counts of Anjou. To the comfortable, imposing castle set high above the city, Eleanor had transported her household from Poitiers. Troubadours, poets, and chroniclers soon followed. Here, free from restraint, disapproving eyes, or malicious tongues, she set about creating her own court, infusing it with all the enthusiasm and gaiety of her Aquitainian heritage. Much as she missed Aquitaine, she was gratified to hear that Angers was responding favorably to her presence.

Shortly after her conversation with Petronilla it became evident that Bernart's attentions were crossing the boundaries of propriety.

In song he accused Eleanor of first enticing him, then spurning his advances. She was, he sang, noble and sweet, tormenting his dreams, causing him to suffer the most appalling agonies. When he sang of offering himself as her bedside slave to draw off her boots when she retired, Eleanor knew he had gone too far.

Before she could act, however, a message finally arrived from Henry to say he had arrived at Wallingford and was preparing to do battle with King Stephen. In his letter Henry also mentioned, casually enough, that he wanted Bernart de Ventadour to come to England at once and exhort his men to battle by composing stirring *chansons de geste.* Did Henry have unknown eyes and ears spying on her? The possibility made Eleanor uneasy.

"Is it necessary I go?" Bernart asked Eleanor, as he knelt before her in the great hall of Angers Castle.

His crisp black hair curled appealingly over a high pale forehead. Liquid brown eyes gazed longingly up at her. Really, he was quite irresistible, but she was proof against his charm. In fact, her husband's summons very neatly removed a potential dilemma: how to get rid of Bernart gracefully, without calling attention to the fact.

"The count of Anjou has ordered you to England; naturally you must obey."

Eleanor experienced a momentary regret. There was a side to her nature that basked in the chivalrous admiration Bernart showered on her. Secretly she thought it a shame that a woman was not allowed to indulge all the diverse aspects of herself. As men did. To expect one lone male to provide all one's needs was, perhaps, asking too much. She dismissed the thought. After all, she loved her husband to distraction and he was riding into grave danger to win them both a crown. The loss of her favorite troubadour was of no importance whatsoever.

"That Norman duke has the soul of an acquisitive merchant and the predatory instincts of a greedy hawk," Bernart cried. "He can never love or understand you the way I do. Like most men he regards you only as a prized possession, somewhere between his favorite gyrfalcon and his champion hound. Secretly he considers you his inferior. It is typical of such a knight."

"Be careful how you speak of my lord," Eleanor retorted, glancing round to make sure no one had heard him. "What you say is nonsense. Thus far he has treated me like an equal."

Bernart raised his brows. "Tell me, Lady, what was the name of

Charlemagne's queen, empress, whatever? Or the paladin Roland's wife?"

"Really, who can remember? If I ever even knew."

"Exactly. What was the name of Charlemagne's sword?"

Eleanor shrugged impatiently. "Everyone knows that. Joyeuse."

"Roland's?"

"Durandel—oh!"

"I see I have made my point."

Only too well, Eleanor thought, rather shaken.

"I will immortalize you, Domna, in my verse and song. Centuries from now, your name will still be remembered."

"For which I will always be grateful. Your songs, they please me well. But my husband does not regard me as some chattel, I assure you."

Bernart lowered his voice. "I did not think to find you so blind. Duke Henry will never think of you as an equal. That does not bode well for one who believes herself superior to all men."

Color flooded Eleanor's face. "You go too far, minstrel. It is high time you removed yourself from my court. A journey to England will cool your hot blood and muzzle your impetuous tongue. If I find you have been unwise enough to repeat such slanderous thoughts elsewhere . . ."

Bernart bowed his head in submission. "Divinity, I am your devoted slave. Never would I be so indiscreet—" He deftly caught the purse of silver coins she flung at him.

He left the next day. Eleanor knew she would miss Bernart's worshipful attentions but it was a relief to have him gone. Man's superior! How had he divined those secret thoughts that lurked, half-formed, in the hidden recesses of her mind, when she herself had never fully viewed them? It was disquieting.

A sennight after Bernart had gone, another troubadour appeared, sent by the master, he said, with a song for her.

> She said in accents clear
> Before I did depart,
> "Your songs they please me well."
> I would each Christian soul
> Could know my rapture then,
> For all I write and sing
> Is meant for her delight.

Yes, indeed. She would miss that impudent rogue.

Meanwhile she had her unborn child to occupy her mind, a civilized court to preside over, her own lands to keep a watchful eye on, and Henry's safety to pray for. Not that Eleanor doubted his eventual success. Every instinct told her that the Angevin star was in the ascendant.

On the seventeenth day of August Eleanor gave birth to a son in Le Mans. He had a patch of russet hair and blue-gray eyes. Beside herself with triumph and joy, she kept examining the tiny pink evidence of his sex, hardly able to believe what she saw. She named him William, after the great Conqueror, and the Troubadour, as well as her own father. At long last she was vindicated. The stain of her two failures to bear Louis an heir was wiped clean.

Two months later, in October, Eleanor's mother-in-law, the Empress Maud, requested her to come to Normandy. There had been no word from Henry since early September, when he had written that battle was imminent. Since he had been at Wallingford since July, this made no sense to Eleanor. She also had misgivings about going to Rouen until she realized that when Henry did return he would undoubtedly go straight to Normandy. Not to mention that whatever news did manage to float back across the Channel, Henry's mother would receive it first.

When William was strong enough—he was a weak babe who ailed frequently—she would most certainly go to Rouen.

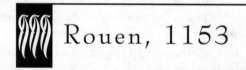 Rouen, 1153

"What do you mean there was no battle? What has everyone been doing at Wallingford for the last three and one-half months? Making faces at each other across the river?"

Eleanor, surrounded by her women, sat in her mother-in-law's solar in the ducal palace at Rouen. She looked quizzically at the messenger, a cleric, who had arrived this chill November morning to inform her and Henry's mother of the most recent events in England. The cleric, who claimed to be an archdeacon of Canterbury, had been closeted alone for over an hour with the Empress Maud, who only two days ago had herself just returned from a rather mysterious journey to Anjou, she claimed. Eleanor tried to stifle the unworthy prick of resentment that rose within her breast. I am Henry's wife. It is I who should have seen this man first.

Ever since arriving in Normandy last month, Eleanor had bent over backward to accommodate her formidable mother-in-law, knowing it would please Henry. In the main, although wary of each other, they had gotten on surprisingly well, discovering they had as many similarities as differences. But when all was said and done this was the empress's domain, and never before had Eleanor been forced to yield pride of place to another woman. She knew it was a question of protocol and courtesy, entirely proper that Henry's mother should have been told the news first, but still it rankled.

Beside her the wet nurse crooned to baby William as she rocked him in her arms. It was another rainy day, so bleak that the charcoal braziers could barely warm the chamber. Ivory tapers flickered wildly in the howling wind that penetrated through the cracks in the stone walls. Outside, torrential rains lashed the towers and ramparts. Eleanor shivered. Sweet St. Radegonde, how she missed the sunlit warmth of Aquitaine.

Overall though, she knew she had little cause for complaint. Ever since giving birth to her son, she had been petted and spoiled, the center of attention in both Anjou and Normandy. Unfortunately, the babe was still not strong, and continued to ail. Eleanor felt protective toward little William and fussed over him—something she had not done with her two daughters. When she heard that Louis and the Frankish nobility were reeling from the shock that the Norman succession was now assured, her satisfaction knew no bounds.

The black-hooded cleric from England, who had not been sent directly by Henry but by the archbishop of Canterbury, returned her quizzical look. His unblinking eyes, dark as mulberries, were set close together in an arresting face dominated by a nose beaked like a hawk. This gave him something of a predatory aspect. Eleanor had the grudging thought that it was a face you would look at twice—and once seen never forget.

"If you will allow me to explain," the cleric said in a deep voice that was probably meant to be deferential but instead sounded condescending.

"Do so." Eleanor wondered why the man, personable and well-spoken as he was, should put her back up. Maybe it was because she had suddenly remembered her father once telling her that you could never trust a man whose eyes were set too closely together.

"Duke Henry and King Stephen both wanted to do battle, Madam. It was the barons, supported by the clergy, who refused. Led by my master, his grace of Canterbury, and the bishop of Winchester, a peace was finally negotiated that proved acceptable to both sides."

"A wise decision yet one that amazes me," Eleanor said. "Henry so looked forward to defeating Stephen on his own ground. And the English king has sworn time and again that he would never make peace."

"I believe that his exact words were he would never make peace unless his son Eustace inherited."

Eleanor curbed her irritation. He was right, of course. "But now that Eustace is dead . . . yes, I see, that would change matters. So—both King Stephen and my husband were persuaded of the advantages to be gained by a legal settlement rather than by power of the sword. I'm greatly relieved that the war in England is finally at an end."

"So are we all. Of course, our Heavenly Father also intervened by sending Stephen an evil omen." The cleric crossed himself.

"Something other than Eustace's death?" Eleanor leaned forward with interest.

The cleric nodded. "While Stephen was marshaling his troops, his horse reared and almost threw him. Not once but thrice. He took it as a sign from heaven."

"The poor beast probably slipped in the mud." Eleanor's women tittered. Ignoring the disapproving look that crossed the cleric's face she lowered her voice. "Tell me, is it really true that Prince Eustace actually choked on tainted fish?"

"So I understand."

"How fortuitous. Do you expect me to believe that no one helped him to a most timely end?" Eleanor placed a hand over her heart. "I promise to be the soul of discretion. Come, tell me how it was done."

The cleric looked down his beaked nose. "There is naught to tell. Many may have wished Eustace dead, one cannot deny that. But in this instance there is no evidence of murder."

"So you say." Suddenly restless, Eleanor rose and walked to the copper brazier, stretching her hands out over the coals. "The whole matter concerning Stephen's change of heart is so—so—unlikely. I cannot help but feel there is more to this tale than has been told, though I doubt we shall ever know the truth of it. Well, go on."

The cleric bowed his head. "Stephen acknowledged Henry's heredity right in England and named the duke his heir. Duke Henry in turn said that Stephen might hold the kingdom until his death. In fact the two have adopted each other as father and son . . ."

Eleanor turned around. "Sworn enemies adopted each other as father and son? Now does the lion lie down with the lamb! Extraordinary."

Ignoring her outburst, the cleric continued. "The barons and bishops then agreed to bind themselves by oath that Henry should succeed to the kingdom peacefully."

Eleanor laughed and returned to her seat. "An oath sworn by the magnates of England is as binding as water. The empress's struggle to become queen of England is living proof of that."

The cleric's lips tightened and a muscle in his jaw twitched. "It was further agreed that the rights of the crown which nobles everywhere had usurped were to be restored and—"

"I'm sure all the details were quite in order." Eleanor knew she was being provoking but could not seem to stop herself. "Thank you. Did my husband have a personal message for me?"

The cleric fumbled in the scrip at his belt. "As I left in rather a hurry I did not actually talk with the duke myself, madam. In fact I have yet to meet him. My master, the archbishop of Canterbury, gave me this for you from Duke Henry." He unwound his blackclothed body from the stool and handed her a square of sealed parchment. "It was His Grace who arranged for me to deliver these glad tidings to you and the empress."

Courteous as he was, there was a sanctimonious air about the cleric that continued to irritate her. In addition he was so tall that Eleanor had to arch her neck to look up at him.

"Please wait in the hall. I'll have an answer for you to take back."

"I'll be glad to act as scribe for you, Madam."

"How kind. But I can write a fair hand myself. In several languages, as it happens."

The cleric flushed. For a moment he seemed nonplussed then swallowed his surprise as she walked with him to the door of the solar.

"Do you have any idea when the duke will be returning to Rouen?"

The cleric gazed down at her with those strange unblinking eyes. "No, Madam. It might be a few months yet. Duke Henry is to return with the king to London so that he may acquaint himself with the workings of Stephen's realm."

"I see." A few months! Eleanor made no effort to conceal her sharp disappointment.

She missed Henry so much, and he had never even seen his first-born son. Still, the arrangements made political sense and even she could see this was not the moment for him to leave England. After all, what they both longed for had come to pass: Henry would be king and she queen.

The cleric opened the door. Eleanor watched him stride down the passageway, his black robe billowing out behind him like a dark cloud. Suddenly curious, she called out:

"How are you called?"

He turned his head without breaking stride. "Becket, Madam. Thomas Becket."

# CHAPTER 24

# London,

# 1154

"My lord, do you wish to comment on the fate of the Flemings?" Theobald of Bec, archbishop of Canterbury, who presided over this meeting in his well-appointed council chamber at the Bishop's Palace in London, regarded Henry with an inquiring look.

Henry felt his blood stir. Since last November and the signing of the Treaty of Wallingford, he had been confined in one wretched council chamber after another: Wallingford, Winchester, now the Bishop's Palace in London where he had arrived with King Stephen two weeks ago. Increasingly frustrated with these endless discussions, it was all he could do to keep his temper on a tight rein.

"The Flemings, you say? Indeed I do, my lord archbishop. Indeed I do! If I had my way all Flemings would be blinded, castrated, and paraded around England in chains."

"A bit harsh, my lord," said one of the English barons seated at the table. "After all, the Flemings were hired by King Stephen in time of need and served the realm well."

"Rape, looting, murder, torture of innocent civilians unable to defend themselves—God's eyes, this is your idea of serving the realm well?"

The bulk of the magnates and ecclesiastics attending the council shifted uncomfortably in their seats and would not meet Henry's eyes. In truth, the chamber was so crowded with former enemies that he felt stifled by the air of hostility that seemed to clog his very nostrils. The burnished copper braziers, thick tapestries depicting scenes from the crucifixion, and heavy silver candleholders only added to the suffocating atmosphere.

"My cousin, the earl of Gloucester, was very nearly quartered like a chicken by one of these whoreson Flemings, weren't you, William?"

William, seated next to him, looked startled. "You have an excellent memory, Cousin."

"An inheritance from my grandfather, the first Henry, the last *rightful* king. I pride myself on never forgetting a good turn—or an ill one." Henry scrutinized each peer. "It passes my understanding that Stephen could even hire such knaves. But then, everything he has done passes my understanding."

Stephen's brother, the all-powerful bishop of Winchester, rose to his feet. "It is not very charitable to attack a man behind his back, my lord duke. Today Stephen ails and is not present to defend his actions."

"How can one defend eighteen years of criminal negligence? It is more than sufficient to make one ill." Henry met the bishop's indignant gaze with a grim smile. "Ill unto death I shouldn't wonder. As God is my judge, I wouldn't have Stephen's conscience for all the gold in the Knights Templar coffers. Considering the widespread damage he's inflicted, I have grave doubts as to whether he is even fit to remain as king."

The bishop's voice rose. "My lord, you agreed Stephen should remain king until his death!"

"Did I? God's eyes, I must have been flown with wine. Or mad. Or both. It's obvious he is unfit."

"My lord archbishop," the bishop said, green eyes blazing. "This is an outrage. King Stephen and Duke Henry have sworn to adopt each other as father and son!"

A moment of shocked stillness followed this exchange. Henry could feel everyone's horrified gaze upon him, including the two clerks perched on high stools, wax tablets and styli poised in their hands. In the midst of the silence, someone snickered. Henry, baffled by this reaction, could not see from whence it came. Then the nobles all raised their voices at once. Henry winced. The uproar sounded exactly like a pack of angry yelping hounds.

"My lords, my lord bishops, order, order if you please." The archbishop of Canterbury held up a palsied hand. "By the Mass, are we here to hurl recriminations or forge a workable set of rules that will guide us in restoring peace and plenty to this wounded land?" He sent Henry a reproachful glance. "It behooves us all to remember that every man has the right to face his accuser."

The magnates quieted. Henry gave a reluctant nod. If it weren't for the unflagging support of the archbishop of Canterbury, who had championed the Angevin cause for the last five years, he would not be here now. He had no wish to antagonize the worthy Theobald. But at least he'd had his say. Or part of it. Henry let out a deep sigh of irritation. How much longer could he stand this kind of imprisonment? Whether well-appointed, such as this one, or barely furnished, all the chambers he'd been in since November looked alike to him. Walls lined with chests filled with crumbling sheets of parchment. Even the smell—dust, moldering wood, and sealing wax—was the same. Henry's backside was sore; his patience wearing thin.

"The Flemings, my lord?" the archbishop reiterated with a weary sigh.

"Force them to quit England," Robert of Leicester said quickly. "Banish them to their native land."

Henry gave a reluctant nod. Unaccountably there flashed into his mind a picture of a bloody, eyeless head nailed to a gate and Flemish soldiers kicking a youth along London Bridge.

He thought again of that sudden snicker; there had been something obscene and totally uncalled for about the sound. How he wished he could have detected its source.

The monotonous voice of the archbishop droned on and on over points already covered in the proposed treaty.

". . . the clergy allowed to enjoy peace and be relieved of all exorbitant demands . . ." Whether famine, pestilence, fire, flood or war—trust the Church to think of herself first. ". . . Farms must be supplied with husbandmen . . ." Who else would they be supplied with, vintners? ". . . thieves and robbers punished with death, soldiers to exchange their swords for ploughshares." Henry could just see some ham-fisted sergeant trying to cultivate a field. ". . . their spears—" The archbishop paused, obviously searching for the right phrase. "Ah—yes, their spears exchanged for—pruning hooks . . ."

Pruning hooks? God save us! Henry drummed his fingers on the polished oak table. He knew these were vital details in the treaty that would help restore the ravaged land to the condition of prosperity it had enjoyed under his grandfather. But why must it go on so long?

As the days and weeks passed, he had grown more and more impatient with these magnates and bishops who had so ill served their king and country. Throughout the civil war they had changed sides with such dizzying rapidity it was enough to make one's head spin. One day they supported King Stephen, the next, his mother, the Empress Maud. Who among them could he trust now? In all fairness, Henry knew he could not blame the king alone for the sorry state of the land. And, if he were totally honest with himself, he acknowledged he quite liked Stephen personally. But liking a man did not mean one forgave him his evil deeds. Justice must be served.

Henry's attention was distracted by the whining voice of a northern baron complaining that the woods adjoining a castle he had recently built were overrun with poachers and the sheriffs did nothing to prosecute them. What safeguards were to be made for unprincipled sheriffs?

Henry's eyes narrowed. "Is this an unlicensed castle you built? Without the king's leave?"

The man turned red as a beetroot, obviously wishing he had kept silent.

"God's eyes!" Henry thrust forward a pugnacious jaw. "Scum like you are just as responsible for the state of my realm as is Stephen." One freckled fist pounded the table. "My courageous mother endured scorn and vilification because of traitors such as you. As did all my loyal followers in England. She was the rightful ruler but forced to flee for her very life to escape your treachery." His fist was now pounding the table with such force the flesh scraped raw.

"My lord," began the archbishop.

Henry, his face gorged with blood, jumped to his feet and began to beat the table with both fists. "No! Let them hear the truth. While the land suffered, you greedy tubs of suet feasted comfortably in your halls, ignored what little royal authority there was, turned your back while my people were crushed, built unlicensed castles, and coined your own money!"

The rage welled up in his throat so thickly he feared he would choke.

"None can deny these accusations," said Robert of Leicester in a soothing voice. "However, the weal of the land is of greater urgency, my lord, I think you will agree. We are all aware that justice must—and will—be served. At the proper time."

There was a murmur of assent.

Breathing heavily, Henry sank back in his seat. He knew if he continued he would fall into one of his tantrums and lose control. This was not the time to give way to his rage. No doubt these magnates already thought him an untried youth. Someone they could lead round by the nose, as they had Stephen. Well, they would learn. By Christ, they would learn.

Every bone, muscle, and sinew he possessed was in a fury of impatience to set about his task of reforms. He could hardly wait to master these nobles' arrogance and grind their pride into the dust. But he must bide his time. Until he was king he would not have a free hand. To relieve his feelings he grasped the pewter goblet of wine in front of him and ground the stem into the table.

The hairs on the back of his neck prickled as he felt someone watching him. Raising his head he met the quizzical gaze of the archbishop's cleric, who had today for the first time attended Theobald at the council. The cleric frowned and shook his head, pointing with his finger. Henry saw that he had dug the edge of the goblet into the satiny finish of the table, leaving a ragged scar in the gleaming wood. God's eyes!

Immediately he put his hands into his lap and gave the cleric a rueful smile. The man returned the smile, which warmed his rather serious face like a ray of sun lighting a wintery morning.

"Does anyone have anything to add?" Archbishop Theobald glanced round the table.

The black-robed cleric whispered something in his ear.

"Yes. Thank you. I think this might be a good time to address the matter of the debased coinage. My lord duke?"

"The cure is very simple: There can be only one standard of money—minted by the royal treasury alone—as there was in my grandfather's day when the coin of the realm meant something. The number of licensed mints will be reduced and continuously inspected. I will have an honest penny in my kingdom or know the reason why."

"An excellent point." Theobald glanced down the table at the other barons, most of whom flushed and avoided the prelate's gaze. "We must enforce that. Vigorously."

Henry repressed a smile. Of course anything that would help fill the Church's coffers must be enforced. Vigorously. Only four of the lords nodded agreement: his cousin William of Gloucester, the earl of Leicester, his bastard uncle Reginald of Cornwall, and a young man called Richard de Lucy. De Lucy had never sworn allegiance to Henry's mother but had come to power under Stephen and now held the post of justiciar. An unassuming man with a broad open face and mild manner that inspired trust, Henry had immediately taken a liking to him. De Lucy, like Robert of Leicester, would be one of the men to bridge the gap from one reign to another.

"Now then—" the archbishop began then stopped as the black-robed cleric whispered something else in his ear.

"What's that? Ah—it has been pointed out to me that the matter of unlicensed castles mentioned earlier has not been dealt with."

"Thank you, Your Grace," Henry said instantly. "All such castles must be razed at once. With no exceptions."

The archbishop nodded his agreement as did a handful of barons. The rest of the magnates glared at Henry with undisguised hatred. No doubt he had made some new enemies in addition to his old ones. It mattered little. They could hate him or love him, as they chose—so long as they obeyed him.

He sent a glance of gratitude to the cleric who had reminded the archbishop of two vital points. As their eyes locked, Henry felt a chill of recognition race down his spine. Had he encountered another harbinger of his fate? And if so was it for good or ill? But, as in the case of Eleanor, it hardly mattered. Between this cleric and himself a tenuous bond was already forming.

Henry turned his head to meet the thoughtful gaze of the archbishop, who had obviously observed their brief exchange.

The talk at the table continued until the Vespers bell sounded. Henry was the first to leap up from his seat.

"After Vespers we will take supper and then resume for an hour or two," said Theobald.

"I must be excused, Your Grace." Henry walked with Theobald out the chamber door. "I will go from my wits if I have to face the walls of this chamber for another moment. Pray excuse me at tonight's meeting. In truth, my head is stuffed so full of facts and figures it's fit to burst." He paused. "I intend to see something of London tonight."

Theobald frowned. "We can easily postpone the next meeting but you are unfamiliar with the city, which is still not safe in these lawless times." He glanced at his cleric gathering up sheets of parchment from the table.

"Thomas would be most happy to take you on a tour of the safer parts of London and see you come to no harm."

With a smile the cleric turned. "I would be honored. Although from everything I hear the duke is well able to take care of himself. We could meet after supper if that is agreeable?"

Henry nodded. So—the cleric not only knew what points needed to be covered in the treaty, but also how to flatter. Well, he had no objection to flattery—especially when it was deserved.

The archbishop smiled fondly at the cleric. "This is a most valued member of my household, Archdeacon Thomas Becket. He's been traveling to Rome and Normandy on your behalf, my lord, and returned only two days ago."

"The cleric who visited my mother and wife in Rouen? Thank you for the messages you brought back. My family appears to be faring well."

"Very well indeed. Your son looks the very image of you. I will see you after supper then?"

Henry felt absurdly pleased to hear that his firstborn son looked exactly like him. And his spirits lightened considerably at the prospect of exploring London in the company of a man who—he paused. A man who what? After all, Thomas Becket was a man of the Church and, as such, somewhat suspect. Although an archdeacon was usually an administrator in minor orders, and not necessarily ordained as a priest. In truth, Thomas did not have the look of an ecclesiastic, on the contrary—ah, a man knowledgeable enough to understand what must be done to salvage this ailing realm? A man who might share his hopes and dreams for the future of England? Henry was determined to find out.

# CHAPTER 25

# London,

# 1154

*B*ellebelle watched while her customer, Miles, Lord Crowmarsh, dressed himself, left several coins on the oak chest, then walked stiffly to the door with the aid of a silver-headed cane.

"Thank ye, my lord," she said.

"Thank *you*, my dear. Not ye." Lord Crowmarsh wagged a reproving finger. "Remember what I've taught you. You're doing much better in your speech. Keep working at it."

"Thank *you*, my lord," she repeated.

"Take care of yourself, Belle," he said.

She forced a smile, almost screaming with relief when the door finally closed behind him, then collapsed onto the bed. With a grimace she examined her naked body. Streaks of purple wine had dried on her breasts and belly; the sheets had wet patches. It was a good thing Lord Crowmarsh was a nobleman and very rich—the other whores at Gropecuntlane called him Old Money Bags—or she would never put up with his peculiar ways.

A nice-looking man for his age—fifty if he was a day—and well-spoken, he had taken a fancy to her and wanted to improve how she talked. She looked like quality, why not talk like quality? Bellebelle didn't see how this would benefit her but she was willing to try. Hawke also encouraged her.

"I can pass you off as a daughter of a good family fallen on evil times," he said. "Forced to sell her body to support her destitute parents. Now that's a teary tale as should appeal to those of my customers who feel guilty going to a brothel. You be worth more."

Because Lord Crowmarsh was soft as a wet rag these days, his favorite sport—his only sport—was to slowly pour wine over her whole body and lap it up like a dog. No harm in it really but there was always such a mess to clean up after. Fortunately he was her last customer and the rest of the night she could do exactly as she pleased.

With a sigh Bellebelle got up and went to the iron cauldron of water warming next to the charcoal brazier. Taking a clean linen towel from the pile nearby she dipped it in the water and began to scrub off the wine stains. In truth, she'd rather have toothless Miles and the wine than the boastful wool merchant from Lincoln who stank of sheepskin, or the Italian scribe from the Temple in London who chewed garlic all the time so that the smell lingered for days after.

She dried herself with another towel, slipped on a linen chemise, then began to straighten up the chamber. First she changed the sheets, grateful, not for the first time, that Hawke's brothel had a goodly supply of sheets and towels, plenty of coals for the brazier and a more gentlemanly type of customer than what she had seen in Southwark. The chamber itself, though small, was larger and more comfortable than the one in Gilbert's establishment. The scarred furniture felt more solid, the bed wider and covered with a bright red, moth-eaten coverlet, its fur lining almost worn away. She'd found it on a trash heap but any one could tell it had belonged to quality folk.

While she made the bed, Bellebelle noticed that her supply of vinegar and water was running low; she'd have to ask Hawke for another full bucket. Also, she must remember to tell the brothel-master that the bunch of dried nettles hanging on the wall needed to be replaced. One customer wanted to be beaten with these but last time he'd complained the nettles had lost their sting.

The bells rang for Compline. Still early. Bellebelle walked to the pole protruding from the wall and took down an old blue kirtle. Thank the Holy Mother, Hawke had given her permission to go out after Miles left. She had been servicing customers all day; if she stayed inside one more moment she felt she would jump out of her skin. A walk to the cookshop on the corner was just what she needed. She'd have a pork pasty, treat herself to a half-tankard of ale at the tavern, and exchange natter with the other whores sure to be there. It was what she did every night Hawke allowed her out.

Bellebelle dressed listlessly, wondering who tomorrow would

bring. Every day seemed the same now; sometimes she could no longer distinguish one from another. Or the months. Was this January or February? January. Not that it mattered. Recently she had begun to understand why Gytha always swilled ale. It made the time pass quicker, and the weary world look brighter. Thus far she had resisted following in her mother's footsteps but when she thought of her future—what lay ahead? Age, sickness, an early death? She could hardly remember the happy dreams she had once cherished. When all was said and done, she was still a whore in a brothel-house.

Never mind. Mustn't grumble. Bellebelle hated it when she felt sorry for herself. Especially when she thought of all she had to be grateful for: her escape from the Flemings, leaving the Bankside stews behind her and being taken on by Hawke. All she had to do was remember what happened to Gytha and she felt herself the most fortunate person in the world. As Morgaine had always said, life were never meant for them as had a wishbone where their backbone ought be.

Ever since coming to Gropecuntlane four years ago—or was it five? Bellebelle had been careful not to cross the river into Southwark. Not only was there the risk of being recognized—although that incident was probably long forgotten—but she could not bring herself to stir up painful memories by going back. Although she would never forget Gytha and Morgaine, that part of her life, particularly the near-murder of de Burgh, was something she wanted to bury forever.

She thought of herself as being born on the day she arrived at the brothel-house in Gropecuntlane.

Bellebelle slipped the coins under the slops bucket. More than half went to the brothelmaster but there still was some left over which she would dutifully save. She pulled on her red and blue striped cloak with distaste, hating the fact that she always had to flaunt her profession when she left the brothelhouse. Mustn't grumble, she chided herself again. She had a night to herself; there was the pork pasty, a half-pint of ale, and good company to look forward to.

In the purple twilight, Thomas Becket and his charge, Duke Henry of Normandy, walked their horses through the streets of London. They were followed by a guard of four men-at-arms who carried torches. It was unusually mild and Thomas watched the duke breathe the crisp January air with relief.

"What's this place?" Henry asked as they came upon a maze of open stalls where a babble of different languages assailed their ears. "I recognize French, Italian, Spanish—where are we?"

"West Cheap," Thomas said. "The merchants are probably just closing up for the night."

"God's eyes, a veritable rat's nest of noise! You can hardly hear yourself think. And what a stink of slops."

Thomas felt a tightness in his chest. Before he could stop himself, he said, "It may seem like a 'rat's nest' to you, my lord, but this is where I was born and, despite the stink of slops, spent a happy youth."

An instant later Thomas was appalled at his own audacity. He had trained himself never to lose control and now . . . What had gotten into him? He had thought himself no longer bothered by his humble origins, and reprimanded himself for the sin of pride. He had so wanted to make a good impression. What would the Duke think?

"Well, I didn't mean to offend you, Thomas. You've obviously come a long way since then. We're none of us bound by our past."

A long way indeed from the poverty of Cheapside where the Beckets, the only Normans in a small area thick with families whose roots went back to Saxon times, were looked down upon. Poverty, mingled with the knowledge that he was different from the other lads who teased and hounded him, had set Thomas apart. On the other hand, having to survive in the rough and tumble of the London streets had made him strong, good with his fists, and willing to fight. No, not bound by the past but bound to it, Thomas wanted to say.

"My father was a poor but well-respected Norman burgher," he said instead. "My mother was the finest woman who ever drew breath. Although my blood may not be royal, my great-grandfather fought with the Conqueror's foot soldiers at Hastings. I'm not ashamed of my origins."

He sounded defensive and touchy even to his own ears.

"Why should you be?" Henry looked around. "Tell me of this area. It appears to be most unusual."

Thomas swallowed, knowing the duke was trying to put matters right by changing the subject. "Indeed. A veritable Tower of Babel, my lord, as you noted, filled with different races and people." He had his voice under control now. "You can find anything here: the best goldsmith's work in England, ginger, nutmeg, embroidered vestments, trinket boxes from France. London has everything."

"So I've heard." The duke smiled and spurred his horse forward. "The one time I was in London I gawked like a country bumpkin from the provinces—which is exactly what I was. Right now I'm not in the market for goods though, but sport."

"I didn't know you were ever in London, my lord."

"Only once as a child." His voice was dismissive. "Now, what taverns can you recommend?"

Thomas slowed his horse to avoid a pile of rubble in the street. "Taverns? Ah, well, I'm not too familiar with—" He sounded like a prude, and changed his tactics. "There's Billingsgate where the wine shops are. But such places are frequented mostly by sailors and other lowlife."

Thomas found it hard to keep the distaste from his voice. "There's Southwark, but it's more dangerous than any area in London. Filled with loose women, robbers, cutpurses, and other knaves who'd as soon slit your throat as give you greeting."

"A veritable sewer of villainy to hear you tell it. I hadn't realized we were in the very heart of Sodom and Gomorrah."

Thomas felt himself flush. "I didn't mean to give that impression at all." He had been so drawn to this young duke and now he couldn't seem to put a foot right. What had happened to his usually calm and diplomatic demeanor?

"It's all right, Thomas, I was only teasing you." The Duke paused. "Tonight—tonight, Thomas, I'm in the mood for a touch of sin, as it happens." He reined in his horse. "Look, down there—"

The Duke pointed toward a lane that turned off the street. At the far end could be seen a tavern sign painted with a blue cock. In the flickering light of a torch carried by one of the men-at-arms he peered at the name scrawled on the side of a wooden building. "Grope—cuntlane? Now that sounds most promising. A willing doxy or doxies is just what I need."

Thomas kept any feeling of revulsion out of his voice. "Ah— well, the name is familiar, of course, but I've never set foot in Gropecuntlane. In truth, it has a most unsavory reputation, and at night—"

"Unsuitable for an archbishop's cleric, I know, but it holds no terror for me. In fact, the very place for what I have in mind. However, you're excused if you don't want to accompany me. Or perhaps you can recommend a better place? A friend of mine in Angers, also a cleric as it happens, always knew the best taverns and whores in the city."

Thomas recognized he was being tested in some fashion, away from the safety—and sanctity—of Canterbury's influence. Tested for what? he wondered.

"It isn't that I don't want to accompany you, my lord—"

Of a sudden Thomas was ten years old, a student at Merton Priory outside London, being dragged from sleep in the middle of the night while his bed was searched for nocturnal pollutions. Tears pricked his eyes now as they had then. He could still feel the agonizing sense of shame when such pollutions were found and he was forced to sing seven penitential psalms right then, with another thirty in the morning. The snickers and taunts and mocking looks of the other boys—it had happened so often—Dear God, why, why should he remember this now?

"You were saying, Thomas?"

The duke's voice forced him to pull his thoughts together.

"Yes. Even though I'm not a priest, my lord, I've—I've—sworn myself to celibacy." He steeled himself for the response.

The duke laughed. "God save us, I won't hold your virginity against you. I've known enough holy men who preach against the sin of fornication with one hand while fondling doxies with the other. It's a rare privilege to meet someone who actually practices what Holy Writ preaches. Just don't tell me you abstain from ale as well?"

Surprised and relieved, Thomas felt a glow of affection spread through his body. "No, my lord, not in moderation. I'll gladly share a peg-tankard with you. What says Holy Writ? 'Take a little wine for thy stomach's sake.' "

"Amen to that."

Thomas laughed, joined by the duke, the feeling of camaraderie strong between them.

They rode down the street, dismounted before the tavern and tied their horses to the wooden post. The sound of raucous laughter and voices raised in song reverberated on the night air. Leaving the men-at-arms outside, Thomas and the duke approached the tavern.

· · ·

Henry paused just inside the tavern doorway, one foot across the threshold. The air was so thick with the mingled fumes of sour wine, smoke from the tallow candles flickering in iron cressets around the walls, and the sweat of bodies pressed close together, that he felt queasy. A long counter stretched half the length of the room. On the wall behind it a variety of cloaks and tunics, hose, and even a pair of leather boots hung from short wooden poles. From the center of the room came the rattle of dice and the calls of the dicing players. Through an open doorway echoed the sound of a lute and drunken voices raised in song.

It was Henry's first experience with a London tavern; the air of expectancy pulsing through the room was contagious.

There was a moment of silence when they entered while everyone's eyes turned in their direction. This was followed by hoots of laughter as they walked toward the counter.

"Where you be from, Curtmantle?" called a voice. "The Welsh hills?"

"Brought your priest with you, did you?" shouted another. "How about your mam? Does she know you've left home?"

Henry's face grew red. He had worn an old tunic, scuffed black boots, and a brown cloak especially made for him in Poitiers.

"Why is everyone making sport of us?"

"It's your short cloak, my lord," said Thomas in a low voice. "Cloaks are much longer in England than on the Continent. It makes you look conspicuous. I should have warned you."

"But short cloaks are the latest style, according to Eleanor. Everyone in Poitiers wears one."

"This is London, my lord, and London is the world to these people. It might be best to remove it."

"I'll not have them laughing at me, by God. I've a good mind to tell them just who I am."

"I suspect it's just as well they don't know who you are, my lord."

"Well, I've no intention of removing my cloak."

Henry, spoiling for a fight, pugnaciously pushed his way through the men crowding the counter. They gave way, eyeing him askance.

"A peg-tankard of ale," he said between his teeth, "and be quick about it."

"Yes, Sir Curtmantle." The tavern keeper behind the counter gave him a toothless grin as he pushed the tankard toward him. "Right away, your lordship."

The men at the counter snickered.

Before Henry could take action, Thomas grasped his elbow and steered him firmly away from the counter.

"Pay no attention to these rogues, my lord," Thomas said, after they had made a place for themselves on a bench at one of the trestle tables filled with drinking men. "They're just playing with you now. But they'd like nothing better than an excuse to start a fight. Don't give it to them. Best we drink up and then leave."

Seething, Henry took a deep swallow of ale. "Don't call me by my title. Henry will do for tonight."

Thomas nodded, then, to Henry's astonishment, pulled a short-bladed knife from the scrip at his belt and tucked it into his sleeve.

"I thought men of the cloth weren't supposed to shed blood," he said, wishing he could take on all the rogues in the tavern single-handedly.

Thomas gave him a faint smile. "We're not. I don't intend to use it—except as I must to defend myself or you. In truth, I prefer using my fists—although it's been years since I tested them—and nothing forbids me to do that."

Henry looked belligerently around the tavern, slightly disappointed to find that no one was now paying them the slightest attention. He turned back to Thomas.

"Good with your fists, are you? You must teach me. Tell me, where does a cleric learn how to wield a knife?"

"At a noble's castle—Pevensey. I've never actually had to use the knife, but I could if needed."

The pride in his voice was evident. "I'm glad to hear it. Pevensey? That's on the Sussex coast, isn't it? What else did you learn there?"

Henry took another swallow of ale then passed the tankard to Thomas who took a small sip.

"Skill at arms; how to ride, hunt, and care for a falcon. How to serve my lord at table; the manners of a gentleman, of course." He paused. "And my place in the hierarchy."

The cleric's lip twisted, and there was an edge to his voice that made Henry give him a sharp look. "After Pevensey?"

"St. Paul's in London, then Paris, training at law—finally a home with my lord archbishop of Canterbury, who sent me to Bologna and Paris again for further grounding in canon and secular law."

"And is archdeacon of Canterbury your place in the hierarchy?"

Thomas smiled faintly. "Perhaps not my final place. It lies in God's hands."

"As well as others. A man with the abilities of a knight, the learning of a clerk, and the cunning of a lawyer, who knows his way about the world—well, that is a rarity indeed."

"So I understand."

The note of pride had given way to complacency. Amused, Henry was not displeased to see that, despite a defensive manner concerning his humble origins, Thomas had a sense of his own worth when it came to his accomplishments. Nor was he above bending a few ecclesiastical rules. Thank God for that. A cleric with no mind of his own, dancing always to Canterbury's tune, could have no place in his administration. Henry was seriously considering the idea of finding room in his household for this gifted cleric. However, it might be worth testing him further.

" 'Evening, Your Worship."

Henry looked up. A hulking man with a black patch over one eye stood over them. He gave Thomas an oily smile.

"Me name's Hugo, Your Reverence, Black Hugo they calls me. I 'as something 'ere as might interest ye."

"I don't think so," Henry said.

"I was speakin' to his holiness, not ye."

Hugo forced a place for himself next to Thomas. "I know as ye'll be interested 'cause this be the genuine article." He took something out of the soiled purse attached to his cracked leather belt and rubbed it against his sleeve. "A lock o' Our Lord's hair." He held out a lock of dirty black hair tied at one end with a piece of string.

Henry raised his brows. "Looks like horsehair to me." He was curious to see how the cleric would handle this.

Hugo shot Henry a hostile glance while Thomas took the lock of hair and made a great show of carefully examining it. "By the Mass, it *is* horsehair. I fear someone has swindled you, my good fellow." He laid it on the table.

"A pity ye can't recognize the genuine article. But mayhap ye'd be more interested in a sliver o' the true cross? Or this?" He dug into his purse and pulled out a shriveled piece of skin.

"What's that?" Thomas wrinkled his nose.

"Foreskin, ye worship."

Henry gave a shout of laughter. "God's splendor! He's got one of his own, I don't doubt."

"It be from Our Lord's circumcision. The genuine article."

"You must be mistaken," said Thomas. "I've seen the original in Rome."

"Rome, did you say?" Henry clapped his hand to his heart. "How could you have seen it in Rome when I saw it in Paris?"

He and Thomas broke into peals of laughter at the same moment.

Black Hugo shoved the relics back into his purse. He gave Henry a long hard look. "Ye with the short mantle, now I ain't seen ye in here 'afore, has I?"

"If you say so."

"I do say so. Black Hugo never forgets a face. Ye looks like a man o' means, a person of some consequence like. How about a toss of the dice for ye? Two silver pennies says I can beat ye three out of three." His eyes, black with enmity, challenged Henry.

"I don't advise this, my—Henry."

Ignoring the concern in Thomas's voice, Henry rose to his feet. His blood was racing and the frisson of danger that ran through him was exhilarating. After weeks of dealing with cautious prelates and shifty nobles, here at last was an enemy he could do battle with.

"Three out of three. I accept."

They followed Black Hugo into the center of the floor where the dicing players made room for them. Several men, obviously Hugo's cronies, knelt on the floor next to him.

"We'll use me own dice," Hugo said, accepting three dice from one of the men.

"Don't play with his dice," Thomas said in an undertone. "I'll get the guards from outside—in case we need support." He withdrew from the circle of players.

"The dice already on the floor are the only dice I'll play with." Henry went down on one knee.

Hugo gave a reluctant nod.

"Well then, let the game begin," Henry said. He was going to beat this scurvy knave. Curtmantle, was it? By God, tonight these people would have cause to remember him.

# CHAPTER 26

*T*here was a heated argument going on between two of the whores, both of them flown with ale, when Bellebelle let herself out the door of the brothel-house. One claimed the other had stolen her customer, and Hawke was trying to make peace. Frightening as he looked, the brothelmaster was not a bad sort. Much better than Gilbert had been. He rarely beat them—he almost never had to as his person was such that few disobeyed him. Nor did he ever cheat them out of their hard-earned wages. With the yowls and threats of the whores still ringing in her ears, Bellebelle trudged wearily down the narrow cobbled street deserted now by all but a few passersby. It was very dark, the moon hidden behind a bank of charcoal clouds, but unseasonably warm for January.

Coming abreast of the Blue Cock tavern Bellebelle stopped. The young girl who sold honey cakes leaned heavily against the wall. Her tray of golden cakes lay on the ground beside her.

"Ye—you be all right?" Bellebelle asked, approaching her with concern. Shivering all over, the girl was coughing into a soiled white cloth.

"Sure and I don't know," the girl gasped, doubling over. "I been walking the streets since Terce. Then cookshop told me they be wanting cakes in the tavern here. Suddenly I comes all over weak like, chilled to me very bones. I be fine in a moment."

"Here. This will keep you warm." Bellebelle took off her striped cloak and placed it over the girl's shoulders. "Let me take the tray in for you. Rest yourself. I be right back."

The cake-vendor nodded gratefully.

The tray, made of stout wood, was so heavy Bellebelle wondered how anyone found the strength to carry it. Inside the tavern she looked about for a place to set it. Amid the crowd of dicing players kneeling in the center of the floor, a youth suddenly looked up. Their eyes met for a brief moment before Bellebelle edged over to a long table and laid the tray down on one corner. Already the small of her back ached and she rubbed it before straightening.

Something about the young man's ginger hair and freckled face looked vaguely familiar but she couldn't place where, exactly, she'd seen him before. A customer perhaps? Probably. She'd had so many over the last five years they were all starting to look alike: a great faceless body heaving and grunting over her. Except for her regulars, Bellebelle doubted she'd recognize a customer for certain even if he ran into her in the street.

As she was about to leave, a loud oath made her turn. Bellebelle recognized several whores from the brothel-house hovering over the players, looking for business, as well as the familiar crowd of ale vats, and the wandering minstrels singing for a penny.

"God's blood," snarled the same voice. "It do be your roll o' the dice."

Now Bellebelle could see that the voice belonged to Black Hugo, whom she'd met on her first visit to the brothel-house. Although she'd never had any personal dealings with him, she saw him from time to time, and knew he was feared by everyone—except Hawke. Along with his cronies, Black Hugo could usually be found gambling in the tavern. A pile of silver coins lay in the center of the floor alongside several peg-tankards of ale. Black Hugo pointed to a player in a brown cloak whose head was bent over the dice. It was the same youth Bellebelle felt she'd met before.

Curious, Bellebelle joined the group of whores. The young man turned the three dice over in his hand, shook them, then shot them on to the floor. A natural seven. There was a mutter of interest from the onlookers as they pressed closer to the players.

"A lucky throw," said one of the girls.

Bellebelle could see Black Hugo's one good eye narrow as he slid two coins across the floor.

"These say ye can't do it again."

She watched the youth blow on the dice, rub them in his hands, then let them go again. Bellebelle leaned forward. Sweet Marie, another seven! Around her she heard murmurs of surprise mixed with oaths. Black Hugo, his eye smoldering like a hot coal, exchanged a few words with his ruffians who looked darkly at the dice lying on the floor.

Bellebelle wanted to tell the player to take his winnings and leave, quickly, before Black Hugo and his cronies turned on him. The youth suddenly leaned forward into the torchlight so that she could see him clearly.

"Fortune smiles on me tonight," he said.

What was it about that voice—not the usual Norman-English or Saxon accent but almost pure Norman—that sounded so familiar? Like a minstrel's song played long ago and now forgotten. But when the chord was strummed again something inside remembered. No question now—she'd met this youth before, not at the brothel-house in Gropecuntlane, but at a totally different time and place. At Gilbert's? No—but Southwark felt right. Suddenly she saw herself on London Bridge with her mother and Morgaine and some of the other whores. Then came a picture of a boy with reddish hair and gray eyes leaning over the rail at London Bridge. Bellebelle gasped aloud. Impossible! Could this really be the same boy? The one who had been so special to her—the only other person besides herself who had actually seen her magic fish? For years she had continued to think of him, then gradually the memory had faded.

What was his name—it was just on the tip of her tongue—he'd said he come back to London and he had. Her heart surged in expectation, then plummeted. Of course he wouldn't remember her. Why should he recall the filthy little urchin he met on the bridge at least nine or even ten years ago?

"Do ye mean to try another pass or not?" Black Hugo's words came out in a low growl. "That be what, we agreed, Curtmantle."

"My name is Henry. Naturally, honor demands I give you another chance to win your money back."

Henry. Yes, that was the name. In the smoky glow of the torchlight, his face was flushed; his eyes blazed with excitement.

Surely he was not going to try another pass? Bellebelle looked around the room to see if he had brought any friends with him. Yes, there were four men-at-arms near the door and a man of the cloth in a black cowled robe, an anxious look on his face, trying to signal Henry. He must now be a person of some importance to have all these attendants with him. Hadn't he told her his father was the duke or count of . . . she couldn't remember.

"Go on then," Black Hugo said between his teeth.

Other players added their coins to the pile. By now everyone in the tavern, even the most hardened drinkers at the tables, had gathered around the gamblers. A tense silence fell over the room as Henry picked up the ivory cubes and muttered a prayer. He rattled the dice then shot them on to the floor. Another seven! Holy Mary Virgin! Bellebelle, who had watched dicing players since she was old enough to walk and learned her numbers as a result, had never seen the like. There was a sharp intake of breath from the crowd. Then everyone began to talk at once.

With a great roar Black Hugo leapt to his feet, a long knife appearing magically in his fist. "The rogue switched the dice. These be cogged dice."

The crowd fell silent. Bellebelle saw all eyes turn toward Henry, not sure whether to believe Black Hugo or not. In one quick gesture, Henry scooped up the pile of coins, dropping them carefully into the pouch attached to his leather belt. Then, as if he had all the time in the world, rose to his booted feet. Bellebelle noticed he wore no sword, only a knife. The crowd moved closer, surrounding him.

"Cogged dice is always the cry of a bad loser, a spoilsport," Henry said. Unflinching, he faced the crowd of hostile faces, the threatening gaze of Hugo's cronies, and Black Hugo himself, knife pointed straight at him.

Bellebelle felt her eyes grow moist. How fearless he looked and sounded. Just as he had in London with the Flemish soldiers. Didn't have no wishbone where his backbone ought be, then, and he didn't now. The crowd noticed it too, she saw, and that held them back. But for how long?

Before Bellebelle had time to think, she heard her own voice ring through the air. "I be standing right behind him. I sees no sign of cheating. Did you?" She dug her elbow into the ribs of the whore next to her.

"Ugh—no. I sees nothing neither."

"See? The gentleman here didn't cheat none," Bellebelle said. "He won by honest means. We do vouch for him."

Black Hugo glared at her and shook his knife. She shrank back.

Henry swung round. His eyes widened in surprise although it was obvious he didn't recognize her. Swords drawn, the men-at-arms closed round him. Even the cleric drew a knife from the sleeve of his robe and shouted:

"Go now, my lord. We'll hold them back."

"This way," said Bellebelle, noting the cleric had called him "my lord." She grabbed Henry by the wrist and battled her way through the crowd toward the front entrance.

"Look at the chicken-hearted cur hide behind that cunt's skirts." Black Hugo's voice bellowed after them like the roar of a bull.

"No whoreson calls me a coward." Henry shook himself free, turned and lunged back, pulling his knife from its sheath.

The cleric sidestepped between him and Black Hugo. Bellebelle again grabbed Henry, this time by the arm, and pulled with all her might while the cleric shoved and pushed at his back. Between them, they managed to get him through the open doorway and onto the street.

Behind them she could hear Black Hugo cursing. At the doorway the cleric turned back. Bellebelle could only pray that he and the men-at-arms would keep Hugo and his cronies from following them until she had gotten Henry to safety.

Henry in tow, Bellebelle raced past the astonished cake-vendor who was still wearing Bellebelle's striped cloak, down the short distance to the brothel-house. She flung open the door, relieved to hear no sound, groped her way up the narrow staircase dragging Henry, stumbled against two customers in the dim glow of the torchlit passage, and finally reached her chamber. Once inside she shut the door behind them. After catching her breath she quickly lit the candle stub in the iron holder that sat on the oak chest.

She saw Henry look curiously round the room and her heart froze. He was sure to catch sight of the nettles and rusty leg irons hanging on the wall. How could she explain these to him?

"God's eyes, is this a brothel? Are you a tart? I thought you were selling cakes of some sort."

Bellebelle, who had just knelt to stir up the coals in the brazier, cringed at the note in his voice. She could not bring herself to tell him she was a whore. But there was no way she could avoid telling him at least part of the truth.

"Me—me friend be a whore. I—I shares this chamber with her sometimes and pays rent to the brothelmaster. When I be out selling she uses it for the customers." It was a feeble excuse but, if he were unfamiliar with the habits of London brothels and whores, he might believe her. She rose to face him. "Ye—you don't remember me, does you?"

Henry frowned. "Someone as lovely as you? I'm sure I would have remembered if I'd met you before."

"It do be about nine or ten year ago now. On London Bridge. I showed you the fish. Remember?"

After a moment's puzzled silence she saw a grin of amazement cross his freckled face. "Of course I remember. God's eyes! Can you possibly be that grubby little rat?"

She nodded.

"I would never have known you. So you sell cakes now? A thankless job I would think." He looked about him. "Is there any wine about? I could use a goblet." He walked over to the wall, fingered the leg irons curiously, raised his brows, then sat down on the bed and began to pull off his boots. "To each his own, but it's a strange place to live . . ."

"At least it be a roof over me head," Bellebelle was horrified to hear herself say. "Have you ever spent your days, rainy or bright, trudging through the muck and filth o' the streets carrying a tray that be heavier than you? I not be ashamed of where I lives."

In the long silence that followed, Bellebelle felt sure she had offended him. What had goaded her to speak so strongly? When she dared to look up she found his piercing gray eyes resting on her in a thoughtful gaze.

"Nor should you be. This is the second time tonight I've caused offense by my thoughtless words. Thank the Lord, I've been spared that kind of life." He ran a hand through his thatch of hair. "Look, I meant no harm. We must all live as best we can with the resources God has granted us. At least you're not a whore like your poor friend. Am I forgiven?"

Bellebelle swallowed, then forced herself to give him a tentative smile. All the warmth and affection she had felt for the young boy on the bridge returned in a flood. Reassured, he lay back on the coverlet and stretched out his arms in a wide gesture, as if embracing the chamber.

"By God's splendor, did you ever see the like? Three sevens in a row. What sport, eh? A game to remember." He glanced over at her. "I think you may have saved me a few scrapes and bruises tonight. What a stroke of fortune to run into you again after all this time. A fortunate night all round." He gave her a crooked smile. "I must confess I don't remember your name, though I remember everything else about our encounter. An odd name, I do recall that. Something to do with a church perhaps?"

"Bellebelle," she said, relieved that he had let the matter of the brothel drop. In truth she had probably saved him more than a few scrapes and bruises. If ever a man had murder in his heart that man was Black Hugo.

"Yes, of course, Bellebelle. But christened something else, I think you told me."

"Ykenai. No one ever calls me that." Fancy him remembering. Pleased, she poured him a cup of red wine from the wooden pitcher that was reserved only for Lord Crowmarsh. Normally she drank ale or mead, wine being a great luxury and kept solely for the customers.

"What you be doing in such a place as the Blue Cock?"

"I'm duke of Normandy now, and heir to the English throne, just as I told you I'd be. I came to London some weeks ago with the king. Today I got impatient with all the formal discussions and legal clap-trap—so I finally persuaded a cleric to show me something of the night life of the city. We stumbled upon the tavern by accident."

She handed him the wooden cup. "I remembers now what ye told me on the bridge, and do be glad you got what you been wanting."

Henry sat up, drank thirstily, then made a face. "The vintner who sold you this should be hung. When I'm king, all the wine will come from Gascony or Bordeaux. The only thing in England fit to drink is ale. You work for the tavern owner?"

"In a manner of speaking I does, but gets me wares from the cookshop," Bellebelle said, trying to remember the little she knew about the cake-vendor's life. "Sells them wherever I can." She was anxious to change the subject. "How soon will you be king then?"

Henry put the cup on the floor, lay back, and closed his eyes. "As Stephen ails so frequently I give him a year or two at the most. Then my wife, Eleanor, and I will be crowned. I also have a son so the succession is assured."

She could hardly believe her ears. "You mean—you be the duke who married Eleanor of Aquitaine?"

"Yes, a year and a half ago now. Why do you look so shocked? I'm a most fortunate man."

He was married to Eleanor of Aquitaine! Tears stung her eyes. "Oh my lord, you do be blessed! You give her flowers once too, ye told me."

"Yes, when she was queen of France. God's splendor, what a

memory!" He gave her a puzzled look. "Indeed I am blessed. But how extraordinary. You sound as if—well, as if you know Eleanor. In truth, I'm surprised you're so well-informed."

People were always sailing back and forth across the Channel, carrying the latest news and gossip with them. Most travelers stopped at the brothels and taverns, so the whores were among the first to hear what was happening. Bellebelle knew that Eleanor's marriage to the French king had been dissolved almost as soon as it happened. News that she had married the Norman duke had arrived in London not long after.

She picked her words with care. "In the streets of London we hears everything that goes on across the Channel."

"I'll remember that in future."

"Shall I look down the street, and see what's become of your men? That cleric now, I hope he be all right. 'Course he had him a knife, and were showing it."

"Master Thomas can look after himself. I'll leave in a moment."

But Henry made no move to go. He had apparently accepted her tale and was too full of himself to notice it was pierced with holes. It was foolish not to tell Henry the truth. After all, she would probably never see him again so what harm could it do?

Yet something inside her winced at the thought of admitting to him she was a whore. She desperately wanted Henry to think well of her, and now he was kindly disposed to her sorry tale of being a seller of honey cakes. But if he discovered she be a doxy? Although they needed them, Bellebelle knew well enough what men thought of whores: a vessel for their lust, like Morgaine had often said, to be used at will then discarded like an old wooden cup and tossed on the dung-heap 'til the next time they needed a willing furrow to seed. One of her customers, a prosperous farmer from Kent, had told her he came to London only to seed her furrow. It had made her feel like that was all she was, a strip of dirt.

Bellebelle felt Henry watching her through half-closed lids. Even in the dim light of the flickering candle she recognized the look.

"Come here," he said, patting a place beside him on the bed.

She walked over to the bed and sat down. Henry stroked her hair, winding a long black ringlet round and round his finger. For a long time he said nothing.

"What I remember most about you on the bridge was how easy it was to be with you, how effortless to talk to you. Everyone I know is always judging, weighing my words, looking for significance in everything I say." He gave her a sideways glance. "Do you still see the fish?"

"No, me lord. Not for years now."

"Henry, if you please." He paused. "I'm surprised you never wed. You must have had many offers."

Bellebelle shook her head. "After the hard life me mam led with a shiftless man—me father whom I never set eyes on—well, all I wanted was to get out of Southwark. Be me own mistress like." She was amazed how easily the lies rolled off her tongue.

"God's eyes! Spare me! You sound like my wife. Or my mother. A woman is never her own mistress. She always needs someone to guide and advise her, rescue her from harm, see she's not gulled by some rogue." Henry looked impatient. "But that appears to be something certain women refuse to acknowledge. In truth . . ." He smiled. "You know, you're much too fair to be tramping about London selling cakes."

"I doesn't know about that."

He ran a finger down her neck. "Well, I does. Has it ever occurred to you that your lot would probably be much easier if you were a whore, like your friend?"

Bellebelle looked away so she wouldn't have to meet his eyes. "I doesn't know. It be a hard life too. Ye—you—be scorned and outcast—like that dog in Holy Writ I heard tell about."

"Pariah?"

"Aye, that be the word. Work in a brothel be like being in the Clinke, and the brothelmaster, the jailer. Ye—you—can't come and go as you please, always having to wear—" She stopped abruptly.

"The Clinke?"

"A Southwark prison."

"Go on. You were being very eloquent." His voice was unexpectedly gentle. "I hadn't realized how badly off such poor wretches are."

"No more to say." Bellebelle took a deep breath. "Tell me about your son."

"My son, William?" Henry's face broke into a ready smile. "I haven't yet seen him. Think of it, Bellebelle, Louis of France was married to my wife for fourteen years and had only two daughters. After less than a year of marriage my beloved Eleanor gives me a son. What do you think of that, eh?"

"Ye must have a mighty hammer and anvil with which to forge sons, my lord," she said, "and a willing wife to receive them into her belly."

She was on the point of adding that Eleanor of Aquitaine was someone she had long admired, when Henry burst into a shout of laughter.

"Now there's a bawdy wench! A mighty hammer and anvil, eh? I like that! By God, I've a good mind to show you myself." He pulled her down on top of him in a great hug. "You're right about my wife, though. Willing certainly. Also charming and beautiful and oh so loving. She sparkles like wine from the vineyards of Champagne. I'm going to tell you a secret. I have the feeling you can keep a secret, Belle. I love my wife dearly."

Bellebelle stared at him, not understanding. Henry rolled her away from him and propped himself up on one elbow with a sigh.

"No, no, that's not it. It's more than love. I feel consumed by her, almost overwhelmed, as if—" He sighed again. "I think when people love too much they give up something of themselves, allowing someone to possess them. I'm putting it badly but it's difficult to explain. Anyway, no one knows how I feel. Certainly not Eleanor. Not even my mother."

Bellebelle felt a sharp prick in her heart, as if Henry had just plunged a knife into her breast. Of course he would love such a woman. It was only fitting, and she didn't begrudge Eleanor the tiniest morsel of Henry's love. Why then did she ache inside? Were it because no one had ever loved her like that and probably never would?

"But why doesn't you tell her how you feel?" she asked finally. "Surely it would please her."

"Indeed it would. Nothing would please her more. But it would also give her power over me. If you give away your power, people use it against you. Love is a dangerous weapon in the wrong hands."

Bellebelle thought for a moment. She had only loved her mother and Morgaine, and a stray three-legged dog she fed for years. "But surely you can trust her not to harm you?"

"Can I? No one can be wholly trusted, Belle. Didn't you once tell me you were raised on the streets of Southwark? I would've thought you had learned that as the first lesson of survival."

Bellebelle, who never expected anything of anyone, could not think of what to say. Such matters never occurred to her. But considering it now—in truth, she neither trusted nor distrusted; you just accepted what was there and accommodated to it. That was how she had survived. How to explain that to him?

Henry was watching her, his eyes shiny with that same look of carnal lust she saw every day of her life. Strange. The lust never seemed to be connected with her even though it was released through her. Nor had she, herself, ever felt it—or met a whore who had. The whole idea of what men wanted and so eagerly sought remained something of a mystery. Vaguely disappointed and almost without thinking she rolled down her woollen stockings and pulled off her blue dress.

"How did you know I wanted you to do that?" Henry looked surprised. "I knew you couldn't still be a virgin . . . not living in these parts and doing what you do." He undid his belt, and laid the pouch on the floor.

She gave him a half-smile, making no objection when he slipped off her chemise.

"Trust," he repeated, pulling off his hose and tunic. "It's important to have someone close to you whom you can trust." He rolled her over onto her back, almost as if he were thinking of something else, and, without preamble, slowly entered her. "Someone to confide in who isn't involved in your ordinary life." She winced at his size, larger than what she was used to. "Someone—am I hurting you? Sorry." He slowed his pace. "Someone who is absolutely safe, who can cause you no harm, offer no threat."

Bellebelle wondered if he wanted her to lie absolutely still, as some did, or move with him, or call him sweet names. Dare she interrupt his flow of words to ask? There were tricks she'd learned that would increase his pleasure but if she were too artful he might suspect. Best to do nothing at all.

"That cleric I met, Thomas, I've taken to him, but with a churchman . . ."—his breath quickened—". . . you can never be wholly sure . . . and Eleanor . . . I always wonder . . . will she be more loyal to Aquitaine . . . than to me? Nothing is more . . . important . . . than loyalty." Suddenly he spent his seed and his body sagged against hers. For a moment he was silent.

"Well," Henry said, brisk again as he rolled off her. "That was sorely needed. It helps to air one's thoughts." He kissed the tip of her nose. "I must find my men. Poor Thomas will be beside himself with worry by now."

He jumped off the bed and began pulling on his hose and tunic.

"I have a proposition for you, Bellebelle. It saddens me to think of all the deprivations such a gentle creature as yourself must endure day after day. How would you like to stop selling honey cakes, leave these detestable lodgings, and belong entirely to me? Be at my disposal when and as needed."

Bellebelle slipped on her chemise while she searched his face. Was he jesting? Could he be so cruel?

"I would like nothing so much," she whispered, her heart in her mouth. "Do ye mean this, my lord?"

He sat down to pull on his boots. "Henry. I only say what I mean." He winked. "But do I always mean what I say? In this case I do. Give me some time to arrange my affairs here. If I were already king it would be a simple matter but as I'm not—in any case leave it to me." He leaned over and nuzzled her neck. "It won't all be a bed of roses, you know. People who find out will call you the king's whore. Revile you for that. Be jealous of you. Are you prepared to live with these thorns?"

"Oh yes. But your wife, the queen to be. What will—she say?" The idea that she might in any way cause Eleanor pain or sadness was like a heavy weight pressing against her chest. She would rather stay where she was.

"This has nothing whatsoever to do with Eleanor. Still, she must never know." Henry gave her a stern look. "Never. And if you're discreet she won't. After all you're not likely to move in the same circles, are you? However, eventually it might be best to move you out of London entirely." He stood up and fastened his scruffy leather belt around his waist. "It behooves a king to have a mistress, you know. Or even more than one. A testimony to his manhood. My grandfather had upwards of twenty bastards."

Bellebelle felt tears well up in her eyes. Henry, hardly pausing for breath, did not notice but strode to the door still talking.

"Can you be found here or in the tavern?" he asked, opening the door.

"Leave word at the tavern," she said quickly as she pulled on her chemise.

Henry stormed through the doorway like a whirlwind and strode down the passage, never once looking back. She could hear him jump down the steps whistling a tavern tune. When he left, Bellebelle collapsed on the bed in a flood of tears. Was it really going to happen? Would she truly be free of whoring at last? She had once

believed her dream of having a better life would be fulfilled in
Gropecuntlane. Matters had not turned out as she expected. But
this time—this time it seemed as if the dream were almost within
her grasp. She wanted it so badly that she felt her heart would break
into tiny splinters if she were denied it now.

On the other hand, how could she bring herself to do anything
that might hurt her idol, Eleanor—who had saved her in the Lady
Chapel at St. Mary Overie? But Henry does love her, she argued
with herself. He doesn't love me, he just wants me to listen and bed
with him sometimes. What she has is much more precious. I'm not
taking anything away from her.

Bellebelle suddenly thought of Hawke and caught her breath.
How could she persuade him to let her go? Everything seemed
against her—Suddenly she saw the pouch with the coins Henry had
won.

Bellebelle looked for her cloak before remembering the cake-vendor still had it. She grabbed the pouch from the floor by the bed and
dashed down the passage and staircase. Clad only in her chemise,
she stepped out into the street. At the far end of Gropecuntlane a
group of horsemen were just disappearing around the corner.

Voices raised in song echoed from the tavern. A drunken customer dressed only in shirt and hose lurched through the open
door. A sudden gust of wind made her shiver; the tavern sign with
its painted blue cock creaked back and forth on leather hinges.
Three men darted out of a narrow alley and ran down the street
chased by the watch shouting threats. From an upstairs window
came the sound of a grunt followed by a squeal.

Bellebelle rubbed a hand over her still-wet eyes and stumbled
back into the brothel-house. The entire evening felt so strange.
Mayhap she'd only dreamed it. Only in dreams did a Southwark
whore ever become mistress of the king of England.

# CHAPTER 27

"*B*less my soul, he's not yet crowned and already Henry of Anjou is causing trouble," said the archbishop of Canterbury to Thomas Becket after Prime the following morning, as he handed him the gold crosier of his office.

They were in the sacristy and Thomas was helping Theobald remove the gold-embroidered dalmatic, alb, and gem-encrusted miter that he had worn for the liturgical services.

"First he puts everyone's nose out of joint at the council meeting, then risks his life in a gambling den, finally disappears with an unsavory cake-vendor," said Roger de Pont l'Évêque, the archbishop's chief secretary and a man of some consequence in the Primate's household. "Couldn't you have stopped him, Bailhache?"

Thomas stiffened but refrained from comment.

"Might as well expect Thomas to grab a wild boar by the tail, Roger. What a merry chase this prince will lead us." Theobald sniffed. "Typical Norman behavior." He put on the black monastic robe Roger handed him.

Thomas repressed a smile. Despite the apparent mildness of his manner, Theobald, Norman down to his toenails, exhibited all the flinty stubbornness of his race. Thomas continued to ignore Pont l'Évêque. A scion of an old and honorable Norman family, he wore a perpetual sneer on his face. The two had been rivals for Theobald's favor since Thomas first came to the archbishop's household in January of the year 1144.

Theobald left the sacristy, followed by Thomas and Roger, and walked stiffly to his own quarters in the Bishop's Palace. At the door, he turned to Roger.

"Leave us, my son. I would speak with Thomas alone."

Pont l'Évêque bowed and shot Thomas a venomous look which Thomas rewarded with an icy smile.

"I'm not easy in my mind about Duke Henry, Thomas, but we'll get to that in a moment," said Theobald, seating himself in his cushioned wooden armchair and indicating a stool for Thomas. "First I wish to ask you about the details of your trip to Normandy . . ." He let his voice trail off into one of his long silences, grown more frequent of late.

Used to Theobald's habits, Thomas looked enviously around the resplendent chamber with its vaulted ceiling. Elaborate tapestries depicting the Nativity in blue, white, and scarlet wools hung on the walls. Enameled reliquaries, several gold caskets, a large book bound in ivory and metal that Thomas had long coveted, were laid out on polished oak tables. A huge silver crucifix blazing with pearls, rubies, sapphires, and lapis lazuli dominated the chamber from its place of pride on one wall. Two goblets of wine and a silver platter of honey cakes rested on a table in front of them.

Thomas thought of Duke Henry but an image of Roger de Pont l'Évêque's face imposed itself in his mind and would not budge. Bailhache he had called him; the name still rankled even after ten years.

Thomas saw an image of himself at the age of twenty-four, trying to mask his excitement as he approached the archbishop's residence at Harrow. He owed this wondrous opportunity to his father, who had been a childhood playmate of Theobald in Rouen. Fresh from the lecture halls of Paris, he was eager to begin his duties in the Primate's household. It was Epiphany, and Thomas was nearing the manor house in company with a Saxon woodcutter who, visiting in London, had been told to escort the new clerk to Harrow. The woodcutter had complained of a pain in his arm and asked Thomas to hold the new ax he was carrying.

Thus, when Thomas entered Theobald's residence he had the ax in his hand. A group of clerks loitering in the hall greeted the woodchopper with familiarity and condescension.

"What have we here? The woodchopper's son?" A short slender youth of about Thomas's age, with sandy hair and arrogant blue eyes, had looked him up and down. "Wipe your boots before you take a step further, my good fellow."

Thomas crimsoned to the roots of his hair as he repressed a surge of anger. "I'm Master Thomas of West Cheap, a lawyer and a clerk, asked by the archbishop to work for him."

"Cutting wood?"

The other clerks grinned.

"He's expecting me."

"Indeed? Well, who would have thought it. West Cheap, you say. Are people actually from such places?" The clerk waited for the laughter of his fellows to subside. "I'm his chief clerk, Master Roger de Pont l'Évêque. I can't think why you brought the hatchet except to cut firewood. Is that what they're teaching student lawyers in Paris these days?"

The other clerks snickered.

Thomas handed the ax back to the woodcutter as if it were a live coal, fearful he might slice Pont l'Évêque's face in two. The bastard had obviously been expecting him and knew perfectly well who he was.

"This way, Bailhache," said Roger.

Bailhache. The ax-bearer. Thomas had never hated anyone in his life as much as hated this sneering clerk. The name Bailhache had stuck. He and Roger had detested each other ever since.

"What was I saying?" Theobald's voice recalled him to the present moment.

"You asked about my trip to Normandy."

"Ah yes. The finer points. Now, I want to discuss—tell me, what is your impression of the duchess Eleanor? I understand she is a great beauty, very well informed, with opinions on everything."

"She is all of that, Your Grace. In truth, I believe her to be a far more dangerous source of trouble than her headstrong husband—who has impressed me most favorably, by the way. Because she is older, was a queen for so long, and has a free hand in Aquitaine, I think she may exert a great influence on the less experienced duke."

Theobald held up a triumphant finger. "Just as I suspected. A meddler in the affairs of men. When I remember the trials Abbé Suger and Bernard of Clairvaux—may God give them rest—underwent at her hands." He crossed himself. "And poor Louis of France was a mere shadow of his former self, a mere shadow, by the time he was persuaded to rid himself of her. Not to mention how that libertine wrecked the holy crusade. She is no friend to Holy Church."

"That was my impression as well," said Thomas.

Theobald leaned forward with a discreet cough. "In his innocence, I doubt our duke is even aware of his wife's sin against nature."

"Sin against nature?"

"The—the unfortunate business with the uncle in Antioch."
Theobald's face flushed with distaste. "Rumor, of course. Still,
Louis believed it to be true, or so he told the pope, who told Bernard
of Clairvaux, who told me. All in the strictest confidence, of
course."

"Of course." Thomas had already heard the rumor but discounted it. Now he wondered.

"When I think of the Conqueror's noble wife, Thomas, and
Stephen's saintly queen, my heart is filled with disquiet at the
thought of this unprincipled creature wearing the English crown.
Even that virago, the Empress Maud, whatever else you may say of
her, was a woman of unsullied reputation."

"The Lady Eleanor is highly valued in her duchy, Your Grace,
which is of some advantage to England regardless of the fact she is
no friend to Holy Church."

"We are all aware of the wealth of Aquitaine. But it does not appear to have occurred to anyone that the Lady Eleanor's marriages—first to France then to England—may have serious,
far-reaching consequences. The Normans and the French have always been at each other's throats." Theobald sighed and shook his
head. "And now . . ."

"Eleanor's marriage to Henry of Anjou may sow the seeds of future conflict?"

"Not may but *will*, Thomas. We must ask God, without whose
favor our efforts are of no avail, to guide us in this matter so that in
time, Louis may come to regard the duke as ally rather than enemy."

Thomas looked attentively at his master's grave face while
Theobald picked up a goblet of wine then set it down again.

"You know what the duke told me? That the crown was his by
heredity right and the last true monarch was his grandfather, the
first Henry. He says that because Stephen was never legally king, he
will annul all the acts Stephen has passed, regardless of whether
they were just or necessary—"

The archbishop paused for breath before again picking up his goblet and sipping ruby-colored wine. "Thus virtually every legal decision of the last eighteen years becomes invalid at a single stroke."

"But chaos would result. No man could hold a clear title to land." Thomas was genuinely shocked that Henry, obviously a man of insight and intelligence, did not see the disastrous consequences of such a course.

"Exactly. However, I may have persuaded the young hothead of the dire results of such an action." He set down the goblet with a firm hand. "The point is that left to his own devices our impulsive Angevin would have followed such a course when he attained the throne. Ergo, he must not be left to his own devices."

Intrigued, Thomas waited. If he knew his master, and he flattered himself that he knew him very well indeed after ten years in his service, he had already arrived at the solution before presenting the problem.

Theobald rose painfully to his feet and began to hobble back and forth in front of Thomas, his frail hands clasped to his breast.

"The duke has much to recommend him—a fine, educated mind, an ability to lead and inspire, and an instinct, I feel, for true justice. Something this realm needs desperately. He has the makings of a great king, and the necessary support of the baronage, the clergy, and the administrative services. Now, having said that, let me hasten to add that Henry's judgment is still undeveloped, and he lacks experience. He will need guidance."

The archbishop paused in front of Thomas. Their eyes met in a long look.

"Not the guidance of an Aquitainian wife," Thomas said slowly.

"Whose loyalty is to her own duchy first, as she proved again and again with Louis, and who is hostile to the interests of Holy Church."

And to me personally, Thomas was about to say before thinking better of it. He had not told anyone of the instant enmity that flashed between himself and Henry's wife.

"Like her whole family before her," Theobald continued. "Root and branch. She has a spirit rife with rebellion—just like the land she rules. The Aquitainians imbibe heresy and pleasure with their mother's milk. Under her influence our future king may draw to himself unwise influences who do not serve the interests of the English crown."

Theobald lowered himself onto his seat. "Precautions must be taken. One of our own must be close to the king to counter this pernicious influence."

"A spy within the walls is better than an army without?"

"Just so, Thomas, just so."

Thomas reached for his goblet of wine. "Who do you suggest?"

"When he becomes king, young Henry will need a chancellor. One skilled in administration and loyal to Holy Church. Who better to fulfill this position than yourself?"

Thomas gasped and almost dropped his goblet. "I? Chancellor of England?" He knew he was staring stupidly at the archbishop but could not help himself. "I'm only the son of a poor burgess in Cheapside," he blurted out. "I hold no land. I've only served in your household. I'm not worthy to be chancellor!"

The archbishop gave him a dry look. "Tut, tut, excessive humility ill becomes you, my son. Do you tell me you are not ambitious to better yourself?"

"But—am I qualified for such a post?"

"How many men have been educated at schools in London and Paris? Studied law in Bologna and Auxerre? Tried cases before the Curia? I think we both know the answer to your question."

Stunned, Thomas could not yet credit the enormity of the good fortune bestowed upon him. He knew himself to be an efficient lawyer with a gift for negotiations, but chancellor of England! An opportunity to work with the young duke with whom he had already formed a bond of friendship! It was beyond anything he had ever dreamed for himself.

"Be discreet in this matter. I have said nothing to the duke as yet, but I feel sure he will be guided by me. It was obvious he took to you right away." Theobald rose to his feet, signifying the interview was at an end. He accompanied Thomas to the door of his chamber.

"The Lady Eleanor will not like this," Thomas felt bound to say.

"Why should she object? You will hardly be at the duke's side as a representative of Holy Church, which, I agree, she would not like. You will be a member of the new king's administration, like his marshall or his chamberlain. You will ride with him, hunt with him, accompany him on such misadventures as last night—it was this escapade, in fact, which decided me. It should be an easy matter to insinuate your way into his confidence, inspire his trust, guide his decisions, and counter all undesirable influences."

Theobald blithely rolled these off as if they were talleys or revenues rather than the daunting challenges Thomas knew them to be. He was again tempted to tell the archbishop of the hostility between himself and the future queen but held his tongue. Such a revelation might prompt Theobald to change his mind and recommend someone else for chancellor. Here was his chance to leap into prominence and show the world what he could do. He had no intention of losing this golden opportunity.

"Your Grace, I will endeavor to serve Holy Church to the best of my abilities."

"As you have demonstrated time and again." Theobald patted him on the arm.

Still in a pleasurable state of shock, Thomas withdrew. He could hardly wait to see the expression on Roger de Pont l'Évêque's face when he heard the news.

When Thomas left, Theobald sank exhausted onto his chair, then passed a trembling hand over his veined forehead. Had he made the right decision? One that would truly serve Holy Church? He had acted on some deep instinct, sensing the empathy between the duke and his archdeacon at the council meeting last night.

Becket was a model of efficiency with a fine legal turn of mind and modest eloquence. In addition, the man had risen well above his humble beginnings and was anxious to better himself. He shouldered responsibility with ease; kept the Commandments, and prayed conscientiously. What more could one ask? But at the back of Theobald's mind lurked a faint reservation. Was it the hastiness of his decision? Or something more deep-seated? In truth, something had always disturbed him about Thomas. What was it? His overly formal manner? The reserve that kept others at arm's length? The sense that he always held himself under a tight rein? Perhaps all of these.

The answer eluded him and Theobald closed his eyes with a weary sigh. Although Stephen was still nominally king, in Theobald's mind Henry's monarchy had already begun. It was now that all the pieces on the board must be set in place so that there would be a smooth transition from one reign to the next. He and Henry had privately discussed various nobles to occupy the principal posts in the new administration, and had already decided as co-justiciars, Robert of Leicester and Richard de Lucy, both holdovers from the last reign. John the Marshal, whose grandfather and father before him had also been marshals of England, was another one. But until that moment in the council when he had seen the spark ignite between the duke and his archdeacon he had never thought of Thomas Becket as chancellor.

The post did not officially rank as importantly as chief justiciar, who represented the king when he was absent. Even the posts of constable, marshal, steward, and chamberlain stood higher than that of chancellor of England. But that position held the greatest potential of power. The chancellor was the king's personal assistant and secretary, always at his side. Privy to all decisions. For an ambitious man there was no limit to the influence he might wield.

Becket was the perfect man for the post in every way, Theobald argued with himself. Then why was he questioning his own judgment? He sat up straighter. Of course. The truth was that though he trusted Thomas, was fond of him, and relied upon his judgment, the archdeacon's true character, complex, remote, had always eluded him. And though scrupulous in abiding by the rules, he was not a man who served God for love of Him. Yes, he had it now.

Unlike some of his other deacons, Theobald knew Thomas to be chaste—not, he now suspected, because he was in minor orders and had taken a vow of chastity—but because his essentially cold nature had no inclination toward joys of the flesh. He had not given up anything that he really wanted in the first place. Did Thomas feel strongly about anything or anyone? If so, Theobald had never seen evidence of it. What then was the main spur that goaded his archdeacon? Self-interest?

It was a disturbing throught.

Yet he had no doubt that Thomas—who could be all things to all men—would make an excellent chancellor. His very lack of spiritual fervor would be an advantage, and probably endear him to the future king. Henry would need a strong man beside him to help govern an empire that stretched from the Scottish marches to the Pyrenees. Thomas already served Holy Church with unswerving zeal and loyalty. There was no reason to suppose he would not serve the English crown, the Angevin realm as a whole, in like manner. Unlike the duchess Eleanor, who would always put the interests of Aquitaine first.

He *had* made the right choice. Theobald gave an audible sigh of relief, pushing aside the persistent niggle of doubt that refused to be stilled. He could put his mind to rest regarding the future king of England. That left only the unsolved question of the lady of Aquitaine.

# CHAPTER 28

*O*n an evening in mid-March, two months after she had met Henry again, Bellebelle walked down the street toward the Blue Cock. Business was slow tonight and when the bells rang for Compline, she had decided her working day was over. Bellebelle had made it a point to visit the tavern every night after her last customer was gone, to see if Henry had left word for her. Hawke had not objected, when she told him she was trying to solicit customers. She would tell him the same tonight—if he should catch her there.

About to enter the tavern, Bellebelle came to an abrupt stop. Through the open door she could see the beak-nosed cleric Henry had called Thomas sitting at one of the tables. He seemed to be alone, at least Henry wasn't with him as far as she could tell. Was the cleric waiting for her?

If the cleric saw her in her striped cloak he would at once know the truth about her. Bellebelle quickly slipped off her cloak and hid it behind the wooden post used for tethering horses.

The moment the cleric saw her enter he beckoned with an impatient finger.

Her heart thumping, Bellebelle threaded her way around the dicing players in the middle of the floor, and pushed past the drinkers at the counter.

"I've been waiting for you. No cakes tonight?" the cleric asked with a dark unblinking stare.

"I—I sold them all. Left me tray at the cookshop."

"My lord duke of Normandy asked me to find you. He's very busy at the moment and soon returns to Rouen, but he has not forgotten you and, in fact, has made arrangements for your future welfare."

The cleric's disapproving expression, the scornful note in his voice made it all too clear what he thought of these "arrangements."

Speechless, Bellebelle nodded.

"I've found temporary lodgings for you in a decent quarter of London near St.-Martin-le-Grand. If you can be ready the day after tomorrow, someone will be waiting for you at the tavern by Nones."

So Henry had not forgotten about her! Filled with joy, she even wanted to throw her arms around the cleric.

"Yes," she said. "I be ready."

The cleric rose to his feet, towering over her like a thin black crow. "It is a great honor for someone such as yourself to become the paramour of a future king. I hope you realize your good fortune and will conduct yourself accordingly."

"I do," she whispered. "Oh I do, Father, and I be ever so grateful. Please tell Henry—the duke what I said."

"I'm an archdeacon, not a priest. My name is Thomas Becket."

Bellebelle wondered what she should call him.

The cleric gave her a curt nod, then handed her a buckskin pouch jangling with coins. "Should you need to provide yourself with any-thing—"

"I still has the money Henry won," Bellebelle said. "He left it be-hind but I saved it all for him. Every penny."

"Very commendable, I'm sure. Nevertheless, my lord duke wanted you to have this. Are there any questions?"

She shook her head. The cleric gave her another look that made her feel less than the dirt beneath his feet, then walked out without a backward glance.

"Who gave you leave to come here?" The sound of Hawke's voice made Bellebelle jump. She hid the bag of coins behind her back.

"No customers since Vespers. I thought I—might find one here. Like I been doing. You didn't say anything before."

"No, and I haven't seen any customers either, and you been here most every night." He paused. "But looks like you did well for yourself just now." Hawke pulled at his chin. "That churchman do look familiar. I knows I seen him somewhere before. You servicing him later tonight, Belle?"

"No."

It was not surprising that Hawke should be in the tavern; he came almost every night. It was just her ill fortune that he should have seen her encounter with the cleric.

"What'd he want then?"

"He—he wanted to know if there be boys at the brothel. Then—then he quick changed his mind." It wasn't true, of course, but if the cleric *had* visited the brothel Bellebelle felt certain he would have asked for a boy.

Hawke spat on the floor. "Them clerics! Full of the same unnatural vices as the rest of us but hiding their sins behind their cassocks. Makes me fair sick it does." He paused and shook his head. "Can't place where I seen him, but I knows I have. A tankard of ale might perk up me wits." He gave her a sharp glance. "Go on then, get back to the house. You never know who might turn up, even this late. I'll be along shortly."

He went up to the long counter and Bellebelle quickly left the tavern, retrieving her cloak outside. How was she going to tell Hawke she was leaving? She didn't dare say that the future king of England would be providing for her. For one thing Hawke probably wouldn't believe her but if he did, there be no telling what he would do. In order not to lose her services, Hawke might see to it that Henry learned the truth about her whoring—which could easily destroy this one chance of escape. Not that Hawke hadn't been fair with her over the years. He had been. But he was first and foremost a man of business and wouldn't want to forfeit the money she brought him.

Bellebelle decided to pray to the Holy Virgin/Eleanor—still one and the same in her head—and ask for guidance.

When she reached the safety of her chamber and lit the candles, Bellebelle sat on the bed and, pulling the drawstring of the bag, poured a handful of shining silver coins on to the faded coverlet. Holy Mary, this was more money than she had ever seen in her life. This, combined with Henry's winnings—She gasped. The answer lay right in front of her. Mary/Eleanor had guided her without even being asked.

There came a knock at the door. Quickly she gathered up the coins and dropped them back into the bag, sliding it under the coverlet.

"Bellabella, *mia cara*," called a voice through the door.

It was the Italian scribe from the Temple who often came late in the evening. The thought of his pounding away at her, crying out to Santa Maria in the heat of his lust, plus the overpowering stink of garlic, made her flesh crawl. As of this moment she was no longer a whore and the sooner everyone found out the better.

"I be unwell," Bellebelle called out. "Get another whore tonight." When she had her courses she refused to service anyone. Now she held her breath.

The scribe shouted a stream of Italian—it sounded like curses—then stomped off down the passage.

A short while later, without any warning, Hawke burst into the chamber. "What pig's piss is this about being unwell? You been with customers all day. Signor Luigi, he's very upset. He's a good, steady one, Belle, and I won't have his nose put out of joint."

When Hawke was disgruntled his scar seemed to quiver like a crimson snake. He walked over to the bed, hands on hips, and glared down at her.

"He's not the only one complained today either. That vintner from Charing, he says you didn't look interested when he showed hisself to you. I had my work cut out to calm him down."

The vintner from Charing, who only wanted to abuse himself in front of her, demanded that she watch him every second as if she enjoyed it.

"I seen him so many times how can I keeps on pretending I enjoys it? Especially when I doesn't."

"Because he's paying you, girl, that's why, and don't you forget it. You're not his judge, Belle, and whether you enjoys it or not got nothing to do with anything. Business is business." Hawke gave her an exasperated look. "What's got into you lately? Your mind not on your work these days, and that's a fact."

"I—I has other things to think about."

"Such as what? I'm losing patience, girl. I'm going to tell Signor Luigi you're ready now and it was all a big mistake. When he comes you apologize, hear?"

Trembling, Bellebelle got to her feet. "No. No more customers, Hawke. I—I be leaving."

Hawke gave an incredulous laugh. "Leaving? Are you daft? To go where? This be the best brothel in the city."

"I know." Bellebelle took a deep breath. "I—I got me a steady customer who wants to set me up private-like."

"Who? Why didn't he ask me? You're my property and you can't go nowheres without my leave." Hawke unbuckled the heavy leather belt studded with silver that he always wore around his ample girth. "You be lying to me, girl, I can always tell. Now, I never touched you, has I? Not once in all the time you been here. But, by Christ, I'll beats the truth out of you if I has to."

Bellebelle backed away. "I not be lying, I swears it. There do be someone who wants me to belong only to him."

Hawke lifted the belt, then brought it down so that it fell within a hair's breadth of her shoulder, hitting the floor instead. Terrified, she thought her heart would stop, and held her hands out in front of her in a placating gesture.

"Hawke, please—"

"The truth, Belle." Hawke lifted the belt again then slashed it directly across her hip.

She screamed; the sharp bite of the studded leather cut right through her gown and chemise into her flesh. It burned like fire. If he continued to beat her, her body might be so marked that Henry would become suspicious. That mustn't happen.

"All right! It's the king."

Hawke, his arm raised, slowly let it fall. "King? What king you mean?"

"He not be king yet. Duke Henry of Normandy."

Hawke eyed her suspiciously. "Better not lie to me, girl, I'm warning you."

Bellebelle turned, ran to the bed, and snatched the pouch from beneath the coverlet.

"Here. I be going to give this to ye—you—anyways to make up for me leaving. You can see I not be lying." With shaking fingers she held out the pouch.

Dropping the belt to the floor, Hawke grabbed the pouch and examined its contents. "By Christ, someone wants you mighty bad that be for sure." His voice had changed.

For a long moment Hawke stared at her, the candlelight casting shadows across the hairless head and puckered face. Then he snapped his fingers.

"That cleric I saw you with be Thomas Becket, archbishop's deacon. Now I remember. They do say he's to be the next king's chancellor. It's all beginning to come together. Well, well, who'd a thought it, eh?"

He bent to pick up his belt and, holding the pouch in his teeth, buckled it round his middle. "You should have told me right away,

Belle. Where'd you meet Duke Henry of Normandy? I never seen him here."

She told him about her first meeting with Henry on the bridge, how they had met in the tavern, and she had sneaked him into the brothel.

"That be the whole tale, I swears it." Bellebelle gave Hawke an apprehensive look. "But you won't tell him, will you?"

Hawke didn't say anything. She could see him turning the matter over in his head, wondering what would best serve his interests. Bellebelle felt the sweat gather under her arms. After a long pause, during which she felt her life hang in the balance, he slowly shook his head. She almost wept with relief.

"Well, you're a sly one all right, and that's a fact. It not be in my interests to tell the duke about you. It be more in my interests to have you become his private doxy."

She frowned. "But then you lose me services."

"Use your wits, girl. While she lasts, a duke's—or king's—whore be a person of consequence. When you comes back here I can sell you for more. A lot more."

"But I never coming back!"

Hawke gave her a pitying look. "Don't be daft. How long you think Duke Henry's going to stay interested in one tart? You smarter than that, Belle. You better pray King Stephen dies soon, that's all I got to say. The sooner the duke becomes king, the better for you."

Bellebelle stared at him. Henry wouldn't tire of her. He might amuse himself with other whores, as all men did, but he would always come back to her, she'd make sure of that.

"You be a good girl, Belle, never caused me no trouble, and I like you," Hawke continued, "so's I'll give you some advice."

Bellebelle wanted to shut her ears to anything else he might have to say.

"May be the duke wouldn't like you being a whore, but lying to him be worse. Men don't like to be lied to, see, makes them feel like fools, like someone took advantage of them. One day the duke'll find out. No telling what he do then. But you tell him straight out, see, and you'll last longer. Now that's a fact."

Bellebelle smiled. She had no intention of telling Henry anything about her past.

Hawke held up the pouch of coins. "I'll take half for my trouble in replacing you. You best keep the rest in case you gets asked why you spent so much so fast with nothing to show for it."

There was no reason to tell Hawke she still had Henry's winnings. Bellebelle watched while he poured a third of the coins onto the bed. "Take that with you. The other third I'll put aside for you when you comes back." He paused. "If you still got your looks, o' course, and not be infected. You might need the money then. Can't say fairer than that, now can I?"

Bellebelle walked with him to the door. "I won't need the money, Hawke," she said. He was going to let her go without trouble and she felt dizzy with gratitude. "Or ever have to come back, because Henry says he'll take care of me. But I'll never forgets you letting me go like this."

Hawke shook his head. "Too trusting by half, Belle, that's your trouble." His wintery eyes warmed for an instant. One hand lightly brushed her shoulder in a gesture that was not quite affection. "Money'll be here when you needs it—and you will."

He left, closing the door softly behind him. In the next chamber someone started laughing. The sound of drunken singing wafted up from the street. A door banged shut. Hawke was wrong, Bellebelle thought. She felt lightheaded, her spirits flown with confidence. She would never need Hawke or the brothel or the money ever, ever again.

# CHAPTER 29

# Rouen, Normandy, 1154

*E*leanor watched with concern as the physician laid his hand on Henry's forehead.

"A high fever," he said. "The duke must be bled, then purged."

Henry groaned. "No . . . too much to do . . . not ill." He struggled to sit up but immediately fell back on the pillow.

"Of course you're ill," Eleanor said, trying to hide her alarm. She had never seen Henry so weak. "You must do as he says."

They were in her mother-in-law's solar in the ducal palace at Rouen, which had been turned into a sick room for Henry's benefit. After more than a year in England, he had finally returned to Normandy in late April. A month later she had accompanied Henry on a trip through Aquitaine which had been cut short to handle an uprising in Anjou. This was followed by a skirmish with King Louis's forces on the Vexin border, from which Henry had just recently returned.

It was now mid-October and for the past three days he had been lying ill of a fever, refusing to allow Eleanor to call in the physician. The Empress Maud was away, visiting the abbey at Fontevrault, so Eleanor had no one to consult. This morning Henry had not been able to get out of bed; his skin was so hot that Eleanor, fearing for his life, had overrode his protestations and called in the physician.

Under her watchful eye, the physician placed leeches over Henry's body, relieving him of a half-pint of blood, then proceeded to mix the purge. In the fifth month of her second pregnancy, Eleanor gagged when the physician lifted Henry's head and poured the evil-smelling concoction down his throat. Within an hour it proved effective as a purge, but the fever did not abate.

Despite continued bleedings and purges, Henry grew steadily worse. His wasted body and incoherent gibberish drove Eleanor to the point of distraction, increasing her fear. Hourly she was on the point of sending to Fontevrault for the empress, but stubborn pride made her hesitate. Her imposing mother-in-law was the only woman who had ever made Eleanor feel inadequate. If she could not care for her own husband . . . what kind of a wife would the empress think her? What kind of a wife would *Henry* think her?

How she wished she had listened more closely when her mother, aunt, and other relatives in Aquitaine had tried to teach her about brewing herbs and simples. It had all been written down, some in Provençal, some in Latin, she remembered. Surely she must have taken some of that material with her when she left Poitou. In France she had never nursed Louis or anyone else, leaving such care in more skilled hands.

After searching through various unpacked boxes, Eleanor finally unearthed some leaves of parchment bound together that contained various jottings on how to handle fevers, swellings, and other ailments. One remedy seemed appropriate for Henry's condition. She decided to mix the brew herself.

Since all household duties had remained in her mother-in-law's capable hands, it took Eleanor a while to locate the kitchen. In the pantry she found a goodly stock of herbs and mixed dried febrifuge, verbena, and root of sassafras in a mortar, then ground them together with a pestle. Next she emptied the mortar into an iron pot, filled it with water, and brought the whole mixture to a boil over the fire.

"Lady, let me add a dried bat's wing to that potion," said one of the cooks who was watching. "The empress always says there be nothing like dried bat's wing for bringing down a fever, so I keeps a supply on hand."

"Yes, all right. If you think it will help." The redoubtable Maud seemed to have an inexhaustable supply of useful knowledge, for which Eleanor was duly grateful. But sometimes she felt like closing her ears when someone prefaced a sentence with "The empress says . . ."

The cook added the bat's wing and a pinch of salt, then said the Pater Noster seven times while stirring vigorously. After the mixture had boiled, it was cooled and strained into a silver goblet.

Eleanor returned to the solar and gave Henry the potion. For a while he continued to toss about uneasily, then gradually became less restless and finally dropped off to sleep. The physician said this was a most favorable sign, so Eleanor, who had sat up with him for several nights, lay her aching body down on a pallet beside the bed and immediately fell asleep.

When she woke to the sound of the Prime bells ringing, the chamber was filled with pale sunlight streaming through the narrow window slits. Shivering, Eleanor rose, rubbed her aching back, and walked to Henry's bedside. He was still sleeping quietly. Placing her hand on his forehead, she found it cool and damp. Praise the Holy Mother, the fever had broken. She was so relieved she decided she would actually attend the next Mass and light a candle to express her gratitude.

The coals in the brazier had burned down to ash so Eleanor opened the door of the chamber, ordered the servitor who slept across the threshold to bring fresh coals and some warmed wine, then pulled up a cushioned stool. She took Henry's hand in hers, laid it against her cheek, and tenderly gazed down at his slack face. It was so rare to see him weak and helpless. Always energetic and spirited, Henry was constantly in action, never needing or wanting to be looked after. How often, in the few times they had been together since their marriage, had she longed to nurture and care for him. Far more than she had ever wanted to nurture her two daughters by Louis, or even her infant son. Eleanor knew that her maternal feeling for little William was inextricably bound with the political significance of the birth of an heir.

It wasn't that she wanted Henry to be ill or unable to care for himself. Of course she didn't. But still, now that he lay in such a sorry state, she found herself treasuring every moment that he depended upon her. If only he would do so more often. Especially where Aquitaine was concerned. The thought of her duchy reminded Eleanor of the sinister incident that had occurred at Limoges during their progression through Aquitaine the previous June . . .

She and Henry had traveled into the Limousin as far south as the craggy landscape of Gascony. Everywhere Eleanor journeyed she was followed by her entourage of poets, women, knights, and troubadours. Henry had been very affable and relaxed, not in his usual tearing hurry to be somewhere else. He hunted and flew his falcon, drank sparingly of the hearty Bordeaux wines, joined in the constant merriment, and made no objection to the ever-present songs of courtly love and story-telling. Despite the thinly veiled antagonism of some of Eleanor's vassals, he kept his temper in check—until they reached Limoges. After a rapturous welcome by the townsfolk, they had pitched their pavilions outside the city walls for the night.

They had been eagerly awaiting their supper when the cook in charge of the ducal kitchen tent approached Eleanor in her pavilion.

"Lady, the town has failed to send us the usual customary provisions."

"It must be an oversight," Eleanor said. "I will tell the abbot of St. Martial's. He deals with such matters."

"No, let me go." Before she could protest Henry had bounded out the pavilion door.

When he returned thirty minutes later his face was flushed, his eyes blazing. "You know what that smirking abbot had the gall to tell me?"

Eleanor, along with her women, had been reclining against a pile of cushions listening to a troubadour. Now she held up a hand for silence. "Smirking? That doesn't sound like the abbot."

"Indeed? Listen to this: The town is only obligated to victual the duke and duchess when they lodge within the city's walls. Did you know that?"

"Of course I knew that." Eleanor shrugged. "Sometimes they victual us anyway, sometimes—they need persuading. Those are the Limousins for you. Unpredictable and self-willed. Since time out of mind." She smiled. "Let me have a word with the abbot myself."

"You're missing the point." His flush deepened. "Is this the town's idea of obedience to their duke and duchess?"

"Henry, this means nothing. Just a little show of resistance." She rose to her feet. "That's all."

"That's all? That's *all*? By God's splendor, they need to be reminded who's master here." His face was now gorged with blood.

"They're more apt to do as we wish if reminded who is mistress."

There was a moment of tense silence while she and Henry stared at each other.

"Mistress or master, I won't allow either of us to be insulted."

"Henry, no insult is intended. I understand these people and they mean no harm. Humor them."

His face was slowly turning a deeper crimson; one hand clenched his sword hilt. Eleanor could feel his hot gaze upon her as one of the women brought her a cloak to throw over her shoulders.

"I will be back shortly," she said, and opened the door of the pavilion.

Outside, enveloped in a warm purple dusk, she had started toward the abbey when there was a strangled cry, then the sound of something falling. This was followed by the screams of her women. Eleanor rushed back inside.

For the second time Eleanor witnessed Henry in the grip of a fire-breathing rage. Shrieking, kicking, and cursing, his hands pounded at the floor, his eyes rolled back into his head. The women's screams increased; the troubadours backed as far away as possible from his thrashing body. Swords upraised, a handful of knights raced into the pavilion. If one added a troupe of jugglers and acrobats one might take the whole business for a mummers entertainment.

Except the scene being played before her eyes was hardly entertaining. It was terrifying.

Though this fit was no less violent than the one in Poitiers, it was over far sooner. With the aid of the knights, Henry was helped to his feet. After swaying back and forth, he recovered sufficiently to down a goblet of wine before staggering out of the pavilion. Eleanor could hear him shout that the walls of Limoges must be destroyed. Aghast, she did not know how to stop him. The refusal to provide food *was* an affront to her authority, this could not be denied. But, left to herself, she would have handled the matter with tact and diplomacy, charming the abbot and leading citizens into giving her whatever she wanted. Her grandfather had done it his whole life as a matter of course. That was the way the more successful dukes of Aquitaine handled their unruly subjects.

"Now we are no longer outside the town," Henry said cheerfully, when the walls were razed. "The townsfolk must provide food. This will teach them a lesson they won't soon forget."

Indeed it would. If her vassals had been hostile before, what would they be once news of the incident spread? Eleanor wondered. Since their arrival in Aquitaine she had been the center of attention; the adoring southerners making a great to-do over her, and paying little heed to Henry. He had initially appeared to take this in good humor, but after Limoges Eleanor was less certain.

"I will see you are recompensed for the walls," she told the abbot privately. "The duke is truly a good man but hasty of temper."

The abbot gave her an incredulous look. " 'Hasty of temper'? Is that how you see it, Madam? May God forgive me, but what I see is that you have liberated us from one tyrant only to yoke us to another. He intends to be master here. Take care that this firebrand who so readily kindles others does not torch you as well."

Was the abbot right? Did Henry basically resent her power in the duchy—as Louis had? Was the show of force against her subjects a foreshadowing of the future? The prospect was so unconfrontable that Eleanor immediately dismissed it. The abbot had spoken in the heat of the moment. She loved Henry beyond reason. Surely, surely, she would, over time, imbue him with the same love, the same understanding of her people that she possessed.

Henry slowly opened his eyes. For a long moment he gazed up at her. "Nell." His fingers closed weakly round her hand. "I thought mayhap I was dead and a beautiful angel was ministering to me."

Eleanor, her dark thoughts banished in the instant, blinked back tears of relief and moved his hand to her lips.

From that moment on Henry's strength began to return, although he was still too weak to leave his bed or even sit up. Eleanor was hard put trying to keep him entertained. He wanted her with him constantly and complained every time she left the chamber. She spent hours telling him stories, massaging his back, feeding him tempting dishes to stimulate his weak appetite. At first he lay quietly, his hands frequently on her stomach so he could feel the baby move.

"That was a lusty kick. I'm sure it's another boy. Bring William to me," he said, a few days after the fever had broken.

A wet nurse brought in the baby, now over a year old and still ailing, and laid him beside Henry.

"He looks like me, don't you think?"

Eleanor smiled. "I've always thought he resembled your mother far more than you."

"Thomas Becket said he was the very image of me." Henry watched the baby's dimpled fist close round his finger.

The name sent a tingle of resentment through Eleanor. Henry

talked frequently of Thomas Becket since returning from England. Why he was so taken with this cleric, who had all the charm of a cold trout, she could not imagine. Henry had told her that the archbishop of Canterbury suggested Becket would make an excellent chancellor when he became king. To Eleanor's amazement, Henry had given his agreement. Even the Empress Maud had voiced her doubts about that, but Henry, who usually listened to her advice—if he listened to anyone's—had ignored her. He seemed determined to elevate this Norman of low birth into a position of power—which, in Eleanor's view, the archdeacon had neither earned nor deserved. With a shrug she thrust the unwelcome thought of Becket aside. Now she had Henry to herself—sharing him with the empress, of course—although sometimes their relationship reminded her more of two kings joined in a common campaign than a mother and son.

"*I* think he looks like me."

"William is well-membered," Eleanor said in a dry voice. "He certainly resembles you in that respect."

"Hah!" Henry beamed, and over the protests of both Eleanor and the nurses, unwound all the swaddling bands to examine the evidence with his own eyes.

"What a son this will be, Nell! As heir to the throne he must, of necessity, be educated primarily in England, of course. It won't hurt to engage his tutors now. One from Normandy and one from Anjou, to start with at any rate. Send to the bishops of Rouen and Angers for suggestions."

"No tutor from Aquitaine?"

"Really, Nell, he isn't going to be a poet or a minstrel, heaven forfend."

"Let us hope they can teach him to be more civilized than the average Norman I've seen," Eleanor said. "All Aquitainians are born civilized."

"This uncivilized Norman is creating an empire, have you thought of that?" Henry sat the baby on his stomach, dandled him in his arms, and played with his downy patch of russet hair. "This Norman is also bored. Amuse me."

"What would you like to do?"

"Surely such a civilized creature as yourself can think of something."

Eleanor was perplexed. In Aquitaine, if a member of the family was ill, he or she immediately called for a troubadour to soothe their spirits. Her grandfather had actually believed that the sound of lute and voice helped exorcise the body's foul humours. Perhaps this would work for Henry. Eleanor knew she did not dare recall Bernart de Ventadour. In England, Henry had intercepted a letter the troubadour had written to Eleanor, claiming that he hated the northern clime and wished he was a swallow who could fly back to her "across the wild, deep sea." Bernart was now back in Aquitaine seeking a new patroness to worship.

She missed him. There was no denying that he appealed to the wildly romantic side of her nature that loved to be adored.

Eleanor sent for another, less gifted troubadour she had brought with her from Aquitaine. After he had played and sang all her grandfather's songs, Henry yawned.

"I'm more scholarly than musical, Nell," he said in a peevish voice. "Read to me. Something I haven't heard before."

At her wit's end, Eleanor sent for the bishop of Rouen, who suggested she call for a particular reading clerk from the cathedral at Caen. The clerk, a Master Wace, was in the midst of translating into Latin an old Welsh manuscript about the ancient kings of Britain.

When Eleanor finally received the Latin portions of the manuscript, she began reading the book aloud. Henry was entranced by the tale of King Arthur, but all too soon it was finished.

As Henry grew strong enough to sit, his demands increased. "Get into bed with me, Nell."

"I don't think you're well enough."

"Perhaps not for everything but for some things. Like this."

He insisted she remove her gown and sit with him in her chemise so that he could pull it down over her shoulders and caress her breasts. He never tired of looking at them, squeezing them together, taking her nipples into his mouth and sucking on them. By this time they were both so aroused that Eleanor forced herself to get up and put on her gown.

"This is the last time I let you start something you can't finish."

Henry made a face at her. "All right, bring over the chessboard. I haven't beaten you at chess in a long time."

"You've never beaten me at chess."

"Haven't I?"

"We've never played before."

Eleanor looked around for the chessboard, praying her mother-in-law would not return home in the immediate future. The empress's well-appointed, immaculate solar now looked as if a storm had swept through it leaving vast amounts of debris in its wake.

In addition to the usual presence of William, his nurses, and various attendants who came and went, extra tables had been brought in and were littered with food, pitchers of wine, and rare books bound in wood and ivory. There were candleholders perched everywhere and the wax had dripped onto the polished tables, over the rushes, even staining the scarlet wool coverlet the empress had had especially woven by Flemish weavers in Arras. As if all this weren't enough, Henry's favorite greyhound bitch had chosen to whelp her pups at the foot of his bed.

Every day now, Henry insisted on conducting all the business of Normandy and Anjou, so rolls of parchment, sheets of vellum, wax tablets, and styli were strewn over the bed. Each morning Eleanor read aloud all the documents and relayed the pertinent news. Henry, aided by subtle suggestions she added from time to time, would then make the decisions which two clerks recorded on wax tablets.

In truth, Eleanor enjoyed doing this activity almost more than anything else, and not only because she was actually sharing in Henry's work; it also gave her a far greater understanding of how Henry's mind functioned, the scope of Normandy and Anjou's problems, and how he proposed to deal with them. Eleanor had thought herself a good administrator. But listening to Henry's incisive decisions on how to increase revenues, conserve expenses, what to look for in appointing bailiffs, measures to take with rebellious nobles, or, particularly impressive, how to dispense justice to lawbreakers, she was awed by the caliber of the man she had married. So vastly different from poor ineffectual Louis.

And also vastly different from how he had behaved in Aquitaine. This Henry and that one, like devil and angel, were virtually impossible to reconcile.

When a servitor placed the empress's prized chessboard of inlaid wood covered with squares of gilt and silver upon the bed, Eleanor picked up the ivory figures and turned them over in her hands, marveling at their workmanship.

"This was given to my mother by her first husband, the Holy Roman Emperor, who taught her the game when she was only a child,"

Henry said. "I think I told you that my father always beat my mother at chess. She let him win to make up for the incident at hawking where he felt so humiliated."

"I remember. Well, I give no quarter," said Eleanor. "Skill will triumph."

"Which is why I'll win. Prepare yourself for a bloodbath, Nell."

"You'll eat those words. I've told you, you can't expect me to pander to male pride."

"Of course I expect it—if I weren't naturally superior to you."

Eleanor stuck out her tongue at him.

For several hours they matched wits until she made a move with her queen that she knew would win her the game. While Henry alternately gazed at the board with suspicious eyes, glowered at her, and tapped his teeth with an angry forefinger, Eleanor sat back on her stool with a complacent smile.

Suddenly Henry threw back the scarlet coverlet and sent chessmen and board tumbling to the floor.

"Henry! Why did you do that?" Eleanor could not keep the note of irritation out of her voice.

He gave her an innocent smile. "Do what? It was an accident."

"Accident? You know perfectly well you did it because I was about to beat you! Sweet St. Radegonde, you're such a child."

Henry put his thumb in his mouth and made a gurgling sound. He looked so comical Eleanor could not help laughing. Suddenly there was an urgent knock on the door and the steward burst into the solar.

"My lord, a herald has just arrived from Canterbury. King Stephen is dead."

Eleanor leapt up like a startled hare; Henry, open-mouthed, looked at the steward then at her.

As Eleanor watched him, she fell prey to a tumult of feelings—satisfaction, excitement, and others less easily defined. Whether for good or ill Henry had diligently pursued that star which was now within his grasp, and she was happy for him—and for herself. But how vastly their lives would change, she realized with a sudden pang of regret that surprised her. Not that this would make the slightest difference. To reach for that which you sought, to finally attain it, for an instant or through all eternity, whether it brought joy or bitter pain—surely that was all that mattered?

"Jesu, Nell! Sweet Jesu! I am King of England! King of England!" He grabbed his head with both hands. "I cannot believe it."

Suddenly he looked so terribly young, so vulnerable, so astounded that Eleanor's heart melted within her breast. She sank down on the bed and gathered him into her arms.

"Duke of Normandy and Aquitaine, Count of Anjou, the father of one son, with another on the way; husband of an adoring wife. Now King of England. You've achieved it all, my lord."

Henry drew back and gave her a tremulous smile. When Eleanor gazed deeply into his pewter eyes she saw, for the first time since she had known him, that they sparkled with tears.

# CHAPTER 30

# England, 1154

*E*leanor's first impression of England was not at all what she expected. Hearing about the state of a realm was a far cry from seeing it for yourself.

First there had been the wild crossing from Normandy, with the convoy of ships being blown like a feather across the unruly Channel. Quite as bad as her voyage from the Holy Land to Sicily, and then she hadn't been seven months gone with child. Mercifully, the voyage lasted only two days. When Eleanor believed she could not endure one more moment, her ship suddenly pitched forward on the brow of a towering green wave, crashed down, then—there it was. A white ridge of coast surmounted by hanging gray clouds that overlooked a large harbor thronged with ships.

"Dover's cliffs," said Henry beside her, unruffled by the voyage. He put a steadying hand on her shoulder.

Eleanor, who had several times voided the contents of her stomach into the sea and feared a too early birth, smiled weakly as she clung to the wooden railing.

"Let us hope the other vessels have found safe harbor somewhere along the coast," said the captain, trotting past them. "By me faith, a voyage to put the fear of God into you, my lord."

"I fear neither God, man, nor the Devil," Henry shouted at his retreating back.

"Only women. Very wise." Eleanor groaned as the ship plunged once more, and his answer was lost in the sound of the rigging thrashing in the wind.

The vessel was moored in the shallows. Burley sailors carried

Eleanor ashore and sat her upon unsteady feet just as the bells from Dover Church rang the hour of Sext. The air was wet and freezing cold. A cruel wind pierced everything it touched. She shivered.

They spent two days at Dover, then, after hearing that the missing vessels had washed safely ashore further up the coast, took the road to London. The weather was still inhospitable, but the ride gave Eleanor a chance to catch her breath for the first time since hearing of Stephen's death. It had taken Henry another six weeks to fully recover from his illness and set his affairs in order in Rouen, while she and the empress organized the travel arrangements, did all the packing, oversaw the loading of the carts and horses, and the subsequent unloading onto the ships. Then violent Channel storms had prevented an immediate crossing, until Henry had had enough.

"Tomorrow," he announced, "is the sixth day of December, the feast of St. Nicholas. As he is the protector of sailors and travelers, we sail, regardless of the weather."

Defying the elements, they had sailed. As always, Henry's fortune held.

Now, riding a palfrey, fourteen-month-old William in a litter with his nurse and grandmother behind her, Eleanor looked about her eagerly.

Several leagues out of Dover, she gave a little cry, as the ruins of a church and half-burned manor house came suddenly into view. Circling hawks overhead indicated the dead bodies of man or beast somewhere in the vicinity.

"Yes, I know," Henry said with a grim look on his face. "I saw it all when I was here last year. When the monks at Peterborough said Christ and all His Saints slept during Stephen's reign, you can understand why."

"Indeed."

Despite everything Henry had told her, Eleanor was still not prepared. Having known only the gaiety and affluence of Aquitaine, the intellectual stimulation of Paris, the exotic beauty of the East, the mellow ease of Anjou, and the rugged security of Normandy, she could not believe the savage evidence of her own eyes. One ravaged field followed another. Towns and villages were burned to the ground, some still smoking. Bodies of slaughtered beasts were strewn everywhere.

"You never told me this violence is still going on."

"Over all, it isn't," Henry said. "Just pockets of resistance here and there. As soon as I'm officially crowned something will be done, I promise you."

Glimpsed in passing, the castles perched on hills looked either deserted or like shuttered fortresses. What inhabitants they met were hostile and wary; some ran for refuge when they sighted mounted knights. Eleanor could have wept for the devastation of what once had been, by all accounts, a great and prosperous land.

It began to snow. Henry, riding beside her, reached out and squeezed her hand.

The next day as they drew closer to London matters improved. Their procession was joined by local barons and prelates, even townsfolk, obviously curious to see this new king who had braved the winter storms to become their sovereign.

When they rode through London it was obvious the city had fared far better than the outlying areas—until they came to Westminster, the official royal residence. Before they could dismount, Robert de Beaumont, earl of Leicester, appeared in the snow-covered courtyard and prevented them from doing so.

"My lord," he said to Henry with a bow, before turning to Eleanor. "Lady, you must forgive your poor welcome. But the legacy of the strife that has beset this land for nineteen years has reached into Westminster itself. The place has been so desecrated by Stephen's men that it is not fit for habitation. Even the abbey is in lamentable condition, although every effort will be made to render it suitable for the coronation."

Henry did not respond but his face began to turn red. Eleanor, concealing her shock, could see he was trying to get control of himself. For once, if he fell into a fit of rage, she could not blame him. The looming gray structure in front of her looked more like a prison than the seat of royal power in England. Whatever she had expected it was certainly not this dingy excuse for a palace. Even France . . . She crushed the disloyal thought.

"It doesn't matter, Henry," she said gently. "There is so much to be done here—we must take it one step at a time." She turned to the earl, a crippled, fair-haired man, with discerning blue eyes and a sensitive mouth. "What arrangements have been made for us? We have our son and Henry's mother—the empress—with us, and I am to deliver another babe in two months time. We must be quartered in reasonable comfort."

"Of course. We have arranged for you to stay in an old Saxon castle across the river in Bermondsey. Not a sumputous dwelling but it must serve for the moment."

"I am sure it will," Eleanor said, so tired now that she would welcome any place to lay her head.

Henry, who had swallowed his spleen, sent her a look of passionate gratitude.

"I am sure you did your best, de Beaumont. Thank you."

Hardly a castle, Bermondsey turned out to be an ancient manor house with very few amenities. Quite primitive, in fact, by her standards, Eleanor thought in dismay.

An anxious steward, apologizing for the meanness of the manor house, showed them over the modest quarters. When he came to a large chamber, obviously hastily refurnished and cleaned, a look of pride came over his face.

"The Conqueror himself slept in this very chamber I have prepared for you, my lord." He looked at them expectantly. "I hope this will make up for any other—inconveniences."

Eleanor, repressing a desire to laugh like a madwoman, assumed a reverential expression. "What an honor."

Henry, the corners of his mouth twitching, nodded gravely. "Indeed. By God's splendor, you have done well."

The steward visibly relaxed and hurried away to see that their supper was prepared. When he was gone, Eleanor sank down on the bed and fingered the moth-eaten, faded blue coverlet.

"Probably the Conqueror's bed and coverlet as well."

Henry flung himself down beside her, took her in his arms, and they rocked back and forth, overcome with exhaustion and laughter.

"Sweet St. Radegonde, what a country this will be to rule," Eleanor said.

Eight days later it was another tale entirely.

On the morning of December 19, 1154, an English chamberlain, silver wand in hand, conducted Eleanor slowly down the short flight of stairs to the courtyard of Westminster Abbey. Three pages carried the heavy folds of her gold-embroidered train. Two Aquitainian ladies and four English noblewomen brought up the rear.

A column of knights walking in pairs led them across the cheering, crowd-filled courtyard to the west entrance of the abbey. Inside, the sound of a choir of monks echoed sweetly from the vaulted ceilings. Eleanor, her heart thumping, knew that every eye was fixed upon her, the new queen. Her coifed head held high, she glided up the center aisle to the choice pews facing the altar. Settling in the seat that had been saved for her, she rearranged the folds of her purple fur-trimmed pelisson and looked cautiously around her. The abbey was filled to bursting with knights, barons, and their ladies, shimmering in a vast array of vermillion, green, and sapphire, their velvet mantles lined with ermine, vair, or fox. Gold and silver chains, jewel-studded clasps and brooches reflected the light of hundreds of glowing tapers. The effect was dazzling.

What would these English and Normans, her new subjects, think of her? Would they hate her, as the Franks had done? Or love her as the Aquitainians did? And how would she feel about them?

There was a rising murmur of expectation. Eleanor turned. A procession entered, led by the archbishop of Canterbury. Eleanor had not yet met the worthy Theobald but knew Henry thought most highly of him. In the two months between Stephen's death and their arrival on English soil, the archbishop had ruled the land in Henry's name.

"Do you know, Nell, that this is the first time in ninety years, since the Conqueror in fact—excepting William Rufus—that the crown will devolve peacefully?" Henry had said this morning. "No protests, no armed demonstrations, no plots to supplant me with another candidate. That's quite an achievement on the archbishop's part."

"You do realize the implications of what you've just told me?" At his questioning look, she explained: "At this moment the Church is the most powerful force in the country."

He gave her a penetrating glance then shrugged. "That will change. I know how you feel about the Church, Nell, but I do expect you to get on with old Theobald."

"Of course. After all I get on very well with some ecclesiastics."

"Name one."

"The abbess of Fontevrault, the archbishop of Bordeaux—some of the time . . . let me see—my old tutor in Poitiers, most of the time . . . hmm."

"Not a very impressive list, is it? Be that as it may, you're to make a special effort with old Theobald, just remember that."

The archbishop was clad in a gold-embroidered chasuble, wearing his gold-encrusted miter and carrying a gold crosier winking with jewels. His head shifted slightly in her direction; Eleanor held his gaze for an instant before he moved on. Behind him, led by the archbishop of York, paced a score of bishops and abbots, crimson, gold, and blue robes brushed with fire from the candle-glow. Behind them she caught a brief glimpse of the tall figure of Thomas Becket.

Next came Henry, striding beneath a canopy of purple silk held on the gilded points of four lances borne by those peers of the realm whose hereditary right permitted them to perform this function. Henry stopped at the chancel and the service began.

A screen was raised when the time came for him to be anointed with the consecrated chrism from a crystal bowl. When Eleanor saw him again, he was led to the throne clad in silken tunic, embroidered robe, and a scarlet cloak edged with ermine. The archbishop administered the coronation oath and the Conqueror's golden crown was formally placed upon Henry's head. The Lord Marshal of England made a sign to Eleanor. She rose heavily and moved toward the throne, taking her place beside Henry. The archbishop placed another crown upon her head. She and Henry were now king and queen of England.

The great bells in the tower rang with lusty abandon; a swelling roar of approval echoed both inside and outside the abbey. She caught a quick glimpse of the Empress Maud, her eyes bright with tears. Henry turned and with a broad smile winked at her. His dream for so many years was now fulfilled. But for how long? Eleanor knew that Henry's appetite for more land, more power was not appeased, only lying dormant like some sleeping giant. Had he not told her only last night that the entire world was but a paltry prize for a brave and powerful ruler?

And for herself? More than fulfilled, Eleanor was ecstatic with what she had achieved: She had rid herself of an unsuitable husband; survived two formidable enemies, Abbé Suger and Bernard of Clairvaux, the latter's demise last year having stilled the most influential voice in Europe. Oddly enough, Bernard's death had not brought her the same sense of satisfaction she had felt when Abbé Suger died, or her first marriage had been annulled. On the contrary, she had experienced a sense of emptiness—Bernard had been . . . what was it about that charismatic holy man whom she had so intensely disliked? Yes, a worthy opponent; extraordinary, for she had never admired an enemy before. She would actually miss him. Strange, but the links created by hate could be almost as strong as those created by love.

Most important, though, she had kept Aquitaine inviolate, safe from harm. Not only that, she had brought—or so Eleanor hoped—the spirit of her pleasure-loving sunlit duchy to this bleak and desolate country. England would never be the same again; in time, she would see to that.

Henry and Eleanor followed the archbishop out of the abbey. Outside, a splendid litter drawn by four white horses waited for them. They rode out of Westminster and moved slowly along the Strand, surrounded by the approving cries of their subjects. While she waved and smiled, Eleanor caught sight of a young girl, big with child, standing in the forefront of the crowd. The litter paused for a moment against the surging throng. The girl was now close enough for Eleanor to reach out and touch her.

Her beauty was so arresting, it was impossible not to stare at the gleaming raven curls, milky skin, and huge dark-blue eyes that blazed with something close to adoration. There was a quality so heartfelt, so passionately admiring in her glance that Henry, who never missed a pretty face if he could help it, must be returning the girl's attention. Eleanor looked at him but his gaze was studiously fastened in another direction.

Who was this lovely creature staring at? After a moment, with a shock of recognition, Eleanor realized that it was herself. Oddly moved, she impulsively stretched out her hand in a gesture of acknowledgment. The girl seized her fingers and brought them briefly to her lips. The litter moved on. When Eleanor looked back, the girl had tears running down her face.

Henry, who had not witnessed the incident, now turned and squeezed her hand. Their eyes met and Eleanor felt the familiar jolt of blood rush through her body. Giddy with joy she wanted to weep, to laugh, to sing, to cry aloud for the sheer wonder of being in this place, at this rapturous moment in time. She was on the threshold of a glorious future, about to help rule an empire with a man she loved more than anything or anyone in the whole world. Twice a queen, mother of a son and heir, was woman ever so blessed?

# Part Two

Heir to thy grandfather's name and high reknown
Thy England calls thee, Henry, to her throne.

—Henry of Huntingdon

# CHAPTER 31

# England,
# 1157

*T*here was the far-off murmur of voices. Someone was shaking Eleanor's shoulder. Henry. "You're insatiable, my lord," she said drowsily.

"I beg pardon?"

Eleanor opened her eyes. A torch flared, blinding her.

"You must get up, Madam. The chaplain just woke me to say the king is ready to leave." It was the voice of Emma, one of her women.

"Now?" The tiny room was in darkness but for the pool of light cast by the flickering torch. "At supper the king said we would not move on until noon at the very earliest. Have the bells rung for Prime?"

"Not yet, Madam. The first cock was crowing just a moment ago. The king wishes to move on at once."

The first cock indeed! Eleanor started to laugh then groaned aloud. Sweet St. Radegonde, it seemed like she had just fallen asleep. "All right. I will need a moment to dress properly."

Sometimes, she suspected Henry took a perverse delight in unsettling everyone. She sternly reminded herself of his oft-repeated dictum that a king must know his country and his people; the only way to accomplish this was periodic visits to outlying parts of the kingdom. Since Eleanor wholeheartedly agreed, she had little cause for complaint.

Emma lit the candle in its iron holder then wakened the two women sleeping on straw pallets. Eleanor sat up and yawned, shivering in the chill of a September morn. Her limbs ached, her neck was stiff, but she felt warm and peaceful inside. It hardly seemed possible she had made love on these straw pallets on the dirt floor of this—well, hovel was the only word for it.

When, as now, the court was on the move, many wagons carried all the administrative records, bedding, furniture, plates, pots, hangings, and linen, to make habitable the chill interiors of remote stone castles or primitive wooden halls. But last night, at Henry's whim, the enormous royal train of 150 had been forced to camp in the middle of a forest, where none of these amenities were of any use. Indeed, Eleanor had witnessed several knights draw their swords over who would sleep in a tiny, evil-smelling hut that swine would have disdained.

"See if you can find some water to wash in," she said to her women who, rubbing the sleep from their eyes, had stumbled to their feet. "And something to drink. It is too much to hope for a crust of bread."

Uncomfortable as she was to have been awakened so early, it came as no surprise. Not after almost three years of living in England. When she and Henry were at one of their royal residences—Westminster, Windsor, Clarendon—life was invariably hectic, as Henry hurled himself into one activity after another, on his feet from morning until night, and expecting everyone around him to do likewise. But touring with him was unpredictable and chaotic in the extreme. After the birth of her last two children—another son, named Henry, born in 1155, two months after his father was crowned, and a daughter born the following year, called Matilda in honor of Henry's mother—Eleanor had vowed she would no longer accompany him on these impossible tours. But when Henry cajoled her, she always gave in, her resistance melting like wax before flame.

Although Henry always promised to be consistent in his itinerary, the pattern never changed. If he announced to his vast entourage that they would leave at daybreak he was sure to change his mind and leave at noon. If he ordered everyone to be ready by noon, he would decide, like today, to depart at cock-crow. What a difference from the leisurely progresses of her grandfather and father, where every stop was carefully planned and adhered to, so as to ensure maximum comfort for everyone. The very idea of missing a well-prepared meal, at home or away, was unthinkable. "The Franks to battle, the Provenceaux to table," was a common maxim.

Outside, Eleanor could hear the usual racket as the members of Henry's traveling household bustled to load packhorses and mule-carts, saddle the riding horses, and grab something to eat from the remains of last night's meal—if they were lucky.

"Are you up, Nell?" The familiar figure, clad in a short green mantle with draped green hood, and scuffed brown boots, burst into the hovel like a whirlwind of energy. "God's eyes, you're still abed." Henry strode over to the stack of pallets, knelt down on one knee, pulled her to a sitting position, and gave her a great hug. "You're not ill?" He felt the rounded curve of her stomach, just beginning to bulge with their fourth child.

"No, no, I'm fine. But you said we wouldn't leave until noon."

His lips lingered on hers. "Did I? Hmm. I must reach York before Vespers, catch the sheriff there off-guard, and see if he's attending to his duties in the proper manner."

"York! Where are we now?"

"Somewhere in the wilds of Yorkshire, I should think. Does it matter? Up, my lady, up, up, up! Make ready. No time to waste." He jumped to his feet, pulling her with him. "What a sour look! You should be purring like a tame cat after last night."

He was gone before she had time to protest. But he was right. She did, indeed, feel like purring.

An hour later, followed by a long line of creaking wagons, they were on the road—if one could call this muddy, deeply rutted track left by the Romans a road. In wet weather it would become an impassable bog. When she was carrying a babe, Eleanor sometimes felt more comfortable riding in a litter, but this morning the thought of being jolted up and down through such terrain was more than even her hardy constitution could bear, and she had opted to ride a gentle mare.

Riding next to Eleanor on a large bay stallion, Henry talked earnestly to Thomas, the chancellor, who rode on his other side. She had fervently hoped that Henry would leave him in London, but he had not done so. Eleanor knew Henry took Becket with him everywhere, implicitly trusted his judgment on every issue that concerned the realm, and, generally, regarded him as a boon companion. Although she had made successful attempts to get along with her husband's chief magnates, such as the co-justiciars, Richard de Lucy and the aging Earl Robert of Leicester, as well as the nobles of Norfolk and Salisbury—even the archbishop of Canterbury had somewhat thawed toward her—the initial dislike between the Norman chancellor and herself had only increased since Henry's coronation.

It was ridiculous, but Eleanor forced herself to face the humilating truth: she was jealous. It was not an emotion she had experienced before Henry, and when she recognized its true nature, she was shocked. In her exalted position, there was something shameful in feeling as she did about Thomas.

She did not harbor such feelings about the scholars and wise men—John of Salisbury, Gilbert Foliot, bishop of Hereford, Hugh of Lincoln—whose interests Henry shared and who were always to be found about his court.

Nor did she feel the same about the various doxies she knew Henry dallied with when he was away from her bed and on his own. Jealousy would have been justified in those instances. Except that Eleanor's sense of pride would not allow her to be seriously troubled by them. Casual fornication, a practice most men indulged in away from their wives, was without significance, and better ignored. After all, Henry was still insatiable where she was concerned, she reflected. In truth, she had never even felt curious about the lowly creatures upon whom he slaked his lust.

Eleanor shifted uncomfortably in the saddle, wishing she had something more substantial than sour ale and last night's tough game and half-baked bread in her stomach. Well, it would just have to sustain her until Henry chose to stop or they came to a town or village. From the look of this God-forsaken country, that could be hours away.

The rolling green downs and grassy meadows of the midlands had changed to desolate untamed moor pocked with brown gorse, purple heather, and rocky crags that thrust upward from the earth like giant fingers. The weather had held for the last few days but in the pink light of dawn Eleanor noted banks of dark clouds gathered menacingly on the far horizon that could easily result in one of those fierce drenching rains for which the region was famous. A brisk wind whistling down from the Scottish marches had a sharp bite to it that penetrated the heavy cloak lined with red fox fur Henry had had made for her. Holy Mother, how she missed the balmy air of Aquitaine.

"I would have thought the queen would prefer the comfort of the litter," Thomas said, sliding his dark eyes toward her.

Clearly he resented her presence and would have preferred to have Henry all to himself. So would she.

"Eleanor is a remarkable woman, Thomas. How many wives bounce back from childbed with such ease, travel everywhere while carrying a new babe—another son I feel sure—sleep uncomplainingly in the most wretched hovel, and still manage to look as beautiful and fresh as a rose in bloom?"

Henry's freckled face broke into a broad grin and he reached out his hand to squeeze hers. Eleanor's heart turned over. The uncomfortable nights and exhausting days, the dismal food and undrinkable brown ale suddenly became mild pinpricks because he had praised her for enduring them.

The look on Thomas's face would have curdled milk, she noted with pleasure.

"This will be my third son," Henry continued, "while poor Louis of France, who has not yet recovered from the loss of Aquitaine—or Eleanor—has only just now married again. I wager he'll have only more girls with this Castilian wife. Was ever man so cursed?"

Ever since he became king, Henry appeared to gloat over every misfortune that befell Louis. Although it was true that as Henry's star continued to rise Louis's descended, Eleanor felt it unseemly to take such satisfaction in his rival's ill luck. No good would come of it. Now she crossed herself, almost ashamed of her superstitious forebodings.

Unaccountably, the wind died; a pale sun rose into a slate blue sky; the dark clouds vanished. Like everything else in this strange land, even the weather was unpredictable. Off to the right, Eleanor could see the white spire of a church; to the left a small castle hugged a distant hilltop.

Henry turned toward Thomas. "I think it time a stable peace was negotiated between Louis and myself. Something to my advantage, naturally."

Thomas nodded. "Indeed. I will think of a plan."

As she listened, a sudden inspiration came to Eleanor. "Henry, I've just thought of something. If Louis—"

Thomas interrupted her with an indulgent laugh. "Do you leave the affairs of the realm to us, Madam."

Ignoring him, Eleanor continued: "If Louis does have another daughter with his new queen—why not offer him our son, Henry, in marriage to her? Then as her dowry, ask for the Vexin back." She had not suggested their eldest son, William, as the boy, now four, was weak and sickly; despite their constant prayers neither she nor Henry expected him to survive.

"By God's splendor, what a bold idea!"

Eleanor knew that Henry had always resented giving up the Vexin, that much-prized Norman border territory, as the price for being recognized duke of Normandy.

"Think of the implications," Eleanor said. "If Louis continues to produce nothing but daughters—who will ultimately reign over France?"

Henry caught his breath. He clapped a hand to his head. "Of course, of course! Henry III, Plantagenet, as the princess's husband. Our son, king of France and England! What a political genius you are, Nell." He laughed. "Thomas, you had better look to yourself lest I replace my chancellor with my queen."

Eleanor was delighted at Henry's response. At the glance of icy resentment Thomas sent her, she gave an inward shrug. Let the chancellor look to his own laurels. She pushed back the hood of her dark blue traveling cloak. Late morning now, the sun was growing warm.

"How far must we go?" she asked.

"Not far now. We've just passed Kirkstall, I believe," Henry said, pointing to the south, "and are approaching the environs of York."

Eleanor stifled a sigh of weariness. By Henry's reckoning, "not far" might mean anything from two to seven hours.

Ahead lay a village of thatched cottages. Behind the village rose a large manor house. On the outskirts of the village a crowd of people were gathered before a huge oak tree with spreading branches whose leaves were just starting to turn a mixture of rust and gold. Under the tree a man sat in a high chair draped with scarlet cloth. He was flanked by two men seated on stools. Behind them stood a priest holding a box. Next to him was a young monk clad, like the priest, in a cowled white robe.

Henry drew rein near the tree then held up one hand. Behind him the long procession ground slowly to a halt.

The man in the chair glanced at the red-and-gold banner with three lions, rampant, carried by the herald. He leapt to his feet and approached Henry with a fawning bow.

"Your Majesty, it is a great honor to have you pass through our humble domains. I am Raoul de Fiennes, lord of this manor, at your service."

With his long face and large yellow teeth, he reminded Eleanor of a horse.

Henry glanced around him. "What's happening here that draws such a large crowd?"

"This morning I dispense justice, Sire. Nothing of importance, only the crimes of village folk." He gestured to the two men sitting on stools. "Here are my steward and my marshal who will act as advisors. Behind them stands Father Joseph of the Cistercian monastery at Fountains Abbey, ready to administer any oaths on his box of relics."

"Indeed, I am impressed. No wise man acts without counsel," said Henry. "Now, my lord, we have not yet broken our fast this day. Do you think you will be able to provide nourishment for my entourage?"

De Fiennes looked at the vast train of men and horses, visibly paling as he managed a sickly smile. "Of course, Sire, we will do our best to oblige. My men will return at once to the manor . . ." He turned to his men and said something in an undertone. They sprang up and ran toward the village.

Henry smiled. "Excellent. Meanwhile Thomas and I will advise you in their stead."

"There is no need—"

"But I insist. Justice is one of my great interests, and my chancellor, Thomas, has studied law in Bologna. Fortune smiles on you today, my friend." He beckoned to one of his clerks.

Eleanor repressed a laugh. The poor man did not look at all pleased with what fortune had brought him. Shortly thereafter she was seated on a rough wooden bench while Henry and Thomas occupied the stools of the absent men.

They would never get to York at this rate, Eleanor thought with a yawn, untying the strings of her cloak. She looked with distaste at the rumpled skirts of her dove gray tunic. How she had looked forward to sleeping in a proper bed, soaking her limbs in a tub of hot water, and changing her clothes. She had seen Henry try important cases in the Curia Regis, the English royal council and court of justice, and had tried enough herself in Poitiers to find the prospect, at this moment, not even mildly interesting. Why Henry would waste precious time in this backwater she could not imagine. Her belly rumbled and she wondered what they would be given to eat.

"No, I do not have the right of high justice, the power of life and death over my people," de Fiennes was saying in response to some question of Henry's. "That belongs to the provost in York. But I can administer floggings and imprisonment as I deem necessary."

"In truth, the law in these parts is a veritable jumble," said the priest. "The royal—"

"But much improved since Your Majesty came to the throne close to three years ago," de Fiennes added hastily. "Before that lawlessness abounded everywhere—"

"As I was about to say, my lord, the royal sheriffs have been among the worst offenders," said the Cistercian, oblivious to de Fiennes's warning glance.

"Unhappily, there is still much to be done." De Fiennes glared at the priest.

"Despite my reforms, it is the same in many parts of England," Henry said, adding in an undertone to Thomas, "Royal sheriffs in York. Don't forget." He nodded at de Fiennes. "Criminals go unpunished, innocent men are hanged. It will simply take more time to put these matters to rights. In my mind, there is only one way to bring order out of this chaos: ultimately one standard of law must apply everywhere."

De Fiennes gave an incredulous laugh. "A law common to all men? Forgive me, Sire, but that is impossible. Why, the law often differs from village to village! Here, for example, we follow the customs of Normandy. In other parts of Yorkshire you will find traces of the old Danelaw, and not ten leagues away they follow yet another tradition."

"A daunting task, I agree, and change will hardly occur overnight, but by the end of my reign you will see sweeping changes in the law, mark my words."

Eleanor smiled to herself. Exactly the sort of challenge Henry thrived on. The clerk, she noted, had taken it all down.

By the time the bells had rung for Sext, the steward had produced a meager repast of dried apples, ale, hard wheaten loaves that had already begun to mold, soft white cheese, and cold boiled mutton. Eleanor forced herself to eat; there was no telling when the next meal might be forthcoming. Henry ate heartily, indifferent as usual to what went into his belly; Thomas, after one look, disdained all food, asking only for well water.

By the time they finished eating, the size of the crowd had doubled. De Fiennes's men were still feeding the royal party and Henry, impatient as ever, suggested they start the trials.

The first three cases were commonplace and the crowd grew restive. The fourth case involved a rape. The crowd immediately perked up. A local knight paraded his buxom, teary-eyed daughter before the court.

"This girl claims to have been a virgin before being raped by this monk from Fountains Abbey," de Fiennes said to Henry. He pointed to the young brother who stood next to the old priest. "The monk says she is lying."

"The monk must be handed over to the local abbot," Thomas said, glancing at the priest. "He cannot be tried by a lay court."

"The monk is not yet on trial, my lord chancellor," said de Fiennes.

Henry frowned. "Indeed, why not?"

"Well, it must be determined first if the girl speaks the truth. The father says that because she has been soiled he will not be able to make a suitable marriage for her. He demands recompense from the abbey because the monk has violated her."

"There is no proof of that," the priest said quickly.

"This surely is no light matter," Henry said. "If the monk were an ordinary man he could be castrated and even blinded for raping a virgin."

De Fiennes's lip curled. "Before the ecclesiastical court, he will get off with a penance and mayhap a flogging."

"That is hardly justice." Henry gave Thomas a hard look. "If it is a lay crime he has committed, he should pay the same penalty."

"I must contradict you, Sire," Thomas replied with heat in his voice. " 'Render unto Caesar that which is Caesar's and unto God—' "

"Yes, yes, I'm aware of all that. Don't preach at me. But that is not justice, Thomas, and well you know it."

Eleanor looked from one man to the other. For an instant there was an unaccustomed tension between them she had not seen before. Henry broke it with an outward shrug.

"All right. The monk is not on trial here so we waste time. How will the maid prove she is telling the truth?"

"She will carry a bar of heated iron for three paces before witnesses. If, at the end of three days, the burn is no more than half the size of a walnut she will be accused of bearing false witness."

Eleanor was outraged. "Has a midwife examined her? This is barbaric." She had no right to speak at this court but could not keep silent.

"That has been done, Madam," said de Fiennes. "That she is no longer a virgin has been verified, but the girl may be protecting the real culprit by accusing this monk."

What reason would the girl have to wrongly accuse the monk? Eleanor wondered, but dared not protest further.

When the bar of hot iron was placed in the girl's hand she ran three paces, screamed, then dropped the bar and fell to the ground in a swoon. Her father picked her up and carried her off toward the village. The monk had a sly look on his face. Eleanor felt sick to her stomach. She fervently hoped that the burn was the size of at least three walnuts, thus proving her innocent.

The fifth case involved three mercenary soldiers said to have invaded a large neighboring farm, stolen a horse, a pig, and several chickens, insulted the women, and severely beaten the farmer and his son. One of the men was caught while two escaped. The captured man, his hands tied behind him, vehemently protested his innocence.

"Pure and guiltless indeed," said de Fiennes with a sneer. "The unvarying plea of the accused."

"Perhaps he is telling the truth," Henry said.

"Not likely. My men found him in the forest in company with the other brigands," said de Fiennes. "It is his misfortune that he was caught and they escaped."

"I don't deny these men are my comrades," the accused cried. "In truth, I was waiting for them. I knew they had gone into the village for food but I did not go with them, nor did I know what they had in mind."

"But you know where they're hiding, I'll wager," de Fiennes said.

The man shook his head, his eyes darting anxiously from Henry to de Fiennes. It was obvious to Eleanor he was refusing to betray the lair of his comrades, but whether he was guilty of the crime as charged she could not be sure.

"Ordeal by water will determine the truth or falsehood of what this rogue says, then a severe flogging should produce the whereabouts of his accomplices." De Fiennes summoned a guard. "Prepare the cask."

"Such practices prove nothing," said Henry. "How can the size of a scar prove whether someone is lying? Is the water to know whether this man is guilty or not?"

At his words a ripple of interest stirred the crowd of onlookers. De Fiennes looked shocked. "But Divine punishment will be meted out to the perjurer. It is well known."

"It is blasphemous to suggest otherwise," said the Cistercian priest, crossing himself. "It is how God makes His will known to us. Like nobles fighting in single combat to prove their guilt or innocence."

"In the belief that God will grant the decision to the one whose cause is just." Henry shook his head in disgust. "Another foolish custom I deplore."

A huge cask near the tree was filled with water, a wooden board set across its top. As a child, Eleanor had once witnessed an ordeal by water, a custom now fallen into disuse, in Poitou at least, for the very reasons Henry had given. The accused was bound with a rope attached to his shoulders and dumped into the cask. If innocent he was supposed to sink; if guilty he would float. Of course by the time he was hauled up he was often more dead than alive so his proven innocence did him little good. This had been the case in Poitiers.

Two guards started to bind the man with rope; the priest came forward with his box of relics to administer the oath of innocence. Henry rose slowly to his feet.

"Wait! There must be a better method to determine the guilt of this man, one closer to the Divine will. As I recall, the Saxons had a way . . ." He thought for a moment, rubbing his chin.

Slowly he walked over to the crowd who fell back at his approach. "You, you, and you," he said at length, pointing at three men. He turned and singled out four more, then pushed his way into the crowd and indicated five others, all of different ages. "Twelve of you—the number of the Apostles as well as the tribes of Israel—should be enough." He smiled at the priest. "It was enough for Our Lord. Come with me."

The bewildered men followed him to a place on the far side of the tree.

"Stay there, don't move," Henry said. "Now, bring this man here and let him stand thus—" he indicated a place in front of de Fiennes. The accused was led to the spot Henry indicated. "Good, good." He reflected again, frowning.

Eleanor watched both de Fiennes and the priest turn rigid with disapproval at this variation in custom. Thomas looked interested. What in heaven's name was Henry up to? Some old Saxon custom not used since before the Conquest? In the midst of a tense silence Eleanor felt a stir of excitement, aware that the crowd felt it too, as if everyone present were going to witness a startling event.

"All right," Henry said at last, "bring forward the farmer and his son who were robbed and beaten, the women who were insulted, and anyone else who claims to have been wronged by these mercenaries."

"Majesty, at the risk of offending you, I strongly protest this grave departure from tradition," said de Fiennes, no longer able to contain his outrage. "This contravenes the law of both God and man. My own guards saw this man with his comrades before they escaped. The others had the stolen chickens and pig in their arms. This man was holding the horse's headstall!"

"They had just that moment put the rope in my hands!" the accused shouted.

"Silence." One of the guards gave him a shove and he fell to the ground. The guard hauled him roughly to his feet.

"As my lord de Fiennes has said, this goes against all custom and violates God's law as well," the priest said, sputtering in his anger. "My lord chancellor, it is not our place to—can you not explain matters to the king?"

Thomas looked from the priest to Henry. "He has a point, Sire. After all, this *is* their territory and we but trespass here. Would it not be best to let them manage affairs in their own way?"

It was indeed a valid point. Eleanor saw Henry hesitate. She did not know why but she was convinced he must not stray from the path he trod.

"Henry," she called out. "If customs forever remain the same, how can England change its laws?"

It was the support he needed. "No, Thomas, in this instance I must override all of you. What the queen says is true, but there is another, more important, point to be made. Man has the ability to reason, to judge right from wrong. Is not this God-given? Surely Our Lord expects us to use His gift so He does not have to directly intervene at every turn."

Henry surveyed the twelve men. "Are any of you related to this man by blood or marriage? Do any have aught to gain if this man prove either innocent or guilty?"

They all shook their heads.

"Do you all swear to Our Heavenly Father that you speak the truth?"

They all swore that they did.

"Then let us proceed. Now, I may ask questions of the relevant parties, your lord will ask questions, and my chancellor may ask a few. When the questions and answers are complete, you will discuss the matter among yourselves and pass judgment, although the final decision, of course, rests with your lord. Do you understand?" He impatiently eyed the group, who appeared dumbfounded. "On the evidence presented you will determine if the accused lies or speaks the truth, is that quite clear?"

"It is clear to me," said one of the men.

"Good. You will be the spokesman for the group. Let us begin."

Eleanor found herself spellbound by what was happening. The farm women, the farmer and his son, the Lord de Fiennes's men were all brought before the court and interrogated. It soon became clear that the man was telling the truth. All the farm people denied ever having seen the accused on their property; only the guards gave incriminating evidence, having caught him with his comrades in the forest.

The twelve men talked together for only a few moments.

"We are ready to pronounce judgment," said the spokesman to Henry.

"Are you all in agreement?"

"We are."

"How do you find?"

"We find he is telling the truth."

Henry turned to de Fiennes. "You are the arbiter of justice here, my lord. What say you to this verdict?"

De Fiennes, his nose clearly out of joint, gave a reluctant nod. "The man is innocent. Untie him—but he must still tell us where his comrades are hidden."

The accused burst into tears and fell to his knees in front of Henry.

"Oh, my lord, Sire, I am your man forever. As God is my witness, I will be your grateful servant until my death."

"God's eyes, get up, man, no need for such a display," Henry said in a gruff voice, clearly embarrassed. "And don't tamper with your good fortune," he added softly. "Tell what you know."

The accused nodded and was led off by de Fiennes's guards.

Within moments the crowd had surrounded Henry, doffing their caps, even daring to touch him with a kind of shy reverence. Their affection and respect was palpable.

"Our king executes swift justice with a strong hand," Eleanor heard a fervent voice say. "May God bless and keep him for many a long year."

It was the very highest praise. Tears filled her eyes; her heart swelled with love and pride.

The moment—afternoon sun glinting through the burnished leaves of the stately oak; Henry, looking absurdly young, enveloped by the adoring throng—was etched in her mind like a pen stroke on parchment, transcending time and place.

De Fiennes had a sullen look on his face. Eleanor was sure he disapproved of the whole innovative procedure. Not that it mattered. Instinct told her that what she had witnessed today—no, not merely witnessed, but contributed to—however crudely done, would one day transform the realm.

# CHAPTER 32

# Bermondsey,
# 1158

*S*now coated the roof of the White Tower, blanketed London Bridge, shrouded Billingsgate and the steeple of St. Botolph's. A chill wind blew gusts of wood smoke from the bonfires smoldering along the Thames embankment. Across the ice-covered river in Bermondsey, Bellebelle, holding her three-year-old son Geoffrey by the hand, trudged down the frozen road that led to her cottage. Suddenly Geoffrey stopped.

"Be something the matter, Son?"

"Look, Maman," Geoffrey said, pointing excitedly. Her gaze followed the direction of his finger.

A group of boys, shinbones of horses tied to their feet, iron-shod wooden poles in their hands, were skating on the glazed surface of the river.

"You'd like to be doing that, wouldn't you, lad?"

Geoffrey nodded vigorously, his eyes shining.

Bellebelle squeezed his hand. "One day you will. When you be older I'll find someone to teach you."

They continued on their way. A curve in the road took them out of sight of the river. Here the road followed a gentle incline then wound through fields on one side and a dark woodland on the other. The village they lived in was on the outskirts of Bermondsey, considered part of Bermondsey, but in fact lay in the next parish. Sometimes of a Sunday, like today, Bellebelle would take Geoffrey walking by the river just to catch sight of London on the other side. How she missed it; more than she had ever believed possible.

Bellebelle had just passed the house of her nearest neighbor when something hard suddenly hit her in the small of the back. She staggered, lost her footing, and slipped to the ground. Behind her she could hear muffled laughter. Turning, she caught sight of two boys, snowballs in hand, leering at her from the garden fronting their cottage. Geoffrey picked up a stone by the side of the road and started running toward the boys.

"Geoffrey, no!"

Terrified, for there were two of them, both bigger than her son, Bellebelle scrambled to her feet, more shaken than bruised from her fall, and ran after him.

"Son!"

He ignored her, drew back his arm, and threw the stone. It landed on the shoulder of one of the boys, who immediately set up a howl. Good for Geoffrey! Bellebelle could not resist a rush of intense satisfaction which turned to outraged disbelief when she spied the grinning face of the boys' mother peeping out the cottage door.

"Whore," the woman said, and spat at Bellebelle through rotting teeth.

"Why don't you leave us alone!" Bellebelle cried. "What harm we ever done you?"

"King's cunt! King's cunt!" the boys taunted in unison before scuttling inside the cottage and slamming the door.

Geoffrey picked up several other stones and threw them, one after the other, at the closed door.

"Leave off that now." Bellebelle grabbed the resistant Geoffrey by the wrist and, pulling him after her, began to run, her feet slipping on the icy path.

"Why do they always call you cunt or whore?" asked Geoffrey in a tight voice, looking up at her with Henry's stormy gray eyes. "What does that mean? Why does everyone hate us?"

"You not be old enough to understand."

"You always say that. When will I be old enough? I'm going to tell Father. He'll make them stop."

"You are to say nothing to anyone. T'wont do no good and might make things worse. Henry's got his realm to worry about, he don't need our troubles as well. Just leave it be."

Bellebelle's heart ached for young Geoffrey. Never, she wanted to say, not if you live an entire lifetime will you ever be old enough to understand the hurt some folks like to cause others. Ever since she could remember she had been the butt of taunts and jeers. It had been hard to bear when she was a child, but then she had had her mother and the company of the other whores to help share the pain. At twenty-three—or whatever she was—being treated like a—what was the word? yes, pariah, was still hurtful but now she had to face it alone, and protect Geoffrey as well.

This family, and many others in the village, either shunned or tormented her in small, mean ways, such as throwing snowballs or calling her names. They didn't dare do more than that, knowing she was under the king's protection. Although it had been all of four years since she left Gropecuntlane to become Henry's mistress, sometimes Bellebelle wondered how much had really changed. She still felt helpless, not daring to fight back for fear of causing trouble. She only wished with all her heart there was just one person she could talk to.

Another fifteen minutes brought her to the small stone-and-wood house Henry had had built for her two years ago. Surrounded by a stone wall, it lay on a croft of land just off the road, backed by a stretch of thick woods. Along with the house there were sheds, a vegetable garden, and animal pens; outside the croft lay a stone well Henry had had dug for her. The gate was ajar and she scurried through the small flower garden, the earth stiff as oak in this freezing month of February. She pushed open the door and with a sigh of relief shut it firmly behind her.

Geoffrey pulled off his wool cap and cloak then ran off to warm himself by the hearth. The huge gray wolfhound that had been sleeping by the fire rose, yawned, and stretched his back legs. Bellebelle closed her eyes for a moment, leaned against the stout wood of the door, and drew a deep shuddering breath. She was home; the dangers of the outside world could not touch her in the warmth and safety of this refuge Henry had provided for Geoffrey and her.

"Light the candles," Bellebelle said, "there's a good lad."

Geoffrey obediently lit the three-branched pewter candlestick that stood on the oak chest near the door. The hall burst into light.

Even after two years Bellebelle could hardly believe that this house belonged to her. Her gaze passed wonderingly over the hall, which also served as kitchen, stopped at the narrow staircase that led up to the bower, moved on to the thick walls hung with heavy linen cloth dyed blue, and decorated in red and green around the borders. From the wooden beams of the low ceiling bunches of herbs had been hung to dry. The room was filled with the combined smell of savory, basil, and rosemary.

A loud banging sound hurt her ears. Bellebelle turned to see Geoffrey standing in front of the fireplace where an iron pot hung from a rack over the burning logs. He had taken an iron poker and was beating first on the pot, then the black cauldron and kettle that stood on trivets before the hearth.

"What's got into you?" Bellebelle ran over to him. "You'll make me deaf, lad. Leave off that noise now."

"I hate them," Geoffrey cried. "I hate everyone in this village." He started kicking the spit and skewer leaning against the chimney.

Bellebelle pulled Geoffrey tightly against her. "Hush now. I know," she said softly. "I know how you feel. But hating don't make the pain go away none. Don't be letting the other folk bother you so much."

"I want to knock them down and kick them and beat at them." Tears of frustration blurred his eyes.

Bellebelle rocked him back and forth, her eyes on the stone chimney built into the wall, one of the very few in all of Bermondsey, remembering how proud of it she had once been. Until the day the alewife, a stout red-faced woman who brewed and sold ale in the village, had shouted at her that it was plain indecent that the king's slut should have a chimney while respectable, God-fearing women did without. Now every time she looked at it she felt a surge of guilt. A fine one to preach at Geoffrey, she was.

"Why can't I tell Father? Why?"

"I told you why. Now, go play with the chess set your father give you," Bellebelle said, kissing the top of his head.

"Will it always be like this?"

"Of course not," she said, wishing she could believe her own words. "One day soon we'll—we'll live somewheres else and folk'll like us. You'll see."

"Why can't it be now!"

"Because it can't. You must learn to live with the way things be." She tilted Geoffrey's chin up and stared down into his tear-bright eyes. "You mustn't have no wishbone where your backbone ought to be, Son. Always remember that."

She released him and watched while he ran off to fetch the chess set.

Like her son, Bellebelle was miserable in the village but didn't see how she could ever bring herself to leave her home. Henry, who complained the space was so small he could not breathe, had no sooner seen this house completed than he wanted to build her another, grander one, but Bellebelle had told him that, for her, this house was grander than any palace.

Now she took off the cloak lined with ginger fox fur that Henry had given her last Christmas, and hung it carefully on the wooden pole protruding from the wall. She walked back to the hearth. This evening they were having for their supper the remains of a stewed partridge, cooked with onions, cabbage, and parsley. Bellebelle took the long-handled spoon Geoffrey had left on the floor and stirred the bubbling mixture in the iron pot.

When she had first moved to the village, a year after giving birth to Geoffrey in the lodging near St.-Martin-le-Grand in London, Bellebelle had not known the first thing about how to care for her new house. She had almost ruined the garden by pulling out all the vegetables and leaving the weeds, then forgetting to water the flowers in the hot weather. The animals terrified her; even the prize wolfhound Henry gave her made her uneasy. She had been convinced the hens would attack and feared to collect their eggs. The first time she tried to milk the nanny goat Henry had brought her, the beast kicked over the bucket and butted Bellebelle in the stomach. She had run screaming into the house. Henry had laughed 'til he cried.

When he discovered she could not sew, embroider, weave, make simples, or brew herbs to heal, he was dumbfounded. Bellebelle could not tell him that all she was able to do was please men, cure certain ailments of a female's private parts, or prevent babies—the last never wholly successful, her son being ample evidence of that.

Since all her meals in Southwark and Gropecuntlane had been fetched from a nearby cookshop, she had been, as Henry put it, hopeless in the kitchen—almost burning down the house in an effort to light a fire in the hearth and trying to grill a rabbit without first skinning it. Henry had promptly ordered the steward of his Saxon manor house in Bermondsey to hire a local couple to help her several times a sennight. The woman cooked, laundered, tended the garden and animals, and helped with the inside chores while her husband split the logs, did the rough work outside, and brought in the food. This left Bellebelle with little to do and often she thought she'd go witless if she didn't find something to occupy her.

Henry seemed amused rather than offended by her clumsiness and ignorance.

"God's eyes, what a terrible wife you'd make someone, Belle," he told her. "Now Eleanor, who was brought up in the most luxurious surroundings, with hordes of servants at her beck and call, can do anything and everything women are meant to do, and what most men can do besides—not that I'd ever tell her so. It's not easy living up to such a paragon, let me tell you."

At her look of dismay, Henry had grabbed her by the waist and swung her up into his arms with a resounding kiss on the tip of her nose.

"Not to fret. You survived by hawking your wares around the streets and there's not many of us who could do that. Anyway, poppet, you're the perfect *maîtresse*—restful, serene, always willing to listen and to please—" He winked at her.

Bellebelle was not really offended when he compared her to Eleanor. It was only fitting that the woman she worshipped above all others would be able to do everything perfectly. But how she wished her early life had been different; how much better she would feel about herself if she could do the things ordinary women did so easily.

Bellebelle did not like the couple who still came each sennight, and wanted to be rid of them, but she could not bring herself to tell Henry. What reason could she give? They did their work well enough, but were taciturn and sullen, speaking only when spoken to. It was from these two, Bellebelle guessed—although she had no proof—that talk about Henry and herself must have spread to the village. It struck her as being wicked that those who took Henry's bounty should serve him so ill by gossiping behind his back.

Bellebelle never told Henry how the villagers treated her—the men eyeing her with hot glances, the women jeering and spiteful, the folk who ran the market stalls looking down their noses at her—and he was never there long enough to see for himself. Sometimes she would not see him for months on end. When he did come, he grew restless after a few days and was soon off again. Their times together were so brief and precious, he had been so good to her, she hated to spoil them with complaints.

Mustn't grumble. She was safe, no longer had to whore to earn her bread, and had Geoffrey to love and care for. When she felt the aching loneliness, badly missing the company of the whores, the jolly banter, even the excitement of the tavern, she had only to think of the mindless drudgery of her life at Gropecuntlane to be reminded that she was blessed, the most fortunate whore in all England.

From time to time Bellebelle felt tempted to tell Henry the truth about her past but somehow she never could find the right words to explain why she'd lied to him. It had been a small thing to start with, but over the years she had buried the truth beneath a blanket of half-lies. Sometimes she herself couldn't remember what was true and what she'd made up.

She took two earthenware plates from the stack on a wooden bench beside the hearth, filled them with stew, and set them on the trestle table. Next she fetched a clay jug of ale, two wooden cups, a straw basket of oat cakes, and two bone-handled knives.

"Time to eat, Geoffrey," Bellebelle said, pulling up two wooden stools.

He nodded and came to the table, three of the heavy chessmen clutched in his arms. Although only three, Geoffrey was well advanced for his years and Henry was already starting to teach him the game. One day he had appeared with a board of inlaid wood covered with gilt-and-silver squares and the ivory chessmen. When Bellebelle asked him where it came from, Henry had told her it belonged to his mother whose first husband, an emperor, had given it to her when she was not much older than Geoffrey. The boy played for hours with the king and queen in ceremonial robes, the knight fighting a dragon, and, his favorite, the bishop with his miter.

Misty-eyed, Bellebelle watched him. When she'd discovered she was carrying Henry's child, only a month after he had set her up as his mistress in London, she had at first decided to try and rid herself of it, terrified that Henry would turn her out. But, to her surprise, he was pleased, urging her to have the child. He had taken it as a sign of his manhood, reminding her that his grandfather had had a slew of bastards.

A smaller version of Henry with his russet hair and gray eyes, Geoffrey was strongly built and already tall for his age. A studious child, he was self-willed, sometimes quick to anger, though without Henry's violent temper. The prior at the priory school where Henry had arranged for Geoffrey to be educated when he turned three, had told her that he was unusually intelligent for his age, extremely apt at his lessons, and would go far in life. Bellebelle was not sure whether the prior—always courteous but ill-at-ease in her presence—had said this to flatter her, knowing whose son Geoffrey was, or because he really believed it.

Certainly *she* believed he would go far, and was determined to make Geoffrey believe it as well. Geoffrey spoke nothing like she did, thank the Holy Mother—although her speech was continually improving, Henry said—but like his father and the other nobles she'd met. Even a bastard could move up in the world, Henry said, and a king's bastard had a deal more opportunity than most. After all, hadn't his great-grandfather the Conqueror been a bastard?

Geoffrey smiled at her and began to eat his food with pleasure. Bellebelle loved her son so much that sometimes it was like a throbbing ache in her heart. Despite the pinpricks that plagued her, time and again she thanked the Holy Virgin for sending her this precious gift.

Two days later Henry arrived in typical fashion: unannounced. Unexpected. With all the fury of a summer storm. The usual entourage accompanied him, most of whom he dispatched to the Saxon manor house in Bermondsey or one of his lesser manor houses, leaving the rest to shift for themselves in the village or camp in the freezing woods.

"You look more fair than ever, poppet," Henry said to Bellebelle as he entered the hall, then bent his head to kiss her on the mouth. "Here." He thrust something soft and silky into her arms.

Bellebelle shook it out. It was a cape of blue samite, a fine silk threaded with gold, and the loveliest thing she had ever seen.

"Oh, Henry," she whispered, laying the silk against her cheek. "How can I ever thank you? But samite! It do be so costly."

"*Is* costly. The treasury can afford it these days. Come here, Son."

Geoffrey ran eagerly to his father, who picked him up and ruffled his hair. "Wait until you see what I brought for you!"

Through the open door Bellebelle could see knights, squires, and clerks milling about the garden. Near the gate stood a fair-haired knight with a pointed beard leaning on a thick oaken stick. He was talking to Thomas Becket, who frequently accompanied Henry on his visits. The chancellor was always polite in his words, as he had been when she first met him at Gropecuntlane. His manner, however, still conveyed what he really felt: she was the king's doxy, less than the dirt beneath his feet, and Henry would tire of her soon enough.

Bellebelle's gaze again passed over the fair-haired man talking to the chancellor then returned. The hairs at the nape of her neck prickled; her heart jumped. Why? Only a glimpse of his profile was visible yet something about him seemed terrifyingly familiar. Had she seen him before in Henry's retinue? No. He was someone new. The man shifted his weight slightly, turning toward her. A ray of sunlight glanced off a large silver medallion set with five emeralds hanging round his neck. Where had she seen . . . Stifling a cry, Bellebelle shrank back from the door, slammed it shut, then ran over to the stairs. Her body trembled violently and she had to stop herself from rushing up into the bower and hiding under the bedclothes.

It was Hans de Burgh, the Fleming she had almost killed. The man who had murdered her mother.

CHAPTER 33

Thomas Becket, having accompanied Henry to Bermondsey and seen him settled in for a day or two with the minor whore, returned to London. He arrived shortly after Vespers, in time for a late supper. In his mind he always referred to Bellebelle as the minor whore, to distinguish her from Eleanor, who was the major whore. The other whores Henry used Thomas dismissed as temporary conveniences, like the necessary woman who emptied the chamber pots. On the whole he preferred the minor whore. She was compliant, submissive, and knew her place.

When Thomas entered his private quarters at the chancery, his secretary was there to greet him, as well as his body servant and a page.

"A pleasant journey, my lord chancellor?" his secretary inquired.

"I would hardly call a visit to a bawd's house—even a royal bawd's house—pleasant."

"No, my lord, I only meant—"

"I know what you meant, William."

Thomas smiled. To be addressed as "my lord" never failed to send a frisson of enjoyment down his spine. "Are there many guests tonight?"

"The hall is packed to overflowing." The secretary paused. "The queen is here. She heard that some missives had arrived from Aquitaine and had not been sent to her—despite repeated requests. So she came herself."

Thomas stopped in the process of discarding his riding clothes. "The queen is here? Now?"

"I put her in an antechamber to await your return."

The body servant helped Thomas don a silk shirt of a pale gold color, while the page held up a silver mirror.

"By the Mass, does the queen imagine I exist solely to be at her beck and call? That every time a missive or two arrives from Aquitaine I'm meant to drop everything and rush over to Tower Royal to put them personally into her hands?" He gave the secretary an accusing stare, as if he were to blame. "Does she think I have nothing better to do than pay court to the puffed-up idea of her own self-importance?"

He knew he was working himself up into a state of self-righteous indignation but chose to continue. "Is the woman unaware of the difficulties of my office? The endless work, the worry, the plots and snares connived at by my rivals?" If someone had asked him about the specifics of these plots and snares he would have been unable to supply any details, but he felt certain they existed.

Thomas remained motionless while his servant slipped over his head a long red tunic embroidered with the golden lions of Anjou—to match the shirt—then his red hood and mantle.

"Sometimes, William," he said to the secretary, "my life is so wearisome that I would glady give up the vexations of court life and retire to an abbey." He sighed. "To think there are those who envy me! If they only knew . . ." Facile tears sprang to his eyes.

"Indeed, my lord chancellor, but think of all the good you accomplish. Without your help, the administration would fall to ruin. Without your help, how would the king ever have brought peace to England?"

The secretary's words soothed him as Thomas remembered the first hectic year of Henry's reign, when together—sometimes, unfortunately, accompanied by the queen—they had subdued an unruly kingdom, divided in its loyalties, torn asunder by nineteen years of strife and bloodshed. Never would he forget the burned villages, the folk dying daily of starvation, once-prosperous men reduced to begging in order to survive.

Week after week, from dawn until far into the night, Thomas had followed the young king to remote castles, far-flung abbeys, and walled towns, covering the length and breadth of the English realm. It was said that no other ruler, not even the Conqueror himself, had ridden as far and wide as Henry had done, and still did for that matter. Not one corner of the kingdom was neglected, Thomas could attest to that. Wary at first, the country had eventually welcomed their new master; even the powerful magnates who had done as they pleased under Stephen had been brought to heel, forced to acknowledge the presence of a truly strong king.

Over one thousand unlicensed castles had been torn down, the Flemish mercenaries banished, criminals punished, men wrongfully dispossessed reinstated to their manors. The roads were safe again; folk no longer needed to lock their doors at night; cattle and sheep grazed in peace.

"Henry Secundus is a mighty king, who sees justice done," men said of him.

It gave Thomas an intense feeling of satisfaction and pride to realize what a significant contribution he had made in creating this happy state of affairs. He and Henry were as well suited to one another as a hand that fits perfectly into a leather gauntlet.

"Oh yes, my lord chancellor, I almost forgot," said William. "Word came from Canterbury. The archbishop wishes to see you—when you can be spared from your duties, of course."

With a twinge of guilt, Thomas sat on an embroidered stool while the page and body servant pulled on red boots of soft Spanish leather. He had ignored several summons by Theobald in recent months. It was just that he was so busy he simply couldn't find the time to make the five-hour ride to Canterbury. In truth, Thomas knew that was not the only reason. Theobald had more or less planted him as a spy in Henry's administration. After three years he no longer felt like Theobald's man but Henry's. It created a certain awkwardness between himself and his former master.

"Write the archbishop that I will visit him as soon as may be, always his devoted son et al—you know the form, William."

"Yes. The queen, my lord chancellor . . ."

"The queen can wait. No one asked her to come."

Thomas looked down at the new boots, aware that Theobald would not approve of them. Perhaps the summons was to chastise him. I realize this is not the way a cleric would ordinarily dress, he argued in his head with an invisible Theobald, but it befits my station as chancellor of England. What about your abundantly stocked stables, well-equipped ships, luxurious chancery, and nobly born pages—like the one now struggling with your boot? echoed Theobald's reproving voice. It does honor to the Church, Your Grace. And to yourself, my son? Thomas could not deny that. It flattered him that so many great families fought to place their sons in his dignified and elegant household so that they might learn courtesy and manners. Some even tried to bribe members of his household to recommend their children.

"I must find time to visit Theobald," he said aloud. "He wasn't at all well last time I saw him."

There was a knock on the door. William opened it a crack then turned to Thomas. "A page. The queen is aware you have returned and wants to know how long you intend to keep her waiting."

All thought of Theobald vanished. Thomas flushed at the rebuke, glancing at himself in the silver mirror held up by the page, not displeased by the gold-and-scarlet reflection that shimmered back at him.

"Now. I will see the wretched woman now." He sighed. "Bring me the dispatches."

When he arrived at the antechamber, Eleanor, accompanied by two Poitevin equerries, was pacing up and down. She was sumptuously dressed, as usual, in a dark blue cloak lined with gray fur, over a crimson tunic bordered in green and blue. She carried a pair of leather gloves in one hand. Her face—which, against all nature, seemed to grow lovelier with each passing year—was taut with suppressed anger. Thomas was not surprised. He had deliberately kept her waiting; the insult was not lost on her.

"I understand you returned from Bermondsey an hour ago. Do you know how long I've been kept waiting?" she asked in an icy voice.

"Alas, I was not told of your arrival, Madam," Thomas said, shutting the door behind him. It was an obvious lie and would not fool her. But he did not care.

"Not told? What a slovenly household you run, Master Thomas. Who would have thought it?" The queen looked him up and down with no attempt to conceal her outrage—or dislike. "Where are my missives from Aquitaine? I know you received them some time ago."

Thomas felt the heat rise to his face. Did she have a spy in his household? Arrogant Aquitainian whore! She had the tongue of a viper. "Only a few days. My secretary is bringing them now. Perhaps you will tell me what they contain? If any concern the king's business . . ."

"You will be the first to know."

William entered the chamber and handed the dispatches to Thomas who handed them to Eleanor. Without looking at them, she gave the sealed squares of parchment to one of the equerries, pulled her cloak tightly about her shoulders, slipped on the furred gloves, and walked to the door. The equerries followed.

"Did the king say when he would return?" She asked over her shoulder.

"No, Madam. But he should not be gone long. A day or two at the most."

Eleanor opened the door. "Some business in Bermondsey?"

"Business? You could say that, Madam. Indeed, that would be one way of putting it."

For a moment Thomas saw her hesitate, sorely tempted to ask more questions. Then she strode out without a backward glance. Let her wonder what Henry was up to, Thomas thought spitefully. Had he dared he would have dropped even less subtle hints. His hatred of the queen, which grew stronger with each passing year, sometimes caused him to behave without his usual circumspection. Any disquiet he could cause Eleanor filled him with satisfaction, and he had to guard himself whenever he was around her.

Sometimes Thomas felt that he and the queen were in a perpetual clash of arms, two champions in the lists, each parrying and thrusting in an effort to outdo the other and win the prize—Henry. He had just won the last bout.

Repressing the unwanted thought that his behavior smacked of childishness and was unworthy, Thomas paused at the entrance to his hall. Filled as usual with visiting dignitaries, guests, as well as his own staff, he gazed with pleasure at the elaborate tapestries, brick hearth and chimney, the fresh straw laid down daily so that those who could find nowhere else to sit might repose comfortably on the floor without spoiling their clothes.

Knowing all eyes were upon him, Thomas strode majestically through the crowd until he came to the high table, laid with gold and silver plate, savory dishes, and fine wines from Bordeaux and Gascony. He seated himself in the center of the table. While others indulged their appetites, Thomas ate sparingly of roast wildfowl and pickled salmon. Ecclesiastics were not permitted to eat any four-footed creature. Unlike many a gluttonous priest, Thomas followed that rule to the letter. While others drank heartily of ruby wine and brown ale, he sipped only boiled water flavored with fresh mint. Aware that he was the center of attention—as well he should be—Thomas made a great show of how abstemious he was. What did it matter if people whispered in corners that his life was unsuitable for an ecclesiastic—even one in minor orders; that his show of wealth and magnificence indicated an inappropriate worldliness.

He, Thomas Becket, was the second man in the realm, next to the king, and he intended no man should forget it. In time, perhaps, few would remember that he had been poor Thomas of West Cheap, a hard-working cleric of modest origins. Once dependent upon the bounty of great nobles and powerful churchmen, these men were now dependent upon him! Truly, it illustrated the teaching of the Gospel.

Later, after his guests had left or retired for the night, Thomas dismissed his secretary and attendants, then withdrew to the privacy of his own chamber where only a monk in black cassock and sandals awaited him. In his hands the brother held a supple green birch rod; Thomas felt the monk's gaze on him while he removed his mantle, tunic, and gold shirt. When he had stripped to his drawers, he knelt shivering on the cold tiled floor. The monk handed him a silver crucifix which Thomas held pressed to his lips, while under his breath he began to recite the first of thirty penitential psalms.

Bowing his back, Thomas tensed for the first blow. When it struck, like a flame searing his shoulders, he felt a bolt of sensation, an agony that was almost pleasurable, shoot through his whole body. While this ordeal was not something he enjoyed as such, Thomas had spent so many years subjugating his true feelings while he followed the orders of the great and powerful that these beatings often provided a new, heightened awareness of himself. Any sensation that he allowed himself to experience—even pain or hatred—was better than constant repression. Thus Thomas subjected himself to this ritual at least three times a sennight. He deemed the chastisement necessary, for he knew himself guilty of the sins of pride, of believing himself superior to other men, of excessive worldliness in his enjoyment of luxury, of not loving God sufficiently, of never having felt His presence—defects of character he quite readily gave up to his confessor.

But the main reason he endured flagellation was the secret sin he had deeply buried, never confessed, barely even acknowledged to himself: his passion for Henry; his need to battle the queen and take her place in Henry's heart—a need he did not understand, and one that, *au fond,* filled him with horror. Depraved and shameful in Thomas's own eyes, his unnatural longing, this compelling drive, must be scourged from him. Only then would God show Himself to him, the most unworthy of His servants.

That same night after Henry had bedded her, Bellebelle lay next to him staring up at the oaken beams of the ceiling. Over the years she had managed to suppress the incident concerning her mother. But all day, to her dismay, she had been reliving every grim detail of her struggle with de Burgh in the Southwark brothel-house, her midnight flight through the twisted alleys of Southwark to St. Mary Overie, and only half-listening to Henry, who, propped up on one elbow, was describing his recent adventures with his usual gusto.

It never failed to surprise her that Henry seemed to prefer talking to bedding her, actually expecting her to listen and discuss matters with him, something no customer had ever asked of her.

Henry commented frequently on the current state of the realm, his desire to see justice done, his constant troubles with France, his less-frequent problems with unruly Aquitaine. Most often, however, especially since the death of his first-born son, William, six months ago, he talked of his family: his mother in Normandy, his rebellious brother in Anjou who was demanding that Henry turn the county over to him per their father's will, and, unceasingly, Eleanor.

Bellebelle could never hear enough about Henry's queen and their growing brood of children. She thought a lot about Geoffrey's two half-brothers and sister. How she wished her son could meet the elder son, Henry, born three years ago, the only girl, Matilda, and the younger boy, Richard, born a year ago, in 1157.

Tonight, however, she felt so preoccupied that it was an effort to listen to Henry.

". . . knew I was right about him."

"Who?" She had totally lost the sense of what he was saying. Something about Louis of France. Bellebelle forced herself to listen.

"You haven't been paying attention. I was telling you about my latest triumphs."

"Over Louis of France. Yes, I were listening."

"*Was* listening. I told everyone he would have a daughter with that Castilian wife, and now he has."

"Why be that a triumph for you?"

"*Is.* Ah, you may well ask. I intend to marry my son Henry to that daughter, Marguerite, I think they call her. Now if Louis will only continue to produce daughters, my son will one day rule both France and England. Think of that, Belle! In June I plan to send Thomas to France to make an official offer for the girl."

Bellebelle managed a smile. "Be—is there another triumph?"

"Another—ah, so you were listening. Yes, I've finally subdued the Welsh barons."

Welsh. Bellebelle thought immediately of Morgaine and touched the necklace of blue stones which she still wore faithfully.

"I'm hardly a novice at warfare, Belle," Henry said, "but I've never seen anything like the Welsh. They never heard of rules or chivalry, won't fight on level ground, and prefer to cut off their enemies' heads rather than hold them for ransom." He shook his head. "But a truce has finally been declared, thank God. I doubt I or my troops would survive another campaign."

When Henry talked of war and fighting she wondered why a Fleming like de Burgh was still in England. Despite the risk involved in asking such a question she had to know.

"When you fight a . . . a campaign, does . . . do you still have the Flemings?" She tried to make her voice sound as if she were only mildly interested.

In the glow of a single candle Bellebelle could see a puzzled look cross Henry's face.

"What a question! Of course not. I got rid of all that scum during the first year of my reign just as I told you I would on the bridge in London. What made you think of the Flemings?"

Bellebelle's throat felt dry and she hesitated. Unless she said she recognized de Burgh, she would never know the reason he had not been banished. His presence threatened not only her whole new world, but perhaps her very life; she *had* to know. Heart pounding, she took a deep breath.

"I thought as I recognized someone in your party from me days selling honey cakes in the tavern. No one I knows, mind, just someone as used to come into the tavern to—to play dice and drink ale. He—was supposed to be a Fleming."

"You must be mistaken. There are no Flemings in my entourage." Henry fixed her with one of his unblinking stares that made her feel all trembly inside. "What man do you refer to?"

"The fair bearded one who wore the silver medallion inlaid with all them emeralds."

"The fair man with the silver—oh, you must mean the one that's slightly crippled—I can't think of his name just now." He paused, frowning. "By God's eyes, you're right, you know, he *is* a Fleming. Half anyway. His mother is of good Norman stock, I hear, and her family are distant relations of my marshal of England." Another pause. "Yes, I remember now that John—he's the marshal—interceded on this man's behalf. Very convincingly as I recall. As a result, I didn't banish him with all the others. I've never even spoken to—I think his name's de Bragh or de Brugh, something like that—he's just one of the marshal's knights. In fact, this is the first time he's accompanied me." Henry continued to watch her intently. "What a memory you have. This man must have made quite an impression for you to remember him all these years."

Bellebelle squirmed under his close scrutiny, hiding her fear behind a crooked smile. "It were—was—the silver medallion with all them green stones."

"It certainly is distinctive." Henry yawned, blew out the candle, rolled over on his back, and within moments appeared to have fallen asleep.

Trembling, Bellebelle let out a long breath. Now, at least, she knew why the Fleming was still in England, and even half-remembered her customer, Ralph, saying something about de Burgh being part Norman. The danger however was just as real. If he continued to travel with Henry's entourage, then sooner or later he would be sure to recognize her and tell Henry what she had done to him. Henry might see that she had acted to save her mother, and not hold that against her, but her life in the Bankside brothel and then at Gropecuntlane would be sure to come out. How would he feel about the mother of his beloved Geoffrey having been a whore?

"Is something on your mind, Belle? You seem troubled, unlike yourself."

Henry's sleepy voice startled her.

She hesitated. Now was the moment to speak out but the words caught in her throat. "I be fine. Tired."

"Then God rest you, poppet."

"God rest you, Henry," she whispered.

Her heart beat so fiercely she was sure he must hear it. Carefully she turned over on her side. You could never tell with Henry. Sometimes she felt as if he had eyes in the back of his head that could see right through her. Bellebelle understood him well enough to know that he wouldn't like her lying to him over the years. There was no telling how he would take it. Unless she avoided de Burgh, he was sure to find out. For a time, perhaps, she might be able to stay out of the Fleming's sight. But one day . . .

CHAPTER 34

*T*wo days after he had left Henry in Bermondsey, Thomas sat at the head of a long table in his chancery by the Thames, a stone's throw from the gray hulk of Westminster.

On one side of the table his secretary, William, read aloud dispatches from all the far-flung reaches of Henry's vast empire: Northern England, Normandy, Anjou, Aquitaine. There were applications for opening a lawsuit; a missive from Henry's lieutenant in Poitou, complaining that the Poitevin lords paid no attention to his orders; letters from scholars seeking benefices; venomous notes from bishops accusing the king's judges of encroaching on their jurisdiction. If true, a very serious charge indeed. Lay judges had no business interfering in ecclesiastical courts.

In a separate pile were several unopened missives, newly arrived from the seneschal in Poitou, addressed to the queen. Probably complaining about Henry's lieutenant. The documents were carefully sealed with a special red seal, and it would have been obvious if they had been opened. By rights all such documents should come directly to the chancellor, and Thomas considered it a bypass of his authority that he could not read them first. But the queen had made a point of demanding that all such dispatches addressed to her should initially be read by her; Thomas did not want a repeat of the scene of two nights ago.

Henry, who officially ruled in Aquitaine, allowed his wife to still believe she was the dominant authority. One day, however, Thomas hoped that Henry would stop indulging his queen. Her receipt of special payments from the exchequer—referred to as the Queen's

Gold—was shocking enough, a complete break with precedent. Whatever degree of unofficial control Eleanor managed to retain over her duchy was even more intolerable.

In Thomas's opinion women had no place in the administration of government. He even questioned the wisdom of allowing the Empress Maud, virtually acting as regent in Normandy, to actually sign charters without royal authority, in her and Henry's name! But as her son lived in a state of unqualified admiration regarding his mother, Thomas, like everyone else, tread carefully where the tough old empress was concerned.

In England, at least, he did his best to see that the Aquitainian whore was relegated to the background. Not too difficult, since she had been kept so busy performing her primary task of producing children that she had little time to meddle in state affairs.

On the other side of the table a set of clerks copied the minutes of decisions taken in the royal council: grants of land awarded, marriages of royal wards—every decision of the king's that must be recorded for posterity. A clerk brought Thomas a pile of his own dispatches to be sealed, along with the great Seal in its wooden box, and the container of sweet-smelling green beeswax. Thomas sealed all his own letters; he enjoyed the ceremony of affixing to parchment this emblem of his power.

"Here is a letter from a knight in the north country," said William, scrutinizing a square of parchment, "reminding the king that he was promised a good-sized fief."

Thomas raised his brows. "Presumptuous of him. What service did he render, pray?"

William cleared his throat. "This knight is the father of Mistress Margaret. You may recall—"

"Yes, yes, I remember now. When you draw up the grant be discreet. Don't mention the services rendered."

A clerk down the table snickered.

Thomas fixed him with a steely glare. "Does something amuse you, Master Paul? It is well to remember that charters are available to the public and can be seen by anyone. We don't want tongues to wag any more than they already do."

He repressed a sign of irritation. If only Henry's personal life were not so undisciplined! Thomas had little fault to find with Henry the king; he worked hard enough for ten men. Even Henry's passion for hunting and hawking took second place to that of keeping the peace in his far-flung realm. Although he was greedy of gain, jealous of his power, and sometimes harsh—only to be expected in a son of Normandy—the prosperity of his subjects and his desire for justice and order were Henry's greatest concern. A good king now; in time, with his, Thomas's aid, possibly a great one.

"This foolish business with women will be the king's undoing if he does not prove more discreet," Thomas said in an undertone to his secretary. "I do not speak of doxies, or bedding a village girl for a night. These matter little."

"I understand, my lord chancellor. Even establishing a mistress of low birth and acknowledging her son as his own can be explained away. You refer to the king's habit of seducing young women of good family."

"Extremely dangerous." Thomas sighed.

"Thus far, no irate father has objected," William said in a barely audible voice. "All have quietly accepted the wages of their daughters' sins."

"For which we must thank Our Heavenly Father. I live in constant fear that one day His Majesty will go too far and bring down upon himself, and the realm, some grave trouble that a fief will not assuage—nor a wife eleven years older than her husband, forgive."

Nor a wife, forgive, Thomas repeated to himself. If such an opportunity ever presented itself—Thomas's gaze met his secretary's and he looked quickly away. "*Benedicite.* Sufficient unto the day, William, sufficient unto the day . . . I cannot silence every tongue in England."

William nodded and perused the next document.

While Thomas watched the clerks stitch newly made copies to the great roll of the pipe, he thought he heard the nearby clatter of hooves. Impossible. It sounded as though the horse was inside the chancery. Thomas looked toward the entrance to the chancery, and half-rose from his seat.

By God's wounds, a horse *was* standing in the entrance to the large chamber! The clerks jumped to their feet.

"Sit still everyone. We can clear you if you lower your heads and don't move."

Henry, crouched flat over a small brown palfrey, leapt neatly over the table. The horse's hind hooves grazed a corner, scattering stacks of parchment to the floor. The clerks scrambled to retrieve them while Thomas, seething, forced himself to smile. Henry knew that his chancellor hated to have his morning routine disturbed, yet how typical of the king to play such a trick. To bring a horse inside the chancery! By the Mass, he was still such a child at heart. Thomas eyed the palfrey with wary eyes, but the well-trained beast was standing perfectly still in a corner of the room.

"I have a new lady love, Thomas, a gyrfalcon fresh from Iceland, and I want you to help me fly her. No one is better at luring a falcon than you, my friend." Henry lifted his head and gave Thomas one of his engaging grins.

"I would like to oblige, Sire, but I have to plan for my June trip to Paris, then there are some dispatches for the queen, just arrived, that I must deliver—"

"Excellent. We can discuss the Paris journey while we fly my new lady. I haven't seen Eleanor myself for several days so we can both pay a visit to her when we're done."

"I hadn't expected you back from Bermondsey so soon," Thomas said. He had a full morning's work ahead of him and the prospect of flying a new falcon was far from welcome.

"I grew restless so I left at first light this morning. It's a fine day, not a breath of wind. Perfect for flying. You mustn't be overly zealous in poring through musty documents, Thomas. I won't take no for an answer."

Thomas picked up a sheet of parchment with fingers that twitched in suppressed anger. Overly zealous! Poring through musty documents! Is that what Henry thought he was doing? Jesu! It wouldn't hurt to remind the king exactly in whose vineyards he labored.

"Poring over musty documents would not begin to describe—I was just drafting an answer to the father of Mistress—let me see—" Thomas held the sheet close to his short-sighted eyes. "Mistress Margaret of Ripon. It seems you promised him a fief."

"Good God, did I really? Mea culpa. In truth, I barely recall the man, much less his daughter. Hardly what you'd call a memorable experience, eh? A plot of land with a few sheep and pigs will most certainly suffice. The wench wasn't worth an entire fief."

Henry grinned again at Thomas. "However, such matters are best left in your capable hands. What would I do without your expertise, my friend?" He glanced at the table of clerks who had been watching this exchange with bated breath. "What would we all do without our beloved chancellor, eh?"

The clerks nodded vigorous agreement.

By God's wounds, the man was totally impossible. But how could he resist? Against his will, Thomas found himself smiling at Henry, his anger dissipating as he succumbed, yet again, to the king's infectious charm. "Yes, all right, I'll be with you in a moment. While you're here, Sire, perhaps you would glance at this letter to your brother in Anjou—"

"My lady from Iceland cannot wait upon my brother Geoffrey's ambition, which will keep, I've no doubt. We can discuss that renegade later. See you outside."

Before Thomas could protest, the palfrey jumped over the table again and Henry vanished.

"Do what you can without me, William," Thomas said in a resigned voice as he picked up the sheafs of parchments for the queen and stuffed them into the scrip attached to his belt. "I probably won't be back until tomorrow."

East of London, on the outskirts of a marsh, Thomas watched while the Icelandic gyrfalcon, a fierce white specimen with an impressive wing span, soared upward into a cloudy gray sky. She circled in a dazzling display of loops before targeting her prey, a heron, flying well below her. The gyrfalcon towered for an instant before stooping in a vertical dive to the kill. Her speed took Thomas's breath away.

"God's eyes, have you ever seen the like?" Henry, standing upright in the stirrups, his eyes shining, was transported. "She's magnificent, one of a kind. I've called her Eleanor."

Thomas gave him a sharp glance, but Henry was entirely serious and obviously meant it as a great compliment. Privately he thought the name all too apt. Eleanor struck him as having the potential for being as predatory and rapacious as any gyrfalcon.

Recovering the bird was a tedious business for she was willful and slow to lure. Even Thomas could not bring her to him. The peregrines that Thomas owned were far less colorful, their performance not as impressive, but they were easier to control and more like sporting partners. He preferred the serviceable, more practical birds, who were biddable and less arrogant. Hunting with a gyrfalcon was like accompanying a wild creature while it stalked its prey, and held no allure for him. But gyrfalcons alone were a symbol of monarchy. Thomas knew that anything that reminded young Henry that he was king—still new and exciting after three years—was immensely satisfying. Not to mention Henry's penchant for the untamable, his love of risk, his inability to refuse a challenge.

By the time the gyrfalcon, her feet tangled in the long leather jesses, was lured and hooded, even Henry's patience was sorely tried, and Thomas could cheerfully have wrung the creature's snowy neck. The king's party then headed for the Tower.

Riding across East Smithfield at dusk, their attendants some way behind them, Thomas noticed a lame beggar bent over a crooked stick barring their way. His garb was so threadbare that patches of bare skin showed through the filthy rags.

"Can you spare a penny, good sirs?" the beggar asked. " 'Afore God, but it's a cold night." Henry reined in his stallion. "Where do you hail from, fellow?"

The beggar paused, searching Henry's face with a sly look. "Why—Le Mans, my lord. Came to London as a mere youth then—reduced to begging as a result of King Stephen's plundering Flemings, God curse the lot of them."

"Le Mans is my own birthplace! And I too came to London as a mere youth. As for the Flemings, well, I couldn't agree with you more. Do you know who I am?"

"A great and noble lord, even a beggar can see that."

Thomas eyed the beggar, who had a ready tongue and a cunning eye. Le Mans indeed! A likely tale if ever he'd heard one. He doubted the rogue had ever set foot out of London in his life, and he was quick-witted enough to know just the right tale to appeal to the king—whom he'd obviously recognized. Henry was naive enough, apparently, to be taken in. Thomas held his tongue, not averse to letting this knave take advantage of Henry's inexperience with London's wily poor.

"On this bitter night wouldn't a warm mantle be of more use to you than a penny?" Henry smiled at the beggar. "As you can see, my own cloak is a poor thing, almost as threadbare as yours. But the chancellor here, Archdeacon Thomas Becket, of whom no doubt you've heard, has a magnificent mantle lined with gray squirrel. You can see for yourself. As he is also the most charitable of men, greatly inclined to alms giving, I feel certain he'll have no objection to letting you have his cloak."

Henry moved his horse so that the two beasts stood neck to neck. He twisted sideways in the saddle and tried to pull the scarlet mantle away from Thomas's shoulders. Dumbfounded, then suddenly outraged at this wanton encroachment of his rights, Thomas grabbed Henry by his sinewy wrists in an effort to stop him. The horses plunged and reared while the two grappled. Henry's stallion, snorting in alarm, arched his neck. Henry, already half out of the saddle, lost his balance and slipped; pulling Thomas with him, he tumbled to the ground. The beggar backed well away while Thomas and Henry wrestled on the frozen earth. By the time their attendants had galloped up, torches in hand, the two men were laughing so hard they could hardly draw breath. Finally they collapsed on top of each other. Henry rolled over then sat astride Thomas.

"Do you yield?" His voice rang out in the clarion call of a knight triumphant in the lists.

"I do, my lord, I do."

"Sir beggar, take your spoils."

Henry stood up and pulled the cloak off Thomas's shoulders. With a flourish he handed it to the beggar, who bent to kiss Henry's hand then bounded away—without the use of his crutch, Thomas noted.

"If that fellow's from Le Mans I'm from the bogs of Ireland. He's a lying rogue but I'll forgive a quick wit anytime." Henry chuckled. "For a tall stick of a cleric you've a power of strength in you, my lord chancellor." He helped Thomas to his feet and gave him a playful punch on the arm.

Thomas brushed himself off with a lofty smile, trying to hold back tears of joy by adding a layer of dignity. Despite their close working relationship as chancellor and king, this was the very first time Henry had actually behaved as if he were a true companion— an equal.

"I'll order a new, more splendid cloak from the finest tailor in London, Sire," Thomas said. "Then put it down in the records as a debt of the king for grievous assault."

Henry threw back his head and shouted with laughter. "God's eyes, you've an answer for everything!"

"Naturally, or I wouldn't have come as far as I have."

"Nor would you be my chancellor."

They grinned at each other, then mounted their horses. They continued on their way to the Tower, the bond of fellowship strong between them.

. . .

Night had fallen by the time Henry and Thomas reached the royal residence. They climbed the spiral staircase to the topmost floor of the Tower, entered the chamber, and found the queen, attended by two women, sitting up in the royal marriage bed. An ever-present troubadour was softly strumming his lute while the official court reader, Master Wace from Normandy, read aloud from his own Anglo-Norman translation of the story of King Arthur.

Observing Eleanor amid the lace-trimmed pillows and fur-lined coverlets piled on the bed, Thomas could hardly believe she was thirty-four years old. Her skin was as fine and smooth as that of a damsel of eighteen; her hair, which was usually confined in a wimple, fell in a shimmering chestnut cascade over her shoulders. When one looked at her body, it was impossible to believe she had borne Henry four children, and Louis, two. Her waist was still supple and slim, her breasts high and firm, clearly outlined through a beribboned silk robe lined with ermine.

Thomas noted that Eleanor looked first at Henry then at himself, as if sensing the new-formed bond between them. Henry seemed unaware of her scrutiny, but Thomas felt a wave of guilt wash through his body, almost as if she could read the dark, secret thoughts that disturbed his nights.

After a moment the queen dismissed the troubadour, reader, and attendants, nodded curtly to Thomas, and patted a place beside her on the bed. Henry sat down; he took her white hand with its tapering jeweled fingers into his own grubby one and brought it to his mouth.

"In bed already? Are you unwell?"

"Nothing of import."

"What ails you?"

"My stomach is queasy, slight chills, and the most rapid palpitations—"

Henry put his lips against her forehead. "There's no fever." He laid his hand across her chest; Thomas saw his fingers involuntarily spread toward the peak of her breast. "But your heart still beats like a hammer."

Eleanor smiled. "Now that you're arrived it's grown far worse. Are you surprised?"

Henry's face became flushed; a finger touched her nipple thrusting against the fabric of her robe.

Feeling like an intruder, Thomas saw their gaze lock, the passion between them so intense it was like watching a streak of lightning pass from one to the other. He was sure they had forgotten him. Yet only moments ago he and Henry had been so close . . . Despite a stern admonition to his will, Thomas felt his treacherous loins stir with impossible longings as carnal images rose, unbidden, to cloud his mind. The scourging was obviously not enough. He must tame his body with longer work hours, continued fasting, more strenuous activity. Temptation must be beaten down again and again and again like the savage beast it was.

After a few moments Thomas regained control. Observing that Eleanor and Henry were still engrossed in each other—she was now whispering in his ear and Henry's face lit up like a candle at whatever she was saying—he wondered, as he had so often before, what insidious demon drove the king to pursue other women. Obviously this imperious creature was the one he loved—in his fashion—the one whom he still fiercely desired, which Eleanor obviously returned with equal fervor. Even the minor whore in Bermondsey, whose claim on Henry's affections baffled Thomas, did not cast the same heady enchantment as did the Aquitainian. Why then did Henry continue to behave as he did? It boggled the mind.

Thomas coughed. "I've brought some recent dispatches, Madam."

His words broke the spell. Henry, breathing heavily, hastily rose to his feet.

Eleanor reached out her hand for the documents. "Thank you."

"Perhaps you will tell me what the dispatches contain? If it concerns the king's business . . ." Thomas stopped at Henry's barely perceptible frown.

"I'm aware of all that. We had a similar conversation several days ago, I believe."

Did the king hear the antagonism in her voice?

"What have you been up to in Bermondsey, my dear?" Eleanor asked Henry. "You can't know how I've missed you."

Henry smiled. "Some matter I needed to attend to concerning the manor house there. Today Thomas and I have been hawking, Nell. I have a wondrous new gyrfalcon I've named Eleanor in honor of you."

"I long to see her." The queen turned her head toward Thomas. "Was there something else, my lord chancellor?"

Thomas felt skewed by those compelling eyes. "No, Madam." Henry glanced first at him then at Eleanor. He *must* be aware of their mutual animosity. The question was—what would he do about it?

"I'll see you back at Westminster, Thomas," Henry said quickly. "Probably by tomorrow morning. Thank you for an adventurous day. Oh, you'll be pleased to hear that in September I'm to be the father of another son. Eleanor has just told me the wonderful news."

"Wonderful news," Thomas echoed. "Congratulations, Madam." He bowed, then walked to the door of the chamber. Henry followed him. At the top of the staircase, the king half-closed the door.

"The queen is out of sorts due to her condition. Forgive her brusqueness." He paused. "There was something I almost forgot," he said in a low voice. "A confidential matter. I want you to get me whatever information exists on one of the marshal's knights, a distant relative I believe. He wears an emerald-studded medallion and his father was Flemish, his mother Norman. This man's recent activities don't concern me, just what he did during the last years of Stephen's reign. Particularly the period when he may have been in London. There's no urgency about the matter, merely—curiosity on my part. But for my ears only, you understand?"

Mystified, Thomas nodded. Henry went back inside the queen's chamber, shutting the door behind him.

All the way back to Westminster, Thomas raged. The Aquitainian whore would pay for summarily dismissing him like an errant schoolboy. There would come a time when she would rue the day she had humiliated the lord chancellor of England.

# CHAPTER 35

# Paris,

# 1158

*T*he following June Thomas left London for Paris, on what would be his most important mission, thus far, of Henry's reign.

He had not spent more than a day or two in France since his student days, and upon entering Paris, Thomas experienced a sense of boundless gratification—something he rarely allowed himself to feel. How different was this arrival from his unheralded days as a scholar when he could barely scrape together enough deniers to feed himself or pay for his lodgings.

From the many hundreds of awestruck faces gazing up at him, it was obvious that the French had never witnessed anything quite as magnificent as the procession now wending its way across the bridge leading to the Île-de-la-Cité. Judging by the size of the crowd, the entire city must have turned out in force to witness the spectacle that, he, chancellor of England, had personally created.

Henry had entrusted to him the task of persuading King Louis that his vassal for Normandy, Anjou, and Aquitaine wanted lasting peace between France and England. The peace was to be solidified by the marriage between Louis's daughter, Marguerite, now six months old, and Henry's eldest son, aged three and one-half years, with the Vexin as her dowry. Thomas's grand appearance was to be followed by a personal visit from Henry himself—the very first time the king of England would meet the king of France face-to-face on friendly terms since Henry had been made duke of Normandy seven years earlier.

The crowd surged forward with cries of wonder and delight as each segment of the procession passed by. First came those on foot: two hundred-and-fifty pages and squires in squads of sixteen, marching to the strains of Welsh and English songs. Next came the hunting-train: fewterers with the finest hounds on gilded leashes, falconers bearing hooded and jessed falcons on their leather-gloved wrists. Then came the wagons drawn by five black horses, led by a grandly dressed groom with an enormous mastiff trotting beside him. The lead wagon, sumptuously decorated in gilt-and-scarlet hangings, boasted a portable chapel for Thomas's own use. The last two wagons contained barrels of brown ale—it was time the French learned there was something besides wine for civilized people to drink.

Following the wagons came the pack mules, each with an ornate chest roped to either side and a long-tailed monkey cavorting in between. Every time the procession halted—and Thomas had arranged for many stops—the chests were opened to show their contents: gold and silver plate, spoons, ewers, jeweled goblets. The hostlers leading the mules were all dressed in identical garb, the livery of the king of England. Next came the men-at-arms marching in precise formation, then the knights in gleaming armor riding huge destriers, and holding aloft the royal scarlet banners with their golden lions. Squires carrying their shields walked in step beside them.

Thomas had elected to bring up the rear, dressed more magnificently than anyone else, in brocaded velvet, astride a snow white horse whose trappings were of gold and silver. He heard someone in the crowd shout "If this be his chancellor what must the king himself be like?" Exactly the effect he wished to create. Abandoning his usual air of dignity and pride, he permitted himself a gracious smile, reveling in this moment of glory.

If he never did anything else for the realm—and God knows he had done enough to defy number—Thomas knew he would always be remembered for the spectacle he had created and organized. This balmy morning in June of the year 1158 would be engraved on the memory of anyone who had watched the procession. Not only that, if each chronicler in every French and English abbey also noted the event, it was bound to be talked of years, perhaps decades, even generations, later. Posterity would know that due to his brilliant chancellor, Henry Plantagenet had become one of the most powerful monarchs in the West.

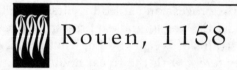

# Rouen, 1158

"This year of 1158 is surely the most glorious of my four-year reign," Henry said to Robert de Beaumont, earl of Leicester and co-justiciar of England. "Thus far."

"You say that every year, sire."

"Well, it's true every year. But *this* one is quite exceptional. Admit it, Robert."

"Gladly."

It was late September. Accompanied by grooms, squires, huntsmen and fewterers, Henry and de Beaumont were riding through the Verte Forest which lay outside Rouen. Turf flew from under the horses' hooves. A blood-stained knife dangled at Henry's belt, a yew bow was slung over one shoulder, an ivory horn around the other; a wolfskin cap covered his tawny head. Having just brought down a five-branched stag, he was filled with that special glow of achievement which always accompanied a successful hunt.

Through the rusted leaves the light was beginning to fade. Henry and his party rode into a clearing, scattering piles of damp leaf-mold, carefully skirting the old wood hunting lodge where his grandfather had died—it must be all of twenty-odd years ago now.

"I keep meaning to tear that eyesore down," Henry said, pulling his horse to a stop and pointing to the crumbling wooden structure. "Every time I ride through here I get a chill—as if a wolf stepped over my grave." He looked at the aging earl, whose face had a shuttered look, as if he were suddenly on guard. "You were there when my grandfather died, weren't you?"

"Indeed," said de Beaumont, signing himself. "I cannot pass this lodge without remembering not only that untimely death but also its tragic aftermath."

And the upheaval of my own life, Henry added silently. There still remained for him an element of mystery concerning the origins of the bitter struggle for the crown between his mother and her first cousin, Stephen of Blois.

"My mother avoids talking about those days," Henry said.

"No one cares to dwell on evil times, Sire," Leicester said, obviously choosing his words with care. "The glories of *this* reign are much more felicitious. At long last you've subdued the Welsh, dispensed strict justice, kept the peace, and managed to persude the king of Scotland to do homage for his English estates. No mean feat."

"Surely that's not an end to my glories." Henry raised his brows.

The earl laughed uneasily. "No indeed—ah, how about inspiring increased confidence in the populace by minting a stronger, sounder coinage? Then there—"

"That will do." Henry held up his hand, aware that Leicester was trying to divert his attention.

By God's eyes, there *was* some mystery to be solved, one he had sensed for as long as he could remember. Not that he had any intention of probing. On the contrary, instinct told him it was best to let sleeping hounds lie. Henry spurred his mount and, followed by the hunting party, rode quickly through the clearing.

Thoughts of what he had accomplished continued to stir in his mind. In midsummer, after Thomas's successful negotiations with the French king, he had himself gone to Paris to collect the baby Marguerite so that she could be brought up as a member of her future husband's family. Louis had permitted her to leave on condition that Eleanor had no hand in her upbringing. Both he and Henry had agreed that until the two children were old enough to marry, the disputed Vexin would be held in pledge by the great military order of the Knights Templar so that neither king might put a garrison to it.

A few weeks later, Louis had decided to make a pilgrimage to the Abbey of Mont-St.-Michel in Normandy. Henry had given him permission to travel freely throughout his duchy, and even joined him. Despite the shadow of Eleanor that, inevitably, fell between them, he had been surprised to find how well he and Louis had gotten along.

"You know, Louis of France is not a bad sort," he said aloud to Leicester. "Although I can see why he would never have suited Eleanor."

"Pious as plainsong and an absolute saint—but not someone I would totally trust."

"With the possible exception of my mother, there are none whom I *totally* trust," said Henry. "Perhaps one other."

"Only one other? Who might this be?"

"No one you know. An old friend I met on London Bridge, as it happens. During the days you still supported King Stephen."

At the startled expression on Leicester's face, Henry smiled. Let the earl make of that what he would.

The party slowed as they came to a thickly wooded copse covered with dense green brambles and fallen branches. A faint mist rose from the moist earth.

The most recent occurrence of the year concerned his mischief-making brother. Geoffrey had suddenly stopped intriguing against him, having at last found an outlet for his ambitous nature. The Bretons, having driven out their overlord, had asked him to take over Brittainy. Unfortunately—for Geoffrey at least—he had died within weeks of becoming their count. Last month, in August, Henry, as his brother's heir, had promptly requested Louis of France to grant him the title of seneschal of Brittainy. It was a test of their newfound friendship and Louis had readily complied.

The hunting party crossed a burbling stream, came to an opening amid the stately golden trees, and emerged onto the road that led to Rouen. Dusk was fast approaching. Through the blue haze of evening wood smoke, a red-and-purple sunset streaked the sky. Ahead, Henry could see the spires and roofs of the city, crowned with flame by the setting sun. The air was still, the pungent scent of the verdant forest mingling with the wild beast odor of the dead stag roped to one of the horses.

Beside him, Henry could see the earl of Leicester crouched over his mount; behind, he heard the sound of horses' hooves beating a steady rhythm against the hard track, the hounds giving tongue as they strained against their leashes.

His senses honed to a sword-edge, Henry was jolted outside himself into a crystalline awareness of the passing moment. There was nothing unusual about the ordinary events of this ordinary day except an aching desire to hold it fast. Why was he always rushing toward achievement, racing like one of the mythic furies toward a future that lay just around the next bend in the road? Why was time his enemy? Always eluding his grasp, trying to rob him of the chance to reach fulfillment. Stop, he wanted to shout. It's all going by too quickly . . .

The trumpets sounded as he neared the city gates. The moment abruptly vanished. In the twilight he could see the scarlet-and-gold standard, showing the duke was in residence, flying from the castle keep. Outside the gates the road split, one leading away from Rouen.

"If you don't need me, I'll ride on to Beaumont, sire," said Leicester. "My greetings to your lady mother."

Henry watched him turn down the road that led to his estates at Beaumont, another three hours' ride. A wise counselor, an able justiciar, the earl was one of the old guard, a lone remnant left from an infamous reign, and, in fact, one of the few men that Henry did trust. Not that he ever intended Leicester to know that. Better to keep him—and everyone else—slightly off balance. Ever green in memory was his mother's oft-repeated admonition that an untamed hawk, when raw flesh is offered to it and then withdrawn, becomes more greedy and therefore more ready to obey.

Inside the ducal palace Henry went straight to his quarters and called for a wooden tub of hot water perfumed with aromatic herbs that would relieve aching muscles. He had been soaking in the tub for some time when Thomas Becket unexpectedly entered the chamber. Henry frowned. He had only left England two weeks ago.

"Greetings, Sire."

"This is a surprise. When did you arrive? Is anything wrong?"

"I arrived just now and nothing is wrong. On the contrary."

"Good! Then I'm glad to see you, Thomas." Henry stood up while a servant rubbed his back with a long linen towel. The chancellor quickly averted his eyes. "What are these glad tidings?"

"The queen has produced another son, Sire, who thrives mightily to judge from his lusty cries."

"By God! By God and all His Saints!" Henry spun round in the tub, splashing water over the sides and onto Thomas's red tunic, drenching the servant. "Another son! How is the queen?"

Thomas hastily backed away. "She is well. As always, she drops her babes as easily as a brood mare."

Henry gave him a sharp look. Sooner or later something would have to be done about the bad blood between Nell and Thomas—when he had the time to confront and deal with it. It was intolerable that his closest friend and his loving wife should be always at odds. Especially when he was the ground over which they waged their subtle warfare.

"To her great credit, Thomas. It behooves you to give the lady her due."

Thomas colored at the rebuke and patted the scrip at his belt. "She sends you a message."

Henry could not stop himself from grinning. There was young

Henry, Richard, Matilda, and now—"We must call this one Geoffrey, after my late brother—and my father too, naturally."

His eyes met Thomas's, who looked away first, both of them well aware that this was not the first son called Geoffrey.

"Madam the queen thought you might wish to call him Geoffrey, and that is the name he will be given at the christening ceremony. She hopes to join you in Normandy within the next month or two."

"What an amazing woman. The Channel lies between us yet she discerns what is in my mind. Extraordinary." Another son! He was filled with a sense of well-being.

When he had been rubbed down, Henry sat naked on a wooden stool while his face was shaved and his hair combed. To his amusement, Thomas, ill at ease, his face flushed, continued to gaze at everything in the chamber but himself. Too prudish for his own good. Henry wondered what the austere chancellor might do if ever confronted with a situation where he was sorely tempted. It might make an entertaining exercise . . .

"All is well in England? The Welsh are still quiet?"

"Yes, Sire, to both questions. Everyone rejoices at the birth of a new son."

"And how fares my family in Bermondsey?" When he was not in London, which was much of the time, he always asked Thomas to keep an eye on Bellebelle and their son, whom he dearly loved.

"I send one of my men at frequent intervals; mother and child fare well." Thomas paused. "Which reminds me—touching upon the matter of that Flemish knight you asked about some months ago—his name is Hans de Burgh, by the way—sorry to have been so long about this business but what with the journey to Paris and all, I've had very little time to pursue any inquiries personally."

A servant slid a blue tunic over Henry's head. "I'd almost forgotten, it's been so long."

"One of my clerks looked into de Burgh's past. The main thing about him seems to be a reputation for excessive violence. This penchant for brutality led to a singular incident in a brothel-house—"

"In London?"

"Southwark, about ten years ago—"

Henry, pulling on a pair of black leather boots, stopped. "Southwark, you say?" Bellebelle was from Southwark.

"In a brothel-house, as I was about to tell you, Sire. Apparently de Burgh had attacked a whore and was stabbed by her daughter, also a whore as it happens—his limp is the result of that wound."

"Extraordinary." Henry grew thoughtful. "Unusual behavior for a whore, wouldn't you say? She must have been sorely provoked."

"Indeed. In the event, the whore—the mother that is—was ultimately killed. By de Burgh himself, I'm told."

"By God's eyes! Was he ever brought to justice?"

"For the murder of a whore? Hardly, Sire. But it was during the final years of Stephen's reign, remember, a time of great lawlessness, as you well know. In truth, it seems a sordid, tangled affair, and my information is hearsay and what little the sheriff's records show."

From the distant past a memory surfaced. Henry saw himself on the London Bridge with Bellebelle. Nearby stood a group of women in striped cloaks, one of whom was her mother or so she had said. Whores? It seemed likely. On the other hand, Bellebelle had never said her mother was a whore, and until this moment he had forgotten all about the other women in the background. A terrible suspicion crossed Henry's mind which he instantly dismissed. Impossible. Bellebelle would have told him the truth about her past. There was not a lying bone in her body. He would stake his life on that.

Although it made no sense, in many ways he regarded Bellebelle as a wife and Eleanor as a mistress. Bellebelle was safe, loyal, and absolutely to be trusted. Eleanor was passionate, volatile, ambitious, and—it wasn't that he didn't trust her exactly, but underneath the sparkling surface he sensed secret depths unknown to him—even, perhaps, to her. Strange. Henry was suddenly reminded of the story of the Greek, Odysseus, Eleanor had told him about. Only who was the wife, Penelope, and who was the siren, Calypso? He gave an involuntary shiver, which meant a wolf had walked over his grave—for the second time.

"What became of the whore, the daughter, who stabbed de Burgh? Was *she* ever brought to justice?"

"No. I'm given to understand she escaped. A search was conducted but the doxy was never found," Thomas said. "De Burgh almost died of the wound and spent a long time recovering with his mother's people in Kent."

"I trust he's stayed out of trouble since that incident?"

"Apparently. As a mounted knight, his limp does not impair his skill with sword or bow, and he is known as a ferocious warrior who gives no quarter. John the Marshal has only good things to say of him. That's all I was able to discover."

"Which is a great deal more than I expected. Thank you. Not that it's of any importance now." Henry stood up and roughly shook Thomas's shoulder. "Not compared to a third son, eh? Tell me, who does he favor?"

But the picture of Bellebelle and the women in striped cloaks stayed in his mind. Instinct told Henry that this affair was not over, and of a sudden he wished to high heaven that he had never pursued the matter. No good would come of it.

# CHAPTER 36

# London,
# 1158

*E*leanor stood up, hugging herself in an effort to ward off the December chill that still managed to seep through the cracks in the wall, despite the lined tapestries and two burning charcoal braziers.

"How many more left, Master Matthew?"

The chaplain, Henry's old tutor, who acted as her secretary, scrutinized the sheaf of parchments that lay on a small oak table before him. "Two more, but if you're tired, Madam, they are not urgent, and can wait until the morrow."

"Weather permitting, I leave for Southampton to take ship for Normandy in the morning—if we can get the packing finished by then, and the treasury pays what is due me." She glanced round the disordered solar, at her women folding gowns, mantles, headdresses into open boxes and saddlebags; piling roped bundles one on top of another.

There was a tiny yelp. Eleanor glanced down. At her feet, young Henry, almost four, and Matilda, age two-and-one-half, were teasing a greyhound puppy. Baby Geoffrey, now well over two months and sturdy as an oak sapling, slept in his wooden cradle; fourteen-month-old Richard, clutching a wooden knight in his chubby fist, dozed on the blue-canopied bed. Eleanor's gaze rested lovingly on Richard, whose corn gold hair and bright blue eyes were so like that of her father and grandfather.

She loved her other children by Henry, relieved to find she was capable of maternal feelings after all, but when Richard had been put into her arms and she had met his milky blue stare, it was as if he had reached out and clutched her heart. An instant bond was formed, stronger than any she had experienced with the others.

At his birth, the chroniclers resurrected an ancient prediction of Merlin the Magician: "The eagle of the broken covenant shall rejoice in her third nesting." They had interpreted this prophecy to mean Eleanor, because she spread her wings over two realms, France and England. This son, they claimed, would strive in all things to bring glory to his mother's name.

To her surprise Henry had taken strong exception to the fact that Richard was singled out.

"By my reckoning, if you count Louis's daughters, our William— who is no longer alive to bring you glory—Henry, and Matilda, Richard is your sixth child," Henry had said, "not your third nesting. How can civilized Christians believe such pagan nonsense?"

"Don't take the matter so seriously," she had said. "He is the third nesting if you leave out the girls—which most chroniclers, being male, are prone to do."

The result of this was twofold: first, the English began to call her "the eagle," even as they referred to Henry as "the lion," a flattering reference to his grandfather, the first Henry, as well as the arms of Anjou. The second result was that Henry conceived a resentment against Richard. Tender and attentive with his other children, he ignored Richard. Henry will get over this dislike, Eleanor told herself without any real conviction. She had observed that once Henry decided how he felt about someone, he rarely changed his opinion. Thus he was steadfast and loyal to those he saw as friends, and bitterly opposed to those he perceived as enemies—whether deserved or otherwise.

"Madam?"

With a yawn, she strolled over to the narrow window. "What next?" There was a light fall of snow covering the courtyard where, despite the cold, people milled about, clapping their hands, hugging themselves, and blowing on their fingers to keep warm.

"The monks of Reading complain that they have been robbed of certain lands they own in London. The sheriff ignores their plight, they say."

In the gray light of this December afternoon, Eleanor could see the great minster across the way, and a stretch of road that ran through the village of Charing to Ludgate. The road was thick with people on foot, men driving carts drawn by horse or mule, and riders on horseback coming from and going to London.

"Tell the sheriff of London—" she began. "Let me see—yes, tell him that he is to look into this matter, and should it be true, ensure that these lands are returned to the monks without delay so that in future I shall hear no more complaints about deficiencies in law and justice. Farewell." She frowned and turned away from the window. "Too harsh?"

"Not to my way of thinking, Madam. The sheriff needs to be reminded of his duties. Let me get that all down. A moment." The chaplain bent his head, picked up his stylus, and began to write on his wax tablet, which later would be transferred onto parchment. When he had finished he picked up another letter. "Now—this last one is from the abbot of Abingdon, who complains that certain services owing to him have not been performed."

"What services?" Eleanor walked back to one of the few chairs in Westminster with arms.

"Some quarrel about statute labor. Not very specific, I'm afraid."

"Let the chancellor deal with him."

"He's still with the king in Normandy, isn't he?"

"Is he? He should be back by now."

When Henry and Becket were both away at the same time, Eleanor issued many documents in Henry's name, frequently in both their names together, rarely in her name alone—which sometimes rankled. In addition, at Henry's side, she meted out judgment at the official courts which were held every year in one or another of their cities: Bordeaux, Poitiers, Le Mans, Bayeaux, or London.

While Eleanor appreciated the fact that Henry allowed her some participation in the administration of the kingdom, he still remained unwilling to appoint her regent in his absence.

"You let your mother act as regent in Normandy," she had told him.

"When you're as experienced as my mother, we will discuss the matter again," was his response. "I share quite enough power with you."

Eleanor had stifled further comment, knowing it would only lead to an argument—which she would not win. But she could not stifle the seeds of resentment growing within her. She had done very well in Aquitaine ruling alone—and Henry knew it.

Meanwhile, when the king was absent from England, the co-justiciar, Richard de Lucy, acted as regent. Becket and Leicester, as well as others, dealt with important affairs of state; she was left the crumbs, dull, routine tasks that others were glad to shunt aside. Like this dreary business with the abbeys.

Always jealous of his authority, Henry, Eleanor had observed, delegated responsibility only when forced to do so to serve his own self-interest. His empire was far too large for him to supervise personally, and he was careful whom he chose to wield power in his stead. Eleanor was sure Henry trusted her, not only as his wife, but as someone who would not shirk her duties. With his propensity for hoarding power, she sometimes wondered if he also recognized—although he would never admit it—that she was capable of ruling as well as any man he had appointed to office. Was this why she was given only minor matters to deal with?

"Are you wool-gathering, Madam?"

Eleanor smiled. "Indeed. All right, Master Matthew, to work! Ah—hmm—to the knights and men holding land and tenures from Abingdon Abbey, greetings." She paused. "Tell them—tell them that I command they provide the abbot with those same services which—which—"

"Their ancestors provided in the days of King Henry the First?"

"Yes, very good. Add, grandfather of our sovereign lord. If they will not obey, the king's justice will force obedience and so on. That is the gist of it. I leave it to you to fill in the details."

"I understand."

There was a knock on the door which then opened. Eleanor looked up to see framed in the entrance the Poitevin clerk she had sent to the treasury an hour earlier.

"They say the Queen's Gold has been paid, Madam."

"Who says so?"

"One of the clerks in the treasury," he said. "I told him we hadn't received it."

"Did you check the Pipe Roll?"

"Oh." The clerk colored. "I didn't think of that."

Eleanor stood up. "Always check the Pipe Roll when in doubt. The chancery clerks generally keep the records current. Paid, was it? Well, I shall go myself and see what has happened to the gold. After Christmas, the king and I will probably tour Anjou and

Aquitaine. Who knows when I'll return. I need my portion now and cannot wait upon a dilatory clerk."

She turned to Master Matthew. "I had best take care of this matter."

"Indeed, Madam, we are through. A good journey on the morrow."

Eleanor smiled as he slowly gathered up sheafs of parchment, stylus, and wax tablets, then hobbled out. She took her doeskin bag from the clerk, pulled on a fur-lined hooded mantle, left her quarters, and started across the courtyard to the chancery. The snow had been trodden down to slush and she had to pick her way with care. As she greeted well-wishers, Eleanor wondered if someone in the treasury was trying to deceive her. After all, they had been paying her—albeit reluctantly—since the first year of Henry's reign. Although her payment was often late, this was the first time it had not arrived at all.

Her entrance into the chancery caused a minor uproar. The clerics sprang to their feet, mouths hanging open.

"I wish to check your records," she told the chancellor's secretary, William Fitz-Stephen. "The treasury clerks claim my gold has been paid and it has not. You should have a record of payment in the household expenditures."

"Yes, of course, but this is most irregular." He stopped and swallowed. "What I mean, Madam, is that there is no need for you to check yourself. I will be glad to do it for you."

"I prefer to do it myself, thank you." She looked around the chamber and spied the Pipe Roll on a large oak table.

"But I must ask the lord chancellor's permission—"

"Pardon? Did I hear you say, ask the lord chancellor's permission to let the queen of England—"

"Let her look, William."

Eleanor glanced up as Thomas Becket, magnificently clad in scarlet robes, stepped into the chamber.

"Thank you, Thomas. I'm surprised to see you, having just heard you were still in Rouen. How fares my lord?"

"Very well, Madam. You leave for the coast tomorrow?"

Eleanor walked over to the table. "Yes."

Fitz-Stephen, obviously in a quandary, followed on her heels, then stepped directly in front of her, blocking her access to the Pipe Roll. "My lord chancellor, I really feel it would be better for me to—"

"Stop dithering like a blue jay, William. Let the queen do as she wishes."

"But, my lord, you don't understand—" There was a note of desperation in the secretary's voice that caused Eleanor to glance sharply from one man to the other.

"I understand perfectly," Becket said. "Now do as I say, and step aside."

The secretary, his face white, fell silent and stepped to one side. Sweet St. Radegonde, what bees' nest had she stumbled into? Obviously Fitz-Stephen feared she might see something in the Pipe Roll; Becket was not concerned whether she saw it or not. Eleanor's skin prickled with a sense of foreboding.

She felt the chancellor's gaze penetrating her back as she unrolled the stitched parchment sheets and began to peruse the recent entries. She went back for several weeks, then months, but could find no entry for her payment during the last three months.

"There is no record of gold to the queen," she said aloud. "You can see for yourselves."

"If there is no record then it has not been paid," said Becket. "We pride ourselves on keeping all household expenditures current, don't we, William?"

"Indeed, my lord chancellor."

Puzzled, Eleanor could see nothing written that would have caused the secretary such agitation. She spread out the sheets so that they could be rolled up neatly, when an old entry caught her eye. ". . . for cloaks and hoods and for the trimming of two capes of samite for the clothes of the queen and Bellebelle."

Bellebelle? Why was that name coupled with her own? Who was she? The date was last February, a little over ten months ago. Eleanor's head felt like an iron helm enclosed it; there was a tightness in her breast.

"Who is Bellebelle?" she asked Fitz-Stephen.

His eyes shied away from hers. "I . . . that is to say—" he looked imploringly at Becket.

"You can tell her, William, it's all right. This creature is a distant relative of my secretary," Becket said in a voice that reminded Eleanor of honey oozing from the comb. "A—seamstress by trade, isn't she, William? From Bermondsey, I believe."

The secretary, in an agony of embarrassment, muttered something unintelligible. Poor man. She could almost feel sorry for him.

Eleanor felt her face grow hot. Did Becket think she was a fool? A relative, indeed. Did he really expect her to believe such a blatant lie? Bellebelle. Why, the very name had a decidedly carnal ring to it. She met the chancellor's gaze squarely. Something like enjoyment flashed in his dark eyes; his lower lip twisted into the mockery of a smile. Chilled, Eleanor realized Becket didn't expect her to believe him. Quite the contrary. He had *wanted* her to find the entry, with all its damning implications, waited for her to find it so he could gloat over her discomfort. Well, she would not give him the satisfaction.

"How thoughtful of you to provide so well for your relatives, William Fitz-Stephen." Ignoring Becket, head high, Eleanor walked slowly out of the chamber, smiling at the clerks as she passed.

Outside the chancery, Eleanor took a deep breath to steady her trembling knees before turning toward the treasury. She didn't know with whom she was more outraged, Henry or his devious chancellor. A blast of icy wind twisted across the courtyard that almost sent her reeling. From the very moment they met, she had known that Becket disliked and disapproved of her. But to deliberately sow discord between Henry and herself . . . It suddenly occurred to Eleanor that Thomas Becket might not be merely an irritating antagonist but a potentially dangerous enemy.

As for Henry . . . Ahead loomed the south wing of Westminster where the accounts not housed at Winchester were kept. No time now to deal with the continuing throb of mingled anger and savage jealousy over this Bellebelle.

Inside the stone chamber, there was the usual bustle of activity as the treasurer and his clerks, overseen by several chamberlains, reckoned sums on talley sticks and arranged counters into one or another of the columns on a black-and-white chequered cloth resembling a chessboard that sat atop a long table.

"According to the Pipe Roll, my gold has not been paid," she said to the treasurer.

"So my clerk later discovered, Madam. It was his error, for which I humbly apologize. We have it right here." The treasurer gave her a rueful smile. "Treasury people are worse than moneylenders. If they can find an excuse not to pay they won't."

Eleanor forced a laugh, gave him the doeskin bag, and waited impatiently while he filled it with silver coins from a wooden coffer. In truth, this habit of strict accountancy was one of the reasons for the

success of Henry's monarchy. When she recalled the appalling negligence of Aquitaine—not to mention her own—where money was
concerned, she could not but admire this miserly approach.

By the time Eleanor left the treasury, the tide of jealous rage had
not abated, nor had it increased. It was just there, a dull ache in her
heart. Climbing the winding staircase up to the solar, Eleanor remembered the flash of enjoyment in Becket's eyes, the smirk curling
his lip, and knew that a sense of pride must never permit her to
mention the incident to Henry. If she could keep from it. After all,
she was a royal queen, a great duchess. How could she allow herself
to be troubled by the bawds Henry bedded for his temporary convenience? Such feelings were beneath her.

Yet the name lingered in her head, insistent as a wave pounding
upon the shore. Bellebelle. Samite was a very rich and costly gold-
threaded silk. Henry had brought her a cape of the same material.
Had he had them both made at the same time? Try as she would,
Eleanor could not stop the thoughts that tumbled about like a frenzied troupe of jongleurs. Bellebelle. Was she a night's pleasure or
the companion of weeks? Even months? Was the girl fair to look
upon? And, the most dreaded question of all, was she young?

# CHAPTER 37

# Cherbourg, Normandy,
# 1158

*H*enry intended to hold his Christmas court at Cherbourg on the Normandy coast. He was still in Rouen when Eleanor arrived in mid-December, bringing with her for the first time young Henry and Richard, leaving Matilda and the baby, Geoffrey, behind. Henry had sent Thomas back to England with some signed charters to be put into immediate effect, and instructions to return no later than February so that he might accompany the royal entourage on a progress through Anjou and Aquitaine. Then he rode to Cherbourg to join Eleanor.

The queen had retired for the night, Henry was told, when he arrived at Compline; he raced up the winding staircase of the small castle and burst into the chamber. Eleanor, in a furred robe, was sitting up in the crimson-canopied bed while one of her women rubbed her hair with pumice so that it gleamed like bronze in the flickering candle-glow. Between her exposed breasts, twice their normal size, Richard lay asleep. One of his fingers curled round a jutting coral nipple.

"Out, out, out," Henry shouted, startling the ladies who scattered at his coming like so many frightened sheep. He wrenched the baby away from his nesting place and thrust him, howling with rage, into the arms of one of the women. "Take him with you."

Henry knelt by the bed and gathered Eleanor into his arms, kissing her cheeks, the tip of her nose, and finally her lips, which opened gently under his. "The boy is too old to be sleeping with you like that. Unseemly at his age. Such pampering will only make him soft and girlish."

"Sweet St. Radegonde, he's only fourteen months old! And there's no danger of his becoming soft and girlish, believe me. He's the most like you of any of your sons, and already has the makings of a young warrior—which you'd know if you ever paid the slightest attention to him."

He squeezed her tightly against him, drinking deeply of her mouth.

"Be careful," she whispered against his lips. "I'm very sore. The wet-nurse's milk disagreed with Geoffrey, and I had to nurse him myself for the last two months until a new nurse whose milk did not upset him could be found. The milk has not yet dried up. Generally, he's been fussy. I hope this is not a harbinger of his future behavior."

Henry lay down beside her, carefuly nestling his head in the crook of her arm. "It's hard to believe that just four years ago we set out from this very spot for my coronation," he said, tracing the outline of her breast with a lazy forefinger. "What a long road we've traveled since then—"

"Without a single failure—"

"—and now we're in control of all our possessions on both sides of the Channel."

"With four children as the embodiment of our hopes for the future," Eleanor said with a yawn. "Think how they will extend our power across Europe. A Plantagenet in every major duchy and county."

"Young Henry will rule Normandy and England, of course, and mayhap France as well. Richard—"

"Duke of Aquitaine, naturally."

"Perhaps. We can discuss it later."

"No, Henry, I must insist. Richard will be duke of Aquitaine."

Henry bit back his retort. No point in making an issue of Richard now. Let the future look to itself. "And Matilda?"

"Only the most high-born husband. A duke—"

"For my daughter? A prince at the very least."

Eleanor laughed. "Or even a king—if any are still available."

"What about Geoffrey?" Henry felt his eyelids grow heavy.

"Why should he not inherit Brittainy?" Eleanor kissed the top of his head.

"I have not yet fully secured Brittainy."

"No, but you will."

"Do you realize, Nell, that if we have another son, I will have run out of territory to give him?"

Eleanor groaned. "Sweet St. Radegonde, we've just had a son and you're already talking about another! You must think my insides are made of old boot leather. Does your ambition know no bounds?"

"None. Does yours?"

Eleanor pulled his hair. "Now, if I still had Toulouse this unborn son could become its count. It was once part of Aquitaine, you know, and all the vital trade routes still run through it. It was my grandfather's dream to recapture it for his heirs."

Suddenly awake now, Henry propped himself up on one elbow. "I'd forgotten about Toulouse. Go on."

"Well, it has all the Roman roads and waterways that connected Aquitaine to the Mediterranean. At one time it had a brilliant court, just like Poitiers and Provence. My father was born there; his mother, my grandmother, Philippa, ruled there. I've always considered it part of my rightful inheritance."

In the light of the flickering candle, Henry could see her face glow with excitement. "Yes, but it hasn't belonged to your family for fifty years at least." He lay back with a sigh. "What I do not need is another rebellious territory. I already have more land than I can easily manage."

Eleanor leaned over to brush her lips against his. "But you wouldn't have to. I would be happy to manage it."

"Didn't Louis make an attempt to conquer it?"

"Oh, Louis. Trust him to botch everything he touches. Toulouse is a rich prize; its count, Raymond, is weak, inefficient, and on bad terms with his vassals. Not only that, he is at odds with his wife—"

"Who is also King Louis's sister." Henry yawned. "This is a totally foolhardy venture. Has anyone ever told you that you are an exceptionally greedy woman, Nell?"

She laughed softly. There was something about the way she laughed—warm, sensual, challenging. He butted his head between her breasts, his favorite place to sleep. "Enough talk of conquest. Let me think on it."

How good it was to lie here with his loving Nell, dreaming aloud of a golden future. England at peace; the acquisition of northern Brittainy; the Vexin one day to return to the Plantagenet fold. Perhaps, in the future, Toulouse? That would certainly round off his holdings. It really had been a most glorious year, Henry thought drowsily, as he gave a contented sigh.

"Henry?"

"Hmm?"

"Who is Bellebelle?"

The question so shocked him Henry's blood froze. For a moment he wondered if he dreamed the question. He pretended to be half-asleep. "Ah—the name is not one I recognize—why?"

"I saw it in the Pipe Roll."

Why was she looking in the Pipe Roll? God's eyes, the woman had the nose of a bloodhound! On the other hand, what fool had put Bellebelle's name in the records? "I don't know the name. Let us sleep, Nell."

Eleanor kissed the back of his neck. "Let us indeed."

Jesu! She knew how to pick her moment. Did she know more than she was saying? Henry experienced an unaccustomed spurt of guilt.

It was not a good omen. With a sense of doom, he wondered if the year that had begun so well would end that way.

After Mass the next morning, Henry received word that the Empress Maud would be arriving the following day, having set out from the abbey of Fontevrault a week ago, where she had spent the past month in retreat.

"This is the first time my mother has been able to attend a Christmas court since my accession to the throne," Henry said to Eleanor as they strode down the passageway from the chapel to the hall. "She hasn't seen any of her grandchildren since young Henry was an infant. We must make much of her coming." The incident of last night might never have occurred. Nell was warm and loving, her usual carefree self. Still wary, Henry allowed himself to hope that she had believed him.

Eleanor wrinkled her nose. "Don't I always make much of your sainted mother? Playing the Old Testament Ruth can be a great strain."

Henry chuckled. "Yes, you're very good with her, Nell. Sometimes it isn't easy, I know."

They walked into the drafty hall, so much smaller and less prepossessing than the one in Rouen.

"In the expectation that she might come, I've invited several of her old friends from the past—Earl Robert of Leicester, his twin brother, Waleran of Muelan, and the bishop of Winchester," Henry continued.

"Old friends?" Eleanor raised her brows. "Old adversaries, would be more apt. Particularly Bishop Henry, Stephen's brother."

"Oh, I think all those fences are mended now. And if not, it's high time they were."

The evening of the empress's arrival, Henry gave a great feast in her honor. She seemed delighted to see her old associates, and they talked away until well after Compline.

"Now does the lion lie down with the lamb," Eleanor whispered in Henry's ear, observing them.

"Not a lamb among them," Henry said with a grin.

The following morning, accompanied by Eleanor and his mother's three old friends, he took the empress to see his heir, young Henry, who was at his lessons with his tutor. Henry was foolishly fond of his eldest son. A captivating boy with laughing green eyes and honey brown hair, it was impossible not to spoil him, so great was his charm.

"Maman, here is the eldest sprig on the ever-growing Plantagenet tree," Henry said. "Henry, your grandmaman—"

There was a strangled sound. Henry turned. His mother clutched her throat and swayed on her feet. He, de Beaumont, and Bishop Henry all sprang to her side, fearing she would fall. Between them they half-carried her, white and trembling, to her quarters.

"What could have upset her?" Henry later asked the three men.

They shook their heads, avoiding Henry's eyes, yet he had the feeling they all suspected the cause. It was maddening.

The next day, claiming that she was ill, the empress insisted on returning to Rouen, allowing only Bishop Henry to accompany her. While Henry did not believe she was ill, it was evident that she was very badly shaken. By what?

"I suspected our son had a lethal charm but I didn't think it would fell his own grandmother before he even opened his mouth," Eleanor said.

Under leaden skies, they watched the empress ride out of the courtyard in a litter.

"I can't understand it." Henry had been brooding on the incident ever since yesterday and could not shake off a feeling of unease.

"Why would she react to young Henry that way?"

A brisk Channel wind flipped the edges of his short blue cloak; rain began to fall. Hastily they walked back inside the castle keep just as the bells rang for Terce.

Eleanor looked thoughtful. "I had the impression that he reminded your mother of someone and it shook her."

"Yes, that makes sense. But who? Why?"

"I can't imagine. William—may God rest him—looked like your mother." She signed herself, as she always did when her late son was mentioned. "Matilda favors you more than me. Richard resembles my father and grandfather. But now that I think on it, young Henry doesn't look like anyone I know."

Henry stared out the half-open door of the keep, wondering if he should attend Mass. The bishop of Rouen was going to officiate, and he tended to drone on forever no matter how many times he was told to keep the sermons short and to the point.

"It's bound to cause talk, Nell, my mother's leaving like that. Everyone will wonder why."

"I wouldn't let it worry me. People always find something to gossip about."

"Well, it is worrying me. It's unlike her to behave so oddly."

The castle steward shuffled by, aided by a knobbed stick. A grizzled man of mature years, he had been at Cherbourg since time out of mind.

"A moment, please," Henry said.

"Eh?" The steward stopped. "Did you speak, Sire?"

Henry raised is voice. "Young Henry, does he remind you of anyone?"

"Who?"

"My son and heir, young Henry. Does he resemble anyone you know?"

"Your eldest son?" The steward scratched his head, frowned, then broke into a pleased smile. "Now that you mention it, my lord, indeed he does. Why, he's the image of the Old King of England."

Henry stared at him. "My grandfather?"

"No, no, Sire. Like Stephen of Blois he is, to the very life." The steward gave a creaky bow and shuffled away.

"There you are. Our son reminded your mother of her cousin Stephen, her greatest enemy. Naturally she would react—Henry? Henry! Are you all right?"

Henry, who felt as though a stallion had kicked him in the belly, was incapable of speech. Eleanor put a hand on his arm. He shook it off. The steward's words threatened to open the floodgates of the past, unloosing a tide of half-forgotten memories that he had thought washed away forever.

He pulled his wits together. "I'm fine, fine. I think I will attend Mass."

"You don't look fine. Such a long face." Eleanor paused, her hazel eyes wide with concern. "Come, sweet love, only last night you were telling me how wonderful the past year has been. The next will be even better. Put this trifling business with your mother from your mind and let us make this Christmas a joyous affair."

Nell was right. What was the matter with him? He had garnered success upon success and there was no reason why it should not continue. Yet Henry could not shake off a feeling of doom. All too similar to the one last night. Had his years of unbroken triumph come to an end?

# London,

# 1159

homas Becket was halfway out the door of the chancery before he remembered Bellebelle. "By the Mass, I knew there was something I'd left undone. That whore's money!"

There was a startled silence in the chancery.

"Ah—which whore is that, my lord chancellor?"

"By the Mass, that's very good. Which whore indeed." Thomas gave a grim smile. "You may well ask, William. I intended to take care of it—" He slammed a thick sheaf of parchments against the oak table. "Well, mea culpa, there's no help for it now. I must get to Southampton while the weather holds. If I don't take ship for Normandy within the next few days I could be delayed for weeks by winter storms. The Bermondsey whore has not yet been paid this month, and—" He looked around the chancery. "I put the money down somewhere, intending—now where in God's name did I put the wretched thing?"

One day, Thomas promised himself, one day he would tell Henry straight out exactly what he thought of his goatish behavior: the extra work it caused, the lies it required, not to mention all the stipends to be paid out.

"Is this what you're looking for, my lord chancellor?" One of the clerks held up a calfskin bag clanking with coins.

"God be thanked, there it is. I must leave this in your hands, William."

The secretary looked overwhelmed. "Yes, my lord chancellor, I understand, but we have so much work here today—I'm not sure I can do it until the end of the sennight."

"Too late. It's already overdue, and the king sets great store by that—creature." Thomas swallowed an impatient sigh, forcing a smile. "In truth, I don't see why you need take it to Bermondsey yourself—though it's not a task can be given to just anyone, is it? Servants gossip like the plague and discretion is—Ah! I have it. A troop of the marshal's knights have recently returned from the Welsh marches. I've seen a few just idling about, seemingly with little to occupy them. Get one of them to do it for you."

"Of course, my lord chancellor, you can safely leave the matter to me."

Accompanied by William, Thomas left the chancery. Outside, his retinue was waiting with the saddled horses, three sumpter beasts, and two carts filled with all the documents and records needed for a traveling court, as well as his own personal belongings. He might be gone on progress through Henry's domains for as long as six months—one never knew—and nothing must be left to chance.

"The money will be there today, William? I intend to tell the king as much."

"Indeed, as God is my witness. A safe journey."

William Fitz-Stephen was about to return to the chancery when he saw across the courtyard one of the marshal's knights. On impulse he hailed him. This one would do as well as another. The man turned and limped toward him. Around his neck a silver medallion set with emeralds caught fire from the rising February sun.

"I wonder if I could impose upon you, sir—that is if you're not on duty at the moment?"

"No. You're the chancellor's secretary, aren't you? Vhat is it you vant?" The man spoke with a Flemish accent.

"It's a favor for the chancellor." William lowered his voice discreetly. "In truth, it's really for the king—that is to say the queen. Would you ride over to Bermondsey with some money for his—Her Majesty's—seamstress? We're very pushed in the chancery just now, and I'd be most grateful. I'll give you exact directions."

The knight gave a gutteral laugh. "No need. I know the place, though I never saw this—seamstress. It's in the next parish to Bermondsey, I believe. I accompanied the king there about a year ago—the chancellor vas there." He winked. "Don't vorry, I can hold my tongue."

"Good. It's a delicate matter . . . If you'll give me a moment

I'll get the money. I'm much obliged to you."

"No trouble. Alvays glad to be of service to the chancellor."

A few moments later William returned with the bag of silver coins which he handed to the knight, who stuffed it into his tunic.

"I'll get my horse and leave at vonce. You vill be sure to tell the chancellor it vas I who did you this favor, yah?"

"Naturally—if you tell me your name."

"De Burgh. Hans de Burgh."

When the priory bells struck None, Bellebelle opened the door of her cottage and stepped out into the garden. The wolfhound, tied to a wooden post by a frayed rope when he was outside so he wouldn't get after the chickens, was curled into a woolly gray circle. Seeing her, he thumped his tail on the hard ground.

Bellebelle turned her face up to the fading rays of sunlight before glancing down the path for a sign of Geoffrey returning from his lessons. Since he had turned four and was so big for his age, Bellebelle allowed him to walk the three leagues to and from the priory school by himself, but did not draw an easy breath until she saw his sturdy figure trudging home.

After a moment she saw her son running down the path toward her. She caught him in her arms and hugged him tightly before leading him inside the cottage.

"One of the boys said a two-headed calf was born in the next village," Geoffrey said, removing his cap and cloak. "What do you think of that?" His eyes were round with wonder.

"Well, I never. Saw it himself, did he?"

"No. But he heard tell of it by someone who had. Is Father coming tonight?"

Bellebelle, cutting a chunk of wheaten bread from yesterday's loaf, sighed. "Now Geoffrey, you know he still be gone on progress to the Cont—the Contin—"

"The Continent. I thought he might be back. How long does it take to travel through one's domains? I miss him."

"So do I, Son, but the king has lots of land to inspect. Could take a very long time. Con-ti-nent," Bellebelle repeated. "Continent." Her speech continued to improve but was still far from perfect.

It seemed like years since she had seen Henry, but in truth it was only the end of last August. She should be used to his long absences by now, but she wasn't and knew she never would be. Bellebelle set steaming wooden bowls onto the table. It was the first day of Lent so they were having pickled herring, covered in a hot parsley sauce to hide the salty taste.

Geoffrey chatted about what had happened at the priory while Bellebelle listened, encouraging him to share his day with her. When Henry was gone, her son's company was the only thing she had to look forward to. Halfway through the meal there was a brisk knock at the door.

"Go see to it, Son. It must be the woodman come with more logs. We been running low."

Geoffrey ran to the door; she could hear a low murmur of voices.

"It's a knight from the chancery, Maman."

"That be—is a relief. The money's late this time."

Bellebelle wiped damp hands on her brown kirtle. With a smile on her face she walked toward the door then stopped in her tracks. In the open doorway facing her, eyes blazing in a face the color of death, stood the man she most dreaded to see, her worst nightmare come to life.

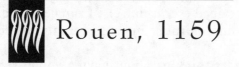

# Rouen, 1159

The strange incident with the empress at Cherbourg had unforeseen consequences. That occurrence—or Eleanor supposed it was that—had unsettled Henry to the point where he came dangerously close to making a fatal error in judgment.

It was late February of the new year, 1159. She and Henry had left Cherbourg for Rouen, where they awaited the arrival of Thomas Becket who was to accompany them on their progression through Normandy, Anjou, and Aquitaine. Since the incident with young Henry and his mother, Henry had come to her bed nightly. Eleanor had discerned an inner tension in him, a mounting uneasiness against which he was seeking protection. Just the contact of her warm body seemed to calm and soothe him.

If Henry was unsettled, so was she, Eleanor realized. Again and again her mind would return to the entry in the Pipe Roll. The name

Bellebelle continued to haunt her. She had known Henry was lying when he denied knowing any such person, an indication that there might be something special about Bellebelle. Perhaps she meant more to him than the other bawds he used. The possibility was like a dagger twisting inside her.

Hurt, angry, and not a little jealous, Eleanor's natural impulse was to make an issue of it with Henry, and thus relieve her feelings. Yet another part of her held back. He was so preoccupied, and did she really want to know the truth? After all, Henry had not changed toward her in any way whatsoever. He was as loving, as tender as always. He obviously needed her. In the past, Eleanor had not allowed herself to be bothered by his other women, but then they had posed no threat. On the other hand, she agonized, it was inconceivable that some tavern wench or lowly village girl could pose a threat. Round and round her thoughts churned. She had no one to talk to, no one to advise her, no one to comfort her—as Henry had. If only they dared communicate truly with each other, give full vent to the doubts and fears that festered inside.

In the end, Eleanor decided to do and say nothing. Like Pandora's box in the Greek fable she had heard about, it seemed wiser to leave well enough alone—for the moment. In any case, Henry's bizarre announcement wiped everything else from her mind.

It occurred one morning in late February while they were in Rouen.

"We must start thinking about having young Henry crowned," Henry said to Eleanor, without preamble.

Along with the empress and Earl Robert of Leicester, they stood on the banks of the Seine watching a crowd of workmen hoist wood plankings in the construction of a new bridge across the river.

It was such an extraordinary suggestion that Eleanor stared at him in amazement, noting out of the corner of her eye that his mother, suddenly pale, was gazing at him in a kind of horror. There had been no warning, no hint of any kind that such thoughts weighed upon his mind—unless—could his need to seek comfort from her be related in some way? It seemed impossible.

"He's only four years of age—a bit young, and I don't see the need, Sire," said Earl Robert, who was due to leave for England to resume his post as co-justiciar as soon as the chancellor arrived.

"Not to mention the fact that you're bursting with good health." Eleanor could not understand what lay behind this astounding statement. But she knew Henry well enough to know that something drove him.

With a brooding expression on his face—one that had become increasingly familiar since the Christmas court—Henry gazed out at the brown water moving sluggishly under an iron-hued sky.

"It is never too soon to begin thinking about ensuring the succession," Henry said. "The practice is common enough in France, and other places on the Continent."

"This is not France, I'm thankful to say. You have three sons, Henry. The succession is secured."

"I must agree with the queen," de Beaumont said. "Such an action serves no purpose at this time, and has no precedent in England. As you are well aware, Stephen of Blois attempted to have Eustace crowned in his lifetime—without success. The archbishop of Canterbury absolutely refused, if you recall, despite Stephen's threats. After all, Sire, where is the urgency? You are not yet twenty-six years of age!"

"Next month." Henry turned to his mother. "What are your thoughts on the matter, Madam?"

"I have no thoughts on the matter," she said in a terse voice.

Eleanor observed that Earl Robert kept stroking his short, pale beard or touching the hilt of his sword in an aimless manner, betraying some inner agitation. He and the Empress Maud avoided looking at each other. Something was afoot here, but what?

After a moment's silence, Henry shrugged dismissively. "All right. Perhaps the decision was hasty. We can discuss the matter again when young Henry is older."

Eleanor saw him make a visible effort to collect himself. "Well, de Beaumont." Henry forced a smile. "What do you think of my plan regarding Toulouse?"

Henry appeared to have forgotten that, initially, Toulouse had been her plan. But then, like a great many ideas she had originated, Henry had adopted it as his own. At the moment, Eleanor thought it politic not to remind him.

"An excellent plan, Sire," de Beaumont said, obviously relieved at this change of subject. "Of course, you will need to get King Louis's agreement on a campaign there, since he is the count of Toulouse's overlord, as well as your own."

"Not too difficult." Henry turned to Eleanor. "Didn't you tell me Raymond of Toulouse abuses his wife, Louis's sister?"

"It is common knowledge in Aquitaine."

Leicester pursed his lips. "Unfortunately, the count's wife is his property to treat as he will. Louis cannot interfere—officially, that is. Count Raymond is still the king of France's vassal, and Louis is honor-bound to protect him from attack, just as he would you, Sire."

"The matter of his sister aside, Louis and I are allies now," Henry said. "Why would he contest this venture? Or take Count Raymond's side against mine?" He shrugged impatiently. "Until I hear otherwise, when we get to Poitou I'll start assembling an army."

They continued to walk along the banks of the Seine. Whenever she thought of the impending campaign, Eleanor could hardly wait for it to start. It had been easy to convince Henry. His appetite for conquest remained unappeased no matter how much land he gobbled up. To regain control of Toulouse had been her family's dream since before she was born, for it was the gateway to the south—Provence, Barcelona, the Mediterranean. Without it, Aquitaine was more vulnerable to her enemies; with it, the duchy was virtually impregnable. Furthermore, whether he gave her credit or not, she *had* suggested the campaign to Henry. Eleanor saw his response as a propitious sign, a sure indication they were joint comrades in all ventures. It took some of the sting out of the Bellebelle affair.

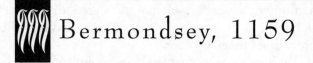

# Bermondsey, 1159

"I knew von day I'd find you," said Hans de Burgh, stepping inside and closing the door. "Und now, at last, I have."

It was the first time Bellebelle had ever heard him speak. Before her eyes he became another person: a cruel glitter appeared in his pale blue eyes; his lips stretched over his teeth into a mockery of a grin, reminding her of a death's head. A scream died in her throat; her legs felt frozen to the floor.

Unable to find her voice, she put out a trembling hand to her son, who was staring at de Burgh as if he could not believe this was the same man who had been at the door.

Bellebelle gestured wildly. "Geoffrey—run—get help—quickly," she managed to whisper.

"Stay vhere you are—Geoffrey is it? Your vhelp, yah?"

Geoffrey looked first at her then at de Burgh.

"Go, Son."

Geoffrey made for the door. De Burgh grabbed him around the waist and held him fast. "I said stay."

"Leave him be," Bellebelle cried.

"Let me go." Geoffrey tried to shake himself free but de Burgh only held him tighter. "You're hurting me—stop."

Released from his spell, Bellebelle flung herself at de Burgh and began to pummel his shoulder. He let go of Geoffrey, caught Bellebelle by her arm, and threw her to the ground with such force that for a moment she could not breathe. Geoffrey was out the door like a streak of lightning. De Burgh made no attempt to follow. His eyes were filled with a reddish glow, crazed with hate. They never left her face.

"Bitch. Filthy cunt," he said, hissing between his teeth like a serpent. "Every step I take is like a knife in my hip because of you." He rubbed a hand over his side. "You'll pay for it. Oh yah, whore's brat, you'll pay."

"You murdered my mother," Bellebelle said, her voice rising. "First you tortured her and then you murdered her!"

"The cunt deserved it! She had the burning sickness. I could have died."

De Burgh drew back his booted foot and kicked her in the hip. With a scream of pain she tried to scramble away but he blocked her path.

"The nights I've spent dreaming of this moment, thinking, planning all I vould do to you." Slowly he drew out a short-bladed knife from the sheath that swung at his leather belt. "You remember vhat I did to your mother, yah? First I do that to you—" He chuckled, that same blood-chilling sound she remembered from the brothel-house in Southwark.

For the first time in years an image of her mother's blood-stained body flashed before Bellebelle's eyes. De Burgh came closer, impaling her upon his madman's gaze so that once again she felt terror constrict her. He dropped down on one knee. With a quick thrust he slashed the bodice of her kirtle, then ripped it open, exposing her breasts. Suborned by the intensity of his hatred, she was powerless to move, her mind unable to function.

There was a low growl. De Burgh ignored it. Bellebelle twisted her head. Geoffrey stood in the doorway holding the wolfhound by the rope.

"You touch my mother and I'll set Valiant on you. I've trained him to attack and he'll do so at my command."

De Burgh turned his head. The wolfhound bared its pointed teeth and snarled while Bellebelle hastened to her feet, clutching the torn pieces of her bodice together. Valiant had only attacked small game, but the Fleming wouldn't know that. De Burgh's arm, which had shot forward to stop her, hung poised in midair.

"Oh, Son. That—that be quick thinking," said Bellebelle in a quivering voice, her chest heaving.

Geoffrey's entrance had broken her bondage; she could think again. "But we need not set Valiant on this scum. He forgets who I—who we belong to. What you think the king'll do if ought should happen to me?"

She saw the red haze of madness fade from de Burgh's eyes. His jaw hung slack; his arm dropped; he rubbed a hand over his eyes and stared at her as if he had never seen her before—which in a way he hadn't, Bellebelle realized.

"You mean—you are—*Gott in Himmel,* of course." He signed himself. "I did not think—" He rose to his feet and reached inside his tunic. "Here." He flung a pouch of coins onto the floor.

"Get out," said Geoffrey. "Don't ever come back. When I tell my father what you tried to do to my mother . . ."

De Burgh gave a shaky laugh. "Your mother passed you off as the son of a king? You could be a butcher's bastard for all he knows, yah." He eyed Bellebelle as if she were vermin to be put down. "I vonder now, does King Henry know vat you vere? That you tried to kill me?"

"O' course he do," she said quickly, too quickly, dropping her gaze.

De Burgh gave her a long speculative look, his composure gradually returning. "I suspect he knows nothing— and vhen he finds out, for I vill tell him, you can be sure of that—how long you think you vill last?" He snapped his fingers. "That long. He von't care vhat happens to you. Then I'll be back, yah. To finish vhat I started."

"The king is gone, he's on the Continent," Geoffrey said, his face white, his gray eyes enormous.

"But he'll be back. In time. I can vait."

With an evil grin, de Burgh slid out the door, his eyes on the wolfhound. A few moments later Bellebelle heard the sound of horse's hooves trotting away. Geoffrey ran to the door.

"He's gone."

Suddenly Bellebelle began to weep. Gone. How long would it be before her life with Henry was gone too?

# CHAPTER 39

# Toulouse,

# 1159

*F*or Eleanor, the next few months slipped by in a flurry of preparation for the war in Toulouse. First Henry solicited contributions from towns, sheriffs, moneylenders, even the Church. Anticipating an outcry, he ordered Thomas Becket personally to collect from the abbeys. In the spring, Henry issued a summons to his vassals in England, Normandy, and Aquitaine to assemble at Poitiers by the end of June. He then went to Paris, confident Louis of France would support him. But, to Eleanor's consternation, Louis was noncommittal. The count of Toulouse was his vassal; his sister's safety was involved. He preferred to remain a bystander.

"What is Louis up to?" Eleanor asked Henry the day after he had returned from Paris. "I don't trust him." For the first time she was experiencing a niggle of doubt about this enterprise. "He should support you, not remain aloof. This holier-than-thou attitude is typical of him. Does he forget his disastrous attempt to take Toulouse eighteen years ago?"

Henry shrugged. "What does it matter? He hasn't said anything either way and in his case a wink's as good as a nod. I've an unbroken string of victories to my credit. Toulouse will be no different."

Nor could Eleanor see any reason why Toulouse would be different, yet Louis's apparent unwillingness to take sides continued to trouble her. She insisted on accompanying Henry on the campaign and he agreed.

On a day in late June, Henry's army left Poitiers. His brilliant host included not only barons from his own domains but the king of Scotland, the count of Barcelona, and several of the count of

Toulouse's dissatisfied vassals. By early July they had encamped outside Toulouse's walls and settled in for a long siege.

Henry, as usual, had brought his clerks, and, with Eleanor's help, busied himself with the constant administrative chores of his empire: issuing writs, reading over judicial cases, and even listening to those subjects persistent enough to follow him to the gates of Toulouse.

In September, Louis revealed his true colors.

He suddenly appeared before the city gates, unattended by troops or guards. Like a penitent, he humbly asked permission to enter the city to safeguard his sister. Had she been present, Eleanor knew, she would have seen through this ploy. But she had gone to Foix for two days to visit a distant relative. When she returned, she found, to her horror, that Louis had been allowed to enter the city, and Henry was planning to call off the siege.

"But you cannot do that," she said, unable to believe either that Louis had been so wily or Henry so willing to back down. "To have come this far for nothing—no, you must go through with it."

"How can I? Louis is my overlord. If I attack him, what sort of example do I set for my own vassals?"

Thomas, an unlikely ally, sided with her for the first time. Having brought along seven hundred knights of his own household—which indicated the size and wealth of his own establishment—Eleanor suspected that Thomas hoped to make a great military showing. It was becoming more and more obvious that the chancellor thought himself a great baron, preferring to forget he was ever an archdeacon in holy orders.

"Louis has aligned himself with your enemies and deserves no consideration, Sire," Thomas said. "You will be the laughingstock of all Europe if you end the siege now. Everyone will say Louis has outwitted you."

"Not in my presence, they won't." Henry's face grew purple, and Eleanor expected that any moment now he would fall on the floor of the pavilion in one of his uncontrollable rages.

To her surprise he did not lose control, but she could tell that he was adamant, and argument was useless. In some way she had never been able to grasp, Henry had developed a curious affection for Louis whom, by turns, he had outfought, outwitted, yet made friends with. Why he would throw away all his advantages on the threshold of a successful siege was beyond her comprehension.

"We will never again have this chance," she said. "We will have lost Toulouse forever." That dull, pious Louis should have been the cause of this loss was like gall and wormwood in her heart.

"We? We? I never wanted it!" Henry shouted. "*You* wanted it, *you* gulled me into it! This whole thing was your idea from first to last. Did I not say right from the start that this was a foolhardy venture?"

Eleanor was taken aback. So he did remember where the idea had originated—when it suited him. He *had* said the venture was foolhardy, but not with any great seriousness, as she recalled.

Henry threw his sword on the ground, kicked several shields across the floor, then stomped out of the pavilion. Thomas followed on his heels, still urging him to continue the siege. Outside, she could hear raised voices as Henry and his chancellor got into a heated argument, the only serious breach between them that Eleanor could remember.

Although Henry was hungry for power, she had long suspected that he had no real taste for bloodshed or war, preferring to win by other means, if possible. Even worse than the loss of Toulouse was the fact that it should be Louis who had shown her husband to be less than invincible. It was the first visible chink in Henry's armor.

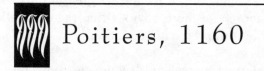

# Poitiers, 1160

Five months later, back in Poitiers, Henry pounded the table with an iron fist. Silver bowls rattled and the salt cellars fell over. "Raze the viscount's castle."

Eleanor gasped aloud. "Henry, you cannot mean—"

"Oh, but I do mean," he said, raising his voice so it could be heard by everyone seated in the great hall of the Maubergeonne Tower on this unseasonably warm evening in late February. "I said raze the castle and I mean just that."

A tense silence fell over the assembled crowd of Aquitainian vassals, barons, and prelates. Six Norman knights seated at the high table immediately rose to their feet.

"God's eyes, not this instant, you hotheads."

The knights resumed their seats.

"But this lord has not deserved such treatment," Eleanor said. Her heart hammered against her ribs as she strove to keep her voice steady, her demeanor calm. "You have already ejected him from his lands at Thouars."

Henry, his face set, did not reply. She saw his eyes rove distastefully over the platters of boiled carp, pike, roasted wildfowl, pheasant, and partridge. He plunged his dagger into a silver bowl set in the middle of the high table, and speared a piece of fish awash in a thick sauce. He gazed at it suspiciously, then sniffed it, like a wary hound nosing at a carcass.

"I don't care for the smell of this."

"All the fish on the table were freshly caught this morning or yesterday. Those stewed lampreys were just made."

He threw the offending piece of eel to a foraging hound. "I won't touch lampreys, Nell. You know that."

Henry's grandfather had died as a result of eating stewed lampreys. Of course she knew that Henry refused to eat the dish. How could she have neglected to remind the steward? Like everything else she had done since leaving Toulouse, she could not seem to put a foot right.

"I'm sorry, Henry. It slipped my mind."

He nodded, finally cutting himself a leg of wildfowl cloaked with fried parsley.

"My dear, please," she said, picking up the threads of their discussion. "Won't you listen to reason?" Aware of every eye fixed upon them, Eleanor lowered her voice. "Such an act against the viscount will only create more strife among my vassals."

"*Your* vassals, Madam? I thought they were mine."

How could she have been so tactless? "*Our* vassals, naturally."

Eleanor's stomach plummeted. He was going to continue being difficult, as he had been ever since they had left Toulouse. In truth, whenever they made a progress through Aquitaine, Henry was apt to be difficult, but this time he seemed compelled to exercise his authority with increasing force—as though trying to prove something to himself after having backed down before Louis of France. Although, despite her initial objection she had not continued to reproach him, Eleanor knew he sensed her withdrawal. It was unjust, perhaps, and not deserved, but she couldn't help it. Henry had allowed Louis of France to get the better of him and his golden luster had slightly dimmed. Now he was making Aquitaine pay for it.

In Limoges, where they had just spent the better part of a week, he had made the young baronial heir his ward, then turned over the reins of administration to two Normans. Didn't he understand that appointing outsiders to important posts only reinforced her vassals' opposition? In Bordeaux he had accepted the homage of her vassals to himself and their sons, Henry and Richard, then taken hostages to guarantee the vassals' fidelity, a clear sign of how little he trusted them.

Visits to her duchy were infrequent, which caused Eleanor much sorrow; on the other hand, Aquitaine always proved such a source of friction between herself and Henry that perhaps it was just as well. There had been a time when she hoped they might live for long periods of time in her beloved domains. But it was now painfully evident that she would never be able to live in Aquitaine with Henry.

"More strife hardly seems possible considering the disorders that constantly beset Aquitaine," Henry continued. "England, Normandy, and Anjou are under my control. *Your* duchy alone continues to be a source of unrest." He finished chewing the wildfowl and began to pick his teeth with the point of his knife. "My policies, my reforms—everything I've done with great success in other parts of my realm—is unsuccessful here. Every region in Aquitaine is suspicious of every other region. The Gascons mistrust the Poitevins; the Poitevins look down on the folk of Limoges, and so on. No one part of Aquitaine agrees with any other part."

Was this any different from how the Welsh felt about the English, or how the English regarded the Scots? Eleanor wished she dare say what was in her heart: There is one thing everyone in Aquitaine does agree on—their resentment of you and your attempts to curtail their independence.

How many times had she told him that, since time out of mind, the dukes of Aquitaine had tried to institute a central form of control over the turbulent duchy—all to no avail. Again and again she had urged a loose rein, a benign presence, a willingness to allow authority to rest with the local lords—this was the only way. But now, smarting under his recent lack of achievement, Henry refused to listen.

"Not to mention those that don't agree with the doctrine of Holy

Church, Sire," said Thomas Becket. "Heresies run rife here. Provençal society in particular is a breeding ground for every spiritual plague imaginable."

Eleanor bristled. This was Bernard of Clairvaux and Abbé Suger all over again. "What exactly do you mean by that? Aquitainians are all Christians. A few minor deviations here and there do not mean they worship the devil."

"Minor deviations?" The chancellor sent her a withering look. "One is either a true believer in the Faith, a heretic, or an infidel. Arabs, Jews, and Cathars abound in this duchy. The Albigensians, some of whose leaders, I understand, are actually women—" he glanced pointedly at Eleanor—"make many converts, I've heard, even among the nobles. What says Holy Writ? 'He who is not with me is against me.'"

Henry shrugged dismissively. Although Eleanor suspected that despite his apparent disdain for religious matters Henry strongly favored orthodoxy, he was not of a mind to suppress heretical cults or persecute Arabs or Jews so long as they did not openly oppose his policies.

"The Cathars and others do not pose a threat, Henry," she said quickly, ignoring Becket.

"I never said they did. But your vassals do. God's eyes!" He glowered. "You ask *me* to listen to reason. Do your vassals behave reasonably?"

She could not deny that all too frequently they behaved either like witless dolts or reckless barbarians.

"Henry, I realize what you are trying to do here and I support your efforts, you know I do. But to bring all these disparate elements under one central authority will take time. These nobles and their ancestors have done as they pleased for three hundred years. It is bred in the bone. I beg of you, do not move hastily."

Henry glanced at her. She gave him a winning smile while her eyes implored him. After a moment he sighed impatiently and stuck his knife into the wood of the table; the blade quivered back and forth.

"All right. All right!" He looked around the table and threw up his hands. "I ask you, how can you deny a woman anything when she looks at you like that?" There was a murmur of tentative laughter. "The castle will not be razed—at this time."

Eleanor let out her breath in a long sigh, knowing she dared not argue further now. At least she had bought her vassal a reprieve. Not that the arrogant fool deserved it.

Down the table there was a discreet cough. "Ah, Majesty, if I may remind you?" Thomas Becket slid his eyes sideways toward Eleanor. "This vassal of the queen's," he emphasized the word queen's, "this vassal has long been a troublemaker in the duchy. It might be well to recall that he sided with your late brother, when Geoffrey attempted to rebel against you."

"By God, that's right! I'd forgotten."

"If you fail to make an example of him it will be said you are no longer master here. After Toulouse, Sire, it would be unwise . . ."

"You're right, Thomas." Henry fixed Eleanor with a hard look. "The viscount's castle must be razed, Nell. There's an end to it."

Eleanor saw a brief smile cross the chancellor's face. At this moment her hatred of him was so intense she almost choked on the carp she was chewing. Thomas Becket, without whose advice Henry would not make any important decision, was a constant intruder, his dark shadow continually falling between herself and her husband, deliberately sowing discord between them.

Eleanor had come to terms with the dominating influence of Henry's mother, but this friendship with Becket was altogether different. The empress, however grudgingly, fully acknowledged Eleanor's role in Henry's life. But in his covert way, as in the matter of the Pipe Roll and now, not to mention countless others, Thomas sought to undermine and exclude her.

Although, on occasion, Eleanor was still able to influence Henry, she could never control him as she had Louis, even without Becket. She was wise enough now to know that she had as much chance of harnessing a thunderbolt. When Eleanor remembered her early conversation with Master André before her marriage, how, in their innocence, they had both thought she could mold the young duke, she didn't know whether to laugh or cry.

The bitter truth was that, thus far, she had gained neither the influence nor power that was her due. In principle she was supposed to be *regalis imperii participes,* a sharer in the kingship. In truth, she was given the illusion of power but none of the substance. These same thoughts which had occurred to her in England kept returning again and again with increased intensity.

England, of course, was not hers. But Aquitaine was another

story. Here she was still duchess-regnant, and her authority should reign supreme. Of course she had spent the last five years bearing children; yet that aside, if it weren't for Chancellor Thomas Becket, Eleanor felt she might have achieved an almost equal position without poaching on Henry's preogatives. Neither Abbé Suger nor even Bernard of Clairvaux had proved so redoubtable a rival. She picked up her goblet of wine then arrested it halfway to her lips. A chill ran down her spine. Rival? Why did she always fall back on that bizarre choice of word? As though Thomas were an actual contender for Henry's affections. Like the unknown Bellebelle.

The royal party was due to leave Poitou the following day. For the first time, Eleanor was anxious to be gone. She could no longer bear the reproachful glances of her vassals and knights, no longer endure the feeling of helplessness that oppressed her in the overwrought atmosphere of Poitiers.

Later that evening her uncle Ralph de Faye, seneschal of Aquitaine, came to the chamber where Eleanor had just finished putting Richard and Henry to bed.

"The Plantagenet is becoming more high-handed each time I see him," Ralph said.

"It is the chancellor's fault this time, not Henry's." Her uncle always referred to Henry as "the Plantagenet," no matter how many times Eleanor corrected him. "Sometimes I wonder if I haven't lost my duchy altogether. My marriage, my children, my crown—I have paid a great price for them, Uncle."

Ralph took her hands in his. "You can never lose Aquitaine, for that would be like losing your very soul. In truth, you have done remarkably well balancing the duchy, your motherhood, your responsibilities, and your husband—your love for him still burns as brightly as ever?"

"Brighter."

"Well, that is something—for you. It was not too long ago that if someone had told me the frivolous, spoiled coquette of Aquitaine would become the woman of substance you now are—I would not have believed him." Ralph shook his head. "And the Plantagenet cares as well, though he attempts to hide it with his overbearing manner. At first I thought he had married you only to possess the duchy, but over time I've come to see there's far more to it than that."

Ralph strode over to the bed and gazed down at the sleeping faces of her two sons. Eleanor followed him.

"What do you mean?"

"I am not sure myself. Only, perhaps, that to a man like the Plantagenet, love is an adversary to be conquered, not a pleasure to be courted and enjoyed." He shook his head. "Idle words. They mean nothing."

Eleanor brushed a golden ringlet from Richard's creamy brow. "Since Toulouse Henry has certainly been more hostile—" She stopped. The incident with the Empress Maud and the wild talk of crowning young Henry passed through her mind.

Even before Toulouse Henry had not been himself, she realized, behaving with more antagonism, even falling into one of his wild rages in Le Mans over nothing at all. She had to confide in someone. It was no longer possible to keep her thoughts and feelings contained. Eleanor hesitated. Ralph de Faye was not the most trustworthy of men but he had proved loyal to her and to his post. If she did not speak she would go from her wits.

In a lowered voice she told Ralph about the entry in the Pipe Roll and the Empress Maud's initial reaction to her own grandson.

Ralph said nothing for a moment. When he did speak Eleanor had the feeling that he chose his words with care.

"There was talk at one time—oh, many years ago now, before you married Louis—that the empress would sooner have had Stephen of Blois as her paramour rather than her enemy. Even talk that the heir of Anjou was Stephen's son—not that anyone believed such far-fetched rumors."

Eleanor was dumbstruck. "I never heard such tales, nor can I credit them." Her head whirling, what she did not say was that this rumor would explain why Count Geoffrey left Anjou to his second son should Henry inherit England, as well as the empress's reaction to a grandson that resembled Stephen.

"Pure speculation, after all," Ralph said, with a dismissive shrug. "Put no stock in it. I find it hard to believe this the cause of the Plantagenet's ill temper. He must have heard the rumors before now. Why would they disturb him at this late date?" Ralph shook his head. "Nor does it signify one way or another as far as Aquitaine is concerned. What *does* signify is the chancellor's influence as opposed to yours."

"He will advise anything that makes less of my authority in the duchy. Sweet St. Radegonde, how I hate him," Eleanor burst out.

Ralph put a finger to his lips, indicating the women in a far corner of the chamber. "Prudence. Prudence. At the moment you can do nothing about him, Niece."

He left the bedside and walked over to the casement window. Eleanor followed.

"My hatred for—that person is only equaled by his hatred of me," she said. "He is highly dangerous—not just to Aquitaine but to my welfare. He *wanted* me to see that entry in the Pipe Roll."

"I don't dispute that." Ralph threw a quick glance toward the women, their heads together, busily working on a square of tapestry. "Do not let him bait you. What does it matter if the Plantagenet dallies here and there? Turn a blind eye—as my mother—your grandmother, Dangereuse, did. The Troubadour always came back to her in the end. By allowing him his freedom she bound him with threads of steel."

"I will try to do that, Uncle. In truth, what disturbs me most is that Henry and Beck—that person are bosom companions in the business of the kingdom, in riding, hunting, hawking—there is little they do not do together except bed! He has cast some sort of spell over my husband, who consults him on everything. It's intolerable."

Ralph sent her a sharp glance. "Henry honors your bed as regularly as ever?"

"Of course." Eleanor gave him a puzzled look.

"Then our friend does not have what he wants the most. Rest content."

Speechless, Eleanor stared at her uncle. "You mean—? Uncle, you cannot expect me to believe—" She simply could not accept what he was implying. "It's impossible. You must be mistaken."

"Perhaps. But the signs are all there." Ralph laughed and shook his head. "I would never have believed you to be so innocent, so unworldly. Truly, you never once suspected?"

"Never. But Henry—"

"Undoubtedly ignorant of his chancellor's hidden tastes, which I'm quite certain will never be revealed. Even to himself he may not admit they exist—though I suspect he knows. So you see there is an underlying reason for his enmity toward you."

Eleanor was astounded. It was the last thing she would ever have imagined, and it certainly gave her a rather different view of the situation. It would explain her jealousy, why she felt Becket was a rival. Always supposing her flamboyant uncle was correct in what he surmised, of course.

Ralph, who had been watching her, chuckled softly. "You must be more observant. Keep your eyes open to what is going on around you, not fixed on the Plantagenet like a besotted maid." He wagged a cautionary finger. "Bide your time, Niece. You must be clever enough never to act precipitously toward Becket. Impetuous action has been the downfall of the dukes of Aquitaine for centuries. But women have always known how to wait. Mark my words, one day he will overreach himself. Your hour will come." He reached out and squeezed her hand. "Meanwhile do nothing rash. You have Aquitaine to think of."

When had she ever thought of anything else? Eleanor wondered. She had just learned two things of vital interest: Becket's predilection for Henry; the Empress Maud's dark secret—if both were even true. She turned them over in her mind. If Henry were not Geoffrey's legitimate son he never would have been permitted to inherit either Anjou or the English crown. Suppose his bastardy were discovered at a later date? Could an annointed king be dethroned? She did not know. Certainly, his children would be tainted by illegitimacy. It was extremely doubtful if they would be permitted to inherit the English crown—the freewheeling days of the Conqueror were long gone, and Holy Church would no longer support the issue of a bastard. Henry's enemies, what remained of the adherents of the House of Blois, and others, would not fail to seize the moment and turn it to their own advantage. Eleanor realized that she did not know the actual legalities that pertained in such a situation, and it was far too dangerous to ask. Not that legalities would matter. Just the rumor, widely circulated, would be sufficient to create havoc.

The resulting scandal could rock the House of Normandy to its foundations. The House of Aquitaine would be equally affected. Would her people accept a misbegotten duke—or one of his sons as future duke? At the very least, there would most certainly be more outbreaks of rebellion, unrest, uprisings in Aquitaine, perhaps in Anjou as well, even another civil war in England. The implications of Henry not being the count of Anjou's legitimate son were so overwhelming they boggled the mind; Eleanor rejected the possibility as being too preposterous, the result of her upset with Henry, her resentment of Becket, a figment of her fevered imagination. She must have been mad to have ever seriously considered such an outlandish idea.

However, should there ever come a time when, her back against the wall, her duchy's survival at stake, she, personally, needed a weapon with which to protect herself, another string to her bow, as it were . . . not that she ever would, of course, still . . .

She smiled at her uncle. "No. I will do nothing rash."

# CHAPTER 40

# Bermondsey,
# 1159–1160

After her encounter with de Burgh, Bellebelle did not believe that life in the village of Bermondsey could continue on in its usual placid way. But it did. Swallows came in the spring; sheep were sheared in summer; hay harvested in the fall. Always on edge now, she saw no further sign of de Burgh but knew he was just biding his time, waiting for the king to return to England.

When her money was next brought from the chancery, and each time thereafter, the chancellor's secretary delivered it. She never mentioned de Burgh and apparently the Fleming had said nothing to the secretary about her.

At first Geoffrey pestered her with questions about de Burgh: Where had she known him and why did he want to hurt her? Had he really murdered her mother? Was that why she had tried to kill him? Bellebelle told her son half-truths, vague about the details, never mentioning that she had been a whore, fairly certain, now that he was five, that soon he would no longer be ignorant of such things. What she did make clear was that she had been less than truthful with Henry about her past; it was possible the King would be displeased. After all, Geoffrey's life might be turned upside down; he had a right to be forewarned.

"What do you think Father will do?" he asked.

"I don't know, Son, and that be the truth. Henry do have a hot temper, you know that as well as I does."

"Do. But he loves us, Maman—doesn't he?"

"Aye, he do—does—that. But sometimes he does things without

thinking them through like, then be sorry later."

Geoffrey's flint-colored eyes filled with tears. "That wouldn't be fair to you, would it?"

"Mustn't grumble, lad. Henry's been good to us, and life not be fair or unfair. It just be like it is. We'll be all right whatever he does." She had no certainty of that but felt the need to reassure him. "Haven't I told you time after time that you can't have no wishbone where your backbone ought be?"

Geoffrey, still full of questions, was not satisfied, but seemed to understand there was nothing more she could—or would—tell him. Tall and bright for his age, he increasingly reminded Bellebelle of a youthful Henry. She had come to rely on him for almost everything: companionship, help about the cottage, and, ever since de Burgh's visit, protection.

The day after the Fleming left she had told the couple from the village she would not need them any more. Terrified de Burgh might return, she did not want the couple spreading gossip about the village that might hurt not only herself but Geoffrey as well. It had been nothing less than a miracle that they had been gone when de Burgh came. Her son had struck up an acquaintance with an old woodman who cut wood for the priory school, and had persuaded him to bring kindling and logs to the cottage. A kindly soul who felt sorry for Bellebelle, the woodman, Old Ivo, had taken Geoffrey and her under his protection.

"You know, Belle," Ivo told her one day when he was delivering a load of wood, "as you leads a quiet life, minds your own business, and doesn't give yourself airs, people in the village saying you be none so bad."

"I noticed that although most everyone still shuns me, a few greet me pleasantly. Sometimes they even stop to pass the time of day with me."

Ivo nodded approvingly as he laid the pile of logs on the ground near the front door of the cottage. "That be a good sign. Won't be long before they accepts you."

So long as they never found out the truth. In time, the king's doxy might come to be tolerated. But Bellebelle knew that growing up in a brothel, life as a practicing whore, and attempted murder were things respectable folk wouldn't stand for. If they found out, and with Henry gone, the village folk might even try to drive her off— or worse.

"Why they take against me so?" she asked. "I never do them no harm."

"No fault of yours, Belle," Old Ivo said, straightening up with difficulty. "Comes from long before your time, it does. When I be a young lad, in the time of the Old King—the first Henry that is— there was a sickness swept through the village, mostly affecting the young ones. Many died, God rest them. There was a woman who lived alone in the woods, sold herbs she grew, and supposedly had the gift of healing. She were known to be the leman of the lord of the manor. Folk blamed her."

"But why?"

Ivo shrugged. "She were different. The lord's whore. No one protected her when he wasn't there."

Bellebelle stared at him. "What happened?"

"The village folk stoned her for a witch. In hard times, Belle," said Ivo, "when folk be afraid, they turn back to the ways of their forefathers, the old gods."

Bellebelle felt her skin prickle with goose bumps. It was a terrible tale and she wished she had never asked.

Now that the couple were gone, she cooked all the meals, having learned by watching the woman. Bellebelle knew she was not very good at it but at least they weren't starving. With the woodman's help she learned how to plant and weed the garden, milk the goat, snatch eggs from the hens, and even lay the fire properly. She was clumsy and had no feel for such work, but she was making do. When a few stunted cabbages, lettuces, and turnips appeared in her vegetable patch, she was filled with pride. The pear and quince trees bore fruit; the flower garden grew purple sweet-smelling lavender; parsley, sage, mint, and a rosemary bush thrived on their little plot of earth.

Bellebelle had bought herself two piglets last year and was going to have one of them butchered come Christmas. The woodman found a villein from the manor lands who was willing to help her for a fee. He had built a wattle fence around the cottage, which gave her a feeling of safety. She even made friends with the wolfhound, Valiant; after all, by his presence alone he had partially saved her life. Yet despite the fence, the wolfhound, and frequent visits from Old Ivo, the sense of threat remained, under the surface, like thunder in the air with no storm to be rid of it.

With Henry gone, Bellebelle received all the news of what was happening in the outside world from either Geoffrey, the woodman, or the village folk. Thus she knew that Louis of France's second wife had died giving birth to his fourth daughter, called Alais, sister to Marguerite who was betrothed to Henry's eldest son and heir. Folk said she was an unlucky child to have killed her mother and would come to grief. A month later the French king married his third wife, sister to the count of Blois-Champagne.

When Bellebelle stopped by the alehouse one October morning, in the year 1160, for her pitcher of ale, two women were there gossiping about the event.

"Such haste be shameless," said one with a sniff, eyeing Bellebelle with hostile eyes.

"Oh, aye, that it be," said the other, turning her back as if Bellebelle didn't exist.

"T'won't do no good neither." The woman who brewed ale, a stout body of middle years with a red-veined nose and a ready tongue, shook her head. "The devil's curse be on King Louis, else why do he have only girls instead of the sons he do need?"

All three women crossed themselves then made horns with their fingers. Bellebelle recognized the horns as the sign Morgaine had often made to avert evil. She had always been wary of the woman who brewed ale ever since she had called her the king's whore in front of a whole crowd of people and shouted that Bellebelle had no right to a chimney. It was wise to tread carefully around the alewife, as the woman was a wealthy widow, of some importance in the village. One son ran the blacksmith's forge next door, a dark cave with showers of sparks at the back of it. Another son was the reeve, chosen by the village folk to oversee all the work done by the villagers for the steward of the manor.

"Look what happened right here in England when the Old King had no sons," the alewife was saying now. "Nineteen long years of trouble there was, when Christ and all His Saints—or was it angels?—slept, priest told us. Lord be thanked Lion and Eagle have so many."

"Lion even have some on the wrong side o' the blanket." One woman nudged her companion with a knowing titter.

Bellebelle looked from one to the other in confusion. "Who be the Lion and Eagle?"

The alewife raised her brows. "King and Queen. Where you been keeping yourself?"

Bellebelle had never heard either Henry or Eleanor referred to by such names before, and suddenly flushed, realizing they had been talking about her own Geoffrey as born on the wrong side of the blanket. While the other two snickered at her obvious discomfort, the alewife's beady blue eyes raked her face, missing nothing. Suddenly the alewife planted meaty arms on her ample hips and glared at the two women.

"You lot reminds me of two cats with their claws out. I say this poor lass be no worse than many another if truth be known. With her face and form I reckon the Horned One tempted her more than most. I dare say as them that points the finger at her would have been no better than what she been if they'd had the chance." She raised an arm and one plump finger shot out jabbing the air. "I don't see no king as coming after you two snaggle-toothed, skinny-shanked hags for his pleasure, now does I?"

The two women grew red and dropped their eyes.

"Didn't mean no harm," muttered one, and they scuttled away.

"Never you mind them old cats," said the alewife, patting Belle-belle on the arm. "Jealous they be, plain as a pikestaff."

Overcome, Bellebelle swallowed. "Thank you," she whispered.

"That be all right." The alewife paused, a wistful look crossed her face. "I never seen no chimney before."

"Oh please, you be welcome in me house anytime. I'd be proud to have you."

"Would you now. That's right neighborly. You can call me Elf-giva. Old Saxon name, that."

"I be Bellebelle."

"So's I've heard. That's not a proper Christian name, if I does say so."

"I was christened Ykenai. Me Mam, her name was Gytha. She was Saxon too." Bellebelle looked down. "Me father was Norman."

"Saxon names, right enough. Well, if that don't beat all."

Elfgiva's eyes met hers. They smiled shyly at each other.

"Anyone as gives you trouble in the village you just tell me, hear?"

Bellebelle nodded happily and left with her pitcher of ale. Elfgiva was the first female friend she had ever made who was not a whore.

One day in late November while Bellebelle was clearing an overgrown section of the garden with the weeding crotch, Geoffrey burst through the gate, beside himself with excitement.

"You'll never guess what's happened! My half-brother's married to the French princess, Marguerite. I heard at the priory that my father arranged it in such secrecy that Louis of France never even knew until it was too late. What do you think of that?"

Bellebelle straightened, rubbed the small of her back, and stared at him in bewilderment. "Your half-brother?"

"Prince Henry, my father's heir."

"But he be only five years old, and the French princess be mayhap two or three? What does it mean?"

"It means that my father has checkmated the king of France," Geoffrey said, his eyes shining. "Now the Vexin will be returned to him, and he'll get his own back for having to back down at Toulouse. He's outwitted Louis yet again."

"Well, I don't see as why two children so young should marry just for a piece of land. Even Gilbert said he wouldn't have no girl in his house 'afore twelve year."

"Oh, Maman, you just don't understand." Geoffrey paused. "Who's Gilbert?"

Bellebelle froze. How could she have been so careless? "Someone I knew long ago. And you're right, I don't understand. But you think what Henry did be clever?" she added quickly. "What be checkmate?"

"Oh, Maman, my father's more than clever, he's—he's—" Unable to find the right word, Geoffrey frowned in frustration. "Checkmate is—like in chess. I've explained it to you, remember?"

"Oh, aye."

Bellebelle watched him with a fond smile. Geoffrey was fascinated by anything to do with political intrigues and affairs of state. Sometimes she was in awe of his effortless grasp of matters that seemed unnecessarily complicated to her.

A gust of wind swept through the garden, rattling the bare branches of the pear tree, and setting the rosemary bush to quivering like silvery green spray.

"What else did you hear?"

Geoffrey thought for a moment. "The queen is back in England. At the priory they say that the king and his chancellor may return soon because the archbishop of Canterbury is ill."

"Henry will be back? When—" She caught the note of alarm in her voice and stopped abruptly. There was a look of dread on Geoffrey's face.

"*He's* not been back—has he?"

Geoffrey did not have to say who "he" was. She shook her head. Both of them knew that when Henry did return, de Burgh would speak to him.

Geoffrey sniffed the air. "Is something burning?"

"Oh! The mutton pottage." Bellebelle ran inside the cottage and quickly removed the smoking cauldron from the fire.

She hadn't seen Henry in over two years; he had never been gone so long before. Bellebelle wanted him to return more than anything in the world, but when he did she had no idea what might happen. Would he understand? She prayed every night to the Virgin Mary–Eleanor that he would understand. But suppose he did not? Suppose he felt she had betrayed him? Suppose—suddenly she grabbed Geoffrey and hugged him as if her very life depended on it.

# Canterbury, 1161

Theobold of Bec, archbishop of Canterbury, knew he was dying. Tended by his devoted clerics, he lay in his palace at Canterbury, heartsick that the obscure clerk he had befriended and helped to power should ignore the messages he regularly sent to Normandy, Angers, or wherever the chancellor might happen to be. Yet Thomas Becket made excuse after excuse, pleading that the king could not spare him from pressing duties. To Theobald, it was quite unthinkable that the youth whose royal mother he had so wholeheartedly supported should ignore him in this hour of his need, denying him the company of the man that he, the archbishop, had made chancellor.

In his last missive Theobald had explained that there would soon be a vacancy in the See of Canterbury and as an archdeacon of Canterbury it was Thomas Becket's duty to come at once and help him choose a possible successor. In vain. It was now March of 1161 and he had last sent to Thomas just after Twelfth Night.

Theobald fingered the silver crucifix on his breast and signed himself. Such base ingratitude was beyond his comprehension. Without his help, Henry Plantagenet would never have mounted the throne. Who was it kept England safe when Stephen died? Arranged the peaceful transition from one reign to the next? How could that thoughtless boy deny him such a humble request during his last hours on earth?

"Put not your trust in kings and princes," he said aloud. "Now we must add chancellors of England. My flesh is worn, my limbs wearied with age, and the end of my days is at hand. I ask only that I look upon Thomas's face once more. Is it too much?"

"No, Your Grace." One of his clerics sitting on a stool beside the great bed leaned forward.

"Perhaps I have not earned the right," Theobald said in a quavering voice. "Perhaps I judge Thomas too harshly. Underneath my archbishop's robe beats the heart of a simple monk, not a worldly prelate. The chancellor's magnificence, his preoccupation with the trappings of power, such a life seems unworthy to me." He shook his head and signed himself again. "I saw Thomas's faults; I was never blind to his ambition, his lack of holiness, but there was good in him, surely I was not wrong about that?" He knew he was rambling but could not seem to help himself.

"No, Your Grace." The cleric held up a goblet of wine to Theobald's lips.

The archbishop sipped, feeling the cool liquid soothe his parched throat.

"But Thomas has done things that have disturbed me. He should never have agreed to tax the abbeys for the war in Toulouse. Never. It goes against our Order, whether or not it is right in law. Master Thomas never fails to side with kingly authority; he is devoted to Mammon, not God." Taking strength from the wine, Theobald sat up straighter against the pillows. Indignation warmed his body.

"Get pen and parchments," he said to the cleric, pleased with the note of determination he heard beneath the quiver in his voice. "I will send to Normandy once more. This time I will order Thomas to come, not beg him. If common humanity will not move him, threats may."

• • •

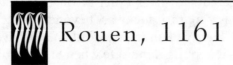

# Rouen, 1161

"I think I should visit Theobald, Sire," Thomas said. "After all, he's sent to me I don't know how many times by now. My conscience is beginning to trouble me."

"As I've already told you, there's no need," Henry said in a lazy voice. "Archbishops are always issuing summons as though they're the foremost canonical authority in Christendom."

On this late March evening, they were seated round a fire in the clearing that housed the Old King's hunting lodge in the Verte Forest, outside Rouen.

Thomas laughed. "I doubt Theobald aims so high."

When, early this morning, Henry had suggested they go hunting together, just the two of them, Thomas had eagerly accepted. Since the ill-fated venture in Toulouse, which marked the first time they had had a serious quarrel, Thomas sensed a withdrawal on Henry's part, subtle but unmistakable. They had been together numerous times on official matters concerning the realm, but there had been virtually no social intercourse between them. Thomas hoped that this invitation to hunt might be Henry's way of healing the breach and restoring their friendship to its former intimacy. The question of whether or not to heed Theobald's most recent summons had been under discussion for several days.

"Theobald has no standing here in Rouen," said Henry. "As far as conscience goes, well, that is a luxury any chancellor of mine can ill afford."

"Even at the risk of excommunication?"

Henry shrugged. "Theobald will never excommunicate you, Thomas, I think you know that. His bark is loud but his teeth are drawn."

Thomas, watching Henry from under half-closed lids, thought he was probably right. The king, clad in a green hunting tunic girded by a belt with silver clasps from which dangled a knife in a leather sheath, blended perfectly with the silent, secret beechwoods that surrounded them. Only the ivory horn, dependent from his neck and swinging round one shoulder, looked out of place.

There was a sudden burst of flame as fat dripped into the fire from the haunch of doe threaded on a wood spit across burning logs. Above treetops brushed with gold, the sun was sinking in the west, the shadows lengthening across the clearing. The evening air was filled with the acrid tang of gray-blue wood smoke mingled with the scent of roasting meat. Three bloodhounds lay stretched before the fire, soft muzzles buried in their paws. At a distance from the fire two huntsmen were talking in low voices, testing birchwood bows and counting the number of arrows left in the quivers. A groom curried the horses tied to several trees at the far end of the clearing.

"Regardless of my conscience, Sire, or lack of it, and leaving the threat of excommunication aside, Theobald is gravely ill. I owe him a great deal—"

"So do I, Thomas, so do I. But I have need of you here. The near-dead—if, in fact, that is how matters stand—must give way before the living. The worthy archbishop is not above exaggerating his condition for his own ends. You know what these old churchmen are."

In truth, the selfless Theobald never acted for his own ends, only those of Holy Church, thought Thomas. But there was little point in telling that to a ruler who acted almost entirely to serve his own ends. As well as the weal of the realm, of course, although in Henry's mind he and the kingdom were one and the same, their interests identical. What was beneficial for one must, perforce, be beneficial for the other.

What Henry failed to observe, however, was his own possessiveness, his need to be at the center of everyone's attention. Affection for him must exceed affection for anyone else. How often had Thomas seen Henry's jealous glance follow Eleanor, when she thought herself unobserved, noting whom she talked to, for how long, and with what degree of pleasure. Thomas had noted that Henry even resented the queen's particular love for her son Richard.

Even the slut in Bermondsey was not exempt. Thomas had long suspected that Henry' s unusual interest in the Flemish knight, de Burgh, was connected in some way with Bellebelle—although he was not sure what the connection might be.

Now Theobald had become a target merely because Thomas wanted to visit him on his deathbed. No matter Henry's justifications, Thomas, pricked by guilt, knew it was uncharitable to ignore the summons of his former master who had taken him in when he was a poor cleric with no prospects. Not only that, it was Theobald who had started him on the road to power when, seven years earlier, he had been planted as a quasi-spy under the guise of Henry's chancellor. Not to visit his aged benefactor was an act of disloyalty; certainly that was how Theobald would view it. In a surprising twist of fate, Thomas had switched his allegience from the archbishop to King Henry. This was where his loyalty—and his interests—now lay. Was it any wonder he felt guilty? Well, one could not serve two masters equally. He had chosen King Henry.

Dusk fell. The sky turned mauve then deep purple; the sun sank beneath the trees. A huntsman took the haunch from the fire and cut it into thick slices.

"I wonder if Theobald has an actual successor for the See in mind." Henry took a swallow from a silver wine flask and held it out to Thomas.

"Unlikely he has a candidate for Canterbury, Sire. This was one of the reasons he wanted to consult me." Although Thomas rarely indulged in wine, tonight he felt the need of some fortification. Was it the image of a dying Theobald? He could not tell, but moved close enough to Henry so that their shoulders brushed. He took the wine flask.

Venison juice dripped upon Thomas's tunic as he carried a chunk of meat to his lips. During the past two years, whenever he was with Henry, he had started to eat the flesh of four-legged animals, a far cry from his earlier adherence to only fish or two-legged creatures, as prescribed by the Benedictine Order.

From Rouen Cathedral came the far-distant sound of the Vespers bell. The horses whinnied softly; the hounds awoke; soon they were snarling as they fought for scraps. The sky grew darker, a pale sliver of new moon appeared.

"I will send a message to Eleanor at Westminster and ask her to pay a visit to the archbishop," Henry said in a conciliatory tone. "She's a past mistress at diplomacy and will know how to explain why I can't spare you."

"I'm sure Theobald will appreciate it, Sire." The very idea that the sensuous queen, whom, incredibly, Theobald had actually taken a liking to, would be a suitable replacement for himself was an affront.

There was no reason he could not be spared, Thomas wanted to say, irritated with himself for not doing so. At the moment matters fared very well indeed for the bold Plantagenets.

After the fiasco of Toulouse, Henry had at one stroke restored his prestige by secretly marrying young Henry to Louis's eldest daughter by his late wife, while the French king, desperate to get a son, was hastily preparing for his third wedding to the count of Blois's sister. The fact that Louis was making an alliance with the House of Champagne-Blois—which had produced King Stephen—threatened Henry's sense of security, and he had acted with dispatch. Despite Louis's subsequent rage and threats at the loss of the Vexin, which was restored to the Plantagenets upon the occasion of young Henry's wedding, there was little he could do except make a feeble attack on Henry's lands in Touraine—which Henry thwarted by a successful counterattack.

In fact, the French king's marriage to a daughter of the House of Blois posed a minor threat, if any, as far as Thomas could see. But Henry's virtual obsession with anything that concerned Stephen of Blois, his almost overpowering need to obliterate any and all reminders of this unhappy monarch, was a source of puzzling concern to Thomas. Along with his philandering and extreme possessiveness, it hinted at yet another unstable element in the king's complex character.

"I keep meaning to tear this lodge down, as I told de Beaumont some time ago, but something always stops me." Henry took another swig from the flask and passed it back again to Thomas.

"A link with the past perhaps?" Against his better judgment, Thomas took another long swallow before returning the flask to Henry. His head was starting to swim and his voice sounded thick.

"That must be part of it," Henry said.

Thomas saw the huntsmen and groom wrap themselves in blankets some distance from the fire and curl up to sleep.

"You could spare me if you so desired," Thomas said suddenly, amazed at his own audacity. It must be the wine. "I'm due to leave for England shortly in any case."

There was a short silence.

"I daresay I could but I don't choose to spare you, Thomas. Theobald can wait a while longer." Henry reached out and roughly slapped calloused fingers across the back of Thomas's hand. "What would I do without my boon companion, eh?"

Henry's fingers seared him like flame. Before he knew what he was about, Thomas turned his palm up, his fingers opened, crossed, then interlaced with Henry's. He could feel Henry's start of surprise and initial withdrawal. Thomas grasped the harder and Henry let his hand rest.

"I thought you were still angry with me," Thomas said in a throbbing voice he barely recognized as his own.

"Well, I was, Thomas, I was, no doubt of that." With his free hand Henry took another pull at the silver flask and passed it again to Thomas.

"Yet it was only your honor I sought to preserve outside the walls of Toulouse." Thomas took the flask, noting that his fingers shook.

"I don't doubt it. But you know how I hate to be thwarted once I've made up my mind. One of my weaknesses, I fear—one of my many weaknesses. I'll warrant you know them better than I do myself. Mea culpa, but you'll forgive me my trespasses, I hope?" He gently withdrew his hand and gave Thomas an affectionate punch on the arm. "But that's all over and done with now. We are like brothers again, eh?"

That was the incredible thing about Henry: he could disarm you so easily with his uncanny ability to confide his own faults. Thomas closed his eyes. He could feel a pounding in his ears. Was it his heart? He took another draught of wine, emptied the flask, then laid it aside.

"Are we brothers then?" he said in a low voice.

"Have I not just said so?"

"Blood brothers?" It was too dark to clearly read the expression on Henry's face.

"I'm not sure I understand you, Thomas." The king's voice was edged with a kind of wary surprise.

"Shall we make a vow of blood brotherhood?"

Thomas was shocked, amazed, horrified at his own words. What had made him voice such an outrageous idea, suggestive as it was of sorcery, faith, passion, chivalry, even pagan ritual?

"The blood bond between brothers-in-arms? Didn't the housecarls of the Saxon kings so bind themselves?" Henry paused. "The Knights Templar formed such a bond after exposure to the infidel during the first crusade."

"A bond of comradeship, yes, that cannot be destroyed or disavowed." Thomas didn't add that it was also a pact of flesh and spirit, such as legendary lovers like Tristan and Isolde were said to have made; what one possessed belonged to the other, and they were sworn to protect one another. Sometimes they did not survive each other.

Henry laughed. Thomas thought he detected a trace of uneasiness.

"You never cease to surprise me, my lord chancellor. I'm sure your saintly Theobald would call such an act heretical. Isn't there some sort of ceremony involved?" His words sounded a bit slurred.

"I believe so but I'm not familiar with the ritual. Of course, if you're fearful—"

"I fearful?" Henry instantly withdrew his dagger from its sheath. "We'll make our own ritual." He pulled up the sleeve of his tunic and shirt, gashed his forearm with the sharp blade. In the glow from the fire, Thomas could see beads of blood spurt from the wound. "Give me your arm."

Slowly Thomas pulled up the sleeve of his tunic and shirt and extended his arm. He choked back a cry as he felt the knife bite into his flesh. Henry pressed his wound against Thomas's so that their blood dripped and mingled together. Thomas felt the violent leap of his heart. His head reeled with the fumes of the wine; the concealing darkness; the intense intimacy of the moment. Overcome, arms outstretched, he leaned yearningly toward the king. His fingers brushed the king's hair.

"We're joined by blood now, Thomas," Henry said, jumping to his feet and pulling down his shirtsleeve. "Though I'm not sure what that means and I wouldn't go trumpeting it to one and all." He yawned. "Well, I'm suddenly very tired. It's too late to return to the castle tonight."

He strode across the clearing to his horse, opened one of the saddlebags, and took out a heavy blanket of unwashed wool. He returned, spread out the blanket before the fire, lay down and rolled himself up in it. "See you in the morning, blood-brother."

Within moments he seemed asleep. Henry's capacity to sleep anywhere or anytime reminded Thomas of a cat's. The Lion, well named. A trickle of sweat ran from his forehead down his cheek. Had he gone mad? What demon had prompted him to so lose control? With trembling fingers, Thomas pulled down the sleeve of his tunic. In the darkness, lit only by the glimmer of the fire, had Henry seen that telltale motion, that outstretched longing toward him? If he had seen it, would he know what it meant? In truth, what did it mean? Nothing, Thomas told himself. It meant nothing at all.

Yet something inside him writhed in an agony of humiliation. He would never forgive himself for such a lapse. Never. To reveal, even for an instant, such a damning weakness was intolerable. No one, not his confessor, not the monk who scourged him, knew of his dark and hidden desires.

But if Henry guessed, even suspected—the possibility was unthinkable. Thomas had always been on his guard, never by word or look or gesture revealing his true feelings. That he should have so exposed himself . . . Tears welled up in Thomas's eyes and he began to weep, hating himself. Because Henry might have witnessed his secret shame, he could feel the seeds of that hatred start to extend to the man he loved.

# CHAPTER 41

# England, 1161

On a mild April morning in the year of 1161, Eleanor approached the city gates of the cathedral town of Canterbury. She rode through the bustling streets and came upon the cathedral itself just as the bells tolled for Sext. John of Salisbury, an important member of the archbishop's household and the most respected Latinist in England, was waiting for her in the courtyard.

"You have arrived too late, Madam. Our saintly Theobald, may God give him rest, died shortly after Terce this morning."

"I'm so very sorry." Eleanor signed herself, and with the help of two grooms awkwardly dismounted, aware of the shocked expression on John's face at the sight of her body, already cumbersome with the child she would bear in September.

"I had no idea Theobald was so seriously ill," she continued. "I'm truly shocked."

This was the truth. The archbishop's death, a blow to her, would be an even greater blow for England. The former monk from Bec, known for his humility and piety, was loved by all. Although Theobald had been against her at the start of her marriage to Henry—due to gossip from France, Eleanor felt certain—they had taken an unexpected liking to one another. Despite her antipathy toward churchmen in general, Eleanor had greatly respected the archbishop.

"Madam, you shouldn't have come in your—condition," said John, averting red-rimmed eyes. "I did not know—that is to say, I appreciate—my master would have appreciated your concern. But should you be riding this far from London?"

"Only a two-day ride, pray do not worry," said Eleanor, noting the man's hostile expression soften somewhat. "I'm heartsick at our great loss. The king will be devastated when he hears of it."

John gave a mirthless laugh. "That would indeed surprise me, Madam. Theobald has sent many times to the king and his chancellor, begging them both to visit him. His deathbed wish was to look upon Thomas Becket's face one last time—a wish not granted. According to the chancellor, the king could not spare him. We at Canterbury are no less shocked by such base ingratitude."

Taken aback at this outburst, Eleanor did not know what to say. It was a harsh judgment and far from politic for John to voice it, but she decided to overlook his indiscretion in light of the tragic circumstances. It came as no surprise to her that Becket, having used the archbishop as a stepping-stone to greater heights, should abandon him when his usefulness came to an end. That others might blame Henry was another matter entirely. She would have to find some way of smoothing John's ruffled feathers.

She took him aside to a less crowded part of the courtyard. "In truth, matters have not gone well in Normandy and Anjou; Brittainy causes trouble, even my own duchy is restive. I know you will be discreet in this matter?" When John nodded, she continued. "The king dares not leave the Continent lest war break out with Louis of France."

John's face cleared. "I had no idea—nor did the archbishop—that matters had come to such a pass. On the contrary, we believed that the king's affairs prospered."

"Quite the reverse. The king did not want to worry Theobald while he was ill. That is why he sent me—despite my condition—as his representative. I return to Normandy almost at once. The king prays you will understand."

"Of course, of course. By the Mass, that puts a different face on matters. It was most thoughtful of the king to send you. Please tell him I said so." John's voice had warmed considerably. "This explains why Becket was unable to visit the archbishop. I wish he had told us how matters stood."

Eleanor shrugged. "I cannot answer for the chancellor. Only the king."

There was not a word of truth in what she had told John but that could not be helped. Nor was Becket's reputation her concern; only Henry's.

A day later, after she had paid her respects to the dead and left the late archbishop's grief-stricken household, Eleanor wondered if Henry had thought about Theobald's successor. It was not a matter they had ever discussed. In theory, of course, the monks of Canterbury elected their own archbishop, but the king's candidate was invariably the monks' choice. She remembered a dispatch she had seen, one that Henry had written to the monks of Winchester, which, at the time, had greatly amused her: "I order you to hold a free election, but nevertheless I forbid you to elect anyone except Richard, my clerk, the archdeacon of Poitiers."

Next to the king the archbishop of Canterbury was the most powerful personage in England. Who would Henry choose?

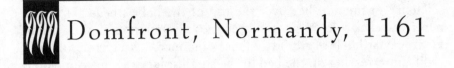

# Domfront, Normandy, 1161

In early September, Eleanor gave birth to her sixth child at Domfront Castle near the Normandy-Maine border. It was her second daughter by Henry, and the babe had been christened with her own name in an elaborate ceremony performed by the same Italian cardinal who had married young Henry and the French princess, Marguerite.

"I've never seen anyone with such a remarkable ability to recover from childbed," said Henry, holding the baby in his arms, a month after the birth. He had just ridden in from Angers and was still covered with the dust of the roads.

Eleanor stiffened but managed a laugh. "What do you know of such matters? How many women have you seen recover from childbed?" She watched him covertly to see how he would react.

"You know the answer to that." Henry kissed the top of the baby's downy head. "This little beauty looks the very image of her mother."

"You can't possibly tell at this age."

He was being evasive; she could always tell when he had something to hide. She had heard rumors of his bastards but knew nothing about them—or their mothers for that matter. Now, for the first time, it occurred to her that Henry might actually have been present either at one of the births or shortly thereafter. The very possibility sent a stab of jealousy through her. If, in fact, this was the case, she did not want to be told any of the details, Eleanor realized, retreating from such unwelcome thoughts.

So long as she did not actually *know* anything for certain, she could persuade herself there was nothing to know. That had been the trouble with seeing Bellebelle's name in the Pipe Roll. Eleanor had managed to put the thought of this bawd from her mind—most of the time. Now she wondered if Henry had had a child by her, but could not bring herself to ask.

"*I* can tell this fortunate child will look like you." Henry examined the babe's sleeping face. "A veritable Helen of Troy. Now—if only she has my disposition—"

"*Your* disposition? What's wrong with mine, pray?"

Henry grinned at her over the top of the babe's head. "I would never survive two imperious beauties in my household. Thank Heaven Matilda is of a mild and meek manner—as a girl should be."

Eleanor, resting on the bed in the small solar at Domfront, could see that Henry was pleased with this new daughter. It never ceased to amaze her how affectionate and indulgent a father he had turned out to be, spoiling and petting all his children—with the exception of Richard, whom he continued to ignore.

Handing the babe over to the wet nurse, Henry walked to the bed, sat down, and took Eleanor in his arms.

"You grow more beautiful each year, I swear you do," he said, nuzzling her neck. "Do you practice some secret spell or other witchcraft to still look so young and desirable?" His hands curved round the outline of her breasts. "You certainly continue to bewitch me."

"Flatterer." She patted her stomach muscles, still loose and weak from the birth. "This is hardly young and desirable. It will take weeks of riding and hawking to harden."

"Then you won't mind returning to England when you're fully recovered? I've lots or riding for you to do there."

"England again? Not without you. I absolutely refuse. Send your beloved Thomas."

"I've other plans for my beloved Thomas." Henry gave her light little kisses all over her face and neck. "I need you in England."

"What plans?"

Henry said nothing but continued to fondle her breasts. Eleanor felt herself responding to his ardor and, knowing he was attempting to distract her, resolutely removed his hands.

"That won't cozen me." She searched his face. "What schemes are you up to? Tell me."

"God's eyes, you're like a bloodhound worrying a bone." He bit his lip and sat back. "You must not speak of this to anyone, especially to Thomas."

"I never talk to him unless I must."

"As you know, since Theobald's death last April, the See of Canterbury has remained vacant. The pope is pressing me to fill it. He favors Gilbert Foliot, Bishop of Hereford."

"A good choice I should think. His entire life is a model of rectitude: never imbibes wine or eats meat, and keeps a most austere household."

Henry nodded his head impatiently. "Not to mention being a great scholar, a distinguished politician, and noted for his high moral standards of behavior. I know all of this."

He rose and began to pace up and down beside her bed.

Eleanor followed his movements with a puzzled look. "Well? What more could you ask?"

"I'll tell you what more." Henry swung around and jabbed a finger at her. "Gilbert Foliot, this prince among ecclesiastics, swore allegiance to my mother when he was ordained, yet broke his vow by later doing homage to Stephen for his temporal possessions. Do you tell me this is not perjury? It is. No matter how valid his excuses."

"That was a long time ago. He has served you well since, has he not?" Eleanor had long noted that Henry was unrelenting toward anyone who had broken faith with his mother to serve Stephen. It was an obsession with him. Her uncle's words flashed briefly through her mind.

Henry came to rest beside the bed. "I never forget an injury."

"I was just thinking that."

"Then our minds run a similar course." He paused. "In any case, it is in my mind to appoint"—he paused and took a deep breath—"Thomas Becket."

Eleanor was mystified. "Appoint him what?"

"Archbishop of Canterbury."

She could not have been more stunned had he named her. "But he's your chancellor! You can't mean that."

"I always say what I mean. The advantages are—well, they defy number. You know I've always followed an aggressive policy in any conflict between Church and sovereign. Thomas has never failed to side with me. To have as archbishop someone who is also chancellor—"

"Ensures you of Church support under all circumstances. I well understand the situation." Eleanor had such a sense of foreboding that the whole chamber suddenly felt shrouded in a thick gray fog of doom. "Henry, listen to me. In theory, what you propose is every monarch's dream, but there are problems—"

"The Holy Roman Emperor's chancellor is also the archbishop of Mainz. From what I hear—and my mother still has contacts in the empire—there are no problems." Henry sat on the bed.

"This is *England,* not the empire! Has there ever been a chancellor here who was also archbishop?"

"A first time for everything."

Eleanor pulled herself up higher against the pillows. "Like crowning young Henry while you still live? You seem set on breaking one precedent after another. Not that I object when there's need, like trying that case in York, but this . . ." She threw up her hands.

Henry suddenly dropped his eyes. "I refuse to be strangled by hidebound traditions."

Eleanor raised her brows. "How many times have I heard you refer to the good old customs of your grandfather? You cannot have it both ways."

"I don't see why not. You'll have to do better than that, Nell."

"All right. Canterbury does not like Thomas. He was an archdeacon who worked in Theobald's household, where he was known mainly as a lawyer and diplomat. Now he is your chancellor. By Church standards he is not suitable. Worldly, ambitious, hardly a pious man, these are but a few of the epithets leveled against him by the monks. You will have trouble if you attempt this. I was recently at Canterbury and I know whereof I speak."

Henry rubbed his chin. "I believe you." He sighed. "I should have seen Theobald before he died. I should have let Thomas see him. It was not politic."

"Not politic? Sweet St. Radegonde, it was cruel! You broke that old monk's heart."

Henry frowned, and scratched his head. His lips were pursed in a pout, and guilt was writ large on his face, like a small boy who has been caught in the act of misbehaving. She knew the expression well.

"Mea maxima culpa. I can be vicious sometimes. When I want something—or fear it—" He shrugged and rose to his feet. "There's naught I can do about it now. The monks of Canterbury must make the best of it."

As usual, his unblinking look at the less favorable aspects of his character disarmed her. Her voice softened. "Henry, I know you believe this to be a shrewd stroke, but if you make Thomas archbishop you will regret it to the end of your days."

Henry resumed his pacing. "I'm not blind. I'm well aware you have never liked him, nor he you, for that matter. In truth, he has served me, and the realm, very well indeed. Give me one specific reason, a fact not based on your personal bias, and I will listen."

Eleanor searched frantically for some incident or fact that would move him. "How do you know he shares your views on, say—need for reforms in matters of law? There's always conflict between the civil and Church courts. You told me yourself that the corruption and greed of many Church officials was widespread. Also he's not a priest."

"You're clutching at straws, Nell. Thomas has been scrupulous in his attempts to win back for the royal courts all that had been lost to the Church courts in Stephen's reign. As for not being a priest— that's easily remedied." He gave a dismissive wave of his hand.

"As your chancellor he has supported the crown. What will he do as archbishop of Canterbury?"

Henry paused in his pacing. "But he'll be both! It won't do, Nell. You have no valid reason for disputing my choice. In fact, I thought you would be pleased to have him out of our lives and safely tucked away at Canterbury." He sat back down on the bed and took her hand. "I will see much less of him. In fact, I will be losing my blood brother and you will have less occasion to be jealous."

Eleanor flushed. Had her jealousy been so obvious? "Blood brother?"

"Last spring, before Theobald's death, we were flown with wine and bonded ourselves as blood brothers." Henry paused, frowning, as if he would say more.

"Was there something else?" Her heart skipped a beat.

"Not really—nothing specific. I do regard him as an elder brother in many ways, a father and mentor even. After all, he was with me from the first day of my reign."

"Yes, I know. So was I." Eleanor felt vaguely disquieted but did not know why. Blood brotherhood. She knew very little about such bonds. "Before you make a final decision, please consult your mother."

The Vespers bell rang and Henry rose. "I never expected to hear you say that, but I intend to. I need not decide at once. Will you attend evensong?"

"I think not. I still feel very weak."

Eleanor watched him walk toward the door, stopping for a moment to chuck his little daughter under the chin. It would indeed be a relief to have Becket at Canterbury, but she knew with an absolute certainty that to appoint him archbishop would be a fatal error. If only she could have thought of . . .

Suddenly she remembered her uncle Ralph's suspicions about Becket's veiled desire for Henry. Should she tell him? He had reached the door now. She hesitated. Ralph's opinion was not based on known fact. Nor was her uncle a man Henry held in high regard. He might think that jealousy prompted her, a desire to destroy Becket's reputation. What should she do? By the time Henry had opened the door and left, the moment had come and gone.

The weeks passed and Eleanor was soon back on her feet, feeling fit and filled with her old energy. Henry had still not finally made up his mind about Becket, and in November she allowed him to persuade her to return to England. Still a prey to unease, Eleanor set sail for Dover, taking baby Eleanor and two nursemaids with her. Henry stood waving on the shore. As his figure grew smaller and smaller, she wondered if the day would come when she would regret her silence concerning Thomas Becket.

# CHAPTER 42

# Rouen,
# 1161

*I*nitially, it had not been Henry's idea to tempt Thomas Becket into losing his virginity, but when a knight in his entourage had suggested it, he had given his wholehearted agreement.

The day after seeing Eleanor off to England, Henry returned to Rouen in the company of his chancellor and three knights. He had decided to say nothing about the vacant See of Canterbury until he had talked to his mother. As he had told Eleanor, there was no hurry. After all, while the See remained vacant, those revenues flowed into the coffers of the king's treasury—although the pope would start complaining in earnest if the appointment were delayed too long. At the moment his domains remained quiet on both sides of the Channel and he was filled with a sense of well-being and accomplishment.

As Henry approached the gates of Rouen this windswept November morning, he hoped Eleanor was having a gentle voyage to England. The weather was uncertain this time of year when the Channel was often troubled by autumn gales—although he doubted there was a storm in heaven daunting enough to challenge the redoubtable Eleanor of Aquitaine. He smiled at the thought. Odd. His wife had been queen of France and was now queen of England. Yet he always thought of his Nell as Eleanor of Aquitaine.

Henry was struck by the realization that whenever she was gone he sorely missed her, although it was a great deal quieter in her absence. No challenges, no adversarial confrontations, no threats to his authority. No excitement either, for that matter. In fact, the atmosphere was dull as plainsong—or would be if Thomas weren't here.

Despite Eleanor's stubbornness, her attempts to control him and his affairs—especially where Aquitaine was concerned—her obvious ambition generally to get above herself, he loved her with the same passionate awe and loin-tingling excitement that he had at the beginning. The number of children she had borne had not, in his eyes, diminished her beauty or desirability. Of course she looked older than when he had first met her, and her body, though still slender, was no longer taut as a whip, but it never failed to arouse him as no woman's ever had. Just thinking of her now sent a pulse of heat through him and he knew he would be visiting a bawd tonight.

Trumpets sounded; guards flung open the gates. Henry rode into the streets of Rouen. Thoughts of Eleanor turned, as they often did, to thoughts of Bellebelle. God's eyes, how he missed her as well! He had not seen her in over two years at least, nor little Geoffrey. He now had many bastard sons—or so the various wenches claimed—but Geoffrey was his favorite by far. He loved this son as much as his children by Eleanor, and the mother too if it came to that.

His feelings for Bellebelle were vastly different, of course, than his feelings for Eleanor. But no less loving, no less meaningful to him. If Eleanor was fire and storm, unpredictable and challenging, Bellebelle was a cool forest stream, nurturing, soothing, and always predictable. He had rescued her from a life of degradation and poverty; she owed him everything. Eleanor, on the other hand, had come to him as an equal. Sometimes he felt that she did more for him than he for her—when it should be the other way round. There was nothing so gratifying than to know a woman was totally in your debt.

The ducal palace lay ahead, the gold-and-scarlet banner flying from the battlements to show the duke would be in residence. A light rain started to fall.

"Can you recommend a bawd?" he asked a knight riding beside him. "Someone new. I grow tired of the same old strumpets."

"There's a skilled tart called Millette, my lord duke, young and mettlesome, newly arrived in Rouen from Brabant. She plies her trade in the old quarter not far from the cathedral."

"Sounds promising." After being called Sire or Majesty in England, Henry always found it strange, at first, to hear himself called Duke in Normandy, or Count in Anjou.

Riding beside him in full mail, three blackbirds emblazoned on his shield, his helm on the cantle of his saddle, Henry could feel Thomas stiffen. The wave of disapproval that radiated from him was almost palpable.

"I sense you disapprove, Thomas?"

"It is not for me to disapprove anything Your Majesty chooses to do, but I believe your time would be better spent in more uplifting pursuits."

"Oh come, don't be so sanctimonious. What harm is there in a night's sport? Next you'll be telling me I set a bad example."

The three knights who accompanied them laughed.

Thomas flashed him a dark look. "In truth, my lord, you do. It's not the doxies that worry me, but the girls of good family I object to."

"Do you indeed." Henry paused. "Have you ever noticed that these 'good families,' so called, have something in common?"

Thomas frowned. "Something in common?"

"I mainly seduce the daughters of those nobles who supported Stephen—or were suspected of supporting him. Some of these treacherous knaves were clever about hiding their allegience."

He could hear Thomas's sudden indrawn breath. "In truth, I had not made the connection. It is still a poor excuse, my lord, unworthy of you."

"I have no need of excuses, I'm merely explaining. The girls—and their fathers—are usually well-compensated, as you know. I receive a certain satisfaction, not necessarily of the flesh, mind, but—" He shrugged. "I don't know. Worthy or not, it pleases me."

"Is the world your trough, my lord, to wallow in as you please?"

"God's eyes, Thomas, but you can be a self-righteous prig!" They were riding on the edge of the cathedral square now. "The trouble with you, chancellor, is that you're almost forty years of age and still a virgin. You're not a priest. No one could say you violated your holy vows if you fell from grace. It would do you a power of good, you know."

"I've taken my own vow of chastity, as you are well aware. Nothing could tempt me to break it. Now—if you have no further need of me at this moment, I have some business to attend to at the cathedral."

"By all means." Henry reined in his horse. Thomas trotted off in the direction of the cathedral, his back stiff with indignation.

"Tut, tut. Someone's nose is twisted out of joint."

"He'd loosen up, I warrant, if he'd yield to his natural inclinations," said the knight riding beside him.

"We all admire the chancellor, my lord, but he's a cold fish when you come right down it," said another knight. "Perhaps he doesn't have natural inclinations."

A picture of Thomas in the Verte Forest popped into Henry's mind. "Oh, he has them, I have no doubt of that."

Why he had no doubt was not something Henry cared to dwell on. He had been flown with wine that night, the events were hazy, but there was something about the experience that made Henry uncomfortable, something other than the bizarre blood ceremony he and Thomas had performed: a faint shadow, ephemeral as gossamer—whose exact nature he had no desire to explore. At the time, the ceremony had offered all the forbidden excitement of two boys indulging in a secret ritual, playing at being one of the Knights Templar, but now . . .

As a result of that night, Henry was aware that a different kind of bond, however tenuous, had been formed between Thomas and himself, a bond to which he could put no name except blood brotherhood. He was still not sure of the implications involved, but whenever the word came into his mind he felt a wolf walk over his grave.

"It is easy for a man to say nothing would tempt him to break a vow of chastity when he's never been tempted, my lord." The knight beside him gave Henry a goatish smile. "He should be put to the test."

"Indeed he should! Why didn't I think of that? This Millette now, a comely trollop is she?" Henry spurred his horse forward in the direction of the ducal palace.

"A true wanton," said the second knight with a wink.

"A man would have to be be dead not to respond to her wiles," added the first knight.

"Bring her to the palace tonight. Discreetly. I will see that Thomas stays there and not with the monks at the cathedral." A slow smile spread across Henry's face. "Well, my holy archdeacon, let us see how you fare in the face of this Eve. Will you refuse to taste of this forbidden fruit, I wonder?"

It had suddenly become of paramount importance to him that Thomas be tested.

• • •

That night Henry waited alone in his large bedchamber. Half-asleep, he sat on a wooden chair draped with scarlet cloth, the arms and legs of which were carved in ivory to represent the head and feet of a wild boar. Outside, a November storm beat heavily against the stone ramparts; howling gusts swept through the cracks in the walls, causing the tall white tapers to flare in their silver holders. Despite the number of copper braziers warming the chamber it was still very cold. He fervently hoped Eleanor had arrived at Dover by now.

Where were those blasted knights? It must be well after Compline. Thomas had come in about an hour ago and gone to his own chamber. He had planned to sleep in the guest house attached to the cathedral, but Henry had insisted he stay in the ducal palace.

The greyhound curled up at Henry's feet whined, and Henry rubbed his booted foot against its back. He felt disgruntled and out of sorts, having had a most unsatisfactory discourse with his mother. He knew the empress had never liked Thomas Becket, but he had not been prepared for the violence of her reaction when he told her that he was planning to make the chancellor archbishop. They had argued off and on most of the afternoon, and all through supper, with no resolution in sight. Arguing with his mother was like poking at a spitting wildcat with a short spear.

Her reasons for not appointing Becket made no sense at all to him, and it was unlike the shrewd, practical empress not to make sense. The gist of it—similar to Eleanor in fact—was that, as chancellor, Thomas did the king's bidding; as archbishop he might be far less amenable. After all, then he need only answer to the pope. Who could predict what Becket would do, given so much power? Power altered men in the most unlikely ways imaginable; there was sure to be conflict between Canterbury and the crown. So on and so forth, God's eyes, he feared she would continue all night.

Henry was beginning to chafe against the cords these two powerful women in his life were so ready to bind him with. He hated being wrong, or told what to do, even when he asked for advice. That was the wondrous thing about Bellebelle. She never made him wrong or asserted her own ideas to challenge his own. Although Henry sensed that Bellebelle joined his wife and mother in her dislike of Becket, at least she had the good sense to keep her tongue from wagging.

There was a soft knock on the door. At last! Two knights entered escorting a third person heavily wrapped in a cloak. The cloak was removed to reveal Millette, a tall, saucy-looking bawd, with white skin and masses of pale red hair curling around her face and down her back.

"You know what's wanted of you?" asked Henry.

"Yes, me lord duke, I does indeed." She tossed back her mane of hair. "I've had me many a priest, in secret, and they's no different than anyone else when I gets through with them. All tomcats is gray by night."

One of the knights grinned. "Take your clothes off, wench, and show the king your wares."

The girl sauntered over to one of the charcoal braziers, removed her cloak, a blue shawl, red kirtle, and chemise, then, mothernaked, strutted up and down in front of Henry. She was certainly well-formed. Although Henry's taste was for slender, slim-hipped women, her swelling hips, round belly, and creamy thighs were beguiling. To be unmoved by her bosom a man would, indeed, have to be either blind or near death. He felt his loins stir.

"Do you lie down, Sire, and let Millette show what she can do. Resist her—if you can"

Henry got up, removed his clothes, and lay down on the wide bed. Millette slithered over to the bed like a sinuous serpent and leaned over him. He lay absolutely still, trying not to respond. First she swung her hair over her head and swept his face and chest with the silky mane. She climbed on top of him, pressed her breasts against his face, then brushed a nipple across his mouth. Henry could feel himself becoming even more aroused but kept his lips firmly shut. She pried open his mouth and thrust a large pink nipple inside.

"That's it, Millette, don't let up," cried a knight.

Accompanied by further shouts of encouragement, the bawd took Henry's hands and cupped one around each heavy breast while she leaned over him. After a moment she squirmed down his body until she reached his member. Taking it between her breasts she swung them back and forth until he was gorged with blood.

"Eh, you've a proper belly-snapper, me lord, and look at the size of it."

The knights gave a ribald laugh. Henry, breathing heavily, was having a difficult time now but still forced himself not to touch her. Next she slid up his body and crouched on her knees right in front of his face. She took her middle finger, licked it, then ran it up and down her moist sex. Henry's excitement grew; he could not look away but remained unmoving. Suddenly she slid backward, raised up and slowly impaled herself upon him. The sight of his stiff member slowly disappearing into the patch of carrot hair inflamed him. With great effort Henry managed not to respond. It was now a matter of pride that he keep control. But Millette knew a few tricks he had not counted on. Within moments he had lost all mastery as she rode him with such skill he was soon helplessly bucking and tossing under her while she drew his seed out of him as if she were drawing water from a well. He was chagrined to realize he could not have stopped her no matter how hard he tried.

"Well, I don't see how Thomas can resist you," he said, at last, drained, but wanting her to be gone.

The lush body now looked like overripe fruit, and Millette's overblown breasts were as appealing as his daughter's wet nurse's. This was the way he usually felt when such brief forays were over. In truth, he much preferred seducing to being seduced and found himself resenting the fact that she had more or less forced him into a response against his will.

"That's what we thought, my lord," said one of the knights. "Some of us have put a wager on it. But we can't hardly find anyone to wager that the chancellor won't succumb."

"For the sake of argument I'll wager two silver pennies that he will resist her." Henry quickly put on his clothes.

Millette gave a throaty laugh while she dressed.

The plan was to have her slip into Thomas's chamber and then into his bed. A knight was to stand guard by the door, and early in the morning, before Prime, Henry would burst into the chamber and catch his chancellor in flagrante delicto. An inspired thought came to him. Although he wanted to see his priggish chancellor humbled by the needs of the flesh, his pride in tatters about his feet, at the same time he wanted Thomas to resist. It was like a toss of the dice, just the sort of gamble Henry loved. If Thomas did indeed resist—he would make him archbishop of Canterbury. If he succumbed . . .

Henry was awakened by one of the knights shaking his arm.

"Cock-crow, my lord. Prime will sound any moment. This is the time to catch Becket."

Henry rolled out of bed, splashed water on his face from a silver basin, and pulled on his drawers, hose, and shirt. A taper still burned in its holder, casting long shadows over the chamber.

"What happened?" he asked the knight.

"We led Millette to the door of the chancellor's room, she slipped in, and nary a peep since. Jocelin and I took turns guarding the door but no one came out. She's done for him, m'lord."

Henry felt both relieved and disappointed. When tempted, Thomas was obviously like other men—so be it. Why then did he feel let down? No matter. He had lost the wager with himself and must look elsewhere for an archbishop.

He followed the knights out the door and down the passageway to the small chamber Thomas occupied. Henry burst into the room, throwing the door wide. A single glance told him the narrow wooden bed had not been slept in. At the far end of the chamber, Thomas and Millette, fully clothed, knelt in prayer in front of the prie-dieu. They turned, startled. Thomas rose to his feet and lifted the bawd to hers. Millette's face was pale but composed; her hair scraped back and covered with her shawl. She looked so different from last night that Henry was not sure he would have recognized her on the street.

"I'd like the wages due me, me lord, so's I can pay a dowry to enter a nunnery," she said in a subdued voice.

Thomas gave her a benign smile and patted her on the shoulder. "Wait for me in the chapel, my child, and I will bring you your money."

Millette nodded dutifully, looking up at him with a reverent, grateful smile, then walked past the dumbfounded knights, an amazed Henry, and out the door.

"Another lost ewe returned to the fold," Thomas said, a look of triumph crossing his face.

Foolishly pleased, Henry shouted with laughter. He turned to the two knights. "I've won my wager so you two can pay what is owed me as well, then escort her to the chapel. I'll send Sister Millette to no less a place than Fontevrault, by God!"

The knights, still unable to believe the evidence of their own eyes, handed Henry two silver pennies each, then hurried after the tart. Henry, digging into the pouch at his belt added several more then poured the shining silver into Thomas's hand.

"Was this your idea?" Thomas gave Henry a quizzical look.

"No, as a matter of fact, it wasn't, but I didn't discourage those who wanted to put you to the test. After all, when you consort with lusty young warriors, such practical jests must be borne with good grace."

Thomas looked deeply into his eyes. "You did not really believe I would fall victim to that temptress of Satan, did you?"

Uncomfortable under his intense scrutiny, Henry turned away. "You heard how I wagered. I merely wondered if you would resist temptation when faced with it; you did. There's an end to it."

He felt an overpowering need to get out of this chamber, away from the burning look in Thomas's eyes. Quickly, he strode to the door, opened it, and stepped out into the passage.

"When you're finished with our new novice, Thomas, attend me in the hall and we will break our fast together. See to it our future nun remembers me in her daily prayers."

Henry started to walk down the passage then stopped. He took a deep breath, turned back, then hesitated. This was the moment of decision. A parade of images marched before his eyes: Thomas at his side in meetings of the Great Council; Thomas approving while he dispensed justice; Thomas successfully dealing with Louis of France, skillfully negotiating treaties, drafting carefully worded documents. Henry remembered their hunting together with hound and falcon, their adventures in taverns, the first moment their eyes had met in the council chamber at St. Paul's before he was king.

He had known from the beginning Thomas was a harbinger of his fate. Whatever the outcome, he knew as certain as he drew breath, that their fates were bound together.

"I have an interesting proposition, Thomas . . . one that might intrigue you."

# CHAPTER 43

# England,
# 1161

*E*leanor, after seeing her new baby safely ensconced at Tower Royal in London, took to leading a wanderer's life once more, this time in the south of England. She rode through meadows, over streams, stopping at castles, manors, towns, and abbeys issuing official writs and documents. The yellowing stone roofs of Sherbourne, ancient abbeys, the iron-gray hues of Cornwall, the rust-colored battlements of castles in Devon were fast becoming almost as familiar to her as the castles and villages of Sarlat, Niort, and Blaye. The weeks of riding, while often tiring, did not bother her. On the contrary, she believed the constant exercise kept her body slender and firm after her many childbirths.

Not only that, but Eleanor took genuine pleasure in her accomplishments. After all, the fact that the roads in England were now safe, the sheriffs conscientiously dispensing justice and collecting taxes, was due as much to her endeavors as to Henry's and Becket's labors. If one counted all the months since Henry ascended the throne, she had probably spent more time in England than he had, although she was still considered only Henry's surrogate and never recognized in her own right.

Now she was on her way back to London. Watling Street, this day in late November, was lined with crowds come to see royalty pass by. Although Eleanor was never greeted with the same rapturous acclaim as in Aquitaine, there was always a cordial response to the Eagle, the king's "foreign queen." How she hated that misnomer, forcing herself to remember that it probably meant no more than that, since time out of mind, she was the first English queen not born and bred on English soil.

Eleanor waved and smiled, slowing her palfrey to greet people, letting them crowd around her and even fearfully touch her garments in superstitious awe. She noted that they looked prosperous and content, a far cry from the miserable wretches she had seen when she first arrived in England almost seven years earlier. Something else she could take pride in.

As she rode on, Eleanor also observed that the cattle in the meadows looked fat and sleek; they should fetch a good price at market. Had the number of monks working in the abbey fields increased since the last time she had passed this way? Or were the abbeys amassing more land? Cassocks tucked up around their knees, the brethern paused in their labors to gaze at the royal cavalcade riding by.

The sight of sheep grazing on the hill crests filled her with a sense of satisfaction. Surely the flocks were growing each year? Lots of sheep meant more bales of wool leaving the port of London, just as row upon row of Bordeaux vineyards meant casks of wine stacked in Channel ports. Eleanor had heard that the demand for wine in the English inns and taverns was starting to compete with that for ale.

All this prosperity spread out before her eyes bore witness to how the realm was expanding, not only in England but on the Continent as well. She had persuaded Henry to build new city walls and bridges in Poitiers, add a spacious hall to the ducal palace, and plan for the construction of another cathedral. He had also decided to build a new palace at Bures in Normandy, so vast that hundreds of oak trees had already been felled. There were also additions to the castles at Angers and Rouen, a royal park, and stronger fortifications along the Maine and Normandy borders. Together, she and Henry had had built several hospitals and a leper-house at Caen, and encouraged the abbess at Fontevrault to found similar abbeys at Eaton and Westwood in England.

All their endeavors prospered—with the exception of Toulouse, the loss of which still rankled. Louis, however, had had little time in which to gloat. The wind had been taken out of the French sails with the hasty marriage of young Henry to the Princess Marguerite, and the recovery of the Vexin. In fact, Louis of France had once again foundered on the shoals of Plantagenet ambition and cunning—

Ambition and cunning? Why was she thinking like that? Eleanor passed a hand across her forehead. She felt as if she had just eavesdropped at the door of her own thoughts. *Her* thoughts? Sweet St. Radegonde, she was looking at the world exactly the way Henry or Thomas Becket might look at it.

There was a time when she would have simply feasted on the beauty of the landscape, reveled in the glory of an autumn morning. Now all that was translated into cattle prices at market, wool for export, wine for import, the abbeys desire to gobble up more land, not to mention Henry's and her own drive for building and improving their vast holdings. It was a sobering realization, an unwelcome indication of how far she had come from the carefree, joyous maid she had been in Aquitaine.

Now, deliberately, Eleanor looked with new eyes at the rolling green downs that stretched on either side of the winding road. She became aware of the brisk wind that throughout the morning had brought sudden flurries of rain and bursts of sunlight on its wings. The air was redolent of moldering leaves and damp earth. Somewhere a bird sang. A flock of geese soared across a slate sky patched with charcoal gray clouds.

It was late afternoon when Eleanor rode through Bermondsey, where she had a manor house she hardly ever saw, then across the river to the Strand in London, and, finally, back to Tower Royal again. She arrived just after Compline, exhausted, and went straight to bed.

It was not until the following morning that Eleanor discovered that sometime during the three weeks she had been traveling, young Henry and his wife, plus their entire household, had been moved to the quarters of the chancellor in Westminster.

"But the chancellor is in Rouen, surely?" There must be a mistake, she thought. It was inconceivable that without consulting her, his mother, young Henry had been removed from her custody. Not to mention the fact that she had grown attached to the little golden-haired Marguerite.

"No, Madam," the steward informed her, "the chancellor returned five days ago, with the king's writ in his hand, ordering the prince and his household to be transferred."

She could not believe it. After breaking her fast and greeting her other children, Eleanor ordered a litter, and, tired though she still was, rode through London to Westminster. It was a cold blustery morning the first day of December, and despite her fur-lined cloak and additional coverlets piled over her, she shivered throughout the tedious journey. How could Henry have done this? Only a month ago they had been so close, so in harmony—or so she had thought. What possessed him to change from a loving, appreciative husband to a near-tyrant? How could he so totally ignore her wishes or feelings? It must be due to Becket's influence; nothing else could account for . . . the litter came to a shuddering halt.

Without waiting for a groom to help her, Eleanor jumped down and marched across the courtyard to the chancery. For a moment she was brought up short. Surely it had been completely rearranged since her last visit several years earlier? Two guards with long pikes now flanked the entrance. The cheerless hall was lined with long benches filled with petitioners, and the antechamber was crowded with at least fifty clerks working at rows of long tables. The secretary, Fitz-Stephen, directed her to a small stone apartment that led directly off the antechamber.

Eleanor paused outside the open door. From where she stood, she could see that the walls were lined with ornate crimson-and-blue tapestries, the chamber filled with copper charcoal braziers, two polished oak tables, and embroidered stools. From a seven-branched silver candleholder, slender white tapers burned brightly. The room was warmer and more comfortably appointed than any other administrative office Eleanor had ever seen.

A frown on his face, the chancellor was seated at one of the small tables piled high with quill pens, containers of ink, sheets of parchment and vellum, and scrolls sealed with wax emblems. He was listening intently to a light-haired knight with a beard who leaned over the table, talking rapidly in a low voice.

Without preamble, Eleanor stepped into the chamber. "What is all this nonsense about young Henry being moved to your household?"

The knight looked up and abruptly stopped talking. It was obvious from the concerned looks on both their faces that they were fearful she might have overheard them.

"Attend me later," Becket told the knight with a dismissive gesture.

The knight nodded and limped away. Eleanor noted that he wore an unusual silver medallion set with emeralds.

"Who was that?"

"A petitioner. How may I help you, Madam?"

"Why has Prince Henry been transferred to your household without my knowledge or consent?"

Becket looked genuinely surprised. "I thought you knew, Madam. After all, the boy is well over six years old now, married, and should have begun his formal education long before this. As heir, young Henry must succeed to the king's wisdom and learning as well as his throne. I have under my care many noble youths whom I educate in letters and knightly accomplishments. Surely you expected such an arrangement to occur sooner or later?"

What could she say? Every noble youth was educated in the household of another noble. "Naturally I expected it, but no one consulted me as to where, or with whom, young Henry would be educated. Now it is a *fait accompli*. I cannot but regard this as an affront to my position as both mother and queen."

"I deeply regret any offense you may have been caused, Madam, though I assure you none was intended. It is your son's future at stake."

The chancellor's cool demeanor enraged her, the more so because Eleanor knew he was right.

Becket looked down at his littered table, a pointed reminder of how busy he was. "Please bear in mind, I'm only following His Majesty's orders. If the king did not see fit to consult you, Madam, I can hardly be blamed. I suggest you take the matter up with him. He should be arriving within the next few weeks, in time for the Christmas court."

His casual arrogance took her breath away. Even she hadn't known that Henry planned to hold his Christmas court in England. There was a slight but significant change in Becket's manner that could only mean—Holy Mother, had Henry already offered Becket the plum of Canterbury? She prayed he had not, but there was a look about Becket, reminding her of a sleek, self-satisfied cat that's swallowed the cream. Eleanor already found him insufferable as chancellor. What would he be like after attaining the highest church office in England?

Feeling like a fool, Eleanor realized there was nothing more to be accomplished here. Young Henry was lost to her, and she must make the best of it. "I wish to see my son."

"Of course. Whenever you like."

Eleanor could tell Becket was enjoying this.

With a lofty smile, he rang a silver bell on his table, and when several clerks came running, gave orders that the queen was to be taken to his private household.

"Not too long, Madam. We have young Henry on a strict routine now. Best not to disturb it."

Refusing to dignify that with an answer, Eleanor turned and stalked out of the chamber. On her way out of the chancery Eleanor saw the knight with the medallion lounging against the wall. His glance shifted away from her. Something about him—his wary stance, his reptilian eyes—chilled her, and she hugged her cloak closer about her shoulders. She wondered again who he was and what business he had with the king's chancellor.

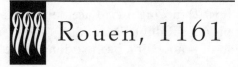 Rouen, 1161

"Have you seen my chessboard, Henry?"

Henry looked up sharply to find his mother's eyes upon him. "Chessboard?"

He and his mother were seated in the great hall of the ducal palace at Rouen, dawdling over the remains of an early supper. Most of the ducal mesnie had left the hall, and they were virtually alone at the high table.

"The silver-and-gilt chessboard with the ivory figures, you know, the one the emperor gave me. It appears to have vanished," the Empress Maud said. "I asked Eleanor before she left for England but she hadn't seen it."

"You probably mislaid it. When did you notice it had gone missing?"

"I'm not in the habit of mislaying things." She paused. "Let me see . . . I'd promised the bishop of Rouen a game, and I was mortified when the board and men couldn't be found."

"A bishop playing chess? How have the mighty fallen."

"That irreverent tone doesn't suit you, Henry. Have you seen it?"

Some time ago, Henry had taken the chessboard to England and impulsively given it to his bastard son, Geoffrey, about whom his mother knew nothing. There was no immediate way now to return it, but he could hardly tell her that. In truth, he had assumed she would not notice its absence.

"I'll look for it," he said, avoiding her eye. "It may have gotten mixed in among my own possessions." He paused. "Perhaps it got shipped to England by error. Surely you have another chess set?"

"That's hardly the point, is it? That particular one is all that remains of my life in the empire; I should hate to lose it."

Lying to his mother was not easy—she could see through him like water—and Henry wondered how he could get her off the subject. There must be a way to divert her attention. Something controversial perhaps?

"I offered the See of Canterbury to Thomas," he said, after a lengthy pause.

The empress, a silver goblet of wine in her hand, arrested it halfway to her lips. "Ignoring my advice not to do so."

"Your advice is not infallible, Madam."

"How would you know? It's been so long since you listened to me."

"Let's not quarrel." Henry sipped from his goblet of red wine and made a face. It had recently arrived from Bordeaux and was already turning bitter. "You'll be interested to know Thomas refused it."

The empress arched her brows in disbelief. "Refused it? Such cat-and-mouse games on the chancellor's part don't fool me for an instant. He'll ultimately accept the post if you're still foolish enough to keep it open."

"You're probably right."

"Of course I'm right. By the way, what was that disgraceful business with Thomas and the Rouen drab all about? The ducal palace is not a brothel, and I won't have you turning it into one."

"God's eyes, you sound as prudish as a Cistercian priest. It was just a bit of tomfoolery, a test to see if Thomas practiced what he preached. How did you come to hear of it?"

She gave him a withering look. "When the day comes that I don't know what goes on in Rouen you can dig my grave and bury me. What reasons did Becket give?"

"For not bedding the whore?"

"Don't be impertinent. I could have told you he wouldn't bed her—or anyone else for that matter, if anyone had had the foresight to ask. What reasons did he give for refusing Canterbury?"

Henry shrugged. "None very valid. He was a worldly cleric, he said, as everyone knew, not even a priest if it came to that. He had far too much work to do in the chancery and could not possibly hold both chancellor and Canterbury as well, and so on and so on." Henry thoughtfully scratched his chin. "He also mentioned that if he became archbishop he feared it might destroy our friendship. Which made no sense at all."

"Thomas Becket said that? Well! I didn't think he was so discerning. But of course he's right." His mother nibbled on a leg of guinea hen.

Henry frowned. "I don't see why promoting him to the See of Canterbury should make the slightest difference in our friendship."

"Yes, well, if you don't see why, my telling you won't help, will it?"

There was a brief silence while Henry cursed himself for having been fool enough to broach the subject of his chancellor. He had gone from the cauldron directly into the fire.

"Is it true you're putting young Henry in his household to be educated and trained by him?" The empress put down the leg of guinea hen.

"Yes. He's been there some weeks by now." God's eyes, was there anything she didn't know?

"What does Eleanor say about that?"

"I haven't told her yet, but when she returns to London, if she hasn't already done so, she'll know soon enough. Why? You sound as if you think she will object?"

"Why? Why? Sweet Marie, she's his mother! She has a right to be consulted on the plans for her eldest son's education! If Geoffrey of Anjou had dared to send you somewhere without first getting my agreement . . . I don't say Eleanor will object, only that she should have been asked, or at least told!"

In the back of his mind Henry noted that she did not say "your father" but Geoffrey of Anjou. He tried to remember if she had ever referred to the count as "your father."

"Sometimes I think there is a female conspiracy in my household against poor Thomas Becket, the brightest jewel in my administrative diadem. You disparage him; Eleanor despises him, even Belle—" he stopped abruptly.

His mother pushed away her trencher of food and fixed him with a level gaze. "Even Belle what? Who is Belle?"

"No one of importance." Henry could feel himself flushing and quickly downed his wine.

Uncomfortable under his mother's scrutiny, Henry looked around the hall.

"I am very proud of you, my son." The empress placed a veined hand over his. "Your accomplishments have exceeded my wildest hopes, and I am the last one to advise you in matters about which I know nothing, but do be circumspect."

"Point taken." Henry took her hand and lightly kissed the gnarled fingers.

A servant passed round a silver basin of water and white linen towels. The empress washed her hands and wiped them dry.

"On the other hand, there are some matters upon which I feel very confident in advising you."

Henry inwardly groaned.

"Thomas Becket," she continued, "like many a man of humble origin, is highly ambitious. He cannot resist power. You have offered him the most powerful post in England—excepting your own."

Henry laughed. "Do you, of all people, tell me ambition is restricted to those of humble origins?"

"I've told you not to be impertinent." She paused. "In this matter, my son, heed me. There is a difference between those born to power and those who must fight every inch of the way to achieve it. What I do tell you is, beware of men such as Thomas Becket when they are given too much power." She began to twist a gold ring set with an emerald stone round and round on her finger.

"At heart, Madam, you are a royal snob. All right. You've told me your thoughts on the matter and I've listened." Henry yawned. He was tired of sitting and impatient to be gone.

"Take Becket at his word, that your close friendship will be destroyed if he becomes archbishop." The empress gazed at him with a troubled expression and sighed. "You court disaster by this folly. I've done my best to teach you how to rule, guided you down the path of judgment—with some success, obviously. But in this instance—well, a fool's bolt is soon shot. In the end, blood will tell."

The empress's goblet clattered to the floor. She had pulled the gold ring with the green stone off her finger and was clutching it in her palm. In the deathlike silence that followed what Henry suspected was a fatal slip of the tongue, he could hear his mother's sharply indrawn breath. For a moment their eyes met; in hers, he saw a reflection of his own grave alarm. Then her lids folded down; her hands clenched into white-knuckled fists.

Watching her fight for control, a variety of thoughts stirred in Henry's mind. The Empress Maud was approaching her middle sixties. Though her wits remained as sharp as a spear point, she ailed frequently and spent long periods in retreat at Fontevrault. More and more often she spoke of taking the vows of a nun before death claimed her. This worried him greatly. Ever since the unfortunate incident with her grandson at Cherbourg, Henry had meant to have a long talk with her about the past. If, before her demise, his mother had matters on her conscience that needed to be expiated, far better that she unburden herself to him rather than someone else—even her confessor.

Unwittingly she had just presented him with the perfect opportunity. But now that the moment was at hand, Henry found himself curiously reluctant. Did he really want to know the truth? What purpose would it serve? Yet such an opportunity might never come again, and he felt driven to know.

"As you often remind me, Madam, the Normans have always been known for their wily ways and quick wits," Henry said while he still had the courage. "Geoffrey of Anjou, may God assoil him, however unsatisfactory your relations with him may have been, however reluctant you are to refer to him as my father, was a person of sound judgment, perhaps the shrewdest man I ever knew." He paused. "To whose blood do you refer?"

The fateful words had been spoken; Henry steeled himself for the answer.

It was an answer he never received. Pale as a ghost, his mother suddenly staggered to her feet, calling for her women.

"I'm unwell—quite faint—unable to continue—I pray you, excuse me—" Several attendants sprang to her side.

Both relieved and frustrated, Henry watched in grudging admiration as she was half-carried from the hall, taking her secrets with her. Old now, scarred by too many battles, and preparing for death, the empress was a cunning campaigner to the last, able to defend herself with all the wiles and weapons of her sex.

Henry, who knew perfectly well he ruthlessly used women for his own interests at every opportunity, had never, ever made the mistake of underestimating the formidable power they could wield.

The empress had once told him pigs would fly before any son of hers would get the better of her. At the time, she had been referring to his late brother, Geoffrey, however . . .

Henry knew he would never reopen the matter. How could he ask his mother, straight out: Was Geoffrey of Anjou my real father? Especially when, in the deepest recesses of his soul, he feared what the answer might be.

His mother, dignified, elegant, and redoubtable, had been a remarkably beautiful woman—one need only look now at the bone structure of her face to see that—but Henry remembered her in the full flower of her russet-haired, pewter-eyed beauty. It was exceedingly difficult, as well as uncomfortable, for him to imagine her in the throes of a wild, all-consuming passion with her cousin, Stephen of Blois. Was he the result of a single night of incandescent desire? Or brief moments of rapture stolen over the years? There was no question in Henry's mind that his mother must have loved Stephen deeply. Only such a love would have caused her to dishonor her family's crown and jeopardize the royal succession.

For the remainder of his stay in Rouen, Henry agonized over and over again: Whose son was he?

To have believed yourself the legitimate scion of an acknowleged union between two great houses—Anjou and Normandy, whose roots stretched back hundreds of years—then suspect you might be the secret by-blow of a forbidden love . . . It was like teetering on the edge of a vast bottomless pit.

Henry left Rouen in mid-December, parting from his mother on amicable but formal terms. He was accompanied on the voyage across the Channel by his cousin William, earl of Gloucester, and his two favorite bloodhounds. The sea was calm until dawn the following day.

From then on it was a rough voyage, typical for December. A brawling wind chased dark clouds across a flint-colored sky and whipped the sea into green-capped swells. The vessel pitched and tossed. While William voided last night's supper into the sea, Henry, an excellent sailor, rode easily with the rocking waves. He felt an overpowering need to ask someone about the past, someone of his immediate family whose history he shared. But the subject was fraught with potential danger; he must guard himself against revealing his doubts to anyone—even those to whom he felt the closest: Thomas, Eleanor, and Bellebelle.

Henry could hear the sound of the captain shouting orders and the men answering. A scarlet sail bellied wildly in the wind. The prow of the vessel, carved into a dragon shape like the old Viking ships, climbed up a rising wave then shot down the other side like a stooping falcon.

Even the weather could not dispel the doubts that continued to torment him. Henry remembered his first council meeting in London, that disparaging snicker when someone pointed out that Stephen and he had adopted each other as father and son. But even before that, there had been subtle hints—his parents had lived in an atmosphere of mutual dislike and bickering, but underneath his mother's iron control, Henry had sensed a deep-seated sadness, a sense of loss that was always present.

The ship bucked and twisted; the wind howled. Strange, but he was not afraid. With that sense of destiny strong within him, Henry knew he would survive. In truth, whatever had or had not occurred between his mother and Stephen of Blois, how could it threaten him now?

It couldn't. He had been an anointed king for seven years; a successful ruler of a vast empire. Who would dare to circulate rumors about his paternity, brand him a bastard? Yet even the whisper of such a rumor could throw the entire succession into jeopardy. His enemies would ruin his mother's reputation. Taint the House of Normandy with scandal. Provoke uprisings. Cast doubt on his right to have ascended the throne. Perhaps set in motion a move to topple him from power. And to put such a potential weapon into the hands of Louis of France . . .

A green wave rose up to spray Henry's face. The shock of the icy water was bracing. Why was he allowing himself to fall prey to idle fancies? There was nothing to be concerned about, except his own fears. And the cure for his fears—groundless though they were—was to ensure that young Henry was crowned as soon as he was old enough. With Thomas as archbishop of Canterbury there would be no problem in crowning him. His demons would be laid to rest.

While the crew shouted excitedly that there was land over the bow, Henry realized that for the first time in his life, he actively resented his mother. As far back as he could remember, he had put her on a pedestal. Now he felt she had betrayed him. It was like a knife thrust into his belly. How could she have—

Of a sudden, the curtains of the past drew apart, and he saw himself when he was fourteen years old, standing in an English wood at dawn, looking up at a comely knight who smiled down at him then tossed him a bag of coins—his safe passage home. That single foolhardy act of generosity had cost King Stephen—and his heirs—the crown. Henry's jaw clenched; his hands gripped the vessel's rail. Blood will tell indeed! His mother was wrong; never in his life had he behaved—nor would he ever behave—so foolishly, so outrageously . . .

Ahead now he could make out the coast; white cliffs surmounted by lowering clouds. The busy port of Dover would soon be in view.

Titles, possessions, the acquisition of wealth, the exercise of power, the crown, kingdoms, even the heirs of his blood were of no account without his lineage. Lineage defined you, gave you an identity. Without it . . . Desperately, Henry tried to conjure up the red beard and cornflower blue eyes of the man whom he had always believed to be his father, the only father he wanted: Geoffrey of Anjou. But the image that stayed to haunt him was the golden smile and emerald eyes of Stephen of Blois.

# CHAPTER 44

# Bermondsey,

# 1161–1162

**I**n the village, placid day followed placid day. Each afternoon when Geoffrey returned from priory school, Bellebelle asked him if he had heard any news of when his father might be coming back to England.

"I don't know, Maman. The prior says that Father is too busy to return. He's strengthened all of his castles on the borders of Normandy, repaired castles in Aquitaine, Touraine, and Anjou, and built new ones as well. In England he's going to rebuild everything with stone."

Bellebelle smiled down into Geoffrey's shining eyes. "Think of that. But no word when he be coming back?"

"No."

When Geoffrey ran off to play with a new greyhound puppy Old Ivo had brought him, Bellebelle felt giddy with relief. She was reprieved for a while longer.

The following week, on a brisk day in mid-December, she walked into the village and stopped for a natter with the alewife and to buy a pitcher of ale.

"The king be back."

Bellebelle dropped her wooden pitcher of ale.

"Now that be a clumsy thing to do, Belle." Elfgiva surveyed the pool of brown liquid soaking into the ground. "I just finished brewing a new batch."

"I know. I'm sorry." The smell of barley-malt was particularly strong today.

"Ye'll have to pay for another quart. I not be in this business for charity, mind."

"No." With trembling fingers, Bellebelle dropped another coin into Elfgiva's stained palm. "Are you—certain about the king? Geoffrey said nothing about it."

"O' course I be certain. Come for the Christmas court, he has, not two days since. Me son, the one that be reeve over to manor, said he had it right from the steward's mouth." She gave Bellebelle a sly poke in the ribs. "Ye'll be seeing him soon yeself, like as not. Been—let's see—nigh on over two years now as I recollect?"

Bellebelle nodded, picked up the wooden pitcher, and waited while Elfgiva filled it to the brim. "Well, I best be off. Thank you."

"Anything wrong, Belle?"

She forced a smile. "No. Nothing wrong."

Elfgiva gave her a sharp look then shrugged as she set up her alestake, a long pole with a bush on the end, so customers would know a new batch of brew was for sale.

On the way home Bellebelle wondered how long it would be before de Burgh saw Henry. Then, how long after that before Henry would come riding over to Bermondsey and—do what? She had no idea, that's what was so fearful. As she had warned Geoffrey, in the heat of an upset Henry was capable of anything. She was not afraid of him hurting her—not her body. Whatever his threats and angry moods, at heart Henry was not a man of blood. How many times had she heard him say that only a dolt ruled by force rather than reason? But she knew he would not readily forgive her lies. Not right away. She could only pray to Mary-Eleanor and hope against hope that Henry would not abandon her and Geoffrey.

Shortly after Twelfth Night, in the new year, 1162, on a sun-drenched morning that felt more like April than January, Bellebelle finished collecting the hens' eggs into a straw basket hooked over one arm.

"To see you now it's hard to believe you were once afraid of the hens."

Bellebelle froze. Heart hammering, she slowly looked up. Henry was standing outside the gate. Alone. Some distance away, well out of earshot, three knights milled about, their horses tied to a tree. She hadn't even heard the beasts approach. A brown hunting cap covered Henry's head, a short green cloak swung from his shoulders, and his boots were the usual scuffed brown adorned with red spur-leathers. He looked just the same and her heart turned over. Perhaps—her eyes met his and she saw they were like ice on a winter pond.

He knew.

"Aren't you going to ask me in?"

Bellebelle quickly opened the gate and led him into the house. The wolfhound and the greyhound puppy, now trained to not attack the hens, growled as Henry approached. When he stooped to pat them their tails began to wag.

Inside she laid the basket of eggs on the table and stirred up the fire in the hearth with unsteady hands. Henry removed his cloak and looked around him.

"Nothing has changed in—is it over two, almost three years? Except you're more beautiful than I remembered. Thinner though, and fine drawn. Tight as a bow-string. Like you looked when I first met you. Aren't you getting enough to eat?"

"I—I've not been very hungry of late."

"Perhaps your conscience troubles you?"

Bellebelle felt her lower lip tremble. Holy Mother, was he going to bait and badger her first? "I missed you, Henry. Geoffrey missed you."

"I understand he's doing very well at his lessons, and highly thought of at the priory." Henry paced restlessly around the room, touching the chimney, running a finger down a long wooden spoon hanging on the wall, reaching up to swat a bunch of drying herbs. "I missed you too, Belle. And Geoffrey. God save me, that's the bloody trouble, how much I missed you."

He walked up to her and grabbed her chin in iron fingers, tilting her face up. "I never expected treachery from you, of all people. Even now, looking at you, I find it hard to believe." He let go her chin and ran his fingers up her cheek. "You skin is like the dew on a rosebud; your eyes such an unusual blue—serene as a summer evening when the light fades from an unclouded sky. Such an innocent expression. Such a sweet nature."

"Henry—I—" She suddenly began to cry.

"It won't do," Henry said in a savage voice, his hand dropping to his side. "God's eyes, you think to cozen me with tears after the japes you played on me? To think I harbored a filthy whore, a near-murderer!" He slammed his fist down upon the table so hard the eggs rattled. "Worst of all, you lied to me! You lied to me!" he suddenly shouted. "To me! To your king, the man who took you in from the stews of iniquity, who protected you, asked nothing of you save that he be allowed to visit you from time to time. You didn't trust me enough to tell me the truth!"

Bellebelle fell to her knees at his feet on the dried rushes of the floor. "How could I tell you? I was afeared of what you might do," she said, through her sobs. "I loved you so much—how could I tell you what I been?"

"Tell me now. All of it. I heard what that Flemish swine had to say—Thomas brought him to see me. Let me hear your version of the tale. But it better be the truth this time . . ."

Bellebelle took a deep shuddering breath and told Henry everything that had happened to her from as far back as she could remember, through her meeting with him on the London Bridge, her encounter with de Burgh in Gilbert's brothel-house, her mother's death, her flight to Gropecuntlane, her meeting with him in the Blue Cock, and why she had been carrying the tray of honeycakes without her striped cloak.

"You took me for a vendor of honey cakes and I let you think I was—I doesn't—don't know why. Didn't want you to think ill of me for being a whore."

Henry again banged his fist on the table. "How do you think I feel now?" His voice was like a growl in his throat, his face slowly turning a deep red. "It hardly pleases me that my son's mother is a whore and a felon, reared in a stewhouse, and I knew nothing about it!" He glared down at her.

Bellebelle threw her arms around his booted legs. "Can you forgive me?"

"What's forgiveness to do with it? It's trust. How can I ever trust you again?" His eyes, gray pools of bitterness, were the eyes of a stranger; he gave a sudden wild laugh that sent a chill through her. "Except for my children, and possibly Thomas, I've only truly loved you, my mother, and late father—" He suddenly paused, a spasm of pain contorting his face which was now a strange purplish color. "And Eleanor. Two of you I can no longer trust."

Who was the other one? she wondered. His mother? Or Eleanor? What could they have done?

Without warning, Henry fell suddenly to the floor. His body jerked uncontrollably, his head arched against the rushes. He began to gnash his teeth; his lips, flecked with white foam, were drawn back in a wolfish snarl, reminding her of a mad dog she had once seen that had terrorized Southwark. Incoherent sounds issued from his throat.

Afraid to touch him, Bellebelle did not know what to do. She had never seen anyone have a fit before, and was petrified he would die in front of her eyes. Scrambling to her feet she ran out the door, bolted through the gate, and shouted for the knights. The hounds began to howl. The knights came running and burst into the cottage.

"Be—is he dying?" Bellebelle could barely get the words out. Henry's thrashings had subsided somewhat, his face was slowly losing that awful puple color, but he was still mumbling senselessly.

"No. Just one of His Majesty's rages," said a knight, unruffled by what he saw. "He'll have to be bled is all." Between them the three knights lifted Henry in their arms and carried him out the door.

"You must have greatly angered him," said another knight, giving her a curious glance over his shoulder. "I haven't seen one of these in at least two or three years."

Numb with anguish, Bellebelle watched the knights carry Henry to his horse and lift him onto the saddle. His head had fallen forward onto his chest and he seemed to be asleep. A knight climbed up behind him and held Henry round the waist. Another knight untethered the king's stallion and, after mounting his own, led the animal by the bridle. The third brought up the rear. Soon the party was lost to view behind a bend in the path. She was alone.

Badly shaken, Bellebelle said nothing to Geoffrey who, having heard at the school of the king's return, eagerly awaited his father's visit. She had heard tales of the king's rages—Henry had even warned her in jest about his fearful temper—and he had on occasion been short with her. But Bellebelle had been totally unprepared for what she had witnessed. Never had she caught so much as a glimpse of that violent, crazed side of him. Now, having once seen Henry in that demonlike state, she knew she would never forget it.

When the king failed to return, Bellebelle knew that all her earlier fears were justified. Would he ever be able to forgive or trust her again? Time and again she had heard him say that he never forgot a good turn nor an ill one. Geoffrey was desolate and cried himself to sleep each night until she gave him a greatly altered explanation of Henry's visit.

Each day Bellebelle expected something dreadful to happen. What form would it take? Guards suddenly arriving and forcing her to leave the house, shattering her life-long dream of being safe and secure? This was her recurring nightmare.

But nothing occurred. Bellebelle heard the king was on progress through England with plans to improve the castles of Windsor, Arundel, Oxford, Scarborough, and many others. January passed into February. The chancellor's secretary brought her money as usual; on the surface everything seemed the same. In early March she heard Henry had returned to London.

One day in the second week of March, Geoffrey did not return home from the priory school. Bellebelle waited until she heard the Vespers bell, which meant he was an hour late, and then, carrying a lighted torch, she set out in the chilly darkness to look for him. It was difficult to believe that harm had befallen him. After all, Geoffrey was over seven years of age, knew the path and the village as well as she did. He must have been kept at the school for some reason. Any moment now she would see him trudging down the path.

When Bellebelle got to the church, it looked deserted but through the narrow stained glass window depicting the healing of the lepers she could see a dim light. She pushed open the wooden doors and walked inside. By the light of two tall tapers set into huge gold candlesticks, she saw the prior kneeling in front of the great silver crucifix above the altar. He signed himself, rose to his feet, turned and walked down the aisle. He stopped short when he saw her.

"What brings you here, my child? Evensong is over."

"It's Geoffrey, Father, he didn't come home," Bellebelle said. "School be closed surely. Where could he be?"

The prior looked at her in surprise. "Why—merciful heavens, Daughter, didn't you know? The king himself came and took Geoffrey away—oh, just after Sext it was."

Bellebelle felt the breath leave her body. She swayed on her feet. The prior ran toward her, grabbed her torch, and caught her by the arm.

"Are you ill? Let me get you some wine."

She shook her head. After a moment she was able to stand. Slowly the breath came back into her body.

"Where—where did the king take him?"

The prior frowned. "Let me see . . . I think he said . . . was it Westminster? No, Tower Royal, that was it. He was going to have the boy educated in London, he said, by the canons of St. Paul. A great opportunity, a sign of the king's favor—" He stopped. "You didn't know?"

Unable to speak, Bellebelle shook her head. She pulled her cloak closely about her and stepped outside.

The prior followed, handing her the torch. "Are you all right? Please, remember how fortunate you are that the king takes such an interest in your son, a bastard after all. You should be grateful that God has seen fit to smile on this child of sin."

His voice followed her, a ghostly echo in the darkness. The thought flashed through her mind that in the very worst moments of her life she was always in a church. Stunned and disbelieving, she stumbled down the path that led to the cottage. Halfway there she dropped her torch, and started to run. She could hear the beating of her heart, the sound of her feet pounding against the frozen ground. On either side of the path the bare trees, like lonely black sentinels, seemed to close in on her. A full moon lit up the clear night sky. Gasping, she reached the cottage.

Inside, Bellebelle lit the fire and poured herself two cups of ale, downing one after another. On the table lay Henry's mother's silver-and-gilt chess set, the ivory figures laid out neatly on the squares just as Geoffrey had left them. The sight was like a knife twisting deep into her breast. Without her son, the cottage at this hour was like a tomb. How could she bear it night after night?

"Geoffrey!" Bellebelle grabbed the bishop, his favorite figure, and clutched it to her heart, screaming his name aloud over and over again.

The ale made her head swim and she finally dragged herself up the stairs to the bower where she fell, fully clothed, onto Geoffrey's trundle bed next to her own. Henry had taken his revenge. He had done it in his usual clever way, for if she protested he could accuse her of denying her son the opportunity for a princely education.

But the thought of being without Geoffrey filled Bellebelle with such an overpowering anguish that she did not see how she could bear it. She must not let it happen; she must find some way to appeal to Henry. He was not all revenge and cruelty; he was capable of great goodness. She knew that he was. Help me, as you always have, she prayed to Mary-Eleanor. Please, help me to get my son back, please . . . Darkness descended. Still clutching the ivory bishop, Bellebelle slept.

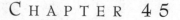 CHAPTER 45

*T*he next morning Bellebelle woke before Prime, feeling
as if her head were stuffed with goosefeathers. A protective veil enclosed her, like the dull gray mist of a Southwark dawn where nothing seemed real. Not unpleasant, it was a welcome relief from the
black despair of the night before. Although distant, she could sense
that anguish lurking quietly in the dim corners of her mind, like a
wild beast in hiding, ready to spring without warning.

Setting about her morning chores in a mindless fashion, Bellebelle decided she would go to Tower Royal and beg Henry to allow
Geoffrey to come home.

By now Henry's anger would surely have lessened. All she need
do was explain that Geoffrey was the whole of her life, except for
him—Henry. She accepted that Henry was lost to her, unless he
would allow her to make it up to him in some way. But if she lost
both him and her son she would have nothing left to live for. She instantly rejected that possibility. Of course, he would allow Geoffrey
to come home. She was sure she could persuade him.

If she couldn't, she would appeal to her idol, Queen Eleanor. She
was a mother, after all, and would surely understand. An image of
Henry's contorted purple face and thrashing body whisked across
her mind, but she hastily retreated from the terrifying picture. Today he would be his old self once again. He would let her son come
home.

"Geoffrey be—is coming home today," she told the hounds as she
fed them.

Filled with confidence now, Bellebelle hummed a tune as she put on her best clothes: a new green kirtle over a cream-colored gown, the fox-fur cloak Henry had given her, woolen stockings, sturdy black boots, and a dark blue shawl to wrap round her head and neck. Underneath her chemise she tied a small cloth bag containing some of the silver and copper pennies she had saved. After a moment's thought she took the silver-and-gilt chess set and ivory figures and placed them on top of Geoffrey's bed. They would be the first thing he would see when he climbed up to the bower.

In the early morning hours carts left for London with produce to sell, and Bellebelle hoped to catch a ride with one of them. She broke her night's fast with a thick slice from a wheaten loaf and a chunk of sheep's cheese washed down with mead, then wrapped the rest of the loaf and cheese in a clean white cloth and put them into a straw basket to take with her. At first light she let the dogs loose in the garden. She carried the hens one by one into the back shed with the goats, bolted the garden gate, and started down the path that led to the village.

After a quarter of an hour's walk the path curved; the trees grew sparse and Bellebelle could see the distant ploughland shrouded in a heavy silvery-green mist under an arching gray sky. The air was chill and moist but there was no sign of rain. Just the thick swirls of mist. A few yards further brought her in sight of the oak roof of the mill, whose blurred outline jutted up above the vague shapes of a few cottages. Before she reached the village green, where the road to London forked, she heard the sound of bleating kids and the wheels of a cart rumbling by, although she couldn't yet see anything.

"Can you take me anywheres near Tower Royal?" she called out. "I can pay." She heard the cart pull to a stop.

"Aye. Hop in—if ye can find room," said a cracked voice. "Tower Royal be my first stop as it happens. Cold as a witch's teat this morning, not a day to be walking."

As she approached, Bellebelle could see that the voice belonged to the driver of the cart, a white-haired old man from the village who made regular trips into London. She made a place for herself in the straw, pushing aside stacked wheels of white cheese, tubs of butter, and covered wooden buckets of milk. In addition to three kids tied together, there were ten geese in large crates and a sow in pig. She petted the kids, who stopped bleating.

"What be ye going to Tower Royal for, lass?"

"To see me son. He's been visiting his father and I'm going to bring him home." Still surrounded by that protective veil of fog, the words came easily, increasing her feeling of confidence. "He wants to send him off to school at St. Paul's, but I think he be too young to leave his mother. In time, of course, I know he have to go, but not yet. When he do go to be educated proper arrangements can be made for me to see him regular."

The old man turned and gave her an odd look but only grunted in reply.

"Here we be, lass," said the driver. "Tower Royal. Lower bailey near the kitchen."

Bellebelle, who had dozed off, now woke with a start, rubbed her eyes, and looked up. A pale sun shone through gray clouds. She had a hazy impression of a garden with fruit trees, vines, and a small fishpond. Crates of squawking hens and other birds were stacked against one white-washed wall. The old man was unloading tubs of butter and buckets of milk, half the cheeses, and all of the geese. An important-looking man with a gold chain around his neck marked off the items on a wax tablet while servants carted off the goods. The man paid no attention to Bellebelle in the cart, and left as soon as everything was unloaded.

"Not yet Terce so's we made good time," said the driver. "If ye wants a ride back I be leaving from Smithfield just after Nones."

Bellebelle jumped down from the cart, gave the driver a copper penny, and thanked him. The clamor of noise had brought her fully awake, but she still felt dull-headed. The courtyard was a beehive of activity: scullions washing utensils in an outside trough, grooms sweeping horse-droppings off the flagstones, servants emptying pots and basins, others catching fish in a net from the pond. Bellebelle saw a laundress pounding sheets in a huge tub of water; another picked up dried sheets and clothes from a grassy plot, and folded them into a large wooden crate.

A few of the servitors eyed her curiously. Fearful lest someone ask her to leave, Bellebelle approached the laundress folding the sheets.

"Can you tell me where the children be?"

The laundress turned and glanced at her. "The older ones be at their lessons, the wee ones with their nurses." She stared at Bellebelle's breasts and frowned. "Not the new wet nurse, I hope?"

"Oh, no."

"Well, that's a blessing. The poor babe'd fair starve if ye was. Are ye here to help with the young ones? I doesn't recollect seeing ye 'afore, but then so many comes and goes, I can't hardly keep tally, now can I?"

"No," said Bellebelle, avoiding a direct answer.

The laundress gave an indifferent shrug and picked up the crate of dried laundry. "I'll be taking this lot up to the chambers. Ye can follow me."

Bellebelle followed her through a back door and down some steps into an enormous kitchen. Kitchen boys turned carcasses of beef and mutton on a spit, while others stirred long spoons into great iron cauldrons hung by huge hooks and chains over the fire. Cooks chopped vegetables at long tables, drenched slabs of meat into wooden bowls of salt, or plucked feathers from a mountain of dead birds. The floor was covered with blood, offal, feathers, and vegetable rinds. The air was filled with the pungent odor of roasting meat, animal flesh, and ordure, and the babble of many voices talking all at once.

Bellebelle had never been inside a castle before, and if she hadn't been in such a hurry to find Geoffrey she would have liked to spend more time looking about. Instead, she hurried after the laundress through the kitchen, then a room where casks of wine were stacked on wooden racks and loaves of bread neatly laid out on tables. Soon she was in a dark passageway, up a winding staircase, down another passage.

"There be the children's quarters, where they has their lessons," said the laundress, pointing to a door. "In the chamber next to it you'll find the little ones." She continued on her way, turned a corner, and disappeared.

Through the open door, Bellebelle could hear the chanting of the children's voices. She noticed the door was open a crack and cautiously pushed it open further. Inside a large chamber, a young boy with curling golden hair, a girl, a smaller boy, and Geoffrey were seated round a long table. A cleric stood at the head of the table over a gilded psalter. He read aloud in Latin; the four children repeated the words after him.

Geoffrey looked content and at home, quite at ease in these surroundings. In truth, he and the girl—who must be Henry's oldest daughter, Matilda—had the exact same solid build, russet hair, and wide-set gray eyes. The golden-haired boy must be the second son,

Richard, the small boy Henry's youngest son, also Geoffrey. No one
looked around or appeared to have noticed the open door. Bellebelle
watched for a moment, noting that her Geoffrey repeated the Latin
phrases with great ease while the other children spoke haltingly,
stumbling over words. She could not bring herself to tear Geoffrey
away when he was doing so well, outshining the royal offspring. She
would see Henry first, she decided, then come back for her son.

Bellebelle gently pulled the door almost shut, paused, uncertain
what to do next. The Tower was such a warren of passageways and
winding stairs she had no idea where to look for Henry. The laundress had turned a corner at the end of the passage; she would follow in her footsteps.

The passage was freezing cold and Bellebelle shivered, pulling the
fox-fur cloak closer about her shoulders. She rounded the corner
and from the far end of the passage heard raised voices.

Something about the clash of those voices—angry, bitter, accusing—warned Bellebelle that a violent quarrel was in progress, and
not to approach. But she was drawn to the sound like a homing pi-
geon. She crept silently down the passage and almost stumbled into
the chamber, pulling back just in time.

The door was flung wide. Bellebelle had a fleeting impression of
a large chamber, green wall hangings spangled with gold and silver,
a table, stools, and a huge green-curtained bed. Her eyes were immediately drawn to the two people in the center of the room. One
was Henry, his face twisted into a scowl. Facing him was Eleanor,
whom Bellebelle had worshipped as the Queen of Heaven ever since
she had seen her face on the statue of the Virgin in St. Mary
Overie's. She had glimpsed her at the coronation, even kissed her
hand for a brief ecstatic moment, and seen her a few times thereafter when she happened to be in Bermondsey as the queen rode by.
Each time she had thought Eleanor the most beautiful creature she
had ever seen, her radiant vitality blazing like the summer sun.

The queen, slightly older now, was no less lovely, but not the gracious, smiling woman that Bellebelle remembered. Her face, framed
in an ivory wimple covering her hair and neck, was deathly pale; her
tall slender body clad in a purple tunic decorated with pearls and
feathers visibly trembled. With rage, Bellebelle realized.

"How dare you ask me to take in this bastard and raise him as if
he were my own son! How dare you!" The voice, husky and vibrant,
penetrated every corner of the room. "Where is he now?"

"He is at lessons with the other children. I had him with me at Westminster last night, then rode over with him this morning."

"He is *here*? *Now*? Without my permission?" Her voice rose in disbelief.

"Where else could I bring him? It will not be for long. Soon the boy will go away to be educated at St. Paul's." Henry paced back and forth. "In truth, Eleanor, I do understand how you feel—"

"If you understood how I feel, you would never ask me to do this thing. Never, never, never!"

Holy Mary Virgin, they must be speaking of Geoffrey! For a moment Bellebelle felt faint and had to lean against the wall.

"I refuse to abandon this child," Henry suddenly shouted. "I will not throw him into the gutter!"

Eleanor crossed her arms over her chest. "Give him back to his mother, this—this London harlot. He must leave here at once."

Her cheeks burning, Bellebelle felt as if she had been slapped across the face. The queen might have been speaking of a hound-bitch that roamed the London streets.

"I cannot. She has betrayed my trust, lied to me. Geoffrey has promise; he deserves better."

Eleanor shrank back as if she had been dealt a physical blow. "Why—why you truly care for this mongrel, don't you?"

"Of course I care. What do you take me for?"

"I don't think I wish to answer that. And the mother? This vile whore?"

"I care for her too. Or did." Henry stopped pacing and glared at his wife, his jaw thrust forward in a threatening manner. "Do not speak of her in such terms."

"How touching. In what terms should I speak of her? What makes you think the brat is even yours?"

"He's the image of little Matilda."

"What?" Eleanor's voice was incredulous. "Do you dare to tell me this whore's brat resembles *our* daughter? I refuse to believe it. This conniving creature has somehow convinced you the brat is yours."

Henry approached the queen and held out his hands. "If you would only see him for yourself—"

"Don't touch me!" She took a deep trembling breath. "Never! I will never set eyes on this misbegotten vermin. Or on any of them!" She gave him a look of such contempt that Bellebelle found herself shrinking from it. "How many bastards do you claim now, or have you lost count?"

Henry put his hands up to his temples. "Jesu. What does it matter? That's not the issue, is it?"

He looked ill, Bellebelle thought. Henry's red-rimmed eyes had a haunted expression; his clothes were rumpled, as if he had not slept in weeks.

"It's not the boy's fault, Eleanor, none of this coil is his doing. Don't punish him."

"What is that to me?" Eleanor walked over to Henry and viciously slapped him back and forth across one cheek. He did not flinch; her hand left a crimson welt on his face. "You still have the effrontery to expect me, the queen of England, to care for your slut's by-blow!" Eleanor's arm drew back as if she would strike him again. "Does my humiliation mean nothing?"

This time Henry caught her hands and held them in a grip of iron.

"Of course it means something!" He swallowed. "Let me remind you that I could order you to do this and you would be forced to comply. Instead I have humbled myself to ask you to be charitable. But do not push me too far."

"Do you now threaten me because I will not grovel at your feet?" She twisted back and forth, trying to free herself from his grip. "How long have you know this creature that means so much to you?"

"Since I was ten years old. I—" He suddenly let go her hands and gingerly touched the welt on his face. "I hold—held—her in great affection. You, I love. She takes—she took nothing from you, Nell, I swear it, but she has been like a part of myself—"

"Since you were ten?" Eleanor's eyes glittered with tears; her voice dropped to a whisper. "You have known this tart since you were a child? Why, she knew you before I did!"

Henry jammed his thumbs into his belt and thrust his head forward. "No, I knew you first, remember? I was only three or four when you first bewitched me at your wedding feast in Bordeaux, an awed little boy, so smitten by the great lady that he gave her flowers by the roadside."

They stared at each other for a long moment before Eleanor spoke again. "The boy is only a little older than young Henry, you said.

You must have bedded her in London before you were crowned, while I was still in Normandy?"

"Yes, yes, yes! Mea maxima culpa! What does it matter now? As you must know, there have been others—there will always be others. None of them important. Only this one whom I have known for so long."

Henry turned away as if he could not bear to see the queen's face, frozen into a mask of pain. Eleanor tried to speak but no sounds came forth.

Watching them, Bellebelle felt her own heart must break.

"However, the bitch has betrayed me, and I intend to root her out of my heart. But the boy is not accountable for her actions! He did not ask to be born, and he must not suffer for it."

Eleanor had found her voice. "His suffering? What about my suffering? Must I have this mongrel under foot as a constant reminder of your faithless nature?"

"God's eyes, if you would only let me explain the circumstances . . ."

Bellebelle had heard enough. More than enough. She backed away from the door and staggered down the passageway. The protective veil which shielded her had been torn aside; she felt like a raw open wound. To have been the cause of the naked anguish she had seen in Eleanor's eyes, the open enmity between Henry and his queen, filled her with so much guilt she did not think she could bear it. If only she could weep, there might be some relief, but she felt beyond tears.

She was at the end of the passage now. Hesitating, she wondered which way she should turn. The scene she had just witnessed—no, not just witnessed but been a part of—swam before her, blurring her vision. She fell back against the wall.

There was no possible way she could ask Henry to return Geoffrey. Not now. From all he had said, and how bitterly he had said it, Bellebelle doubted if Henry would ever be willing to see her again. She could either take Geoffrey away by stealth, some time in the future when Henry was not in London, and try to make some sort of life for them both, or leave him to be educated by his father who, from all she had heard, would do right by him.

She could try to take him away now, of course, but she was sure to be stopped and questioned. She felt so shattered, so filled with pain, she did not know what to do. The thought of losing her son was more than Bellebelle could support. But what would be best for Geoffrey? She must have time to think, to decide . . .

Right now all she wanted was to escape from Tower Royal and her overwhelming sense of shame. If only she could flee from the hateful words that still rang in her ears, blot out the rage and hurt that still stung . . . Behind her she heard voices.

Bellebelle darted round the corner then down another passage. The winding staircase lay just ahead. She half-slid down the stairs, almost falling in her haste, ran along another passage that looked familiar, then through the pantry and kitchen, out the door into the courtyard. She raced all the way around the side of the white stone walls to the front courtyard of the Tower. Guards were stationed by the keep and next to the open courtyard gates. A line of traffic—knights on horseback, clerics, and richly clad burghers on foot—came and went across the wooden drawbridge that spanned the moat.

Bellebelle joined the crowd, crossed the moat, then found herself in the outer bailey. Within a few moments she was through the outer gates and onto the road that would lead her into London.

Bellebelle vaguely recalled that Tower Royal lay not too far from Aldgate. Not that it mattered where she was, or what road she followed. The thoroughfare into London was thronged with carts, horses, and people on foot. With no destination in mind, she let the crowd carry her aimlessly along, jostling her this way and that, through the massive city gates, which she barely glanced at, into the heart of London.

She was only half aware of the gray shroud of smoke hanging in the air, the soot covering the cobblestones. Had the city always been this dirty? She couldn't even remember the last time she'd walked London's streets. Bellebelle had no idea how long she'd been walking until the tangy odor of roasting chestnuts brought her up short. Ahead lay a cookshop; she was at the Strand, near the foot of London Bridge. The open stalls filled with bolts of cloth, strings of onions and garlic, the lilting London voices—all were now achingly familiar.

Bellebelle started to walk across the bridge, pushed along by the crowd. There was a slight movement at her skirts. Looking down she saw the grimy, birdlike face of a street beggar, a practiced pickpocket by the way he'd sidled up to her. Habit made her tighten her hold on the basket, and ensure the purse of coins was still tied safely under her skirts, before shooing him away. At the far end of the bridge two women in striped cloaks called out to the men going across. The sight added to her pain, unexpectedly calling up memories of Gytha and Morgaine.

Bellebelle turned away and stopped to lean over the rail. A line of wool barges floated downstream. She could hear the familiar call, "Through, through." There were the tilting boats, the wherries that carried passengers up and down the river. Why it must be years since she had crossed the bridge on foot, not since she'd lived in Southwark, in fact. In Gropecuntlane she'd been afraid she'd run into the Flemings. In the village, fearful of being recognized by an old customer, she had avoided going to the Strand or the area of London around the bridge. Occasionally she'd made trips to St.-Martin-le-Grand, where Geoffrey was born, but that had been years ago.

For something to do, Bellebelle listlessly unwrapped the cheese and bread from the basket and took a bite, not really tasting the food. A few feet away she caught sight of the ragged little pickpocket again, eyeing her with hungry eyes. He must be about Geoffrey's age or even younger, but looked old and hardened by the wicked world of the London streets. She held out the bread and cheese; he approached her warily, like a wild badger she'd once seen in the woods behind her house, snatched the food from her hand, and wolfed it down before disappearing into the crowd.

Was that how she had looked—was it really seventeen years ago?—when a well-dressed boy, a very prince to her innocent eyes, had given her a pork pasty to eat? Close to this very spot he had boasted what he would do when he became king of England. A great deal of which he had actually done. The earlier desolation, which had receded for an instant, now flooded her. Drowning in anguish, Bellebelle watched the muddy water swirling beneath her. She was now twenty-eight years of age, or thereabouts, and she felt as if her life had come to an end. She could think of no reason to go on living.

At some point between leaving the Tower and where she now stood, Bellebelle realized, a decision had been made: she would leave Geoffrey where he was. Henry could make the boy's fortune; what right had she, a former whore with no prospects, to spoil her son's future? No right at all. What could she offer him? Only a vast love that accepted him exactly as he was, with naught wanting. It was not enough. Despite the damage she had done—the terrible pain and shock she had caused the queen, Henry's rage and distrust—Geoffrey must not suffer. Henry was right about that. If her son came back to her, in time he would grow ashamed of what she had been and want nothing to do with her.

But with Henry he would have the chance to truly better himself, the chance she had never really had, the chance that wretched street urchin would never have. There was no question in her mind that Henry would either persuade or force the queen to take Geoffrey in. Eventually, even Eleanor would come to see Geoffrey's worth. Would the queen mistreat him, take out her anguish on the boy? No. Bellebelle felt certain that was not her way of dealing with matters. Despite the violence and bitterness of Eleanor's reaction, Bellebelle could not find it in her heart to blame her.

Bellebelle finally understood that powerful as she might be, Eleanor was human after all, not a painted statue of the Virgin, but a mortal woman who had been hurt to the quick, just as she, Bellebelle, was hurt. Underneath they were the same. Two women who loved Henry and suffered at his hands.

If she, Bellebelle, did nothing to interfere, Henry would see to it that Geoffrey flourished and prospered. Perhaps, one day, he might become a knight, or a merchant, even a scholarly clerk, for already he could read and write. There were no limits to how high the bastard son of a king might rise. If her life were finished, the boy must still have his chance.

On a sudden impulse she leaned over the rail and threw her basket into the water. It bobbed for a moment or two then slowly sank between the tiny waves. Such an easy way to disappear really. The jumping off would be hard but then, like the basket, you would feel nothing, just slowly pass from view into the deep river and be carried out to sea. So easy—Bellebelle took a deep breath and leaned far over the rail.

It was then she saw the long silver fish with big green eyes.

# CHAPTER 46

"Very well, explain. I'm listening. How did you first meet this strumpet?" Eleanor clasped her hands tightly in front of her bosom, as if, by so doing, she could hold back an enraged demon struggling to burst through the confines of her flesh.

"She was no strumpet then. Bellebelle was about ten years of age—her birth date is unknown—when I first met her on London Bridge . . ." Henry frowned, walked over to the open door and shut it.

Bellebelle! Sweet St. Radegonde, she might have known!

Listening to Henry's explanation, each word deepening the wound in her heart, Eleanor still could not believe that he had dared to impose this whore's bastard upon her. Rumors about his lecherous behavior, gossip about his misbegotten offspring, even specific knowledge of one or two that Henry had taken an interest in was painful enough. But at least she had been spared any actual contact with the children involved—or their mothers. There was no direct threat to *her* world.

Eleanor could just imagine the salacious comments and ribald remarks—all at her expense—that would circulate through the court. Her pride was so outraged at the possibility she could barely contain herself from screaming her fury aloud.

With a supreme effort of will, she forced herself to listen to the tale of Bellebelle's degrading life in a Southwark stewhouse, her attack on a Flemish knight, the mother's murder, her flight into London and another brothel, then, over ten yeras later, the hostile confrontation with the Fleming in her home.

"Apparently young Geoffrey had the wit to loose the wolfhound on that Flemish scum," Henry said, "and thus saved her from his savagery."

Despite her anger and hurt, Eleanor was moved. "You met her again only by chance?"

"In a tavern, long before I was crowned. Where she rescued me from a band of ruffians." Henry shook his head in amazement. "The incredible part of this is that I myself only discovered the real truth about her life within the last two months. Can you believe that she actually deceived me all these years?"

"Which only goes to show that she is far, far cleverer than you have given her credit for—and you more gullible."

"Apparently. But I still cannot easily accept that she lied, that she can never again be trusted."

"*You* lied to *me!* Are you no longer to be trusted?"

Henry, standing by the window slit, swallowed. "An omission is hardly a falsehood. There is a world of difference."

"Is there? I call it splitting hairs. In any case I don't intend to play whore's advocate." Eleanor walked over to an oak table and poured herself a goblet of wine from a silver pitcher. She took a sip of the ruby liquid and set it down again. "You truly don't intend to take up with her again?"

Henry put his hand to his heart. "You have my sworn word. I will take an oath, if you wish, on any sacred relic you care to name."

"Why is it the Normans are so eager to swear a sacred oath and so little inclined to abide by it?"

"You cannot accuse me of that, surely?"

Eleanor no longer knew what to believe. From the way Henry spoke about this doxy and her son, she knew that they had deeply touched his life in some inexplicable way that was no less painful because she could not comprehend it. What she *could* comprehend—it kept staring her in the face—was the galling realization that this Bellebelle was Henry's age while she was eleven years older. There was no avoiding the fact that the gap between eighteen and twenty-nine, when they had married, was easily bridged. Between twenty-eight and thirty-nine lay the edge of a chasm that would yawn wider with each passing year.

Henry came up behind her and warily slid his arms around her, moving his hands up to cover her breasts. "Nell—"

In a violent gesture, Eleanor thrust his hands away. How dare he try to cozen her in such fashion! She turned around; Henry seized her hands.

"God's eyes, your fingers are like ice." He rubbed them between his palms. "Do not punish the lad for the sins of his parents," he said softly. "Please, may I bring him to you?"

They were at an impasse. She was not winning the battle with the tactics she was now using. Might she be better served by agreeing to see the boy? She was not wholly convinced that this child was Henry's, regardless of whom he was said to resemble. He could be anybody's by-blow, one that this very clever tart had foisted off on Henry as his own. Yes, perhaps by seeing the child, she could persuade Henry it was not his own. Also, truth to tell, by now she had grown curious.

"Very well. Bring him to me."

Henry left the chamber. While she waited for him to return, her thoughts churned like a bubbling cauldron. What must Bellebelle be like to have held Henry's interest all this time? By his own admission, most of the women he bedded, even those who bore his bastards, were short-lived encounters that meant nothing to him. What, then, was so different about this one?

She distractedly picked up the silver goblet then set it down again without drinking. An open psalter combined with a Book of Hours lying on the oak table caught her eye. It showed the Last Judgment and the Fall. Eleanor noted the furrowed brows and fierce expressions on the green-shaded faces, a perfect mirror for the emotions roiling inside her.

Henry opened the door of the chamber. He led by the hand a small boy and was followed by a servant. So great was her shock that Eleanor staggered back against the table, nearly knocking over the pitcher of wine. Facing her was an almost exact replica of the young Henry she had first seen in Bordeaux. This misbegotten child more closely resembled Henry than any of his legitimate sons. The whore would not have had to convince anybody; the evidence was there for all to see. Eleanor could barely hold back the tears that sprang to her eyes.

Henry prodded his son. "Here is the queen of England, Geoffrey."

"*Deus vobiscum*, Madam," said the boy, obviously fearful but determined to put a good face on it.

Eleanor was speechless. She could tell from the ease of his delivery that this bastard was fairly fluent in Latin. Young Henry, heir to the throne, was hopeless at his lessons. Had Henry told the boy what to say? What point was he trying to make? That this whore's brat was superior to hers? She hardened her heart.

"Thank you—" She could not bring herself to say Geoffrey.

"When Geoffrey is a little older, I'll offer him as an oblate to the monks of St. Paul."

"An excellent opportunity," Eleanor said in an icy voice. "Every father should have a son in the Church—to pray for his sins. I'm sure he will make an excellent priest."

Geoffrey looked from her to Henry and back again. "I don't want—" He grew pale, swallowed and bowed his head.

With sudden insight Eleanor realized that the boy did not want a career in the Church but was incapable of telling this to his father. She had a moment's identification with his plight. He was as much a victim of Henry's subtle tryanny as she.

Henry nodded to the servant, who took the boy by the hand and led him out.

"*Pax vobiscum,* Geoffrey," she said impulsively.

She was rewarded by a tremulous smile as he blinked back tears. The sight moved her more than all of Henry's words.

"I didn't think the Church was of a mind to accept bastards these days," Eleanor said as the door closed.

"A king's bastard is not the same, is he? He won't be with us long, Nell."

Henry walked over to her, put an arm around her shoulders, and pulled her to him. She knew he was trying to make amends, but she could not respond.

"You offer the boy as an oblate. And the mother? To whom will you offer her?" Eleanor shrugged off his arm and walked to one of the braziers, turning her back on him.

There was a moment's pause. "That arch tone is unworthy of you, Nell."

"Please forgive me. What tone would suit you better? Do you think you can wipe your boots on my heart and expect me to turn the other cheek?"

"It is only your pride I've wounded." Henry let his breath out in a long sigh. "I intend to see Bellebelle is provided for, naturally. She can keep the house in the village near Bermondsey—"

Eleanor turned swiftly. Only her pride wounded! Was the man

blind? "You gave her a house near Bermondsey, where *my* manor is located? You didn't tell me that."

"You didn't ask." Henry jammed his thumbs into his belt and began to rock back and forth on his heels. "Where did you think she lived?" he suddenly shouted, his face growing red. "In some gutter or rat hole? In the name of God, Nell, be reasonable. It's over and done with. Finished."

"Is it?" After a pause, Eleanor, her body shivering with cold, turned back to the brazier. "But the boy will be here, a living reminder of—of—"

"Don't say something you'll later regret. I've asked you not to blame the boy. Blame the mother, if you must blame someone."

She swung around and confronted him with an icy look. "I know who to blame. How like you to lay the guilt at her door. Is that why you've punished her?"

"I, punish her?" Henry looked bewildered.

"Do you really believe a house will compensate for the loss of her son? A son you took without warning? Cruel and heartless punishment I call it!"

Now Henry looked shamefaced, like a small boy. It was one of his most endearing looks, she thought coldly. "Well! I was angry at her deception. Very angry indeed. I admit it was—as you say—cruel and heartless. Yet what's done is done. I cannot turn back the hourglass."

Eleanor was not surprised at this facile admission of wrongdoing. Henry was equally endearing when he confessed his sins—after the fact.

"You will still see the whore from time to time, when she comes to visit her son. Won't that stir up—"

Henry shook his head and spread out his hands in a gesture of finality. "She won't be coming here. Ever. I don't intend that she see Geoffrey."

"You cannot mean—"

"I can and do mean that the more distance between Geoffrey and his unsavory background the better. I intend the boy to go far."

Under ordinary circumstances, Eleanor knew she would have protested this harsh judgment. These were not ordinary circumstances. At the moment, she had not an ounce of pity to spare. Eleanor stretched out long, slender fingers sparkling with jeweled rings toward the burning coals. She had always thought her fingers were particularly graceful. For the first time she noticed the prominence of pale blue veins on the backs of her hands. How ugly they suddenly looked. And old. Quickly, she withdrew them, hiding her hands behind her back.

"Geoffrey, obviously not satisfied with Bellebelle's explanation, asked me why the Fleming had tried to hurt his mother," Henry continued. "What could I say? That she had been a whore? This would only open the door to even more questions. Does he really need to know that his mother was raised in a Southwark brothel among the dregs of humanity? That *her* mother had also been a whore, and God only knows who Bellebelle's father might be—a man of noble blood, she was told. The truth will never be known." Henry shook his head. "Let the boy be spared all that. A clean break is best. He'll thank me for it later."

Did he expect *her* to act as the boy's mother? Eleanor wanted to ask. "What will happen to the Fleming?" she asked instead.

"He has been tried and found guilty of willful murder a sennight ago." Henry began to pace the chamber again.

"Will you hang him?" A rushed trial, with a foregone verdict. Not that the Fleming didn't richly deserve his fate.

"In England, it is not the usual custom to hang men of noble blood."

So he would be beheaded. Perhaps already had been. Eleanor, watching Henry stride back and forth like a caged lion, a ferocious expression on his face, retreated from pursuing the matter further.

"The children must have thought it peculiar when you appeared with a complete stranger this morning. What will you tell them?" she asked. "What will you tell others?"

"The truth, what else? Young Henry, Matilda, and Richard are old enough to understand. I have other bastards—"

"None who live with us, whose mothers are whores."

"You make too much of nothing. My grandfather had a slew of his bastards, including my uncle Robert, brought up at his court. My father had several. So did yours. Time and again you've told me how fond you are of your misbegotten half-brothers."

"This is different," Eleanor said, although she knew it wasn't. "Does it not matter to you that I, your queen, will be the butt of sneers, crude jests, and snickers behind my back?"

"Who would dare?" Henry walked over to her, grabbed her arms and pulled her resisting body close to him. "On the contrary, people will praise your generous spirit." She pushed him away. "Be reasonable. Take the boy in. Do this for me willingly, Nell, and I'll never forget it."

Bitterness rose, clogging her throat. "Henry, there won't be any more—surprises of this nature, will there? I swear by the Virgin I will not—could not—tolerate this a second time. I do not mean some casual encounter when you are on campaign but—"

"I know what you mean." He reached out for her again but Eleanor evaded his grasp. "Never. Never. Never. I vow and swear. Can we leave it now, Nell?"

"There is one thing I would know. What—what was there about this creature that kept you enthralled for so long?"

Henry threw up his hands then savagely jammed his thumbs into his belt again and kicked at the dried rushes. "God's eyes, why can't you just let it be? She took nothing away from you, Nell, I swear it. Nothing."

"Do you answer the question."

"I don't know—" He shrugged helplessly. "Let me see—for one thing she was a good friend, I had always thought. Loyal. Trustworthy. Ha! Easy to talk to." He glanced at her pointedly. "*Her* tongue never wagged overmuch."

"What do you mean by that?"

"I never felt on guard, or concerned that a careless word might be remembered or repeated in the wrong quarter or used against me." He paused.

"Well, go on. There must be more."

Henry ran impatient fingers through his hair. "She was—ah—attentive to my needs and asked so little in return—"

"Carnal needs, you mean?" Not really wanting to know but compelled, despite her pride, to ask. "A practiced whore, with a barrel full of tricks at her disposal must have made good sport."

Henry thrust out a pugnacious jaw. "Don't put words in my mouth! No, not carnal—I bedded her out of habit more than desire, I swear it. There is no woman in the world I desire more than you—or who satisfies more completely."

Eleanor scrutinized him closely. Could she believe him? He met her gaze without flinching but was he lying? Trying to avoid hurting her any more than he already had? It was impossible to tell.

"It probably comes down to this close-knit bond between myself and Bellebelle," he said slowly, "forged when we met as children. Who can explain the inexplicable?"

Eleanor did not trust herself to speak. She been a fool to ask. "All right, I understand."

But having started, Henry could not now be stopped. "The other thing—I know this will be hard for a woman of strength and independent spirit like yourself, a queen and duchess, born to power and affluence, to fully comprehend—but Bellebelle was so utterly helpless. So dependent. She needed me, you see. Bound to a hopeless life of filth and poverty. A pathetic victim of unbelievable wretchedness. You and I cannot imagine what such a life would be like." He crossed himself, obviously much moved. "Without me, she had—has—virtually nothing. Nothing at all."

He looked at her and sighed. "Now, are you satisfied?"

Far from satisfied, Eleanor was heartsick. Suborned by the force of his will; desperately loving him, desperately afraid of losing his love, was she not equally dependent upon him? Were her needs no less important? Perhaps Henry thought she had none.

It was on the tip of her tongue to reveal what lay in the depths of her heart but if she so exposed herself, would she not be totally at his mercy? Like the whore was now. She shrank from the possibility.

Henry seemed quite oblivious to the fact that there was another side to this pathetic victim, Bellebelle: she had been quite capable of attacking a knight to protect someone she loved. This wretched, dependent creature, a felon any way you chose to look at it, had somehow had the wit and resourcefulness to evade capture by her enemies, survive the rigors of a London brothel, convincingly deceive Henry about her past, manage to get him to provide handsomely for her and her son, and, moreover, keep him ensnared for eight years!

Utterly helpless? Holy Mary Virgin!

Henry threw her a cautious glance. "You will take the boy in and treat him as one of your own?"

Eleanor looked at him for a long moment. The battle was far from over, but she would not win by directly engaging Henry in the lists, so to speak. She must appear to accept defeat gracefully, and play a waiting game. An image of the boy hiding his tears came and went. Yes. The child she could force herself to accommodate. It was the threat of the mother that still terrified her.

"When have I ever refused you anything you wanted?" She gave him her most artful smile to conceal the rage she must now suppress.

"Nell—I will never forget this." Henry strode toward her with outstretched arms, his face slack with relief.

"Don't touch me. I'll do as you ask. That must suffice. Do you expect me to love you for it as well?"

Leaving him with a glum mouth and empty arms, Eleanor stalked out of the chamber. Despite his reassurances, could she trust Henry not to see the whore again? That might be *his* intention—but would the temptress who had beguiled Henry for so many years let him go so easily?

Eleanor closed the chamber door behind her and walked slowly down the passage. If this sordid *affaire du coeur*—or whatever it was—was to end, *she* would have to end it. Once and for all. Somehow, somewhere, the means would present itself.

# CHAPTER 47

*B*ellebelle watched the fish rise to the surface of the water then slowly sink. She drew back from the rail. When she looked again the fish had disappeared. But she *had* seen it. In the very nick of time—just at the moment when all seemed lost and life of no account.

There was no easing of despair; her sense of desolation was every bit as agonizing as it had been moments ago. But throwing herself off the bridge no longer seemed an answer. Bellebelle took a hesitant step in the direction of the Strand, then stopped and looked over her shoulder at Southwark. Which way should she go?

Bellebelle felt just like a wolf-bitch Old Ivo had trapped in the forest behind her cottage, unable to move in any direction. She could not go on as before; Henry had seen to that. Ahead lay a black void, a life filled with loneliness; no one to care for, no one to accept the love she needed to give as much as she needed to breathe.

Behind lay the remnants of her shattered childhood dreams. The safe secure life she yearned for had eluded her, she realized. Even while she thought she was living that life, danger had always lurked in the shadows. She had lived a lie, deceiving Henry, deceiving Geoffrey, her friend Elfgiva, and herself most of all. Even at this very moment she felt threatened. What would Henry do next? Now that the king was no longer her protector, de Burgh might think he could have a free hand with her. Menace seemed to lie in wait around every corner.

What she wanted right now, more than anything else in the

world, Bellebelle realized, was to be comforted. Arms to soothe her; voices to reassure; a safe harbor. Where to find this?

Without conscious thought, she turned from the rail and began to walk across the bridge toward Southwark. It was just possible that Morgaine still remained in Gilbert's brothel-house. The Welsh whore would help her, give her the comfort she so badly needed. She began to run.

When she reached Southwark, Bellebelle recognized the gray stone mass of St. Mary Overie on the left. She turned right and, slightly breathless now, ran along the Bankside, then darted down a narrow street. Nothing had changed. Heaps of refuse still lined the street; slops and rotten fish still stung the nostrils. Skinny wide-eyed children dressed in filthy rags scrounged in the dirt for a scrap of food. She threw a handful of pennies at them.

Bellebelle turned into an alley, then ran down another street. Over the roofs of hovels and buildings, she glimpsed the spires of St. Mary's and St. Margaret's. She must be getting close. Twice she slipped and almost fell into a pothole. Any moment now— Suddenly she came to a dead stop, then slowly retraced her steps. Had she gone past the brothel without recognizing it? Surely it had stood just here?

But where the tavern and brothel-house had been lay a heap of rubble, the crumbled remains of wood and stone. She stared down in disbelief.

An old woman hobbled by, carrying a wooden bucket of water.

"What happened to the—tavern as used to be here, Old Mother?"

"Burned to the ground it did, and the brothel-house too, good riddance to that, I says. Though there's plenty more to take its place." She crossed herself.

The woman's dialect was so broad Bellebelle could barely understand her. Had she really sounded like that once? She hadn't become aware how much her speech had improved over the last few years.

"When—how long ago?" It should be no matter for surprise. Fires were common in Southwark, all over London for that matter. But Bellebelle found herself unable to accept the evidence of her own eyes.

" 'Round about when new king be crowned. Mayhap seven or eight year. Can't remember exactly."

"How did it happen?"

The old woman crossed herself again. "God struck them down like he did Sodom and Gomorrah. That be what Father Sebastian at St. Mary Overie's say when it happen."

Father Sebastian! Bellebelle gave a start of recognition, "What—what about the people inside? Be any still alive?"

"I doesn't know. Fire started in the brothel-house first, they says, then spread to the tavern. But all the whores and customers gone to their doom, every last one of 'em, I heard. They'd burn in hell anyways, so what be the difference if they burns now?" She gave a loud cackle.

"Do you know where the whores be buried?"

"Now how would I knows that? In unhallowed ground like as not. Why ye asking?"

She gave Bellebelle a suspicious look, then hobbled on her way, water sloshing over the rim of the bucket. The bells from both churches rang for Sext at the same time. Bellebelle looked once more at the ruins at her feet. Her past was truly gone now; everything she had known turned to dust and rubble.

Almost with a will of its own, her body turned and began to retrace her steps. The woman had mentioned St. Mary Overie's. Bellebelle let her feet lead her along the twisted alleys and narrow streets of Southwark, past the Clinke, and the bishop of Winchester's ornate house, until she came to St. Mary's. Perhaps Father Sebastian, the priest who had helped her once before, would know where the whores had been buried. At least she could pay her respects at Morgaine's gravesite, and her mother's too.

Bellebelle stood irresolute by the wooden doors, then pulled the blue shawl up over her head and walked inside.

A young priest she had never seen before stood in front of the altar while a long line of supplicants filed by to receive the host. After a moment's pause, she walked listlessly down the aisle to the Lady Chapel.

There were a few women kneeling at prayer. Bellebelle slipped inside an empty pew. Here too nothing had changed. The cool interior was dimly lit by flickering candles. Before the altar stood the statue of the Virgin in her gold-encrusted blue robes, the jeweled circlet atop her wimpled head. Mary looked just as Bellebelle remembered. It seemed impossible now that she had ever confused the Virgin and Eleanor. She held no grudge, no resentment against the queen, but Bellebelle had seen the woman behind the crown.

In her hour of need, seeking comfort and succor, she had arrived at St. Mary Overie as she had once before. But what could this place possibly give her now? Her mother and Morgaine were gone. Eleanor's power had disappeared; Henry had abandoned her and taken Geoffrey with him. Who was left?

The figure of the Virgin, surrounded by a halo of light, blurred before her eyes. What was happening? She opened her mouth but no sound came forth. Once again the Virgin merged into Eleanor as Bellebelle had first seen her, radiant and confident, to become the shocked, tortured face in Tower Royal. Then the face merged into her mother's, then Morgaine's, her words echoing loudly in Bellebelle's ears: Life was never meant for them as had a wishbone where their backbone ought be. Morgaine's face passed into that of the alewife, Elfgiva; into the laundress in the courtyard of Tower Royal; the old woman she had just seen by the ruins of the brothel. Then to Bellebelle's shock and amazement the face became her own, smiling back at her, serene, at peace, radiating a power of comfort and love.

She had not been able to cry but now the healing tears streamed like a benediction down her face as she wept and wept and wept.

Bellebelle had no idea how long she had been in the Lady Chapel before she was able to collect herself and slip from the pew. She felt drained; shaken, but calm. Before leaving St. Mary Overie's, she deposited several silver pennies in the poor box, then walked quickly outside. She had given away almost all her money except enough to pay the driver of the cart. The air had turned colder and the sky leaden. She took a deep breath, drinking in the freshness in huge gulps. If she was not going to miss her ride back to the village, she would have to hurry to get to Smithfield by Nones. Bellebelle walked back over the bridge. When she reached the Strand, she stopped to look around before continuing on her way to Aldgate, where she must pass through the city gates to get to the market site of Smithfield.

Surely the colors were brighter? The smells—roasting meat, hot bread—more fragrant? The citizens of London, had they always smiled so much? The red roofs of the city—had she ever seen them this clearly before?

There was so much to think about, so many decisions to make. But the main thing, despite the ache in her heart for her son and Henry, which would probably always be there, the main thing was that now she had hope. She knew, with absolute certainty, that she would survive, and with good grace.

Bellebelle crossed Newgate Street; ahead lay the familiar double swinging-doors of heavy oak reinforced with iron: Aldgate. There was the usual crowd of people, horses, and carts leaving and entering the city that there had been earlier, the same guards armed with spears pacing atop the mighty stone walls.

Suddenly Bellebelle was unable to move. Before she could prevent it, a scream issued from her throat. People eyed her curiously; a few even slowed their pace to see what had happened. One man asked if she were all right.

Oblivious to everything else, Bellebelle only had eyes for what she saw surmounting the gateway: the severed bloody head of Hans de Burgh. Passing through the same gate earlier, beset with anguish and loss, she had not noticed it. The Fleming's head must have been cut off fairly recently. Perhaps even this morning or yesterday; the blood was not yet dried solid. A cluster of black ravens hovered atop the gate. As Bellebelle watched, one large raven swooped down and began to peck at an eyeball.

From across the span of years came the voice of a confident boy: "When I'm king of England there won't be any need for bloody heads on the gates." In truth, there had been very few.

Bellebelle had thought herself too drained to weep again, but the tears now gathering in her eyes were vastly different. She had not been abandoned after all.

Henry had taken Geoffrey—but he had given her justice.

# CHAPTER 48

# London,

# 1162

"*Y*ou remind me of a coy virgin, Thomas, who says no but means yes."

Thomas Becket, wearing a new scarlet tunic, glanced down to admire the pearls embroidered in the cuff of the sleeve.

"Virgins are something you know more about than I do, Sire, but where you are concerned, coy seems inappropriate."

"Ha! Do you imply that in my presence they don't remain virgins very long?" Henry turned his face up to the pale rays of the sun this balmy April morning.

"Did I say so?"

"That is what you meant. Confess now."

"By the Mass, Sire, if I must always say what I mean—where will it end?"

"Where indeed?"

They grinned at each other. Seated next to Henry on a stone bench, Thomas lazily watched the stir of activity thronging the northern courtyard of Westminster. Huntsmen sharpened hunting-spears and polished horns; fletchers tested bow-strings and checked arrows; grooms curried chargers and palfreys, falconers sunned their hooded birds, fewterers aired shaggy wolfhounds, heavily built liams, and wiry greyhounds. A stream of clerks, pages, sergeants, and men-at-arms came and went through the north gate in the outer walls of the palace.

"The See of Canterbury has been vacant a year, Thomas. The monks of Christ Church as well as the pope are pressing for a new archbishop."

"The entire Church, not to mention your lay magnates, would be shocked if you chose your chancellor."

Henry frowned. "What is that to me? Canon law says the canons of a cathedral chapter meet to elect a new bishop—in this case archbishop. In theory anyone is eligible—if I give my approval."

"They expect you to appoint Gilbert Foliot, bishop of Hereford."

Henry gave him an incredulous look. "Allow the Canterbury chapter to elect Foliot, who supported Stephen, as first magnate of the realm?"

"Head of the clergy, Sire."

"You should know your history better than that, Thomas. Ever since Archbishop Anselm publicly rebuked my great-uncle, King William Rufus, for sodomy in the last century, Canterbury also represents the people." Henry gave a mock sinister smile. "Against the tyranny of an absolute ruler. Or that is what Theobald once told me. A warning perhaps?"

Thomas felt himself flush; it was an ill-suited example and heresay at that. Why had Henry chosen it? "Our pious Theobald was apt to idealize the influence of Canterbury. And it's St. Anselm," he added, signing himself.

"There you are. An impressive posterity to look forward to." Henry impatiently smote his fist into an open palm. "We've been over this a hundred times."

"What will happen to my chancery?"

Henry shook his head in mock disbelief. "Not again! You will be both. The Holy Roman Emperor's chancellor is also archbishop of Mainz."

"So you keep reminding me, Sire, but the empire is—"

"Not England. If I hear that one more time I refuse to be responsible for the consequences."

Thomas was well aware of the problems involved in holding both positions. Two separate viewpoints were needed to hold Church and state in equal balance. God and Caesar. Surely Henry knew that? But what he knew and what he wanted were at odds.

Thomas slid his gaze sideways at Henry, particularly pleased today by what he saw. Henry's piercing gray eyes radiated warmth and merriment. For a wonder, even his clothes merited approval: the short reddish-brown mantle clasped at one shoulder with a gold brooch actually matched the gold-embroidered crimson tunic and tight-fitting crimson hose. Surely the russet boots of Cordovan leather were new? The queen must have had a hand in this new garb.

"You know Eleanor leaves for Dover later today?" Henry asked, as if he had read his thoughts. Not an uncommon occurrence when they were in harmony with one another. At Thomas's nod, Henry continued. "She will stop by to pick up young Henry, then on to Normandy where I will join her within the sennight. And I expect your presence at the Easter court, as well."

"Of course."

"I'm bound to say Eleanor took that business with Bellebelle better than I had expected. She was most upset, of course."

"So you said." Upset was an understatement. Thomas had heard that since the incident over the bastard, Henry and Eleanor had been sleeping apart.

"Well, she had every right to be upset. Every right in the world. Nor is she over it. But early days yet. I fear I made rather a dog's mess of it." Henry gazed broodingly at a groom pacing his charger back and forth. "Women can be the very devil, Thomas. What it is to be a husband, a father, a king."

"St. Jerome called women 'the gate of the devil, the patron of wickedness, the sting of the serpent.' "

"Sounds like that old arch-misogynist. Hardly my view."

"The boy, Geoffrey, thrives at Tower Royal?" Thomas asked, to distract Henry from the irritating subject of Eleanor.

The king smiled. "Indeed. Twice as bright as Richard, I'm told. How is young Henry progressing?"

"Charming, as usual. A pleasure to educate." In some ways this was true. Thomas hesitated. "Of course, young Henry is no—ah—scholar, mind, but then—" He spread out his hands.

"The makings of a good warrior, though, eh? Excellent already at the quintain. Seen him myself." Henry tapped a ringed finger against the side of his nose. "That's another reason for you to be archbishop, Thomas. As I've told you, I intend to crown young Henry in my lifetime as they do in France and Germany. Since only an archbishop can consecrate a king, if there is trouble on this score—after all it's never been done successfully in England—you will be there to support my intentions as efficiently as you've done everything else."

The business with young Henry was not "another" reason but, perhaps, one of the main reasons Henry wanted him for the See.

Thomas knew, as few others even suspected, that the king lived in almost obsessive fear that his heirs would not succeed to the throne. Whether due to England's lack of a regulatory system to provide for the succession, his mother's bitter experience in being rejected by magnates sworn to uphold her claim to the throne, Henry's own struggles to achieve the crown, or some other factor entirely was anybody's guess. But the constant need to be assured that his heirs would inherit haunted the king.

Young Henry. Thomas sighed. What could he say? That England's heir was spoiled, lovable, and inattentive to his lessons? That he possessed more comeliness and charm than was good for him? That he traded on these not inconsiderable assets to get his own way? Of course the boy was only seven. Plenty of time for him to grow into his vast responsibilities—or so Thomas fervently hoped. When thinking of the young prince, however, he was uncomfortably reminded of King Alfred's dictum: Unlettered king, crowned ass.

"You favor the base-born Geoffrey, don't you, Sire?" Thomas asked now, to avoid any further discussion of Prince Henry.

Henry gave a rueful smile. "In some ways. Although I adore young Henry as well." He scratched the sleek head of a liam that had escaped its keeper to place its two front paws on Henry's lap. "It was awkward explaining to Geoffrey that he might not be seeing his mother for a while, but he seemed to accept it."

The liam leapt up and licked Henry's face. "It's Joyeuse, isn't it?" He laughed, twisting his head away from the wet tongue.

"I can barely tell one hound from another," said Thomas. "It never ceases to amaze me how you recognize each dog you've hunted with."

"Well, Joyeuse is used for starting the quarry. Notice how heavily muscled he is compared to the others?"

Thomas, who could see little difference, nodded absently. He felt an unaccustomed spark of sympathy for Henry's bastard son, removed so precipitously to alien surroundings.

"What else could the boy do, Sire, but accept his fate? What choice did he have?"

"Well-spoken, Thomas. Indeed, children are little better than pawns of their parents; parents are the pawns of House and lineage. We devise the rules then become prisoners of our own devising." Henry sighed, patting the hound's deep tan chest. "Are any one of us free to choose, I wonder? Are we not all the pawns of circumstance? Can this hound choose where or when or even what game he will hunt? It is a hard lesson Geoffrey must learn—the earlier the better."

"God has given us free will, Sire. Some of us do not use it as wisely as we might."

"There speaks the artful lawyer! Nor do I dispute that, but I fear I'm not up to a philosophical debate with you, Thomas. You usually win." The berner came to retrieve his charge, who was led protestingly away. "I expect Geoffrey misses his mother; God knows I do."

"The Southwark whore?" Thomas was honestly surprised. "Heaven only knows who she might have taken up with by now."

Henry scowled. "Before I leave for Normandy, I had thought of paying her a visit to give her news of her son. But if she's taken up with someone else, I'll have her out of that house and without support so fast . . . do you know this for fact?"

"No. Just speculation. Once a whore, so to speak." Thomas would have liked to say otherwise but did not dare. In truth, he had no idea what the little doxy was doing, nor did he care. That Henry still cared was only too obvious.

Sometimes Thomas wondered if Henry ever thought of their vow of blood brotherhood, and what else might have occurred beside the fire in the Verte Forest. Often—far too often—his thoughts returned again and again to the desires evoked that night—and forcefully repressed. Because he would never know Henry's true feelings he felt vulnerable, at risk. Had Henry guessed, suspected, what lay in Thomas's heart? The possibility tormented him. Outwardly, Henry seemed the same: trusting, comradely, affectionate. But it was impossible to tell what lay beneath that jovial exterior.

Thomas hated uncertainty, the need to keep watch and ward over all that he said and did. As primate of all England, he would not feel disadvantaged but almost Henry's equal. His own man, so to speak, with only the pope to answer to—and the Holy Father was conveniently tucked away in Rome. But the unique quality of the relationship between Henry and himself, their close friendship and bantering camaraderie, would undergo a change. How drastic a change, Thomas could not predict. It was this uncertainty which made him withhold acceptance.

As well as the doubts about remaining Henry's chancellor despite the king's blithe assurance to the contrary. Strange that Henry did not perceive the pitfalls so readily apparent to a discerning eye. But then, the king had his blind spots. He charged ahead like a wild boar after its prey, seeing only the goal, not what lay beyond or on either side.

"What deep thoughts disturb my chancellor's mind?" Henry put a hand on his shoulder. Thomas could feel that touch all the way down his arm to his fingertips . . . Jesu.

"Yes or no, Thomas? I would have an answer now or I *will* offer the post to that dry stick, Foliot."

"Suppose a situation arose, Sire, that put the intent of Holy Church in direct disagreement with royal policy? What then?"

"That is exactly why I want *you* in Canterbury—a foot in both camps so to speak. Then such a situation would never arise."

"Let me put it another way. Holy Church already believes you presume too much in her affairs. Suppose Canterbury itself were in opposition to the crown? Think of the strife that others could foment between us."

Henry jumped up, stretched, and gave a sigh of exasperation. "Suppose we were all struck by a bolt of lightning within the hour? God's eyes, anything is possible. But we have always agreed— Toulouse was an exception, I grant you. Why should our paths diverge once you are primate? You will be head of the Church and also tending to state affairs, thus leaving me free to devote more time to my Continental possessions. No matter the issue, you and I, together, can seek a resolution." He rocked back and forth on the heels of his boots. "No more 'What ifs.' Yea or nay?"

The king was no longer to be denied. Thomas imagined himself as archbishop of Canterbury. Primate of all England! Second only to the king himself in greatness. To attain such heights of power . . . his mind reeled. But within the depths of his soul, Thomas knew himself for what he was—not a man single-mindedly devoted to God. In good conscience there was only one answer he could give Henry.

"I accept." It was not what he had intended to say at all. Astounded by his own audacity, Thomas waited for a sign.

The world did not tumble apart. Lightning did not strike him down. The courtyard still bustled with activity. All was as usual. In the face of Henry's broad grin of pleasure, the hand pounding his back in a burst of goodwill, Thomas drew a trembling breath. The words could not be retracted—nor did he wish to do so. Whether for good or ill, matters would fall out as God ordained they should.

"Madam?"

Eleanor, in the midst of helping the nurses get all her children into two litters in the front courtyard of Tower Royal, turned distractedly to see the steward's troubled face.

"There is no time for me to deal with anything now. I'm trying to get the children settled so we can leave for Westminster, pick up Prince Henry, and proceed to Dover."

He said something, but there was so much noise and confusion she could not hear. The courtyard of Tower Royal was filled with the sound of grooms still loading carts and strapping saddlebags onto sumpter horses. Baby Eleanor was crying. Matilda and her younger brother were quarreling over a wooden doll; Richard was sulking because he could not ride in the same litter with her.

"What? Speak up."

The steward raised his voice. "That woman is here again. In the kitchen courtyard."

Eleanor, about to climb into her own litter, paused. "What woman?"

The steward appeared embarrassed. "The—the bastard Geoffrey's mother."

Eleanor stiffened; her heart jumped a beat. She felt the familiar knot of anger and jealousy tighten in her chest. "What do you mean *again?* Do you tell me she has been here before?"

"Indeed, Madam. This is the third time in the last fortnight. I did not want to disturb you with the matter. Each time she comes, I faithfully relay the king's explicit instructions that she may not see her son. Each time a guard escorts her out and tells her not to return. Only this time—" He hesitated.

"Only this time?"

The steward flushed with irritation. "This time, somehow the boy was outside. In all the commotion no one noticed. He saw his mother enter the courtyard, and now he is clinging to her and stubbornly refusing to let her go. Naturally, the guards are hesitant to forcefully lay hands on either of them. Since the king is at Westminster, Madam, I came to you for advice."

"Yes. I see. All right. I will do what I can. She is in the kitchen courtyard, you say?"

"Yes."

"Very well. Leave this business to me. See to matters here until I return. I won't be long."

Eleanor felt her whole body tremble in anticipation. So the enemy was at Tower Royal. Now. Never again might she have such a splendid opportunity. She adjusted her black cloak lined with ginger fox fur and took a deep breath. Head high, she marched across the courtyard as if going into the lists, invisible lance in hand, shadowy sword and buckler by her side. The whore was persistent, she would give her that. So was her son. Eleanor thought about Henry's bastard.

Despite her bitter resentment, she found it impossible to hold a grudge against the little chap. Geoffrey was so bright, so personable and eager to please, surprisingly well able to defend himself against the hostile forces arrayed against him.

These forces consisted of Richard, who had immediately taken against the newcomer in a rage of jealousy that was quite unlike him, and her own Geoffrey, a devious child at three, who covertly stirred up trouble between the boy and the other children. Matilda, a gentle child, might have welcomed him if she weren't so intimidated by Richard. Young Henry, ensconced in Becket's household, had yet to meet him.

When she arrived in the kitchen courtyard, Eleanor found herself confronted by an amazing spectacle. Directly in front of her, ringed by guards and curious household servants, stood a slender young woman with a thick braid of curly black hair hanging over one shoulder. Geoffrey was holding on to her as if his life depended upon it.

The crowd fell back at Eleanor's approach. She came to an abrupt halt, unable to move. Her heart felt as though it would burst inside her. So this was Bellebelle. The whore had skin the color of new cream and enormous eyes of an unusual dark blue. Her lips, the stain of crushed summer strawberries, were tightly clenched in a face taut with defiance. She looked impossibly young. With a start of angry surprise, Eleanor saw that she was wearing a black cloak lined with ginger fox fur, exactly like her own! Henry must have had two made, as he had the samite cloaks she had seen listed in the Pipe Roll.

She was not sure what she had expected but certainly not this exquisite creature that looked like a doe beset by hounds, vulnerable enough to break your heart.

Without warning, all of Eleanor's doubts and fears surged up in a huge threatening wave. Regardless of what Henry said or promised, or truly intended, could he really give up anyone as lovely as this?

Bellebelle had gone deathly pale when she saw Eleanor, but she held her ground, tightening her grip on Geoffrey.

"I don't mean to take him away," Bellebelle said in a tremulous voice that held the lilt of the London streets overlaid with a refined veneer. "I just wants to see him sometimes."

Was it only Geoffrey she wanted to see? Or was she hoping to meet Henry as well? Did the whore still think to get her claws into him? Despite Bellebelle's air of helplessness, Eleanor was filled with distrust. Silk over iron was probably a more accurate assessment.

"Leave us," she said, dismissing the guards and the crowd of scullions, laundresses, cooks, and other servants. "Return to your chores."

They dispersed. Eleanor could just imagine the gossip that would run like wildfire through the Tower, then spread to the court. Well, there was no help for it.

"I would talk to your mother alone, Geoffrey. Do you wait over there—" She pointed to a far corner of the courtyard. "Nothing will happen to her," she said, noting his fiercely anxious look. The boy had not been clinging to his mother, she realized, but protecting her.

Geoffrey looked up at the whore who nodded; he ran off. Eleanor watched until he was well out of earshot. She had quickly determined exactly how to foil this threat and thus ensure her own security.

"I know who and what you are. Henry has told me all about the—liaison and how it began," she said, "so don't try to gull me."

Bellebelle stared at her in silence.

"Now," Eleanor continued, "I'm willing to make an arrangement with you."

A wary look flitted across Bellebelle's face. "What kind of arrangement, Madam?"

"You must undertake never to see the king again. I want your solemn promise."

Bellebelle shook her head in obvious bewilderment. "But Henry won't have nothing to do with me anymore. Not after—not after all that's happened. He doesn't trust me."

"That is what he says now. If you know him as well as I think you do, then you also know that Henry is impulsive and unpredictable. He can blow hot or cold at a moment's notice."

Bellebelle gave a reluctant nod. "But I don't think he will change his mind about me. He never forgets an ill turn, he says. My lying to him . . . no, Madam, it do be finished between us. But even when he were—was keeping me, I never be a threat to you. Never for a single minute. He loves you, Madam."

Eleanor stiffened. "I don't need reassurance from the likes of you about how my husband feels." She swallowed her resentment. "If you agree never to see him again, I will arrange matters so that you may see your son. If you break that promise—and I shall know if you do—you will never see Geoffrey again."

"Of course I agree," Bellebelle whispered unhesitatingly. "If Henry do come riding up to the cottage I can't stop him, but I never bed him again if that be what you really mean. Though he never be interested in me like that, except as a way to remind himself he be a man. Like it be expected of him."

Eleanor was surprised at this unexpected directness—and the whore's astute perception of Henry. "Yes. That is what I meant."

She stopped, at a sudden loss for words, aware that it was becoming harder and harder to see this whore in the guise of a foe. She was losing control of this encounter and must get it back.

"If you need money as well to persuade you—" Eleanor began.

Bellebelle looked affronted, as Eleanor had intended she should.

"No. I gives you my word. I never do anything to cause trouble for Henry, or make you hurt, or try to come between you. I never did come between you. Not for a single moment, I swear it. If only you believe me." Her eyes glistened with unshed tears.

It struck Eleanor with all the force of a winter gale that the whore—that Bellebelle—loved Henry, just as she did her son. Truly loved Henry. Every bit as much as she did, and far more selflessly. She suddenly felt ashamed. In that instant, the knot of anger and jealousy dissolved. Here was no enemy, no calculating, formidable rival out to gull her or use Henry. A mixture of courage and cowardice, strength and helplessness, submissiveness and independence—Bellebelle was, in truth, simply a woman. Just like herself.

A great burden began to lift from her shoulders. Relief and understanding slowly started to replace resentment, jealousy, and fear.

"Forgive me," she heard herself saying, "I now understand why Henry wanted you for a—friend all these years. He was—most fortunate."

Impulsively she held out her hand. A transformation came over Bellebelle's face. With a radiant smile she seized Eleanor's hand and pressed it to her lips. Her gaze contained such heartfelt admiration that Eleanor, dazzled by the light, had to look away.

She beckoned to Geoffrey, who had never taken his eyes off them. He came running over.

"Your mother may see you whenever she wishes. I will arrange it with the steward, but I caution you both to be discreet. Don't mention this to your father, Geoffrey, or anyone else for that matter."

His eyes shining with relief, Geoffrey nodded and hugged his mother. Bellebelle whispered something in his ear. He turned to Eleanor and hugged her about the waist. As she bent to return the embrace, Eleanor's eyes met Bellebelle's. For an instant they shed their separate identities of queen and whore, as they exchanged a look of triumphant complicity. Each had had her own private battle with Henry; together they were about to secretly outwit him in overturning his thoughtless injunctions. Not a major triumph, perhaps, but no victory, however small, was to be wholly discounted where Henry Plantagenet was concerned.

Bellebelle turned to go. "Thank you, Madam. I should have known you be the one to help me. Just like you always did."

Much moved, Eleanor watched her cross the courtyard, a brave little figure who cast a shadow that was larger than life.

"What did your mother mean," Eleanor said to Geoffrey, as they walked around the Tower to the front courtyard, "about my having helped her before?"

"Oh, when she was very young she admired you so much, Madam, that she thought you and the Virgin Mary were the same person. She used to pray to Mary-Eleanor, she said. Of course she knows better now."

"I'm sure she does," said Eleanor, staring at this miniature Henry with tearful eyes. "I'm sure she does."

CHAPTER 49

*T*he day after Eleanor left for Dover to set sail for Normandy, Henry decided to ride over to Bermondsey. While there he would stop at the village and see Bellebelle one last time. He would give her news of Geoffrey and persuade her not to attempt to see the boy again, aware that in the past fortnight she had made several attempts to do so. He must put a stop to it.

While he sorely missed Bellebelle's soothing, nurturing presence in his rough-and-tumble existence, he still resented the fact that she had kept her unsavory past a secret for so many years. Women were such able dissemblers, far better than men, now that he thought about it.

He left before dawn, taking a few huntsmen and hounds with him, hoping for some sport in the forest behind the village. By the time Henry rode through Bermondsey, the morning mist had cleared. Sunshine splashed across a land coming into bud this April day. Valley, marsh, woodland, and strip-patterned fields, all wore the fresh green livery of spring. In the meadows, ewes and their lambs grazed on young shoots; cows and heifers lowed in the byres. In one of the orchards belonging to the manor he had given Eleanor, villeins were already at work pruning plum and apple trees. They doffed their caps and called out greetings. Henry waved in return.

He was not breaking his promise to Eleanor by this visit, he assured himself, nor had he any intention of doing so. They had been estranged ever since Geoffrey came to Tower Royal, and Henry missed her badly—her warmth, her gaiety and wit, the sheer excitement of her presence. She was so infinitely satisfying that when he was actually with her he never thought about other women. If only he could get her to understand that. When he was gone, of course, it was another matter entirely, which she had seemed to accept.

Yesterday morning, when Eleanor stopped by Westminster to pick up young Henry and take him to Dover, he thought he detected a thaw in her icy attitude toward him. God's eyes, he certainly hoped so. Matters between them could not go on as they were. He had not even told her yet that Thomas had agreed to become archbishop of Canterbury.

Henry came upon Bellebelle on her knees in the garden, planting seeds in a furrow. There were smears of mud on her cheeks, dark wisps of hair had come loose from the single braid she wore, and her hands were smeared with earth. An apprehensive look crossed her face when she saw him standing outside the gate.

"I leave for Normandy tomorrow," Henry said without preamble. "Before I left I wanted to tell you that Geoffrey fares very well."

Her face was pale as she rose to her feet, brushed the dirt from her hands, and opened the gate.

"I—I be glad he's well. Do he go with you?"

"No. I hold my Easter court at Falaise, and it would not be politic to have him there—at the moment. When he's older, of course, he can accompany me everywhere."

She appeared ill at ease, unwilling to meet his gaze; unusual for her. Well, it was an awkward moment, after all.

"Will you not offer me a cup of ale?"

He followed Bellebelle into the cottage where she poured him a cup of foamy brown ale from a wooden pitcher. He drank it off at a single gulp then prowled restlessly about the narrow space.

"See here, Belle, I may have acted hastily when I took Geoffrey as I did. However, I was very angry with you at the time. But now—I see that the matter could have been handled very differently. And should have been." He stole a glance at her from the corner of his eye. She was very still. "Having said that, let me add that the deed is done and I honestly believe it best for the boy to stay where he is. He has a fine mind and I want him educated at St. Paul's with an eye to a career in the Church."

Bellebelle frowned. "Geoffrey be—is more of a warrior inside than a churchman. Such a life might not be to his liking."

"How can he know his own mind at this age? There is more to

being in the Church than preaching at the pulpit. Look at Thomas. Lawyer, statesman—why, the possibilities are limitless. I will decide what's right for Geoffrey. Now, without intending any offense, Belle, I really believe it's in the boy's best interests if you don't see him—not until he is much older anyway, and understands about—your early life."

"That I were a whore, you mean?"

"As well as the unsavory business with your mother and de Burgh. But yes, generally, that is what I mean. I want to give Geoffrey the chance to rise above his early origins. Make something of himself."

"You think I hold him back?"

"I did not say that. It is—well, the Church frowns on accepting bastards these days. He'll need all the advantages I can give him." Henry gave her a winning smile. "Meanwhile, you can stay in this house as long as you wish, and I'll see you're provided for." He paused. "By the way, I know you've tried to see Geoffrey. The steward had orders to forbid it. He still does."

Bellebelle grew red. When she poured herself a cup of ale he saw that her hands trembled. "You be bribing me to stay away from Geoffrey and not cause no trouble?"

Her directness was unsettling. "It is not how I would have put it—"

She gave him a crooked smile. "I knows you for a long time, Henry. In Gropecuntlane, you once told me you say what you mean but don't always mean what you say. It sounded like gibberish at the time. Tell me then, how would you put it?"

"Don't try to make me feel sheepish, Belle."

"Then stop trying to pull the wool over me eyes."

Henry burst into unwilling laughter. "By God, that was close to the mark! All right then, that is how I'd put it. *Quid pro quo*. It's the way of the world. Satisfied?" There was something different about her, a subtle change he could not quite identify.

She poured him another cup of ale. Henry sipped it. "If I were you I'd put Gropecuntlane and your life there behind you now. Unless, of course—" He raised his eyebrows.

"No. That life be—is finished. After knowing you how could I ever . . ." The tearful note of finality in her voice could not be questioned.

"I'm relieved to hear it."

"But I not be ashamed of that life anymore." Bellebelle's eyes suddenly flashed in a way he had never seen. "I did earn me keep and that be better than begging in the streets."

"It is indeed." Henry put his cup down on the table and took her hands in his. They were warm and still trembled slightly. "Let us part friends, Belle. I've no wish to hurt you. As I said, this house is yours." He brought one of her hands to his lips. "You've earned it. Putting up with me all these years—well, it can't always have been easy."

Her dark blue eyes glistened. "Never had no cause for complaint." She swallowed. "Until I decides what I going to be doing, I'd be grateful for somewheres to stay."

"There is no need for you to do anything, or go anywhere. You now own this house. It will be so stated in the parish records. I said I would take care of you, and I will—providing you keep your part of the bargain, and not see Geoffrey."

Bellebelle pulled her hands free then turned away, picked up a long knife, and began to cut thick chunks from a loaf of maslin bread. Henry took her silence for assent.

She offered him a piece of bread; he took it.

"I saw the Fleming's head on Aldgate, Henry. Thank you. Now, finally, that whole coil be—is over."

"De Burgh got a better death than he deserved. Oh, I almost forgot." Henry fumbled in the purse at his belt and pulled out a silver medallion set with five emeralds. "Here. This is yours if you want it. A *memento mori*."

Bellebelle stared at the medallion then slowly reached out her hand. "Me—memento what?" She examined it cautiously, as if it were a viper that might bite her.

"Remember death. This death in particular. De Burgh's paid the debt he owed you for your mother." Henry took a bite of the bread. Made of mixed wheat and rye, it was coarse and chewy, not what he was used to.

To his surprise Bellebelle slipped the chain over her head.

"I never forget you gave me mam justice, Henry. Never."

He looked away, embarrassed at the intensity of her gratitude, glowing like a candle in her eyes. "I miss you, Belle." Henry was surprised at the gruff note in his voice. "In my own way, I love you—still. I imagine I always will."

"I knows. I feel the same."

Their eyes met and held. Henry reached out his hand, then, with a deep sigh, let it drop. Too much had come between them. They could never be as they were. There was no need to explain, for in the wordless way he and Bellebelle had often communicated, he knew she understood.

"I would like to do something for you," he said, to cover his sense of loss and inadequacy.

"You done so much already. If not for you I still be lying on me back to earn me bread, still be almost like a prisoner to some brothelkeeper, having to wear what they tells me, do what they tells me— no better than some poor serf chained to the land."

"It does seem unfair when you put it like that."

"Whores deserves justice too," she added with a flash of indignation, then clapped a hand over her mouth. "Listen at me, will you?" Her face grew rosy. "Mustn't grumble, I'm out of all that now."

"You were very eloquent. Well, I must be off, Belle." With an effort of will, Henry walked to the door and out into the garden. He would never have believed how hard it was to leave her. Bellebelle followed. "I'll see you get news of Geoffrey, of course, and remember, this is your home."

At the gate he turned. "I still think of you—I will always think of you—as one of my closest confidantes, the very first friend I met in London."

Tears ran down Bellebelle's face, making narrow tracks in the mud smeared on her cheeks. At the moment she looked almost like the dirty urchin he had first met on London Bridge.

Henry walked through the gate and closed it behind him. "Should you find yourself in any difficulty, the chancellor's secretary, Fitz-Stephen, will know what to do, where to reach me if I'm available. He'll also bring your money each month."

"Thank you." Bellebelle wiped her eyes. "Oh! A while back I walked across the bridge and saw the fish. I never believe he still be there. I meant to tell you right away."

"The fish?"

"Never mind. I wish you good fortune, Henry."

It seemed a fitting note on which to take his leave.

Henry did not turn around; no purpose was served by looking back over your shoulder. Filled with a vast regret, a hollow ache in his heart, he mounted his roan stallion, whistled to the hounds, and, followed by the huntsmen, rode off in the direction of the woods.

He and his party entered the forest. The hounds started to bark and point their noses to the ground.

"They've scented game, Sire," said one of the huntsmen riding up beside him.

Suddenly Henry drew rein. "The fish! God's eyes, how could I have forgotten?"

"What fish do you refer to, Sire?" The huntsman peered closely at Henry's face. "Your eyes are watering. A branch must have brushed across them. Do take care."

# CHAPTER 50

# Falaise, Normandy, 1162

*E*leanor was seated in an armchair in the solar at Falaise, in the midst of dictating a letter to her uncle Ralph, seneschal of Aquitaine. Unaccountably, she had been plagued by a sense of doom ever since landing on the Normandy coast a sennight ago.

Henry was due to arrive tomorrow, and the prospect of seeing him oppressed her still further. She had not really talked to him since her confrontation with Bellebelle, and she could not decide exactly how she felt. Ambivalent. Certainly she had made her peace with the girl, unexpectedly establishing a bond of affection and respect between them, and she intended to do what she could to make the bastard Geoffrey's life as pleasant as possible before he went to the canons of St. Paul.

Despite her understanding of the situation between Bellebelle and her husband, it was Henry she had not made peace with, Henry whom she had not yet forgiven. Try as she might, she could not let go her feelings of rejection and resentment.

"Read that last back to me, Master Roger," she said to the clerk who served as scribe whenever she was in Normandy.

He picked up the wax tablet. " . . . 'the king wishes to nominate Thomas Becket as the next archbishop of Canterbury, while still keeping him as chancellor of England. My own feelings—' "

Her own feelings. Ralph knew her feelings, just as Eleanor knew what Ralph thought of Thomas Becket—details of which she had never repeated to a living soul. She recalled how her uncle had predicted that the chancellor would one day overreach himself. Thus far he had not done so, going from triumph to triumph without placing a foot wrong. But Becket in a position of power comparable to the king's . . .

Eleanor sighed. There was no point in burdening her uncle with her own doubts—and that is all they were, doubts; no basis on which to pass judgment. Ralph knew only too well that she was jealous of the close comradeship between Henry and Becket, her feeling of exclusion when they were together. No, it was not a time to heap more coals on the fire. Especially as Ralph was having his usual difficulties with Henry's lieutenant, the earl of Salisbury, in Aquitaine. She must continue to encourage him not to act precipitously. This was a never-ending attempt on her part to keep the situation in her duchy, always simmering, from actually boiling over. Sometimes she felt like a juggler with one too many balls in the air—which might all come crashing down upon her head.

"Rub out that last about my own feelings," she said.

Restless, Eleanor rose to her feet, stretched, and glanced down at baby Eleanor asleep in her cradle. Then she briefly examined the huge altar cloth her women were embroidering for the cathedral in Rouen.

Presided over by the Empress Maud, the altar cloth would be an exquisite piece of work when finished. Her formidable mother-in-law's exacting eye for perfection would not let it be otherwise. This morning the empress was sitting in the only other armchair, besides Eleanor's, in the castle. With her ivory-colored wimple, purple tunic, and heavy gold cross hanging from a golden chain around her throat, she looked very regal, very correct.

Eleanor walked over to the recently enlarged window slit. Outside it was a gray and windy morn. The last day of April. In the courtyard below she could see her three sons—young Henry, Richard, and Geoffrey—engaged in their usual activity when they were all together: fighting. It needed at least two sergeants-at-arms to keep order among them. Matilda and Henry's little French wife, Marguerite, were sitting decorously on a stone bench, watching the fray. Eleanor's fondness for the princess continued to increase—despite her resemblance to her father, Louis of France.

Inside the solar it was dark and chill. Not even the brightly lit tapers gusting in their silver holders, the colorful blue, green, and crimson arras tapestries that hung over the thick stone walls, or the soothing sound of women's voices could dispel the gloom that hung over her like a pall.

"Madam?" The clerk gave her an inquiring look. "Did you wish to add something more?"

Eleanor turned distractedly from the window. "I haven't decided yet, Master Roger. Why don't we leave the matter for now."

The cleric nodded, picked up his stylus and wax tablet, and with a bow, left.

"Has Becket agreed to be both primate and chancellor?" The empress spoke for the first time. "I hadn't heard that, but then Henry tells me very little these days."

Eleanor hesitated. "I know no more than you, Madam, but as the See has been vacant for so long and the pope is pressing for it to be filled, my feeling is that Henry has persuaded Becket to accept the post. I imagine he will announce it at the Easter court."

"Yes, I thought it would come to that in the end." The empress gave Eleanor a sharp glance. "I detect you have the same reservations I have. A man who tries to serve two masters equally—king and God—falls prey to conflicting loyalties."

Disconcerted by an observation that mirrored her own, Eleanor left the window slit, crossed the solar, and stood by her mother-in-law's chair.

"Becket has been of immense help to Henry," she said, out of her usual sense of duty to support her husband. "Much of the realm's success has been due to the chancellor's influence."

"Naturally, he has served the kingdom like any loyal servant of the crown. So have you, for that matter."

"I serve the crown? You mean the children."

"Tut, tut, my dear, don't look so stunned. And no, I don't mean the children, though one is not ungrateful for such a large brood. It was your other contributions I had in mind." The empress raised her brows. "Ignored by some, perhaps, but I have not forgotten that it was you who attended Theobald's obsequies at Canterbury when it should have been the king and Becket. I know how many times you have traveled through England on Henry's behalf, often big with child, issuing writs and charters, writing to nobles and prelates, settling disputes. Oh yes, I am well aware of the hospitals and convents built at your instigation, your untiring efforts to reconcile differences between the crown and Aquitaine."

Eleanor could hardly believe her ears.

"Nothing has gone unnoticed," her mother-in-law continued,

"or unappreciated. By your subjects; even by Henry himself." She paused. "But of course he does not mention all that you've done. Merely takes them for granted."

"As well as sole credit." The words came out before Eleanor could stop them, and she could have bitten her tongue off. How like a whining victim she sounded.

Unperturbed, the empress squinted at a corner of the altar cloth. "Naturally. Henry is a great king but obsessed with the need to control everything in sight, to be the source from which all blessings flow. Whatever else he may be, fierce in his hatreds—and his loves—unfaithful, selfish, both loyal and treacherous by turns, he is certainly no woman's minion, nor will he bask in her reflected glory. You do the work in the name of the crown; the glory is his." She gave a delicate snort. "Really, my dear, what kind of man did you think you were marrying?"

What kind of man indeed! Eleanor was speechless. Henry's mother had never spoken to her like this before.

"Louis never even let you do the work, remember. At least give Henry credit for that. What you accomplish must be its own reward."

Eleanor tried to feel gratitude for being Henry's dogsbody—without success.

"Don't expect acknowledgment as well. Bear in mind that you are married to a great king, and sacrifices must be made."

"I do bear that in mind, Madam. All the time." If she ever forgot, someone—usually Henry or his mother or one of his privileged staff—were sure to remind her.

"Now, having said that," the empress continued, "let me also say that my son possesses blind spots of which he is totally unaware." Her hands fell idle in her lap and she stared, unseeing, into the distance. "There are times when he fails to act in his own best interests. This business with Becket may be one of them." She sighed. "You must be aware of his frailties, these lapses in judgment, Eleanor, and do all you can to help him."

"You ask *me* to mount guard against such faults in Henry's nature—"

"When he asserts his will and is oblivious to consequences, yes."

"If only I could." Eleanor stared down at her mother-in-law in disbelief. "But in this matter with Becket—it may well be the wis-

est decision he has ever made. I pray that is how matters fall out."
Eleanor walked back to her chair and sat down. "In any case,
Madam, you have far more influence on him."

The empress rose to her feet. Straight as a spear she stalked over
to Eleanor.

"Not any longer. My day has come and gone." She looked down
at Eleanor with unfathomable gray eyes. "You are mistress of his
heart, regardless of what he says or does to the contrary. Oh yes, I
know all about the little Southwark doxy and her son—the son that
Henry has asked you to raise. It takes a woman of generous spirit to
do what you have agreed to do. But these little lapses of the flesh
mean nothing. Nothing! Don't spoil your life together by continuing to punish him."

"Would you have done it, Madam?" Eleanor asked boldly, stung
by the reproof, even as she wondered if the empress had ears and
eyes planted everywhere in the realm. "Would you have done this
for Geoffrey of Anjou?"

The empress smiled coldly. "Never. But that was a different circumstance, as I'm sure you know. In any case, what is the use of
growing old except to help others avoid your mistakes?"

Eleanor felt her face flush. How much did the empress know
about her flirtation with Geoffrey of Anjou? Not that she had done
anything she regretted. Still . . . this was the only time in almost ten
years that she had ever had an intimate conversation with her formidable mother-in-law. She doubted there would be another. There
were so many questions she wanted to ask her—Eleanor remembered her uncle Ralph's insinuations about the rumors concerning
the empress's amorous leanings toward her cousin, Stephen of
Blois; the speculation about Henry's paternity . . .

But what difference did all that make now? Had she herself not
fallen victim to enough vicious gossip and intrigue to last a lifetime? Let the past stay dead and buried, where it belonged.

"I—I saw Henry's little mistress. He refused to allow her to see
her son. I arranged for her to do so."

"Of course you did. Quite right too. My son can be so thoughtless."

To her amazement, the undemonstrative empress suddenly
picked up Eleanor's hand and held it between clenched fingers.

"Listen to me, Eleanor. I have few years left. Soon I go to my account. No, no," she said, as Eleanor started to protest. "I have lived

a full, long life. Most of that life has been spent in serving Henry's cause—and mine too, of course."

Abruptly, she dropped Eleanor's hand and began to pace the chamber, reminding her so strongly of Henry it was uncanny. "For years, you know, I felt crucified on duty, a slave to responsibility—as I'm sure you do. But you have the love I lacked."

She walked back over to Eleanor. "However imperfect, you do have such a love. When I am gone there will be no one else Henry can absolutely trust to watch over his interests, except you. Be clever enough not to let him know that is what you are doing." She paused, swallowed, and took a deep breath. "I did not want him to marry you, you know."

"I know." Their eyes met and locked.

"I was wrong. *That* was the wisest decision he ever made in his life. Let us pray that his decision to make Becket archbishop of Canterbury is another." A wry smile rippled across her stern features. "You and I are much alike in some respects. Unique women, who will always survive. When all is said and done we have our inner resources to fall back on. Whether triumph or tragedy—we owe our life to no man's goodwill."

"Yes—it is so easy to forget that," Eleanor whispered.

"One must guard against ambitious natures, however."

"Guard against them, Madam?"

"Have you not noticed that those gifted—or cursed—with ambition too often possess the seeds of their own destruction in equal measure to their desire to create and manipulate events?"

Was the empress referring to Henry? To Becket?

"What men do you refer to?"

"What makes you think I was referring only to men?"

The arrow hit the mark. Much shaken, Eleanor watched the empress turn, march back to the circle of sewing women, and resume her seat.

Henry's mother had given her much to think about.

She had spoken of ambition, of power, of loyalty, and of love. Not to mention burdening Eleanor with yet more responsibility—and resentment. Was she to spend the rest of her days dancing attendance upon a faithless husband who would not share credit or truly delegate power? She was sick and tired of basking in Henry's power, shining in the light from his reflected glory.

Feeling as if she might jump out of her skin, Eleanor bolted from her chair and prowled about the solar. She was thirty-nine now, and somewhere during the years of her marriage to Henry, she had lost her own life.

*This* was the source of her resentment, the true cause of her bitterness. Henry was merely its object.

We owe our life to no man's goodwill, the empress had said. Holy Mary! How could the queen of England forget what Eleanor of Aquitaine had always known?

"Any doubts since we last talked at Westminster?" Henry glanced at Thomas from the corner of his eye.

They had just left the St. Prix Chapel at Falaise Castle after evensong, and this was the first opportunity Henry had had to talk to his chancellor since his arrival from England this afternoon. Henry himself had only arrived two days earlier.

"If you mean by that, Sire, have I changed my mind about accepting the See of Canterbury, the answer is no," Thomas replied.

"I didn't really think you would. Tomorrow I will announce the momentous news to the court at a special feast I've planned. An envoy from His Holiness will be attending."

"I'm impressed, Sire. You've thought of everything."

They walked down the long passage that led to the great hall. Nobles and prelates who walked by them bowed.

"You took care of that matter regarding the Southwark stews before you left, Thomas?"

Thomas reached into the scrip at his waist and handed him a roll of parchment. "Here is a copy. The council approved it and it has already gone into effect. Although I still fail to understand why an ordinance is required to give Southwark's brothels—the most notorious in all England—status and protection. Why not just suppress them and be done with it?"

"And leave the worthy bishop of Winchester virtually penniless? Without the Southwark brothel rents he would have to beg his bread in the streets." Henry laughed, although Thomas was obviously not amused. "No, the brothels should not be suppressed, but why not regulate them? All of them. This—" Henry unrolled the parchment and quickly scanned it—"may refer directly to the Bankside stews, but any brothelkeeper in London and elsewhere with an ounce of sense in his greedy head will take heed and follow its rules." He read through the document then handed the parchment back to Thomas. "Everything appears to be in order. Very good."

Clearly disapproving, Thomas rolled up the parchment then tucked it into the scrip at his belt. "An extraordinary document."

"Not so extraordinary." Henry repressed a smile. "Were you aware that the Roman prostitutes had their own guild?"

"Such vital information was not included in my studies of Roman law, Sire."

"Pity. God's eyes, such a face, my friend. Sour as vinegar. I thank you for seeing to this matter, regardless of your reservations."

"One of my last acts as chancellor."

"As *only* chancellor, you mean. You will still be my chancellor when you become primate, remember? That is the whole point of your becoming primate."

"Yes, Sire, something I could hardly forget."

Despite the glum look on Thomas's face, Henry entered the hall with a renewed feeling of security. He wondered what Bellebelle would say when she heard about the ordinance. How he would love to see the expression of wonder on her face. He sighed. At least he had the consolation of knowing that his conscience would rest easy now. He had seen justice done and paid his debt of honor.

"If I lay dead in my shroud," said Henry to Richard de Lucy at the noon feast next day, "would you do your utmost to secure the throne for my son and heir?"

Despite the chatter at the high table in Falaise's great hall, the voices of the troubadours raised in song, Henry was sharply aware of the long look exchanged between his mother and Eleanor—with whom he had barely had time to do more than exchange greetings since his arrival. He took note of the startled glances, surreptitious whispers, and raised brows that passed between the nobles who attended his Easter court.

"With my very life, Sire, if need be," replied the co-justiciar, de Lucy, a fervent note in his voice.

"By God's splendor, one can't say fairer than that, my lords."

Henry held up his heavy silver goblet; his gaze swept the hall in one compelling glance.

The talk at the high table, the laughter and raucous voices coming from the castle mesnie seated at the trestle tables below abruptly ceased. The troubadours' hands fell suddenly idle on their lutes; servitors and pages, sprinting back and forth from hall to kitchen, froze where they stood. Within moments a vast silence descended upon the assembled throng. Henry knew he had full attention, as if the inhabitants of the castle, nay, even Normandy itself, held its breath, spellbound, for what would come next.

"Then I charge you to strive just as hard to make my chancellor, Thomas Becket, archbishop of Canterbury." Henry's voice rang through the hall piercing as a clarion call to arms. "Rest assured that I have the papal blessing in this matter."

He indicated his guest, the cardinal of Pisa, a special envoy from the pope, whose presence, he hoped, would lend weight to the announcement.

It was evident from the shocked expression on many faces that this was the very last thing most members of his court expected to hear. Not surprising, as only his very closest associates knew his intentions concerning the See of Canterbury. Every eye turned to Thomas Becket, who smiled in acknowledgment. Today, the chancellor was extravagantly clad in a tunic of his favorite scarlet cloth trimmed with sable, red leather boots fastened with silver spurs, and several gold chains around his neck. Henry frowned. Not the most politic choice of garb for the occasion.

Richard de Lucy bowed his head in agreement. "I will set sail for England as soon as may be and tell the monks of Christ Church, Canterbury, that the king has nominated his candidate and they have the royal permission to proceed to election."

"The king may nominate his candidate but the monks are supposed to have a *free* election, I believe?" It was the voice of Master John of Salisbury, a member of the late archbishop's household, sitting with other clerics at one of the trestle tables below.

Trust that grave scholar of Canterbury to let everyone know that he, for one, disapproved the choice of Thomas Becket.

With a bland smile, Henry faced the castle mesnie and guests seated below the dais. "A free election, Master John, naturally. What else? As king, I can only offer my nomination." It fooled no one but preserved the formalities.

Henry downed the last of the wine in his goblet and resumed his seat; the inhabitants of the hall renewed their talk, the servants brought platters of food; the troubadours commenced to play and sing. But the air in the hall now bristled with expectancy. More than one face continued to glower with the disapproval voiced by John of Salisbury.

Henry had always been aware he charted a dangerous course in these troubled waters, therefore he was not overly surprised by the reaction of his magnates. He knew his choice of Becket might prove unpopular, that there would be those—both in and out of the Church—who would strongly oppose his will. Although he would have his way in the end, as he always did.

"De Lucy, you and Thomas must leave for the coast without delay. It would be best if I remain behind."

"But your assent is needed at the election, Sire," de Lucy said with a frown. "You must return with us."

Henry hesitated. This was true— A hand touched his arm.

Eleanor, seated next to him at the high table, bent her head and said in an urgent whisper, "I don't think everyone has entirely grasped that your *chancellor* will also be primate of all England. The sooner this election is brought to a speedy conclusion—without your presence—the better for all concerned."

"But as de Lucy said, my assent is needed," Henry murmured under his breath.

"Send young Henry in your stead, my lord," said Eleanor in a loud voice. "It is high time the prince performed his first official function as the king's deputy by giving assent in your name."

Henry sent her a passionate look of gratitude. "An excellent suggestion, don't you think so, Thomas? De Lucy?"

"Indeed, excellent." Thomas bestowed a lofty smile upon everyone at the table.

The co-justiciar nodded his agreement.

Henry felt the tension drain from his body. He had now taken the decisive step that would set in motion those series of events that would result in Thomas being elected primate.

Eleanor, bless her, had supported his decision despite her reservations concerning Thomas. Not to mention her quick wit in helping him out of a tight corner. He stole a glance at her from the corner of his eye. She looked very lovely today in a new cloth of gold tunic, the sleeves cut with increasing width from elbow to wrist, their open ends trailing on the rushes. The inside was lined with sapphire silk. Eleanor's manner toward him appeared to have thawed considerably. As soon as the feast was over he intended to take her off somewhere and repair whatever damage still remained over the business of little Geoffrey and Bellebelle. He was prepared to make any necessary amends—within reason, of course.

With a sigh, Henry turned his attention back to the inhabitants of the hall. How he wished it were within his power to change Nell's attitude—as well as his mother's—toward Thomas. If only he could get her to see what he and Thomas had accomplished together in terms of reformed laws, prosperity, peace in England, power and prestige on the Continent! This was one of Nell's few blind spots.

Now that the matter was almost as good as settled—he could envision no obstacles—Henry felt such a sense of freedom, he was so light-hearted, he could hardly contain himself. With Thomas safely installed at Canterbury, he knew that both Church and realm would work peacefully together, nominally apart but, in truth, under the control of one viewpoint—his.

With Thomas as primate, young Henry would be crowned within his lifetime. If it was a break with precedent—well, precedents, as well as rules, were fated to be broken. Hadn't all his family done just that? William I had taken England by conquest; William Rufus, a sodomite, had thumbed his nose at the Church; his grandfather, the first Henry, had named a daughter his heir to the throne. Let his enemies do their worst, spread what vile rumors they liked. Although this had not occurred, Henry felt prepared for any eventuality; the succession would be assured when young Henry was crowned king. It was one thing to usurp a disputed throne, quite another to depose not one anointed king but two! At last, at last, he could draw an easy breath.

He felt like getting up, jumping on the table, and doing a Moorish dance.

When the feast was over, Henry grabbed Eleanor's hand.

"Meet me within the hour just outside the gates." At the look of surprise on her face, he said, "Your king commands you. And *don't* bring any of the children."

A short while later he and Eleanor were strolling on the banks of a broad stream that ran outside the walls of Falaise Castle. On the battlements above, guards and archers kept watch. The weather had totally cleared on this third day of May, and apart from a brisk wind, the day was fair, a bright sun swimming in a pale blue sky streaked with shreds of white cloud.

"I've missed you," Henry said.

"Usually, I didn't think my absence bothered you."

"Usually it doesn't. But we have never been seriously estranged before. Not for more than a day or two anyway. To my surprise, I found my attention returning to you again and again."

Eleanor gave him the ghost of a smile. "I think of you frequently when we are parted."

"It's what women are meant to do. But how can you expect a man to run a kingdom thinking about some woman all the time? It won't do." He took her hand and brought it to his lips. "All the same, I'm glad you're here and—no longer angry?"

"No longer angry, no."

From the out-flung branches of several apple trees, clouds of pink apple blossom floated on the swirls and eddies of the stream and carpeted the green path where they walked. Henry had always liked Falaise, an ancient huge fortress of the dukes of Normandy, flanked by fourteen towers that dominated the tiny village set in a ravine marked by scattered rock spurs. It seemed to him that the immense square keep, perched on high ground with great flat buttresses, was haunted by the memory of his great-great-grandmother, Herleva, and the misbegotten son she bore, who first became Duke William Bastard of Normandy and then Conqueror of England.

"Did you know, Nell, that just here, in the last century, was where it all began?"

She raised her brows in a question.

"My ancestor, Robert the Fearless, son of Duke Richard, first saw Herleva washing clothes in this very stream. The Chronicles say she was very beautiful and, despite being the daughter of a simple tanner, she found favor in his eyes. When Robert, in turn, became duke, he did not forget her—nor their bastard son, William."

"Yes, of course, I remember now. It's a lovely tale."

"You know what Thomas said when I told him?" Henry drew himself up, looked down his nose, and said in a deep voice reminiscent of the chancellor: " 'And from such humble beginnings sprang a great dynasty. It clearly illustrates the teaching of the Gospel.' "

Eleanor burst out laughing. God's eyes! What a treat it was to see her laugh like that.

"Obviously readying himself for his new calling," she said, "Thomas Becket, man of God."

They walked along in companionable silence.

Some elusive quality—to which Henry could put no name—concerning the Conqueror and his origins filled him with a sense of fate this morning.

"Sometimes, Nell, I marvel at the strange, unforeseen ways in which our destinies are forged. Because a duke's son glimpsed a fair maid in the stream and desired her, because they conceived an illegitimate son who became duke of Normandy, because that duke followed a dream and conquered England, I was fated to expand that dream into an empire."

"The Conqueror would be proud of your accomplishments, Henry."

"Do you really think so? Well, what I have done—what we have done—is only the beginning. After all, I'm far from dead yet, eh?"

Thoughts of his illustrious forebear led Henry to thoughts of his own well-beloved bastard, Geoffrey. A gifted, highly intelligent child with Bellebelle's easy, affectionate nature. What would he, in turn, accomplish?

Henry stopped by an apple tree and took Eleanor in his arms. "Is that coil all behind us now? Am I forgiven?"

"Yes to both."

He looked down into her hazel eyes, whose unfathomable depths were as darkly green as a forest pool this afternoon. "But something still troubles you, doesn't it?"

"I'm not very good at hiding things from you, am I?"

"I would hope not. What have I done now?"

"This is not to do with you, Henry, but me." She broke away from his arms and leaned back against the twisted trunk of the tree. "I'm not sure I can explain."

"Try."

"I feel—as if I have lost myself. Like a wanderer in the darkness without a beacon to light the way."

He stared at her. "I don't understand."

"Nor do I, entirely."

Henry ran his hands through his hair. "What do you want of me?"

She took a deep breath. "I want to go to Aquitaine."

"Now?" What in God's name was the matter with her? "But I

need you here. With me. More than ever. Thomas will be leaving shortly, there are so many—"

"You always need me, and there will always be so many things far more vital for me to do than visit Aquitaine. Let me go, Henry. It will not be for long. This is something I *must* do."

"If it is only a short trip then I will go with you. I haven't been to the duchy since Toulouse."

"No!" Eleanor closed her eyes for an instant. "No." She walked over to him. "I would go alone. Without you or the children. Think of it as a pilgrimage. As if I were going to a Holy Shrine. You cannot begrudge me this one request."

"But why? *Why?*"

"I told you I couldn't explain."

"I have never known you to be inarticulate before."

"During all the time I was in France, all those miserable years I spent with Louis, when those oppressive churchmen were trying to control me and my duchy—despite the terrible tragedy of Vitry, the outrages committed in Poitiers, the senseless death of my uncle Raymond—I never lost sight of who I was. Now I no longer know."

Henry laughed. "What nonsense. But of course you know. *I* know. You are my queen. Mother of the royal children. A woman of incomparable beauty and knowledge, without whom I could not run my kingdom or expand my empire."

"That is exactly what I mean."

Henry saw the suspicion of a tear in her eye. "I fear you've lost me."

"Henry—"

"Dearest Nell, I refuse to let you go—" Henry swept her into his arms and began to kiss her with such passion that after a few moments her body began to respond.

Her lips opened under his and her arms twined themselves around his neck. The familiar urgent rapture overtook him, as it did her, blotting out everything but the hot intensity of the moment. To Henry's surprise she forcefully pulled herself away, breathing heavily, and placed her hands against his chest.

"No," she said in a gasping voice. "This will not make me change my mind." She took a deep breath and with a hand on her heart steadied herself. "I love you. I want you. I have not and will not desert you—but this I must do. Whether you understand or not—

allow me the grace to do what I must." She paused. "I long for your agreement, but I am prepared to go without it."

Open-mouthed, Henry stared after her as she turned and began to walk along the edge of the stream back toward the gates of the castle. A pilgrimage to Aquitaine? *Now?* God's eyes! Women were the very devil! If he lived to be a hundred he would never understand them.

# CHAPTER 52

# London,
# 1162

One morning in mid-May, a month after she'd last seen Henry, Bellebelle rose before dawn. She put on a rose-colored kirtle, making sure the medallion of emeralds was tucked under her chemise and would not be seen. She wore it every day, right on top of Morgaine's necklace of blue stones. She had thought touching anything of the wicked Fleming's would be hateful to her, like holding a talisman of the Horned One. To her surprise, she had derived a curious strength from wearing it, almost as if it were a holy relic.

She broke her fast with bread and ale, then walked to the village green where she hoped to find a cart going to London. She was planning to see Geoffrey then continue on to Gropecuntlane and collect the money she had left with Hawke eight years ago. As always, the prospect of going to London excited her. In her heart she was really a city lass, the sights, sounds, and smells of London more to her taste than the dull country quiet.

Although there wasn't a day she didn't think of Henry, nor an hour that passed when she didn't miss him, the pain had settled into a dull ache that was bearable. Bellebelle felt a slight twinge of guilt about going to see Geoffrey, but really there was no reason for it. After all, she hadn't actually *promised* Henry she wouldn't see her son. He had assumed she wouldn't, but was that her doing? Besides, she had queen Eleanor's agreement, didn't she? That was what counted. When she thought about the queen a smile came to her lips. If she never saw her again, Bellebelle knew she had found a true friend; Geoffrey would always be safe in her keeping.

A cart rumbled by, and she persuaded the farmer and his wife to let her ride with them. She crouched down amid baskets brimming with red and green cabbages, strings of brown onions, fragrant bunches of leeks, yellow turnips, and baby carrots.

The farmer could not hide his interest. All too frequently he kept turning his head to look at her. The farmer's wife, round and solid as a wine cask, eyed her with dislike and suspicion throughout the journey.

Bellebelle ignored both of them, her thoughts still turning on Henry. Sooner or later he was bound to find out about her secret visits to Geoffrey. Even the queen wouldn't be able to protect her if that happened. Her heart jumped at the possibility. What would be the worst he could do? Make it impossible for her to see Geoffrey? Turn her out of the house and no longer provide for her? And if he did? Well, she didn't have no wishbone where her backbone ought to be. Not anymore she didn't. But she intended to be prepared—which was one of the reasons she was going to see Hawke.

The bells rang for Terce just as the cart pulled to a stop in East Smithfield near Tower Royal. Bellebelle thanked the farmer, then, ignoring his outstretched palm, deliberately put a silver penny into the goodwife's hand. She was rewarded by an amazed smile and an invitation to return with them to Bermondsey. They would be leaving, said the goodwife, sometime in the very late afternoon between Nones and Vespers.

Bellebelle walked slowly toward the gleaming White Tower, its four turrets touched with fire in the morning sun. The goodwife's whole manner had changed after Bellebelle paid her. Not for the first time, it occurred to her that folk were willing to overlook how they truly felt if money were involved. Once she had taken Geoffrey to St. Ethelred's in Bermondsey for Sunday Mass. The priest had preached a sermon about how much easier it was for a camel to pass through the eye of a needle than for a rich man to get into heaven. Bellebelle had found that strange and still did. Anyone who lived in Southwark knew that money was akin to lifeblood. With it all things were possible; without it you might as well be dead. Even Geoffrey had not been able to explain the sermon to her satisfaction.

Later, when Bellebelle asked Henry about it, he had called it a parable, not meant to be taken literally. He had pointed out that animals always did peculiar things in Holy Writ. Still, it had puzzled her. If what the priest said were so, why had she never seen anyone with wealth, including Henry himself, try to get rid of it, like money was truly a bad thing to have? Did people not want to get into heaven then? If the parable about the camel was not meant to be followed, why did the priest bother to tell people about it? It made no sense.

Yet something about the tale, as in all the tales she heard in Holy Writ, found a response within her. Perhaps Holy Writ wasn't at fault—but that hardly no one ever followed what it said. Now wasn't that a thought to be going on with!

Geoffrey was pleased to see her and boasted of how he had almost finished learning the Trivium and would soon graduate to a study of the Quadrivium.

She had no idea what he meant, but he looked happy and confident, which was all that mattered.

"Are you lonely," Bellebelle asked, "what with the queen and everyone gone to Normandy for the Easter court?"

"No. I'm too busy. I have Master Adelhart, the tutor, all to myself, and by the time Father comes back I'll have learned ever so much more."

"You must go now, Mistress." The steward approached them, glancing anxiously around him.

Although Bellebelle had been there a fair while, she felt she had just arrived. She and Geoffrey always had so much to say to each other.

"I understand. I'll leave now."

"You know you're not to speak of seeing your son, or ever show yourself while the king is in residence."

"No. Never."

"If you don't mind—someone might see you and ask awkward questions."

They were in a deserted section of the kitchen courtyard, and the few people she could see were paying no attention to them. But the steward was not satisfied until he had seen her safely outside the gates of Tower Royal. Poor man. She felt sorry for him, trying to follow two opposing orders—Henry's and Eleanor's.

Bellebelle passed through Aldgate and into the city proper. De Burgh's head, still on the gate, could no longer be recognized; the ravens had picked it clean. Bellebelle knew she should feel pity for him, but she was glad he'd gone to his doom, and there it was.

On her left a group of lepers begged for alms. She dropped a few silver pennies into a filthy hand that was half-eaten away. The sight moved her to pity and gratitude that she was not in such a horrible state. There was the familiar sight of Holy Trinity Priory on her right, a small Benedictine convent and cemetery on her left, then the street of market stalls selling fresh strawberries, mulberries, plums, and cherries. From the next street over, a shoe-smith's forge rang so loudly she thought her ears would burst; the sight of a barber carrying a basin filled with blood made her sick to her belly.

She turned off onto a narrow street intersected with many lanes, slipped into a sinkhole, then fell almost ankle deep into a torrent of filthy water running through the deep gutters. Snapping dogs and hollow-eyed urchins, crawling with vermin, preyed upon piles of garbage. Two ruffians shouting curses ran down the street, almost knocking her down. The overall stench was enough to put you off your feed for days.

But this was London. As much a part of her as her own bones and blood. She felt truly alive for the first time in—well, she couldn't even remember how long.

Bellebelle found herself on Gropecuntlane without at first recognizing it, the street had changed so much in the eight years since she'd been here.

"Is this near Gropecuntlane?" she asked a man carrying a bucket.

"This *is* Gropecuntlane. Or used to be. *Groppecounte*lane is what we calls it now." He winked. "Come up in the world it has. Just like the tavern down the street." She followed his pointing finger to where a brand-new sign had replaced the Blue Cock sign. "Lion and Eagle be the new name." He eyed her. "From around these parts, was ye?"

"I was." She looked at him unblinking. "I were a whore. On this very lane."

He appeared startled, then smiled and passed on. Bellebelle felt foolishly pleased with herself. Such a relief to tell the truth straight out like that.

Now she looked around her wonderingly, hardly able to believe her eyes. To think this prosperous and respectable street was Gropecuntlane. The tavern seemed brand-new, freshly painted, with another small building added to it. The houses glistened with coats of red and blue paint. There was an alehouse now, and a new pie shop with a long line of customers right next to the cookshop. Her eyes returned to the scarlet sign with its rough likeness of a gold lion and eagle. The same tavern where she and Henry had met again, now bore his—and Eleanor's—name. How he would laugh at that. She must be sure to tell him, she thought, before remembering, with a stab of pain, that she was no longer in a position to tell him anything.

She swallowed the tears that welled up, and stared at the top of the street. Also new were the row of stationary carts where people were buying wood, charcoal, and water. She began to walk slowly along the street, then stopped.

Where was the brothel-house? Sweet Marie, she was standing almost directly in front of it. The house was almost unrecognizable with its rich new color of blue paint, plum-colored hinged shutters, and fancy curlicues decorating the door casement.

Her heart beating like a drum—she was still fearful of the brothelmaster, she realized—Bellebelle knocked on the door. It was opened by a neatly dressed young man.

"Yes?" He eyed her up and down. "Applying for a position?"

"I be here to see Hawke."

"Who wants him?"

"Just say—someone as would like to see him."

"Wait here."

After a few minutes Hawke appeared, filling the doorway. He had grown stouter. Scowling, he glanced down at her, his scar livid and fearsome as ever.

"Well, what you want, girl? Looking for a position, are you?" He was dressed like a man of means, in red leather boots and black tunic. A black velvet cap covered his hairless head and a heavy gold chain lay on his chest.

"We're full up at present, but—" His wintery eyes narrowed. "Don't I knows you from somewhere? Worked for me, did you? I never forgets one of me girls. Seems like . . . wait . . . it's right on the tip of me—by the Mass, it's Bellebelle, isn't it?" He gave her a brief smile that showed rotting teeth. "Come in, come in."

Inside everything looked clean and freshly painted, with green rushes on the floor—unheard of in her day. Bellebelle followed him down the narrow passage into the chamber she remembered so well. This too had been painted, and now boasted a large polished oak table set with several pewter goblets, a silver pitcher, heavy pewter candlesticks with tall white tapers. In one corner stood two iron-banded chests, and there were several cushioned stools scattered about. Hawke pointed to a stool. Bellebelle sat down, her fingers laced tightly together.

"Marry, but I expected to see you back here years ago." He actually seemed pleased to see her. "You looks sweet and toothsome as ever, but I would have taken you for a country lass in that garb. Come back to work, has you?" He stood over her, arms folded across his chest, head cocked to one side, lips pursed.

"No. I be finished with whoring for good."

"Shame. I could sell the services of the king's former whore for a bloody fortune, I could." Hawke walked over to the table and poured himself a goblet of red wine from the silver pitcher.

"So's you once told me." Bellebelle shook her head when he offered her a goblet.

"Speaks right proper now, I notice, don't you?" He peered at her. "Found out about you, did he?"

Bellebelle nodded and glanced down at her fingers.

"Now you can't say as I didn't warn you. But he probably would've grown tired of you anyways. It's the way of the world, and that's a fact. Men always wanting new furrows to seed. But you lasted nigh on eight years, a long time for Henry Plantagenet from all what I hear about his lecherous ways. Even has a son by him, don't you?"

"How'd you know all this?"

"You been gone too long, girl." Hawke wagged a playful finger at her. "The brothels and taverns hear everything first, remember? Lion leave you well provided for? Reckon he must have or you'd be wanting work."

"I've got a bit put by. Won't starve anyways."

Hawke snorted. "You always did have a head for money, Belle. But you let your heart be master just like all cunts does." His eyes grew speculative. "Come for what you left then, I suppose?"

"Yes."

Hardly daring to breathe, Bellebelle watched while he walked over to one of the iron-bound chests, squatted on his knees, unlocked it with a large rusty iron key, opened it, and lifted out a stained leather pouch, the same one Thomas Becket had given her in the tavern so long ago. He shook it and Bellebelle could hear the coins jangling. She closed her eyes and let out her breath in a long sigh. Thank the Holy Mother, Hawke had not played her false.

"There's more here than you left," he said, lumbering to his feet.

"I borrowed your money so's I wouldn't have to go to Hakelot the Jew and pay usury. Want to count it?"

She shook her head. "I trust you. Why'd you need it?"

"Expansion, naturally. I bought the tavern next door, see, and the cookshop, put up the money for the pie shop as well, and have half-interest in the alehouse too. Of course, someone else has the running of them." Hawke eyed her curiously.

"You be a woman of means now. What're your plans then, Belle?"

"I don't rightly know—yet. Me son, Geoffrey, going to be educated by the canons of St. Paul's, then a career in the Church, so he don't need me no more."

"I should think not. His fortune's made, I'd say. You're free as a bird then, and still got your looks. Who'd a thought it, eh?" He shook his head in wonder. "Born under a lucky star you were, Belle, and that's a fact. Thought about your future at all?"

"I was thinking that if I puts all me money together I might have enough to—" She stopped.

"To what?" Hawke prompted her. "Enough for a marriage dowry, mayhap? Plenty of men overlook you being a whore with enough silver to help them forget."

"Never want to have a husband. Not for anything. Don't need no one to care for me." She paused. "I wants to do something for meself. Something of me own. That no one can take away."

Hawke gave a short laugh. "You don't want much, do you? Eh, it's a weary old world, Belle, for the likes of you and me. None of us gets what we want, and most of us settle for what we do get, and that's a fact."

Bellebelle was reminded of the conversation she had once had with Morgaine on the steps of the brothel-house in Southwark. What she had wanted then—to get out of the stews, to belong to only one man, to feel safe—had all come to pass. Some of it at least. Although not quite in the way she had imagined.

"Perhaps nothing ever be like you dreamed it would be," she said slowly, "once you has it. That be what you mean?"

"Aye, that'll do. You getting wiser with your years, girl, I'll say that for you."

From upstairs there was the sound of a heavy object hitting the floor; the ceiling rattled. Hawke gave an impatient sigh.

"By Christ, now what? Someone always be causing trouble."

He walked to the door. "Best look into it." He gave her the pouch. "You'll find your money, like I said, and a bit extra for the use of it. I'm not a wealthy man, mind, but I pay me debts proper."

Above, there was another loud noise. A female voice from one of the back cubicles shouted for quiet. From directly above, someone raised a drunken voice in song followed by a squeal of laughter. Bellebelle smiled at the familiar sounds that called up memories of Southwark, of Gytha and Morgaine. She rose and followed Hawke slowly to the door.

"Might build me an inn next," Hawke said. "Somewhere outside London. After all, country's at peace, thanks to the king, and growing all the time; trade's increasing back and forth across the Channel. Means more travelers, which means more inns be needed, which means more customers wanting service, right?"

Bellebelle nodded. As Hawke opened the door for her, two young whores ran down the stairs and brushed by them.

"We be off to the cookshop, Hawke," said one, over her shoulder. "No more customers to service. Won't be long."

Bellebelle watched them walk down the street talking and laughing. Something was different about them. What was it?

"They just left without asking you, Hawke. And weren't wearing no striped cloaks!"

"Bloody whores don't know their place, no more, they don't. That's 'cause of the new ordinance come out." He raised his scraggly brows. "You mean you don't know?"

"No." Bellebelle was still staring at the whores in bewilderment. "What ordinance?"

"Well, it's mostly meant for the Southwark stews 'cause most of the brothels be located on the Bankside, but I follows the new rules for brothels and whores just to be on the safe side."

"New rules? I don't understand."

"Well, let's see what I can recollect exactly. 'That no stewholder . . . should let or stay any single woman, to go and come freely at all times when they listed. No stewholder to keep any woman to board, but she to board abroad at her pleasure . . . No single woman to be kept against her will that would leave her sin . . .' It goes on with how much money I can take from the whores, how the whore has to lie with a customer all night if he pays, the bailiff has to inspect the stew every sennight, no married women or nuns to work here, and so forth. Marry, but there be over thirty items. Protects the whores and the customers too. Even I gets protection long as I be licensed."

"You mean that whores don't *have* to live in the brothel-house? They can *leave* whenever they wants?"

"Aye. That be part of it. Not like the old days, Belle, and that's a fact." He grinned. "Want to change your mind?"

"No." Bellebelle felt a lump in her throat. "The king did this?"

"Aye. His council recently approved it, and the ordinance just been issued." Hawke grunted. "Best see to the trouble upstairs now. Fare well, girl."

"You too, Hawke."

Bellebelle walked down the street in a daze. Her heart felt so full she thought it would burst. All those things she'd told Henry about her life in Southwark and Gropecuntlane—to think he'd actually listened, then gone and done something about it! She could hardly believe what Hawke had told her. At the top of Gropecunt—*Groppecounte*lane now, she must remember that—Bellebelle turned for a last look. The tavern, the brothel-house—all behind her now. For good. She felt like singing aloud.

She passed the Strand, looked with a smile at the bridge bustling with foot-traffic, and walked back toward Aldgate. She passed the cemetery, then slowed her pace by the Benedictine convent. The bells from St. Paul's rang for Nones. If she didn't hurry she'd miss her ride with the farmer back to Bermondsey. Not that it mattered, she could always find another cart and driver to take her. There was no rush to return.

The convent had a small garden in front enclosed by a low wall of weathered gray stone. Odd, she'd never noticed that before. A nun in black habit was on her knees pulling out weeds. She smiled at Bellebelle, who came to a halt. The walk leading up to the convent door was paved with uneven flagstones scrubbed clean. Although located right in the heart of London the convent was very quiet, with a kind of soothing stillness.

Bellebelle had never been in a convent yet it felt so familiar, as if she had always known such a place without ever having been aware that she knew it. Impulsively, she turned up the walk. Elfgiva would say she was well and truly daft. Hawke would too. Even Henry would be astounded—but he would see the justice in it. Geoffrey would understand. So would Queen Eleanor. Even Morgaine, if she were here. Bellebelle knew she had enough, more than enough, for an ample dowry—and not for a husband. She smiled.

She had been avoiding this step all her life, Bellebelle realized, only to have come full circle. She had found what she had always been looking for, only to recognize it for the first time.

She had come home, safe, at last.

# CHAPTER 53

# Normandy,
# 1162

*I*n late May, Henry and Eleanor accompanied Thomas Becket, Richard de Lucy, young Henry, and their entourage on the two-day journey to Barfleur. Here, Thomas, de Lucy, and young Henry would take ship for Southampton. It was a day of sparkling brightness which, to Henry's mind, boded well for the voyage and events in England. A frivolous wind chased snowdrifts of cloud across an azure sky, dappling the sea in green and blue patches.

Henry and Eleanor took turns kissing and hugging their seven-year-old son, then lowered him carefully into a small boat. De Lucy climbed in after him; bulging saddlebags and roped bundles followed. A berner, two howling brachets clutched under each arm, jumped in behind them; lastly, a falconer, a hooded Icelandic peregrine anxiously clawing his gauntleted wrist, carefully slid down into the ship. This was Henry's gift to his young son, who was overcome with the ecstasy of owning his first falcon, the excitement of the journey, and the anticipation of representing his father.

"Do as the chancellor and justiciar tell you, my son," said Henry, gazing at his heir with affection.

To his great relief, as the boy grew older his body had become stockier and his hair had turned tawny-red, more like his own. With the exception of the green eyes, his earlier resemblance to Stephen of Blois became less pronounced with each passing year . . .

A sailor pulled on the oars; the small boat headed toward the hoy which, rigged fore and aft, lay bobbing in the white-capped shallows.

Eleanor turned to Henry. "I will wait for you down the quay, so

that you may have a few words alone with our new archbishop-to-
be."

"Thank you, Nell." He watched her walk down the quay, well
out of earshot. "What a woman for tact, eh, Thomas?"

"Indeed."

Waiting for the boat to return, Henry and Thomas stood close together, mantles billowing in the brisk Channel wind. Sunlight
danced on the surface of the shining sea.

Impulsively Henry grabbed his chancellor by both arms and
roughly shook him. "Well, my dear friend, when next we meet you
will be the archbishop of Canterbury!" He made a great show of
sniffing the air. "God's eyes, do I already detect an odor of sanctity
about you?"

Thomas laughed and tried to free himself from Henry's grip.
They wrestled briefly before Thomas freed his arms.

"How I will miss your witty tongue and our contentious debates.
Who else can cross swords with me on virtually every subject? My
boon companion, how large a hole you will leave." Henry gave a
mock sigh. "Well, you will still be my chancellor, I mustn't forget
that. We need not forego all our adventures together." He chuckled.
"Do you remember the time we wrestled near Tower Royal and that
cheeky beggar ran off with your mantle? Or the time we had our
first adventure together in that tavern on Gropecuntlane? What
was the name of that rogue who wanted to sell you Our Lord's foreskin?"

"Black Hugo."

"What a memory. By God's eyes, will I ever forget that
night . . . all those sevens I threw, one right after the other . . ." He
shook his head in wonder. "Fortune has rarely deserted me since,
now that I think on it."

Thomas gazed at him with an unfathomable look, then dropped
his voice. "Do you also remember the night we swore a blood
brotherhood?"

"What I recall is that we were both somewhat the worse for wine
that night."

"*In vino veritas* . . ." Thomas began.

"We must catch the wind, my lord chancellor," called the sailor
who had rowed back to the quay.

Slowly Thomas reached out his hand; Henry clasped it, then
threw his arms around his friend in a hearty embrace. For an in-

stant Henry was aware of a current pulling between them, an inner tension that gripped him from head to foot with all the force of a Channel undertow. He stepped back.

Thomas girded his scarlet robe and mantle up about his knees, and let the sailor assist him into the rocking vessel. The prow of the tiny boat headed for the moored ship.

On the quay Henry was acutely aware of the breadth of sea and sky, sunlight glancing off the breakers, Thomas's scarlet figure upright in the prow, braced against the swing and surge of the boat against the green waves. All of it etched clear and fresh as a newly minted coin.

Suddenly, he was no longer alone. Eleanor stood beside him.

"Nell," he began, and found, to his surprise, he could not go on. Sweat beaded his brow; the breath felt clogged in his throat. What in God's name was the matter with him?

Eleanor clasped his hand in hers and squeezed it. The tightness in his throat loosened. A wave of understanding and tenderness flowed from her with such acute force Henry could have wept. There was no need to explain. Her very presence was enough—almost enough—to fill the sudden void. Henry had not expected to feel this—this inexplicable sense of emptiness. It was like losing father, elder brother, mentor, and merry companion all in the same moment.

Shaken yet comforted at the same time, Henry put his arm around Eleanor and kissed her softly on the lips. "I must rely on you now, my love, for all that Thomas gave me. You will be my confidante, my trusted advisor, my boon companion—as well as my heart's love."

"As always, my lord." Her eyes swam with tears.

They stood thus, arms entwined, watching on the quay until the ship was only a blur on the far horizon. By the time it vanished, Henry had almost entirely recovered. What had gotten into him? There was naught to mourn, everything to celebrate. A renewed burst of confidence swept through him. All was well in his world, and not just in his world alone, but also those dependent upon him for survival.

Bellebelle was safe and secure. Their misbegotten son, Geoffrey, child of his heart, Henry recognized, was being raised as a royal prince.

His dear friend Thomas had been given the chance to achieve the power and success Henry knew he had always craved. Perhaps the demons of Thomas's humble origins would be exorcised at last; he would grow into the greatness that Henry had long suspected lay buried within him.

Then there were his legitimate children. Richard would inherit his mother's duchy of Aquitaine; Henry was already investigating the possibility of having his youngest son, Geoffrey, marry the heiress of Brittainy. Soon he would be looking to form illustrious alliances for his daughters, thus continuing to expand his empire.

His heir, young Henry, whom he intended to crown king of England while, he, Henry, yet lived, would establish the succession beyond any doubt or future breach of faith from others.

Best of all he had his dearest Eleanor, now nestled within the crook of his arm, her cheek against his chin. She was still the enchanting Circe who had captivated his heart, stirred his loins, and challenged his intellect. But she was becoming more like Penelope as well. Steadfast as moonrise, dependable as sunset, she was part of him—breath, blood, bone, and sinew. All the threads of his life had come together now, rewoven into a glittering new fabric.

Henry felt his spirit take flight on invisible wings. He knew that he would remember this moment of pure, unadulterated joy all the days of his life.

*Since I feel a need to sing,*
*I shall write a poem of sorrow;*
*never again will I be love's slave*
*in Poitou or in Limousin.*

Eleanor sang aloud the words of the song composed by her grandfather.

How the road to Poitiers rang out so melodiously beneath her palfrey's hooves. How the June air she breathed, the balmy sunlit Poitevin air, how deliciously scented and sweet it felt. All around her the countryside bloomed: the pink and blue and yellow wildflowers by the roadside, the tender green leaves that adorned the trees, the grassy meadows that formed the gentle landscape of Poitou.

Behind her she could hear the steady pace of her entourage—Norman knights, carts, grooms, sumpter horses, female attendants in the litter in which she, herself, had started out the journey from Normandy. Eleanor had wanted her sister to accompany her, but Petronilla, who had taken refuge in a convent several years after her husband's death, had turned her back on the things of this world.

With regret—she would miss her—Eleanor pushed all thoughts of her sister aside. She was too excited to feel sorrowful, just as she was too impatient to be enclosed by the cumbersome litter. In truth, she would have liked to set a faster pace on her palfrey, jump the roadside hedges, and gallop away across the verdant grass, the breeze at her back, embraced by the warm sun of Aquitaine.

Domfront, Le Mans, Angers, Touraine, then crossing the Loire. The road to Fontevrault over on the right, following the Vienne River by Chinon, Châtellerault—all had formed the various stages of her journey. Like a pilgrimage through the past, journeying back through the scenes of her life. At each stage she had shed another title, another responsibility, another identity. Queen of England; countess of Anjou and Maine; duchess of Normandy—all were left behind along with Henry, her children, and the whole tumultuous mélange of court intrigue, politics, power, and ambition.

Of course Eleanor knew that she must return. Love, honor, responsibility, and the siren call to once again take her place in that intoxicating world where men and kingdoms were made and lost, would lure her back. But now she needed to replenish herself, nourish her roots at the wellspring of her beloved Aquitaine.

She had left Henry desolate, so he said, at the loss of both his right and left arms—Thomas Becket and herself—when, in truth, he had lost neither. He had wept, thrown a tantrum, begged and threatened. After sharing a night of passionate love he would not soon forget, Eleanor thought with satisfaction, she had simply departed.

By this time, she had no doubt, Henry would be happily creating new laws, hatching new plots to acquire yet more land and more subjects. He would be pondering what kings and emperors to ensnare in his web as potential husbands for his daughters to marry. It would not even surprise her to learn that he had a new intrigue afoot to install some tame prelate of his into the papacy! And, of course, he would be mourning her absence at the same moment he was lustfully eyeing some lovely young damsel.

She would never change him.

But Eleanor knew that she had come to terms with the way things stood. To transform what she could, and accept Henry and her life for what they were. Both enemy and lover, friend and foe, sometimes rivals in power—she knew Henry loved her in the ways that he was capable of loving, as much as she loved him.

So long as she never lost sight of herself, who and what she was, and had been, she would survive with good grace.

A group of Poitevins trudged by—women, children, and men. One old grandfather led a mule laden with pannier baskets filled with chickens, eggs, and white cheeses. They all drew aside to let her party pass.

"Wait!" One of the group called out.

Eleanor drew rein and turned her head.

"By St. Radegonde, it do be the duchess Eleanor!"

"Our duchess! Welcome, welcome!"

The Poitevins crowded around her palfrey, doffing their caps, grinning with pleasure, grasping her hands, lifting small children so they could see her, some even trying to kiss the hem of her purple cloak.

She was conscious of a great sense of joy. What remained of the present burden of power and love, the uncertainties of the future, were lifted at a single stroke.

Eleanor of Aquitaine had come home.

TO BE CONTINUED . . .

# AUTHOR'S NOTE ON THE CHARACTER OF BELLEBELLE

At about the time that Eleanor gave birth to her first son, William, a son had been born to an English woman of the streets, called Ykenai. According to Master Walter Map, an archdeacon of Oxford in the twelfth century, she "was a common harlot who stooped to all uncleanness,"\* and, in Map's opinion, had conned Henry into believing the child his. "Without reason and with too little discernment,"\*\* says Map, Henry accepted the child as his own and called him Geoffrey.

It is also a matter of record that early in Henry's reign, Eleanor accepted the boy into her own household. No reason is given.

This is *all* that is known of Ykenai. In the Pipe Rolls of Henry's reign (some years later than I have depicted it in the novel), there appears the entry: "For clothes and hoods and cloaks and for the trimming of two capes of samite and for the clothes of the Queen and Bellebelle, for the King's use . . . by the King's writ." There has been speculation that "Bellebelle" was the king's mistress. I put the two—whore and mistress—together to create the character in the novel.

Henry II showed great favor to the illegitimate Geoffrey (whose fortunes will be detailed in Book II of the story of Henry and Eleanor). An additional note, and I quote from *Harlots, Whores and Hookers*, a history of prostitution by Hilary Evans: "It was, extraordinarily, in England, that the earliest European laws aimed at regulation rather than suppression were formulated. The regulations passed by Henry II . . . to control conduct in the stews of London's Bankside are a key document in the history of the subject."

Speculation regarding a whore/mistress whose son was raised in the royal household, coupled with a set of laws regulating the notorious Bankside brothels, resulted in the fictional character of Bellebelle.

Additional note: Gropecuntlane actually existed.

*Walter Map. *De Nugis Curialium (Courtiers Trifles).*
**Ibid.

# POSTSCRIPT

Research in England was done at Guildhall Library, Aldermanbury, London; Southwark Cathedral, Southwark; the York Minister Library, the Foundation Museum, St. William's College, City of York; the Salisbury Public Library, Old Sarum, Salisbury; Wallington Public Library, Wallington. In the United States, research was conducted in Los Angeles at the UCLA Research and College Libraries, the Brand Music and Art Library in Glendale, the Glendale Public Library, and the Pasadena Public Library.

Of the many history volumes consulted the one I relied on most heavily was Marion Mead's superb biography of Eleanor of Aquitaine. The following were also particularly helpful: *Eleanor of Aquitaine,* by Desmond Seward; *Eleanor of Aquitaine,* by Regine Pernoud; *Eleanor of Aquitaine and the Four Kings,* by Amy Kelly; *Eleanor of Aquitaine,* by M. V. Rosenberg; *England Under the Angevin Kings,* vols. I and II, by Kate Norgate; *The King and Becket,* by Nesta Paine; *Henry the Second,* by A. S. Green; *Henry II, King of England,* by Geraldus Cambrensis; *Henry II Plantagenet,* by John Schlicht; *My Life for My Sheep,* by Thomas Duggan; *Life in a Medieval City, Life in a Medieval Castle, Women in the Middle Ages,* all by F. and G. Gies; *Daily Living in the 12th Century,* by Urban T. Holmes, Jr.; *Pilgrims, Heretics and Lovers,* by Claude Marks; *Life on a Medieval Barony,* by W. S. Davis; *The Survey of London,* by John Stow; *Medieval London,* by Timothy Baker; *Harlots, Whores and Hookers,* by Hilary Evans; *Beds, Bawds and Lodgings,* by C. J. Burford; *Sex in History,* by C. Rattray Taylor; *The Women Troubadours,* by Meg Bogin; *Songs of the Troubadours,* edited and translated by Anthony Bonner; *The Conquering Family,* by Thomas Costain; *De Nugis Curialium (Courtier's Trifles),* by Walter Map, edited and translated by Frederick Tupper and M. B. Ogle; *The Middle Ages, A Concise Encyclopaedia,* edited by H. R. Loyn; *Henry II,* by W. L. Warren.